BLOOD & KIN

An Empire Saga

SINCLAIR-STEVENSON
LONDON

Also by Andrew Sinclair

FICTION

The Breaking of Bumbo
My Friend Judas
Gog
Magog
King Ludd

NON-FICTION

Prohibition: The Era of Excess
The Better Half:
the Emancipation of the American Woman
Jack London
The Other Victoria
Dylan the Bard
War like a Wasp: the Lost Decade of the Forties
Francis Bacon: His Life and Violent Times
The Sword and the Grail
Jerusalem: the Endless Crusade
The Discovery of the Grail
The Secret Scroll

First published in the United Kingdom by
Christopher Sinclair-Stevenson in 2001
3 South Terrace, London SW7 2TB

ISBN 0-9540476-3-X

Cover by DVA Ltd, Bramley, Hampshire
Printed and bound in the United Kingdom by
St Edmundsbury Press, Bury St Edmunds, Suffolk

This book and THE SECRET SCROLL (book and
video cassette) by Andrew Sinclair are
available from Web Order Sites:

www.clansinclair.org
secretscroll@beagledirect.co.uk
tel. UK: 01933 443862

THE FAR CORNERS OF THE EARTH

Chapters

		Page
Prelude	AN ADVANTAGE OVER SHEEP	1
1	THE WARNING OF THE DOMINIE	7
2	TO CATCH A FISH	12
3	THE BRIGHT BUSHES	16
4	THE CLEARING OF THE GLEN	23
5	THE HARVEST OF THE WEED	31
6	THE CASTLE AND ITS KIND	39
7	THE CROSSING	44
8	THE BURSTING AT GROSSE ISLE	51
9	A FOREIGN EDUCATION	56
10	THE MOUNTAINS AND THE STONES	66
11	THE SERVICE OF THE FOREIGN QUEEN	78
12	A VISIT TO MISS NIGHTINGALE	87
13	BLOWN FROM THE GUNS	94
14	THE SEA OF THE TREES	102
15	THE WASTE OF IT	114
16	DANGER OF SURVEY	127
17	IRON ROAD AND WAYWARD PATH	141
18	A SORE WHILE	153
19	ALIEN LANDS	161
20	THE GREAT MOTHER	169
21	THE FAR FILAMENTS	182
22	COMING HOME	191
23	REVIEW	204
24	ALL THE CORNERS OF THE EARTH	213

THE STRENGTH OF THE HILLS

Chapters

		Page
1	BLACK WEEK	225
2	A BARE TABLE	240
3	POUND THEM DOWN	252
4	PAST IT	257
5	BURNING TIME	269
6	A MATTER OF CONCENTRATION	275
7	ALWAYS NOWHERES	287
8	RAJ AND TREK	304
9	SOCIAL GAMES	315
10	A LONG LABOUR	325
11	A MINE	335
12	TO SHOOT A DUCK	344
13	NOT PROVEN	355
14	TEA, GRIT AND CARBOLIC	365
15	A VOICE WITHIN	375
16	WITH WINGS	384
17	SWEATED WOMEN	393
18	FIGUREHEADS	401
19	MEAT CLEAVER	415
20	POT SHOT	427
21	WAR AND CHRISTMAS	436
22	MY ENEMY, MY FRIEND	448
23	MURDER BY MACHINE	458
24	THE STUTTER OF THE GUNS	472
25	FIRE FROM HEAVEN	480

THE SEAS ARE HIS

Chapters

		Page
1	PEACE, WHAT!	486
2	THE MUSIC OF THE SPHERES	497
3	ESCAPE FROM BLEWSBURG	506
4	BACK TO BACKS	517
5	CROSSED LINES	526
6	NO SIEGFRIED LINE	533
7	UNPHONEY WAR	546
8	MESSING ABOUT IN BOATS	558
9	WALLS HAVE EARS	570
10	BLITZ FOR LOVERS	578
11	BYE, BYE, SINGAPORE	587
12	OPS ROOMS	596
13	MINEFIELDS	605
14	A SCALDED CASE	613
15	THE SIXTH COMMANDMENT	625
16	A WINTER'S TALE	634
17	FAREWELL, ANNANDALE	640
18	NO COLONY THERE	646
19	MUSHROOM CLOUDBURSTS	650
20	WHAT HAVE WE DONE?	658

THE PEOPLE OF HIS PASTURE

Chapters

		Page
1	NORTH OF SUEZ	663
2	FALLS	672
3	REMEMBRANCE DAYS	679
4	JACK THE NIPPER	689
5	THE SUMMER OF QUESTION	703
6	THE POISONED LAND	714
7	ARM'S LENGTH	722
8	A FAMILY PORTRAIT	738
9	DRESSING DOWN	747
10	BEARING WITNESS	756
11	POLL TAX	767
12	EASTWARD HO!	779
13	RED NOSES	786
14	HONOUR AND PORTRAITS	796
15	HIGHLAND MILLENNIUM	807

The
SINCLAIR
Family Tree

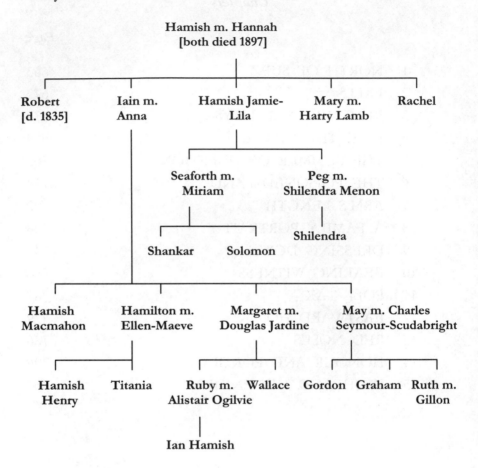

Hamish m. Hannah
[both died 1897]

Robert [d. 1835] — Iain m. Anna — Hamish Jamie-Lila — Mary m. Harry Lamb — Rachel

Seaforth m. Miriam — Peg m. Shilendra Menon

Shankar — Solomon

Shilendra

Hamish Macmahon — Hamilton m. Ellen-Maeve — Margaret m. Douglas Jardine — May m. Charles Seymour-Scudabright

Hamish Henry — Titania — Ruby m. Wallace Alistair Ogilvie — Gordon — Graham — Ruth m. Gillon

Ian Hamish

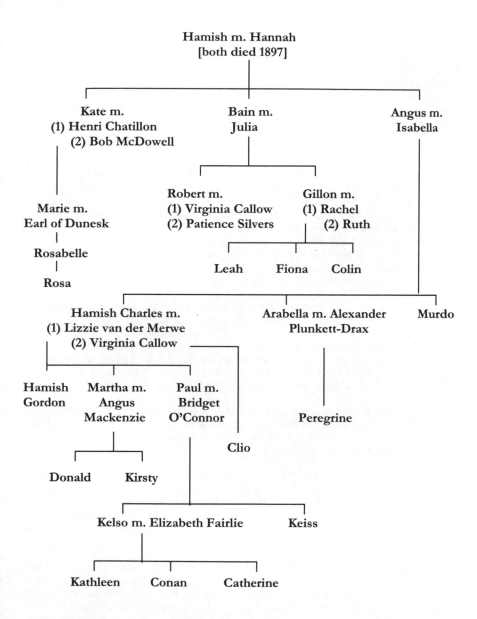

Hamish m. Hannah
[both died 1897]

Kate m.   Bain m.   Angus m.
(1) Henri Chatillon   Julia   Isabella
(2) Bob McDowell

Robert m.   Gillon m.
(1) Virginia Callow (1) Rachel
Marie m.   (2) Patience Silvers (2) Ruth
Earl of Dunesk

Rosabelle   Leah   Fiona   Colin

Rosa

Hamish Charles m.   Arabella m. Alexander   Murdo
(1) Lizzie van der Merwe   Plunkett-Drax
(2) Virginia Callow

Hamish   Martha m.   Paul m.
Gordon   Angus   Bridget
       Mackenzie O'Connor   Peregrine

                     Clio

Donald   Kirsty

Kelso m. Elizabeth Fairlie   Keiss

Kathleen   Conan   Catherine

THE FAR CORNERS OF THE EARTH
by Andrew Sinclair

With this new novel, the first in a series called "The Empire Quartet", Andrew Sinclair introduces a project of epic scope: the history of the British Empire and its friends and rivals (which is to say, most of the world) from the mid-nineteenth century to the present day. Such a vast subject needs some sort of linking theme or framework to keep it within manageable proportions, and Sinclair has opted for the historical novelist's standby, the family saga; in this case, a family of displaced Scottish crofters called Sinclair.

So, even before we begin, we are offered a puzzle calculated to distract us from the book in hand. Are these Sinclairs Sinclair's inventions? The dust-jacket promises us a blend of fact and fiction. Are they, then, fleshed-out individuals from his own family history? Are they *real*? Is the story *true*?... We soon realize that the question is irrelevant. Only the unique, the weird and the coincidental rely on proof for their interest. This novel deals with the probable, the universal: its essentials would have remained unchanged had the protagonists been a Hindu family, or a Chinese or African family, or any family whose lives were disrupted by the cancer of imperialism and whose descendants, scattered to the four corners of the earth, changed the natures of the lands they settled.

The impetus for the Sinclairs' diaspora comes from the Highland Clearances. Once set in motion, they are unstoppable: they travel from Peking to British Columbia, cheat death at Sebastopol and Cawnpore, find long-lost kinsmen at Gettysburg, marry Peruvians and half-blood Amerindians, become soldiers, nurses, farmers, doctors, surveyors and music-hall artists. To do full justice to the events they took part in would have required an encyclopaedia. What Sinclair offers us instead is a sort of new Bible: the Testament of the Wandering Scots.

> Strange it was, that the small population of two inconsiderable islands off Europe had spread themselves so thin and so wide across the globe and had webbed and netted the seven seas. There might be a divine purpose in it, there must be a heavenly intervention.

This is liquid history, history as a river that will either sweep you forward, like the Scots, or submerge you, like Crazy Horse and his Sioux. It eschews all causality except the law of motion and the hand of God. Even colonialism, "the urge to kick and lunge into new territories", is seen as no more than the national expression of this natural instinct to expand or perish, seeking rational justification only because it cannot be resisted.

The form of the novel carries us forward on this flood through a series of richly detailed vignettes told in an almost biblical style, smooth with conjunctions: "And then"; "But yet"; "For when"... *The Far Corners of the Earth* deserves an honourable place on the shelf of serious historical fiction. More than a costume drama or mere chronicle, it offers the attentive reader thoughtful consideration of the relationship between history in the making, and the people who make it.

This book is dedicated to all the soldiers and sailors and pilots and engineers and surveyors and doctors and nurses and other servants of the Empire, who found their work and duty was a long way from home.

Although *An Empire Saga* is a work of fiction, my great-great-grandfather was cleared from the Highlands, my great-grandfather served in India and wrote its school histories, both of my grandfathers fought in the Boer War and in the Great War, my father served in South and West Africa, in Palestine and Tanganyika. The Sinclairs are still scattered across the Commonwealth – and this one had their story to write.

ANDREW SINCLAIR

THE FAR
CORNERS
OF THE EARTH

AN ADVANTAGE OVER SHEEP

1835

Sir John Sinclair of Ulbster looked like a giant dragonfly. Tall and erect, even in his old age, he stood in his green-and-black tartan trousers and long scarf, thrown over his scarlet jacket, with his yellow cuffs and waistband shining above his sporran. He was holding a book in his hand, his own *Analysis of the Statistical Account of Scotland*. He had stopped reading it to the Countess of Sutherland who had been widowed two years before and now sat on the sofa with her embroidery and looked to him for advice. But he was looking down from a round turret in her castle to the formal gardens which she was trying to grow on the east slope down to the shore. The straggling circles and squares of the low hedges did not seem to prosper in the sea wind. Was there any use in trying to put some sort of order onto this savage land? Sir John Sinclair pointed his straight nose back into his book and read on.

> The introduction of sheep must, of course, diminish the tenants in particular districts. They require a smaller number of hands to tend them than black cattle; – they can graze in places, where cattle cannot venture; – and they yield a greater produce. While it may appear a pernicious measure to drive away the people, by depriving them of their possessions, the strength of a nation cannot consist in the number of idle people which it maintains...

Sir John stopped reading again. His words seemed dry to him. But they were right, and he was right. He was proud of his reason and his vision. He was not a man for sentiment and cant. The countess believed in showing tenderness to her clansfolk, but with more than a million acres in the Highlands to consider, tenderness should be interpreted as a proper degree of firmness. The countess wanted his advice about what she should continue to do with her vast estate, already partially cleared for sheep. He would be delighted to give his counsel. Such a handsome woman still, even in her old age, her stoutness only serving to emphasize her puffed and hooded eyes as bright as an osprey's above her fine beak of a nose, as she bent over her needlework, stitching in the detail of the pattern.

"I fear I am boring you, my lady."

"Pray, Sir John, read on, unless it bores you to read what you have written. You must already know it. But for me it is very instructional."

"What you have done is right, my lady."

"I know that," the countess said, "but it is also comforting to find a learned man of the same opinion. And a practical man. All the improvements you have done to Thurso. Those houses in Janet Street are really quite elegant, although the Scots I am afraid will never be Palladian. And that handsome temple at the end of Sinclair Street! You have left a monument to your name."

Sir John Sinclair shrugged.

"We do what we can. I have done little compared to your useful improvements. That distillery you have built at Bora – it has changed your tenants from criminals into respectable men. Instead of selling their grain to the makers of all that bog whisky, they sell it to you to make legal spirits. And you feed pigs off the spent grain from the mashing. Most laudable, dear lady –"

"I am not sure," the countess said. "We have still put half the crofters out of work with the spread of the sheep. And they leave us, they emigrate."

"Not all of them. Many become sailors or fishermen. They take to the sea, that is true, but not to leave Scotland for ever. Why, in a creek at Ulbster, a whole fishing industry has developed. The men catch the herrings, the women carry them up the steps in creels on their heads–"

"How many steps, Sir John?"

Sir John closed his eyes for a moment. He saw a vision on the back of his lids, a line of women winding and toiling up the stone steps of the deep crevasse, bowed under with heavy burdens. As they passed him at the top of the cliff's edge, they would not bob to his rank, but only glare at him in weariness and contempt. He opened his eyes to the sight of the countess stitching on her sofa.

"Three hundred and fifty steps down and the same up at Whaligoe Harbour."

"A woman can do that? How much fish does she carry?"

"Up to a hundredweight."

"Your Highland women don't seem the fair sex to me," the countess said. "Porters and climbers. Do you really think they wish to do it?"

"It is a useful employment," Sir John said confidently, as if to reassure himself. "And it is steady work. There was no profit in the crofts, herding the black cattle and growing potatos and neeps. Men must work."

"And women too."

"And women too. So many of the families you have sent away because of the sheep are all employed now in Glasgow and Greenock in the bleach-fields and the cotton-mills, which also train the children to do something useful. And there is all the building work in our growing ports and cities, and the fetching and carrying of our manufactures. Your acts have done nothing but good by encouraging people to move from a brutish life to an economic one."

"Damnation," the countess said. She had pricked her hand with her needle. Now she sucked her finger like a small girl in search of consolation. "This embroidery – it is hardly worth it. I have quite spoilt my Garden of Eden by dropping some blood on the Tree of Knowledge."

"Perhaps," Sir John suggested, "you have merely added another apple for the serpent to offer to Eve."

"I doubt if she would eat it," the countess said. "But what else can a woman do to pass the time of year in Sutherland?"

"You are doing valuable work in improvements. Your name will go down through the ages, dear lady –"

"As a benefactor? Is that what you are telling me?"

"A great benefactor. The uplifter of a whole people –"

"Then why do they resist? Why do they write such terrible things about me in *The Scotsman*? I am most pained."

"Do not be. I have dealt with this in my book."

"Then pray continue, Sir John."

The baronet turned the page to find the passage he was seeking.

> The partiality in favour of former times, and attachment to the place of their nativity natural to old people, together with the indolence in which they formerly indulged, misled the Highlanders in drawing comparisons between their past and present situations. But indolence was almost the only comfort they were accustomed to enjoy. There was scarcely any variety of wretchedness to which they were not compelled to submit. They often felt what it was to want food; their scanty crops were consumed by their cattle in winter and spring; and little remained for the sustenance of themselves and their families in summer. During a great part of the year they lived wholly on

milk, but sometimes they were reduced to such extremity, that they were obliged to bleed their cattle and subsist upon the blood; and even the inhabitants of the glens and valleys repaired in crowds to the shores to pick up the scanty provisions which shell-fish afforded them They were miserably clothed, and the huts in which they lived were dirty and mean beyond expression...

"I have visited their huts," the countess said. "Frankly I would not put my dogs or my pigs in them."

"How different is their situation now!" Sir John read on. "They enjoy the necessaries, comforts, and even some of the luxuries of life in abundance. Even those who live on parish charity, feel no want..."

"Enough, Sir John. Shall we walk in the garden? I need the benefit of your advice about my hedges."

Sir John Sinclair bowed slightly.

"Topiary, my lady, is a speciality."

"Is that what it is called? Hedges are quite good enough for me."

A garden in the French style had been attempted outside the castle on the slope down to the sea. Carved stone parapets and steps led down to a round fountain with flowerbeds enclosed by privet and clipped bushes. There had been efforts to trim the greenery into birds and beasts, but the winds had made the foliage moult, so that a leafy pelican was as thin as a stork and a verdant elephant was without a trunk or hind legs.

"What miracles you have wrought here, my lady," Sir John managed to exclaim. "Why, Versailles in the north!"

"Stuff and nonsense," the countess said. "Nothing grows here except foul weather. Now what do I do about those hedges?" She considered a mouldy green monkey. "Do I put them out of their misery?"

"In time, in time —" Sir John said.

"In time we are all dead," the countess said, "and we two all too soon. I am viewing the miserable species now."

"They seem a little unaccommodated."

"What does that mean, sir? Plain English, if you please."

"Out of sorts, my lady. But there is a blight in the land. It is called *Phytophthora infestans*. It has attacked the potato in Ireland and may cross the Irish Sea in time."

"But these are hedges. Does it make hedges rotten too?"

"There may be a connection," Sir John said judiciously. "In diseases there is often an affinity between one illness and another."

"But if the potatos are blighted, all my people will starve."

"No more than usual," Sir John said, "if they stay in the Highlands."

A footman came hurrying from the castle along a gravel walk which sprayed about his feet. There was something askew in him, one white stocking in a wrinkle on one knee, his wig crooked, his face purple, dust on his yellow coat.

"One simply cannot get them to wear livery," the countess complained. "They simply do not understand."

"My lady," the footman said , "there is a petition the now."

"There is always a petition," the countess said. "And always now. It can wait –"

"The minister came with it. It has come all the way from the Gorval."

"Is there no end to this botheration?" the countess wailed. "Is there no peace on this earth?"

"Instruct the minister to say his prayers," Sir John said to the footman, "until the countess is ready to receive him."

The footman opened his mouth, but he said nothing and turned on his heel and walked away, crunching the little stones of the path. His stocking had fallen about his ankle.

"You must stand firm," Sir John told the countess. "You must persevere."

"What can I do?"

"What you have been doing, that shall you do," Sir John said. He pointed to the far moorland on the hillside above the castle. "Look, the sheep have already improved the land. It is green now where previously it was black and barbarous. A firm persuasion will make the people go for their own good to the towns and the factories or to the sea. You know of the kelp. It did sell for twenty pounds a ton, and a man and his family may gain two pounds a week by gathering kelp for the manufacture of glass and soap."

"But my people do not want to be removed to the factories and the sea."

"Your people, my lady?" Sir John posed the question like an advocate. "When did your people last serve you?"

"At the time of the rebellion. Ninety years past, when we chased that wicked young Stuart Pretender out of the land."

"And since then, your people have not served you as soldiers for their tacks of land."

"With reluctance," the countess said angrily. "And with disobedience. I had to make threats when the recruiting officer could not sign enough of them in the Ninety-third, my regiment, against the French."

"And what was it you said then, my lady? Those famous words of yours."

"Oh then," the countess said. "Well, they were true words about my clansmen."

Sir John smacked his lips as if on a buttered radish, and then he quoted, "They need no longer be considered a credit to Sutherland, or an advantage over sheep or any useful animal."

"I said that?"

"You did. And you brought in the sheep."

"Poor men," the countess said. "If they did but know their own good."

"If they did, my lady," Sir John said, "they would know you for the good countess, who removed them for the good of us all."

"If there is another famine, I shall help them."

"To emigrate, my lady. Not to move them on to another patch of land like your previous tenants. You merely sent them to another miserable glen. Charity is often the enemy of industry."

"I do not know," the countess said. "I shall be dead soon and lie beside my dear departed husband. Anyway, I have to leave the castle. My son, the second duke, wants it for his wife, Lady Harriet. Can you believe it, Sir John, as if Dunrobin was not good enough" – her hand swept in a motion towards the tall white turrets with black conical hats surrounding the fortified house – "my son is employing the man who is building the Houses of Parliament like a Gothic nightmare to rebuild this place. It will look like a gingerbread palace – something out of *The Thousand and One Nights!* It is a simple Scots castle, and we have lived here for four hundred years. And it is good enough for another four hundred years –"

"Whatever the duke does," Sir John said diplomatically, "I am sure he will do well. But he will never be remembered as well as you."

"I wish I were as sure as you are," the countess said. She turned to look out to the wrinkled grey North Sea at the end of her unkempt hedges, where sheep also grazed on the salt grass on the far side of the garden wall. "We have both done so much, Sir John. But have we done so well?"

And Sir John Sinclair was dead that same year, and the countess five years later.

1

THE WARNING OF THE DOMINIE

1846

"I hit it."

"You lost your marley."

"I hit the plunker."

"You did not."

Angus hurled himself on Simon. It was always the same. Sinclair against Mackenzie, someone was cheating, someone was robbing, someone was raiding. Clan took on clan, and the devil and the stranger took the profit. The two boys grappled, held, twisted, tried to throw and dump and fall and wind each other. Then the big Hamish Jamie was behind his small brother, breaking his grip by holding his elbows and wrenching him loose. Then Simon Mackenzie swung a fist and blood was bright on the nose of Angus.

"Foul, Mackenzie."

The third of the Sinclair boys rushed in. Bain lashed out at Simon, only to have his blow taken on the arm of a second Mackenzie. Then the other Macs all came in, Mackay and Macdonald and Macleod, with only the Frasers aiding the Sinclairs, and the girls keening at the edges of the shinty without sticks. Then, louder, the voice of the dominie, shouting:

"Ha, you wee devils! Break it now! Or it is the strap. The rod will chastize –"

The boys split and turned to face the tall and stooped dominie in his black robe, bent like a hooded crow in judgement.

"And I will have them," he demanded. "I will have them all. Give me your bools."

He held out his clawed hand in a begging bowl of the flesh and the boys filed by, dropping in it their burned clay piggers and fired red marleys and the slate balls they called sclaiteys. The marbles filled the dominie's hand until he had to bring up his other palm to make a bigger pouch for receiving them. When the last boys had given up their treasures and the dominie's hands were heavy, he led the way back into the schoolroom and dropped the marbles under the open lid of his high desk.

"And here they will stay until you see the sin in the fighting over toys and baubles. Woe is he that shall harden his heart and raise his hand in the sight of the Lord."

For Angus, wiping the blood off his nose with his fingers, the squatting on the rough bench behind his scarred desk was worse than enduring the broken chairs in the converted tent where the Free Church minister preached to them from the Gaelic Bible on a Sabbath day. Angus could never abide the sitting for more than a minute, it was fidget, fidget all the time with him. He would rather be niffering and bartering his piggers and marleys, he wanted to spin his peerie and throw the beechwood top so its iron point struck the cluster of the other boys' tops and scattered them wild. He could watch the teetotum fall all the days of June, shouting its numbers and trading on the open face of the single dice. Or he would be after the birds, yelling at the crows that their mother was away and there was powder and lead to shoot them all, or he was calling at the cuckoo:

"I see the gowk, and the gowk sees me,
Between the berry bush and the apple tree."

Or there would be the counting game in the ring of boys with the teller saying words that came from a time before time, words long gone with the Picts and the Druids dead in the peat bogs What did they mean?

"Eenerty, feenerty, fickety, feg,
El, del, Domin, egg –
Irkie, birkie, storie, rock,
An, tan, toose, jock –
Black face, white trout,
Gibbie ga – you're out."

And out of the dream that was in his head, Angus heard a voice saying: "You're out, Angus Sinclair, out of your head, you have not been listening to your dominie, what was I saying now?"

Angus felt the blush on his cheeks hotter than the blood from his nose.

"You were saying –"

"And what was it?"

"The good Lord –"

"Was it not the bad laird?"

"I was meaning the bad laird."

"But the Lord is good and the laird is meant to be."

"I did not hear you true, dominie."

"Then you will hear this."

And the dominie was down the space between the benches and the desks, then the flat of his hand hit Angus's ear with such a crack that the rafters shook above and a mouse fell from the roof and stunned itself on the planks of the floor. And the girls shrieked at the little thing and stood on their desks, but Hamish Jamie bent and picked it up by the tail and swung it round and threw it through the one little window under the thatch. And everybody laughed until the dominie spoke in thunder again.

"There is the wee slicket cowering timorous beastie, and now it is gone. And so shall you be gone. For the Lord giveth and the laird taketh away. The Lord gave us this glen and the growing things upon it. He gave us the fish of the river and the sea, the black cattle and the fowls of the air. But the laird says the land is his land and he will give it over to sheep, not men. He will throw down your houses and your dwelling-places. He will burn your barns and your byres. And he will send you to cut and burn the kelp weed and to till the furrows of the sea and to pass beyond it to all the corners of the earth. As he has done to Ross and Cromarty and Sutherland, in Lewis and Skye and the Western Isles, so shall he do here. We have been cleared before and now it shall be for the last time. And this school shall be a kennel for the dogs that chase the deer and the hare, and where your roofs are, there shall be ravens under the heavens."

The dominie paused in his speech as he looked round the silent children of the glen that ran down towards the sea. He saw their faces crowned with raggety hair, some round and some pinched, all pink and red with play, and he saw their poor shirts and tousled smocks, their slate pencils and torn books, one primer between each four of them. They did not seem to be afeared, but to listen, even to accept. A dry rage burned in the dominie's throat so that he coughed. This damned obedience to laird and to established minister, this bending to the law and to things as they were and should not be at all.

"When will this be?" Bain held up his hand, but he asked the question before the dominie gave him the right to speak.

"Too soon."

"I will not let them. Not the Sinclair house."

Hamish Jamie was standing and speaking, already Highland tall, more than six feet at sixteen years of age, a down of hair on his bare legs below his kilt, dyed black over the pattern on it. For who should dare to wear the old dress since it was banned after the butchering of the clans by the guns of the House of Hanover at Culloden, except for the dwarf Queen at Balmoral with her German prince, all decked up in red stripes and green squares in fancy tartans like sweetie stands at the feeing market.

"*You* will stop the baillies, Hamish Jamie, and the constables and the keepers with their shotguns. And what will you use? Your bare hands and your bare feet? Or will you fall on your bare knees and ask them to spare you?"

"I will beat them."

"Then they will beat you, my boy. There are hard times to come."

The dominie looked at the stone fireplace, where no fire burned. Peats and whin-roots and pine knots and broom kindling were piled around the hearth, all brought by the pupils instead of fees. His gaze moved up to the rafters, which had been boarded over to make a loft. Other offerings were stored there, potatoes and oatmeal and salted fish for the winter months. But he would not see the cold weather here. Even by the summer, they would be gone.

"On your desks, laddies. Open the trap door. And take out from the loft all you find of the food there. You gave it to me, and I will not be needing it, and you will be wanting it. Take it down now."

As Hamish Jamie led the reaching and the scrambling into the roof, the dominie walked back to his high desk. Behind it on the wall hung a Blackie's world map, creased and stained. The little Angus had come to look at it. The dried scabs of blood on his nose were as black as the faded patches of the red British Empire that made an occasional quilt across the paper earth.

"Are we there?"

Angus stuck his fingernail on the map that was Scotland pointing up to the north from the weight of England below.

"Aye, we are there, Angus."

"We are awful small."

"A sparrow in the sight of God is as big as an eagle. And the Scots, well you know, Angus, they have travelled all over the world. It was a Sinclair now who first went over the seas to America a century before Christopher Columbus."

"There."

Angus drew his dark finger across the dull blue paper that reduced the Atlantic Ocean to several inches wide.

"Henry Sinclair was an earl of Scotland," the dominie said, "and a prince of Norway. He brought the Orkney and the Shetland Isles to us."

"We have our own folk there."

"And he sailed with seamen from Italy across the ocean, and he came to Canada, which he called New Scotland – Nova Scotia in the Latin."

"And do they have salmon there? And potatos?"

"The potato comes from there. And the salmon too, Angus. The fish go there to mate and make more salmon, then they come back to our rivers."

"I like fish. My brother Iain –" The face of Angus reddened, making black smudges of his freckles.

"Where is your brother now? He is not in the school today."

"Iain is gone after the fish. We have not a one –"

"He must stay at the learning."

"He is eighteen. He is a man."

"You will never make your way in a wicked world without the learning."

With the noise of grapeshot striking the barricades, potatos bombarded the desks and planking. Pellets and slugs and lumps bounced and scattered dried earth on to the boards. The harvest was hitting the floor.

"Will you not be careful then?" the dominie shouted. "Will you spoil the gifts of God? Get on down and take care."

Bain had come up to the dominie's desk to join his brother Angus. Both of them were now peering over the rim to contemplate the marbles trapped among the stubs of chalk and the pens and the primers. Neither boy dared to ask, but they looked up at the dominie with wide eyes. This was no day like other days. There might be a mercy in the master.

"I should not," the dominie said. "What is the matter with me? I must be daft." He scooped out a few clay marbles and put them in Bain's hand. "You can have your bools. And there will be no school more today. Get you back to your homes and to the wool cleaning. You will need to be ready for the coming of the laird's men, when they do. Get away with you."

2

TO CATCH A FISH

Iain lay on the flat rock, his left hand trailing in the narrows of the river. The water broke his arm at the wrist. Below the bent bone, his four fingers and thumb moved as thick pink weeds, waiting. The brown speckle-backed oval moved on transparent fins over the stones and stayed short of the waving lure. The mouth of the fish seemed to suck at the tips of the flesh, then it moved over the palm of Iain's hand. His skin tickled the cold scales of the trout's belly, then his forefinger and thumb jerked up into open gills and flipped the fish high in air. It arched and sparked silver and fell against Iain's free hand, which knocked it sideways up the bank, where it humped and flapped.

"Guddled you," Iain said with satisfaction.

There had been three trout guddled that morning, but Iain was set on bigger game. In the shallows of the dark pool upriver he had seen a shadow move above the stones as large as his forearm. There was a chance, a small chance, if he could chase the big fish into a tuck of the bank, he could break its head with a rock. Iain picked up the last trout, now still but gasping, and forced through its gill and mouth a dry rush that plaited it to the two other fish that he had caught that morning. And whistling "Will you no come back again" out of tune, the young giant walked up the glen towards the dark pool. Stepping over the mosses on the roots of hazel and pine, Iain strode against the current that splashed and brawled down the vast cleft in the mountains. Through the trees, the heather was already painting the slopes of the hills in streaks of blood, while lichen scored the flanks of the black crags that trimmed the blue sky. Ahead, a belt of birches drooped their green feathery wings near Iain's hunting place, where the salmon was resting on its bed of stones.

Iain dropped his ring of trout in the crotch of a broken tree. Then he bent and worked out of the ground a boulder half the size of his head. Carrying it in both hands, he trod on wildcat's feet towards the water's edge. For a man so large, he walked as delicately as Agag of the scriptures. The sun between the branches streaked his ruddy face, for he was careful to front the light so that his shadow was cast behind him, not upon the shine of the ripples. And his slow approach had its reward. For he could see the long charcoal shape of his prey set in the sombre-bright waters against the granite stones on the bed of the corner of the pool, the big fish at ease.

For a while, the young man watched the salmon. He moved no more than a tree stump moves. Yet each half minute, he would take one step closer to the bank, his heart in his mouth that the fish might take fright and glance aside. But the sun seemed to shower its gold upon his luck, for the salmon also swung to face the sun, so that the split rudder of its black tail was nearmost. Now Iain could take the last two paces and bend under the weight of the boulder as if bowing to a good fate.

"God speed you," he breathed and heaved the lump between his hands, up and away.

The stone flew in a lazy arch in the air and fell into the water in a spout. For a moment, Iain knew that he had missed his quarry, but then the thrash of blazing foam glittered off a stricken leaping thing, and he was plunging into the pool and slipping on the wet rocks and falling with one hand out and another bunched in a fist to knock the flying salmon further up the shallow into the bank. Iain gashed his knee and bloodied the water, but he lunged and scrabbled after the salmon, which was flailing in a flurry of spume, broken at the neck. The man clasped the fish in his arms that were thicker than the stakes that held up the nets in the waters, but the fish's head struck the man's chin in its death throe, then bucked in a last desperation onto the mosses by the pool. Crying and laughing with pain and exultation, Iain threw himself on the earth by the great fish and opened his arms and lay on his back in his glory in the light of the sun.

A black metal pipe was pointing down between his eyes. At the top of the barrel of the fowling-piece, there was the spotted face, all whinberry and oatmeal, of Donald Mackay, the chief servant of the laird, the keeper of the glen and all that swam and ran and flew in it.

"And where will you be taking that fish, Iain Sinclair?"

The young man sat up and pressed his hot forehead against the chill kiss of the muzzle of the gun.

"I took the fish, Mackay, and it is to take now where I please."

"It is the laird's fish."

"He did no take it. I did."

"It is still the laird's fish."

"And did the laird make the fish?"

"He did not make the fish. But you know it is his fish."

"I know he did no make it, and I will take it."

"You will not."

Mackay kicked the body of the salmon with his boot. It jerked again at the shock and slithered six feet along the bank into the ferns.

"That is my fish," Iain said.

Mackay raised the barrel of his gun to point at the innocent sky and shook his head.

"You are a daft laddie," he said. "You are big and bonny, that is a fact —"

Iain now rose to his height. He dwarfed the bulky figure of Donald Mackay as a heron over a cormorant.

"But you do not ken the world, Iain. If the laird put you in the sessions, you would be sent for seven years to Australia where the men and the boys go for the catching of the game."

"And you will tell him, Donald Mackay."

"I will and I will not."

"You speak like a Mackay. I will and I will not."

"I will tell him, for I have taken the oath to him and to his own which are my own. But I will not tell him until after you are gone from the glen."

"That will never be."

"It will be very soon."

"That will no be."

"Iain, Iain —" The keeper Mackay put down his gun on its wooden stock and thrust his blotched face up at the young man's. "Will you not listen? As your own mother and your father came to this glen after the coming of the sheep to the Highlands and the Isles, this is but a waiting place for them and for you. Now after the sheep, they want the moor and the forest for the deer. Not a village now, but a park for the stags. And down by the sea, they want the folk to toil at the kelp weed and hunt the silver herrings. There is no dwelling for the men now, but for the beasties. Not one at all."

"I will fight against it."

"You cannot fight your laird. You must fight for your laird."

"I will," Iain said, "if he asks me. And if he grants me the land and the river which is mine."

"He cannot ask you now. It is the English and the colours of their regiments that do the asking. It is not the chiefs and the clans that ask any more. It is for the foreigners and for the foreign wars that we are fighting. But you ken I fought the good fight at Waterloo."

"Aye," Iain said. "I ken that."

"They came at us all day, and we could not charge. First we were near a farmhouse among the trees. And they came and we fought, and they came on and we fought, and with bullet and with bayonet and with claymore and with dirk we fought them away. And there were dead men on that field, Frenchmen and our men, lying in their blood with their arms round the one the other, and their steel still stuck in the one the other. And there was a keening of the wounded as the sea wind keens in the roof. And there was a blanket of the bodies as the broom on the moor. And since that day I have never lifted hand to man, and I will never murder my fellow creatures again."

"But you are the keeper here, Donald Mackay. You will kill the beasties and the fish."

"Aye, but these are the living creatures God gave us for our eating and our stay."

Iain laughed. "Then we shall eat the fish. The laird has muckle enough to eat."

"You shall keep the fish, Iain. But it is the last fish you shall keep. It is not for you or your folk. It is the fish of the laird of the glen."

Iain walked across to where the body of the salmon lay among the ferns. He picked up its slippery length that had begun to ooze slime between its scales.

"It is the fish of the Good Lord of the glen," he said. "It is so."

"Get away with you," Mackay said. "And do not you be catched on the way home. You hide that fish, do you hear me?"

"I will stuff it down my shirt," Iain said. "And all will think I am having a wee bairn soon."

Mackay laughed.

"You are a fine big laddie," he said. "If Boney had seen you at Waterloo, he would have run for his life."

"You are a tolerable fine man too, Donald Mackay. Like that Nelson, you can turn a blind eye the now."

Iain dropped the great fish in the pouch of his open shirt. Its cold weight lay on his belly above the waist band of his drenched kilt.

"What shall we call it now?" he asked. "Mary – or Donald after his father?"

"Get away," Mackay said, and Iain went laughing down the glen with his salmon in his shirt and his ring of trout in his hand.

3

THE BRIGHT BUSHES

The bushes by the burn were bright with blankets and kilts and cloaks and coverings. The pine knots and the peats burning beneath the great three-legged iron cauldron filled the air with their acrid sweet incense, and the butterflies seemed like scraps of garments as they wafted from heather to broom to bracken The soaking tubs still full of the woollen stuffs stood on their rollers, trundled from the cottages for the annual cleansing. Young women with kirtles up to their thighs were stamping on the blankets in the tubs, their eyes fearful and wanting the spying gaze of the hidden men. Mary Sinclair was waiting with a basin of hot soapy water for any peeping Thomas, and she had doused two in the morning already. Her small sisters, fair Rachel and red-haired Katie, were giggling and singing along with the women at work at the washing of the clothes.

> "They that wash on Monday
> Have all the week to dry –
> They that wash on Tuesday
> Are not far by –
> They that wash on Wednesday
> Are not so mean –"

Mary saw her large brother coming from the river along the burn. The wet bulge in the front of his shirt made him waddle with his bare feet splayed out to take the forward weight. His kilt was a hitched skirt, but red bloodied knees and legs like birch trees would never do for a woman with child. All the same, Mary ran towards him with her basin of suds, followed by the screaming Katie and Rachel.

> "Get away, peeper,
> Fly away, spy,
> Or you'll get a dousing,
> Never go dry."

And all the while, the young women at their treading of the sodden wool in the tubs were singing:

> "They that wash on Thursday
> May get clothes clean –
> They that wash on Friday
> They have muckle need –"

Now the big Sarah Macdonald saw Iain coming, *ach* and she had always had her eye on him, he was certain and big enough for her, there was no gainsaying it. And she pointed and screeched and hoisted her kirtle higher to show the tops of her legs, whiter than snowbanks.

> "They that wash on Saturday
> Are dirty dogs indeed!"

Iain had stopped short in his tracks, faced with the shouting and the laughing of the young women and with the clothes and the blankets spread in a woollen harvest on the bushes. He turned as if to run, but Mary was upon him, throwing the soapy water up and over his red hair and the yoke of his shoulders. Rachel and Katie scampered to grab one of his knees, the gashed or the whole one. The young women sang fit to deafen a raven:

> "They that wash on Sunday
> Are the devil's breed!"

Iain wiped the soap from his eyes with his free hand. Then he pulled off Katie and dropped the ring of plaited trout round her neck over the flame of her hair. The little girl cried in delight and horror at her sudden necklace of fish. Then Iain reached inside his shirt and plucked out the salmon and mockingly cradled it like a baby in his arms.

> "Chin, cherry,
> Mouth, merry –"

As he sang, he chucked the fish under its jaws and prodded its head with his forefinger. Rachel joined in the game, pretending the salmon was a baby.

> "Nose, nappy,
> Cheeks, happy –"

Now the laughing Mary joined in, taking the cradled fish from Iain's arms and rocking it in hers. It might be her own little one swaddled in silver scales.

> "Eye, winkie,
>   Brow, brinkie,
>   Over the hill and far away."

Mary tossed the salmon to Sarah, who had come up from her stamping tub and was standing over from Iain, laughing in his face. She caught the fish and cradled it, then she stared at him, bold as a brass knocker.

"And is this the only bairn you are able to come with, Iain Sinclair?"

A beacon fire was brighter than the flush in Iain's face that fair dimmed the embers of his own hair. He mumbled and growled, but not a word came from him.

"The poor thing," Sarah said, dandling the slimy slithering creature. "And you with a father that dare not own to you."

Mary laughed with all the young women as Iain turned and plunged away through the bushes. His kilt snagged in thorns and was ripped open. The shrieking was so loud behind his back that it sounded in pursuit, not in glee. He gathered his kilt clumsily around his loins and ran on, mindless of the stones that were bruising his feet. He left the young women mad in their merriment at the great Iain Sinclair come to grief at the cleansing of the wool.

"Come back, come back, Iain," they cried. "We need you the now. For the wringing out."

"I will wring him out," Sarah called.

"To find your ring on him," Mary said to her.

"Ach, I never did think –"

"You think of nothing but how you will get wed to our Iain –"

"I never did –" Sarah's face was now the fiery furnace that Iain's had been. "He's no a pin to me."

"Good on you," Mary said. "As if you did not spend all your day eyeing him like a hen at the grain."

"If you do no hush you –"

Sarah had raised her right hand from cradling the salmon, but the slighter Mary blew her a kiss.

"I did no mean it, Sarah. It is only that everybody says it. But I – no I –"

"You did say it the now," Sarah said.

"Only to say, who might believe it? Our Iain and you – daft. Give me our fish."

Mary snatched the salmon from the crook of Sarah's arm, and she ran with it along the burn. Katie and Rachel went scampering after her. They left Sarah behind them, her legs planted astride, silent and angry. "You will have a bite of our Iain's salmon," Mary shouted to the treaders in the tubs. "And I will bring him back for the wringing. He has more force in him than ten of the other men." And Mary and her sisters ran away towards their home, where Iain had gone before them.

Their mother Hannah was finishing the sweeping. Cleanliness was next to godliness, all the ministers said that. But what use was it, when there were nine of them living in the cottage with its two boardings to separate the bed of the boys from the bed of the girls, and the other section beyond the planks to keep the black cows apart in the byre. The blankets, they were only cleansed once a year, and the fleas and the ticks, they hopped off the cows and the thatch, and there was scratching and itching in the winters, how could you keep a house clean now, with the bairns and the beasties under the same roof, and the fireplace in the middle of the room, so when the wind blew sorely down and the flakes from the peats were driven free, there was a black snow inside powdering away before you could catch it? God – Hannah thought – God Himself could not be so pearly-white and scoured if He lived like He made His creatures live in the glen.

The ache at her back straightened her against the handle of her birch-twig broom, and she saw Iain coming from the burn towards the house that stood topmost of them all in the clachan. Her heart swelled to see him, so big now and so small when she bore him, her Iain, her own, her first son but for Robert, and he was laid to rest before he was weaned, why did she think of the lost one before the living? She threw out her arms and smiled to see her Iain, but instead she saw the blood in a black scab on his knee, and she heard herself scolding him against her thought.

"Come here the now and let me look at that. There is hot water in the pot."

"It is no anything at all, mother."

"That is what you say, and then there will be the poison in it, and they will take the leg off you."

Hannah pushed her son before her into the main room and sat him on the wide pine chair, where her husband Hamish sat when he was home from the field. She dipped an iron ladle in the black pot that was set over the fire, and she took out the hot water and lifted her petticoat and put its hem in the steam and knelt on the earth floor and wiped the hot linen against the hard gash on his knee. It took her a small scrubbing to soften and loosen the scab until she could staunch the red blood by the tear in his skin against the bone.

"Ach now, mother –"

"Hush you. Did you catch a fish?"

"Four. And one great one."

"Where are they now?"

"The lassies have them."

"And what were you doing with the lassies?"

"What were they not doing with me?"

Hannah laughed with her son and stood up, leaving him to hold his finger against the wound on his knee. Then suddenly her eyes stung with the peat smoke or a tear. "Ach, you foolish boy –" She shook her head and walked away. "Were you not seen?"

"Donald Mackay saw me. But he will no tell."

"Will he not?"

"He will not. But he did say, they will be clearing our folk from the glen."

"I have heard tell that. They cannot. Already they have cleared us. Twenty-five years past, before you were born. You know the story, Iain. The countess in the castle, she was telling them to do it. God rest her soul, perhaps she was not knowing what they were doing, but they were doing it for her. We came to this glen, all the folk of the hills, the Sinclairs as your father is, and the Frasers as I am, and the Maclarens and the Macleods, the Mackays and Macdonalds and Mackenzies, and before we did not know the one the other. And they are good folk, now all the fighting is forgotten. We break bread now, and not heads. No more of that foolishness, Iain. But when we were coming to the glen, they said we will not be moving again. And what the now?"

"To send us to the sea and over the sea."

"They will not do that."

"I said that to Donald Mackay."

"They will not do that."

Now Mary was running through the doorway with the salmon in her arms, and then Katie with her necklace of three trout on a rush plait, and then Rachel, crying, "And look what we have." They praised and teased Iain, the mighty hunter. Mary found the sharp knife and took the fish outside. She slit their bellies and scraped out the guts and then ran the blade the wrong way against the lie of the scales until she had scattered around her a silver chaff. And when the fish were ready, she carried them down to the burn and washed them in the water and took them back up to the house. And so she saw her other brothers, Angus and Bain and Hamish Jamie, as they came home from the school.

Hamish also saw his three sons as they passed the field on their way home, carrying in the pouches of their kilts the potatos taken from the rafts of the school. He himself had a small potato in his hand. It was hard and well, firmer than a boiled gull's egg. This should be a good year for that. He had hated the moving from the old hills to the lots in the glen, but there was a blessing in it. The getting of the barley and the oats and the rye was never a certain thing. Sometimes Hannah had stood in the yoke beside the cuddy all the day long, the woman beside braying beast. She had also pulled the ploughshare that he held to drive the furrow. But the new moorland given on lease and by lot was good for the potato, and there was no tacksman now to take the harvest and the rent on its way to the laird above. All was straight now, man to laird with never a middle man. And the potato was a fit brother to the porridge and the brose, the other staff of life.

"Is there no school then?" Hamish called.

"No school at all," Bain called back.

"And what is in your kilts?"

"Potatos."

"We have enough and more."

"Dominie gave them."

That was fair enough, Hamish thought. If he gave potatos to the dominie for the learning of the boys, the dominie might give them back.

"Give them to mother," he called.

"Aye."

As the boys went up the hill to their wood and turf croft with its thatched roof, its hump the first of all that ran down the glen to the factor's house and established church and the blacksmith's and the tent beyond where the Free Church now was, Hamish scratched the side of the potato in his hand with his nail. A white streak appeared under the earthy skin. Water ran in the gouge. It must be wrong, the rumour from the Western Isles. The potatos reeking like dung from the cattle beneath the field. You could never hold by the word of a man from the Isles. They were after telling stories there.

There was never a thing more for a man to do today. The two black cows were in the pasture, the turnips and the potatos were in the ground nurtured by God's will, and in the kail-yard by the house, the gooseberries and the redcurrants were swelling in the sun. What did they say when they moved the men from the mountains to the glen?

You Highlanders, you are born idle, you live on the black cattle, you will never lift a hand except to the whisky or the sword. And look now, we have turned our hands to the roots and the neeps, we have taken the moorland in fee and made it give us our new life. So Hamish made his way to this house in the noon of that warm and soft day.

The potatos from the school were already boiling in the pot when Hamish came home And the fish only needed to be steeped in the salt and steaming water to complete the meal. Mary tried to save some of the salmon for her friends at the cleansing tubs, but there was little left once the men had had their fill, big fish though it might be. There was good reason for Hannah to say grace before the unexpected feast, but Iain was graceless after the meal, for nothing Mary could plead would make him go back among the young women for the wringing. Sarah Macdonald would still be there, and she put more fear than God did in him.

So Mary took back Hamish Jamie for twisting the blankets into thick ropes to squeeze the water out of them. He was strong enough to do the work and just young enough for the women to spare his blushes. But there were too few young men in the clachan now, they were already leaving for the sea and the regiments, there were too many single women left, and they had to be bold if they were looking for a husband. "It was not like this in our time," Hamish said. "I asked for Hannah's hand, not she for mine."

4

THE CLEARING OF
THE GLEN

They came first and early in the morning to the Sinclair house, as it was the topmost in the clachan of all the houses. There was the factor Hector Smith, who had come from England and knew its harsh laws and its ways. He was too red of face from the richness of his blood, but bleak eyes as dull as slate showed no life in the man. With him was a sheriff-officer and four constables, who were fondling their ash-sticks as if they were nervous about the business in hand. Angus saw them coming over the hill, and he shouted to Hannah, "Mother, mother, the men are coming."

Hannah left the pot where the hot water was boiling to make the porridge and the brose for her men and her daughters before they left for their work or their learning. She had to duck under the low door lintel and blink as the sun seared her eyes, and only then did she see the six strangers coming up to her home. She stood, legs apart, fists on her hips, confronting them. She spoke in Gaelic, the tongue of her people.

"And what would you be doing fretting honest folk before they have broken their fast?"

Hector Smith thrust a piece of paper into her hand, although he knew that she could not read it.

"Here, woman," he said in English, his native tongue.

Hannah looked at the paper.

"Angus," she said, "go on in and bring me a burning peat on the spade, and mind you do not burn yourself."

As the boy ran into the house, Hannah stepped forward and rammed the paper into the game pocket of the factor's shooting jacket.

"There's your scrap of paper," she said. "Keep it in your own black pocket."

"You have taken the summons," the factor said. "It is against the law to return it."

He took the paper out and thrust it at Hannah again. But this time she stepped back.

"Why do you not speak," she said, "in words that God-fearing folk ken here?"

"Tell her in her bloody gibberish," the factor said, turning to one of the uneasy constables.

As the constable was explaining to Hannah the meaning of the paper, a summons to evict the Sinclairs from their house because of the termination of their lease, Angus came outside, carrying a spade before him, clasped in both of his small hands. On its iron tongue, a peat was smouldering.

"Will you take the summons now," the factor demanded and pushed the paper at Hannah.

"I will," she said. "Give it me." And she took the spade from her son's hands, and she thrust it out to take the offered summons upon the glowing peat. And slowly the paper began to crinkle and to curdle and to blacken, as the factor would not withdraw it. Then it broke into a little flame that ran along its edge and licked at the factor's fingers.

"Damn you," he cried and stuck his fingertips into his mouth to suck.

Hannah and Angus laughed. Out of the door of the house came the stooping Hamish and Iain and Hamish Jamie, all roused from their sleep. They lined up in their bulk behind Hannah, and they looked down on the constables with their ash truncheons.

"Tell them they have one quarter of an hour," the factor said, "fifteen minutes, to take their goods and their cattle from that black house before it is utterly destroyed. Tell them. And if they resist, there are dragoons waiting in Fort Augustus that will enforce the law. Tell them."

So the constable that spoke in Gaelic told Hannah and her men of the law and the force of the law. The leases had terminated on all of the glen. Some of the land had already been leased to a single southern farmer who would graze his Great Cheviot sheep on the braes, while much of the moor would make a larger deer park for the laird. There was no good in rebelling any more than there had been any good in rebelling from the clearances twenty-five years before by the countess, which had left the survivors of several different clans on their forced march to their present home. The place they had found was still not their own land, and they must leave as they could, where they would. That was the new law of Scotland.

"And for why will we go?" Hannah said.

"And to where will we go again?" Hamish said.

The constable translated to the factor, who only shook his head.

"Fourteen minutes," he said, taking a silver turnip watch from his pocket. "Fourteen minutes, and then we burn this house."

As Hamish Jamie started forward, his father caught him by the elbows and stayed his arms. "No, son," he said, "it is not the way." Then Iain moved past his mother, his fists knotted like twin boles of the Scots fir, but his mother seized him by the wrist. "Heed your father, Iain. It is not the way."

"And will you do the fighting for us, mother?"

"Aye, they will not strike an old woman."

"They will and all."

"Twelve minutes," the factor said. "Will we have roast beef from your cattle for our dinner?"

"Clear the house," Hamish ordered. "Bear everything outside."

"Will we not fight, father?"

"I have done with fighting," Hamish said. "I fought for the countess to keep my tack of land, and I fought against the countess when she had it taken from me. But for this new laird, I will not fight again."

"But it is our house."

"Where we are is our house," Hamish said.

"We made our house here."

"Then we will take it with us on our backs like the snail. To where there is no laird. And we will make a house there where the land is our land, and no laird will say again, 'Do this, do that, this is mine, it is not yours'."

"I cannot," Iain said. "I cannot."

"Listen to your father," Hannah said. "He has seen good men die, and good men sent to the prison ships to Australia, all for the raising of a hand against the factor and the sheriff and the constables."

"Ten minutes," the factor said.

"Clear the house I say," Hamish said and led his sons back beneath the low door, stooping in a kind of obedience.

There was little to carry outside, for it was little they had. The iron pot and the hearthstone, the spades and the pans, the spinning-wheel and the spindle, the blankets that were cleaned on the yesterday and the boards that made up the three beds, the one for Hamish and Hannah and the one for the boys and the one for the girls, the knives and the forks and the spoons and the plates, the best shirts and the cloths and the bonnets and three pairs of shoes, the seed potatos and the sack of oatmeal. The two black cows were driven from the byre, but the ten minutes were already gone and the constables were lighting the torches, yet the deal planking was still on the partitions and the bog pine battens in the roof supporting the thatch between the birch timbers.

"Hold your hand," Hannah said. "Give us the time to take our house with us as we must go."

The constable paused, who already had his burning pitch brand in his grip. But Hector Smith said, "Proceed. We have all the village to clear. Get on with you."

"No."

Iain barred the way with outstretched arms, while Hannah began pushing the smaller boys and girls on to the thatch. "Break out the battens," she cried. "Break them out. And we will have a new house in the morning." And Hamish and Mary and Hamish Jamie began tearing the deal partitions open and throwing the planks out on to the earth.

The constable with the fiery torch stepped forward. Iain grasped the arm that held the burning brand with both of his hands. He wrenched it and wrung it as he had failed to do with the wet blankets, and the constable screamed and dropped his incendiary on the ground.

"I am hoping that I did not hurt you," Iain said.

Now the factor and the sheriff came on Iain, also the constables with their raised truncheons. But he still stood at the door of the house.

"Will you burn women? Will you put the bairns in the roof to the fire? Are you not Scotsmen?"

"You make it sore hard, man," a constable said.

"Are you not a man yourself?"

None would attack Iain at the door of his house, but only Hector Smith. He came at Iain with the riding crop that was hanging from its loop on his right wrist. He cut Iain across the nose, raising a welt of blood. Never strike a Sinclair on the face. Whether it is the shock of the unexpected, whether it is the threat of blinding the eyes, whether it is the trace of the Norse berserker in the veins, a Sinclair struck on the face is a mad bull. Iain hit and butted and kicked, he charged and hooked and lunged, and the red rage was filling his sight as he tried to break the head of Hector Smith against a rock, before the constables beat him senseless with twenty blows raining on his head from their truncheons.

In woe and anguish, Hamish stopped Hannah and Hamish Jamie from running to Iain's help until he lay still on his bloodied back. "Wait," he said. "It may be that we shall escape the gaol. He was struck the first." Then Hannah and her second son ran out to cover the body of Iain with their bodies, to stop the blows. And Hamish picked up the fallen whip of Hector Smith and broke it in two parts and tossed it aside, then he picked up Hector Smith himself and brought him to his feet and slapped his face to waken him and said, "If you ever whip my son again, Master Smith, I will surely break your neck and every bone in your poor body."

And Hector Smith was silent and shook his head and said, "Now let me go, man."

So Hamish let him go, and Hector Smith wobbled on his feet like a new-born lamb, and then he took hold of himself and told his constables, "Burn the house."

So they picked up their brands and set them on fire and put them against the thatch, where it drooped over the turf walls. And the flames ran along the reed and the straw, for it had been a dry June. And Hannah rose from the body of her eldest son and went into the house and plucked down the children from the roof, Angus and Bain and Rachel and Katie, where they had been taking down the battens and throwing them on the floor.

"We must away now," she said, "we must away. Or they will be roasting us for our own dinner."

So they gathered up the battens they had already scattered on the earth and made their way through the smoke and under the low door. And they all stood and watched outside the flames moving up the bristles of the dark thatch as shafts of sunlight move up the bracken through a shifting cloud, and the fires met at the crest of the roof and threw up a pillar of smoke. Then the cows began to groan pitifully, while the sparks and the ashes were flying in the air, until the floating embers came down on to the deal planking and scorched the wood.

Iain was on his feet now, supported by Hamish Jamie, the mark of the whip across his face a fair testament of the reason for his rage. Hector Smith kept well shy of him, he would not go near. And Hamish said, "We will take away what is ours, or it will be consumed in the fire." So he and Hannah and the seven children bore away the few battens and the planks and the household things and the farm tools and the two black cows, and they went down the hill towards the other houses of the clachan. But the factor and the sheriff-officer and the four constables had gone before them, and Hector Smith was already giving his foul pieces of paper to the other families of the glen, and the torches were lit to set fire to the whole of the community.

As in their house, so with the other houses. The men raged and did nothing, the women shrieked and wept, the children wailed or stood in fear, then all hands went to the clearing of the goods and chattels before all was set in a blaze. The dominie came to protest and denounce, but his voice was a piping in the wind. Mewing like a cat with froth upon his lips, daft Ron Mackenzie ran at the sheriff-officer, who caught him with a rope, for Ron was touched in the head, and if that was what the rebellion was, it was sore proof that rebellion was madness. And so the people of the glen found themselves leaving their burning homes to gather in the tent that was their Free Church, to listen to their dominie and preacher tell of God's will and why He permitted the razing of the glen.

"Woe unto them that join house to house – so spake the Prophet Isaiah – that lay field to field, till there be no place; that they may be placed alone in the midst of the earth. Woe until the laird that makes of the houses of his people a waste for the sheep and a wood for the deer, so that he shall dwell in his mansion in the wilderness with strangers for his shooting companions and beasts for his sustenance. It is not your wickedness, my people, that has turned the face of the Good Lord against you. It is the wickedness of the Lords of Sutherland and the Macdonald Lords who have turned their face against the Lord God. They believe that they are the lords of His Creation. Shall they make the land of God in their image? Shall they decree that where God put His Adam and His Eve and the generations of their children to till the good earth, they shall put the beasts of the field to chew the cud and the beasts of the forest to roam and devour? Unnatural – wicked and unnatural. Just as they would not build us a church here, for well they knew that there would be a tearing down before there was a building up, as the Tower of Babel itself was torn down, so they will defy the will of the Lord and make a brae of our gardens and a ruin of our hearth and our homes."

The dominie looked down from his rough platform at the sixty people and a hundred children crowded under the low tarpaulin tent. His mouth was bitter at the injustice of a few men to their fellow creatures. By what right? There was no right any more upon earth, but he had to preach the righteousness of heaven. For there was might indeed in Scotland now, and if might was never right, there was a sore confusion in the person of the laird. He had to speak obedience and gag on the words.

"If the ways of the world are wicked, the Lord God has said so, and His Prophets have said so. But we must not do so. We must turn our eyes to the Lord and praise Him – not for this new trial and tribulation which He in His infinite wisdom has chosen for our affliction – but we must ask Him to change the hearts of the dukes and the countesses and the lords who oppress Scotland so sorely, after they have had their sonsy titles from south of the border, and after they have needed muckle rents from us to pay for their abominations in London town. And if the Lord will not change their hearts, we must go from here, where no proud laird shall harden his heart against the people, where the land is free and the birds and the beasts upon it, so that man can enjoy the fruits of the earth and the fishes of the sea without the bidding of a master. And we will heed always the word of the Good Lord, when He saith Yea and when He saith Nay, blessed be the name of the Lord."

A voice seemed to be torn from the throat of Hannah in the congregations. "And where is God the now? How will He help us?"

The dominie had no answer. But the need of the people made his thin body quiver like a flung knife.

"We shall take up this tent which is His tent. Let us follow Him, for He shall show us the way."

The dominie's words were not too soon. Already the torches were burning through the guy-ropes of the tent, as the people came out to see the destruction. Such was their fury that the constable backed away and allowed the people to undo the ropes and lay down the tent on the ground and stamp the wind out of it and roll it in a bundle and place it to drag behind a cart to pull it away behind a black ox and a cuddy yoked together in front. And behind them walked a procession of the homeless and the wanderers, the men wrapped in their plaids and wearing their bonnets and carrying their infants or their spades in their hands, the women with their scarlet shawls leading their children and driving the few cattle behind the carts, where their smallest ones rode on the household stuff piled above the planks and the battens for the homes they were to make again. But on that sad trail and trial of the people of the glen, hardly a one thought that they would find a home once more, but they would ever be on the rough road to nowhere at all, on foot without end.

The dominie knew where to take them. Five miles on over the hill, there was a ruined church with its gravestones still standing around it. Even the forces of the law would not dare desecrate the lodgings of the dead. They were in the last sanctuary, beyond the writ of law, truly at the mercy of God.

They set up their tarpaulin tent on poles among the stone arks and the marble slabs and the crosses and the urns that marked the names of those who had gone before. Here was AMY ROSS – *Rest in Peace*, there KIRSTY MACLEOD – aged two years, *Abide in God,* and there DUNCAN MACKENZIE – *God Is My Shepherd.* The sides of the shelter were protected with horsecloths and rugs and plaids, while blankets made up the compartments for each family in its sleeping. Outside, the cattle and the cuddies cropped the nettles and the long grasses between the headstones. Fires of peats cooked the porridge and boiled the few potatos that remained. The people of the glen were safe for that night, but for that one night.

In the morning, the man from *The Scotsman* came in his frockcoat and his billycock hat. He was a writer for the journals and the newspapers as all of his trade were, ready to write of the troubles of others as long as he did not fuss himself except for the words. "My articles," he told them, "will make your terrible treatment and your foul wrongs known in all the corners of the earth."

"But will they give us back our home?" Hannah asked.

"I cannot answer for that," the writer said and wrote in his notebook things that might be praise or blame or pity or untruth. Who was to know? But for the true recording, Mary borrowed the little diamond ring that the mother of the mother of Hamish had given to Hannah on her wedding, and Mary scratched on the glass of the one standing window in a church, *Glen is a wilderness – Blow ship to the colony – Mary Sinclair.* It was the only memorial of their passing.

For they could not abide in the churchyard. They had nothing to eat, they could not eat the seed. If they were to kill a cow, they could not have the milk of it. The folk of the near clachans were fee-holders of the laird, and they were sore afraid to help the wanderers, for they might lose their homes and be made to wander as well at the laird's will. People were divided from people in their fear. Then a dark and smiling man came to them. He was saying there was land on a loch by the sea, and welcome to it. They could graze their black cattle and raise their potatos and their oats. There were herrings by the millions for the catching, there were mussels and limpets for the taking from the rocks if all else failed. There was always the harvest of the sea. And there was the working at the kelp weed, when a man and his family might take in thirty shillings a week in the season. For those who were laborious, it was a good life, even if the land had a thin soil, it being by the sea.

"We will take it," the dominie said, "for we have nowhere to go except to the colonies beyond the sea. And we have no money for that. And who knows if it is not a worse wilderness there, and men with harder hearts."

5

THE HARVEST OF
THE WEED

The black knobbles of the weed were better cut below the sea water. The dried bladders of kelp thrown up by the tides on the rocks did not have the sap in them that was needed for the burning out of the extract in the kilns, to be sent down south for the making of the glass and the soap. The brine stung the grazes on Hamish Jamie's legs as he stood waist-deep in a cleft in the cliffs, hacking at the tough plants and dragging the slimy tendrils out of the swell and throwing them up to Angus and Bain on the rocks to spread for drying in the wind and the sun. Hannah was also wading in the sea on a shelving inlet, cutting the kelp with a sickle and lobbing the indigo strands back to Katie and Rachel on the shore. This was the promise, the harvest from the fields of the sea. But it was wet work that tore the hands and bent the back and wounded the legs. It was not work fit for a farming family of the glen.

Mary had the cuddy by the dried patches of kelp. She was packing the creels on either side of the donkey's back with the crop of the sea, so that she could lead the animal up the path of stones and slippery shale to the kilns at the top, where Hamish and Iain were labouring at the burning of this tillage from the deep. There had been no place for them in the black boats, for there were too many displaced men on them, learning the craft, while the catches of herrings were less each year. Even the riches of the boundless ocean would not stretch to the needs of the new folk now come to furrow it. There were places at the kelping and the lime-burning, but at poor wages, where all the family must labour to earn less than a living, but enough for broth and potatos. But then, the potatos – it was not a lie that the Islanders had told. The new crop was diseased and smelled of corpses in the ground. The very earth was sick, as if the rottenness of the ways of men above it had infected the roots below.

In the circular holes of the kilns, Iain put the dried kelp on top of the smouldering peat. With his clatt, he spread the weed evenly over the heat of the dried bog earth, using his long iron poker to stir the seaweed and render it into a tarry mass. The smoke and fumes made him cough and wheeze as if his lungs were old bellows. Soot coated his red face in a highwayman's mask. His bare feet were singed and corroded by flying embers. To his father Hamish, the young man seemed like an ogre in the legends, one of the miners of the underground who smelted metal for the gods of the north. But in the kilns they were smelting an alkaline residue, which cooled into thick crusts of brittle blue. Powdered and mixed in the southern factories, this dust became invisible in window panes or washtub suds – the evanescent gift of the sea.

The hot reek of the kilns tasted more sour than disgust in Hamish's mouth. He tapped his son on the shoulder and nodded towards the low door.

"This is no work for a man, Iain. We'll away."

"Wait."

Iain raked the glue and knit of the surface of the weed with his clatt, then turned to follow his father out of the kiln shed. They stood at the door, looking to the path up from the beach, along which Mary was leading her donkey, loaded with the creels of dried kelp.

"Muckle more," Hamish said.

"For aye," Iain said. "Muckle more work, muckle less pay for it."

"That's the truth, lad. Give Mary a hand the now."

Iain took down the creels from the cuddy's back and emptied the kelp into piles by the kiln door.

"Da," Mary said. "Da, they say the ox is in the pound. There was black cattle straying from the top of the cliffs to Mackenzie's field, and his man has catched them all. And they will no give back our ox until the paying of a fine. Four shilling."

"Four shilling." Hamish gave a dry snort that might be a laugh. "We barely earn four shilling from Gavin Macdonald for four days at the kelping. And if an ox recks there is greener grass than the muck of the common land, how shall the poor beastie know more?"

"Mackenzie says our ox shall no be in his field."

"And tell me, if Mr Mighty Mackenzie cannot build a wee fence to keep out my ox, then how the devil –"

"Don't you, Da –"

"Sorry I am, Mary, but how does Mr Mackenzie expect my ox to stay out of his open field?"

"It's in his pound the now with a great fence about it, and no a thing to eat. Da, you must get it back."

"I will," Iain said. "I will say a word to that fine Mr Mackenzie."

"No, Iain," his father said. "I will say the word. You would say it with your fist."

"And if I did –"

"Mr Mackenzie is a friend of the sheriff and the constables. I will say a word to Mr Mackenzie, and it is not the last word he shall hear from me."

So Hamish Sinclair set off to free his ox from the pound. And as he walked past the crofts by the sea, where sometimes an upended black boat was the roof, with mosses on its keel where barnacles had been, he thought how queer it was the now, the coming to the sea, eating the limpets and the mussels and the crabs, not the berries and the nuts and the eggs, the salt in the taste of the silver herrings that were not sweet and taut as the red salmon or the brown trout. But the oatmeal and the potatos were still the same, the porridge and the brose, and these gifts of the ground were the true living of men, that came so hard from the sea.

As he passed the graveyard by the kirk, Hamish saw the red earth heaped over two narrow graves, slashing the darkling green of the sod and the stone crosses, weathered by time in memory. These were the Mackay twins, never a hope for them when the storm blew up sudden from Barra, their boat caught like a mussel-shell in an eddy and then whirled under, mermaid-deep, so that they might only come back again as seals and dreams, a warning to other farmers never to trust to the waves. Hamish never would. He was a man of the moor and the brae, he could not swim, he hated water beyond his depth. You could not take a man from his natural ground and put him on a treacherous element and call that his own.

"God be with you," Hamish said to the new graves, "but do not go out on the great waters."

A scarlet man was coming down the road, bright red in face and jacket, ruddy of bonnet and knees, only his kilt in green and black and blue denying the general bloodiness of him. Hamish had been hearing of his coming, the recruiting sergeant, giving a guinea to every lad who would leave his home for the service of Her Foreign Majesty.

"And good day to you," the recruiting sergeant said. "And to your family. What would be the name?"

"Sinclair," Hamish said.

"You're new to these parts? Sinclairs here are as rare as eagles."

"We're new the now."

"And your sons, they will be working at the kelp?"

"How else? There's not a thing but that."

"And what age will they be? Bonny and braw I have no doubt."

"They are not for you, Sergeant. Not for the foreign wars."

"Foreign, is it? If seeing the world is foreign, why then it is, and good it is." The sergeant put his finger along his nose. "There's gold in it for you, man. And the Ninety-third Highlanders, why it's the finest regiment that ever fought for God and the Queen, God bless Her."

"Aye," Hamish said, "and where do all your fine lads live now? In the far lands and over the seas. When do your lads come home, if they come home and stay not under the ground? After twenty years of service to a land that is not their land. Once we served our laird, and he gave us land that we held was our land. Now we serve your Queen, and where?"

"Our Queen Victoria, God bless Her."

"And Her laws take the land that was our own."

"You have Her pay, Her glory, Her honour –"

"Her land that was our land, we do not have. Go away with you, Sergeant. My Iain and my Hamish Jamie you shall not have."

So Hamish went away towards the pound to look for his ox, while the recruiting sergeant went to look for his Iain and his Hamish Jamie, named so unwisely by their father. And Hamish heard the lowing of the black cattle and the bleating of the sheep that were penned inside the pound of Mr Mackenzie. And there was a queer stench as if a beast had died and rotted, but more harsh to the nose. And there was the gentleman himself, as if the title would cover such a stout and shifty fellow in tight breeches of yellow pigskin.

"And it's good day to you, Mr Mackenzie," Hamish said, polite as you please and murder in his soul.

"And it's good day to you, Hamish," Mr Mackenzie said, always trying to be the superior.

"Not such a good day," Hamish said. "I hear you have my ox."

"With my grass inside him. He is a great ox to eat of my grass."

"You have grass growing out of your ears," Hamish said, "if you cannot hear the ox complaining he has no grass inside him the now."

"Will you pay the fine for him," Mr Mackenzie said, "or he will eat no grass until you do."

"I will take him with me the now," Hamish said.

"When you pay me four shilling."

"When I pay you four shilling, Mr Mackenzie, for a swatch of grass, it will not be before Judgement Day."

"That will be next assizes, if you do not pay me four shilling."

"Out of my way, man," Hamish said. "You will not make suffer my ox."

"Do not enter the pound," Mr Mackenzie said, "or you will suffer worse than the ox."

"Ach, away with you."

Hamish put a hand on Mr Mackenzie's shoulder and thrust him to one side. Then he opened the gate of the pound and walked inside among the cattle and the sheep. His ox knew him and came towards him and rubbed his face with the slobber on its nose. And Hamish threw his arm over the ox's neck and walked him back to the gate into the pound, which he found closed against him with Mr Mackenzie on the other side. Only Mr Mackenzie now held a fowling-piece in his hands with his factor stood behind him.

"On payment of four shilling," Mr Mackenzie said, "you may leave with your ox."

"And if I cannot pay."

"You cannot leave with your ox."

"And if I will not pay."

"You will not leave with your ox."

"I am leaving with my ox."

But when Hamish put his hand to the gate, he saw it was locked with a padlock, and he had no way out.

"I have not the money," Hamish said, "and I will have the ox."

"Then you must bide with the ox in there," Mr Mackenzie said, "until you have the money."

Behind Mr Mackenzie and his fowling-piece, Hamish could see a column of black smoke rising from the cliffs by the sea.

"That is the kilns," Hamish said. "For drying the kelp."

Mr Mackenzie turned to look behind him.

"Where you work with your sons?"

"There is muckle smoke," Hamish said. "The kilns will be on fire. I must go and see."

"Not without paying four shilling."

"Don't be daft, man. I must go."

"Pay me four shilling. And take your ox."

"I have not four shilling."

Hamish glared so intently through the gate at Mr Mackenzie that he raised his fowling-piece and levelled it at Hamish.

"Give me my four shilling."

"I do not have it, you daft bugger."

"And you are a man of God, Hamish. And would you swear so?"

"There is muckle worse to say of you."

Hamish began to climb the bars of the gate, while Mr Mackenzie followed him with the barrel of his shotgun. When Hamish reached the top of the gate, he looked down on Mr Mackenzie.

"Shoot," he said. "Who dares to meddle with me?"

He jumped down off the gate, staggered and righted himself like a boat after a gust.

"When I have settled the fire at the kilns, I will come back with my sons for the ox."

"You are the daft bugger," Mr Mackenzie said. "Too many of you Sinclairs, too many. Can you not see? Muckle too many. So you must go over the seas or in the army regiments. What else can a Sinclair do?"

"I have a cousin Archibald," Hamish said, "and he went over the sea to fight for General Oglethorpe against the Indians. And now he has land there in a place called Georgia. And many a Sinclair has gone over the sea to fight in Sweden and in France, and in Ireland and in Canada, and they have land there the now. But we will not go."

"You will go," Mr Mackenzie said. "Starve you or emigrate. You will go."

"We will not go."

"You will. Have you not seen the blight?" He pointed to a swill bin at the corner of the pound. Now Hamish could smell the reek that came out of it, the stench of putrefaction and decay. "The cattle will not have them, nor men either. Potatos. All rotten, all foul."

"I do not believe you."

"Go to your fire. And look at that swill on the way."

So it was that Hamish saw the slimy and liquid tubers, their skins black and tattered as the seaweed, in a bin that heaved and belched with bubbles of fuel gas. And he hurried away towards the black smoke, his heart heavy within him.

Hamish met his two elder bairns on the road from the kilns, the giant Iain leading the cuddy with Mary on its back and he still holding the long clatt in his hand. The black smoke was now a pillar in the sky, but Iain looked not back on the evidence of the burning behind him, no more than Lot looked back on the fire and the brimstone that fell upon Sodom and Gomorrah.

"The kilns are burning, son. What is with you?"

"Let the kilns burn and the weed, father."

"You shall be asking what is with Gavin Macdonald, Da," Mary said from the back of the donkey.

"I reck nothing with Gavin Macdonald," Hamish said, "but that he would sooner lose his heart, if he has a heart, than a shilling from his pocket, and he would sooner see us starve than pay us wages for the kelp."

"He was lifting Mary's kirtle, father –"

"Hush, Iain, now –"

"I hit him with my clatt. Look, there's the hair and blood on it."

"God help us, Iain," his father said.

"And he fell down, and I was that mad with us chaving like slave folk for that swick and cheat that I put the peat to the timbers of the kiln shed, and I am taking Mary away home."

"Is he dead?"

"If the devil will have him –"

"And what will you do the now, Iain?"

"Enlist. They do no reck if a soldier is a murderer. And if he is a murderer, he is the better the soldier."

"Never," Hamish said. "Come away to Canada with us."

"The sheriff will find me. But if I take the guinea from the recruiting sergeant –"

"You've met with the red devil?"

"Aye. He's no so bad."

"His clothes," Mary said. "The kilt on him. All the lassies love –"

"Hush," Hamish said. "And if you are a soldier, and if we go to Canada on the ship and find us a home and land, then you can leave the army and come to us, where none shall know you –"

"I will no go to Canada," Mary said. She slipped down from the donkey's back. "I will bide in Scotland."

"And who will see to you?" Hamish asked.

"The laird," Mary said. "I will go to the castle with the dominie. He has written a petition. From the people of the glen. Give us back our land. The laird, he does not know what is done in his name."

"Ach," Iain said and spat. "Damn the laird. You ken what he calls his castle. Dunrobin. Because he has never done robbin' his own folk."

"Hush," Hamish said. "Never say that of our laird."

"I'll take the Queen's guinea," Iain said. "And my chances."

"And who'll be after caring for your mother and me?" Hamish said. "Who will care the now?"

"You have Hamish Jamie, father. Only he wants to be taken for a soldier more than me."

"He never will."

"You cannot stop a son, father, any more than your father might stop you. If he must go."

"No son of mine will fight for a foreign queen and another country."

"A fight's a fight," Iain said. "It's only a better fight if it's for the right." He swung his clatt round and round, making the iron whistle in the air. "It is the blood, father. We like to fight. It is the motto of the clan. Fight."

"What will you tell your own mother?"

"You tell her, father. I will be gone the now. Or they will have me for the murdering of that mean man."

The pillar of black smoke had spread sideways until it was a broad toadstool between earth and heaven. At the top of the cliffs, Hamish could see people running towards the base of the smoke. Among them would be his wife and his children, all of them except this one, who was lost to them.

"You will not tell her. You will be a soldier, and you will not face your own mother." A prickle hurt Hamish's eyes. He would not cry. No Sinclair cried. "You break the family. Ach, you will not do that, my son."

"I must," Iain said. "You will tell mother. Father –" Iain shivered, the huge man that he was, as a fir in the wind. "I cannot. You tell her. I must go, or I –"

"Aye," Hamish said. A tear was now running down his cheek, but he did not brush it away or hide it. "You must go. Or you may be hangit. And it was for your sister."

"Give me your blessing, father."

"God be with you, my son," Hamish said. "Never forget. Your home is always where we will be."

"I will never forget that." Iain bent and kissed his father on the brow, then turned and swung Mary round off the ground with his free arm.

"Don't you go and wed the duke," he said, "though a countess you are, even the now." He kissed her and dropped her head down and twirled his clatt so fast that it made a dark circle in the air, which seemed to draw him away.

"Fight," Iain said, "and I will do that."

6

THE CASTLE AND
ITS KIND

"Scones," said the duchess, "there is nothing better than scones. They're almost worth coming to Scotland for."

"And butter," said the duke, spreading plenty on his hot tea-cake. "But those bloody builders. They will never finish this castle. Sometimes I think they are building one of those new railway stations. They look like castles too."

"Oh, we do not want trains here," the duchess said. "Or passengers. Because that is all guests are. They move through. And all that smoke. It would ruin things. Like the blight."

"I am sorry about that," the duke said. "They say there is famine. But there cannot be. They have the fish now and the sea. My mother moved them there in time. It was providence. Somebody had to compel our backward peasants — and do not call them Highlanders, for they are peasants — into modern existence. My mother was a great improver."

"And you," the duchess said. "The model fishing villages you made. Port Gower and Golspie and Helmsdale."

"And the emigration. I have spent tens of thousands of pounds, my dear, to assist the poor unfortunates to make a better life in a new land, perhaps more suited to their peculiar talents, in order for them to earn a living."

"You are so good. That is why they come to you with their petitions."

"Oh, not another one," the duke said, blowing out a froth of crumbs from his cake. "Just as we were taking our tea."

"Shall we receive them?" the duchess said. "Or it will hang over us." She picked up a small silver bell and rang it in tiny chimes that dropped through the air like breaking china. "I cannot bear something hanging over one like poor people complaining. It takes away the appetite. Ah, Mackay —" She addressed the footman who came into the tea-room. "Please clear away. And bring in those poor people who wish to complain about their good fortune."

"Really, my dear," the duke said, "you do not have to trouble yourself –"

"I am your wife," the duchess said, "and I wish to know all that concerns you. It is my duty and my desire."

The footman brought in a tall and cadaverous dominie in black and a bonny young woman in a plaid skirt and shawl. The man ducked his head in a quick nod, and the girl bobbed up and down like a float struck by a fish on the hook. But there was no bow, there was no curtsy. Abrupt Highland manners, or downright rude.

"If it please you, sir –" the man said in English. "And lady –"

The duke shook his head.

"Where did you learn to address people of quality?" he asked.

"I am a teacher, sir –"

"That is why you are not taught," the duke said triumphantly. "Is this your daughter?"

"No," the man said. "Her name is Mary Sinclair. She is of the petitioners."

"Come over here," the duchess said. And when Mary did not move, she added sharply. "You do understand plain English?"

"An it please you, lady," Mary said in English, the alien words harsh on her tongue. But she still did not move.

"You're not deaf, but you are wilful," the duchess said. "Come here, girl."

Mary moved forward slowly and stood near the duchess, sitting in the floral chintz that Queen Victoria was making popular because she wanted her Scots castle to look homely.

"Turn around," the duchess said.

Mary slowly turned around, her head low, her hands clasped before her, trying to hide her rough fingers. She felt like a heifer at the fair.

"You'll do," the duchess said. "After a scrub and a change. Report to the housekeeper, Mrs Rogers."

"An it please you, lady –"

"It does not, if you repeat yourself."

"I was not thinking ... a position –"

"I know it is too good to be true," the duchess said, "and I know you people find it hard to be grateful, but I do wish to *do* something for you – and it so happens a position is vacant." Then very brightly, "And here you are!"

Mary was silent, wondering how to refuse, when her dominie spoke. "If you wish to do something for us, lady, then you will hear our petition."

"Give it to the duke. It is for him to hear."

"Where is it, man?" The duke held out a hand, on which his polished nails glittered as brightly as his signet ring. "I can read English."

"Pray, may I hear it?" the duchess said.

"You may," her husband said. "Although it may not be to your taste." And he read this:

That the land of your Petitioners was laid waste under your Mother the Countess by the sheepfarming system, in consequence of which your Petitioners were removed to other parts under leases. That these leases now being ended, your Petitioners were removed again to the sea, already overcrowded with a surplus population. That your Petitioners formerly paid their rents by rearing Cattle and by fishing, but now that ten families occupy the place formerly inhabited by one, the rearing of Cattle was rendered unpracticable, and the fishing which at all times is precarious has this year in a great measure failed. That your Petitioners are prevented from improving the little land they Cultivate, not only by not having leases on it, but above all being prohibited from using the sea ware on the coast for manure. For that ware must be made into extract for the kelp factories, and moreover, the potatos have been utterly ruined by the blight. That, in consequence of these hardships there are not in this parish nine families which can be supported for nine months by the produce of their lands, that the young men of the parish, though much attached to their superiors and to their country, are compelled by their grievances to emigrate to Foreign lands, but before they reluctantly leave their native soil they deem it their duty to make their case known to Your Grace.

The duke put down the petition. He said nothing for a time, then he looked at the man in black.

"At least you know what to call me," he said, "when you write. Is this true?"

"It is all true."

"We cleared these Sinclairs originally?"

"Yes. And they have moved on. And now they have no food and nowhere to go."

"I will give you more money, damn it," the duke said without grace. "Another ten thousand pounds to assist their passages to Canada or the colonies or where they will."

"They do not wish to go over the seas," the dominie said. "They wish to remain in Scotland. This is their home – their land."

"My land," the duke said, "which can no longer support them with their idle ways. The hand of God struck down the potato crop, not my hand. Is that not so, teacher?"

"It is so."

"Then tell them that. It was for their sins – in opposing me, and others in authority."

"I cannot tell them that."

"Really?" The duke considered the dominie. "You make it difficult for me."

"They do not wish to leave their own land."

"They must go. I will assist them."

"Aye," the dominie said. "The sight of our folk gone – and gone for aye – it will not offend the view from the castle."

The duke was silent, but the duchess spoke out.

"The view is beautiful now. A garden down to the sea. Sheep in their pastures. A panorama – purple moors, far hills, the noble stags – and no huts."

"No huts, lady, no huts. And no folk either."

"You will take the money and go to Canada," the duke said. "The land cannot support you. You have no option. Or else you will starve."

"If we must, we must go," the dominie said. "But do not fear yourself, we will return." He gave a bob of the head to the duke. "I will tell them that I gave you the petition and you said, 'Get you away to Canada'."

"That is putting rather a strong construction on my words."

"You did not say that?"

"In so many words –"

"In so many words." The dominie turned to Mary, who had stood mutely by the duchess all the while. "Are you coming away with me?"

"She is staying here," the duchess said. "I am offering her a place here in my service."

"Her place is with her own folk," the dominie said. "Not in your service."

Mary flushed. The words that came out of her mouth almost surprised her. "We have no place, dominie. So how can you say my place is with my own folk? They have no place. There is a place here – and it is in Scotland – and I will bide here."

"What will I tell Hamish and Hannah?" he asked.

"I will find them when they have a place to call their own. It is no our fault that we have to leave. It is your fault, their fault. We have no home."

"You shall honour your father and your mother."

"I do – but how live with them when they have no home for me?"

The dominie shook his head and turned to the duchess.

"She will bide with you, lady. Care well for her."

"I trust she will care well for me."

The dominie turned to face the duke. "We will take your money as we have nothing else to take. We will leave the land as you have taken it when it was also our land. But when we return, this land will be as it has always been, the land of God and his children, and never will you take it from us again."

7

THE CROSSING

"There's no decency," Hannah said.

"We be buried," Bain said.

"It is only for the crossing," Hamish said. "Bear with it the now."

They were viewing their berths below the decks of the *Hopeful June*. These were low boxes, one on top of the other, six feet wide and six feet long and two feet one inch high. Just enough for one person or a closely married pair, but these were for four people and devil a matter if they were of the opposite sexes, a place in a berth was a mess of pottage, you took what you could get next to you, a bairn or a lassie or a Herod.

"In here," Hannah said, "there will go Katie and Rachel and Angus with me. And below will go Hamish and Bain and whatever shamelessness the Good Lord inflicts upon them. And Hamish Jamie, if –"

"Mother," Bain said, "you know he's gone for the army and to keep a good eye on Iain there."

"Aye, he loves his brother," Hannah said, "but he will not leave us."

"He will be back," Hamish said. "Just as soon as we have our farm in Canada. Iain will be back, and Hamish Jamie will be back, and we will be one family again."

The emigrants' quarters in the *Hopeful June* were a catacomb in wood. In the thick and fetid air, hutch was piled upon hutch for the thousand souls that were to endure the crossing. Cattle have their byres, horses their stables, even cut corn has its cribs – but the emigrants had their berths as the slaves from Africa had their berths. Human beings were packed as tight as tripe in the bowels of the ship. There was not room to swing a cat, for there was not even room for a cat at all. Bedding, boxes, bundles, shoes, shawls, petticoats, waistcoats, bonnets, hats, pipes, curling-tongs, cut-throat razors, flat irons, corsets male and female, fiddles, swaddling-clothes, nostrums and remedies for all ills filled every crack and cranny and crevice below decks. The one universal was Holloway's Pills, the Greatest Sale of Any Medicine in the Globe. They were guaranteed to cure any ailment including sea-sickness, scrofula, venereal diseases, tumours, the whites and the King's Evil.

"Help me with this, Bain," Hannah said, driving hairpins into a plaid over the wooden hole into her berth. She would be private. "I'll not be a sight for the likes of these."

The likes of these were the other poor folk on the boat, assisted to emigrate beyond the seas. Most of them were young men in their only pair of breeks with a dirty shirt and an old coat of rents and patches and their boots open at the toes. They smoked clay pipes with anything they could stuff into them, shavings, old tea-leaves, wool and coarse tobacco. Their lips were black with swearing. Their red eyes had the look of beaten puppies. They had lost the strut of the cocks of the walk for the crouch of curs.

There were some young women with red raw hands, scarred from the gutting of herring or the lime-burning or the power-looms. Big Kirsty MacNiece, wide at the shoulder as any man, had only the one hand, for the other had been severed at the wrist by a spinning-machine. "Ach, they give me a week's pay and a Certificate for Good Conduct. It was not my fault. So I tore the certificate into wee pieces with the fingers still on me – good and slow – and I threw their certificate in their good faces. Give me back my hand, I said. And do they? They do not, they cannot. Only another poor lassie works the same machine."

They had all to fight for their food, and the weakest did not eat. If eating you could call it. The rations, when they were doled, were never what the book said – a cupful of flour, mouldy rice and oatmeal, biscuit harder than a whetstone, tea and molasses, and salt pork so tough and acrid you might have been eating the kelp itself. The mates swore without drawing breath, "I'll break your bastard head in, God damn your soul." You had to fight with the other passengers to get near the bosuns giving out the stores, and then fight harder to get near the six stoves serving the thousand wretches. And as for getting to the cook without a bribe of money or brandy, or to the ship's doctor, who was only an upstart drunken apothecary, you might as well be climbing Jacob's ladder to heaven, and come tumbling down like the bad angel to hell.

If you could not live like that, you could die like that. The dying started on the fourth day of the crossing, when a child would keep no food down and lay in her mess with nothing to be done about it. And the doctor said it was dysentery and muttered of cholera and typhus under his port-wine breath. And the captain swore he had not a cloth or a canvas to spare to sew up the little body inside. So she was thrown into the waters of the deep without even the benefit of a prayer, for there was no priest aboard. There were only the sailors pulling at the ropes with their song, which was no hymn of praise:

"Haul in the bowling, the Black Star bowling
Haul in the bowling, the bowling haul –"

In the darkness below, the air was thick as brose or milky porridge. Its stenches and smells coated the nose. The candles ran out, and the wicks in the whale-oil in the single lamps guttered and burned black. There was always a battle for supper and the slops. And after the unspeakable visit to the privies at the stern, with the sailors leering through the cracks in the boards, Hannah would retire with her children while there were still the lines of evening light. She would huddle in her wooden tomb until the coming of dawn, having to suck in the foul air only to blow it out fouler, praying for the crossing to be over in just one more day.

But the crossing was never over, and the dying and the sickness went on. There was an old shepherd, Stewart MacPhee, who stood at the bows of the *Hopeful June* as still as a figurehead. He would not be moved. He looked for the land. The agent had said twenty days for the crossing, but it was twenty-four days now, and there had only been the false hope of the sighting of Northern Ireland to the lee. But Stewart MacPhee stood wrapped in his plaid in the bows, watching for that Newfoundland to come out of the squalls and the mist, watching as he had for his sheep in Benbecula, before he and his people had been driven out by the wolfhounds sent by the black Gordon of Cluny, the buyer of the Hebrides. It was not as if the Good Lord gave any man the right to buy islands and make them into the desolation of the wilderness.

"Yes," old MacPhee sang in his rant to Hamish Sinclair, who often stood with him on watch for the Newfoundland, "many a thing have I seen in my own day and generation. Many a thing, O Mary Mother of the black sorrow! I have seen the townships swept, and the big holdings being made of them, the people being driven out of the countryside to the streets of Glasgow and to the wilds of Canada. And many of them died of hunger and plague and smallpox while going across the ocean. I have seen the women putting the children in the carts which were being sent from Barra and Benbecula and the Iochdar to Loch Boisdale, while their husbands lay bound in the pen and were weeping beside the women, crying aloud, and their little children wailing like to break their hearts. I have seen the big strong men, the champions of the countryside, the stalwarts of the world, being bound on Loch Boisdale quay and cast into the ship as would be done to a batch of horses or cattle in the boat. The bailiffs and the ground-officers and the constables and the policemen were gathered behind them. The God of life only knows all the loathsome work of men on that day."

Hamish took the old MacPhee into his berth with Angus, and the three of them held it against any other intruder. Hannah and the three bairns above shifted and knocked, listening to the moanings and the laments of the sick and the dying, the snorings and the cursings of the weak and the living. For the cholera and the typhus had come among them. The illness began with shivering and the grip of the claws inside the forehead, then swelling in the face and muck in the nose and the throat, then the blood in the eyes and the muscles squirming beneath the skin, then the stupid stare of the idiot to show the brain was dull and half dead. The pulse in the wrist sometimes raced in a fever and sometimes slowed to a plod. Then the skin became dark as if burned by the sun.

The name for it was *fiabhras dubh*, the black fever. On the fourth day, sores afflicted the body in large boils. The fever was now a loosening of the limbs, so that the sufferer could no longer move to crush the lice on his berth. Yet if he would live to the seventh day, a sweat might come from him and a smell as from the byre, and he might rise from the black fever weak as a lamb that is born, but in rejoicing. The remedy on the *Hopeful June*, at the cost of one shilling, was a dose of Epsom salts and castor oil. And at the cost of two shillings, thirty-five drops of laudanum were given, and then the face was rubbed with vinegar.

The cures did no good. There were twenty dead on the thirtieth day of the voyage, and forty-one dead on the forty-first day which was a coincidence, but hardly a blessing, except to the dead, who were out of the suffering. By now, there was no water for the poor folk below, but only from the stinking bilges. The salt pork was cooked in water from the sea, making the thirst from drinking the bilge-water even more terrible. So hardly a man or a woman or a child alive was not gripped by spasms of vomiting and running discharge from the bowels. They groped in the darkness of their berths, they fouled their resting-places, they crawled on the decks to breathe some kind of life from the winds that stretched the sails overhead, bringing them to the promised Newfoundland, which never came to them.

And when it did come, it came as ice in the night. The *Hopeful June* struck the berg off Nova Scotia. Her rotten timbers were breached.

The sea water came as a cold wall into the quarters below decks. The screaming of the awakened was drowned by the roar of the flood. Hamish clutched Angus and struggled down to the planks of the floor, the sea rising to his knees. He was struck from behind, nearly thrown over, but held upright. He reached above to bring down Hannah, and Angus reached for Katie and Rachel and Bain.

"Hold fast," Hamish shouted. "Hold tight."

And there was the shrieking and the keening and the cursing of the damned. The weight of the waters pushed the trapped against each other, stirred them into cold porridge in a wooden pot. They clung to each other in the grip of life, which would be the death grip also. And above them now, a flicker of red light jumped through the joins on the decks, a sound of crackling, a whiff of sharp smoke.

"Oh dear God," Hamish said, "the fire."

Two men fought up the companion way, banging at the hatch above. But none could open it. They were penned below to die between the roaring deep, the ice to the side, the fire above. They surged against each other, shouted, implored. And there was a sudden mercy. The blade of an axe splintered the boarding between the steering and the forequarters of the ship. Kirsty MacNeice threw her one hand forward to clench at the splinters and wrench out more wood to widen the gap. And she nearly lost her other hand, with the axe driven through again and again to clear a way of escape for the damned souls below.

The waters were waist deep now, as the emigrants struggled through the hole in the boarding. Three more sick bairns died now, two crushed and drowned among the desperate press of the people, and one small boy broken by a tier of berths collapsing on his shivering body. But the rest of the people struggled out and up the ladders and the steps to the hell above, where the way from the cold salt waters led to the masts of fire and the cables of flame, casting weird shadows and the shapes of devils and imps on the cracked whiteness of the great iceberg, which had stove in the hull of the *Hopeful June*.

Sailors were lowering the two boats that still hung clear on the lee side. But already the ship was tilting with the weight of the inrush of the waters and the shifting ballast and cargo of pig-iron. Hamish and Hannah and the children found themselves scrambling up the slope of the decks, bombarded by loose boxes and lashed by broken cables from the wreckage. And now burning fragments of canvas were bright birds settling on the screeching mob below. Three kneeling figures by the poop were singing a hymn, but they were enveloped by the flames as incandescence ran down and split the rigging and brought it down on their heads in a burning shroud. The stays above shed sparks and ropes were alight, the fibres falling in fireflies on to the shoulders of the men and women, who screamed as they tore off the scorching embers. And old MacPhee slid down the decks to the rail and fell overboard on to the berg, where he hung by his hands until the chillness loosened his grasp, and he vanished in the crack between the ship and the wall of ice.

One boat was lowered and was swamped, the other lurched down the tilt of the ship's side and bobbed on to the waters. Sailors and passengers slithered down ropes into the single boat, until it was loaded to the gunwhales and then cast off. For the rest of the abandoned, they scrabbled up the shelving decks and clung to the lee rail or to the masts or to lashed boxes or to coils of rope. Hamish struggled with his wife and children forward to the end of the jib, which was already crowded with others, clinging for dear life to the spar. Their hands held on to boom or arm or leg. And down on them rained the torches of the burning sails, charring their skins already shivering from the strike of the blast and the sea and the ice.

Now Hamish heard a fearsome cracking and crashing. And he looked back to see the fiery foremast falling towards the berg, carrying with it the fastenings of the jib. And those who were holding the spar were lifted into the air and shook down onto the tilted decks or dropped into the waters between the keeling vessel and the walls of ice or thrown on to the harsh whiteness of the immense berg. But Hamish and his own were still clinging to the remains of the hanging jib, where it had broken from its cables. None of them was hoisted and swept away.

Now Kirsty MacNiece came to their salvation. He red hair black and singed, naked and scorched to the waist, she held the sailor's axe which had broken the partition below. She was wedged against the smouldering stump of the foremast, chopping at a lashed coop of hens, mostly dead, but with two birds squawking and thrashing their wings.

"Get you over here," she shouted. "The good ship *Hopeful MacNiece*."

First Angus let go of the battered jib and slithered across the decks to catch at the coop. Then came Katie and Rachel and Bain. Then Hannah, rolling over and over as the ship lurched sideways ready for its deep plunge down. Then Hamish pitched forward to grasp at the coop as Kirsty's axe split the last of the lashings. Fire fell on them, burning their hair and hands, but they did not let go. And with a

mighty groan and wrenching and rush of great waters, the *Hopeful June*
split apart, shrugging the coop and its human cargo into the ocean by
the cliff of ice. In that terrible cold slap, the breaths stopped in all the
survivors. In the suck of the going under of the ship, they were
drowned in the tomb of the deep that squeezed their lungs flat and
choked them in black brine.

Then God spat them up from the grave of the drowned. He threw
them up upon the mercy of His waves that had no mercy. The coop
and its human limpets were driven against the ice. Only at the last, the
wind blew up a spray that sheered the frail craft past the jag of the
berg to the sea beyond. And by the grace of heaven, the cutter *Ahoy!*
out of Quebec City, saw the wreck and wretches in the water and took
them aboard, Kirsty MacNiece and the six Sinclairs and twenty-seven
others of the thousand and more who were drowned in the splitting
and the sinking of the *Hopeful June*. And they were set ashore at Grosse
Isle with only sailors' clothes from the slop chest on their backs. Katie
and Rachel were hot and shivering with the black fever, although a
cold coming to Canada they had of it.

8

THE BURSTING AT GROSSE ISLE

Doctor George Douglas had served as the medical superintendent of Grosse Isle for ten years. Here the ships had to dock as they sailed down the St Lawrence River on their way to Quebec City and Montreal and Toronto, and here Doctor Douglas inspected the passengers. If he did not like the looks of them, he took them off to the tents and shacks and sheds on the island for a period of quarantine. But naturally they had to be ill, very ill, before Doctor Douglas would take them off their ships. Feeling under the weather was good enough to be passed on down the great river into Canada. Feeling at death's door was just about enough to be landed at Grosse Isle.

There, the sultry late summer was called an Indian summer, though the Indians did not bring it with them or leave it behind them in their forcing to the west. The tens of thousands of poor folk flung from Scotland and Ireland were bringing the fever heat with them, typhus and dysentery. The contagion was spreading with the lice and the flies and the mosquitos that bred on the swampy ground of Grosse Isle which never seemed to dry out, even in the sun which conjured pestilence out of the dank earth, not purgations or curatives.

Once Doctor Douglas had only three people to help him on the quarantine island, Tom Fitch the steward, old Johnson the orderly, and the gap-toothed tyrant Meg Halloran of the black tongue and the healing hand. But this summer there had been more than twenty doctors on Grosse Isle. Whatever their lack of qualifications, they were trying to deal with the plague of mass contagion, the sick lying on bare boards in their bunks in the fever sheds or on straw in the bell-tents. And the doctors were dying as fast as the patients, ten of them expired and five more sick of typhus, and only six gravediggers to bury in the sodden shallow graves over the rock the hundreds of bodies that Doctor Douglas discovered day by day, dead on the open ground or in the huddle of loose stones or under old sail-canvas or

stiff in their berths in the fever sheds that were worse than the
steerage holds from which he had plucked them into this hot fate.

Oh God, dear God, he could not go on, he must go on, he would
go on. He would write to his superiors in Quebec City, but they would
do little but send him one or two more doctors with their mother's
milk still wet upon their lips to die here. The poor folk from the isles
off England were not really the concern of the people of Canada, who
were now learning to hold dominion over themselves. And so Doctor
Douglas went to his quarters in the plague camp, and he penned a
letter to the authorities who would ignore it down the river.

Grosse Isle, Tuesday, 9 a.m.

Out of the four thousand or five thousand emigrants that have left
this island since Sunday, at least two thousand will fall sick
somewhere before three weeks are over. They ought to have
accommodation for two thousand sick at least in Montreal and
Quebec, as all the Greenock and Liverpool passengers are half
dead from starvation and want before embarking; and the least
bowel complaint, which is sure to come with a change of food,
finishes them without a struggle. I never saw people so indifferent
to life; they would continue in the same berth with a dead person
until the seaman or captain dragged out the corpse with boat-
hooks. Good God! what evils will befall the cities wherever they
alight. And as for the typhus and the black fever, they no more
resist it than a lover's kiss. The hot weather will increase the evil.
Now give the authorities of Quebec and Montreal fair warning
from me. And send me, for the love of God, all the doctors and
orderlies and nurses and grave-diggers you may provide to
undertake service on this pest-island. Take these from the gaols if
needs be, for I have need of all servants here in this extremity. I
have not time to write at length, or should feel it in my duty to do
so. Public safety requires it...

There was a large, thick-set man standing in the room, his awkward
boots making the pine-boards creak and groan as a wind in the living
branches. Doctor Douglas had not noticed him enter, but there he
was, freckled and burly as if he were planted there.

"And what would you be wanting?" Doctor Douglas asked.

"A life," Hamish Sinclair said.

Doctor Douglas snorted and shook his head.

"This is the last thing and the least thing you will find here."

"Yet that is what I will have," Hamish said. "This life."

And then he moved as though uprooted. He weighed heavily on the pine-boards with his boots and left the room and was gone but a moment and returned with the body of a child in his arms. Her long fair hair splashed from her lolling head on to his knees. Her mouth was fixed in a gape, her eyes stared wide and blind.

"But she is dead," Doctor Douglas said.

"I will have the life of my Rachel."

Douglas rose and walked round the trestle table where he worked and put his hand on the chill cheek of the child in the man's arms.

"I am no sorcerer or resurrectionist," he said. "I cannot make the living from the dead."

"Her life," Hamish said, "I must have her back."

"Come with me," Douglas said, speaking before he knew what he was saying. "We will find a place fit for her."

The doctor and the man carrying the dead child emerged from the pine-board shack and walked past two large sweltering sheds and five rough tents, pitched to shelter the sick and the dying. The torrid air hung in an invisible sheet, damp with the effluvia of fever. One voice was crying out, "No, no, no...", then fell away. Some bull-frogs croaked from a marsh as if gasping for air.

"We will walk to my farm," Douglas said. "It is over there, by the trees."

"I cannot leave my wife and bairns for muckle time," Hamish said.

"I will show you a place where your Rachel may rest, and then you may bring your family to her."

The farm, which Douglas had on the island, was the only farm. It was his solace and his refuge. Near some maple trees, he had built a cottage out of stone, with a barn for cattle nearby. He had half a dozen cows and an old bull, and there was a vegetable patch at the back of the house. To Hamish, carrying his dead daughter, the farm seemed to be the dream which he had crossed the ocean to find.

"I did not think," Hamish said, "in this isle – where we are cast like dung into a pit..."

"I have to live here," Douglas said. "But I like to think I have made a farm like a farm in Scotland."

"If I had that farm in Scotland," Hamish said, "we would never have crossed the water."

Douglas led the way to the maple trees, their leaves already beginning to show the blood in them. Between the trees, a small grave had already been dug, or what seemed to be one.

"We use it for storing the jars of maple syrup," Douglas said, "when we tap the trees. Perhaps Rachel might rest there, and we might say the prayers to wish her good night."

Hamish stood with his small daughter above the grave. Although he was weeping, the tears did not show among the many beads of sweat on his face. Walking was swimming through the hot clamminess of the atmosphere. At last he brought himself to speak.

"She was a one for the trees," he said. "She will be lying quiet here."

Hamish straddled the gash in the earth and lowered his daughter's body into the pit. Now it lay below ground, enclosed by the earth, it might have been uncovered, as a man might dig up some marble statue of a sprite or an angel of time past.

"She is a beautiful girl," Douglas said. "She will rest easy there. Will you go and find your wife and your children and bring them here? I will be fetching a Bible from my house."

Hamish turned to him and wiped his eyes and his cheeks with the back of his hand.

"Why should you be after caring for us, Doctor Douglas?"

"Death is random," Douglas said. "Thousands are dying. I cannot care for them all. I am failing in my duty. People even say I have a farm on Grosse Isle to sell the produce to the sick in my care. And I do that."

"I was a farmer," Hamish said. "I will be a farmer. We must sell the things we grow."

"I only care for the people one by one," Douglas said, looking down at the body of Rachel lying so whitely in the earth. "This one I care for. Do not ask me why."

Now Hamish also looked down at the body of his daughter, and he raged and cursed and spoke the blasphemy that he had never spoken, not even when Hannah had lost their firstborn son.

"You care!" he shouted. "And God does not care! Why did God give me Rachel and take her from me? He does not care! God does not care!"

Douglas put his hand on the shaking and drenched shoulder of Hamish Sinclair.

"Hold your peace," he said. "God makes me care. For this one, your Rachel, His Rachel. And for you. Do you see that farm? There is no one to work it. All are sick or dead. And I have too much to do and may be sick or dead soon. Go you there with your wife and your children. You are a farmer. Look after the cattle, grow the vegetables.

I will teach you how to take syrup from the maple trees that watch over your daughter."

His eyes red with rage and grief, Hamish stared at the doctor.

"I cannot take that from you."

"Take it," Douglas said. "I can only offer it to one. And it is you."

"I cannot thank you —"

"Thank God, not me."

"I am not in the way of thinking to thank God."

"Thank Him."

"Aye."

Hamish turned and looked down again at the body of Rachel in the little pit. She was so small, but she seemed to trust the lap of the earth with the arms of the soil about her.

"Thank God," he said, "for saving her sister Katie from the black fever. Thank God for preserving us from the sinking of the ship in the ice. Thank God for bringing us to this good man, when I was thinking that there was no good in any man, no, no good at all."

"I am not a good man," Douglas said. "I do not know why you are the one. I simply do not know."

So Doctor Douglas sent away Hamish Sinclair to find the rest of his family and bring them to the burial and to the farm to dwell there. And as he walked towards his small stone house, the only cool place on the island in this Indian summer and sultry fall, he did not know why he had displaced himself for this one poor family among the thousands of families of the displaced, for this one distraught mourner, for this one dead child. He had seen the babies dying and the fathers weeping and the mothers in agony in their tens of thousands in the ships that lined the bay, waiting for him to go out and inspect them before they sailed on to discharge the human wreckage from them. And for some reason that was beyond his understanding, he chose to save this father and his unknown wife and children. Because Rachel had died, because her father had brought her body to him, because he could not live with his guilt at doing so little for so many, because he could do no more, because all we may do on this earth is to save one another one by one. God only knew.

9

A FOREIGN EDUCATION

Iain would never have thought it of the army, but the Sutherland Highlanders which the British had put their number on as the Ninety-third, were like a musket and bonnet and boots. The men formed themselves into a congregation, they chose their own elders, and they paid for a minister in Edinburgh to preach to them on Sundays. It was a queer thing, the soldiers being that way, but most of them came from parishes that were not cleared as the Sinclairs had been, and the worst of the punishments for them not was a flogging of five hundred lashes with the cat o'nine tails, but the threat to post a notice on the door of their kirk at home telling of their disgrace, so that when they did go back to their clachan, why, all would know their shame and none would bear with them for it. For they had taken the guinea and were bound to be a good soldier for their terms of years, even though there was not a tack of land at the end of it now, only the honour of the clan that was not the honour of the regiment, whoever heard of a thing like that?

These were men that matched Iain himself in the size and spirit, Willie McBean was that big, he could look down on Iain and call him a wee man. And when they came to it with the wrestling of hands, Iain could only hold Willie for forty minutes with the blood squeezing out of the tips of his fingers, before Willie put Iain's hand gently down on the scrubbed deal and said, "Toots, wee man, you'll make a tussle of it when you grow." But Tam Ogilvie was a bantam cock with a kick like a cuddy; Iain saw him put four big fellows on their hams with his head butt and his fists in two blinks of the eye. These were hard knocks in little packets, and Tam Ogilvie was the very devil when the blood ran up, for all the pint bottle he was.

When Hamish Jamie came to Edinburgh, it was not to the Sutherlands, for he would have none of them, but only to the regiment from Ross where they had been cleared before the family were shipped to Canada. His was Fraser's Highlanders or the Seaforths, also the Seventy-eighth, but they were a wild lot at the grogshops and the flogging-post as often as not. The meeting of the brothers in the barracks was not easy, but it was done, and Iain heard of the loss of the ship to Canada and the dying of his sister Rachel of the fever and the family in the farm out there, but they had moved west now into the woods to clear their own farm, and not a word from them the while.

"We were in Montreal," Iain said, "and we only came back the now. And we will be in Canada again and see them all."

"If you have the luck, Iain," Hamish Jamie said. "The Seaforths have been in India for years, and they have been dying of the cholera, and that is why they need me out there, more oats for the illness. They say it is as bad as the potatos, you swell and go black and stink like an old fish. And I want the fighting."

"You'll have that," Iain said. "When we last shipped to America, we were at a big river, they say the Mississippi. And the daft officers, they walked us into the American long muskets of the men of the woods –and good Scotsmen all of them, Bowies and such. And every man of them could hit a squirrel in the eye at two hundred paces. So we were soon dead or wounded, though I heard tell it was better in garrison in Montreal, where we had the curling and the bowling. Fine it is to play them."

"I want the fighting."

"Have the playing while you can," Iain said. "The fighting will come surely."

And so it would with the Russian bear striking his claws south to Constantinople, which was halfway to India, where the Russians were also at the Himalayas and wanted to come in. And there was the balloting for the soldiers' wives and the children, "To Go" or "Not To Go" with their husbands to the front. Would they exchange one dark room for a worse wet tent, one scrubbing tub for another, one sick bairn for a sicker one? But if the paper was "Not To Go" it meant a separation for ten years or more. They were not paid a pension, they had to be paupers on the parish. Even a shack or rotten canvas for worry on half rations was better than the workhouse at home. The marrying of the uniform, that was the proud day in a lassie's life. But following the flag was slow dying and shame.

Before his posting, Iain had a letter from Mary, telling him that she was with the duchess in her grand house in London. He was given a leave of embarkation, and since he had no parish and no family in Scotland, he was after taking the new steam train to London to see the great city and his sister there. But Hamish Jamie did not tell his brother of his own troubles with the flesh, how one of the soldier's wives, Meg Robertson, who did his washing and pipe-clayed his straps and leggings, had the eye for him and taught him the things the Bible said were not to do and yet were so sweet to do. And on a foul mattress off the market, where rooms were at rent for twopence an hour, Hamish Jamie learned of love or what was called love. After the thrashing and the cries of pain and the release, there was a time of peace and joy when the lines of labour and sorrow on Meg's face were soothed soft as curds, and she spoke as honey, "My one, my own Hamish," and the smile on her lips was the smile of sixteen, and that was the wonder of it from Hamish Jamie, how the desperate coming together made such a calm and a child out of her weariness. There could be no sin in it, but there surely was, and never did Hamish Jamie meet the eye of Robertson in the mess. And when one night Meg's husband asked harshly for the loan of his kettle and never did give it back, Hamish Jamie never did ask for it, reckoning Meg was worth more than a piece of old tin, even if her man did not.

There was no end to their fifth winter in the woods, although it would be the end of all of them if the spring came not soon. But it did not come, and the chores of staying alive made every day a chill labour with skin cracking in the frost, and fingers and toes turning blue through fur mittens and boots, and the very breath of a man changed to steam in the still air or to crystal if he spat to the snow. There was wood enough for the chopping, in truth there were too many trees. For the forest staked their log cabin round in a bristle of giant fence on fence on fence, as if God Almighty had tossed ten thousand cabers from the sky in some High Heaven Games.

Ice had to be chopped from the spring too, when water was needed, and it froze in the pail as old Hamish toted it back to the cabin door. Inside the smoky and small space, the holes between the log walls plugged with dry mud clotted with twig and reed, Hannah was the abiding miracle of herself. It was sore hard with the penned spirits of the children, Bain and Angus and Katie, fretting at their long confinement, longing to run out over the white wild that at first fall had been snowballs and sliding and laughter, and now was a pale shroud laid across the world.

Yet Hannah tended to the iron stove that the waggon and the ponies had taken with them, giving them less each day of the sour lumps of dough called flapjacks, which were the cold porridge cakes of Canada. The only sweetening was some drops of maple sugar gone into the boiling water until there was a thin syrup with a faint taste of far joy as a love remembered. They were at the bottom of the sack of dried apples and plums, and their teeth were loose in their black gums, while their lips were as white as linen. They thirsted like the moose and the bear and the snowshoe rabbits for the berries and the grasses of spring to make them whole again.

Angus was the first to despair. They had prayed before the meal, a simple Grace and God be thanked for His mercies, and it was an occasion, the last of the bear's bacon, even if it was more rind than lean. But Angus kicked the table on the sudden and fell back on the big bed he shared with Bain and said, "Rachel's lying sweeter than we are in those trees on the island. Why did you bring us to die in the snow, father? For we will."

"God will provide," Hannah said, "but until He does, we must."

"We have the land now," Hamish said. "Thirty acres. Did we have that ever to call our own?"

"Thirty acres of trees," Angus said. "And what do we grow on trees? Nuts and bears?"

"We will bring the trees down," Hamish said. "And there will be a town in these woods, with a kirk and a mill and a store and a school-house. And we will be the making of this new land, for that we were unmade in our own Scotland."

"We had a farm by the river and the sea at Grosse Isle –"

"It was not our farm. It was the farm of the good Doctor –"

"And he gave you the money to come west, and the ministers and the relief. And it was not for the saving of us, but for the ridding of us."

"Hush, Angus," Hamish said. "They were good folk. We should not be here as we are if they –"

"We should not be here as we are." Angus coughed into the smoke that blew back from the stove and could not escape from under the low ridgepole and planks piled with stones and sod that was their roof. "There's no place wants the Sinclairs the now. We are the outcasts – that goat in the Good Book."

"The scapegoat," Hamish said. "Aye, Angus, you have right in what you say. There was no sin in us for what we had to suffer –"

"Talk of himself," Hannah said, "that he does. That's for you to say, Hamish. An' how do we know the now what the Lord saw in us that we did not do right?"

"When the snow's gone..." Katie said.

"If it is ever gone," Bain said.

"Can I have a new dress at the store?"

Hannah's heart bled to see her daughter wrapped in a grey wool blanket with a robe of stitched beaver- and wolf-skins thrown over her to keep her warm. Dear God, were the woods making them the savages that even the braes and the mountains of Scotland never made them be?

"You'll have a fine woollen dress of the red and the white," Hannah said, "an' the men catch enough skins for Rafferty at the store. And you will have them, Hamish, will you not?"

Hamish and the boys spent the winter months in the making of the traps that were their living until they could clear the land. They already knew the art of the snare and the noose and the deadfall and the wooden cages for the skins of beaver and otter and wolf and mink and fox and coon only sold without a ball-mark in them. And they were down to the last of the powder for the old smooth-bore muzzle-loader with a flint-lock that was almost as old as Hamish himself. They had to use their knives to kill and flay the furred beasts of the forests, which God had given for their clothing and their trading. And now the pelts were pegged on their stretchers under the roof in black flags, waiting for the thaw that did not come.

"There's game enough," Hamish said, "for every man. But it takes a pile of skins for Rafferty to cut a dress out of it – if a dress he has at all."

Rafferty's store was a walk through the trees away to the river, where the canoes brought in the goods – new lead bars laid over the barrels of gunpowder, muskets never shot off before, bolts of cloth in all the colours of the rainbow and blankets brighter than lightning, beads and ribbons and bells and rings for the Indian finery; and the knives for hunting with the horn handles, and the axes and the tomahawks, and the iron rails and hammers and steel saws for the cutting down of the trees and the building of the cabins. And the keg in the corner with its spigot and tap, spilling out the sour sharp smell of the whisky that pinched the nose, while the Indian braves sat by, trading their furs for ten mugs of the spirit that made them wilder than the natures God gave them in His mysterious way.

"Rafferty will have cloth for a dress," Hannah said, "if you don't spend all the tally for the skins on knives and blacksmith's traps and whisky –"

"And when did I ever spend on the whisky what was for the family?"

Hannah heard the hurt in the voice of Hamish which was also his defence against a weakness so rare it should be forgot. But she never forgot a weakness.

"It is not that you never, Hamish," she said. "It is that you will not now. And we will have yeast so we will have good Christian bread again with the meal, and we will have that dried fruit paste you cannot tell from chewing leather for the good of our sore mouths – and cloth for Katie's dress. For to look at her, you will think she was a squaw and worse, for they have fine beads and bells on their leggings, while Katie has no shift or shirt to call her own."

She took the last of the flapjacks off the skillet with the flat fork and put it on the plate of Angus.

"Eat," she said. "You will live. We will clear the trees. There will be a fine farm house, but builded in wood, not the stone. But we will have a stone hearth for the winter to come, and another room for the boys, so we do not have to sleep like cuddies, in the barn, and we will plant potatos and corn on the land which God has given us."

"Listen to your mother," Hamish said. "And we will bide this winter."

And the very next morning, there was a noise as of a volley of rifles, and it was the daggers of ice splitting from the rims of the roof and the frozen water cracking on the top of the spring and the frost breaking open at the coming of a warm wind that sang of the hope of the ending of the winter without end.

"Lord, and you think working for the duchess in London was better than being in the army, Iain? But men, they ken only what they do, and they think they have the worst of it. If you think privates and corporals and sergeants and captains and majors and generals are anything to *our* household, you have many thinks a-coming. You no ken what we have to do and every missie keep her place, or it's out on the street, bag and baggage, if there's any you have.

"Work your way up, Herself says, and when they say work, it is *work*. I was starting as a second dairy maid, and out with the cows at the milking before it was light. And then it was under-laundry maid, Iain, and never you saw so much bleach and starch, for they soil their linens and their chemmies just as bad as anyone, for all their ladies' airs that nothing but Paris perfume ever come under their noses."

Mary swept back a strand of her hair which had fallen loose on her forehead. She had to tell her soldier big brother all that had happened to her. That's what brothers were for. They had to listen.

"After upper-laundry maid, I was promoted to under-housemaid, and glad I was to keep out of the kitchen, for cook calls himself chef, and the only thing he had out of France was his sauce, not his sauces, and a temper worse than red pepper. But chambermaid was not so grand, up at dawn to light the kitchen fire and clean the other grates, dust off the night before and prepare the morning after, sweep the hall and stairs, and all before breakfast, and the seeing to the ladies in their bedrooms, their fires and their hot water, and waiting for their rising and their dressing by their lady's maids, so their rooms be aired and their mattresses turned and their sheets put on fresh as daisies every day. And so on until the afternoon, when all is done backwards, for the hours are sixteen every day, and hardly a holy day of rest.

"But the *rank* of it, Iain, and keeping your place, and where you may sit in the parlour and in the kitchen for your dinner, it is worse than the army, even if you and Hamish Jamie say it is not. I no ken if His Grace – and he has not a grace in him – the duke is worse than His Mister Menzies and the Lord High Butler. You would think the moon shone out of his weskit buttons, for bulging they are, and he is worse than the Duke of Wellington to the footmen. And he would tell off the housekeeper, Mrs Rogers, only he is scared she will rap his knuckles with her great bunch of keys, so it is Her Holy Cow who has the minding of us parlourmaids and nursemaids and skivvies and such. And she says to me, 'Mary Sinclair, if you took it upon yourself to be educated instead of remaining as thick as porridge, why, I might recommend Her Grace that you be her lady's maid, after Céline goes back to that God-forsaken country where she was born.' But you have to be French to be a lady's maid."

Mary could see her brother smiling and shaking his head at her, not disapproving, but enjoying the story of her life below stairs. And she could not stop the telling of it.

"We eat in the kitchen, while Mister Menzies and Mrs Rogers eat in their parlour, and we wait on them there. And breakfast for them, Iain, it is what we had for a whole day in Scotland, and better – hot rolls and dry toast and a fancy bread loaf and a common loaf and a pound of butter and a red-hot iron in an urn of boiling water for the making of their tea and a thick coffee that is more of a chocolate you ken. And all of us below the stairs take lunch at one in the kitchen and dinner at six, and if you saw the spread of it, Iain – cold cuts and soles fried with capers, a leg of mutton and a dish of ox, pullets and potatos, rice and rhubarb tart. It would feed an army, that it would.

"And this silk dress I am wearing! I might be the grand lady, for off the back of Her Grace it is. Céline was clever, she was. Pleats and flounces, Her Grace wants them right and neat every time like the Guards on parade, and I do them for Céline, I am a dab hand at the ironing. But this silk dress Céline did, and she burned it and stitched it up poorly and put it on Her Grace and said, "Oh la la, ma'am, it eez not 'vair good, eez bad stitches, look ze dress-maker, kell horror!" So her Grace gave Céline the dress and Céline give it me and I stitch it so it is good as new. And I am the lady now – on my day off, if I get one.

"I got one to see you, Iain, and I got one to see the Great Exhibition. Albert took me, the footman, very saucy, but he's a cockney, and London's like a brae to him, and there were so many folk in the park we never did get inside, but there was this crystal palace shining in the sun like a dream big as our mountain, but all glass with trees *inside*, and it is all took away the now and the trees still in the park, but it was the wonder of the world, and I saw it. But you are took away over the sea to Russia, and you will not come back. Iain, oh Iain, must you go?"

"I must," Iain said.

He had been listening to his sister Mary talk of her life for an hour or more, as they sat in a tavern off the Seven Dials. His tartan forage hat was set on the table before him by his mug of porter, but there was bare room enough to squeeze his knees under the wood, while Mary billowed out in her green silk like a wave over the sawdust. She was bonny now with the oval face of the Sinclair women, and she surely had found her tongue. Talk, talk, talk, it was longer than a sermon, though more lively for all that.

Outside by the Seven Dials, they could hear the ballad-seller shouting, "Awful catastrophe! Awful catastrophe! Only a ha'penny!" And Mary rose in a surge of silk and held out her hand and pulled him up and said, "Come and buy a ballad! Albert takes me here, when he can – and they are an education! I ken they are not holy, but they have a tidy moral. And if a good murder is the subject, why, Iain, there is murder enough in the Good Book – Saul slew in his thousands and David in his tens of thousands –"

"There is killing and killing," Iain said, "and some of it is legal and some of it is not, but for the dead man, he does no care, for he is too dead to care at all."

They went out among the costers at their barrows, crying, "Mussels, a penny a quart! Live eels, three pound a shilling! All large and alive – O, new sprats, O, a penny a plate! Cherry ripe, twopence a pound!" And Iain bought Mary a pound of cherries, which she sucked into her mouth till her lips were stained black with the juices of them, while she stored the pips in her cheek till she could slip them into her glove and drop them while no one was looking. For they were all gawking at the red-faced ballad-seller in his black hat, and coat of pearl buttons, talking of a dreadful murder at the Seven Dials, a father killing his pretty little boy, the sadness and the badness of it.

"No my friends, here you have, just printed and published, half-an-hour ago, a full, true and particular account of the life, trial, character, confession, behaviour, sentence, repentance and execution of that horrible malefactor, J. F. Jeffery, who was executed and hanged after on Monday last, for the small charge of one ha'penny – and for the dreadful and wicked murder of his only son Arthur, pretty and tender and handsome. You have here every particular, that which he done, and that which he didn't. Ain't this just a dodgy country – we loves birds and dogs and flowers, treat them right we do – and we puts our sons and daughters down the mines and up the chimbleys, 'Sweep, sweep, chimbley-sweep!' and we does away with them most unnatural – and for only a ha'penny!"

"I never heard of such a thing," Iain spoke down to Mary from his tartan cap that perched above the crowd as high as the faces of the Seven Dials. "Murdering your own boy!"

"Did I not say it was an education?"

And the patterer went on, as a boy walked round the crowd, offering the pink sheets of the ballad.

"Yes, my customers, to this is added a copy of serene and beautiful werses, pious and immoral, what he wrote with his own blood and skewer the night after – I means the night before his execution. It is addressed to young men and women of all sexes – I beg pardon, but I mean classes – my friends, it is nothing to laugh at, for I can tell you the werses make three of the hardest-heartist things weep – a bailiff, a banker and a copper. And look at that soldier lad, down from bonny Scotland and tall as the gallows what they hanged the horrible murderer on, he'll have this dreadful tale what is tidy moral and highly educational – for the small charge of only a ha'penny!"

And as the boy with the ballads put a pink sheet in Iain's hand while he fumbled in his sporran for a copper with his other hand, the patterer began to sing in a voice like a gurgle in a drainpipe:

> "You kindest fathers, tender mothers,
> Listen to this sad tale awhile,
> Listen, listen, listen brothers,
> To murder in the Seven Dials.
> In Earl Street lived a wretch named Jeffery,
> His trade a tailor I am told,
> His little boy called Richard Arthur
> Was a tot of six years old –"

"Toots, man," Iain shouted, "if this is the best you can do in your great city, the ship to Russia can no come too soon."

"Hush, Iain," Mary spoke up to him. "We will away, then."

And as they pushed through the crowd at the Seven Dials among the crying voices of the costers, they could hear the boy joining the patterer at the end of his song, his piping answering the deep voice of his master.

> "The villain took him to a cellar,
> Resolved his offspring to destroy,
> Tied his little hands behind him,
> Hanged the pretty smiling boy.
> 'Now upon the drop you see me,
> Guilty and heart-broken here!
> Who in Heaven will forgive me?'
> 'I forgive you, Daddy dear'!"

"If that is what you call entertainment – theatre in London –"

"Others there are – The Vic!" Mary said.

"I will never see the theatre again," Iain said. "And if there is to be killing, I will be killing Russian bears and no wee boys. Mary, Mary, how can you bide in a schlorich and a slummock like London?"

10

THE MOUNTAINS AND THE STONES

1855

"All officers are daft," Iain Sinclair said, "for anyone must be daft to buy in to be an officer, but only one of them has a brain to put beside the next –"

"He'll be Sir Colin Campbell," Tam Ogilvie said, running his whetstone along the edge of his bayonet. "Put all the brains of all the officers' mess in the army in one skillypan, and boil 'em, and Sir Colin would have 'em for breakfast, and who'd know the lack of nothing?"

"He must have asked for us," Iain said, "and that's the pity. A river to cross and then a mountain to climb into the Russian guns. So Sir Colin says, 'Send you for the Highlanders. They're fools and they're goats. They're fools enough to fight head on climbing a mountain, but they're goats enough to climb it'."

"More'n they can!" Iain said. He nodded his head towards where the battalions of the Brigade of Guards were waiting in scarlet coats with brass buttons bright enough to blind an eye on. "Them Grenadiers and Coldstreamers, they'll fight on the flat –"

"With the cannon behind them."

"But on the hills ..." Iain laughed. "Why, if they won't fall over their big boots on a wee scree of stones!"

The Highland Brigade was in the second line with the Guardsmen under the heights of Alma. They could clearly see how bad the fight would be. If ever there was a battle lost in advance, this was it. A river to cross, bare scraped slopes to mount towards two great and lesser redoubts hairy like a sporran with cannon, then cliffs with dozens of grey Russian battalions waiting on top. The only good thing was that the Highlanders were not in the front line. That was for the Light Infantry, they that had won so many hard battles for the old Duke of Wellington in the Peninsula against Boney's armies and now were cussing at the pounding from the long Russian guns, lying and waiting for the order to attack until the afternoon. So when it came and they had to struggle across the river, they stopped to drink for their terrible thirst, even though some of them were drinking blood, as the grapeshot and canister cut them down.

Now the Russian guns were reaching them and they were told to lie down too, and Iain felt his own berserker blood surge into his head, as he watched the Light Infantry stumble up the barren slope towards the great redoubt, with the smoke obscuring them from the brushwood fires lit by the Russian scouts. But on they climbed with more and more laying on the slopes, but then, far and away, a hunting cry, "Stole away! Stole away!" And daft it was, the Russian guns, all limbering up and drawing away behind the horses, and the beaten men of the Light Infantry going over the earthworks on to the heights, all because the Russians had stole away.

"Forward, forward," Iain muttered to himself, as he squinted from the ground along the lying lines to where the royal Duke of Cambridge sat on his grey. But the Duke did not budge, he did not speak, he might have already been the statue or the pub sign that would surely become of him. There was no word of forward or backward from him, but the silence of stay where you are, stay where you'll always be, down and out of it. And looking forward again, Iain could already see the grey Russian battalions come in wedges towards the great redoubt to push back the Light Infantry. So it would all have to be done again, as it always had to be done many a time and dead men too many.

And done again it was against the mountains and the odds. Crossing the river was not so bad, although the weight of the water on his kilt dragged Iain down at the knees and the fur fringe of his big bonnet fell in his eyes. And it was luck that hardly a Russian long gun was firing as they picked their way up the left of the slope among the dead and the dying of the Light Infantry, moaning and piteous as curlews on the moor over the sea-shore. The Highlanders were ragged, but faster up the hill, for they were surely used to that. But the Guardsmen, they were a sight for the drill sergeant, their two thin red ranks advancing as if to the pacestick, thirty inches between each pace, and eighteen inches from shoulder to shoulder, how would they keep that order and that perfect distance? And when the round-shot and the musket balls hit a Guardsman and threw him over in a crumpled scarlet shroud, why, the rank closed up from the left, you'd have thought an invisible bar was keeping them straight and an unseen wire was pulling them together, as they marched over the bodies of the Light Infantry and their own. And now it must be over, for four columns of grey Russians, each thick as a man o'war, came over the hill to ram the thin red ranks and sink them utterly.

But now the red ranks halted, and the Minié rifles were raised thicker than the prickles on a hedgehog, and the command came, "Fire!" and the smoke and the crackle came from the muzzles of the Guardsmen, and then they slipped in another cartridge, through the muzzle beneath the bayonet and rammed it home and marched on this devil's parade. The Russians coming down from the heights had stopped, the rear ranks pushing forward, the front ranks stepping back from the wall of their dead comrades lying as heaps of spent kelp before them.

Looking forward, Iain saw two more columns facing the Highlanders in two bulwarks and piers of grey stone. They also fired a volley, but the firing of the volley was not the way of Sir Colin Campbell and the mountain men in the attack, and there was a shout that might be for a charge, but it was lost in the yelling and the wild outcry of the pipes, and Iain was shouting and running up the scree, swinging his rifle and bayonet to the fore, his kilt clapping and sticking at his bare legs. Then the shock as he stabbed home the point of his bayonet into the grey cloth of a man under a shako, and the twist into the wound, and the kick forward on the falling shape to jerk out the bayonet, and the swinging of the butt in a club, and the cheeks and noses breaking open in spurts of red, and then slipping down.

Now he was slipping down himself, and then he was rising at the lunge, and another body was writhing on the bayonet and taking him down so he had to pull it out with a boot on the bloody cheek of the other, then swing the butt, swing and strike, and strike home. All the while, the red mist was in his eyes and the war cry was breaking out of his throat wilder than bulls at the mating, till the white faces in front were grey backs on the sudden, and the bulwark was a broken sea wall, with the kilts and the bonnets streaming through, and the Russians in dull waves on the slipstream away.

And as Iain reached the heights of Alma to see the broken battalions and the Russians in one great ebb tide sweeping back towards the hard walls of Sebastopol, he heard the hurrahs and the shout of triumph to the right, and he looked across to see the earthworks of the great redoubt fringed in the scarlet of tunic and ensign, and he knew that the battle of the Alma was won, if a battle is ever won, for it is lost for some, the wounded and the dying and the dead. And even the terrible Duke of Wellington, was it not he that said, "Next to a battle lost, there is nothing so dreadful as a battle won."

But there is always another battle to lose. And so it looked outside Balaclava, where the generals had got it wrong as they always did, and it was left to Sir Colin Campbell and the Highlanders to save the day, as they always did. There were only five hundred and fifty of them not dead or wounded now, and another hundred sick, and some Turks who were better off at the running than the shooting, for they had poured down from the lost redoubts in front, shouting, "Ship! Ship!" How to get out seemed the only Christian word they knew. And seeing the Russians coming down from the taken redoubts above the valley leading to the port, Sir Colin ordered his men to lie down on their faces in two ranks like Guardsmen on the far side of the hillock that was their position.

So Iain lay down with murder in his heart to take the pounding and the shot of the Russian horse-guns lobbing their shells over the crest. The lying down and the taking it was the bitter part and the British part that was called the discipline, while the real pounding was the blood in his temples redder than his coat and telling him to rise and charge, yelling, forward. And what was that? From the corner of his eye, Iain could see the distant glitter of the Light Horse Brigade to the side, waiting to take the enemy on the flank, but they were wheeling now and going about and leaving the Sutherland Highlanders in the lurch. But what could a Scotsman expect from a bunch of Sassenach dolls on fancy gee-gees who might have been riding on a merry-go-round at the fair for all they knew of war?

Now the Turks were running over the hillock, shouting "Ship! Ship! Ship!" again, and they were scampering like rats in a grain barge back to Balaclava. And it must be the sight of the Russians, and so it was, for the cannon had stopped, and there was the sound of horses in a far trotting that rose to a near clatter, and Sir Colin shouted, 'Rise! Take your aim! Fire!' and they were just like the bloody Guardsmen in their two thin red lines raising their Minié rifles with the bayonets tipping them with steel and taking aim at the four squadrons of horsemen that had halted down the hill, surprised at the sudden view of them.

When they fired their volley at the Russians, the men came down like skittles, the horses like broken stools in a wild whinnying. The rest of the horsemen rode on, but when another cartridge was rammed in, and the order came again to aim and fire, the second volley took the guts and the wind out of them, and they staggered as in the gust of a gale. And Iain started forward with half the Highlanders, but he heard Sir Colin shouting the British number of their regiment, "Ninety-third! Ninety-third! Damn all that eagerness!" And Iain steadied with his line, and he put another cartridge in the muzzle, and he pushed it home and he aimed and he fired on the order, and the third volley broke the Russian cavalry, which wheeled and rode away from the downed and heaving carpet of their own. And a yell split the air over the valley. The Sutherland Highlanders had saved Balaclava, and the stuck-up fellahs on their fairground gee-gees had the Devil to do with it as usual. It was the two thin red lines, and didn't Sir Colin say, "I did not think it worthwhile to form them even four deep."

For Iain Sinclair, that day was the last he had of the fighting in the Crimea. He did not see, he did not know of the charge of the Heavy Brigade against the Russian massed horse and their breaking of the bears with six legs, and he did not see, he did not know of the foolishness of the charge of the Light Brigade into the cannon to left of them and cannon to right of them and cannon to front of them that volleyed and thundered. For it was sure that no poet was to write of the foolishness of him getting his wound, bending over a fallen Russian hussar to strip the helmet off his head as a keepsake for Mary and a dead horseman rising up behind as a solid ghost and shooting him with a pistol through the back, before Iain in his falling dropped him dead at last with a giant fist as heavy as a hammer on his bare skull.

Iain tried to stop the blood coming out of the hole in his chest with his spread hand, but it was no good. He felt his veins pumping out his life through his back, and he could not walk away. And Tam and Willie McBean came, and they plugged the holes in the front and the rear of Iain with wadding and lint for the cleaning of their rifles, and they bound it tight with a sling round his chest, until the red flow of his veins was stoppit, and they made a cat's cradle of their hands, and so it was that they carried him with his arms round their shoulders all the way to the ships at Balaclava. For if Sir Colin Campbell expected his men to die for him, he also wanted them to live for him, and after the fighting, he was the man of all of them to see after that.

The woman, who sat writing in the lamp-light was dressed in white. But her face was not angelic. It was practical and almost dour. She pinched her lips pale as she wrote to her friend Doctor Bowman in England, which seemed at the far end of this world.

On Thursday last (November 8th), we had 1715 sick and wounded in the Hospital (among whom 120 cholera patients), and 650 severely wounded in the other building called the General

Hospital, of which we also have charge, when a message came to me to prepare for 510 wounded on our side of the Hospital, who were arriving from Balaclava.

A moaning rose from below in the Barrack Hospital at Scutari that was not the moaning of the Black Sea. It was more like a moaning from a purgatory below. The woman in white was still writing, but now she wrote about herself.

> I always expected to end my days as a Hospital Matron, but I never expected to be a Barrack Mistress. We had but half an hour's notice before they began landing the wounded. Between 1 and 9 o'clock we had mattresses stuffed, sewn up, laid down, alas! only upon matting on the floor. We have had such a sea in the Bosphorus and the Turks, the very men for whom we are fighting, carry in our wounded so cruelly, that they arrive in a state of agony.

This time she did put aside her pen. How could she write it all? And should she write that the army was killing its own soldiers by its inefficiency and cruelty? The truth pointed itself in phrases through her head, as her lips spoke what she must write.

> Twenty four cases died in the day of landing...
> We now have four miles of beds, and not eighteen inches apart...
> The wounded are now lying up to our very doors, and we are landing 540 more from the Andes...
> And there are two more ships loading at the Crimea with the wounded...
> We have erysipelas, fever and gangrene, and the Russian wounded are the worst...
> I am getting a screen now for the amputations, for when one poor fellow, who is to be amputated tomorrow, sees his comrade today die under the knife, it makes an impression and diminishes his chance...
> In all our corridor I think we have not an average of three limbs per man...

Her pen did not go on writing. She would finish the letter later. The wounded were waiting for her, and the dying. It was a ritual now. "The lady with the lamp," she was called that. But sometimes she felt of no more use than the lamp, casting a light here and a shadow there indifferently, and the wick going out from time to time, which she was never allowed to do.

Walking along the miles of the mattresses, hands were stretched out to her – when there were hands to stretch, and not stumps. It was the gangrene, and the only remedy was whatever sawbones there were, for the surgeons did not relish army pay and stayed in England. There must be a better remedy for the gangrene than draining the green matter and all the hygiene that could be managed; but when the wounded came in from the Crimea, their wounds were already infected. And the nurses they sent her, some of them downed as much *arak* and rum as the male orderlies, who were mostly dead of cholera or *delirium tremens*, and the poor devils getting blind drunk before they lost a limb or two, tied down on the blood bench.

There was no Mrs Roberts, worth her weight in gold, and Mrs Drake, who was a treasure. And that extraordinary Lady Alicia Blackwood, but what about the baggage she had to dismiss all because of the caps she made the nurses wear to show they were also in uniform. "I came out, ma'am, prepared to submit to everything," the hoyden said, "But there was the caps, ma'am, that suits one face, and some that suits another. And if I'd known about the caps I wouldn't have come to the Scutari."

Well, she was gone, and good riddance, to put the wearing of caps above caring for dying men. Four in ten had been dying when she came, and now it was down to two in ten, but two in a hundred would still be too many. But down below in the cellars, those were the worst, where she had sent Lady Alicia Blackwood to cope with the remains of it all, the sewers and the soldiers' wives and the children that the army forgot even more than its men. The rats did better there than the people, but Lady Alicia would have to manage. It would be about time that she learned about life downstairs, Miss Nightingale thought. She herself was needed above.

She passed along the lying men, leaning up to her, mumbling and muttering, shrieking and calling to her or somebody quite beyond her. Only as she came by, she could hear the cursing stop, the foul words end. Armies lived on their swearing, she knew that – not on their bellies or on their boots, as books would have it. But as her lamp threw ahead its little swinging path along the great corridor with its mattresses of the wounded fresh from Balaclava, she only heard "Gi' us ... Tell me ... I'll live then ... Write me mam ... They'll no have my leg ... Water, for the love of God ... I canna bear the pain ... God ha' mercy ... mercy, then ... mercy."

And she repeated her litany in passing, the words they wished to hear, the things she could not do for them.

"Brave lads, we'll look after you ... you will get better ... you're in good hands now ... God has sent you to us ... only have faith ... we are doing all we can ... all we can for you ... God bless you ..."

Why one Scotsman caught her eye rather than hundreds of others in the corridor, Miss Nightingale did not know. It must have been the size of him, for he was a giant, with his bare feet protruding from the end of the mattress. He had shaken off the sheet and showed above a draggled kilt a naked chest bound by a bandage, black with his old blood and red with the new. The bullet must have missed heart and lungs, for he spoke to her with the rough lilt that the Queen herself loved so much in her Highland servant, John Brown.

"Will you be writing me a letter, Miss Nightingale? For as it is, I am sore hurt and no can hold a pen, and I have no pen to hold."

Miss Nightingale stopped and cast her lamplight on the strong, sunken face of Iain Sinclair, his ruddiness drained down into his bleeding bandages.

"If I write for you, I must write for all."

"Write for me," the giant said. "To my sister Mary Sinclair. She is with the duke, and his mother, the countess, she was the laird of our clan. But we are scattered now to the four corners of the earth ..."

"Your mother and your father?"

"Gone to Canada, and the devil alone knows where."

"God knows," Miss Nightingale said. "Have they not written to tell you where they are?"

Iain Sinclair shook his head and winced at the pain of it from his smashed rib bones.

"We are not a writing nation," he said. "But we are a fighting nation."

Miss Nightingale smiled. It was her first smile of the day and the night, and in the lamplight Iain saw a trace of sweetness that could hardly be shown.

"I have read your Sir Walter Scott," she said. "Is his name wrong?"

"We are not a reading nation neither," Iain said. "That is for them as has the time for it."

"I will write to your sister Mary Sinclair, but tell me, what shall I say?"

"Tell her —" The giant paused, but the fever in his eyes struck two sparks from the candlelight falling from the lamp in the lady's hand. "Tell her – she'll be seeing her Iain again in London. An she will wait,

I shall be home again. It is but a wee hole in my ribs and a touch of the heat in my head ..."

The fever, it might come down. The holes in his chest and back, they might not be infected with gangrene. His smashed ribs might mend. He might not catch any of the hospital diseases that spread from bed to bed. He had survived the dreadful crossing from the Crimea to Turkey. He must be as strong as an ox to do that. And perhaps the glint in his eyes was hope as well as fever.

"I will write that you will return," Miss Nightingale said. "And which Duke does your sister serve?"

"Serve?" The giant's loud laugh turned into a cough. "Och, I'll not laugh, it hurts. But no Sinclair serves another. It is all one clan except some do forget it with English ways. I am in the Sutherland Highlanders – and surely that is the Duke's name."

"And his address?"

"Is there not a House of Lords in London big enough to house them all? And find them?"

Miss Nightingale knew she should reprove the wounded giant for his resentment, but she felt a secret pleasure in his words. What were the battle orders of the Duke of Cambridge and the Lords Raglan and Lucan and Cardigan, which had sent him to Scutari in such a sorry state? As if she herself had not suffered from the pig-headed peers who ran the army worse than a slaughter house.

"I will send your letter to your sister Mary Sinclair," she said, "And I will find the Duke. But now, I must go on. And you will be well."

"Aye," Iain Sinclair said. "I will be well now."

And a strange certainty possessed Miss Nightingale that he would be well, not another maimed hope. She found the rest of her rounds less burdensome than she had dared to expect. She even looked forward to seeing Lady Alicia in her office. Whatever complaints there might be from the worse hell of the women and children below, she would send Lady Alicia back to her place and the duty which her class so often preached and so rarely practised.

All the same, she found it hard to answer what Lady Alicia told her. A dead baby had been wedged in a sewer-pipe to stop the muck flowing into the cellars. Was it not too much to bear? How could heaven above allow such a crime?

"I would advize the three P's," Miss Nightingale finally said. "Practicality, a parson and a plumber. Take the baby out, give it a Christian burial and divert the sewage. Do not think about it, Lady Alicia, just do something. I am afraid that we must work now and pray later. God helps those who help themselves – and God help us if we don't!"

God made the world, old Hamish Sinclair thought, but it was certain He put too many trees and stones in it. As if cutting the trees for the clearing of the pasture was not bad enough, the lifting of the great rocks and drawing them aside with the oxen was a worse work. A tree had a use in it, but a lump of stone did not except as a boundary mark. Hannah had her hearth now builded of the wee stones, and under it was a turnspit for the meat, a large kettle and a small kettle on their hooks, an iron skillet and a Dutch oven for the bread baking. And she had a broom of dry brush, tied with rawhide strips to a pole. And the fire was always banked now, if it was not burning, for the phosphorus matches from the store were sore dear, and there was no need for the fire ever to die. And Hannah had moulds for the deer tallow now, melting it in a saucepan and pouring it round the wicks that spanned the shaping. And if there was a blaze of light needed when the buck-skins were drawn tight over the window at night, why, pitchpine would flare on the fire or a twist of rag would flame if it floated in a pie-plate full of bear's grease.

Other women papered their walls with pages from the newspapers and magazines that sometimes reached the store. Then they read the walls. But Hannah would have none of that. The reading in the house was the Bible, and that was good enough, and Hamish had learned to read and write the English when he had served in the army, and now he taught the reading and the writing of the English to Bain and Angus and Katie, for other schooling there was none. Except they learned some of the French down along at the store, because the trappers went up and down river, and many of them only spoke a sort of French and said they were longer in Canada than the Scots were.

But Hannah was afeared as she watched her man and her young men working at the trees and the stones, for Hamish was bending now as an old pine bends to the sea wind, and if Bain loved the land that was at last their own, Angus did not, he was restless for the learning and the wide world beyond the prison palings of the trees. And Hannah knew in her heart that she would not keep him, no more than she had kept her Iain and her Hamish Jamie, gone to Russia and to India in the service of Queen Victoria.

In the fall when the leaves on the trees and down on the ground were yellow as broom and scarlet as blood and bright as cramoisy, Hamish was so wearied that he could not put a spoon to his broth at dinner, and he slouched at the table like a pricked bag of meal. And Hannah spoke her mind, for she could not live without that great bent body near her in the dark.

"If the clearing of the trees and the moving of the stones is more than a body can bear," she said, "we can go west again. They say there are plains there and grass as far as the edge of the sky. It is good for cattle."

"For cattle and men," Bain said. "But bad for women and wood."

"This home is not to your liking," Hamish muttered so low that Hannah could hardly hear him.

"Eat your broth," she said. "This is a fine home. It is not that. I ask you, where are the other homes?"

"The Mackenzies are here —" Bain said.

"More than a mile away."

"And the store —

"Three miles to the river. And there is no minister, no church. That store, you ken Hamish, a woman cannot go in alone, for those drunken Indians and naked children playing with the dogs, and those old squaws liking a dram of whisky as much as the braves."

"But why will we go on west?" Angus asked. "Back east, I say, where there is schooling and opportunity. That is the answer they all speak. Why did you come from over the sea? Opportunity." He threw out his hands to encompass the log and mud walls of the cabin. "This is slavery. Worse than the black men in the South. Slavery. Chained in here all winter. Eaten by black flies all summer while we break our backs on the trees and the stones."

"It is our land now," Hamish said, sitting upright. "And here we bide, until —"

"I want dresses," Katie said. "And the dancing. And who shall I meet in the woods? A big brave and I am his squaw and wear leggings with beads and bells, and never a skirt again."

"Hush that foolishness," Hannah said. There was no keeping children in their growing except they were as her Bain, patient as the ox they hired from the store for the rooting out of the stumps and the stones. "All things come if you wait for them. There will be folks here — our own folk —"

"When I am an old maid fit to knit stockings for the bairns of the neighbours —"

"Soon, Katie, soon. More will come down the river."

"How long, O Lord," Hamish said, "How long?"

"Too long for me," Angus said. "I will go when I am able back down the river. To learn. And to America, it may be. They say that opportunity there –"

"You will bide with us," Hamish said. "Two of your brothers are already gone far away to India, and your sister Mary in London –"

"I will bide here," Angus said, "only as long as I must."

Hamish took a spoon of broth and spoke. "Angus is right, Hannah," he said. "This is no life for a lad who must make his way in the world. The land is for one man, and Bain is the older."

"But others will come. There will be more land to clear."

"In time. In a long time. In too long a time. Have you not seen how it is for the Scots? We never live in our time but in the time of our children. We go out in the world to make the way for others, and not even for our own children." Hamish's voice was powerful now as a surge of white water along a stream. "We do not labour for ourselves but for what will be. Iain and Hamish Jamie, they spread the red empire over the four corners of the earth, and their blood is not counted. Look at them, gone to India for the mutiny of folk who do not want us there. Mary works in the service of our duke and duchess, who do not reckon her, and who sent us away to a wilderness where they have forgot us. We break our bones clearing these trees and these stones for them who will follow us and feast on the fat of the land. It is never the time for the Sinclairs, only a time to work for them who will inherit the earth the Sinclairs have made for them."

Hannah's heart was proud with love for what her husband had said. It was true, but a woman expected that, raising bairns for their sake, not her own. But for a man to reckon that he worked always for other folk, and never for his own ...

"You are right, Hamish," she said. "But you would still be a Scots family, for all that."

"I would be what we are," Hamish said, "and nothing else. But as for the way the world is, I would it were other."

"The world is other," Angus said, "if you will go and find it in other places."

"Hush," Hannah said, "you will bide here."

"As long as I must," Angus said.

"You must," Hannah said. "Your mother and your father and your sister Katie have need of you."

"He will go if he must," Hamish said. "But not before it is the time."

11

THE SERVICE OF THE
FOREIGN QUEEN

"Trust," Hamish Jamie said. "No trust at all."

He had been trying to catch a rat for days, now the rat seemed to be inside his belly, gnawing him to death. It was not so much to bear for him, for he was used to hunger as a child in Scotland, and even in the army in India, on the long marches to nowhere from the cantonments across the plains where the red dust stood up in a brick wall, advancing pace by pace, surrounded by the artillery of the storm, flashing with lightning and belching black clouds and thundering louder than a victory salvo. Then they had been buffeted and soaked and starved for days and nights until the tempests passed, and the soldiers spread-eagled on the ground might resume their weary plod to the ends of the earth.

Now the cannon were manned, the twenty-four- and eighteen-pounders that the Sepoys had captured, and the big guns volleyed and blasted the mud walls of the entrenchment at Cawnpore, they took the heads off men with roundshot or broke both arms of Mrs White carrying her babies, so that she lay on her back in the main-guard, a twin suckling on each of her breasts, and her hands unable to cradle them. Hamish Jamie had been on the sally when they had spiked the Sepoy guns and bayoneted the sleeping gunners, but more had been brought up, you could not stop the thunder of the pandies from killing you.

"But they're sending us elephants," Missie said. "They'll take us to the boats on the river."

Hamish Jamie looked at the scarecrow on his left, who still chirped and hopped after him, lean and moulting in her torn dress, her yellow hair streaked white with dust powder. This was an odd attachment. Her father and mother had been killed when a blazing bolt had struck the thatched roof of the second barrack and incinerated those who were inside. Missie had run out into the resistance to the mass assault, and had hung on to Hamish's bare left leg under his kilt, while he bit off the tops of the greased cartridges stinking of the cow-fat that had started the Mutiny, and he loaded his Enfield rifle with them, and he fired it time and again until the oil spurted out of the stock and burned his hands and the gun barrel glowed in the dark with the Sepoys falling in front of them like herds of sleeping Jacob's sheep for the vultures and the adjutant-birds to consume in the light of the morning.

"If we get to the river, Missie," Hamish Jamie said. "If we get on down to the river."

"I'm thirsty."

"We all are that. Here."

Hamish Jamie pulled the last button off his tunic, gashed and burst on his blackened chest.

"Suck it," he said. "It helps."

Missie popped the button in her mouth and began to suck, while Hamish Jamie peered across the dust and rubble to where the Sepoys ringed them with their tens of thousands and their guns. They had given up the attacks, they would starve them out, dry them out – for one of the wells only provided moist grit, and the other well was full of two hundred and fifty dead from the siege. The defenders had endured for twenty-one days and nights, and now they were to surrender to the Nana. How trust a man with a name like the bogies of the fairy tales, how trust the millions of his pandies that were trying to put an end to the Raj, all because of some cow-fat on the cartridges, and the false tale that every Hindu or Moslem should be massacred or converted by force to Christianity, as if anyone wanted the pandies in the kirks anyway.

"Will you come with me in the boat to Allahabad?"

"I'll not be leaving you, Missie," Hamish Jamie said. "Did I tell you I had a sister like you – Rachel?"

"Tell me again."

"She passed away in Canada, but I have another sister called Katie, she will be grown the now, and she lives in a log cabin in the woods in Canada."

Missie took the button from her mouth and looked at it to see why it had not melted and put it back in her mouth again.

"What's Canada?"

"It's a country full of bears and Indians and trees, lots of trees."

"I like trees. They're shady."

"They don't like trees in Canada. They have too many stones and too many trees. They have to clear them, pull out the stumps, before they can make a field to grow food."

"I want to go down the river now. I want to go with you to Allahabad."

A musket shot pinged in the entrenchment. The heat it was which caused it, nearly one hundred and forty degrees, the ferocious sun exploding the cap on a musket, the molten barrel sizzling off the round. But the enemy believed it to be the end of the cease-fire. Bullets and grapeshot whistled round their heads, throwing splinters of wood and chips of brick and scraps of iron about them. Hamish Jamie threw himself on Missie and held her under his body, feeling her scraggy shape quivering and boiling beneath him.

"It will be well," he soothed her.

And it was. For the firing stopped, and the evacuation was set for the morning. There was no more horse soup now, but double rations of *dahl* and *chapattis*, like the Indian cakes that had appeared just before the Great Mutiny as a signal of the revolt to come. No more lump, thump, whack of slaughtered cow chucked into the stewpot, causing howls at blasphemy from the Sepoys as they saw the holy stew bolted down in sacred chunks. But if they had done such sins and transgressions to the gods of the Hindus, how should they be given safe passage to Allahabad? The Christian scriptures were more unforgiving. Did they not say that stripes shall be meted out according to faults, and death for abominations?

In the morning, sixteen elephants and eighty palanquins drawn by bullocks appeared in front of the battered entrenchment. The Sepoys came out from their emplacements and talked to their old masters. They could not understand how so few had held out against so many, they feared the white devils who had become as burned black as they were with dirt and cordite and dried blood. They said there was a safe passage to Allahabad, that forty roofed country boats stood at the river waiting for their transport. They mourned the deaths of their old officers and carried the little relics that the garrison sought to take with them, Bibles and heirlooms, knick-knacks and photographs and one feathered hat. But Hamish Jamie slung himself with bandoliers of ammunition until he was weighed down like a loaded donkey, and he walked beside the elephant on which Missie Gordon was now hoisted proudly in state.

The river boats were moored in the shallows and sunk down flat on the sand-banks with all the load put on them. For the rains had not yet come to settle the dust and fill the flood, and the Ganges was running low. But as the soldiers tried to push off the boats, all the Indian sailors jumped off and began wading to the banks. Smoke now rose from burning charcoal hidden in the thatch of the roofing of the craft, and as Hamish Jamie brought up his rifle to fire, he saw the barrels of guns appearing from the buildings and ghauts by the landing-place. The mounted troopers who had escorted the elephants and palanquins down to the river now opened fire with their carbines, and Hamish Jamie shot two of them, dropping them from their saddles, careful to spare the horses, which were worth more.

"Push the boat!" Missie shrieked beside him. "Push it!"

Hamish Jamie leapt into the shallow water and began heaving at the loaded craft. Bullets and grapeshot were hornets at his ears and clipped the wooden rails. Every bush was spitting fire, while four nine-pounders were firing canister into the massacre, raking them with shot. The boats burst aflame, all the passengers jumped into the shallow and waded out until only their heads were showing as marks for the fusillade.

One boat alone floated free down the current, and Hamish Jamie plunged towards it. And as he surged on, he looked up to see Missie's body falling down to him. In a vision against the sun, he thought that he was seeing Katie, her red hair flying in the wind. But it was a spray of blood, flung out from her face and chest, exploding in droplets over the air. And he caught her in the fall and held her with one arm and unbuckled his dragging bandoliers with his free hand and began to swim out in the slow dog-paddle that he had learned towards the sole boat escaping downstream. And soon he saw that Missie was dead, and he let her body drift down the holy river, let it redden the waters that receive the dead and take them to a Hindu heaven.

Bullets whipped the surface like jumping trout, serries of shots lashed the water into spume, but Hamish Jamie paddled on. Near him, two brothers swam, but one of them weakened and sank, and the other, Ensign Henderson, was struck in the hand by grapeshot. He put his wounded arm over Hamish's shoulder and swam beside him to the boat, which had stranded on a sand-bank close to the Oudh side of the river. And there they were pulled aboard, the few survivors of the slaughter, and they were still able to hear the far and piteous crying of the women and the children, who were being netted in the Ganges waters and brought to the bank, while the last of the living men were shouting or groaning in their death agonies. Even the blunt-nosed crocodiles shunned the carnage and sheered away. They would return later for the corpses to bury them in the bank for their future store.

Now the last boat swung free and wallowed down the current, slow, too slowly. It was a target until midnight came. The scuppers were filled with the wounded and the dying. A mother standing above her six-year-old boy was struck by a bullet and fell off the stern, and the small child came up to Hamish Jamie, saying, "Mama has fallen overboard. Oh, why are they firing upon us? Did they not promise to

leave off?" But Hamish Jamie was firing back with the Enfield that
was on the boat, and he did not look for the boy for another two
hours, and then he never found the wee fellow again. He never knew
how or why the child was gone.

They could have all died in the morning, but the rains came.
Curtains of water turned the Ganges into a torrent, they wetted the
power of the Sepoy guns, they deluged the attackers who lined the
banks on either side of the river. All the same, the dying went
sluggishly on, four more officers killed and two women and Ensign
Henderson, shot through the groin and begging Hamish Jamie to
finish him, for God's sweet sake, a quick release from all the pain. But
Hamish Jamie said, "No, no, I cannot. I have a brother Iain in the
Sutherland Highlanders, and he is seeking for me even now with Sir
Colin Campbell, and if I kill you, a brother who has lost a brother, I
will no see my brother Iain again." But Ensign Henderson died
towards the evening, his guts spilling out over his torn britches, and
Hamish Jamie heaved him into the Ganges, which always takes the
dead.

But the following morning, the matter was finished. The craft
drifted into a backwater opposite Soorajpore. The Sepoys following
along the banks discovered the boat through the downpour of the
rains and moved upon it in their hordes. And the last surviving major,
shot through both of his arms, ordered the final act of desperation.
"Lieutenant Delfosse," he said, "and Sergeant Grady and Corporal
Murphy" – for he called Hamish Jamie that in his pain – "and you ten
privates of the Thirty-second and the Eighty-fourth, make your way
ashore. Drive off the Sepoys. You thirteen men will rout their
thousands."

And so they did, the thirteen against the thousands. They were
mad, they were berserk, they charged and hacked and stabbed their
way through walls of flesh with sword and bayonet and rifle-butt.
Behind them, they could hear the screaming of their companions as
they were butchered on the boat by the swarms of the enemy. But the
thirteen ran on with a rabble of murder at their heels. Each quarter of
an hour, they turned on their pursuers and dropped to their knees and
fired one volley. That stopped the mob and left a few more corpses
littering the retreat. So the flight and the chase progressed for three
miles by the banks of the Ganges, until the British soldiers spied a
temple set apart against a cliff and took refuge there. Sergeant Grady
was shot through the head and expired instantly, Lieutenant Delfosse
was crippled by a machete swung at his knees and was hacked to
pieces. But the other eleven survivors made their way into the temple

and turned about and fired volley after volley from the dark interior until they closed the open entrance with a wall of Indian bodies.

There was a hesitation, and then the crackling sound of faggots piled outside with the fire being put to them. Smoke bellied inside the dark chamber of heathen worship, followed by a mighty explosion as of the end of the world. A barrel of gunpowder had been put on the flames. Shreds and shrapnel of flesh, burning shards of firewood were blown into the faces of the eleven defenders, who were hurled to the ground. Then Hamish Jamie arose and gave the order, "Fire your last rounds. Then charge the enemy and make for the river." And there were only nine men to obey him, for one had died of a chip of stone that burst his eye, and they fired their final fusillade and charged with fixed bayonets over the burning wood and charred pieces of human remains, and they savaged and stabbed their path through the clawing mass in front of the temple, and three fell to be torn to pieces, but seven fought their way to the river, and one of them was Hamish Jamie.

As the seven men struck out for the meandering current, three were killed by the intermittent firing from the banks. Hamish Jamie and the three survivors paddled or stroked onwards through the waters for five miles through the night, and by the mercy of heaven the crocodiles did not intrude upon their passing, as if the very reptiles were more merciful than men in preserving God's creation.

And on the coming of the next morning, exhausted on a mud-bank, naked and shivering, the four men were found by the washerwomen of Dirigbijah Singh, the rajah of Moorar Mhow, who was still the faithful subject of the Foreign Queen when all had risen in revolt around him. And the washerwomen were not ashamed at the nakedness of the four men, piebald with their blood and bloated skin, blistered with the sun and wrinkled with exposure to the Ganges. They took the men under their armpits, a woman on each side of each man, and supported them severally to their master, who had them bathed and treated and, within the fullness of a month, returned them on a steamer which General Havelock had sent upriver from Allahabad to reconnoitre the Cawnpore region.

What a meeting they had of it, although some of the soldiers were old comrades to Hamish Jamie, the Seaforth Highlanders who had left him at the depot at Cawnpore sick of the fever when they were shipped out to fight the Persian War, and now they had come back to put down the Mutiny. Murdo Maclean called him Murphy again, because he looked a real Murphy in his turban and wide trousers from the Rajah.

"And Murphy I will always be," Hamish Jamie said. "For that a Sinclair never did give up the women and the children before, aye and it is a crying shame that I did it, and a Murphy I am to let it be done."

There was hardly a body who would believe the stories of their escape, how had so few hewed their way through so many? But there the four men were, they were alive, you could touch them or taste them, the proof of the haggis ... "There's a thing the now," Hamish Jamie said, "and I dinna ken it – why thirteen can put to flight a thousand when we are serving the Foreign Queen and the English Empire, and why a thousand Highlanders are put to flight at black Culloden by the Foreign King and the English? Tell me the truth on that?"

"They had the big guns," Murdo said. "They have the big guns."

"No," Hamish Jamie said, "Nana had the big guns at Cawnpore and along the Ganges. It is not that. What is it? Service – foreign service – for a German Queen and Her German husband – why do the Highlanders fight like devils out of hell?"

"Why," Murdo laughed, "isn't that the oath we take! For God and the Queen, which might be to say – for the devil and Her Own."

"You've a foul mouth in you, Murdo."

"You've a black asking head on you, Hamish Jamie."

As Havelock fought his way back to Cawnpore to save the captured women and the children, two hundred and ten of them confined in dark closets worse than the Black Hole of Calcutta, Hamish Jamie followed in the rearguard, watching the terrors of the retribution. Havelock had taken command from General Neill with his heart of flint and noose of vengeance in his hands. Neill hanged any suspect spy, any Sepoy, in figures of eight, nine men dangling in two circles, skinny and rotting as an example to nobody very much. The death of Missie still flew as a red angel in Hamish Jamie's mind, a haunting presence asking for blood and yet mercy, as he marched with his comrades back towards Cawnpore, the vultures coasting and the jackals dying and the pie-dogs yapping about their column, ready for the pickings of war.

Havelock would not let them rest in their work of rescue. In the full heat of July, he marched his Highlanders twenty-four miles in one day through the whirling dust, then made the attack on Nana's troops at Fattehpore. With the screech and the skirl of the bagpipes as wild as the furies, Hamish Jamie ran upon the Nana's guns, his legs buckling under him, his throat dry as a kelp kiln, his feet raw and bleeding in his boots, and he fired and skewered and swung at the pandies, who fell or were chased away and vanished, as nightmares leave at the break of day with the dreamer waking in fear and sweat and exhaustion.

There was no cease to it. Two days later, the Highlanders charged again at Pandoo Nuddy, and the enemy fled once more, leaving their guns and their corpses behind them. On the morrow, the bulk of Nana's army stood before Cawnpore in their tens of thousands with Havelock's brace of regiments facing them. The attack of the High-landers was as a sword entering a scabbard or a dirk making a wound which enclosed it. For the ranks of the enemy enveloped them utterly. They fought hand to hand and bayonet against tulwar for two hours, but Havelock had kept his reserve of irregular horse at the back, and he sent them to wheel round the right flank of the foe and rout them.

The Nana in his flight did as the British had done at Delhi, he blew the magazine so that Hamish Jamie, leaning on his rifle in trembling fatigue among the turbaned dead, as a corn stook shakes in the wind among the fallen sheaves, he felt a pluck at his bare knees in a blast of hot air streaming across the plain, then a banging of pans that seemed to split the burnished sky, then a tongue of fire towards Cawnpore, followed by a vast black balloon in the ascendant. The whole city appeared in conflagration, but when the Highlanders advanced inside the rubble and the destruction the following day, they found that the ruins and the houses and the palaces were still there, but all the white women and the children had been killed in the Beebeeghur.

Hamish Jamie could hardly bear the sight of it. The bodies were gone, thrown to the cleansing of the crocodiles in the Ganges. But the walls were dark with blood, and the ground was stained with blood, and strewn about were collars and caps and round children's hats and combs, locks of long hair and the torn pages of books. Hamish Jamie picked out one bloody Bible, which was inscribed in the fly-leaf, "For dearest mama, from her affectionate Louis, June, 1845." Pages had been ripped out of it, but from a coincidence that was none, the thin papers fell open at the blood-smeared Forty-seventh Psalm, and so Hamish Jamie read:

> For the Lord most high is terrible;
> He is a great King over all the earth.
> He shall subdue the people under us,
> And the nations under our feet.
> He shall choose our inheritance for us.

Now blood obscured the text except for two more phrases:

> God is gone up with a shout,
> The Lord with the sound of a trumpet

and then:

> God reigneth over the heathen

This was no consolation. Missie Gordon and the departed Rachel seethed in Hamish Jamie's mind. He would kill and kill to settle their ghosts. Before the Highlanders were marched away once more to rescue the garrison that was still surviving in Lucknow, Hamish Jamie had heard tell of General Neill's verdict on the murderers at the Beebeeghur. "Severity at the first," Neill said, "is mercy at the end." Each pandie sentenced to death by hanging would be taken to the house of slaughter and forced to lick clean the stains of blood on the walls and the floor.

"For why?" Hamish Jamie said to Murdo. "The Ganges has taken their bodies. Can men's tongues wash away their blood? I do not see the sense in it. They will not come back again."

And there was a kind of recognition of true courage. For when the new Victoria Cross was given to the Seaforth regiment – a piece of copper worth a *lakh* of gold – it was given to the surgeon who had saved many lives under heavy fire. What was the killing after all beside the curing? And what was the fighting beside the needing to eat and drink at the siege of Cawnpore? And Hamish Jamie determined that he could not move to the curing, for he did not have the skill for it, but he could move to the commissariat, which saw to the feeding and clothing of the men. Bullets and bayonets were all very fine, but he had had muckle of it. He would live in the provisioning of the weapons of war, not die in the using of them.

12

A VISIT TO MISS NIGHTINGALE

When the duke or the duchess came down the staircase of the house in Belgrave Square, Mary Sinclair had to step into the broom closet. She could not be visible to her employers. And to pass anybody on the stairs, particularly one of the two Graces, was great bad luck. "You must never be seen or heard," the housekeeper Mrs Rogers told Mary, "unless you are summoned by His or Her Grace. And then you may speak when spoken to, in the proper manner."

"But children can be seen," Mary said, "but not heard."

"You are not a child, Miss Sinclair," the housekeeper said, "even if I am not certain of that at all, by the way you behave."

Life was not bad in the basement and the attics where the servants saw and heard all about each other. There was the comradeship of close encounters with the dreaded quality, the times when one of them had dropped the tea-tray, stumbled over a curtsy, said "Disgrace" instead of "His Grace", frizzled the marchioness's hair with the curling-tongs, burst the laces of the marquis's corset, dropped the hot ash and cinders on the Turkish carpet to improve the pattern, aged the Gainsborough by cleaning it with a wet mop, put a hot iron through the seat of a lady's unmentionables, and generally made a terrible mess of something, without being caught or owning up. "Honesty," Mrs Rogers declared, "Her Grace insists on total honesty in all her staff," and then she would cover for everybody. Within her starched and virgin breast lay a heart of syllabub. She was strict only for show, and she knew which end of the social ladder was which, and she was not on the top of it.

Albert was the bane of Mary's life. He was the marquis's footman and cockney clever, wise off the streets of Blackfriars and Whitechapel, the sound of Bow Bells always ringing in his good ear, for one of his ears was deaf if he did not want to hear something that he did not want to hear. He was bonny enough in the sharp southern way, his nose as thin as the edge of a dirk, his eyes as washed-blue as the sky after rain, and the skin on his face too spare so that his skull shone through its surface, but his sandy moustache and his hot hands made him difficult to evade. He had acquired the arrogance of his masters without their courtesy. Impudence was his excellence. He courted a woman as if indelicacy were a compliment.

"Got yer," he said, as Mary slipped into the broom-cupboard on the sight of Her Grace descending the stairs.

"You've been waiting here, Albert!"

Mary felt Albert's hands crawling over her bodice, his hard stomach thrusting against her back.

"Whisht," he whispered, "or *she'll* hear you."

Mary wriggled under Albert's caresses in the dark closet, but she could not cry out or escape. Her Grace's heels were already outside on the stairway, clip-clop, tick-tock, as if time would never pass by. Mary drove her left elbow backwards and dug Albert sharply in the ribs.

"Wooh," Albert grunted, then changed the noise into a "Miaow."

The tick-tock stopped outside the closet. Her Grace was listening.

"George," she called, "there is a cat in the stairs cupboard."

"Instruct Mrs Roberts," His Grace called back, "to instruct Albert to put it out."

The tick-tock of the heels continued down the stairs. Mary breathed again.

"I'm the mouser," Albert said in Mary's ear. "And I'm going to put it in."

Mary felt her face redden in the dark, but Albert could not see her flush. She hacked back with the heel of her shoe and cut him on the shin.

"Strewth," he swore. "Yer bitch."

Mary shook herself loose and fell forward out of the closet on to the stairway. The light from the Regency windows shone upon the azure carpet by the curling ebony and ironwork banisters that seemed to direct a way to heaven up the stone steps.

"You, Albert, you –"

Albert emerged on to the stairs, limping and grinning.

"Yer like it, Mary," he said. "I knows yer do. I knows women, I do."

"Some women do," Mary said, "and I wouldn't call them ladies. In there it was like that Cawnpore. My brothers, they'll kill you, Albert, when they come home. In Cawnpore, they locked the women and children in dark cupboards –"

"And what they didn't do to them," Albert said. "Course, we're not the ones to know. They'll never say to the likes of us, never say. All women's now like Her Majesty, ain't they? Not bloody human. They ain't got anything to sit down on. Sort of lost under that bustle, only yer not really. Yer a woman, Mary, and a right pink 'un."

"I've got to get the fires out." Mary began to hurry down the stairs, but Albert caught her by the arm and held her.

"Tonight," he said. "I'm going to the 'Orse and Groom. There's soldiers there, back from India. Perhaps, 'ow do yer know, they knows yer brothers —"

"I'll not go to a drinking den with you, Albert Smith —"

"Don't know what yer miss, Miss." Albert grinned. "I'll fetch yer at six."

Mary shook herself free.

"You'll be waiting," she said. "Just because you think you're God's gift to the lassies —"

As she fled down the stairs, Mary knew that she did feel for Albert. There was something in him, rotten and common, but lusty and a man for all that. But it was no good. A girl, a poor Scots girl, there was only one way to make a way in the world. To be a spinster and find a trade. And if marrying there was, it would be marrying a fine man who could give her a home, a house that did not move with the battens in the roof for her and her bairns for aye. No more moving, no more starving, no more, whatever the hot blood in her said on the moment. Hold, Mary, hold you.

At six o'clock, it was the duchess who fetched Mary, not Albert Smith. Actually, it was Mrs Rogers who brought Mary to Her Grace, who was working at her *petit point*. She was stitching a cherub flying above a pink cloud. This was a finger-pricking task she had inherited from her mother-in-law, who intended to fill the whole of the Scots castle with hand-embroidered cushions. Alas for the duchess, it did prove a kind of continuance in the family.

"Ah, there you are, Mary," she said, abandoning her delicate labours. "Well, what do you have to say for yourself? Too much, as usual."

"Begging your pardon, Your Grace — nothing — unless you say what I have to say."

"Impertinence!"

"Not intended," Mrs Rogers said. "Miss Sinclair was trying to say that she does not know what Your Grace wishes her to say."

"She addressed one of the guests. About India!"

"My brothers —"

"You are in service here, Mary. You do not address our guests about anything."

"My brothers –"

"Especially when our guest happens to be the Foreign Secretary. And you ask him about your brothers –"

"An he should know, Your Grace," Mary said, "if he be the Foreign Secretary, he knows of foreign things."

"My dear child," the duchess said, "your simplicity exceeds your modesty. Although the noble lord is responsible for our foreign affairs – and dreadfully he honours that responsibility – sending that abominable weakling 'Clemency' Canning out to pardon all those barbarians and murderers in India – he does not *personally* know the fate of your brothers, however valiantly they are fighting for their Queen and country in India."

"I am sure that Miss Sinclair meant no disrespect," Mrs Rogers said. "A natural concern and affection for her family –"

"Very laudable, no doubt," the duchess said, "but absolutely inadmissible in this household. Mary, I had been considering you as a possible personal maid, to look after my minor requirements ... but now – I really despair at eradicating in you those wild antecedents. To think I plucked you from those unspeakable huts and bogs, and placed you in a position where every refinement of culture and society might instruct you – and then, I am repaid by a total lack of application, an unwillingness to learn!"

"I try to give satisfaction," Mary said, "to be sure I do."

"Trying is not good enough," the duchess said. "It is succeeding, Mary, it is succeeding that matters. You will *never* address any of our guests on personal business."

"And if he falls over dead drunk like that Lord Chalmers," Mary said. "And he near to breaks his leg and he's calling out for help. Can I not go to him and aid him as I did do? Is that not a personal business?"

"We are never drunk," the duchess said, "although we are occasionally ill. We imbibe always with discretion. If a guest may stumble and fall by mischance, you may go to his assistance. That is not personal, it is unfortunate. Mary, you are incorrigible. Uncouth."

"Is that all, Your Grace?"

"It is all. Mrs Rogers!"

"Yes, Your Grace?"

"Put Mary on night duty, perhaps reflection in the small hours ..." Her voice trailed away in the implication.

"Yes, Your Grace."

"On personal business –" Mary said.

"Did I request you to speak, Mary?"

"Tomorrow I am to see Miss Nightingale."

The duchess sat upright in her chair as if Mary had thrust a hot rod down her spine. She rapped her hand on the stuffed arm-rest where she had stuck her *petit point* needle. Her thumb was pierced. She said, "Ouch, damn it," stuck her thumb in her mouth, sucked it and glared at Mary. Then she spoke, "Miss Nightingale? The *nurse!*"

"She sent me a letter, Your Grace. She wrote for my brother Iain, that he was wounded in Russia. Now she herself will see me."

The duchess shook her head. Her laugh was as brittle as rice-paper.

"Miss Mary Sinclair," she said, "you do have ideas above your station. Be careful that you not aspire to more than you may attain."

"It is hard, dirty and dangerous work," Miss Nightingale said. "It has no respect. You know how the nurse is seen in the novels of our time – as drunken, foul and immodest. And you will see sights of men's bodies that no woman –"

"I have brothers," Mary said. "We had a board between us in our croft. Ach, I know the men, how they are."

"I had many Highlanders at Scutari," Miss Nightingale said. "They fought like lions at Sebastopol. They carried the Russian city with a charge. There were many of them with terrible wounds – the grapeshot."

"My brother Iain was with you," Mary said simply. "In the Crimea, he was wounded and he was not lasting among the living. But you saved him."

"Your brother Iain Sinclair. A Highland regiment?"

"The Sutherlanders. They are in India now. Both my brothers are in India fighting the Mutiny."

"A terrible thing that." Miss Nightingale shivered. "There is no respect for women there, not even for nurses. I cannot organize there. It is too soon for the army. They are dying of cholera and typhus as well as gangrene. I have told them, cleanliness and lye soap. But will they listen?"

"Look," Mary said, "I have a letter from you."

She took out of her small handbag a piece of paper, folded into four and worn brown on the edges. She passed it to Miss Nightingale as if it were the Grail. Miss Nightingale unfolded it with great care and read it.

"Yes," she said, "I did write this."

"You wrote it for my brother. You said he would be well again. You had it sent to me in London. It is my treasure."

"I see. You work for a duke?"

"Hard, dirty and dangerous work, Miss Nightingale."

Miss Nightingale laughed.

"I remember your brother. He was a giant. And he made me laugh too. Why is it that you have this sense of humour?"

"We only say the truth," Mary said, "and the English are amused."

"Why is it so hard working for a duke?"

"The hours are sixteen a day, and some nights. The kitchens and cupboards are dirty beyond pigsties, and in the summer, the horse-flies fall off the candles on the chandeliers on to the ladies' bare shoulders like shawls – and we have to clear them away. And as for dangerous, if some young master does not try to put you on your back, his footman will."

Miss Nightingale smiled this time a tight grin that looked like wincing.

"You are very plain spoken, Miss Sinclair."

"I was reared with the cattle on a farm. We see what is there."

"And what do you want of me?"

"I wish to leave service," Mary said. "I will take up your service. Your hard, dirty and dangerous work."

"And will you stick to it?"

"I will."

"For ever, if I train you?"

"Aye."

"And the men, a husband?" Miss Nightingale stared at the handsome young woman. "They will want to marry you."

"You have not said yes, Miss Nightingale."

Again Miss Nightingale laughed.

"And how do you know if they have asked me?"

"I would, an I be a man."

For the third time Miss Nightingale laughed.

"You are too blunt for me, Miss Sinclair. But not too blunt for our profession. For that is what it is. A dedication. A lifelong service."

"I will do that," Mary said. "You have my word."

"That is good enough for me. Give your notice. You may commence at the Westminster Hospital within the month."

"The training," Mary said. "I have my brothers in India. Would I be going there and training there?"

"The service must come before your family," Miss Nightingale said. "You must know that."

"I do."

"Then I shall take you." Miss Nightingale stood upright and held out her hand to Mary, who also rose and took the offered hand in both of hers and held it and said in her gratitude: "I say yes only to you, Miss Nightingale."

13

BLOWN FROM THE GUNS

"Tell me the story one time more," Iain said. "The blowing from the guns. And her."

"I seen her when they were blowing the pandies from the guns," Leish said. "They'd tie the pandies to the muzzles of the howitzers, for an example as it might be. And before they put the match to the powder, why, she would ride out in front of the guns, all in white, mind you. An angel on horseback, as you might say. And as the guns fired, and they fired away the poor beggars sitting on the end of them, why, she rode across all that bright red rain, and the pieces of the pandies flying through the air like robin redbreasts, and she was all dripping with scarlet like a Lancer, and she would ride away the far side. And we never did say a word and we never did know who she was. The scarlet lady of the sorrows, as you might say."

"You never did ken who she was," Iain said.

"We never did ken. I heard tell she had lost a mother and sister at Delhi, and they were bound naked to the wheel of a gun carriage, and there were things done, and she would have her vengeance, she would."

"When a woman wants a vengeance," Iain said, "it is worse than a man."

"That it is," Leish agreed.

"But I will have that woman," Iain said, "for my own. But first, we will find my brother."

This time the Highlanders were marching with the heavy guns, Peel's Naval Brigade and the horse artillery of Hope Grant. They would batter their entrance through the walls and towers of Lucknow to the besieged residency, where Hamish Jamie was caught for a second time like a rat in a trap. "That brother of mine," Iain grumbled, "he's no more sense in his head than porridge. You're caught once, that is bad luck. You're caught twice, that's daft."

"Those were the orders," said the huge Willie McBean.

"They always are," Iain said. "Once you follow the orders, you're caught for life."

Their commander, Sir Colin Campbell, was not of the hurrying kind. He proceeded slowly, trusting Havelock to hold out. The big guns were in the front, blasting the Sepoys away, and the Highlanders were fighting like the redcoats, wearing plumes in their bonnets and practising as if on parade, firing in file one by one, picking off the enemy. There was no charging yet. The final dash would come at the walls of Lucknow.

An Irishman came to them first, one Kavanagh, as absurd an apparition as only an Irishman can be. A green turban over his ginger hair, black lamp-oil on his ruddy face, in orange silk jacket and pyjama trousers, he bluffed his way through eight Sepoy pickets and reached the rescuers outside Lucknow. He worked for the Post Office, and it was the electric telegraph of the Post Office in the new code that had stopped the Mutiny in its tracks. The message was transmitted that saved the Punjab and allowed the British to disarm their Sepoy regiments before the *chapattis* and the news of the first mutiny at Meerut had reached them.

But Kavanagh had also served night after night in the Sappers' counter-mines under the Residency, as the Sepoys tunnelled away to plant their explosives beneath the walls, and when the earth crumbled and burrow met burrow, then Kavanagh had blasted the enemy with his pistol and stolen away their gunpowder from their caverns and galleries. Now, in unlikely disguise, he had breached the enemy lines and would lead Sir Colin Campbell back to Lucknow. His first act was to dress himself for his new part, and that is how Iain saw him, wearing a cotton quilted tunic, corduroy britches, jackboots and a pith helmet.

"Hello, *sahib*," Iain said. "You're very *pukka* for a Kavanagh."

"Only because I cannot borrow your kilt," Kavanagh said.

"You'll have it," Iain said, "when you take me to my brother in Lucknow."

At the Sikander Bagh, the Sepoys were valiant and took the pounding of the heavy artillery and were crushed beneath the broken walls, until the Highlanders stormed the breaches with their bayonets and strewed two thousand dead bodies as a red meadow in the gardens at the back of the fort. And at Shah Najaf Iain found the way to his brother. He crept forward to the walls, where the Sepoys could not fire down on him, and, circling them, he found a breach at the back. He shouted his war cry across to his comrades, the bagpipes shrieked their wild notes, and the Sutherlands poured into the fortress. There in the passages and the halls and the catacombs, they were butchers in a slaughter-house, they were berserkers in a delirium, they were killers of other men who meant no more than beasts to them.

When the red rage cleared from Iain's eyes, the sight and the reek of the blood sickened him, and he heaved and retched and stood, until an explosion outside brought him running to an embrasure, where he saw a black cloud over the Moti Mohal. Havelock was dying in the residency, but the other besieged general in Lucknow, Outram, had blown up the buildings between him and the rescuers and was fighting his way out. And Willie McBean was fighting his way alone into the Begum's palace. With bayonet and fist he killed eleven Sepoys as they came at him, his vast shape lunging and battering as thunder splits the sky, and ending by spitting a havildar swinging a sword as neat as a Christmas goose. He was to get the Victoria Cross for it, which he shrugged away, saying, "Toots, man, it did not take me twenty minutes."

And so the Sinclair brothers met in the fallen city. The troops looked more like pirates than soldiers, the Sikh cavalry in bedspreads and drapes, the English infantry in slate-grey powdered with red dust, the Highlanders in their torn kilts and rakish feathered bonnets, and the Ninth Lancers, still dandy in their white turbans wound round their forage caps. But Iain only had eyes for his brother, and when they saw each other, they fell into an embrace, crying and shouting without sense, their tears streaking the blood and burns on their faces.

"We have found the brandy," Hamish Jamie told Iain.

"And the gold?"

"And the gold for any man who will pick it up."

Time for the looting and drinking now. After the slaughter, the plunder. Through the courtyards surrounded by stucco and gilt palaces, thrusting aside the green jalousies and venetian blinds closing off the pierced windows, smashing the carved door panels with rifle butt and musket ball, the invaders sought their reward. Here Leish was draping himself with a sari encrusted with rubies and emeralds, there Murdo was shattering a jade vase to look for gems within, then he gouged with his dirk a jewel from the stem of an ivory pipe. Their faces black with powder, their cross-belts splotched with blood, the Highlanders filled their tunics with jewel caskets and loose pearls, gold bangles and diamond rings. Hamish Jamie used his bayonet to lever open an iron box which was full of gold-encrusted pistols and muskets with barrels inlaid with silver. He threw aside the weapons in disgust,

"No bloody good to fire," and found a bag of gold mohurs and a swathe of silver brocade. But Iain looked to the little things of great value and found a string of blackish pearls as big as quail's eggs, a butterfly brooch with opal and diamond wings, a ruby locket and an emerald ring in a thick gold setting, the green stone a big as a drop scone with a dark flaw in it, like a hidden tale not yet told.

"The brandy the now," Hamish Jamie said. "To hell with the baubles."

On the spread of the silver brocade, Hamish Jamie and Iain began their drinking. And a deep draught they had of it, swig after swig from the black bottles which had been found in the cellars and the bagpipers coming to join them and playing the old songs, the charge and the lament, the only two moods that the Highlanders knew, a time of fury and a time of tears. And the two brothers became merry, and then they became angry, and then they wept, and then they sang, and then they were foolish, and then they boasted, and then they shouted and wept again, and then Hamish Jamie fell over on his back and lay as if he were dead. And his brother Iain slapped him on the cheeks and blew into his mouth and yelled for a doctor, who was also drunk and the other side of Lucknow, then he fell to keening and wailing in the *coronach*, but Hamish Jamie suddenly sat up and said, "That is one devil of a shindy you are making, Iain," and the two brothers fell again into each other's arms and finished the last bottle of brandy and became insensible for twelve hours until a sergeant-major kicked them awake with the threat of a flogging. And that night, Hamish Jamie went in search of the native women in spite of Iain urging him against coupling with the heathen, but he did not prevail. So Iain was left polishing the emerald ring as large as his thumbnail and wondering what woman would wear it for him.

They could not hold at Lucknow. The enemy in their millions still beset the city. Two relief columns had burst in, but now they must all evacuate under the protection of the wheeled guns. And so a stratagem was set for their retreat. First Havelock's old garrison marched out, breaking their step in case the measured beat drummed a signal to the enemy outside the walls. But Havelock was dead, and only Outram went with them. Then the rearguard followed, the gunners and the Highlanders, passing the Ballie Gate and leaving their camp-fires burning in the ruins of the residency until the embers would die down and tell the foe that Lucknow was again an Indian city.

Nearing Cawnpore once more, Iain was wounded sorely in a storm. The heat had been beyond all description, the sky was an upturned copper cauldron with men broiled within it. Then the tempest broke with the clattering hoofs of ten thousand cavalry horses. The hail beat them with ball-shot, the rain lashed more lustily than the cat o'nine tails. The lightning flashed in streaks, in belts of blazing light, in blue zigzags, in bolts of fire, in split-ended jets, which leapt from tree to tree or ran along the ground in crackers and cobras of fire. The army halted and took cover, and Iain found shelter under a baobab tree.

And there among the down-curving branches, a superb and tall Gwalior man stood, a spy on their progress. And Iain grappled with him, and they struggled as twin oaks might lash one another in the force and twists of a gale. And Iain threw the Gwalior man, who drew his tulwar on the ground and hacked at Iain's leg and hamstrung him, the muscles and sinews cut, so that Iain fell upon his opponent and strangled him to death, pressing the life out with the balls of his mighty thumbs. Then he shouted through the howling storm, "I die. For the love of God, I die."

His fellow-soldiers found Iain and they bound his leg in a tourniquet with a rifle-sling and they carried him to a litter. And there his brother Hamish Jamie found him and said, "Thank you for finding me at Lucknow. You will not die of this wound. You did not from the one in Russia."

And Iain said, "No, there will be a nurse for me as there was at Scutari. It is the same kind of wound. It will have the same cure. Look for yourself, you wee man. How can I be looking for you the now?"

For his recovery, Iain was sent to Nainital, seven thousand feet high by a lake in the foothills of the Himalayas. The mutiny was dying now in its last throes, and dying with it were the mutineers by the tens of thousands and the collaborators in the Mutiny in their thousands, hanged by the neck or blown from the guns, flogged or sentenced to thirty years in chains. "Vengeance is mine!" the Bible proclaimed, but the frightened rulers, nearly swept off a continent, imposed their order again by noose and gunpowder and manacle. Yet in the thin air of Nainital, Iain sat in the garden of the hospital by the lake, where the nights were so cold that his spittle was an icicle on his pillow, and the days so calm and hot that the sweat tickled the bandage on his leg. And down the staircase of the low hospital building, where an old Babu sat in his office mixing the certificates of birth with the certificates of death because he believed that living and dying were the same stream of being, the woman in white would walk, the woman who was to be given Iain's gold ring with the emerald mounted on it.

Many things are chosen, others are fortunate, some are fated, occasional ones are prophecies. There had been an operation that afternoon; the leg of the Lancer had turned green and blue; it had to come off. Sister Anna Macmahon was in attendance. There was no laudanum; the Mutiny had cut the supplies. The screaming could be heard in the mud- and tin-roofed town below by the lake. When Sister Anna appeared, she was wan and had not changed. She walked out into the garden with the red blood still spotting her white dress. Iain saw her, for he was always looking at her.

"Sister Anna," he said, "did you hear tell of a woman in white who was riding out when they were blowing the pandies from the guns?"

Anna stopped short. Her face was as white as her dress, but on her cheekbones, two red spots flared.

"I heard of her."

"You have blood on your dress."

"I was her."

And looking at that pale face with its tiger's eyes and squashed mouth like a split plum, Iain knew that he had found the woman he was forever seeking.

"You lost your sister and your mother in Delhi?"

"I lost them there."

"And you wish for vengeance."

"You can never find it." Anna looked over the silver lake below them, her chin and nose lifted as in a profile on a coin. "There is no vengeance. Only remembering."

"I have been looking for you," Iain said. "I have been looking for you for ever and aye."

Anna turned and smiled at him and came over to move the blanket across his leg that was stuck out on the stool in front of him.

"The men always say that," Anna said. "They all say they have always been looking for me, just because they are in my care."

"But I have been," Iain said. "And I bring this for you, as a pledge."

He looked in his pocket and brought out the emerald ring with the stone as big as a scone and the dark trace embedded in it as deep as a secret.

"I can't take that."

Yet Anna took the ring and examined the gold setting inscribed with Sanskrit writing and turned the green gem to the light to catch the sun in its lozenge.

"It is for you," Iain said. "I will not take it back."

"Then I will have to throw it in the lake."

"Throw it in the lake then."

"I will not!"

A flash of spirit that might have been covetousness made Anna speak sharply.

"You will be rid of it, Iain Sinclair?"

"I will."

"Waste not, want not. I'll keep it."

"It is for you."

"What is for you?"

"You."

"You speak your mind, Iain Sinclair. You know emeralds are not lucky."

"They are for you."

"You're a big man, Iain Sinclair, but why are you in the army? It is no life for a man – and not for his wife either."

It was she who talked of his wife, and Iain smiled.

"I did not wish it," he said. "It was the Highlands and the clearances. My own folk went to Canada. I joined the regiment."

"Yes," Anna said. "We did not wish it. My father, he was a doctor in the army. My mother and my sister and I ... we went with him. We did not have the choice. Except to die out here."

"Anna Macmahon," Iain said, "if you will be with me, I will leave the army, but not India. For I have no place back in Scotland. But there are matters here – the tea, the forests, the railways. This is a great country, and we may make it."

"You are all the same," Anna said. "Wild Highlanders. Why should I listen to one word you say?"

"Because I was looking for you for ever and aye," Iain said. "And you were looking for me for ever and aye."

"You are a clown," Anna said, then she suddenly slipped the gold ring on to her index finger, where it fitted as if it were made for her.

"Look you," Iain said. "As if you did not already know."

"I must change my dress," Anna said. "How should I be talking to you with the blood all over me?"

"You'll be back."

"Perhaps I will," Anna said, "and perhaps I will not." But she was looking back at him as she left him.

She was the scarlet lady of the sorrows for whom Iain was looking. He had found her and he would not leave her. The time for vengeance was over. And if the Scots were best at revenge, they were better at one thing more. They did not forget. Memory was all. And the remembering of what would be, that was sure to be better than the revenging of what had been.

14

THE SEA OF THE TREES

They could not take the fires. Many of the fires they lit themselves in the big stumps, so that these burned away night and day, and did their clearing for them. These little fires went on month after month, the cracks in the cabin walls glowing red in the dark from the smouldering trunks outside. And they set on fire the cut branches and even the great oaks and walnut and maple trunks, because these could not be rolled to the river to float down to the saw-mill. But from the ashes, Hannah Sinclair knew how to boil the lye and then to make black salts out of the lye, and these were sold at the store against the axes and handspikes and saws needed for the cutting of the timber.

The fires they did not start drove them west. One forest burning would have been good, for it would have cleared the brush and made the work of hacking fields out of trees an easier one, as well as the ash being good for the feeding of the soil. But there were five fires that season, and none of the Sinclairs knew the cause of them. It might have been the summer lightning that frolicked in the night like crazy yellow goats. It might have been the Indians, careless with the China matches that they bought in rows at the store, and wanting the white men off their hunting grounds. It might have been the sun shining off a quartz rock and lighting the pine needles piled drier than tinder. But Act of God or acts of man, five fires there were, and the last of them burned away the ripening oats and barley and charred the outer logs of the cabin itself. Fighting the flames turned the Sinclairs into blackamoors, the soot on their cheeks streaked with their tears, the dark powder of the smoke as bitter as defeat in their lungs.

"We will no longer bide here," Hannah said. "We will away to the west."

"Ach no, father," Bain said. "After all this work and the land the first land to call our own, and the earth so black, never used except for the trees."

"And the fires," Angus said. "The next time we will wake to see the roof in a blaze and we will be like quails on a spit."

"Aye, like when that sheriff burned our home with the constables in Scotland." Hannah put a basin of water in front of her husband and her two sons for them to wash away the grime and the smoke-stains. "And when Iain burned the kiln and had to be taken for a soldier. And Hamish Jamie went with him, how could he do that to his mother? And you, Angus, if we go as your father says, to the west because of the fires, you will be coming with us?"

"I will go east," Angus said. "The work on the land is not the work for me."

"But you are hardly grown –"

"Old enough to learn a trade, mother. I ken I am your wee boy, the youngest, but look" – stretching up to touch a beaverskin drying on a rack above him – "I am tall the now."

"Let him go, Hannah," Hamish said, "an he will go. But we would have your help, Angus, on the waggon to the plains. It will be a hard journey."

"I would never come back," Angus said. "It is far enough from here to Montreal. Or to Boston or New York, for there I mean to go."

"Take me with you," Katie said. "I could see the dresses – and go to the theatre –"

"A Sinclair woman has never yet been to the theatre – a low and sinful entertainment," Hannah said.

"But Mary wrote from London that she went to the theatre – and saw a man who sang funny songs – and a man who swallowed a sword and a snake and blew out fire –"

"There –" Hannah said. "Sinful and corrupt. The theatre is an abomination."

"Hush, Hannah," her husband said, wiping his face clean on a strip of coarse red cloth. "You can not judge the theatre, for you have never seen it."

"Nor never will."

"Mother, I will not go to the theatre," Angus said. "I will go to school and be an engineer. I will build the railways. Do you hear, father, what they say in the store? In Canada, they will build a railway from the sea to the sea. Like in America."

"And you will build that?" Bain laughed. "You do have the big notions, little brother."

"And I do them, Bain. You will see."

"We will ride on them," Hamish said. "When we are out west on our fine ranch with all our black cattle –"

"Longhorns," Bain said. "Buffalo. Not black cattle."

"Angus will ride out to join us in his railway carriage, driving the steam engine –"

"He will be shovelling the coal," Bain said. "Blacker than he is even now."

"I will be designing the bridges," Angus said, "not shovelling coal or laying the tracks. I have a head on me –"

"And a tongue in your head," Hannah said, "that gabs nothing but foolishness. You will bide with us, Angus."

"I will not," Angus said. "If you go west, I go east."

"We will eat on it," Hannah said. "We have deer meat. And if it is not the red deer of Scotland –"

"It is good meat," Hamish said, "and we will say a grace for it."

When they had thanked the Lord for what they would eat and sat down to sup from the venison stew thick with broth and corn flour, they found that it was seasoned with the soot that floated from outside. And the savoury smell of the meat did not fill their nostrils, for the sour stench of the burning fields fouled the air. They had only one thing to do. They must leave the trees for the plains or even the Rocky Mountains beyond the plains. There were droughts there – to hear tell – and blizzards, and twisting winds that sucked up men and animals and carried them howling through the sky, but there were also mountains larger than the mountains of Scotland, and Hamish found the forest almost as sad and encompassing as the sea. They were drowned in it as surely as set on fire. It enfolded them and roasted them. It wrapped them like babies in swaddling bands, then burned them like kindling in its oven. The trees and the sea were no places for the Sinclairs to trespass upon. It was the grass and the mountains for the ilk of them.

In spite of its name, Annandale looked like a Swiss chalet. Perched on the hillside above the glen near Simla, it looked down through pines and fir trees and giant cedars to a wooded valley, which was as picturesque as the romantic dreams of Lord Byron or Mary Shelley. In the summer, all the ladies of Simla would ride out for picnics or Fancy Fairs. The valley also had the same name as the house, and the glen in the lowlands of Scotland, but Anna Macmahon said it was named after her, Anna's dale. For she had been born there when her father had built it for her mother, the first house outside Simla. And now her father was dead and her mother and sister gone in Delhi, and she was the heiress of Annandale, and she had married Iain Sinclair that morning, in the stone church at Simla, and the ladies and officers and civil servants were riding out to their house for the reception – those who would agree to come. Most people had accepted, even though they knew Iain was only a common soldier. At the last resort, even in a hill-station, curiosity was stronger than snobbery.

Standing in the hall in his full regimental costume, double-breasted doublet with white pouches, kilt and sporran, long stockings and white leggings, fur helmet with a cockade to the left, Iain knew it was the last time he would be wearing the colours of the Queen. Anna had bought him out. He was still limping and unfit for active service. But he had never wished to be a soldier. It was a rotten life. And though he was sorry to leave his friends in the ranks, especially Tam Ogilvie and Willie McBean, he was glad to be a farmer and forester again among Himalaya mountains wilder and grander than Scotland even could offer. "I do not regret it," he told Anna. "The army is not for me. It is the orders. I cannot take orders. A Sinclair cannot serve."

"And if I tell you do something?" Anna said.

"That is not the same, Anna. I will do it with all my heart. That is love."

"Then I'll ask you. Only what you can give. That is love."

Now they were waiting for their guests. Anna had been all round Simla leaving the cards at the bungalows and villas and chalets with their wooden balconies and porches. She had been carted from door to door in a jampan, which she hated, an upright lurching coffin, carried by four bearers who tripped over the toes of their huge slippers. The first guest, indeed, was being lugged up to Annandale in a jampan, not on the back of the hill-ponies, which Anna could see picking their way up the slope between the trees behind. The jampan must have set off from Simla hours before, and the bearers looked dead on their feet, supporting the weight of the woman inside.

The litter was dumped before the door of the house. A jampanee opened its door. Out waddled Mrs Dalgety in a billow of white lace, as if she was the bride herself at sixty, even though her corset could do no more than make a small dent in her voluminous waist.

"My dear Miss Macmahon," she said, "I beg your pardon, Mrs Sinclair, I do declare," and, appraising the huge height of the kilted Iain, "you have married Mount Jakko."

"I bet you would like to climb him," Anna said.

Iain laughed to see the pale round face of Mrs Dalgety suffused with sudden crimson. He loved Anna for her sharp tongue and true wit. She hated being patronized even more than he did. And as for a matron as formidable as Mrs Dalgety ...

"Your visit to that army hospital seems to have done something to your manners, Mrs Sinclair. We all disapproved, but your poor dear father was not able to restrain you. I suppose that is where you picked up your language and your husband."

"I carried her away," Iain said, "When I could walk, that is."

"A private soldier, I see," Mrs Dalgety said. "Were you never promoted?"

"Too busy fighting," Iain said. "We leave promoting to the officers, they that can pay for their commissions."

"Well, you have married money all right, Mr Sinclair. The only estate in Annandale. You should have been here for the *fete champeter* given by that dear Prince Waldemar of Prussia. Oh, the costumes and the gowns. And then he had to be killed watching the battle of Ferozshar."

"I have seen a few killed," Iain said, "but fighting."

"Watching is very dangerous," Anna said. "Particularly in Simla. You never know when you will be shot in the back by tittle-tattle. The ladies have tongues sharper than bayonets. Ah, Doctor Gillespie –"

Through the door stepped a portly, ruddy man in riding britches and bowler hat. He bobbed up to give Anna a kiss on the cheek.

"You brought back a prize from the wars," he said.

"First prize," she said. "Iain, meet the doctor. The best man north of the Ganges."

"Anna told me of you," Iain said. "You were always her inspiration."

"When there are women doctors," Gillespie said, "Anna should train to be the first. She's got more guts and sense than the surgeon-general. But tell me, Mr Sinclair, what are you going to do with the fine land at Annandale?"

"Grow potatos," Iain said. "Or indigo. And cattle and horses, if I can."

Mrs Dalgety rounded on him. She was horrified.

"You *dare* to plant in Annandale? Why, we shall have a race-course–"

"And we will have potatos," Iain said.

"This is for recreation, for beauty –"

"Nothing is more beautiful," Anna said, "than a spud roasted in its jacket."

Doctor Gillespie laughed and took Mrs Dalgety by the elbow and steered her away, as other guests came through the door to greet Anna in her simple wedding-gown of white silk.

"Come, Mrs Dalgety, we mustn't monopolize the bride and groom. And certainly we mustn't give them advice. They've hardly had time even to get to know each other."

Now the officers in their forage caps and pantaloons were greeting Anna, but they did not know how to treat Iain, the Highland soldier. They hesitated and waited, as if expecting him to salute them. But Iain put out his hand to grasp theirs and crushed their finger bones in his grip.

"It is good to greet you," he said, "off parade. And Annandale, it beats any officers' mess in the land."

The rooms filled behind them with the officials and the officers and the summer ladies escaping from the heat of the plains. Some of Anna's dozen Gurkha servants moved among them, dressed in green jackets and leggings, serving sherbet and cake, white wine and fruit punch. The noise of conversation rose as the sound of artillery rises on an advance towards the guns from a mutter to a chatter to a roar to a thunder. And then as the last of the guests passed by, Iain saw through the open door his brother Hamish Jamie enter in his full uniform of an assistant quartermaster of the Seaforths. And behind him followed an Indian woman, glittering in a sari of red and gold braid. She wore a thin black veil over her face.

"I am Hamish James Sinclair," Iain's brother said to Anna, "come all this way to tell you that you that you could do worse than marry my big brother Iain. And this is Lila Singh. I wanted her to meet the family."

Those near the door fell silent as they saw the veiled Indian woman by the bride. But Anna only smiled and said, "How very good of you both to come to our wedding. It is very good to meet a woman who has no time for all this silly *purdah* business."

"Ach, Lila did not wish to come," Hamish Jamie said, "But I said she must. To get to know you."

"You're a terrible man for breaking the rules," Iain said. "But you and Lila are most welcome here."

As Hamish Jamie and Lila passed through the crowded rooms, people parted in front of them, shrinking back as though they were contagious. Only Doctor Gillespie came up to them to greet them.

"You must be Iain Sinclair's brother," he said. "A race of giants. And you, madam —"

Lila stared at the doctor with black and glittering eyes above the veil.

"Lila Singh," she said in a low voice.

"I am Doctor Gillespie. I admire your courage in coming here."

"That is what Iain's wife said," Hamish Jamie interrupted. "It was my doing. Lila should get to know the family —"

"Why, if I may ask?"

"She is my family now," Hamish Jamie said.

"You are married, then?"

"The Commanding Officer would never give me permission," Hamish Jamie said. "What do they say? White is white and brown is brown and never the two will meet. But they do. Only nobody must see it."

"You think we are all hypocrites, Mr Sinclair?"

"It is the only way to rule India, it may be."

As Iain and Anna left their sentry posts by the door to join their guests, Mrs Dalgety rolled towards them in a monsoon.

"How can you let *that* woman in here?"

Anna smiled.

"As easily as I let you in, Mrs Dalgety."

"But she is an Indian."

"So are we all," Anna said. "I was born here as she was."

"But if you let them into our homes —"

"We already do," Anna said, taking a glass of fruit punch from the tray of the Gurkha servant. "They run our homes for us."

"But socially. It is perfectly unacceptable."

"Not to me," Anna said. "I am glad my brother-in-law has the courage to step over a few of these silly prejudices about colour and caste —"

Mrs Dalgety's face seemed to swell. Iain thought that if he tapped her cheek, it might puncture and pop like a balloon. "Nobody will ever — I repeat *ever* — receive you in Simla again, Mrs Sinclair."

"Not to worry," Anna said, putting her arm through her husband's. "Iain and I, we only intend to see each other for months and months now."

"Sociable," Iain said, "is hardly in my nature at all."

When the last of the guests had gone with a new scandal to pass the time of night in Simla, Iain took Hamish Jamie and Lila outside to watch the sun set in pink and golden rays through the banked clouds that clustered above the white peaks of the Himalayas. The constellations seemed to be shining on the slopes of Annandale, wild geraniums and hill anemones, columbines and pheasant's eye. The wind sang in the tree-branches high and low in a skirl of bagpipes. The trees breathed out resin and pine as they stood to ragged attention down the sides of the mountains.

"You are a lucky man," Hamish Jamie said. "To come to all this."

"It was meant," Iain Sinclair said. "I feel I have come home."

"It is fairer than Scotland, Iain. And I never thought the day would come when I was saying that."

"Where we find mountains," Iain said, "we make Scotland again."

"You will not change these Himalayas. They are too big even for you."

"Who would change them? Look."

And the sunset sent down spikes of light through the clouds and the snow bonnets on the far mountains glittered with white gold and only the tune of the wind in the forest piped its soft airs.

"Hamish go to China," the veiled woman said. "He not tell you. He take me to you for you care for me."

"We have a boy," Hamish Jamie said. "Look after him and Lila. They are sending an expedition against the Chinese Emperor. I am a volunteer in the Commissariat."

"A boy?" Iain did not wonder at the news. "And what will become of him?"

"Not in my world," Lila said. "Not in your world. He has no life. But he is."

"When you need us," Iain said, "Anna and I, we will help you and your boy. And my brother will return from China. Now he is in the feeding game, not the fighting."

Anna appeared at the door of Annandale, a silhouette against the light like the black cardboard outlines cut by nail-scissors for children.

"Dinner," she called.

"We must go," Hamish Jamie said. "It is your wedding-night."

"Time enough for that," Iain said. "Every night shall be a wedding-night for ever now. Come to dinner."

The East Indian Railway was both a dream and a nightmare. Mary Sinclair did not have the money for the first-class fare with sleeping-carriages and leather padded seats, but only for cane-bottomed and wooden-backed compartments in the second-class. To travel third class was out of question in the Raj, with a hundred-and-twenty Indians locked into their compartments for the length of the journey, and their numbers calculated by weight rather than by tickets sold, a black hell-hole worse than Calcutta on wheels.

Mary would have wanted to travel with them, for she had her wish to come to India after her training, to assist the Zenana Missionary Society in its work of looking after women in *purdah* who could not be seen by male doctors, but who were doomed to risk death by dirt and puerperal fever at every child-birth. Florence Nightingale had taken up India as her cause, and letters flew from South Street thicker than bombardments at the civil service and the army, demanding hospitals and sanitation, soap and water for the whole continent, with a woman's hand in it all. She had sent Mary out to work at the only place where women could work in the medical way, and to report back to her so that she could recharge her batteries for more cannonades at the male fortresses of imperial control.

Yet Mary was on the railway to Delhi to visit her brother Iain before she took up her duties in Amritsar. In her carriage were soldiers' wives and clerks in the Civil Service, with the train guards and servants pushing through, and the din of the sellers at the stations during the interminable journey on a vehicle that did not seem to go much faster than the bullock cart she had to take from Bombay. Among the scrum of passengers in *dhotis* trying to pack their way onto the jammed third-class carriages with baskets on their heads, the vendors would cry, *"Hindi pani, Musselman pani"*, because even the water was segregated here, and *"Tahsa char, garumi garum"* for the hot fresh tea that made the travel tolerable, and *"Pahn biri"* for the betel nuts that she could not chew because a lady could not spit. As for the child beggars clinging onto the train windows with the limbs which had not been cut off them, Mary had not learned to take them for granted yet and gave them a few annas, causing a riot and disapproval from the other travellers.

"It only encourages them," a soldier's wife said. "If you give them money and the market's good, they mutilate more children to beg, and it's worse."

"Supply and demand," a clerk said, lighting a huge cheroot. "The good old law of supply and demand. I hope you ladies do not mind if I smoke?"

"Good of you to ask," Mary said, but she did not dare to stop him puffing out more black smoke than the locomotive dragging the train along.

She began to talk to the soldier's wife, whose husband was a sergeant in the Seaforths. Yes, she had met Hamish Jamie Sinclair, whom they all called Murphy now after his escape from Cawnpore. He was doing well and had risen to assistant quartermaster. He was a wonderful organizer. The men had never had such good supplies and always on time. There was talk about him and some Indian woman, and when there was going to be this expedition to China and he applied for it, why, it was thought good he should go to get away from the woman.

"It doesn't do," the soldier's wife said. "I mean, it is bad enough, most of the soldiers having no woman even to speak to for a tour of duty that may be ten years. But if they go to the native women, even for their washing – with the temptation –" a small shudder shook her that was not the heat – "where will it end? A *khaki* continent."

"I am here to work in the *zenanas*," Mary said, "with the Indian women in *purdah*. Four out of ten mothers die having children. Dirt, disease, not able to see a doctor. And those midwives of theirs –"

"The *dais*. They're a caste on their own."

"What they are is dirty, pig-ignorant, superstitious and daft," Mary said. "They even give an English midwife a good name, for she is only gin-drunk and incapable."

The soldier's wife laughed and looked at Mary with admiration.

"Good luck to you. Are you going to your place now?"

"No. To see my other brother Iain. He has married and has a farm near Simla."

The soldier's wife was now impressed.

"And was he a soldier too?"

"He was. In the Sutherlanders. He was wounded and married the woman who nursed him, although she was not trained, but helping."

"My husband says, if he is ever wounded, he would sooner die than let the medicals lay hands on him."

"It is getting better. And when they let women do the work too –"

"As you are –"

"As I will be, in the only place I can be." The carriage jolted and swayed and jerked forward as they left the station. "When will you go away from India? And where do the Seaforths go then?"

"To Canada, as I hear."

"To Canada? And Hamish Jamie off to China?" It was Mary's turn to give a laugh, which turned into a cough as she inhaled the smoke of the clerk's cheroot. "I beg your pardon – ugh." She cleared her throat. "My mother and father are in Canada. My brother is always in the wrong place at the wrong time."

"We all are," the soldier's wife said. "Soldiers always are. My name is Rose Campbell."

"Mary Sinclair," Mary said. "We will meet again. In the end."

The train gathered speed. A blast of hot air threw dust through the window and a gritty smoke layered them with dirt.

"But this journey will never end," Mary said. "So we will know each other, Rose, for ever."

The journey did end thirty-six hours beyond endurance, and then the question was how to find transport to Simla. There were coaches

of sorts drawn by horses or camels or bullocks. And then by *tonga* up
the steep and winding slopes of the cart track that bore the hopeful
name of The Great Hindustan and Tibet Road.

The *tonga* had two wheels and was drawn by two ponies. Riding on
it, Mary felt she was in a scull on a choppy sea, not a curricle on a road
that was one bump after another up to the finish, past precipices and
gorges deep enough to disappear down, never to be seen again. One
way, Mary thought, to oblivion.

But Iain was waiting in Simla, wearing a plaid coat and trousers and
boots now, taller by a head and chest than any of the hill-people with
their flat faces and nose-rings in the *bazaar*. And he took her and her
two bags out to Annandale on a pony-rig, then walked up to the house
with the luggage past new terraced fields among the tall trees. He trod
heavily now, as a man does on his own ground, feeling the weight and
the worth of his property.

As for Anna and Mary, it was communion at first sight. Sometimes
at one looking of the eyes, there is a binding between two people.
Sometimes the few words of a voice spell out a sentence for a lifetime.
These two women knew that they had already met before they had. It
was not the Hindu doctrine of the transmigration of souls, the
meeting in another life. This was this encounter in this life, an
immediate understanding, a mutual recognition of each other. Instant
and everlasting friends, they became so close and so quickly that Iain
was quite left out of it. He had to stop himself becoming jealous about
his sister over his wife.

"You are doing what I always meant to do," Anna said to Mary
over the dinner, the candles on their silver stands making a dozen
spear-points of light in the still air. "You are healing women."

"But you were healing men."

"Unofficially. I was not really allowed. I visited the hospital. But
they had to use me. There was nobody else."

"Miss Nightingale will get women nurses into army hospitals. She
has sworn to it. The day will come."

"It can not come soon enough," Iain said.

"And woman doctors," Anna said. "There is a female hospital in
New York in America. The Blackwell sisters, who studied medicine in
Paris and London, are in charge. And you here at Amritsar –"

"Miss Hewlett there studied nowhere but in books and by experience. The need of the Indian women made her learn. It was so for
Miss Nightingale and for us. The medical schools still will not admit
us. So we must learn in the wards – from the sick and the needy. We

may cure some of them, but the rest are our experiments – which do not always work."

Anna and Iain laughed. The Gurkha servants in their green tunics poured wine into the incized glasses, cut into diamonds and petals.

"Learning as you work," Iain said, "it is the best way."

"You learned to kill," Anna said.

"It was the best way to learn," Iain said. "I am planting now. Potatos. And we have horses. But cattle, they will not last the winter here. And driving them down to the plains is too far. And there is so little water in the Punjab –"

"Water, clean water, that is Miss Nightingale's answer to everything," Mary said.

"She is right. If they would hold the water from the melting snows, if they would spread it across the plains, there would be a thousand villages, a hundred thousand farms, a million people where the dust is. Dams and irrigation, and the Punjab would bloom like the rose."

"If it isn't enough farming in Annandale ..." Anna smiled.

"India gives people big notions," Iain said. "It is the size of the place – and the reason we are here."

"There's muckle to be done," Mary said. "That is what we are saying back in Scotland."

"Aye, muckle," Iain said. "Clean water, then, that's the secret?"

"For everything," Mary said.

"You do not like the wine? Come all the way from France."

"Once in a wee while. But water, that is the true stuff."

"It is," Anna said, "if you can get it where it is wanted."

15

THE WASTE OF IT

The high plains were called the inland sea. Hamish could see why. The red grasses moved in ripples and surges on the eager mind, they stretched to the horizon without end. But there was no peace on the journey because of the Red River cart. It shrieked like a banshee, it groaned as a soul in torment. The wheels were tree sections bound with shrunken rawhide, the axles were unpeeled poplar logs. There was no bear's grease in the hubs because the dust would have stuck to it and clotted the turning axles. The cart with its light hide cover was drawn by only one pony. It carried all the Sinclairs had in the world which they could take from their cabin – mainly traps, for the prairie before the Rockies was still hunting country and owned by the Hudson's Bay Company, not yet by Canada, edging its way towards self-government. Hamish and Hannah and Bain walked with the pony, but Katie sometimes rode. For she had a kind of fever that Hannah said was young woman's fever, the longing for something she did not know, but knew she wanted. But Katie stayed curled in a ball in the jolting and screaming cart, rather than walk the wild grasses of the plains. Hannah tried all the known remedies from the medicine box on Katie, but none had any effect – not sulphur or powdered alum, castor oil or rhubarb, soda or sage tea. It was a growing pain, Hannah said. Katie would bounce out of it.

One day, a roaring ahead was louder than the howling of the cart. It might be a river, with the water cantering down in a clatter of currents and tossing white manes. It might be an angry mob of Indians with their drums, beating out some sinful ritual or portent against the coming of the new people. But the Sinclairs had hardly seen any of the savages on their horses in the long grasses, or dragging their summer camps behind their ponies on two long joined poles. The noise came from the buffalo they had travelled so far to find, the bulls roaring at their mating and at their dying, for that great noise of reverberation over the wavering wasteland announced the presence of the herd and drew the hunters to it.

As the Red River cart plodded and jerked closer to the source of the sound, Hamish heard interruptions to the steady bellowing. There were cracks and yips – the sound of rifles and scavengers. Over the tide of corpses, shapes were moving as fast as the shadows of the clouds scudding on the breeze. Buffalo bulls charged out showing only their tufted woollen heads and horns, then paused and snorted and rolled back to the herd behind. The bare and painted chests of Indian braves swept behind the living hobby-horses of their mounts, as they discharged arrows and musket-balls towards the vague mass of the surrounded buffalo. And now ahead of the pony, Hamish saw timber wolves and prairie wolves yelp away, waiting to feed off the carcasses made by man.

"We could use some hides and meat," Bain said.

"What about them?" Hamish said of the Indians.

"There's muckle for all," Bain said and moved over to the cart and brought down the musket, already primed and loaded against the day. "They do not own that cattle more'n we do."

As the shrieking cart approached the hunt, the buffalo broke and stampeded across the plains. Some of the bulls did not budge, but stayed in a circle around their dead. The Indians on their horses rode away after the herd, yelling and firing. But still there was the steady crack of a rifle fired within the confines of the bulls, and one by one, their shaggy heads dropped below the red sea of the waving grasses.

As the pony and the cart approached, a buffalo bull charged towards them. The pony reared and whinnied, the bull lowered its huge head and stopped and pawed the ground which had cleared into the cropped mounds of a prairie dog town. Bain raised his musket and fired. It was a good shot. The lead ball hit the bull in the back of its lowered head, severing the spine. The great animal fell on its knees, flailing, then it toppled to the side, threshing the air. Bain yelled and ran forwards. Then he stopped at the sight in front of him, lifting his useless musket, before setting it aside. Hamish took the pony by its traces and pulled it forward while Katie got down from the cart to see the goings on.

Only two bulls stood now in the circus ring of slaughter beyond the clearing made by the prairie dogs. Aiming at one of them with his long rifle was a tall figure in a buckskin jacket and wide hat. He fired, and the bull dropped as if a spike had been driven into his heart. Standing untouched in the middle of the ring of dead or dying great beasts, the man seemed to be called among them for their massacre. He was invited for their ending, their chosen slayer, the angel of their deaths. Now he leaned on his rifle and watched the pony and cart come towards him, leaving the last bull to break and run after the herd that was leading the Indians away on its stampede towards safety.

"Easy there!," the buckskin man shouted. "*Gardez à vous!* Gopher! Dog-'oles!"

As he shouted, Hamish stumbled. His foot broke the surface dirt and plunged into a hole. There was a squawk of anger. A small burrowing owl fluttered out of its nest and hopped about in a rage of feathers, trying to get these intruders away from its nest. Hamish pulled his boot free and trod carefully forward with the pony picking its way between the holes. Hannah and Katie walked beside him round the hairy lumps of the dead buffalo, which Bain had already reached on his way to talk to the buckskin hunter.

"Henri Chatillon," the man was saying. "And you?"

"Bain Sinclair. And my family. Hamish and Hannah, my father and my mother. And my sister Katie, the lassie with the red hair."

This was one of the miracles in the Good Book. If it was not the raising of Lazarus, it was the casting out of devils. Katie was instantly well. Her blue eyes had the glint of the sun in them, although its light was at her back. Her face moved with thoughts and smiles more than the grasses.

"Why kill so many of the poor beasties?" she asked. "You canna eat even the one."

"Bulls," Henri said. "Too many bulls. They fight for zee cows." He smiled, his teeth white under the shade of his hat, not black as were those of most of the *métis*. "*Les hommes* fight for you?"

"We are God-fearing people," Hannah said. "Hush, Katie," for Katie was laughing. "We are here for the land and for raising the black cattle."

Now it was Henri Chatillon's turn to laugh.

"What black cattle?" He threw a lazy hand towards the bleeding mounds of the dead buffalo. Already the wolves were moving towards the humans and the pony and the cart with its canopy of hide.

"Buffalo. All we 'ave. *Dans les montagnes*, sheeps *sauvages*. Big 'orns. *Boeufs sauvages*, sheeps *sauvages*. Maybe you come *trop tôt* –soon."

"We care not for the trees," Hamish said.

"We hear there is a railway coming," Hannah said.

"Is under Medicine Line," Henri said. "To river, Missouri River. *Mais il ne peut pas passer les montagnes.*" His hands followed his speech and swept up into the air. "Ver' up. Big, big. No *passer* railroad. *Jamais.*"

"It will be," Katie said. "You canna stop the railway – rail road? I have no seen it, but my sister in London ... my brothers, they have been on it. It will come here."

"*Jamais.*" Henri said. "Buffalo. Red grass to zee Red River. See –"

The blue sky was suddenly alive and grey. Startled by the stampede of the living buffalo, innumerable birds filled the air with rags and scraps of flying things – passenger pigeons and meadow larks, longspurs and little grouse. The beating and twittering of the birds in their hundreds of thousands was a small storm of hail in their eyes.

"'Ow many birds? You count zem? 'Ow many buffalo? An' bears. An' wolves? *Ici, dans les prairies, ce n'est pas l'homme qui compte.* No peoples. All zee *animaux.*"

"We come here to farm," Hamish said. "And we will bide here."

Henri Chatillon laughed and leaned on the muzzle of his rifle.

"Is plenty room," he said. "You 'ave it all. And plenty lonely. *Les indiens* – Crow, Blackfeet, Utes – and *les métis.* I am *métis, ma mère,* she Crow. All we 'ave is no people, no people, so you *les bienvenus. Et le Bon Dieu vous protège.*"

"Where do you live?" Katie asked. "You must live somewhere."

"Where is buffalo, I live. Sometime I see *maman.* Sometime at post on Red River. Trade buffalo robe. Pemmican. Fur."

"So it is all grass country," Bain said. "But there are no cattle yet."

"Right," Henri said.

"And there will never be cattle?"

"*Jamais.*"

"There will be," Hamish said. "And wheat and oats. To there."

He pointed his arm now to the far horizon as a lone branch standing out from a tree stump on the plain while round him flies began to buzz towards the carcasses of the buffalo.

"I do not see so far," Henri said.

"My father," Katie said, "sees far too far. Past his children and his children's children. Somebody else will take it all."

"Hush, Katie," Hannah said. "If we work now, we will have the cattle."

Bain had taken out his skinning knife. He turned back towards the buffalo bull, which he had shot and killed.

"You 'ave two, three my bulls," Henri said. "You need zem. Is ten day to Red River. And zen, you swim. Take wheels away – 'e float, *la chose-là,*" indicating the waggon. "Is post at *village.* But 'er," now opening the palms of his hands and smiling at Katie, "*elle est trop belle pour la frontière.* She too *belle pour les métis et les indiens.*"

Katie smiled at Henri's face under the shade of his hide hat.

"Will you not protect me, then?"

"We can do that," Hamish said.

"Our blessing on you for the meat," Hannah said.

"I 'elp you," Henri said. And while he stripped off the buffalo hides and cut off the choicest part of the meat and the fat and the insides, Katie stayed near to him. Even if his doing sickened her, she could not draw away from him. And when he offered her a small piece of raw liver on the point of his hunting knife, she took it and chewed it and swallowed it as if it was a sweetmeat from the hiring fair. It seemed to put the life back in her that had fluttered and ebbed in that last winter among the trees.

The cry of the baby gave a twist to Mary's heart. As she cleaned the little girl and swaddled her and put her in her mother Lila's arms, Mary felt her own loss of children. All this birthing she did for Indian women – and never giving birth herself. And this new little niece of sorts, for certainly she was the child of Hamish Jamie, what would become of her? Her mother's room off the bazaar was squalid enough in spite of the bright cloths hanging on the walls and the brass lamp and the little charcoal fire, where a kettle had been boiled at least for the purifying of the hot water. Through the single shutter, bars of light striped the bare boards of the stifling place. Little Seaforth Singh, called after the regiment perhaps in the hope that it would adopt him, was in the care of neighbours. The birth of his sister was no sight for him at the age of two. In fact, Mary thought, clearing away the last of the mess on the linen she had brought with her from the midwives' training centre, there should be a neater way of having babies. The process was like an animal, and God did separate men and women from the beasts of the field. He really could have done a wee bit more about child-birth, even for Jesus. How Mary must have suffered in that stable.

"It was lucky I was here, Lila," she said. "Or you would have had one of our *dais*. And we can teach them all we can about hot water and clean linen, but they still have their superstitions – keeping the cord on and leaving it till it falls off, wrapping up the baby's head till the hole is gone, such foolishness, as my mother always did say."

"I not know you come," Lila said. Tears streaked her face as she lay on her mattress on the floor, looking down at her infant.

"Of course I had to come," Mary said with the cheerful briskness that she had learned to use as her armour in this alien land. "Another nephew or niece – how could I stay away?"

"Hamish – he away in China. He not back here."

"Oh, he will be back the now," Mary said. "Scotsmen turn up like bad pennies. Now I will be cleaning you –"

"No. You will not –"

"That is the worst thing here," Mary said, stripping off the stained cover above Lila's body. "They say the mother is unclean for forty days after she had her baby. Forty days lying there without being washed! We did not do that to a cow in our byre! It is not natural – and it smells!"

With a towel dipped in hot water, Mary began to wipe Lila's legs, gradually working her way up towards her stomach. At first, Lila shuddered and her flesh puckered, shrinking back from the touch of Mary's fingers through the wet towel. But slowly she relaxed and lay against her pillow, holding the baby.

"We are unclean," she said.

"Rubbish," Mary said. She rose and changed the stained towel for a clean one, over which she poured the last of the hot water from the kettle. "You are as clean as you wish to be. And certainly as clean as I can make you."

She came back with the fresh towel and continued wiping the brown skin of the Indian woman, who was the mother of Sinclair children, which she would not be, for it was already nearing the time when she would be past her time.

"When the husbands first let me into the zenanas," she said, "it was only because their wives were already dying. Some of the wives were bairns – scarce thirteen years of age. And their husbands old enough to be their grandfathers. Shocking and disgusting – left to die in a cell full of flies – no soap, no water – and if the wee babe was a girl, God help the mother, for no one else would, until Miss Hewlett and I came along, and we were graciously allowed to assist because we were women – despised women – so we did not break the rules of *purdah*."

Mary finished wiping the worst off Lila and threw aside the towel.

"And now," she said, "for the changing of the sheets. It is much more important than the changing of the guard. Shift you to the side, and I will change them. I carried clean sheets with me."

Lila slowly moved across the mattresses inch by inch, holding her baby.

"You do too much, Miss Sinclair," she said.

"My brother does too little, that is sure," Mary said. She twitched the soiled undercover out and bundled it up and tossed it down. "But do you not worry. Hamish Jamie will be back from China and Iain is coming to visit us in Amritsar. He will see to you and your children. He has told me he will."

"We will go to the Himalayas?"

"No, you will wait here for Hamish Jamie to come back." Mary spread the clean sheet across the mattress that was stained as well, but she could not do anything about that. "Iain himself is coming down to the plain in the Punjab. To plan irrigation – bringing the water to the dry land. And the railway. There will be improvements, he said. We are here to improve."

Mary tucked in the corners of the sheet under the mattress, pleating them exactly so they made a triangle at each end. Bed-making, it was the first thing to be taught to nurse and soldier. If you were not squared off, there was no sense in your life.

"You are here to change us," Lila said, giving her breast to her baby for the first time. "And if we not want it, you still change us."

"Improvement must be," Mary said, finishing the tucking of the sheet at the top, forcing Lila to shift back with her baby across the clean linen. "My brother Angus, the now, he writes from New York City in America where he studies for to be a surveyor and an engineer. For he says, the rail roads as he calls them, they will come all over the world." And the sight of the red wrinkled face and tight-shut lids of the baby gasping as it drew back from the breast smote Mary's heart. "And babies too," she said.

"And babies too."

Lila gave her breast again to the baby. There was a sadness in her eyes as well as a sharpness.

"Your brother Iain, he has babies?"

"Two also," Mary said, squaring off the undersheet. "Hamish Macmahon and Hamilton. Two boys they are. But they have a fine mother."

"And I am not?"

Lila looked Mary full in the face. Dark eyes stared at blue eyes that looked away. Mary blushed, and she never did.

"It is not ..." she paused to think. "It is not you are not a mother. It is ... you are not the mother my mother Hannah would wish for the children of Hamish Jamie."

"You do not lie."

"Ach, plain speaking and plain living, that is all the Sinclairs are good for." Mary began to spread another clean sheet over Lila, who had plucked her loose cotton wrap below her knees.

"You not like me."

"I do. That I do. Why am I here, Lila?"

"Duty. That bad word you say."

"Duty?" Mary laughed, then she stopped laughing. "Aye, I am never off duty. There is no end to the women having babies in India and having not a good time of it."

"And you not having babies?"

A dagger went into Mary's heart. It was an assassin's thrust. She did not see the sharp point strike her. But it hurt, it hurt sore.

"It seems everyone is having babies," Mary said. "And someone must tend to them. If we all had babies, where would you find a woman to look for you?"

"You want babies," Lila said. She took up the infant and laid its head over her shoulder. "You want Sinclair babies. You say, why *this* woman? Why not me?"

The truth of it was too much. Mary felt a sudden pain in her womb. It was the time of the bleeding, and it was a time that would not go on for ever. The lives within her were draining away into the cloth between her legs. She crouched down and rocked and blew out her cheeks, panting. The heat was as an oven. The strips of light from the shutters divided the room into brightness and dark. The shouts from the *bazaar* were a nest of wasps. She looked at the brown woman with her baby's head as a lump on her shoulder, lying on the white sheets laid around her.

"Many have babies," she said. "Some of us do not. I give my life to other women. I do not give it to babies."

"But you will."

"I will not." Mary rose, feeling a cramp in her stomach, a dragging down. Then her temper rose. She would not show anything to this woman. "But do not think it is not for the want of the asking. Many men have tried ..." Not many, to tell the truth, but some. So Mary went on, "But I said no. I said to Miss Nightingale, I will ever say no. I am here for the healing, not having babies."

Still with the dragging down inside her, Mary smiled a quick smile of false security, as she went over to Lila and touched her cheek.

"I have seen that the good milk will come to you," she said. "Also there will be rations from the barracks. The commanding officer knows you because I told of you. He says there will be no wedding –" Mary saw the pain upon Lila's face, as the baby began to whimper. "But I said – a mother is a mother is a mother, and this is the child of Hamish Jamie Sinclair, and she will eat, and her mother will eat."

"Thank you, Miss Sinclair." Lila hugged her baby to her. It was more in defiance of her, Mary thought, than in seeking consolation.

"You need anything more?"

"You do too much."

"Yes," Mary said. "I do too much. That is the truth."

"And you like to say the truth. When it hurts."

Mary picked up her bonnet and a hatpin to pin it to the coil of hair on her head.

"It may hurt or not," she said, jabbing the pin home, "but I like to say the truth."

As if the mention of it brought the man himself, Mary found another suitor pressing his hand on her in Amritsar. Erskine Montgomery was a captain in the Lancers, but not the sort who thought that pig-sticking and *chota pegs* before tiffin were the best things about army life. Lean to the point of emaciation with sunken cheeks and luminous black eyes, his mouth was full and unexpected in its lines of humour. Erskine had heard of Mary by reputation and from Rose Campbell, the soldier's wife encountered on the train. But when she met Captain Montgomery at one of the rare receptions she was obliged to attend, Mary found herself caught in the concentration of his gaze. He did not look at the other guests, but only at her. He seemed to be searching something out of her. He spoke as if he had known her for ever.

"Miss Sinclair," he said, "your remarkable work among the women here – what gives you the strength to do it?"

"Because you men who say you are strong," Mary laughed as she answered, "you soldiers – you cannot do it. So I must."

"Because the women will not let us near them."

"Nor will their husbands."

"You are not married –"

"I can look after myself, sir."

"What I see in you" – the Captain's eyes pierced her own – "I see a woman who does not wish to be on her own. What woman does?"

"You do not know me."

"I have always known you. We merely have not met before." Erskine Montgomery was arrogant in his certainty. "But anyway, all women are the same. You – are you different?"

"All women are different, Captain. It is only the men are the same in the approach to the women."

Erskine Montgomery laughed. Mary had to admit that he looked devilish bonny when the mirth was in him. And he still gazed into her eyes as if nothing mattered in the world but herself, not the other officers in scarlet from the cantonment, not their few wives and the poor relations come out from England to marry abroad.

"I trust you will find the difference in me," he said. "I am not as other men are. And certainly not as other lancers are."

This turned out to be true. While his regiment was still quartered at Amritsar, Captain Montgomery became Mary's weekly companion. He would take her off riding on the quiet pony which he provided, and he would show her the ancient Indian temples and sacred caves ignored about the city. Flouting all conventions, he did not treat her as a Victorian woman, but as a comrade with a mind of her own. The erotic carvings in the caverns, the sexual or animal characteristics of the Hindu gods, these he explained to her as if they were natural. At first, she was shocked, but in the end, she took his confidence in her as a great trust. She began to depend on his Saturday appearance at the clinic as her only escape from her dedicated, enduring, frustrating work among the women. His telling her of their religious beliefs, his refusal to think there could only be one God and one way to Him, these began to liberate her from the certainty of her Scots faith and the teaching of the dominie that there was only a single true path to righteousness. And, frankly, Mary was falling in love with this elegant scarecrow with the smiling mouth and the intense, brilliant stare. For the first time, she wanted a man to ask her to marry him, to take her away from the blood and toil and tears of her nursing. But he said nothing, until one sultry Sunday, when he came to her to announce that he was posted to the north-west frontier with his regiment, and he must go.

"The only thing I cannot leave in Amritsar," he told her, "is you."

"Then —"

"I must."

"I have my work," Mary said. "I had it before you came here. How could I go?"

"Your sacrifice?" The smile on Erskine's lips for once made them thinner with mockery. "You would still nurse on and not come with me?"

Was Erskine asking her? Mary did not know. If it was a proposal, it was a queer one. He had hardly touched her on their long expeditions, except to help her down from her pony. Once she had slipped from her saddle into his embrace, but though he had held her to him for an instant, he had pushed her away with a strained joke, as though he had to deny himself. And was this really a proposal? Or only a test of her secret love of him?

"You have not asked me to come with you, Erskine."

"Not in so many words."

"So few. You never have."

Erskine smiled again with his mouth tight against himself or her.

"How I shall miss you," he said. "And you will never know –" He put out his hands and pressed her cheeks between his palms and burned his gaze into her eyes like a brand. Then he kissed her fiercely and briefly full on the lips. And then he put her away.

"Erskine," she said. "What? What will I never know?"

"How I have stopped myself –" He shrugged, his thin shoulders hunched in despair. "I cannot. Yet I love you –"

"Ah," Mary said. "And if it is love, what is cannot to that? Love always can."

"I have a wife," Erskine said coldly. "She is insane. In a superior Bedlam in England. I cannot." Roughly, he took Mary by the shoulder. His fingers were iron claws digging to her bone. "Now you know." His eyes were sudden red with passion like the Indian actors Mary had seen who put crimson dye in their eyes to show anger. "You know now. And I will go." He turned and walked towards the door.

"Erskine," Mary said. "You men are all the same."

"Why?"

"You are always married."

Erskine's laugh was short and dry.

"What a woman you are, Mary. A joke, *now*."

"It is true. And you are always the same, because –"

"What?"

"You are hurt. You have control over yourself. Your pain. Your suffering. Your love of me." Mary was now staring at Erskine with her bright eyes. "What about mine? Did you think of that?"

"Mary, I never –" Erskine started forward. "I could never have hoped –"

"Get away you, Erskine," Mary said. She had meant to sound cold, but her tone was fond enough. "You will never know. Never ken at all."

"Then you do love me." Erskine was suddenly happy. "And you might –"

"Get away with you, man. You will not know. How can you? You are a man like the rest of them."

At the end of the war in China, Hamish Jamie found himself at a plundering and burning worse than at Lucknow. In the Summer Palace at Peking, he burst in behind the French, who had draped silk robes and hangings over their epaulettes higher than their shakos, with gold and jade ornaments falling out of their knapsacks and pockets.

There was so much more gold inlaid in the painted carvings which decorated the palace walls that it looked like brass. Hamish Jamie was prizing a strip out of it when he saw a young captain in the Royal Engineers with a blazing torch in his hand, setting fire to some silk hangings. Flickers of flame ran as red mice up the wall.

"Ach, you're burning gold, sir."

"It's brass."

"Look you."

Hamish Jamie handed over his strip of inlaid metal to the captain who bent it and whistled.

"Gold it is." Then watching the flame run up the silk to the ornate ceiling. "Too late now. But no matter. There are hundreds of other pavilions. And we are ordered to burn it all. They did torture our envoys. Ungodly swine."

"But we'll get the prize money."

"So our commander says. He's given his share back to us." The captain laughed. "Damn fool, but a good general. What's your name, sergeant?"

"Hamish James Sinclair, sir. In the Commissariat."

"Charles George Gordon." He smiled briefly under his black curly hair, but his eyes remained filled with a hard blue light. "I have seen you on the carts. You did a fine job, bringing up the shells."

"I saw you on the pontoons at the Taku Fort. Engineers win wars."

"And transport. To hell with the glory boys. Glory is nine-tenths pishposh or ninety-nine per cent twaddle. Getting there is what matters."

The flames began to roast them and the smoke made them cough. They moved towards the door of the fiery pavilion.

"It's a damned shame burning this," Gordon said. "It's wretchedly demoralizing work for an army."

"Aye," Hamish Jamie said. "The waste of it."

His prize money came to ten pounds. A private received four pounds, and Captain Gordon forty-eight pounds. The Summer Palace was burned to the ground, its ashes its only legacy. And though Peking proved as dirty a city as Cawnpore or Amritsar, Hamish Jamie found a consolation in it. It was filled with concubines and prostitutes, even more than those denounced by the old prophets in Babylon and Sodom and Gomorrah. There was no holding the troops.

Hamish Jamie chose a young woman called Wu, so slight and delicate that she lay in his arms as small as a thrush chick in a nest. Yet when she took the combs out of her hair, its black waterfall covered all of his body as if drowned in her tresses. He taught Wu to say one word, "Love", and she taught him a great gentleness in the touching of her skin. Tracing the line of her leg to her ankle with his thick fingers, he came to her crippled foot, bound to the size of a scone with the bones crushed inward. He stroked the foot and said, "How is it, Wu, the more people are wise, the more they cripple you sore?"

16

DANGER OF SURVEY

They were stuck in a hard sea. In the winter, their sod and timber hut was trapped like a small berg in ice. In the summer, it was becalmed among the blowing grasses. Too cold for most of the year, too hot for a part of it, and windy pretty much all the time. And what winds, when they wanted to take a breath of it! Round the corner of the hut in winter, and you would bend double like a half-open jackknife, as the gust hit you in the vitals with the point of its sword. And in the summer, suddenly out the plains, a tall black tower would rise as a black keep shredding at the edges, and out of it jags of lightning would crackle or split it from top to bottom, with the thunder breaking your ear-drums with the clap of heavenly hands.

So it was to Bain, who wanted to master these new lands. They had three hundred and twenty acres for the taking, and that was an estate in Scotland, they would be the lairds there. But here, it was flying in the face of the ground. Because of the wind, they had to build their hut in a bottom, where the river ran – or did not run nine months of the year. It was not a burn, but a trickle over stones some of the time, a torrent for a month at the melting of the snows, and a dry rock bed for most of the year. And when they ploughed the grasses for the planting of the wheat and the barley, there was no keeping the crop or the soil. For they could not fence the field from the plain. There was not the wood for it nor the time nor the water for the hedges. So the living things came in to eat them out, the prairie dogs and the deer and the pigeon. And one summer with a beating of bronze wings, the plague of locusts came as foretold in the Good Book. They were called hoppers now, and they ate the grain and the grass and all that was green under the moving carpet of their clacking wings. And there was no riddance from them except the burning of them. And that left nothing but a black devastation.

"Was it good to come here?" Bain asked his father. "There is nothing the now. In the trees, there was the timber. And now –"

He spread his hands to the horizon half as far as time away. "We come to nothing. And nothing we have of it."

"There will be the day," Hamish said, "when there will be the wheat to the sky."

"But the buffalo –"

"They will be gone. We are killing them all."

That was truly said. Now that the Indians had rifles to fire from their horses, and now the railways were pushing across the American continent below the Missouri River, the workers had to be fed, and the buffalo hunters went on at their work of massacre as if the killing would never stop because the herds would always be there, which they would not. And Henri Chatillon was little now at the trading post, so that Katie was sore sick at the loss of the sight of him. Not that his courting of her was anything at all – or to his shame, Bain had to admit, Katie's courting of Henri. For she was fair throwing herself at this man. And him half a savage as well as half a Frenchman. And what did they say about the *métis*, the half-whites and half-red men? They took the worst out of both the races.

Yet even Bain would not say that about Henri. At the post, when the other men and women and children ever were drinking themselves into the forgetfulness of the whisky and rum that all craved – perhaps because the furs were being trapped out and the ploughs were beginning to turn the grasses – Henri stood back, leaning on his rifle, making his few comments, or sometimes telling the elaborate tales of the frontier which ended in one final soft joke. He never seemed to fall out of his detached concern. Only once had Bain found him passionate, when he was talking with the trapper Gerald Fitzgerald who had come up from Missouri over the Medicine Line, as sharp and intense as a flung knife.

"Then you will be with us," Fitzgerald was saying. "For he that is not with us is –"

"Not against you," Henri said and laughed. "But I am not for you."

"Only for yourself," Fitzgerald said.

"Is big country," Henri said. "*Ce beau pays est pour tout le monde. Eh,* Bain, you know Fitzgerald. 'E wish we join America."

"You'll no be a friend of the Queen of England," Fitzgerald said. He took a tin mug and held it under the tap of the whisky keg and gave the drink to Bain.

"I am not," Bain said. "But I have two brothers fighting for Her in India."

Fitzgerald spat on the mud floor.

"Wearing the red," he said. "How could you do that? But the Scots are not our friends in Ireland."

"So my father says," Bain answered. "But I have nothing against you."

"In France," Henri said, "*On aime les Écossais. Zee Garde Royale* it was zee Scotsmen. Often, zee Scots fight for France. *La belle alliance.*"

"Then it's time for another *belle alliance*," Fitzgerald said. "The Scots, the Irish, and the French."

"And my mother's people," Henri said.

"The redskins, why not?" Fitzgerald laughed. "One thing we have in common. We all hate the bloody redcoats."

"I was telling you," Bain said, "my two brothers, they wear that coat. Though Iain the now, he has a fine place of his own in India and he's out of it. But my mother and father, they will not have a word against the Queen."

"The more fool them," Fitzgerald said. "And all the murthering she has done in Ireland."

Henri stoked the muzzle of his rifle.

"A woman – a little woman – can she kill so many?"

"Not herself –"

"So she does not kill. So why we join America? Zey kill my brothers and sisters –"

"Redskins –"

"Zey not kill zem 'ere."

"You work for a British Company?" Fitzgerald's lips were as sour as the whisky in Bain's mouth. "You work for the Hudson's Bay Company? And you're French and redskin. They can't keep this Rupert's Land. Canada will have it if we don't."

"*Bon*," Henri said. "But zey look for my brothers and sisters. No wars wid Indians 'ere. Zat is for Americans."

"You will not be for the Fenians then?" Fitzgerald said. "Not for free men in a free country."

"I am free," Henri said, picking up his rifle, and then speaking with hardness. "And I kill zee man who say I am not free. We go, Bain, and see Katie."

Bain put down his tin mug on the rough wooden bar. It still had some of the whiskey in it.

"I would give you back all your whiskey, Fitzgerald," he said, "only the half of it is in my stomach."

"Where it will curdle," Fitzgerald said. "So stupid you are."

Henri seemed to know all the people in the hide tents pitched round the trading-post, the big squaws with a baby clung like a lump on their backs, the lounging braves braiding their hair, the naked children that clung to his leg, and even the thin dogs that did not cringe at his passing, but shivered towards a caress from his hand. Bain was almost jealous at the trust and love that Henri seemed to inspire. But not in him, not in Katie's brother.

"How is your —" Bain paused for the word — "squaw? Wife?"

"I not marry," Henri said. "She is Indian wife. We together ten year. But no boy, no girl. *Et je pense* — is it zee end of Chatillons? *Pas plus les* Chatillons? No —"

"So you think of Katie?"

Henri took Bain by the arm and stopped and turned towards him.

"Bain, you please me. But — Katie and me — is for us. Not for you. I ask your father —"

"He will say no."

"Why? I am not — you say — Protestant?"

"What do you believe in?"

"God. Who else?" Henri smiled and walked on with Bain following. "Crows, Blackfeet, Assiniboins, Sioux, we all believe God. He make zee world. You believe God. He make zee world."

"We don't believe in the same God."

"Same world," Henri said.

"Not the same God," Bain said.

"If zee same world," Henri said, "and many Gods, or same God wid many faces, we live in same world — and God show 'is face to each of us as 'e wish."

"Sounds good," Bain said, "but it is not true."

"Why?"

"Minister says only one God..."

"And I say wid many faces."

You could not help liking Henri, and Bain saw Hamish and Hannah fall under his spell, even though their wills were hard against the buffalo hunter going with their daughter. Katie did all she could to change minds and win hearts, but it was the stubborn bent of the Sinclairs, that once they had set their thought, it was like hot lead in a mould cooling into a bullet. The more she made Henri tell the tales of his courage and cunning in the wilderness, his loyalty and humour in adversity, the more she saw Hamish and Hannah were determined not to let this man of the wild take their daughter as his own. She knew why. He was a half-breed, and her parents would think that he would make a squaw of her. As though being in a hide tent was worse than in a sod hut, which was *all* dirt, if you came to think of it.

Henri took Hamish outside to ask for Katie's hand. It was the time of the setting of the sun. The broad and turning globe of yellow light was balanced on the rim of the land, and the shadows behind the men were a hundred feet long, two giant spokes of blackness across the stubble of the remaining crop that Hamish was able to harvest, barely enough to last them for the winter. The soil was loose and powdery to their feet, and the toes of their boots scuffed up dust.

"I marry Katie," Henri said. "I give you dowry of five hundred beaver skin."

"You do not buy women here," Hamish said.

"I not buy," Henri said, his eyes yellow in the low light. "I give. I wish I give!"

"I will not take from you," Hamish said. "You will not take my daughter."

"She take me."

"She will not go against her father."

"She is of age. She take me."

"You do not fear God," Hamish said. "You will make a squaw of her. A wild woman."

"I build her a big *tipi*. And a cabin – timber for zee winter. She live as Queen – as Queen in England. I hunt for her. I die for her."

The passion of Henri startled Hamish, but he did not show it.

"I will not have it the now," he said. "Did you not hear me?"

"She – her who say," Henri said. "Katie say – Henri, you are my man. I say, Katie – my woman. And you say – no?"

"I say no."

"She say yes. I say yes. And you, old man," Henri stood over Hamish, so that their two shadows now made one black path away across the plains – "you will not stop us."

"I will," Hamish said. "My daughter will bide with us. We have need of her."

"I need her."

"Go back to your squaw," Hamish said. "That is your place. With the savages."

Hamish saw the stooping figure in front of him shaken as a sapling in a gale with a terrible anger. Then the man mastered his wrath and grew still.

"She come to me," Henri said. "I call and she come."

"The devil you do," Hamish said.

"She come."

And Henri Chatillon went now, loping over the plain, the rifle a third leg on him black against the sun, its face orange now and cut in half by the land. And Hamish went into the hut to tell Hannah and Bain and Katie that Henri would never come to the hut again. And for all her red hair and temper, Katie did not weep and storm. She was almost too calm, as if she knew what had to be. Yet she was only biding her time. For at the end of the winter, and come the spring, she was gone at the silent call of Henri Chatillon. And there was no trace of her, no tale of her. She was gone as the wild geese are gone and the wild duck are gone, migrating after their kind.

Angus never knew a survey could be that dangerous. He was the transit man with the axeman in front of him and the leveller behind. He had been slung on a rope with his theodolite in mid-air over the edge of a gorge to make his calculations. He had been swung on a log on chains over a roaring torrent. Now he was hanging by spikes clamped into his boots on an ice-slope with his fingers too frozen to turn the screws of the transit. His eyes were full of tears from the invisible spokes of cold that the wind drove at him. He could not see the angles on his theodolite, let alone record them for the leveller behind him. He blinked furiously and turned a screw and wrote in his mind eleven degrees. Then he jerked out his spikes, turning onto his back and cradling his instrument to his chest. So he slid down the slope to a ridge, where the leveller stood with his assistants and their graduated poles. He was lucky in his scramble down. No snag of rock tore through his clothes or between his legs. But a survey was a pig all right.

"It's murder up there," he said to Donovan, the leveller. "The wind's so sore you can not see through your little telescope."

"You have the readings?"

"Aye." Angus put his mitten in the pocket of his jacket to pull out pencil and pad. "I have them."

Another railroad was being driven across the Appalachians to compete with the two which already ran across to the plains. The market on Wall Street was well watered with stocks sold in tracks to the west that were not yet laid. When Angus had reached New York, he had found work at once as an assistant on a preliminary survey, holding the painted pole as the leveller adjusted his sight and made his reckonings. But the team was working against time and the wastage of men did not matter. The first leveller was lost to dysentery from dirty water, his replacement broke both his ankles slipping down a cliff of shale, while the transit man cracked his skull open when the axeman felled a tree that tumbled down backwards. The accidents were good for promotion, if you were quick to learn. Angus took all of three days hanging around the instruments to study how to set a theodolite and even to level the tripod and turn its small telescope to sight upon the graduated poles. This was just a question of being careful, and some simple subtractions between the levels of the front-sight and the back-sight. As the poles were moved forward, fresh sums established a profile or a backbone line, showing the gradients. Contour lines were made at right angles to the central line, though plotting the path of the railroad was a mazy way through the mountains, doubling back and forth and sideways, always along the easiest slope or through a natural pass, because tunnels and cuttings cost millions of dollars, and why not use God's cracks in nature to ease the path of the iron roads of man?

They were lucky to have an abandoned cabin as their base camp. A mountain family had moved on west in despair. They had hoisted an iron stove onto their pack-mules, so they had hot hash and corn bread for dinner, and the bitter black scalding coffee that made the wheels turn all over America. There was an uneasy truce among the team, different as they were. For they had to labour together, even if they did not like each other. And the work of each one meant the wages of them all.

"There's a better route," Donovan said. "The recce party, they are wrong to be sure."

"It is good," Mencken the axeman said. "Open land. No trees."

"Lazy bastard," Donovan said. "Never lift an axe, do you? Give me some coffee."

Angus poured the last of the tin pot into Donovan's mug.

"They must have their reasons," he said. "To want to go this way."

"Lawyers," Donovan said. "And all lawyers are crooks. They should be hanged, not the people they put on the rope's end. Thieves, every one of them. To be sure, they bought the land cheap that this road will run on, and they sold it back dear to the company."

"That is a fact," Thorvald said more as a statement than a question.

"That is a fact." Donovan mimicked Thorvald's thick accent. Thorvald held the front pole for him and could not answer back. "And there is politics too. Towns are built ahead in the hope the road runs there. Millions of acres are sold in the hope the road runs there. And if it runs another way – what?"

"Ruin," Angus said. "And the poor people moving again."

"We already moved to America," Donovan said. "We poor people."

"Aye," Angus said, "but there is no call to move again when we are here."

"This is a moving nation," Mencken said. "I move."

"You move." Donovan now mimicked Mencken's guttural sounds. "He, she, it moves. We move, you move, they move. Here, it is a declension of move. And what are we doing? We are putting the whole of this American nation on to iron wheels. And that is how they will stay – moving. Rolling up and down the length and the breadth of the land. Rolling like timber, rolling like the river, rolling, rolling till they roll off the Rockies into the ocean on the far edge of this all."

Angus admired the talk that Donovan had in him, although he did not admire the man.

"It's a mighty land," he said. "And do not the people move towards their opportunity?"

"No," Donovan said. Then he swallowed the last dregs of his coffee. "They did fail, and they fail again in this new land. They move from one failure to the next. And our job is to make them move faster. We grease the wheels of failure. We export it to the frontier and beyond."

There was a hush in the cabin. Always difficult not to believe Donovan, but none of the seven men wanted to believe him, for he suggested their failure too. Finally, little Cappeto, the other assistant on the back pole, dared to speak.

"We make opportunity. We build railroad. All go and make west."

"Baloney," Donovan said. "We are spreading the great mistake. Does the west want our rejects? And what will we do in that desert out there? It is fit for Indians, not for the like of us, who can not even make a go of it in a better country."

"My folks are out there," Angus said. "But I willna go. I said, here, come here for opportunity –"

"Then they had a smart one," Donovan said, "to be sure. Except for one matter, Angus Sinclair –" He jerked his thumbs at the dank walls of the cold cabin, which had already wet the pile of their bedding rolls. "Do you say this is opportunity? Speaking for myself – and you know what a religious man I am – I would call it purgatory. We are here because it is nowhere – to remit our sins without a chance of a progress to the heavenly land. We may help to build the railroad, but only for people to pass through looking not to the left of them, and not to the right at this forgotten place where only fools would ever waste their time."

Mencken rose to his feet and stood over Donovan.

"It is work," he said. "Then I go home to Baltimore. Do you have home, Donovan? Your home is in your mouth, I think."

The men laughed at Donovan, and he did not like it.

"Your home is in your belly, Mencken," he said, trying to turn the joke. But his voice was too sharp to raise another laugh. "I speak the truth, but you do not want to hear it. The company – it will kill us or wear us out for a few dollars more. And when the railroad is laid, and all the moving nation – that's what you said, Mencken – when they are all moving upon it, they will never give any thought to them that made the railroad there. We will be dead and gone and forgotten – for a few dollars more. And devil a one will know of the men who made the iron road."

Angus rose now to stand beside Mencken and look down on the plausible Donovan.

"Do you no think, Donovan, that if we do our work, we may no live in that work? That work is ourselves – if we do it well."

"There speaks a canting Scot," Donovan said, and now he tried to mimick the burr of Angus. "By their work you shall know them."

"Aye," Angus said. "And by your mouth we know you."

The other men laughed again and rose. And now they stood around Donovan in an accusing circle, looking down on the voice which made them doubt what they did. But Donovan was not put out. He remained squatting and snarled out his disbelief.

"And how would they build a railroad at all without men with potatos for brains?"

"You have potato in your head," Thorvald said. "Hash potato."

"Go to bed," Donovan said. "Or you'll not be fit for the work in the morning."

"You are no fit for the work at all," Angus said. "For you do not mean to do it."

Now Donovan rose to his feet, lean and hooked forward at the shoulder.

"I mean to do my work," he said, "for a few dollars more. But do not ask me to give my mind to it. That is set on other matters. I tell you, there will be a change here and a war here. And all you slaves to the dollar, even you will be free – if you want it, and even if you do not."

The colonel's office in the barracks at Amritsar was hardly surprising, even if it was not expected. The desk had been brought from England, but it was a military travelling desk in pine and leather, on twin trestles. The paintings were horse pictures, but not the usual ones of ladies riding sidesaddle in pink hunting-coats. Here a tiger attacked a frightened charger, there a mare kicked a wolf attacking her foal. And

Hamish Jamie liked the hoof on the colonel's desk which had been converted into an ink-stand. He had thought that they were foot-soldiers, the poor slogging infantry; but the colonel must have been in the cavalry before he had to get down onto his feet.

"Sinclair," he said, "you know why you are here. Everybody in this camp knows what I am going to do before I know myself."

"Well," Hamish Jamie said, denying what he knew, "you do not mean to make an officer of me."

"I do."

"The Mess." Hamish Jamie came to the sticking point. "The officers' mess. How will they speak to me there?"

"As an officer," the colonel said, "and a gentleman." He paused. "Sinclair is a great name."

"There were Sinclairs fought at Bannockburn. And with the Heart of Bruce, the Sinclairs died fighting the Moors. And at Flodden Field. It is an old fighting clan."

"Your citations from China are excellent," the colonel said. "You are right about supplies. They are the backbone of the regiment. You will accept to be quartermaster. You will be gazetted as a captain."

"Aye," Hamish Jamie said. "That I will. But I will not pay for it, for I do not have the money."

"Buying commissions is on the way out, Sinclair. As for the quartermaster, you were always my personal employee. You had to make your mess bills on the sale of the supplies, but now the government will pay them and another thirty pounds a year, so you need not be a thief. I never liked buying pips. Nobody did. The rich do not always fight the best. Of course, if you are defending your wealth —the price you paid for your commission — you might fight like the devil to save your investment. But there are better reasons."

"Aye, sir. The regiment."

"And Queen and country." The colonel gave Hamish Jamie a long stare. Then he smiled, or Hamish Jamie would have sworn that he did, only the flicker on the thin lips under the grey moustache could have been a sneer or a grimace. "But as we are the Seaforth Highlanders, and as you are a Sinclair — and which side were you on at Culloden? — I think the regiment is a very good thing to fight for."

Now Hamish Jamie could not stop a grin that spread over his face, incorrigible.

"The regiment is a very good thing to fight for," he said. "For it is a very good regiment — the best of the regiments."

"Only because of the men in it," the colonel said. "Including you. But you must understand, Sinclair, there are your fellow officers who may not wish to include you."

"Ach, then I will not include them in the circle of my acquaintance."

The flicker passed across the colonel's tight mouth once more.

"And there is another matter — more serious even. I do not wish to mention it, but ..." the colonel paused. "I believe you may know what it is."

"About me? My habits?"

"About your character. An Indian woman —"

"Ach." Hamish paused to think. He felt the blood in his cheeks and a dirk in his heart. He knew he would betray what he held most dear.

"I have heard tell of that."

"It has been mentioned to me," the colonel said, "that you and a certain lady — even that there are children. A boy, it is said, called *Seaforth* —"

"That would be impossible, sir."

"Impossible, Sinclair? Now I agree. No officer of this regiment could have a child by a native woman. And certainly not called by the name of this regiment. It is impossible. Therefore, Sinclair, as it is impossible, I presume that it is not possible."

Hamish Jamie looked the colonel in the eye with the straight blue stare of untruth. But he chose his words defensively. "As it is impossible, sir, it must not be true."

"I am glad to hear that, Sinclair. It would have been an insuperable impediment, however much we wished you to join us as an officer in this regiment. But as it is impossible, and you have told me it is impossible, I trust that I shall never hear of this impossible matter again."

"That you will not, sir."

The colonel rose from behind his desk. He walked over to Hamish Jamie and put his hand on the epaulette of the sergeant-quarter-master's tunic.

"I will take you to the mess myself," he said. "And I will introduce you. There will be no problems there, if you have courage enough, and I know that you have. And as for what is impossible, that never happened, because it is impossible. The army only has time for the practical, as you do."

Hamish Jamie dropped his eyes. His heart seemed to fall into his belly and drag it down. Yet he had been given all he wanted at the price of his word.

"You may trust me, sir," he said, "to do all that I must do as an officer of this regiment."

He went to Lila the following night, changing his pony-chaise to hide his tracks, in case somebody might be following him. When he came to the open stairway to her room in the *bazaar*, the market children shouted at him in the streets or begged, clinging onto his kilt or his arm until he shook them off and shooed them away. When he sweated up the steps to the wooden door to knock three times on it, he knew that she had already seen his coming. She always did. But then she was shy, and she would be huddled in a corner, fearful of the father of her son and daughter now.

The door opened. A small boy stood at it, so small that he reached only to the knee of Hamish Jamie, who bent and seized him and whirled him round in the air and put him down. Then he walked over to the bed where Lila sat, her purple shawl wrapped around her face, the baby absently crawling over the bedspread of crimson stripes.

"I am here, Lila," he said.

"I think I not see you," she said.

"But here I am," he said. He looked round the dark white walls with their pitiful brightness, the painted woodcuts and the patterned cloths pinned on the plaster, and the shining dragon silk hanging he had brought from the spoils of Peking. "Seaforth –" He picked up the solemn small boy again and looked at him. "You like the mountains?"

The small boy made a face.

"He not know mountains."

Lila dropped her shawl and turned the black beam of her gaze on Hamish Jamie. "You send us to the mountains? To your brother? Why?"

"The air is good," Hamish Jamie swallowed on his lie, "for little children. Here there is dust, flies, illness. In the mountains it is clean–"

"Pah. You send us away."

"I do not." Then Hamish Jamie could not bear his own deceit and went over to Lila and kneeled before her and took her face between his two hands and spoke to her. "I do. My brother will look for you and the children. I am to be quartermaster – an officer. And the Seaforths must away to Canada. I will see my mother and father there. I love you, Lila, but – I must away. And you must away to the mountains."

Hamish Jamie felt the tears prickle at the corner of his eyes. The relief of confessing had provoked a weeping in him that he just held in check.

"So you will send us to Himalayas. You will go from us."

"I am a soldier. You always knew Hamish Jamie – a soldier."

"And liar," Lila said. "We can not go back to Singhs. I am *pariah*, worse than dog to be with you. To have your boy and girl. And you send me to your brother. And I am dog to him."

"You are not." Hamish Jamie was indignant. "You met him and Anna. They loved you."

"They love you. Me they hate. But Seaforth –" The small boy came forward and stood within his mother's arm. "He is of you. Seaforth Sinclair. For him, they love me and they hate me."

"Do not make it hard, Lila," Hamish Jamie said. "I do what I must do. I do all I can for you."

"You make me a dog," Lila said. "You make Seaforth and Peg more than dogs. For who will want them?"

As Lila began to cry the black *kohl* running down her cheeks, the small boy ran at Hamish Jamie. His head was as high as his father's bare knees under his kilt. He began drumming at the man's thighs with his tiny fists like hail on calico. He was shrieking cries that Hamish Jamie could not understand, the sound of the mewing of gulls, so he picked up the little lad by the waist and let him wave his hands in the air and keep on screaming.

"Put him down," Lila said. "Give him me. He is not for you. He is for me."

So Hamish Jamie put him in his mother's arms, and she tried to hold his arm to his sides, but she could not. He flailed away and ran out and clutched his father's leg by the ankle of his white boot. He wound his father tight to him in a ball and chain. And Hamish Jamie stood foolish there, shackled in front of Lila. And now the baby girl began to cry, and her mother took her up and unbound her *sari* and gave her daughter the breast.

Hamish Jamie took money from his sporran in a pouch, and he threw it onto the bed.

"There is for you and Seaforth and the girl," he said. "It is more than enough until Iain and Anna come to find you –"

"Your sister Mary will come," Lila said. "She think you are bad."

"She is my sister yet," Hamish Jamie said. "And never think you or your kin will be between me and my kin. But Mary also will look for you until Iain comes. I will see to that."

"She will see to that – she is a woman."

"Aye," Hamish Jamie said, his leg pegged to the floor by Seaforth. "And I will come again if I can. But the Colonel does not want –"

"You to be with an Indian wife."

"It is impossible, he says."

Lila gave a harsh laugh, the cracking of dry sticks in her voice.

"It was possible for you."

"I loved you, Lila," Hamish Jamie said. "And I still love you. You do not believe it, but I do. But I must go the now. The regiment –"

"Daddy," Seaforth called, holding harder onto the leg of his father.

This was the hardest going that Hamish Jamie had ever had of it. He could not shake off the small boy like a burr. Such was his son. And bending and trying to prize him off was no good. The boy cleaved to him as to one flesh and blood. In the end, he had to break the child's grip by force and drop him yelling on his mother's lap as she fed the baby. And Hamish Jamie had to make a stumbling backwards run from the room, the most shaming retreat of his army life. He would rather have shrapnel and grapeshot whistling round his ears than the sounds of the sobbing. He would rather have been dead than having to walk back to barracks with his own living self, and knowing the wrongs he had done and the sort of man he was.

17

IRON ROAD
AND WAYWARD PATH

"He's drunk and he's slow and he's dumb," Sergeant Hockmeister said. "That's why he's the general."

"He knows where the railroads go," Angus said. "That's why he's the general."

Grant and his army were the wrong side of Vicksburg. His supply barges and steamers had to run past the Confederate batteries to carry his supplies down to Mississippi. His ammunition waggons were commandeered from the local plantations. They ranged from fancy carriages to cotton carts, pulled by mules and oxen with straw collars and rope lines for harnesses.

The armies of Dixie lay north and south and east of them, and the railroads converged at Jackson, from where trains could reinforce Vicksburg at will. The Union soldiers only had five days of rations, hard bread and coffee and salt. "What I do expect," Grant said grimly, "is to make the country furnish the balance."

The foraging parties were scavengers on the face of the earth. They stole the chickens and dug up the buried sacks of seed corn. Grant's subordinate, William Tecumseh Sherman, was driven to living off the land as Moses was, when taking his people from Egypt to Israel. For Sherman, his foragers were God's instruments of justice. He would make the South howl. He would squeeze the soil until it bled supplies for him. And he would burn the rest as an example. For he did not think he was fighting only soldiers, but a whole people, who had to feel the hard hand of war before they laid down their resistance. Devastation was the truest weapon.

Angus could not bear the sight of it, which was worse than his childish memories of the clearances. In the name of God and the right of the North, barns were fired, dirt yards jabbed with bayonets to find hidden plunder, cattle butchered, families beggared and turned from their blackened homes. His duty was with Grant's only pontoon train, which was needed to cross the rivers that flowed into the Mississippi. But he had little to do, while Grant struck at Jackson and took it in a downpour, leaving Sherman to destroy the railroad system there, and Sherman liked to destroy. Grant doubled back towards Vicksburg, driving the Confederates ahead of him to bottle them up in their city. They burned the bridge over the Big Black River, and Angus was called to bring his pontoons into action at Bridgeport. The iron and wood casings were slotted and bolted and roped into place, and Sherman's corps of pillagers crossed over the shaking and makeshift bridge to Walnut Hill, where they set up a base on dry high ground, which would be supplied by the navy from Haine's Bluff and the Mississippi. Vicksburg was doomed.

Yet if Grant cared that his men ate and their ammunition pouches were full, he cared less for their lives. He ordered two frontal assaults on the entrenchments before the enemy city. Angus had never seen such a shooting gallery or skittles game outside a country fair. As the masses of Federal troops ran forward with fixed bayonets, a deadly hush fell on the Confederate diggings. Then out of them rose lines of grey men aiming their muskets and rifles. Deliberately, they fired volley after volley into the advancing troops while another grey line appeared to shoot over their heads at the enemy. Grape and canister swirled like devil dust among the Union men in blue. They were struck down and shaken and whittled away until they fell back, only to be ordered into a second assault which mowed them to the earth as the sickle and the scythe might reap a tall harvest of blood. After such a brilliant preliminary strategy, this was the stubborn folly of mass murder. And Angus could not comprehend it.

Now Grant settled down to a siege. Where marching had prevailed and assault had failed, walls and starving would do the work. The foragers scattered as locusts over the land behind the earthworks, while the troops in the trenches watched the surrounded city that must give in, for there was no hope of relief. War was waiting, Angus knew that. It was very rarely fighting. And when General Sherman sent for him, he knew what to expect. It would be a plan to spread the war behind the rear of the enemy, to destroy the front lines by striking at the back country. A dirty business, but dependent on good communications.

The intensity of the general was almost biblical. There was a preacher in this soldier, and as a surveyor of things, Angus did not relish a sermon in his fighting.

"How mobile can you be, Sinclair?" Sherman asked, pacing up and down his tent as if sitting down were an expression of defeat. "Can you pull those pontoons over country roads thirty miles a day – forty even?"

"I doubt it, sir," Angus said. "You canna depend there will always be mules. And axles break. Fifteen miles a day. No more."

"Too slow. We will have to swim, if they burn the bridges."

"A raid is it, sir?"

"That is my business. But I hear well of you. You raised that pontoon at Bridgeport in less than a day." His eyes radiated light at Angus. "Could you design for me a *light* pontoon – and quickly assembled – a new kind that could go with the cavalry?"

"Aye," Angus said. "I could. But it would take time."

"We do not have time. We have God's work to do, and it must be done quickly."

"Burning the houses of the innocents –"

Sherman scowled at Angus. "I am disappointed in you, Sinclair. I had thought you might have more imagination. And dedication. Do you not reckon? We are not only fighting hostile armies, but a hostile people. We must make old and young, rich and poor, feel our wrath. We can punish Georgia and South Carolina as they deserve. Did they not punish their slaves? And if they are given into the hand of destruction, we can repopulate them. The devastation of them and their roads and their houses and their crops will destroy their armies. For we cannot occupy the South, we do not have the men. So we will burn it. And without resources, their soldiers will perish on the vine." Sherman was influenced by his own dark vision. "So you will make me my light pontoon."

"As I can," Angus said. "But in good time. And I do not think in good time for your black work. I come from a land cleared by the burning of the crofts –"

"But this is a just cause –"

"That is what the lairds said to us."

"God's will and work."

"There is fire from heaven," Angus said. "But it is better direct from the hand of God than from the matches of your men."

And indeed, waiting proved to be the best policy. For Vicksburg surrendered on the Fourth of July.

Angus was assigned to count some of the weapons of the Confederate soldiers as they stacked them in front of their conquerors. The heaps of rifles and swords and long bayonets looked like the horns of a thousand dead elk and stags, their prongs sticking out in futile aggression. The beaten soldiers even had to drape their regimental colours over the tops of the piles of weapons, draping their muzzles and points in a ragged bright blanket of defeat. Angus found the sight too sore for him, a last and unnecessary insult. But there it was. The war must be changing him, too. For he had had precious little feeling for a flag and certainly not for the Stars and Stripes, and now he was feeling that the yielding of a piece of gaudy cloth was a true humiliation.

Later, when Angus was checking the roll of the thirty-one thousand prisoners who had been taken, he fell on the name Archibald Sinclair. And when he found the Confederate officer leaning against a wall, tracing a pattern in the dirt with the toe of his boot, he appeared a reflection of the face of Angus himself – the same long jaw with a cleft in the chin, the parallel sad hollows which ran down from cheekbone and nose, the projecting brow over the sunken blue eyes.

"Kinsman I see," Angus said and held out his hand, which the other man took.

"You are a Sinclair, then."

"Angus Sinclair. Hamish is my father. We were cleared and came to Canada. They are in the west there."

"We came with Oglethorpe to Georgia. We whipped the Spaniards and they never came back from Florida. And we were given fifty asses and five pounds and a year's rations to stay on as settlers. And we did on Saint Simeon's Island, and we built a fine plantation there by the sea. And how it will be now, I dare not reckon."

Archibald Sinclair traced in the dirt with the point of his boot as if he were trying to draw a plan or a map, when there was only a prison camp ahead of him.

"Will your slaves take it now?"

"The *nigras*? No. They like us well. It is a Northern fiction they are not happy with us. Why, they need us. For they'd never look after themselves."

"That is what they said of us in the Highlands," Angus said. "We were too feckless to look after ourselves. Without the black cattle we were good for nothing." He looked at the piles of arms sticking out from under the Confederate flags. "We are good for something."

"To fight each other?" Archibald gave a sour laugh. "Brother against brother? It is not your war, even."

"I have two brothers fought for the Queen in India. I am a surveyor and an engineer. The wages are fair. I build pontoon bridges. I will not hold a gun."

"Would you have some whisky, cousin?"

"I do not."

"If I did not carry a sword," Archibald said, "and I do not now, why I would carry whisky."

"It would do you more good," Angus said. "And I shall get you a dram."

"Spoken like a cousin and a gentleman," Archibald said. "You look like me, you know."

"I do not agree. You look like me."

Archibald laughed. "Do you always have to be in the right, as all the Sinclairs do? Or shall we say it is the same thing?"

"I am in the right," Angus said, "but it is the same thing."

"When the war is over, and I think it is nearly over now," Archibald said, "will you come visit me on my plantation? Saint Simeon's Island in Georgia. They know the name there."

"I will, but first the whisky –"

So the prisoner and the surveyor began drinking together that night, and they became friends where they had been said to be enemies. But they were never true enemies, or so Angus and Archibald reckoned. They went out to do the bidding of their opposite sides, and to be paid or killed for it. All around them, the soldiers in grey were drinking with the soldiers in blue, and one thing was certain in the chatter of accents, the nasal and the throaty, the burr and the drawl, they were all Americans. And by the end of the second bottle of liquor that Angus had found, he also found himself drinking to the toast that Archibald proposed: "To a most civil war."

Henri Chatillon was not as the other men were. Katie knew he would not be, but so many men – or so she was always told by Hannah – reverted to brutes when they had what they wanted from a woman. Henri did not teach her to be a man, or more like an Indian woman. He bought her buckskin leggings and a short skirt and put her astride a pony so that she would ride the tall grasses with him, avoiding the pitfalls of the prairie dog towns and a stumble on to the broken leg of a screaming horse. But in their life in the cabin which he built for her a mile from the fort, he taught her to be a woman, to reach for him in the night under the buffalo robe and make him cleave and cling to her, to be dry with desire as a thirst in the desert, to be soft with fulfilment as a calf in clover, to wait for his coming as for an annunciation and to weep for his going as for a burial. She was always probing into her man, wanting to know and possess all of him, for he eluded her, not holding back the heart of him, but the kernel that kept him solitary and strong. This would never be given to a woman, and she had to have it from him.

He spoke her language better now, for she was not good at learning his tongue, neither French nor Crow. He told her what the Indians called her, Flame Wind, for the red mane of her hair that floated behind her as she galloped across the plains. It was better, Henri joked, than being called Black Buffalo woman. She was the maiden who was causing all the trouble between the Oglala Sioux, because she went off with No Water, a warrior in Red Cloud's group of Bad Faces, and she met with Crazy Horse, the young raider against the Crows with his polished medicine stone behind his ear and a red-backed hunk in his hair.

"He dream dreams," Henri told Katie. "He see Sioux die if all white men not killed. He bring war."

Katie saw him once, when there had been fighting along the Platte River in Minnesota across the Medicine Line, and the United States cavalrymen had been drawn away into their own civil war, and the Sioux and the Cheyennes had taken their vengeance on the settlers and the wives, and now the militia were on them, and they were slaughtering and mutilating each other, children and women scalped and hacked to pieces among the men, and Crazy Horse riding north among the buffalo, which were fleeing the long guns as he was. And Katie saw him on the plains one day on his pony, charging along into nowhere, his long black hair flying out with his calf-skin cape that was spotted with the white hailstones of his angry vision.

After this sighting, Henri kept Katie in their cabin for a week. Crazy Horse and his band of Sioux hated the Crows and the whites. And there was other trouble, raiding American parties coming up to the Red River to compete for the skins and the hides, and to try and drag them into the war in the United States so that they would be incorporated into that land. Slowly, slowly, the British were giving the Canadians their own government, but it might well come too late. And the Medicine Line of the Forty-Ninth Parallel, that artificial boundary splitting a continent in half, only existed in the mind and might never be drawn, and then Western Canada would be swallowed into the snare of America as the north of Mexico had been.

"We will send for my brother Angus," Katie said. "He is a surveyor. He will draw the Medicine Line, and we will be safe above it."

"I do not think you see your brother again."

That was true. When Katie ran onto the red plains to meet Henri and be taken to his *tipi* on his horse, she knew she would not go home again. Hamish had sworn to her that, if she left with Henri, he had no daughter. And Hannah had not winked at her or said soft words to her, but she had spoken as harshly as her father. "If you go in sin we cast you out for ever." Yet Henri did take her to a priest at the fort, a black father in the wrong religion, and there was a ceremony in the Latin and the French, but not a word of it did she understand, with drunken *métis* as the witnesses, shouting fond curses at Henri and trying to kiss the bride, though Henri struck down one of them at the attempt. But it did not matter now, for all the love and need of him that overwhelmed her. Except when he left her alone for the hunting of the buffalo, and she had days and nights of thinking of the other folk dear to her, Hamish and Hannah and Bain and Angus, and the lost ones in India. And she wept bitterly until she found herself smiling in the memory of her new love, who would come back to her soon.

Her wild spirit now ran free. She had always chafed under the orders of Hannah, telling her what the Good Book told her to do, or not to do, which was more often. She would rather have the dirt of the life of a *métis'* wife and the awful lack of privacy – the passing women round the fort pinching the freckles on her white skin, not believing they were red, or begging meal and salt buffalo tongues from her stores. She learned from them the brewing of bitter herbs and wild grasses for teas and purges, the softening of the buffalo robes by pounding and chewing, the stringing of the bright beads and the sticking of the patterns on the supple hides. She even learned to fight, giving better than she got with a squaw who snatched away her best silver spoon and left a handful of dark braid in Katie's hand to show her defeat. Katie loved riding the wind and sending up clouds of the pigeon and the quail with her pony's hoofs and hearing the buffalo bellow in a rumble to the west. Once she saw Bain plodding after the plough yoked behind his oxen in the river bottom, and she found her love for him drowned in a wash of pity. He was doing the wrong thing on the wrong ground, and she had escaped rightly from that sad toil.

When the baby kicked inside her, she put Henri's hand on the walls of her belly so that he could feel the tiny thumping. He smiled and waited with the palm of his hand for the next shifting of the child.

"He is very strong."

"She is, I hope."

"She is very strong. But she have red hair. Then I love her."

"One day my hair will be white."

"After I am gone." Henri rose to his feet and looked down, seeing her hair as embers glowing bright and dark in the firelight in the cabin. "I will go first. I am twenty year more. What you do then? Go back to your people?"

"They will not have me," Katie said. "I am a lost woman now." She laughed. "You dinna know how glad I am to be lost, when it is you who found me."

"I worry," Henry said. "It is not good a woman *sans famille*. When baby come, a woman, her mother –"

"You have to be my mother and father now, Henri. I'll settle for being your woman."

"*Bien*," Henri walked over to the hide hanging over the cabin door and twitched it aside to look out. There was a far noise from the fort of drunken voices, then a shout, then a silence.

"I do not like this war," Henri said. "It come here too. *Je n'aime pas*."

"Come here." Katie held out her arms and waited until Henri lay down and put his head against the swell under her robe, the shape of the life to come. "Hold on. Keep this. And I will see the war never comes to us."

On other plains in the deserts of the Punjab, there was hunger. The five rivers of the Jhelum and the Chenab and the Ravi and the Beaz and the Sutlej hardly watered its barrenness. The wanderers and cattle-thieves who haunted its wastes were called the *janglis*, but even they could starve when there was no rain for years, and the land at the edge of the water bore corn parched in the husk. But there was hope now. The iron rails ran to the Punjab, and the British government no longer used starvation as a weapon to clear the land as it had at home in Scotland and Ireland. For where would the Indian people go, if they were driven from their poor soil? What country would receive such refugees?

Bags of grain filled the extended waggons on the train from Amritsar. Two steam engines pulled and pushed the increased load towards its destination. Packed as tight as the corn sacks in the box-cars, the passengers on the lower tier of the third-class carriages sweltered and suffered from the dust and black grit blowing through the compartment. Lila, shrouded in her shawl, had managed to make a kennel under her seat of wooden slats for Seaforth and his little sister Peg. But there was no way of her moving in the crush, no means of answering the calls of nature. So down below was a moist playground of rank smells, unfit for children. There was nothing else to do. They had to go to Simla this way, the only way for them.

Up the train, Mary lay on the top of her pull-down bunk, also prickling with the heat through her bodice and clammy from the touch of the padded wall of the compartment. Below her, the missionary wife, Mrs Dougal, asked for more tea, which was brewed on the train floor by a half-naked man with a top-knot and a saffron loin-cloth, who appeared between stations offering his scalding brew, the heavenly *char-wallah*. There was a theory that drinking boiling liquid in a temperature of more than a hundred degrees somehow cooled you off. Perhaps. But Mary did not see the logic of it. The tea seemed to pass out directly in drops through her skin, which only then cooled her off a bit.

She was making for the Punjab because disease had followed famine as it always did. Cholera and fever were bringing down the *jangli* women and children, as they had in the camps of the railway workers, and the *jangli* men would not let male doctors touch their sick families. But Mary also knew that Lila and her two children were travelling to join Iain and Anna at Simla as an *ayah* for their four children. She had tried to book Lila on the second class, but caste and expense were too much for her. So she had to settle for the inhuman double-decker flesh-trucks that were called carriages by the Amritsar and Multan Railways. These meat-waggons did not seem to be progress to her, but mere incubators for more contagion. Sauntering along at twenty miles an hour, the Indian trains were a slow route to heat-stroke and a quick exposure to disease. If the sun did not fell you, the filth would.

Entering the new Lahore Station was going into a medieval castle by a tunnel, not a drawbridge. Since the Mutiny, passenger stations were built to be defended. Turrets and bomb-proof towers dominated the outer walls, riddled with loop-holes for rifles, while iron sliding doors stood either side of the tracks, ready to close them off. Strategy was based on the railways now. The metal tracks were the wrought nerves and sinews of the Raj in India. There was not much need to talk the languages or to know the various peoples as long as communications were quick by rail or telegraph. Messages in English were all, and delivery of the goods to the right place in double time.

The howling of the vendors in the station, which seemed to be a roofed *caravanserai* of all the displaced of the south, nearly put Mary off her purpose. The windows of her compartment were blocked off against the maimed beggars, but she rolled down from her berth and bribed the *char-wallah* to fight his way ahead of her along the platform. She was hardened now to the plucking of little hands on her skirts and the strange bright things thrust into her face. She was carrying a wrapped bundle and she had to get through. And looking into the openings on the lower layer of the carriages, she saw a hand wave to her from a shawled woman, and she knew she had found Lila. She passed the bundle through the aperture, food and drink of sorts, *chapattis* and boiled water and limes and sugar.

"Where are they?" she shouted.

"Take them," Lila shouted behind her shawl. "They die here."

There was no choice in it. Mary took Seaforth in her arms, as his mother handed him down, and the *char-wallah* took the shrieking and damp Peg. And the two of them pushed their way back to her carriage. All Mary could think was that she was breaking all the rules, and the Raj ran only on the rules as the rails, and they had to be obeyed, because if the regulations were not followed to the letter, there would be another Mutiny and no Raj at all. Of course, the whole Empire would crumble if two half-caste tots got into a first-class carriage. But there you were. Since Mary had become a nurse, she had really found caring more interesting than ruling. In fact, healing people meant breaking the rules. And Seaforth was even hugging her as if she could defend him against the press of the people and their push and bustle, and the welcome he would receive on the train.

Mrs Dougal took the intrusion of the children in fairly good part. After her first shocked surmise that they were Mary's own little mistakes, she began to warm to them. No question, Seaforth and Peg were a relief from the monotony of the journey. It was even fun finding them hiding-places from the guards and the ticket-collectors and making a game of it. "You go in there and keep very quiet until we say, 'Shoo,' then you come out and get a barley-sugar" – or a sweetmeat that did not appear too toxic.

"I will never tell a lie," Mrs Dougal confided, "but I do not mind a cloth over the truth when it is a matter of children."

And so they reached Multan and the changing of the railways. Mary had to transfer to trains for the Punjab, Lila to transport to the hills. There was no common railway gauge in India any more than there were common peoples. Divide and rule was the British principle, even in the width of iron tracks. Mary kissed Lila on her cheek through her shawl as they said good-bye. This was the first time she had done that, but she had fallen a little in love with the children. Lila trembled to her kiss on that public station, and Mary trembled, too. It was a declaration of what could not be declared, and there might yet be a judgement from it. But there was no other way to go.

At Annandale, Lila was killed with kindness and stifled by diffidence. She could not get it right, because she could not do wrong. Her errors were condemned by silence, her mistakes were pointed out by talking of other things. She could never understand the invaders, or so she thought, because they included and rejected her at the same time. She was their servant, the *ayah* of their children, Hamilton and Hamish Macmahon, Margaret and May. And the children seemed to accept her little children, who were their cousins, that was the truth. But with Anna, for all her warmth and her feeling, there was the barrier, as strict as for the Untouchables of India. She was the lady of the household, and something in her past made her shrink from Lila, who could see Anna's mind fighting against the mutiny of her skin. Iain was easier, but more casual and brutal, the master of the place, even if he was the serf of his wife. For he seemed bound to her as though she were the chieftainess or maharanee of his clan, so great was her hold on him. Often Lila would see the huge man kissing the large flawed emerald on the gold ring on her hand, and bowing before her.

Lila was outside the bedroom door, when she heard the talking that would send her and the children away, only she had nowhere else to go, and she could pretend that she never heard a word of it.

"They are my kin," Iain was saying. "There is nothing I can do about that."

"But people will see," Anna said. "And people will say."

"You welcomed her to Annandale. When Hamish Jamie brought her here for our wedding, you took her to everybody. You were proud that Simla would never ask us again. And now —"

"And now we have our children. And I am proud of them."

"And she is the *ayah* to our children, Anna. And our children play with her children."

"Yes. And that is what they say in Simla about us, Iain."

"And you care about it."

"I do." Behind the bedroom door there was a rustle and a soft slap that might have been a kiss.

"Darling, things change. The government, they think you have done wonders at Annandale. It is your use of the water, the small dams and the ditches. And now in Punjab, where there is a desert —"

"They want lilies." Lila could hear Iain laugh. "But what is the use of it?"

"Out of hunger, you will grow plenty. Out of sand, you will grow wheat. We may even grow the tea. Out of the strong came forth sweetness."

"And out of Lila, we will grow servants?"

There was a silence, then again the sound of the kissing.

"Come to bed. We have taken her in, Iain, for the sake of your brother. But we must not take it too far. Believe me. I know."

Again Lila heard Iain's low laughter.

"One thing I ken from you, Anna. A man's place is always in the wrong."

There was the sound of Anna laughing now.

"Don't say that."

"I do."

"Then a woman's place is always in the right."

"It is."

As Lila stole away from the bedroom door, she knew one thing. Her place was where she would never be wanted.

18

A SORE WHILE

A letter from Hamish was rarer than a white Christmas in India. It almost made Mary weep to have the sealed envelope in her hands. She smiled as she saw her name spelt out by his hand in the careful letters which were not joined together so that they were the more readable. She had worried when he was posted to yet another absurd war in Africa because of his experience with the Commissariat. This time the tyrant Theodore, King of Abyssinia, had made hostages of the British Consul, Captain Cameron, and of assorted German and French missionaries and adventurers. He tortured them from time to time, then proposed to exchange what was left of them for artillery and machinery for making explosives. He wanted the best of western technology in return for some of its representatives. Queen Victoria's government sent the machinery to Massawa in the Red Sea, but by the time it had arrived, King Theodore had lost control of his country and his senses. He threw the captives into the dungeons in his mountain fortress at Magdala. Now it was a question of saving face as well as the lives of the hostages. They must be got out. And Hamish Jamie had gone to do it, although never were so many sent at greater cost to rescue so few.

Mary wanted to know how it was done, and the letter told her. Hamish Jamie wrote:

> To have the prisoners they say the whole thing will cost nine million pounds, which is about quarter of a million a head. Is it worth it? I think our heads were not worth that when we were in Scotland. Probably sixpence each.
>
> We live rough, we have no sugar, no milk, no butter, no flour, no bread, no rum – nothing but water, we get char though, but not much. We eat biscuits, which are like dog biscuits broken up into hard bits, murder on the teeth. And tough beef killed just before being taken. When they brought our ration of it this morning, the muscles were still twitching. This sounds odd, but it is true. Alive, alive-O, like those cockles and mussels in London.

I am writing to say how good the hospitals and doctors are. No nurses yet, but they will come! There is a new stuff called carbolic, and they put it on wounds and scalpels and saws, and now there is not so much gangrene in the soldiers. It seems to kill the rotten stuff, I don't know how. But if we lose only about three hundred men, this is a reward for an expedition like this.

You know what I want to ask. Did Lila and Seaforth and Peg get to Iain's house in Annandale? I know that you cannot let me know, but I want you to know that I do care, even if I do not seem to, because of coming to Abyssinia. But I come to Abyssinia because it is my duty. You know that. Please tell Lila when you see her that this is the only reason. Duty.

Sometimes I do not know what the Army is all about. Sometimes I am back in Scotland, and we are working at the kelp. I know that even my life now is better than the kelping, and your life helping the Indian women, and Iain is doing famously. But I wonder. What we are doing in Abyssinia when nobody wants it, not even the people here? I do not know. And as for our family in Canada – you know I could not find them on my tour of duty with my regiment in Montreal, for they were too far gone across to the west – are we condemned always to be wanderers, never with a home of our own (except for Iain, and that is Anna's)? Will we always work for others and never for us? Is this duty, and if it is, why do we believe in it?

I am only a soldier, my dearest Mary, but even a soldier may wonder just what he is doing. The rain beats down on my tent, the oil is low in the lamp. I must stop. My love to you and Lila and the children and Iain and Anna and theirs. But tell me when we meet again – why do we do what we feel we must do? There are so many other beautiful things to do ...

Louis Riel was young, only twenty-five years old in 1869, but he could inspire and seemed able to lead. When he declared himself president of his Red River republic, he hauled down the Union Jack from Fort Garry and put up his own flag of the *fleurs-de-lis* and shamrocks. For he hoped the American-Irish would come over the Medicine Line to help the *métis* in their rebellion from the British Crown, which had just taken over Rupert's Land from the Hudson's Bay Company and incorporated it into the Dominion of Canada. And Gerald Fitzgerald was in the Fort, as Henri Chatillon knew he would be, and with him a man called Donovan, who said he knew Katie's brother Angus – they had worked together surveying railroads to the west in America. Both Fitzgerald and Donovan boasted that they had been with the Fenians, when fifteen hundred veterans had invaded Canada after the Civil War and again the previous year, when they had been licked at Trout River.

"And if you not make your free republic two time in Canada," Henri asked, "why try now? Third time lucky, you say."

"The French and the Irish," Donovan said, "we're natural buddies."

"Maybe."

"We hate the Queen."

"Maybe."

"You don't want to be free?"

"We are free now," Henri said. "Sometime a Mountie come in red coat, *ça va*. Indians, *mes amis*, zey come 'ere because zey are free. No trouble, only south zee Medicine Line. Louis Riel, our *président* —"

Henri had to laugh at the thought, although the two Irishmen did not.

"He's not funny, Riel," Fitzgerald said. "He's a Napoleon."

"*Alors*, I am Marie Antoinette," Henri said. "I think 'e not fight. When army come from Montreal."

"They'll never get here."

"I think yes."

"We'll stop them in the woods," Donovan said. "Shoot 'em like bears. They can't make it. It's thirteen hundred miles to Toronto. And its murder all the way. I wouldn't even reckon I could survey it. Mosquitos, black flies, swamp. They will never come this far. Impossible."

"My wife, 'er family, zey come 'ere. So will army."

"Then we will kill them," Fitzgerald said. "The French and the Irish, they're the best fighters in the world."

"I do not know," Henri said. "*Ça je vois*."

Sir Garnet Wolseley and his twelve hundred men were already on their way from Toronto to Georgian Bay by the railroad, by steamers along the Great Lakes, by waggons through the forests, and then by foot and portage over river and lake to Fort Garry. Not a man was lost, surprise was complete. Even Henri had not suspected their coming. Then there they were, in scarlet and in line, advancing on the wooden walls of the fort. Louis Riel ran, and Fitzgerald and Donovan. For reasons he did not know, perhaps because of shame, Henri picked up his rifle and fought with two other *métis*. He was not aiming to kill and he killed nobody; but a fusillade ripped through his buckskin jacket, shattering his ribs, shot from the Sneider and Henry rifles that were in the hands of the attackers. And so Henri died in a farce of an action which achieved nothing.

Katie and her child Marie were inconsolable. Her life was Henri, and with his death, she thought she must die, too. Yet she did not. She wept twenty times a day, and she could not sleep for the missing of her man's body not beside her. She took his hunting knife in and out of its sheath, and she even cut her thumb deliberately on the edge of it, practising her killing of herself. But there was always Marie, who loved her and clung to her left ankle, as if she would never let her go. And her mother had to live on because of her, there was no alternative.

Katie found a task, washing for the garrison at Fort Garry, ignoring the scorn of the *métis*. She and her daughter had to live. She might have travelled the hundred miles west across the red plains to see whether Hamish and Hannah would take her back, but she could not. The terrible pride of her family was a hard fist inside her breast. If she went back, she would feel that she had betrayed Henri. And even if he were dead, the memory of him hardened her against her family, which had refused him although she had loved him with all of her nature.

There was always trouble in the west now below the Medicine Line, with the Crows and the Blackfeet and the Sioux moving north to safety across the invisible frontier, where the American cavalry had to rein up and watch their jeering adversaries ride away to safety. Yet the news was that the line which nobody could see was being at last made clear. From the east, the British were sending Royal Engineers and Canadian surveyors, while the Americans had commissioned their Corps of Engineers and a Company of the Twentieth Infantry as an escort. By stone cairn and earth mound and hollow metal pole, a straight line would be delineated across an indifferent continent, and Canada would be defined above its powerful neighbour all the way to the Pacific Ocean.

Angus was in the Canadian party. This was the task of his dreams. Sometimes he would still wake in the night in a quagmire of sweat, struggling against his blanket and shouting, "No, no, I will not leave you, I will not go." His hope had always been to return to his family in proof of himself and in glory. It was worth his desertion of them in their need and his flight and his education in peace and war, his job of mapping the haphazard soil into lines straighter and more rigid than furrows, into frontiers where the writ of one law ran and not another. Thomas Jefferson had decreed a grid map across the whole of the United States, stamping it in theory like a waffle-iron in three-mile squares to the Rockies. Now Angus Sinclair would draw the border

for evermore in the north of America, and all who crossed it would
know he had done so. It impressed an order on nature, where none
was.

The work was fearsome through winter and summer. At first, the
Indian axemen worked in waist-deep swamp water, while the
surveyors fell through the slime in the bogs up to their shoulders. One
previous marker was found six feet deep in the area below the
branches of the birch trees and the tamaracks. When the Indian
summer was over, the temperature dropped to fifty degrees below
zero. They mapped their frontier above the ice and snow, using dog
sledges with brush shelters rather than the skin lodges of the hot
season. Now mosquitos and flies did not make their faces swell with
their stinging venom, but frostbite and scurvy hurt their complexions.
They could not turn the screw on the theodolite without their fingers
sticking to the icy metal; ripping their prints free left blood behind,
which froze at once. If an eyelid touched their telescopes, it held and
had to be eased loose, leaving the lashes to fringe the eyepiece. Yet
they drove the line on, by stake and chain and grit.

By spring, they had reached the Red River, by summer they were in
the plains. Already they met the bleaching bones of the lower buffalo
herds, hunted to near extinction, their old wallows stinking with their
rotting hides. When the sun was high and burned away the clouds of
flies, it was too hot to work at surveying because the air wavered and
danced as it rose from the baking ground. And it was almost the fall
again before they reached the highest plains near the Dakotas, and
there it was that Angus learned of the two parts of his separated
family, Katie and Marie at the fort, Hamish and Hannah and Bain still
trying to plough the dry grasses.

On his scarecrow horse, ravaged by worm and bite, Angus found
his sister in her cabin by the fort. She could not believe her eyes and
wept with joy, pressing Marie into his arms, saying, "Uncle Angus,
uncle, Marie! I said he would come, I said he would come." And
Angus heard of the death of Henri, and he told of his own work in the
Civil War and now on the laying of the Medicine Line, and then he
asked Katie the hardest question of them all, knowing her answer, as
she was also a Sinclair. But then he was a Sinclair also, and he was
returning where he could never go again.

"I am off to see Hamish and Hannah and Bain," he said. "You
must come, too, with Marie."

"I can not. Never." Katie's eyes could not look at Angus, but they
flickered as summer lightning. "They hated Henri. They drove me out.
They said I must never come back."

"They did that to me," Angus said. "I deserted them, when they needed me. But God knows, Katie, they are our mother and father. We canna change that."

"They drove us out."

"We will return."

"Never."

"That is what they say. Never. And if all we can say is never, we can never see each other again."

"Then we never can."

"The heart of a woman —" Angus said, "Hannah always said it was soft. But it is flint — or that new steel they make. You canna forgive."

"I can. It is them. They canna forgive."

"How do we ken until we try them?"

After a night and a day of argument and fears, Angus persuaded Katie to come with him on a new pony he bought for her. It was this gift, perhaps, that persuaded her. Leaving him to hold Marie beside his lean horse, she galloped off across the red grasses, astride in her leather trousers and short skirt. Angus laughed. He had worked so much with the Indians now that he had come to admire the boldness and the freedom of their women, while the soft plump whiteness of the American city belles made him shiver with a slight repulsion. He saw why Henri had loved his sister, and he was proud of her.

As they approached the cabin in its bottom, the earth heaved and moved. On the grasses and the stubble of the crops, ten thousand thousand things with scales crawled and shook and beat their wings. The horse and the pony shuddered as their hoofs crunched the swarm of the insects. The locusts had descended to devastate the land.

"My God," Angus said to Katie, "our family — they never deserve it. Why does the Good Lord give them more than they can bear?"

They found Hamish and Hannah inside a barricaded post with planks nailed across the hide door. Perhaps it was the plague of insects, perhaps it was the fear of dying alone, perhaps it was the true love of their children, but they fell in each other's arms and spoke as if nothing had been said, there was nothing to forgive. Bain was away, looking for an exterminator for the locusts, but there was none, or none yet, only the news of some strange fence of wire that might keep out the buffalo from the crops, if there were any buffalo or crops left after the hunters and the locusts had their fill. But that was forgotten. Now was the reunion and the coming together of people, who believed that they had parted for ever. The hard words were blown away like the dust on the plains, the streams of feeling flowed again in the spring thaw. Even the shy small Marie put her hand in her grandmother's, as if she had always known her, always expected her to be there. In the trust of little children, Angus thought, we forgive all.

"You will not stay here now," Angus said. "You will move again."

"We have moved and moved," Hamish said. "We will not move again."

"But the locusts – the hoppers as they say across the Line –"

"They will not come every year."

"But if they do – and how will you live till then –"

"Hunting and trapping. There are still buffalo, very few – and wolf-skins – and we will bide here."

Angus knew his old father was not to be changed. Too many calamities had at last fixed him where he had landed. Even the tumbleweed, blowing in the wind from thousands of miles across the dry plains, snagged in a bush and sent down its dry roots. Hannah was playing with Marie now, a game which Angus hardly remembered. Perhaps they used to play it with crabs on the beach, and now Hannah had crooked her old hand into the shape of a crab, and her fingers were crawling up the smock of little Marie, who was giggling with glee. And Hannah chanted.

> "Tip tap taisie,
> The tide's comin' in –
> If you run a mile awa'
> The tide will take you in."

And as Marie squirmed away, her grandmother enfolded her in her arms and took her in. Then her old fingers were rain on Marie's hair, pattering down and combing it with her nails:

> "Rainy rainy rattle stones
> Dinna rain on me
> Rain on Hamish Jamie
> Far over the sea –"

Katie was laughing now, and she squatted by her mother, and she said, "I remember them. The old games you used to play with me."

"She's a darling," Hannah said. "Beautiful. You might have taken her to me before."

"It was because –" Katie caught her tongue, but decided to go on to the end. "I thought you would not want us. You would not want ever to see me again."

Hannah was indignant. "I never said the like. Not see my own daughter! I never said it. And this wee darling – Hamish! Tell her."

And Hamish looked at Hannah, and he knew it was no use telling her the truth of what she had said when Katie had run away with Henri Chatillon. She no longer believed she had said it and so she had not said it. If she believed she could never have banished her daughter for ever – for what mother could say that? – then she had never said such a thing. Anyway, at Hannah's age, it was useless telling her that she was wrong, or ever had been. She had the perfect gift of Scots' righteousness. However many times she changed her mind, she had only ever wanted to be steadfast, and that was the way that God approved. She was sure of Him, and so she was always right and always consistent.

"We were ever wishing to see you again. And Angus," Hamish added. "And now you are here, this is a day of rejoicing. And when Bain is home, we will have a feast of it though it only be pemmican and salt tongue and oatcake. And we will have the dancing and the singing – my fine daughter, my clever son, who have been away from us a sore while."

19

ALIEN LANDS

Advancing through the bush against King Koffee was not the sort of operation that Hamish Jamie had ever planned before. Sir Garnet Wolseley was an organizer above all. You could see that in his expedition to the Red River. To him, beating the Ashantis was another kind of routine, this time adapted for the jungle. His three thousand soldiers, spearheaded by the Highland Black Watch and the Royal Welch Fusiliers and the Rifle Brigade and Marines from the Naval Brigade would need three times that number of native carriers. Mules could not pass through the trees and the undergrowth. They were opposed by fifty thousand savages – or so Wolseley thought then – accustomed to draping the entrails of their mutilated prisoners round their ritual slaughterhouses in Kumasi. In his message to his troops, the commander had no doubt about victory against the odds. Technology and discipline would defeat raw courage and numbers.

> Each soldier must remember that, with his breech loader, he is equal to at least twenty Ashantis, wretchedly armed as they are with old flint muskets, firing slugs or pieces of stone, that do not hurt badly at more than forty or fifty yards range. They have neither guns nor rockets, and have a superstitious dread of those used by us.

Wolseley even had one of the new Gatling guns with him, the first of the machine guns, yet its murderous volleys would not be too effective as nobody could see more than a few yards ahead or sideways, in the jungle. The real secret weapon was the superiority of the European over the African.

> A steady advance or a charge made with determination always means the retreat of the enemy. English soldiers and sailors are accustomed to fight against great odds in all parts of the world. It is scarcely necessary to remind them that when, in our battles beyond the Prah, they find themselves surrounded on all sides by

hordes of howling enemies, they must rely upon their own British courage and discipline. Be cool, fire low, and charge home.

 That was the theory of it. The fact of it for Hamish Jamie was that he had been seconded to the expedition because of his experience in Abyssinia, as though Africa was one big similar continent, as far as the War Office was concerned. Actually, the bearers from the coast tribes whom the Ashantis regularly killed and enslaved, ran away as soon as they were paid or approached the enemy. Although the Royal Engineers were hacking a road of sorts towards Kumasi, the advancing troops had to slash their path through the bush and the creepers with swords and bayonets, if they could not follow the narrow ruts which ran between the hidden villages. It was an eerie business. From the tangled forest, the drums throbbed like a wound in the head and horns wailed as mourners and the thunder of the Ashanti muskets full of bad powder and chipped slugs cut swathes of twigs and leaves from the jungle canopy, a green rain on the advancing Highlanders. The whole terrain was a perfect ambush. On the sudden, there would be an onrush of black bodies, a pell-mell waving of spears, then up would go the line of Sneiders and Enfields, and a gust of lead would drop the Ashanti warriors, who would fall back into the recesses of the forest, leaving a few bodies and broken muskets behind. There would be a silence for a moment, then the bugles of the regiments would sound their whereabouts in brazen notes to each other, while the secret Ashantis would signal in bird-calls, followed by war-cries and whooping. Then hundreds of invisible voices would break into a chant that stopped the blood to hear. For even more than the bagpipes of the Black Watch, it foretold certain death.

    The final battle took place before Kumasi, and Colonel McLeod led the Highlanders in short charge after charge, once rockets and canister shot and shell had cleared the way. Finally, the Ashantis fled, even their captains in their ramshorn helmets and plumes of eagle feathers. The wooden lodges of the Asantehene, called King Koffee, reeked of rotten flesh. Ancestral drums were hung with skulls and smeared with blood. Bodies were impaled on stakes or flayed or burned. Even the golden stool of the Asantehene was reddened with sacrifices. Wolseley was outraged. He seemed to have fallen upon the abomination and desolation of the Old Testament, and like a prophet, he ordered the city to be put to the cleansing flame. "All ranks felt they had done a brilliant day's work," he wrote in his dispatch, "and for our victory I am sure many fervent thanks went up to God that night."

Hamish Jamie thought that only God knew why they were in the African jungle at all, which could not be of use to anybody except the Ashantis. As they fell back along the rough road they had cut to Kumasi and over the pontoon bridges across the rivers, they burned every village as an example. But it was all useless. The trees and the creepers, the thorns and the spines, encroached everywhere and overwhelmed them. They were irrelevant, a column of ants on an unnecessary continent. They proved nothing at all to the jungle about them.

Hamish Jamie had soldiered for twenty-five years. He knew the cause of it, but not the reason why. Once he had believed that the orders which sent him to India and China and Canada and Abyssinia and West Africa had a sense, a policy behind them. But he did not think that now. He was helping in the slow spread of the red colour across the map of the world, which he had seen in his first school in Scotland, when the dominie had showed it to him. Yet this urge to kick and lunge into new territories seemed as aimless as the big centipede, which Hamish Jamie had turned on its back in his tent in the camp outside Cape Grant Castle, where he sat, waiting to organize the embarkation for England and a review by the little Queen at Windsor Castle. He had pinned the insect – nearly a foot long – by the point of his sword, and he watched its tiny legs strike out in a flurry of prickles, in a desperate greed for life. All that frenzy of action achieving nothing.

"Poor wee beastie," Hamish Jamie said and put his boot on the struggle of the centipede. If only it were that easy to end the fits and starts of the British Empire.

Lila only heard of Hamish Jamie now through her employers, Iain and Anna at Annandale. He never wrote to her, he had abandoned her to his brother's care. She had sunk from being a sort of poor relation into the position of a servant and an embarrassment. For the society of Simla had spread out to the Sinclair farm in the nearby glen. Where there had been woods and a few fields reaching down the slopes to a rustic valley, there were now formal gardens and a flat playground for polo and cricket matches, and a race course. Anna had told Iain not to stand out against the trend. Frankly, selling a few plots of land was worth ten years of crops of potatos or indigo or tea, if they went in for that. And there was the pressure from Simla, both official and social. This was impossible to resist, with *aides-de-camp* in white uniforms calling from the viceroy himself, not to mention the imperatives delivered like broadsides from Mrs Dalgety and her kind, or rather unkind.

There was also a tacit understanding in a society where straight dealing would have been bad manners, and where the unspoken was an agreement. If some land was yielded at a reasonable price, then Iain's humble origins and the presence of his half-caste nephew and niece in his house would be ignored and the Sinclairs received into Simla society – to a degree. It was not that she cared, Anna insisted to Iain – and of course he did not care. Yet their four children had to go to good schools and make their own way in the world as it was. Hamilton and Hamish Macmahon, Margaret and May, they should not suffer for the sins of their parents or their uncle. It would not be fair on them. They were born innocent, not condemned.

So in the name of his children, Iain made a truce with the world as it was in India. Truly, the better way for a boy to rise was through government service. And as for the girls, if they were to meet the right sort of young men... It was not that Anna had reverted to the position or the caste, from which she had rebelled when she became a pioneer nurse and met Iain in Nainital. Surely, she was the best of mothers, and she wanted with a fierce and possessive pride the best for her children, particularly for the two boys she adored. If Iain sometimes thought of his own hard rearing, he did not mean to inflict that pain on his children, and he never ceased to bless the day of his marriage to Anna, who had brought him all he wanted – and if a little was unwanted such as having to be polite to the ladies of Simla, this was a small price to pay for the rest of it.

When they were small, Anna's four children had loved Lila as their *ayah* and second mother, and they had played with her children, Seaforth and Peg, with that blindness to any variation which most of the little ones have. If the two groups of children slept in different quarters or dressed in other clothes, their games and frolics were much the same in the flowering woods or on the bright snows. But this acceptance was changing now that Hamilton and Hamish Macmahon were youths and trying to grow moustaches, while Margaret and May were always trying to make their mother take them to the haberdashers in Simla for new dress materials and on to Jacob's shop, where he retailed wonders of turquoise and amber necklaces, green jade bangles and peacock-blue draperies, bought from the caravans which still crossed the passes of the Himalayas on the old trade routes to the far east.

In the shyness and doubt of growing up, Hamilton and Hamish Macmahon now avoided Seaforth and were relieved when he went to the missionary school in Simla, reserved for native Indians. Seaforth also began to avoid them, not from delicacy, but from sullenness. His sister Peg remained closer to Margaret and May, but she began to slip into the position of her mother, becoming a ladies' maid in their play and helping them to dress up in their new finery for the fêtes at Annandale, where Peg was never asked and would not be. As for Lila, she knew that she would lose the love of Anna's children as they aged and needed her no more, and she fought to keep the bitterness of his exclusion from Seaforth and the awareness of a false inferiority from Peg. But Hamish Jamie never came back to protect her. She was becoming an alien in her own land, which was not this land of the hill people with their flat dark faces and strange dialect and stranger ways.

Lila also fought the pain when it came, because she would not admit to it. Seaforth and Peg had need of her. They could not live without her. She no longer trusted the members of the family of the father of her children. They did not seem to have the natural love of their own blood. The divisions put upon India had divided the human heart. Family was put asunder from family, kin set against kin, and it was called the Raj. So Lila waited for Mary to visit again, before she could confess to the disease that was wasting her, and when Anna said to her, "Lila, how good you look, so thin and majestic, I wish I could look like that too, but I am becoming a bit of a matron," Lila only said, "I eat less. I do not need it."

Yet when Mary did come at last to tell them all that she hoped to go back to England and study there to be a doctor, for Miss Nightingale had written to her that soon this would be possible, even in London, Lila waited for a week until the evening before Mary left to ask her to examine her. And Mary came to her room and helped her to unwind her *sari* and felt her with cold fingers and asked many questions and then helped her to dress again.

"Do you wish the truth, Lila?"

"I do."

"There is nothing that I may do. It is a wasting disease. It is not consumption, for that is in the lungs, and the air of these mountains would help it. It is the wasting disease that eats you from within, and there is no cure for it. I could say milk, eggs, meat – but you do not wish for food."

"I do not."

"But you do not wish to die?"

"I must live. For Peg and Seaforth. When Hamish Jamie come and take them –" Looking at Mary hanging her head. "He not come."

"His duty keeps him in Africa. He is a specialist now. In the Commissariat, in the military train. There is trouble now in the South. He must go there. It is his duty."

"His duty? And me. And Seaforth and Peg."

"That is his duty too. But it is not what he thinks. Lila, I tell you –" Looking at Lila with her blue stare. "I swear that I will see that Seaforth and Peg are reared well. They will be a credit to you and their father. I swear that."

"But you not can. You are single woman. No family."

Mary smiled so quickly that it seemed a tremor on her face.

"I would rather be a single woman and spin my own yarn. Trust me. Though you have no reason. Trust me over your children."

Lila had no one else to trust. For her own people would never have her back nor her children. So she made a belief of necessity.

"I trust you," she said, and she believed that she meant her words.

Mary rose to her feet.

"I will tell Iain and Anna that you are ill. You will do little. Look after Seaforth and Peg while you can. And I will arrange for their future care. Perhaps, Lila, perhaps, Seaforth would wish to become a doctor, as I will be. Will you ask him? I will help him."

"I must ask him."

"And Lila –" Mary stooped and kissed Lila's cheek. For the first and last time, Lila put out her arms and held Hamish Jamie's wife by the neck with hands that trembled. "And, Lila – trust me. The children will do well."

"Why *you* do this for me?"

"I am a woman, too." Mary took Lila's arms off her, laid them by Lila's side and moved away to the door. "And I am alone. In a world of men, I am a stranger. In a world of married folk – and mothers – I am single. And I am in India, not in my home. Do you not think, Lila, I may also feel apart? And not wanted. And out of place. As you are."

Hamish Jamie did not know what to write to Anna after the disaster. He had sworn to her to look after his namesake, her son Hamish Macmahon, scarcely twenty, a volunteer from India who was longing to get at the enemy and see his first action. Hardly was it the boy's fault that Lord Chelmsford had left him behind in the camp at Isandhlwana, where he was surprised by a Zulu *impi* and stabbed to death along with fifteen hundred other men. It was not Hamish Jamie's fault that he was working in the supply lines for the army, as it moved on Zululand. He only reached the scene of the great defeat two days later on the ammunition waggons and he helped to bury the bodies, all disembowelled ritually, their right hands put where their hearts had been. What could he write of that? Senseless murder caused by a bad commander in a war provoked by an ambitious colonial governor, who wanted more and more. He put down:

Your son fought bravely to the end. You can be proud of him. One of the few survivors, a gunner who got away on a horse, tells me Hamish Macmahon was shooting until he went down under a mass of enemies. His death was swift and merciful. He had a Christian burial. I know his last thought was of you.

As Hamish Jamie penned these false and necessary words, he did not blame himself for the lies, given the real mutilation and the horror, the flies and the mass graves. The boy was dead. He had believed in what his uncle had never believed, glory and honour, a good cause and a just war and a certain victory. That was what his imperial schools in India had taught him.

Yet it was not like that at all. Yes, a handful of our men had won something back by mowing down a few hundred Zulus at Rorke's Drift in a frontal attack on their earthworks. But the truth was that the troops were so scared they fired at shadows as well as Zulus. At Fort Funk, the artillery fired into its own Royal Engineers and wounded five of them. They would have all been shelled to extinction if a bugle had not sounded the call. And Lord Chelmsford's response was as sickening as the sight of the dead at Isandhlwana. He brought up reinforcements and used the local South African mounted volunteers to search out and destroy all the Zulu kraals and stores of grain. All was looted, every Zulu woman and child turned out to starve on the veldt. These were exactly the same tactics which 'Butcher' Cumberland had used after defeating the Highlanders at Culloden. This was not war, it was rational destruction by any means.

The final encounter outside King Cetshwayo's capital at Ulundi was surgical slaughter. The massed chest and two horns of the Zulu charge with the stabbing *assegais* were met by a hollow square of redcoats, behind which the Gatling guns and the seven-pounders and the rocket-tubes poured out a heavy annihilation. The Zulus could not get to close quarters because of the weight of fire. The canister tore through them like a harrow through black weeds. The rockets ravaged them with flaming zig-zags. The machine-gun bullets scythed them in swathes and laid them in the dust. And Hamish Jamie, supervising the pouring of the ammunition from a chained waggon within the square that spat out lead and steel, again thought of his own Highland people in the past century, as they charged the Hanoverian guns with shield and claymore and were laid low by shot and shell on the moors of Culloden.

Yet the Sinclairs were not the mountain savages now. They were the servants of the new machines of death, which had once divided the clans of Scotland into artificial shires on the English model, and were now dividing the tribes of Africa into provinces and territories and protectorates. This was a civilizing mission, to be sure. There was no doubt of it. Hamish Jamie himself was educated now – a major and a quartermaster, a man of dignity with a pension to come, able to write in English and think with the method and the order of Englishmen. And yet he was helping them at their greedy game of covering more of the globe with plots and patches of red. And Hamish Macmahon was dead of their grabbing, and his uncle could not finish that letter back to his mother Anna, trying to tell her that her son had died for something worth his blood sacrifice.

After another week, Hamish Jamie concluded his letter to India:

> We have won a famous victory and the Zulus are broken. They are a fine and fierce people, but they can not stand our guns. As they advance at the run, they wave their painted, pointed long shields – black with white spots, white with red spots – white feathers and cow-tails and monkey-skins shake on their heads and shoulders and legs. It is like the waving of our kilts and bonnets, and I am sad to see it fall down. Hamish Macmahon died bravely for his Queen and Her Empire, and I weep with you for him – and for all the brave men who have fallen here. I am glad Hamilton means to be a naval engineer. We must have no more soldiers in our family. Tell Lila that Seaforth must not enlist. He is better as a clerk than a sergeant or a major like me. Better a live babu than a dead Zulu – for we are all somebody's son.

> My love to you all.

> Hamish Jamie

20

THE GREAT MOTHER

Before the Sioux fled to safety above the Medicine Line, they had their revenge, as the Zulus had before their breaking on steel and lead in South Africa. At the Little Big Horn, the Sioux wiped out Custer's men and seized their carbines and rifles and moved north, a whole Indian nation, driving the buffalo herds ahead of them with the American army and cavalry in pursuit, hardly believing in their defeat by mounted savages, who had taken the gun and the horse from them and now used bullet and hoof to halt their incessant advance. Now the Indians were pouring over the border, Ogdalas and Hunkpapas, Minnecoujous and Sans Arcs, Two Kettles and Tetons under Sitting Bull, but Crazy Horse stayed on with his hostiles in the Powder River country and the Black Hills of Dakota. He would not trust in a Medicine Line or leave his hunting country.

Hamish and Hannah, Bain and Katie feared for their lives on the land by the river bottom. They could hardly believe the courage of the Mounties, which quite restored their faith in a scarlet jacket and a white helmet, even if they were worn by an Irishman, the tough and grizzled Walsh who built a log stockade in his own name with a powder magazine and blacksmith's forge, stables and bakery and quartermaster's store in the valley before the plains met the hills, bristling with jack-pine. Outside it, three hundred families of *métis* and Indians and a few Macleods lived in their log cabins and boasted a hotel as well as a pool hall and a restaurant and a barber's shop. This was civilization, and the visiting Sinclairs riding in from their farm were right glad of it. And they watched with wonder and admiration as Walsh went out with his dozen men to settle the affairs of thousands of fleeing Indians, armed and angry, bluffing them into obeying the law that was hardly there at all.

"I dinna ken how you do it," Hamish told him over the long pipe they were sharing at Fort Walsh. Some of the Indian customs passed on. They were companionable. Smoking cheroots apart was not the same as drawing on a tobacco stem together.

"No more do I," Welsh said. "To tell you the truth of it —"

"What more is there to tell?"

"When I rode in to Wood Mountain, there were three thousand of them – and some scalps with yellow hair drying over the wood-smoke, maybe Custer himself – I did not reckon we would come out alive. My hair tingled on my head as if it was waiting to be lifted off."

Hamish laughed. He liked Walsh for never taking himself seriously although no man was more braw in all the west.

"They were all there, but not Crazy Horse. There was Spotted Eagle and Little Knife, Long Day and Black Moon, and their hunting bands, all waiting to fire those fancy Martini-Henrys they took at Big Horn. But they said they had enough of fighting the war, no food, no peace, no hunting. They wanted to stay in the Great Mother's country above the Medicine Line."

"Great Mother?" Hamish laughed again. "You reckon Queen Victoria would like that?"

"She would like it well," Walsh said. "For that is what she is to all these people in their manner of thinking. And it is the why I am alive. For I say to them, you must follow the law of the Great Mother, and this is the law. You will do no harm to any woman and any child and any man –"

"Thank God for that," Hamish said, sucking on the pipe that he had learned to love, the hot smoke cool in his lungs. "For there are muckle of them and few of us."

"You will steal nothing, not one horse or one cow. You will not fight with the other Indian tribes, for they also love the Great Mother, and Her law is their law. And you will not hide north of the Medicine Line for the winter, and go south and raid in the Dakotas when it is dry. And you will not hunt beyond the Medicine Line, for the beasts of the Great Mother –"

"And she is the mother of the beasties," Hamish said. "And I wish I had known the like in Scotland. The laird said they were his, not Hers."

"The beasts are American beasts. And anyway, all the buffalo are dead here, and you may only hurt their bones. And you will not send guns and bullets to Crazy Horse in the south, for he must fight his own war if he stays there. That is the law of the Great Mother, and you will obey it if you stay in Her land."

"And they obeyed it? How?"

"I do not know," Walsh said. "A dozen of us, and three thousand of them. And all they asked was bullets to hunt the buffalo, for now they could only kill them with lances and ropes. So I gave Jean Louis Legaré the right to sell them bullets, for they must have the meat if they are to live."

"I dinna ken," Hamish said. "They have the power to kill us all."

"I tell you," Walsh said. "If they believe a man will keep the faith, they will help the faith. And they love this land, and they fear we will take this land from them. As we will, but not all of it."

"But enough for ourselves," Hamish said.

"But how many of ourselves will there be? Too many."

Crazy Horse did not cross the safety of the Medicine Line. He was told that he would be given the land of the Powder River country, and he believed in the word of General Crook. When he rode in with his eight hundred braves to give up his rifles, they wore paint and feathers and sang their songs of war. But it was all lies, the usual lies, with the broken promises whatever the pieces of paper said that the chiefs did not understand. And the Powder River was taken away and the Black Hills and Crazy Horse brooded in his despair. He even offered to lend his warriors to fight against the last of the Nez Percés on their long flight east to the Medicine Line. Yet his words that he would fight till the Indian fighters were killed was said to be that he would fight until all the whites were killed. It was a time when only the reverse was true. So when he was brought in to be jailed, he fought, and a soldier of no repute stabbed him to death with a bayonet. And so the pride of the Sioux nation died and his followers were too broken and too jealous of him to follow his spirit, and the Indians of the plains remained humbly on their reservations on rations from the government that sometimes came and sometimes did not.

Angus was working on a railroad survey which would bring the iron tracks across the prairie to the west, and he asked one of his Sioux axeman why the warriors were not filling them with arrows and cutting their bodies into strips to mark out their boundaries. The Sioux told him about crabs, freshwater crabs. There was this Indian, the Sioux said, and this white man, and both had a pail of crabs. And as they walked along, the white man's crabs were always leaping out of his pail, while the Indian's crabs were quiet as could be. So the white man asked why the Indian's crabs were so damn quiet. And the Indian said: "They are Indian crabs. When one big one rise to top, all the other crabs, they pull him down."

North of the Medicine Line, Bain and Hamish were working to make a farm too soon on the high plains. There was no question but that Bain had more than horse sense in him, if horses could be said to have any sense at all, doing all they did for men. He heard of the Glidden wire, and he had the first rolls of it brought up by rail and steam and cart to Fort Walsh, and when the men were unloading it, why, François Dubois near ripped off his leg and lost a boot in its spikes, but on the day of the unrolling, most of the people of Fort Walsh came out to see the sight. And Bain and Hamish had set up the fence posts over a mile round the corner of their land, and they brought out the coils of barbed wire on the Red River waggon, and they put the end of the wire to the first post, and they drove on the ponies and the wire unrolled its spiky length behind them. And every two hundred feet, they stopped the waggon and they braced the wire to the posts. And when they came to the end of the spool, why, they jacked up the hind wheel of the waggon and wound the wire round the hub, and they turned the wheel until the wire was taut and trim. Then they hammered the wire to the posts by staples, and so the spiny barrier was put across the plains that tore into the hides of cattle and buffalo, men and horses, until they cursed the fierce barbs of the iron thing that kept living things in and living things out.

This was a sort of progress, and Bain believed in a sort of progress. When the wind began to blow away the thin soil of the prairies, he made his own invention, as if it had never been made before – a waterwheel with little dangling buckets. And if he harnessed a mule to the wheel, and the beast plodded round in circles several hundred times in a day, a rachet and a crank turned the great wooden wheel with the buckets upon it, and muddy water would be drawn out of the creek from the river, and some of the slops would fall into the crumbling ditches dug into the ground, and a little of the wetness would creep on to the edge of the fields, most of it lost on the way to the arid soil and the dry air. There was talk of sinking wells to find the water underground, and of making windmills to draw it up by the power of the breeze, but this was only talk, and Bain did not have the knowledge or the use of it.

Katie became a field-hand and a hand about the house. Hannah's joints were locking now. She would have to rise three times in the night, crawling out of bed, then levering herself upright, then cracking the bones of her knees and elbows loose, because if she set in one place too long, she set. Katie massaged her with bear's grease and put on hot herb poultices in wet bags to draw out the swelling and the pain, but it was no use. The knuckles of the bones came together again. Maybe the gristle between them was plumb wearing away, like living did to folks in little dribs and drabs. Working the land certain wore a woman away, the bending and the stooping, the weeding and the cropping, the threshing and the binding. The men couldn't do it alone, Hamish was too old for it, worse bent than a scrub-pine in the wind, and Bain was as dogged as an ox, but even he had a limit to him, and by the evening he plodded so slow anyone could see he was tuckered and fit to die.

The nights were the worst for Katie, when she thought of Henri and their love-making, and her skin was on fire and she felt prickly and scratchy with desire, and she had to hold her daughter to her, squeeze the breath out of her for the want of her man in her arms. There were other men at Fort Walsh, but none of them were a patch on Henri Chatillon, none with his grace and his smile and his holding of a woman, his making her feel that she was the only woman. There would be none other – even if there was.

"I will not settle for less," she was always telling Hannah, when she was asked to the dances at the Fort and did not go. "There was only the one of him."

The talk of the railroad was true talk. The Canadian Pacific was building west, and it might come to Fort Walsh. If it did, there would be a city there below the hills. If it did not, there would be a wilderness again. The problem of the tracks coming at all was the gradient of the hills and the swamp by Battle Creek, which was full of dead horses and buffalo and brought the fever and the typhoid down in the water, so it had to be boiled to be fit for drinking. And the Mounties were needed now to look after the railroad workers in their brawling camps, always the fighting over the whiskey and the Indian women, and the Sioux and the Hunkpapas and the Tetons were moving back over the Medicine Line because the hunting was gone. There was talk of the Fort being pulled down, and one day it was true. All the old logs and posts and even the nails were hauled to Maple Creek and Medicine Hat to build stations for the railroad there. And the Mounties were to have a new fort at Pile O'Bones Creek on the main railroad line, and maybe there would be a city there to be called Regina, after the Great Mother Herself.

Angus came to visit at the valley bottom. Dust devils were swirling and scampering over the ploughed fields in little twists and capers. One of them struck Angus on his pony, and he coughed and spluttered and was nearly thrown as his mount snorted and reared and shook its head to clear the blinding dirt from its eyes. "Whoa, there!" Angus soothed the pony and patted its neck and took it on towards the low-lying cabin with its few shade-trees planted beside it to give a relief from the scoured plain. Even the barbed-wire fence had the look of a dried hedge, with the yellow weeds and humps of blown grass hanging on its prongs. This was no country to live in, Angus reckoned. But it never was, wherever the Sinclairs wandered.

"I can do nothing about it," he told his father and mother. "I survey the routes the reconnaissance parties choose. And they choose the easiest way and the way the law says. If we can buy the land – and that isn't the problem in this wilderness – then we take the way that is firmest and has the least gradients and curves. Do you know what a cutting costs through granite? Or a tunnel? We've had parties in the Rockies and the Selkirks scouting for six years, and there have been hundreds of routes suggested. And it's not our final choice. Someone up there decides it, and that's that. And it's no good me crying, we've got to get the railroad to Fort Walsh because my mother and father, they live near there, and they want a town there. Think of the land values. The railroad bosses just say, what's the cheapest way, and what's the easiest way, and what's the best way for the fewest dollars. And in quick time."

"But we came here," Hamish said. "And as we are here, the rail must come."

"You go where the railroad goes," Angus said. "In Ohio, I tell you, there are a thousand ghost towns. And some already over the American west. All because the railroad went to some other place. And here – the railroad won't come here now. It's too late. But it is expanding. Do you know the pace we lay the tracks? One day, in just one day, we laid six-and-a-half miles. That was sixteen thousand ties, more than two thousand lengths of rail and sixty thousand spikes hammered home. Call that track laying! I call it a miracle."

"Hush you," Hannah said. "Miracles are God's work. They are not the work of men who are playing with His work."

"But, mother, you may go on the railroad where you wish. All the way to the Pacific Ocean, when we drive in the last spike."

"And will that be soon?" Katie asked.

"In two years. And then the one shore will reach the other shore, and we will have crossed a continent."

"We have crossed seas," Bain said. "And forests and plains. And the devil a bit of good it did us."

"Hush," Hannah said. "The Lord is with us."

"Some of the way," Bain said. "So we will be left in a backwater, Angus?"

"Aye. There is no help for it."

"And what is the advice of the great engineer?" Bain could hear the sneer in his voice, but he could not help it. His young brother was right, he was the future, and Bain was getting nothing from being a slave to the dry land.

"Where the railroad goes, the dollars will go. Already the land near it increases in value – a hundred times if there will be a depot there. They are already building out through the Rockies and we will meet in two years. The opportunity –"

"That word of yours," Hamish said. "That word that was taking you from us."

"The opportunity is where the railroad goes. Father – Mother – and Katie – go west to the ocean. To Vancouver and Victoria. The land there is like Scotland. Hills and trees and the sea. It is a new Scotland. And there is not only the land, there is all the trade of the East. Go there."

"And who will pay?" Bain asked in bitterness. "Our land is here. You did not ask me."

"Because your land is here, brother," Angus said. "Because you always said you would bide with it. But for old folk – for a young mother like Katie – it is too hard here, too lonely. As an engineer on the railroad, I have a right to a plot of land. And I am taking it up in Columbia, in British Columbia, near the sea and the end of the line, where there will be a great city by Vancouver Sound."

"That is your land," Hamish said. "It is not our land."

"Honour thy father and thy mother," Angus said. "And shall I not honour you in your old age – and Katie, until she shall find another husband again."

"That I never will," Katie said.

"There is another sort of man in Vancouver," Angus said. "With a head on him. Brains. Never in great supply near this creek."

"None of that," Bain said. "Brains are best in haggis or black pudding. You'll be taking the old folk and Katie and leave me alone here on the farm."

"Blowing away in the wind," Angus said. "It is already. You come too, Bain. You are wanted."

"I will bide. This is mine. I will find a woman. We will have sons. We will have a ranch here, a kingdom. Wheat and cattle."

"I will not have the family break again," Hannah said. "Now we have our Katie back."

"There is the railroad," Angus said. "To visit each other – over the Rockies – it will be a day and a night. It is not a season in a covered waggon. It is comfort in a coach."

"We will go," Katie said. "I want the best for Marie. A school. And her learning the piano and the violin."

"What nonsense," Hannah said. "As if the harmonium was not good enough for her!"

"She shall not always play church music," Katie said. "But I will go with you, Angus. And Hannah and Hamish will come, will you not?"

"I do not ..." Hamish said and fell silent.

"The sea air, they say," Angus said, "is good for the bones. In places in Europe – they call them spas – they put old ladies in brine baths, and they come out skipping like lambs –"

"Get away with you," Hannah said, striking Angus's shoulder with her knuckle to show how pleased she was.

"And there are so many salmon in the river, a man has to put a fly through a bent pin, and he has a monster in his lap –"

"Who can hold to a word of it?" Hamish said, smiling.

"Then it is a fact," Angus said. "In two years, when the last spike is driven, you will be taking the railroad to the Pacific, and I will see to it, a frame house is already waiting for you there."

"And if you have a bride –" Katie said.

"She will join us all." And seeing the glower on his brother's face, Angus added, "And Bain shall come every Christmas with his bonny family."

"You are like the dark man himself on Hogmanay," Bain said. "You come with muckle blessings. And they are all smoke up the chimney."

"Steam," Angus said. "From the railroad. It will take us anywhere it goes."

At St Thomas's Hospital where the new school for nurses was established, Mary Sinclair met Harry Lamb. She had a double reason to be there. She had to learn more herself and to teach about tropical diseases, for Miss Nightingale had recommended her most highly. And she had to arrange for the entrance of Seaforth Sinclair to the medical school, what with his mother Lila dead now, and her promise, and the need for him to leave Annandale and India as well, and for his own good.

The voyage home was shorter, but hotter, sweltering in the Red Sea on the steamship and passing through the new canal at Suez. There were the usual problems with Seaforth's accommodation, having to put him in a class below hers, and having to eat apart. He was as tall as any Sinclair, and his father's bones already made hollows in his dark cheeks, and the blue eyes under the jet hair were startling in their contrast and their contact with any inquiry. His politeness was dangerous. He seemed aware of living on a sabre's edge, watching for any slight so that he could strike back with an insidious flick. He put no one at their ease, for he was uneasy in his own skin. If he loved anyone, he loved Mary, and even she found him too self-aware for comfort.

"I was a poor maid," she told Seaforth in the hansom cab on their way to St Thomas's. "I was working for a duke with the manners of a coal-heaver, when Miss Nightingale gave me my chance. Don't think the English won't take every chance they can to patronize you and make you feel the size of a wee mouse. It is a trick of theirs. A trick of power. Making us feel the lower when we are not. We do their work and we are not thanked for it."

Seaforth smiled, his lips a black curve in the grey London light.

"Do not worry, Aunt Mary. You know I do not say what I feel. I know of the hardships of the Sinclairs. You are always telling me – the taking of the land, the clearing you away, the coming to India, the taking of our land –" He looked out at the carved and streaked stone of the newly-built Mother of Parliaments, as they rolled over Westminster Bridge to the hospital. "Losing your land, you take another's land. Or your brother does."

"And we take you back to learn here," Mary said. "You will be a doctor greater than Louis Pasteur. You will cure wounds, or heal the plagues –"

"Is that what I will learn here?" Through the side window of the cab, Seaforth could now look over the parapet of the bridge towards the five projecting little towers of St Thomas's hospital on the far Thames bank. "Or will I learn how to take back our land and clear you once more?"

"You must not think like that, Seaforth. You must not speak like that. We are in London now."

"Naturally I will not," Seaforth said. "But you always told me to tell the truth, Aunt Mary. So only to you –" They had crossed the bridge and were turning towards the gates to the hospital. Through the rear window of the cab, they could hear Big Ben strike the hour of eleven as a repeated summons to the future. "I will not say or do anything to put you out. You know me."

"I do, Seaforth. And I worry. You are discreet. But inside you, I see sometimes – a new Mutiny."

Seaforth laughed. "We must cure bodies first," he said. "Then we can change minds."

Too clever by half, Seaforth was; but that was not what Mary said when she recommended him for the medical school to Harry Lamb. She stressed the need for Indian doctors in India – the trust that the people would have in somebody more of their own kind. She also

spoke of Seaforth's brilliance at his school in Simla, and she did not
deny that she was his aunt. As for Doctor Lamb with his mop of
white curls, he was more humane than his biblical namesake, and as
fearless. He would lie down beside any British lion in perfect
confidence that he would achieve his own soft purpose by his woolly
persuasion.

"Miss Nightingale has spoken to me of you, Miss Sinclair. Of all
the reports she receives from India, she praises yours the most – on
the *zenana* mothers, on the military hospitals, on the famine in the
Punjab. Her regard for you is great enough to give you what you want.
We will admit Seaforth Sinclair into the medical school, and his costs
will be defrayed by one of those charitable foundations which are the
hidden hand of mercy here to the unfortunate. As for you, you will see
what we can do for training nurses now, and you will tell them what
they can do in healing the diseases of the hot countries. And one more
thing –"

"You are giving me too many things –"

"A personal application – or rather, an appreciation –"

"From you yourself, Doctor Lamb?"

"Admiration, really. Would you, Miss Sinclair, allow me to escort
you to the opera? *Così fan tutte*, I believe, and cosy it will be. Some
Italian warblers are gracing our shores and our ears. My sister will act
as a chaperone."

Mary laughed and laughed. And when she had finished wiping her
eyes, she said, "Do you ken, the last time I went to the theatre here, it
was at the Seven Dials. It was a ballad-singer. He told the sad tale of a
father who murdered his wee boy. My brother Iain was off to the
Crimea, where he met Miss Nightingale at Scutari – lying down with a
hole in him. I still have the ballad sheet – that poor dead wee boy."

"And you have never married?"

"I said to Miss Nightingale –"

"She said you had said. But she loses many nurses to matrimony."

"A word is a word."

"To you. Not to all. You do not regret – a boy not born to you –"

Mary was suddenly angry. "You are a prying man, Doctor Lamb.
And who gave you the right? I am not under your medical examination."

"Forgive me, Miss Sinclair. Let me make amends at the opera."

"I have quite enough of children, and I prefer they belong to
others. Seaforth, he is one of them. And why should I add to the
many mouths of this world?"

"You should not. I only ask for your company with my sister as a chaperone."

Mary shook her head. "And if you think in India we have chaperones?" She stood up and looked down at the small and fleecy Doctor Lamb, smiling up at her in delight at her domination. "I have no need of your sister to protect me from you. I have been protecting myself a wee while the now. Unless, of course –" Mary towered over the shrinking doctor behind his desk – "you need your sister to protect you from me."

Now it was Doctor Lamb's turn to laugh.

"Miss Nightingale said you were a bold woman – but I did not know how bold."

"So you will not take me to the opera?"

"Twice over, if I may." Doctor Lamb now rose. His curly head only reached to Mary's shoulder, but his eyes were quick with sympathy and intelligence. "I don't need protection from you, Miss Sinclair. Only your company to shepherd me."

Mary was amused by the opera, although she did not understand a word of it, and she found women dressed as men getting away with it although they sang soprano as silly as fat tenors pretending to be lissom lovers. "To tell you the truth," she told Doctor Lamb, "it's all a great fuss over nothing, and I've heard linnets sing as sweet at no cost at all and hardly the weight of those warblers, as you call them."

That sort of talk made Doctor Lamb more attached to Mary. She could see that he might make a proposal to her, but he was so settled in his ways with his sister as his housekeeper, and how would she let another woman in the house to run the set affairs of Welbeck Street? And there were other troubles. Mary did not love Harry Lamb, as she called him now, although she liked him better than any man she had ever met. And she was past the age of having her own children. And surely that was the point of marrying, to create life and populate the earth, as if there were not enough people in it, anyway. Of course, there would be the comfort of him, and in their old age, the caring for each other, but there was so much to do in India, and the work was never done, as Miss Nightingale always said and did.

So when Harry Lamb managed to pop the question without popping all the buttons of his yellow waistcoat, on their evening at Nicols's new Café Royal, where the crown on the N stood for Napoleon and not for the proprietor, Mary had considered her answer. Yet all the same, she found herself blushing even redder than the two dabs of rouge she had put on her cheeks for the first time in her life. There was no question, being courted did turn a woman to a few vanities of her sex.

"I feel for you, Harry, and I would spend my life with you, but I must not. There is the work to do."

"You have done too much. You deserve happiness."

"Aye, I did think that once." Certainly the dust, the heat, the flies, the smells, the hearing of the pain, the utter fatigue which made her bones ache, she could do without that. Perhaps it was her due to lie down with this lamb.

"But there is work to do yet."

"You are crazy, Mary. You will work yourself into a grave."

"Aye. I will."

"And what profit is that?"

"The grave's."

"Have you no heart in you?"

"Too much a heart. Oh, Harry, I would stop and care for you, but – if I do – what of all the years I worked? Why did I do it at all? Why?"

For the first time Mary saw the sweetness of Harry Lamb's smile cradle into a pucker on his mouth.

"Sacrifice," he said. "Duty. Obedience. I would like to take those three words and hang them like the three gold balls outside a pawn-broker's and say, 'For you three liars, I pawned my life and my heart and my joy, and what did you give me back? A mean loan to keep me alive, and a ticket to happiness I could never redeem'!"

"Oh, Harry –" Mary took his hand across the table and noticed for the first time the scars on his fingers, where the chemicals of the experiments had burned him or the scalpel had slipped.

"I will only say no the now."

"You will give me hope, Mary, that last delusion."

"I mean to come back here for the Jubilee –"

"Three years away. How shall I live that long?"

"For my family have all sworn to come here from all the four corners of the earth. For the Jubilee. And then, if the work is done –"

"It is never done," Harry Lamb said. "My work, your work is never done. There is never a shortage of the sick. When they are better, there are more of them."

"But you will ask me again, Harry Lamb?"

"To hear you say no?"

"I will no say that I will say no," Mary said. "And I will no say that I will say yes. And that is the best answer you will have of me."

"It is both the most honest and false answer I have ever heard," Harry Lamb said. "It is saying no to yes, and yes to no."

"Well, that is what I mean," Mary said. "And you will have to take it or leave it. But I do agree with you, Harry Lamb. Sacrifice, duty, obedience – they are the three worst words ever said, and if they were all hangit, we would be well rid of the pack of them."

21

THE FAR FILAMENTS

They felled two forests to put up the Mountain Creek trestle bridge for the Canadian Pacific, more than one and a half million feet of timber to support the iron tracks. And when the gangs from the Pacific met the gangs from the Atlantic for the driving of the last spike, Angus was there. The portly director of the company, Sir Donald Alexander Smith, took the long hammer, and tried to play the smith at the forge in his frock coat, gasping at each blow on the spike, a slow and unsteady gong to signal the joining of the line. The head of the spike hardly seemed driven down at each flop of the hammer, but now it was nearly level on the top of the track. And Sir Donald Smith raised his thumping weapon for the last time, and the seams of his coat split like old bellows, and he brought down the hammer with a clang, and he drove the spike home. And the thousands of gangers and navvies, surveyors and engineers, train drivers and guards burst into a cheer that was lost in the prairie wind.

Over the hurrays and the hurrahs, a Scots voice was heard, "All aboard for the Pacific." And on that command, the watchers climbed on the carriages linked to the locomotive which stood on the eastern tracks, huffing and puffing at the boredom of the waiting, and the great iron wheels began to turn, and they rolled over the last spike, and the train steamed on to prove the link between the oceans. Canada was one bound land.

Only a month later, Angus took his mother and father and sister and little Marie to Vancouver Sound, where a frame house was already built on land that ran down beneath pine trees to a rocky beach. Bain would not come. His boots in a swirl of red dust, his hide hat in a cloud of flies, he said he would lick the land before it licked him. He was too young to retire or look for a city or a railway job or work on the docks. He was a farmer and he would beat the soil into shape.

Hamish and Hannah had not been settled for a year, running a small market garden to supplement the pension which Angus sent them, when they had a visit from a long-lost son. Hamish Jamie took the railway from his regimental depot in Canada to see the parents he had last left on the western shore of Scotland nearly forty years before.

And now they were on the western shore of Canada. Truly, a great migration, a long separation.

In the middle of his fifties, Hamish Jamie was a fine sight, in his Number One Dress, with his white spats over his boots, and his sporran fronting the pleats of his kilt, and the new yellow facings on the tunics of the Highland units, for they were now the Seaforths without any British number imposed on their origins. Even with wearing his forage cap rather than a bearskin, he towered above his father and his mother, with the trim diagonal hollows that ran from eye to chinbone and from nostril to lip showing him to be the Sinclair that he was. At first, little Marie screamed to see him as if he were a bogeyman, but soon she was sitting in his lap and using his sporran as a muff for her hands, while he adored her as if she were a reincarnation of his unknown daughter Peg in India.

"I have not been a family man," he told Hannah.

"That is the truth of it, my son."

"All these wars, all these foreign places," he said. "And never a place any Christian would wish to be."

"You are no a family man," Hannah said, "and you have a family. And you are a Christian, and yet you did no marry."

"I cannot, mother. The regiment, it did not let me."

"And poor Lila is dead, Lord rest her soul. She was a Christian."

Hamish Jamie shook his head. "She believed in her gods, mother. And Seaforth and Peg, they are Christians. They went to missionary schools in Simla."

"Mary wrote to us that Seaforth is doing well in London. He will be a doctor. She wants that we come to London for the Jubilee of the Queen. It will be a fine show, she says, and all the family will be there. But –"

"Her bones," her husband said. "They dinna move. I dinna think as she can take the stairs. Even the steps into the railway train, we had to pluck her up."

"Go away with you," Hannah said. "A wee bit stiff in the morning. That is all, and at an age as mine, I have to be thankful."

The day before, she had dropped two of the best new china plates as her hands could not hold onto them while they were being washed. She was losing her grip, but she would not admit it. She knew she could do everything she had always done, although she could not.

"I want to go to London," Katie said.

"Me, me, me. Me too," Marie said.

"Of course you will," Hamish Jamie said, holding her. "I will tuck you in my sporran and carry you all the way, such a little thing you are.

And you will meet your cousin Peg, for Mary wants her to train as a nurse in the new school that Miss Nightingale has started. Do you ken, father, there are even army medical schools and hospitals the now, and the medical officers in the regiments are trained doctors, and they say army nurses will come one day, if Miss Nightingale has her way."

"Will Mary be at the Jubilee? And Iain and Anna and their four bairns? Then I will go," Hannah said. "I will be there."

"Three children," Hamish Jamie said. "The eldest boy, he died in Zululand. I saw him buried. He was a fine lad."

"It is too hard," Hannah said. "The wars and the losing of the men. That Henri of yours –"

"He was the finest man," Katie said. "No one can take his place. No one –"

"No one?" Hamish was quizzical. "And what of Bob McDowell?"

"Ach, he's just a fancy bonnet and a watch-chain."

"A friend of Angus from the railway," Hamish told his son. "He has been visiting."

"He can visit till Kingdom Come," Katie said. "But there's not a word I will hear of it."

Yet she did hear of it. For Bob McDowell came to call while Hamish Jamie had not yet returned from his leave. And the Highlander had to admit that Bob was sporting a different sort of uniform. With the scarlet tunic and his ruddy cheeks, Hamish Jamie looked like a lobster after it was boiled, while in his blue train uniform, even with the gold braid on the shoulders and the cap, Bob looked like a lobster before it went into the pot. And the whistle that hung on his watch-chain on the other end of his hunter timepiece, why it was no dirk or grenade, but only a silly thing to blow to warn people you were coming. Bob was a chief Guard on the Canadian Pacific, and he was too tight for his clothes, swelling into them with all the pride of his position. But there was a look in his eyes when he sighted Katie with her red hair spilling in long ringlets in the new fashion that made Hamish Jamie change his mind. Such humble longing, such a look of hurt from the past. His voice might boom, but his gaze was beaten. Life or a woman had given him a terrible whipping. Yet there was a buried charm in him that any clever woman might bring out, if she wanted.

So Hamish Jamie felt pity for Bob as Katie treated him cruelly, declaring herself not at all well on the evening he was to take her to the restaurant with the band by the Sound. Hamish Jamie took him to a saloon instead and heard of a man, who had barely lasted his time as a boy, and had no good to tell of it. Bob was an orphan, and he ran away at fourteen from his institution to be an engine-cleaner.

"We worked nights, two running, thirty hours at a stretch. They'd put us in the firebox of the boiler with the steam still in it, changing the burnt-out firebars, while the heat of the grate scorched our shoes, and the dust filled our lungs, and the black sweat ran off us in rivers. I had a mate got into the furnace of a dead engine to have a sleep, and a stoker put in a shovel of blazing coals not seeing him, and he died screaming. Then I got to be a lighter-up, starting up the furnace four hours before the engine was wanted. Then I got to the footplate, a passed cleaner – I could stoke the boiler of the train when it was moving. Then up to a red ink fireman and a black ink fireman, shovelling coal into that furnace till I swear the blood was near dried up in me, I was bone and not much skin left. Twenty years, and I never did get to be a passed fireman or a driver. So I took the ship over to Canada where the railroads were starting up. And it was the best thing I ever did."

"You make the army sound like a love seat," Hamish Jamie said. "It is a terrible thing the railroads are."

"And over here," Bob said, "I said, No more shovelling the coal into that firebox, I will march up the train and blow the whistle and do the stopping and the starting and I will grow back all that flesh and blood they have been working out of me ever since I was a boy. But look, I am not complaining. For I love the railroad. There is nothing so grand as the engine getting up steam and pistons chump-chumping up and down and the hiss of the whistle and the horn blowing over those great plains and all the power under your feet, you can feel it rumble. I am a train man, although it was near the death of me."

"Have you never told this to Katie?"

"She would not care for it."

"She does not care for you," Hamish Jamie said, "because you never told of it."

Bob lifted his eleventh burning whisky, and he said, "And what gives you the knowing of the women?"

"I had sisters, you did not."

"And you left your woman to be a soldier."

"You will leave yours. You will stay on the train."

"It always returns. It is the end of the line here."

"If you have a place to go."

"But why tell your sister of when I was poor and weak? Women, they love you strong –"

"Ach, they do not."

"Major Sinclair, if you took off that uniform –"

"I would be the same creature as I am." Hamish Jamie laughed. "You ken we wear nothing under our kilt. So why shall we pretend the sporran is the truth over it? We are no bigger than we are, for all that. And that is what the women wish to hear."

"I will tell her then –"

"That you are worse and better than a blue coat and a silver whistle."

"That I was a poor lad –"

"And you still are –"

"That I love her –"

"Not that. There is much better." Hamish Jamie put his forefinger alongside his nose and squinted across it with one eye to make his point to Bob, and to prove he was still sober. "Tell her you need her."

"I need her?"

"You need her."

"But she needs me. To help her raise Marie."

"Yes, Bob. But that is not the logic of the women. For reasons only known to the Lord, their reason is all backwards. If they need you, you must say you need them. If they say they do not want you, you say you want them. And if they say, get away with you, you marry them in the morning." Hamish Jamie took away his forefinger from his nose and pointed it at Bob. "Do not say I did not tell you. I ken women."

"And you a soldier. You have passed all your life with women?"

"I ken women. You need her. Tell her."

And so Bob did, not once, but many times. And soon Katie was smiling at him and allowing him to escort her and Marie to the park, where she would watch the ladies riding side-saddle and laugh to see them teeter so high and so uncomfortable. And kindly treated, Bob became playful and expansive. And when it came the time him to take his train back to Montreal – and Hamish Jamie as a passenger back to his regiment – Katie in her best black silk dress took Marie looking like a church doll in white lace to the station to see Bob standing by the last carriage with its platform at the end, and blowing his silver whistle. And Hamish Jamie could have almost sworn he saw the light of pride in her eyes as he kissed her goodbye, and he said to Marie, "I have not forgot. Next time I see you, I will take you to London in my sporran," and Katie said, "Men will promise anything, but they never mean a thing," and then the whistle sounded for the last time, and Hamish Jamie scrambled onto the train, for the order of the Guard was almost as final as the order of Sir Colin Campbell to advance on Lucknow, "All aboard for the Atlantic."

The Scots might have won all the charges and the battles once, but now they were manning the engines of the ships and the trains that steamed over sea and land, making a web of trade that bound all the world to Britain. Money followed the bayonet. These far filaments were serviced by millions of working hands and legs and heads in a dogged fury of connecting peaks to valleys, and deserts to saddle mountains.

Angus went to Peru now, to advize on the highest railway in the world which ran one hundred and forty miles on a switchback from Callao to Oraya and rose over fifteen thousand feet in the Andes. The project was a madness, but it was made to work on trestle bridges, on the edge of precipices, channelled through gorges and funnelled through mountains, wandering back and forth like a tipsy snail, leaving a whirligig trail behind. In one tunnel, there was even a reversing switch, so in the jet blackness, the engine came to a halt, before shuddering off in the opposite direction, rather worse than the slope on the Bhore Ghat outside Bombay. And they had to use special banking engines and put three cogs with double sets of pinion brakes on each locomotive, each one able to stop the engine in ten inches on the steepest gradient. It made travel safe enough, bar a rock slide or an avalanche.

Yet was it worth it? Angus began to doubt it. Surrounded by the snow-bright peaks with cascades of howling silver torrents beating on the rocks, the eye falling sheer as the swoop of a condor down cliff and crag, Angus found the work pitiful. The Inca roads were still there, the Royal Road with its wood bridges suspended on ropes and its rough paving stones. Mules and llamas were better beasts of burden than steaming engines, and iron trucks inappropriate for such wild majesty. The fact that he met Isabella de Guadalluna because of her father Don Pedro's admiration for his feats of engineering did not make him think he was doing more than ornament the intractable. The line might last for a century or two and then it must revert into the Andes, irrelevant.

"You cannot really think we can conquer this," he said to Don Pedro, as they sat on the balcony of his town house on the square of Callao, looking past the church spires to the taller pinnacles of the mountains. "We are flying in the face of nature. We might live like the old Incas, behind great stone walls. Use natural things to build."

"But you *do* things," Don Pedro said. He nodded to Isabella to pour some more *coca* tea for their guest. "We, we live here – centuries, we do nothing. You have two words, iron and steam. We have two words, *nada* and *mañana*."

"Nothing and tomorrow," Angus said. "I've heard worse words if it is dealing with a landscape like this. Why try to change it?"

"We are trapped," Don Pedro said. "Eh, Isabella?"

Isabella glanced up at Angus, her black eyes huge and brilliant as wet coal against the pallor of her oval face.

"We are trapped," she said. "I learn English. We dream of London—"

"The fog, the grime, the dirt," Angus said. "You must be mad. It's a nightmare, they say. Read Charles Dickens —"

"No. Charles Darwin, Isambard Kingdom Brunel —" Don Pedro said in awe.

"The Royal Society, the Buckingham Palace —" Isabella breathed.

"I do not think the first has much to do with the second," Angus said. "The first deals with the sciences royally, and the second with anything but. All the same, I suppose you will both be wanting to go to London for the Jubilee. Fifty years of Queen Victoria ruling, and it is quite remarkable. She has made — or rather they who work for her have made — of all the oceans an English lake. And of the Andes an excursion trip up the railway line."

"It is my dream," Isabella said. "It is my dream."

"And do you think dreams ever come true, Don Pedro?"

"Men make dreams true."

"And women?"

"They dream of men —"

"Who make the dreams come true?"

"Sometimes." Don Pedro clapped his hands. A Peruvian servant came to collect the tea things. In his quilted hat and woollen tunic, his face flat and dark, he gave Angus a shock. He seemed exactly like the hill people of the Himalayas, who served Iain and Anna at Annandale.

"Did your Indians walk here from India? They are the same as the hill people there."

"They were here when we came," Don Pedro said. "Our Indians."

"I have not been there," Angus said. "But my brother and sister are there. The Sinclairs have been on many of the continents."

"And God make you to come here," Isabella said.

"Or your dream," Angus said.

Isabella looked down quickly at her lap, then glanced up as if surprised and smiled. Her father was smiling too.

"I do not dream of men," she said.

"Not of men only."

Isabella looked down again. She allowed her father to reply.

"We dream of London," he said. "And he who will take us there. But we will not detain you, Señor Sinclair. You have your work, I know. But perhaps, if you have time to come again, to talk to those with *nada* and *mañana* in their mind —"

"I will come again," Angus said, rising. "You did not ask what my dream was. The next time, I may propose it."

The next time, he did propose it, formally to the father, but to Isabella on his knees, as he had read in the books. She did not seem surprised, saying, "I saw you in my dream. I have always known. What took you so long?"

Angus did not let his religion be an issue; to him, a priest was as good as a pastor. His job was to build tracks and bridges, not to pray. He married Isabella within three months, and they stayed at Don Pedro's *hacienda* in the valley among the corn and the *coca* plants and the horses. Angus was wild for her body as the stallions were for the mares, and she was fierce and pliant, for all the softness of her white skin that she always kept from the sun. The children were born every year, Hamish Charles and Arabella and Murdo. And when the railway was laid and the last bridge built and the work was done, then it was the year of the Jubilee. And Angus persuaded Isabella to live her dream, even at the price of abandoning her babies for a year to the nurses chosen by her father.

"This is the Jubilee," Angus said, "and every woman has a right to her dream."

Behind Brunel's behemoth, *The Great Eastern*, the cable unrolled and coiled into the depths of the ocean. On the sea bed it lay, the submarine snake which linked the outposts of the empire by the tapping of the operators, DOT DASH – DASH DOT – the Morse Code that ran along the seven imperial serpents that girdled the bottoms of the seven seas. "Hush!" as Rudyard Kipling wrote. "Men talk today o'er the waste of the ultimate slime, and a new Word runs between: whispering, 'Let us be one'!"

From Annandale, Iain sent his Gurkha runner to the relay station in Simla, and there the message was clicked on the Morse keys by the cable workers, their little punctuations sounding their soft castanets in the night. And the stuttering points and strokes were picked up at Bombay, then sent along the third cable to England through Aden and Suez and Alexandria and Malta and Gibraltar, because the two overland cables went through Persia and Turkey, or through Russia and Germany, and who knew who was listening to what secret? So it was safer to stick to the undersea, where the British navy patrolled above, Hamilton Sinclair in the engine-room of HMS *Repulse*, surveying the oceans and all that sailed upon them.

Mary was already in London for the Jubilee. She had left India early on the P. and O., the good old 'dear and slow', which treated its passengers as though it were a favour to allow them aboard. She never confessed to herself that she might have come home a trifle soon, because she wanted to be there to see Harry Lamb before the rest of her family arrived for their reunion, whether she said yes or no to him this time. But she was none too early, because the cable was already waiting for her at Morley's Hotel on Trafalgar Square, where Harry had insisted that all the family must stay. It was translated from code into letters, and it ran:

ALL COMING TO JUBILEE
ANNA IAIN MARGARET MAY HAMILTON OFF SHIP

That said enough. A word in a cable cost money, and a Sinclair never wasted either one.

22

COMING HOME

The day of the Golden Jubilee of 1887 brought the Queen's weather. Brilliant sunshine bathed the crowds in the streets in yellow light. Her Majesty had turned down a glass coach. She would show herself to Her people in Her open gilt landau drawn by six cream horses. And She would not wear Her crown and robes of state. Her ministers might say that everybody wanted gilding for their money, or that a Sovereign should be grand, or that the Empire should be ruled by a sceptre and not a bonnet. But She would wear Her bonnet, and quite a bonnet it was, all diamonds and white lace. On the way to the thanksgiving service in Westminster Abbey, Her eldest daughter Vicky sat in the landau with Alix, the Princess of Wales, while twelve Indian officers rode in front alongside Her three sons and five sons-in-law, nine grandsons and grandsons-in-law. Her family was on display as well as Herself, and all the gleaming cohorts of Her global realm.

One of them was an apparition on his white charger, the Crown Prince of Prussia, in the white uniform of the Pomeranian Hussars. His helmet with its eagle crest and his silvered breastplate glittered in the sunshine, setting off the sash of the Order of the Garter and the sky-blue of his marshal's baton. Around him rode the princes of Europe and the whole world, the Hussars and Horse Guards. But he was the spectre at the feast of Empire. He was Vicky's husband, but he was dying of cancer of the throat. The Queen knew this and also knew that her grandson William would then become the Kaiser of Germany. He blamed his withered arm on incompetent English doctors called by his mother to assist at his birth, as he would blame his father's death on the same foreign meddlers. He was envious of England. He wanted Germany to do better on the seas and overseas. His dreams were the nightmares of the British Empire, while his father rode, a glorious white ghost, at the Golden Jubilee of the Queen of England and Empress of India.

Watching the procession from the balcony arranged by Harry Lamb, the Sinclairs were in London on their first and last time of coming together. In the streets, all the squadrons and the regiments were parading from all the red quarters of the globe. Those who had been thrust out from Britain when the Queen was young were gathered again to honour Her after fifty years of Her reign. The Sinclairs had been split like quicksilver and had rolled apart, but now they were drawn together again in one mass for this celebration of the ageing monarch.

As she passed below, so dwarfish in the splendour around her, it seemed incredible to Iain that such a dumpy old grandmother could command the allegiance of armies and navies and the respect of the world. All was a fiction, but a necessary masterstitch for the patch-work of dominions and colonies across the earth. He was told that she had built Buckingham Palace in a series of small rooms, so that reaching her was a period of waiting times in one antechamber after another until the final interview did not disappoint the expectation of it, for she was raised on a dais and spoke down graciously to a suitor. In Westminster Abbey, where the gilt coach was heading, she would sit high on the coronation chair above the stolen Stone of Scone, elevated in her littleness to the majesty she did not possess. Such was pageant, making a glory of the insignificant.

The troopers and the horses passed, the mounted bands and the walking pipers, the gaudy palettes of the uniforms and the brassy helmets and the tossing furs and fluttering plumes. And finally at the last tramp of feet, even the cheering stopped in the crowds below, leaving only the piles of dung gently steaming on the cobbles from the horses that had clopped away. And Iain turned and stooped to enter the room behind the balcony through the open French windows. There Harry Lamb had arranged for a feast of cold meats and sylla-bubs, iced wine and fruit punch. And there the Sinclairs had their reckonings to make.

Doctor Seaforth Sinclair looked at the uneasiness of his father, Hamish Jamie, and almost felt a sort of pity wash over his bitter mouth.

"Father," he said, "it has been so long I fear we do not remember each other."

To Hamish Jamie, meeting this thin and tall reproduction of himself was like that strange phrase in the Good Book, watching through a glass darkly, then face to face. But he would never excuse, never explain.

"I hear you have done well for yourself, very well. A qualified young doctor, working under Doctor Lamb."

"I have much to thank Aunt Mary for. But as for you —"

"I could not be at your mother's dying," Hamish Jamie said abruptly, preferring to charge before he was accused. "I was on duty."

"You always were," Seaforth said. "She hated that word from you. It was your excuse for not coming to us."

"You have your duty now. In the hospital. Your roster. Your calls. Do not tell me you fail in your duty, Seaforth."

"Oh, I do not." Seaforth smiled the quick wry smile that he seemed to imitate from his aunt. "I have been taught duty. The only question is – to whom do I owe it?"

"To your patients."

"True. I have no family – yet."

"You have us."

"Some of you."

"We are all Sinclairs."

"I am not sure," Seaforth said, "that all of you recognize that. Have some wine." As he passed a glass to his father, he looked across to the far side of the room to where Margaret and May were ranged beside their mother Anna, as though they were defending their corner of silk and lace and parasol against all comers. Mary was talking to them with an unusual animation, hoping to disguise her nervousness. For once, she appeared out of self-control. Harry Lamb had not spoken to the family yet about their plans, although he had given them all their fruit punch, and now was taking Peg across to her father.

"Peg," he said, "she is a jewel in our crown at St Thomas's. I do not doubt she will do more for India than even her splendid Aunt Mary has done."

"Peg –" Hamish Jamie stood awkwardly, looking down at the elongated oval of his daughter's face, her dark hair off-setting the triangle of the white nurse's cap pinned on it. He put out one arm, then dropped it in a sort of shrug of despair. But then Peg came forward, her dark lips seeking upward, from the shield of her nurse's cloak, and she kissed him on the cheek. He stepped back, as if he was stung by her forgiveness.

"It is good to see you, father," Peg said. " A major – and what a beautiful uniform. You look – alight in that scarlet."

"Yours is better than mine," Hamish Jamie said. "And it does more good."

"True," Peg said. "But not many soldiers would say that."

"Oh, father's very good at compliments," Seaforth said. "Mother always knew that. It is his way of avoiding responsibility."

"Seaforth!" Peg was angry and turned to Hamish Jamie. "Don't listen to my brother! He's always had a fork where his tongue is."

"He has cause," Hamish Jamie said. "As far as I am concerned."

"Saying you're sorry," Seaforth said, "is no excuse. The British are always saying they are sorry in India – but they still keep it."

"Shut up, Seaforth," Peg said and took Hamish Jamie by the arm and aside. "You have a whole life to tell me, so tell me. Don't listen to my brother. He won't ever forgive you for being his father – that's natural. But he forgets – without you as his father, he would not be here. And I neither."

The light from the French windows showed that Marie already had an extraordinary quality at the age of ten. The lithe speed of her movements, the slant of her cheekbones throwing up her wild red hair, the narrow green glitter of her eyes promised a fierce beauty. Iain was entranced with her as Hamish Jamie had been, and he told Katie that he had never seen a child as enchanting. "Like one of the wild faeries Hannah told us of. Born of the mountain dew and the salmon's leap. You must be very proud of her."

"Bob is also," Katie said, looking at her new husband, who stood stoutly in his check suit, looking ready to burst with pleasure and satisfaction. "I think he loves Marie more than me. Or his train engine, which is saying something."

"You'll not say that to me," Bob said, liking the teasing.

"Personally," Iain said, "I prefer an engine to a woman. More reliable."

Katie laughed. "Less fun."

"Don't be sure of that," Iain said. "Talk to Hamilton when he comes. He cannot see a lassie for all the cogs and pistons of Her Majesty's Royal Navy revolving before his eyes. But, Katie, they would not come?"

"They could not come. Hannah's bones – you almost have to crack them in the morning to make them move. And Hamish, his blood, it is so slow –"

"In India, they say the chewing of raw garlic often, it works wonders –"

Katie did laugh now, and Bob with her.

"Hamish reeking of the garlic –"

"Like an Italian waiter," Bob said. "We have one on the train. But I said, none of that heathen smell. Keep it for your pestilential *pasta*. For me plum duff and bread-and-butter pudding."

Iain looked at Bob's girth under his waistcoat. "I can see that. A fine diet. But now garlic, it does speed the blood. But, Katie, our mother and father, they are not in real pain."

"If they were, how would they tell me?" Katie smiled. "You know a Sinclair. If he's hurt, it's a wee nothing. And if he was in hellfire, he would say, 'More coal, more coal, please. I cannot feel it.'"

"If anyone was ever to go to heaven," Bob said, "your parents would."

"For putting up with me?" Katie gave her husband a mischievous smile. "Oh, I know you do, but that's what husbands are for. Putting up with their wives. Do you know, the last time I had a wee fever – nothing at all – Hannah was up in the middle of the night to bring me a bowl of brose. 'Feed a fever', she said, 'feed a fever', when eating is the last thing you can do. Then Hamish came in with what he calls a wee drop of something. 'Not to tell the wife, please, but there's something in there will chase away the chills'. And there was – enough whisky to fill a distillery! I love them both, Iain, and they are as well as may be at their age."

Now Iain looked across the room, hoping to see his son enter, but all he saw was his wife Anna being introduced by Angus to Isabella, dressed in lace flounces even more extravagant than Margaret and May were wearing, and with her hair piled on her head like the pyramid of Cheops. The ladies seemed to recognize each other instantly, friends in their social understanding against the lumps of menfolk in the room.

"Coming to London has been my dream," Isabella was saying. "And to see the Queen in that beautiful hat. A miracle."

"A good hatter is no miracle," Anna said sharply. "Doubtless She can afford it. Most of those diamonds come from India." And looking at the silken pink confection pe1rched on Isabella's head, "And your hatter, he must be very dear."

"He is very dear to me," Isabella said, not understanding why Angus laughed. "But your daughters, they are so pretty. Which is Margaret and which May?"

"This is Margaret," Anna said, introducing the taller girl in her green silk gown with only a small bustle – thank the Lord the crinoline had rolled its last hoops away. "She is to marry somebody in the Indian government on our return. Douglas Jardine. Very well thought of by the Viceroy himself."

"Oh, mother," Margaret said, "Douglas has more than the Viceroy's good opinion. He has mine."

"I don't know," May said, shorter than her sister in lilac with her buttercup ringlets almost violent to the eye. "You could do better. I shall."

"Those two sisters," Anna confided in Isabella. "They truly love each other, though you would never believe it to hear them speak. But it is only play."

"Girls, girls," Isabella said. "I was fortunate. I was an only child —"

"I was the one who lived —" Anna said. "You will inherit everything?"

"My father loves Angus. And our three babies — they are with him."

"Angus, I do declare —" Anna looked her brother-in-law straight in the eye — "you are as shrewd as your brother. You have married an heiress."

"Oh, she married me," Angus said, then saw his wife blush and he added, "or rather, her father married us two. He loves Charles Darwin and Isambard Kingdom Brunel, the great scientist and the great engineer. He has the wrong opinion that I learn from both of those masters."

"And you do," Isabella said. "But if you say you do not marry *me* —" she turned on Anna — "Why, on his knees, he asked me —"

It was Angus's time to turn red, while the women laughed.

"I must say," Anna said with that dry humour that seemed to grow on her with age, "Iain asked me on his back with his leg up. Very romantic."

Isabella laughed and blushed. "But — how can he?"

"Easily. He was wounded. But Angus tells me, you also have Indians in Peru."

"We do."

"We have Indians, of course, it being India. I love them, you know" — her gaze wandered across the room and fixed on Seaforth — "but I will never trust them. Not after the Mutiny. They killed my family."

Anna would have said more, but Hamilton came into the room, resplendent in his naval uniform. And Anna fell upon him, the blue apple of her eye. When he could disengage himself from his mother and his sisters and had shaken hands with his father, he found himself set upon by Angus and Bob with the technical questions and the mechanical talk so dear to that breed of men who lived for their work. Hearing them gab about cantilevers and crankshafts, cog wheels and pressure gauges, Hamish Jamie could only bless the one thing his new position as an army officer had taught him — no shop in the mess.

Harry Lamb brought them all to attention by rapping with a silver ladle on the embossed bowl which held the fruit punch. "I have an announcement to make," he said, his voice tinny and sharp with an odd strain in it. Then he coughed and brought it down to his usual reasonable tone. "And it will be to my new family, whom I welcome here. Mary." He signalled to her to come to stand beside him, and she came forward with reluctance, her face gaunt in its reserve and power with the grey hair scraped back from her forehead to a bun behind. "Mary — she has accepted to become my wife. I have long waited for her to feel that she has done enough for others, but never for herself. And I have persuaded her that her work now lies here — she will be teaching the nurses at St Thomas's — and also that she needs care herself, and love — mine." Now Harry seemed to conjure out of his hand a yellow apple as if by illusion or magic. "And I will show you how Mary and I will always be. I call it the Platonic Apple. It must be cut in a certain way — most delicately. With a scalpel, with a surgeon's knowledge —" And now Harry brought up his other hand to hold the apple, and lo, the complete orb parted into two serrated segments. And then Harry put the pair of them together again, and held up one perfect pippin.

"What Plato said was this. Before we are born, there are two parts of us, one male soul and one female soul. They are severed before birth, born to different mothers. They spend all their lives looking for each other desperately. Only if they find each other will they become whole again — a circle — a oneness — a communion. I call it the Platonic Apple, and that is us."

He gave the yellow fruit to Mary, who looked at it dubiously, not knowing if she was meant to bite it. But then Harry gave her a ring, aglow with red light and blue light and white stardust, the ruby and sapphire and diamonds of the Empire. "And this too, a ring, which will bind us in the Platonic way."

"Platonic?" Iain growled to Anna. "I am not a man for the books, but does that not signify that he will not touch her at all, but he will love her from far away?"

"It was a sweet speech," Anna said, "and the dear doctor did not mean that at all. He said he had been looking for Mary all his life, and now she would make him complete. And it is a better asking than the asking you did for me, Iain Sinclair!"

The smile on Mary's face flickered on and off, brilliant, and then closed. She was full of joy and fear. "I don't know," she said, as Harry put the engagement ring on her finger. "I don't know —" And then she burst into hysterical weeping and then she kissed Harry full on the mouth among her tears. The women all hurried around her, leaving Hamish Jamie again with his son, who was smiling almost scornfully at the aunt he claimed to love.

"She should not have done it. Doctor Lamb, he is not for her. Not for any woman –"

"What do you mean, Seaforth?"

"Nothing," Seaforth said. "Nothing of any consequence. Certainly, he needs a good wife, and Mary will be that. It will even –" He paused and stared at Hamish Jamie. "Where will you go now? Back to your damned duty?"

"To Scotland," Hamish Jamie said. "Iain wishes to go there and see how the land is now. And my regiment, they say... If I go for the recruiting –"

"Recruiting? More cannon fodder for the Empire?"

"My pay," Hamish Jamie said. "It has been keeping you and Peg. I always send the main part of it to Mary. You know that."

"I thank you," Seaforth said. "It is the least a father can do, and you do it. But you were cleared from the Highlands. Will you go back to your shame?"

"It is still our country. And your country –"

"India is my country."

"And Scotland."

"India is my only country. And it is only for Indians."

"Ach, so you will have your father out of you." Hamish Jamie smiled. "You can not, and you ken that. You cannot do it. I will always be the half of you. Like that yellow apple."

"Do not be too sure, father. But Peg, she wishes it. You saw that."

"You are my only son."

"And I do not have a father."

The two men looked at each other, and then Hamish Jamie looked aside. "You will change your thinking."

"I will not."

"The Sinclairs are awful stubborn – but they can change their thinking, if their heads are beaten enough."

"What do you expect to find in Scotland, father? More empty land and broken roofs? Desolation."

"I hear Mister Gladstone has passed a Crofters Act. They have been given the right to their land at a fair rent, and to give it on to their sons. Perhaps I shall have a croft again with my pension – and you, my son–"

Seaforth grimaced in that sudden quick smile of his aunt. "Burning *ghats*," he said, "are more for me. They only passed that Act because there were troubles in Scotland. The Battle of the Braes on Skye ..."

"I heard that," Hamish Jamie said. "So they sent Lord Napier over from India, and he said the crofters will have their land at last."

"There will be more troubles. There have always been troubles in that sad land you come from."

"There are always troubles everywhere." Hamish Jamie looked across the room to where the bright ring of women was breaking about Mary, who now leaned against Harry Lamb, and he put his soft hand round her shoulder and whispered in her ear. "That is why I am a soldier. I stop the troubles. But you do not. There are no troubles here."

"Don't be too sure," Seaforth said. "There will be, and there will be soon."

Never had there been such a feast as when the crofters of Lewis stormed the deer park in that year of the Jubilee and shot the red beasts with their rifles and roasted their carcasses slung over wood fires or boiled the venison in great pots over the hearthstones under the broken roofs of the black houses of Stromas. Iain was welcome among the visitors, and even Hamish Jamie in his regimental uniform was forgiven for the wearing of it. For he had not come to take them. He found the whole affair most paradoxical. For the Earl of Seaforth himself had cleared the crofts for the game park, providing room for the deer as well as men for his regiment. But he had sold it, and now Lewis was in the hands of the widow Matheson, whose late husband had been a partner in the great China firm of Jardine Matheson, with its profits from the opium trade protected by the raid on Peking. The money was lavished on the surviving islanders, who were now biting the hand that did not feed them enough by the taking of the red deer, so sweet in the mouth.

"And will you not be punished for this?" Iain asked an old man from Morvig.

"For taking what the Lord provideth?" the old man said. "There is no jury in Scotland will commit on that."

"That is what I thought and I did when I was a lad," Iain said. "I took the salmon and I blessed God for it."

"And we have blessed God for this deer and said our Grace to Him," the old man said. He pointed to where a pile of blackened stones and mossy rubble showed a building once had been. "And we will build the Church there again at Stromas."

"Will you now?"

The smell of the roasting meat was suddenly harsh in the air, as sour as the rankness of the kelp charring in the kilns or the burning of the imperial palace in China. It was not the scent of plenty, it was the smoke of useless defiance, and Hamish Jamie had to question it.

"And how many now are there in Sutherland and Ross and Caithness? Are they not nearly all gone? A fair rent on the crofts, it is being given too late, for they are broken in and fallen down, and we are all gone away across the earth, and we will not come home again. There are thousands now, where there were tens of thousands and how shall we fill the land again?"

There was the piping that night, and the fiddling, and wild laments sounded from the western island. And on their tour of the Highlands, Iain and Hamish Jamie found a terrible beauty, the brae and moors given back to heather and stag, the sheep close-cropping the grasses of the glens to a stubble unfit to eat, and a wilderness growing where the black houses had been and were laid down. Often as the two Sinclairs gazed over loch and mountain, they seemed lost in their own company, as if no men had set foot there before, and no men would tread there again.

"We do more in Egypt and the Punjab," Iain said. "Where there are deserts, we make the water flow for other peoples. We irrigate the sand and plant colonies there. And here –" He flung out his arm to describe the sweep of the saucer of hills that cradled the loch below. "We have water that makes nothing grow. A few men take the fish from it and the deer drink of it and foul it. We grow gardens and granaries over the seas, and here there is wilderness and game parks –"

"We, Iain? *We?*"

"They. But we serve them."

"You always said a Sinclair does not serve."

"We do their bidding They bid us, and we do it."

Doctor Seaforth Sinclair was also right about other trouble in that golden year of Jubilee. That took place in the heat of the empire under Nelson's Column. There beside the four bronze lions which lounged imperturbable at the base of the column, the vagrants and the unemployed had made their home, and there the socialists and the Irish reunited the core of their mobs of protest. On that Bloody Sunday in November, the people had been called in from South London, from Deptford and Battersea and Bermondsey, and they surged over Westminster Bridge, wearing their red armbands and their green sashes, and singing the 'Marseillaise' or 'Starving for Old England'. A detachment from the five thousand constables called up especially for the occasion blocked the bridge and defended the Houses of Parliament. And under Big Ben, a battle was fought.

St Thomas's Hospital took in twenty-six of the wounded, and Seaforth had to treat them for cuts and contusions, bruises and broken arms. Worried about the Sinclairs who were still staying at Morley's Hotel, he took the horse-bus to Trafalgar Square. From its top deck, he looked down at the milling crowds as the charge of the socialists, carrying their banner, *Disobedience to tyrants is a duty to God,* met with the cordons of police surrounding the Square. The truncheons rose and flailed and struck home sickeningly, but the wedge of the protestors drove through. Some of the crowd were knocking off police helmets like coconuts on a shy with flung cobbles, while others were using little switches on the police horses, which were backing and rearing and bounding and upending the high constables.

But now the Horse Guards appeared at the end of the Square, and they began to walk their mounts slowly round the people. And from the north, the Grenadier Guards came on with fixed bayonets. The troopers quickened their pace to a trot and then to a canter. The booing and the shrieking of the crowd was an assault on the heavens. And now the Guardsmen began to charge, and the people split and ran, screaming in their panic. The horse-bus rocked with the pressure and the rush pell-mell of the fleeing mob. Below him, Seaforth saw the flying hair and waving beard of the radical speaker George Bernard Shaw skedaddling on his way to Hampstead, escaping the disgraceful defeat of the many by the few. Only Seaforth hoped that when his day came in India, the masses would sweep aside the military as poppies before the scythe.

He found Mary safe in Morley's Hotel, while Anna and Margaret and May were on an excursion to the country. "I never thought to see," he said to this aunt, "such scenes in the capital of Empire. I don't know how you can send so many soldiers abroad when obviously you need them at home to keep down your poor."

"Seaforth, Seaforth," Mary said. "This is a most unusual Sunday. Most of us are at church, not in the streets."

"Tell me, Mary," Seaforth said, "how long do you think before India gets its independence? After Ireland?"

"Only when you can run it yourselves," Mary said with some asperity. "And when we are tired of running it for you."

"And an independent Scotland?" Seaforth smiled his thin smile.

"Now why should we need independence," Mary said, "when we Scots already run England and the Empire for the English? You will note, Seaforth, that where you go, it is a Scots person you will meet – doctor and nurse, engineer and guard."

"But not a minister –"

"Ach, we have had kings here – and ministers. But it is not they that matter. It is the Scots that run the real thing – the ship, and the trains and the hospitals. And train you –"

"To make yourself unnecessary." Seaforth smiled again. "How very unselfish of you, Aunt Mary. But I will never understand – I can never understand – why after the clearances you still worked for the English."

"It was our own folk did that wicked thing," Mary said. "And we had to earn our bread. I am not ungrateful. Nursing, it is better than the kelping or being a skivvy. And you, Seaforth, are you not working for the English?"

"I am learning how to get rid of them, Aunt Mary. And they are kindly teaching me."

"And are you not grateful for that, you wicked boy?"

Seaforth laughed at his aunt's fond disapproval, and he took each of her cheeks between the palm of his hands, and he kissed her lightly on the nose.

"As grateful as the crocodile is to the fat sheep between his jaws."

Now he held his aunt's face firmly between his hands, so that she could not look away.

"Do not marry Doctor Lamb, Mary –"

"Do not tell me that. It is too late. In three weeks the now –"

"Men who marry late have their reasons –"

"He never met *me* before –"

"He is a man who has always had to do with men. His life is very private."

"He helps with the nurses in the hospital."

"He loves women – at a distance. Platonic – you remember the apple. And I have seen him – in the dissection of a woman – I would say a repugnance, an aversion."

"But she was a dead woman. I am alive. It is natural to feel averse to a body –"

"Not for a surgeon."

"But you know nothing definite, Seaforth."

"Nothing. Doctor Lamb is discretion itself. I have a feeling – as I have for some of our British civil servants. All smiles on the surface, and unspeakable beneath."

"And you say that of the man who has helped you so much!"

Two bright spots of rage or concern flared on Mary's pale cheeks.

"It is because I love you," Seaforth said, "and I do not want you to make a mistake."

"You are jealous of him," Mary said. "You fear to lose me."

"Let us say that," Seaforth said. "But never say I did not warn you."

He walked over to the windows of Morley's Hotel. Under Nelson's Column, only a few policemen patrolled lazily in the empty square. It was as though no battle had taken place. There were no casualties, only an eerie lack of evidence of what he himself had seen.

"Perhaps nothing will happen," Seaforth said. "Perhaps you will be very happy. I can never believe my own eyes."

23

REVIEW

He was too old to serve, and yet his regiment could not serve in Africa without him. Hamish-Jamie sometimes thought he had been serving the army for nine lives, not just the one the Good Lord had given him; and yet the Seaforths had called him back from his retirement, when he had left the new Army Service Corps after nearly fifty years with the colours. But he could not refuse, he would not refuse to be the quartermaster of his regiment in Egypt and the Sudan. He had a personal reason to join Kitchener's expedition. He had not forgotten the martyred General Gordon from their meeting at the sack of the imperial palace at Peking. Indeed, when Hamish Jamie had heard of Gordon's killing by the Mahdi at Khartoum, he had not been surprised. That man would never evacuate. He could not retreat. He would stay to the bloody end, even if Sir Garnet Wolseley took two days too long to relieve him, struggling up river only to find a headless corpse.

On his belated imperial revenge, Kitchener was even slower at advancing up the Nile against the khalifa and his dervishes from the Sudan. Method was all. Cataract after cataract, he drove his forces forward. When they reached the khalifa's mud capital at Omdurman, they entrenched themselves and waited to be attacked. And when the assault started with the dawn it looked as if the whole of Africa was coming at them staring through the spires of the *zareba* at first light.

Hamish Jamie saw the great sand plain in front of Omdurman covered with dervishes in their white *jibbas* with patchwork colours, their flying turban tails and black and blue and green flags, and the khalifa's guards with their red tunics – a parody of the foe they faced. They waved their long swords and struck them against their round shields and ran forward to the beating drums, shouting, "Allah! Allah! Allah!" Then it was deadly work to watch.

From the corners of the brigades lined up in sections beyond the *zareba*, the guns opened up, pumping out the heavy lyddite shells, while the Maxim guns swung on a slow traverse, cutting down the dervishes methodically, left to right, then right to left, as a machete cuts the dry undergrowth, swinging from side to side. Then Hamish

Jamie saw the Highlanders fix their bayonets and rise and fire section volleys, not a dozen times, but three short of a hundred volleys from their Lee-Metford magazine rifles, pulling the bolts and changing the magazines like workers at the new lathes at the government factory at Enfield turning out the scored barrels and ejection mechanisms of the new standard weapons. Precision had replaced courage, pigeon-shooting was now the charge.

When the order came to take Omdurman, the Highlanders walked over a multitudinous sea incarnadine of bodies, making the dun sand red, with white torn *jibbas* breaking over the billows of the dying. The Maxims had been so effective that Hamish Jamie could count five or six crimson holes in each fallen dervish, while the two heroes who had held up the khalifa's black flag until the last were spilt blood puddings. There was no joy in this for Hamish Jamie, just the sight of the black flies clouding the wounded and the dead and the reek of the mud huts of Omdurman, where the troops in their looting could only find one silver snuff-box, and precious little else.

Hamish Jamie's only fortune or misfortune that night was to meet a young officer of the Lancers, his square face flushed with some sort of triumph, too young in his brash arrogance to see a hollow victory. He was a war correspondent as much as a cavalry officer, and he wanted evidence of how the battle looked from the Seaforths' point of view. He said his name was Winston Churchill – he was chiefly famous so far for breaking down the barrier in the Empire in Leicester Square between the bar and the stage. But Hamish Jamie did not take to him. His voice descended like the slow flick of a lash.

"You Highlanders, you hardly had a thing to do. Stay behind your prickles, pot them like snipe, then walk into town. We had a charge, a cavalry charge. It may be the last cavalry charge ever in the British Army!"

"Why do you say that, Mister Churchill? And you in the cavalry too!"

"Those damn Maxims. When we fight our own kind, how are we going to charge machine guns? With armour on? The bullets will smack straight through. And look at you, firing cool as cucumbers, knocking down ten thousand of them, and losing a dozen or two."

"It was cool work," Hamish Jamie agreed. "But you had hot work in the Lancers."

"Indeed, we did. There were only three squadrons of us – perhaps three thousand of the enemy. And we went straight through them. They did not break. They had these swords and spears – hamstrung the horses, hacked their bellies, cut them with backhanders. Hardly sporting, and when we rode on, they fired their Remingtons at our back, so we had to gallop back. I killed a few, a pistol shot in their faces, and the Lancers, they were giving them a good poke. You know what one of them said to me?"

"And I do not."

"It is nice to put a sword or a lance through a man. They are just like old hens. They say *Quar!*"

Churchill laughed, but Hamish Jamie did not join in his pleasure. He looked at the bulging blue stare of the young man.

"And what is it all about, now we have the Sudan?"

"We shall have the Cairo to the Cape railway. We shall have all Africa, even if we have to whip the Dutchmen in the Cape to get it."

"I have soldiered in Africa, east and west and north now," Hamish Jamie said. "And if my regiment goes to the south – I will look like an old compass. But God help me if I know which direction we are pointing in. I have never understood why we came to Africa at all."

"The route to India. The Cape. The Suez Canal. You must see that."

"We are a wee way from that up the Nile."

"Germany, France, Italy, even Belgium, they are seizing parts of Africa –"

"Let them have it," Hamish Jamie said. "I tell you, Mister Churchill, I do not doubt that Africa will see them out."

"Are you a Little Englander, man? Would you stay in our crowded island?"

"Aye," Hamish Jamie said, "but we were cleared from it, and we cannot go back the now. All that concerns me, Mister Churchill, with your grand strategy, where will you send me before I have my pension? And where will my old bones lie in the end? On what godforsaken shore?"

After the royal review of the one hundred and seventy-three ships-of-the-line of the Home Fleet off Spithead, some of the Sinclairs met at a waterfront hotel in Portsmouth in the Victoria Lounge. The chamber orchestra was playing Elgar and Strauss very prettily, and the aspidistras were almost as well-groomed as the ladies. May was very much the *grande dame*, as only those can be who are to the manner unborn. She queened it over the waiters, protested that the music was vulgar, and dropped the names of great acquaintances like sprinkling pepper. She used the nick-names of friends known only to her and her husband, Charles Seymour-Scudabright, as if not to know them were to be in *purdah*. It was all too much for Mary.

"Pom-pom," she said. "Is that not a tassle on a bonnet? And Dee-dee – ach, that's baby-talk."

"Dee-dee Devonshire," May said in reproach, "is one of the sweetest, kindest creatures –"

"I was not referring to her character," Mary said, "but to her nickname." Then turning on Charles, ablaze in the white uniform and gold braid of an officer on the battleship *Majestic*, "you don't have time for tittle-tattle, do you?"

"My ship keeps me busy, ma'am." Malice sharpened Charles's eye. "But not so busy I had not heard – May we hope to see your husband?"

"Doctor Lamb is extremely busy," Mary said, but she could not help but flush. "His work at the hospital – it detains him night and day."

"At night," Charles said, "I heard that he sometimes roams the streets of London. As Mister Gladstone used to do, rescuing fallen women, I believe. Or not quite rescuing them ..."

"Has that lie, that scandal reached you?" Mary swung on May, who looked away in a flutter. "It must have been you, May!"

"I have never said a word –"

"Oh no?"

"Except that Doctor Lamb was not really interested in women. Not even in you, Mary. Seaforth told me about it. That word he used – an aversion to women."

"He is a good and kind husband," Mary said, red in the face. Water prickled in her eyes. How could her own family betray her? The Sinclairs had always stuck together. What was their life doing to them? And marriage with this superior sort of person, the same sort who had driven them out to wander the earth.

"Your doctor – he may be not much under the sheets, ma'am," Charles said, "if you'll forgive the plain words of a sailor. Yet in a surgery, cutting up people, a sawbones –"

"Then you do credit the lie?"

"Nobody will ever catch Jack the Ripper, ma'am. He was far too clever for that. Too good a doctor to leave any traces."

"I cannot believe this." Mary found herself on her feet with the tears running down her face. She tried to speak down to her niece and the insinuating Charles. "Do you know, there is not a single surgeon in London – not one – who has not been accused of being the Ripper? Just because the bodies were dismembered by somebody with a knowledge of anatomy. It could have been a butcher – a medical student. There are even other lies – the King of Belgium – a member of our Royal Family –"

"It had to be a surgeon," Charles said.

"Then why pick on my Harry Lamb?"

"An odd character," Charles said, "a very odd character. Who does not make my May's aunt happy."

"I have never said that," Mary protested. "I am extremely happy. Harry is so kind, so thoughtful –"

"So damned peculiar he never touches you, ma'am," Charles said. "And how do you explain that?"

"It is not for you to ask, sir. And I will certainly not reply. I came here to see the family – if family they are. But I will not stay to hear the gossip, the scandal, that rules this country. There's not a word of truth in it. Tongues wag, click, click, click. He did that, she didn't do that – all lies. You'd all rather tell lies and bring people down than – Hamilton!"

Through the lounge Hamilton rolled. He had not found his shore legs because he treated the steady Axminster carpets of the hotel like a pitching sea. Making his way carefully towards the family table, he trod as delicately as Agag of the Bible. He was wearing blue service dress, and when Charles rose and put on his braided cap, Hamilton had to salute him, although he made this gesture more of a throwaway of his right hand.

"Hello, Charles," he said. "Hello, May. You didn't have to get up to greet me, Aunt Mary. You weren't going?"

"Of course she was not," May said. "She was so glad to see you come in."

"I certainly was," Mary said. "You stopped me from going." She was trembling with agitation and horror. "I have heard such things. I cannot –"

"What's this?" Hamilton said. "Aunt Mary –"

"It's nothing," May said. "An idle rumour. Quite untrue. It has been a long day, watching the fleet. Do sit down, Aunt Mary. And compose yourself."

Still shaking, Mary found herself sitting down on May's command, while Hamilton enthused to Charles.

"Did you see our ship?" he asked. "The *Turbinia*. Didn't she run? What a lick!"

"I prefer sail," Charles said, seating himself and taking off his cap. "Steam – it's so noisy. I don't know how you hear down there."

"What we hear," Hamilton said, also sitting beside his shaken aunt, "is only the engine going wrong. Nothing else. It's all very well for you up on the bridge speaking down the tube, 'Full steam ahead', 'Hard astern'. Do you know what it's like down there, following those commands?"

"No, I do not," Charles said. "And I do not intend to know. Engine rooms are not for gentlemen. Steam, as far as I am concerned, is a necessary evil, and best left to those who understand it."

"Ship's engineers," Hamilton said, smiling. "The lowest of the low. But then, you can't do without them." He hailed a waiter. "Rum, grog – whatever you call it. And don't say you don't have it – this is Portsmouth. Navy ground."

"It was wonderful, your ship," Mary said. "I saw it pass in the distance. It swallowed up the sea."

"Thirty-four knots," Hamilton said. "Put that in our new destroyers – with torpedos and the new gyroscopes – and it will knock every battleship out of the water."

"Oh, I think," Charles said, his thought the wisdom of Solomon, "our big guns will smash you to matchsticks before you get near us."

"You're too slow," Hamilton said, "and too old, and you still think you can fight like Nelson, broadsides and all that bosh. I have news for you. Nelson is dead! And Sir Charles Parsons has invented the turbine engine." He turned to Mary. "Where's Seaforth? I wanted to see him. He does something useful like I do – being a doctor."

"Have you not heard?" Mary watched as the waiter set down a glass of rum in front of Hamilton as gingerly as if it were an explosive. "Seaforth has gone to South Africa. To Cape Town. I really am worried for him. It may be the wrong choice."

"Why?"

"Well –" Mary was embarrassed, which she rarely was.

"He says – his colour – there are many Indians there – and he will call himself an Indian. He has very strong views. And they have very strong views against the Indians there."

"They call them Coloureds," Charles said. "I have been to the naval base at Simonstown. The Coloureds are a step up from being Kaffirs, though there are those who say they are a mixture of the worst of both races –"

"Or the best of both," Mary said. "As Seaforth certainly is."

"You always loved him too much," May said. "As if he were a son – because you don't have –"

Mary reddened again.

"You go too far, May."

"A wee bit more love in the family," Hamilton said, "would go a long way."

Yet was it love, Mary thought, that had made Seaforth first warn her against Harry Lamb? Or was it jealousy about losing her love? Or both?

"Seaforth said he had more opportunity in South Africa." Mary was still flushed in her defence of her favourite. "There is a sizeable Indian colony –"

"They imported coolies to build the railways," Charles said.

"An influential Indian group," Mary said. "So he has gone there. I think, in a way, Iain was quite relieved. Seaforth and Peg were always a reminder in India – and it is such a caste society, the Hindus and Us are equally bad, I don't know which is the worst. Peg has gone back, of course, and she is doing very well in the hospital at Bombay. But I don't have to tell you, Hamilton. Your father must keep in touch with you."

"Hardly at all," Hamilton said, "except to tell me of his mighty irrigation work in the Punjab. Have you heard from mother, May?"

"She does not write much," May said. "Everybody is well. Annandale is more of a courtesy club for Simla than a home now. Because Margaret's husband is an aide to the Viceroy, and there are the two children, Ruby and Wallace. There is a good deal of entertainment – although not quite on the English level."

"And poor Iain," Mary said, "is banished to his culverts and his drainpipes in the Punjab. He never could stand the Simla ladies."

"I am sure making drains for Indians," Charles said, "is very worthy work."

"Actually it is," Hamilton said. "More worthy than a Review of the Home Fleet."

"Are you suggesting, sir, that the British Navy is not the foundation of the Empire?"

"Only the policeman," Hamilton said, "on his beat. The foundation of the Empire is those who make it tick. Like my father."

As Charles glared at Hamilton, Mary intervened. She had fought down her agitation to a form of control. When there was too much to say, it was best to talk about little.

"And, May, how are your three? Gordon and Graham and little Ruth. In the pink, are they not?"

"Yes. The boys are down for Eton, but Ruth, we shall keep her with us at home. I feel that education quite spoils a girl's femininity."

"Oh," Mary said. "You think I am a male, then? It is the masculine in me, which appeals to poor Harry Lamb."

"You have said it, not I." Charles could not restrain his smile. "Before you came, Hamilton, we were saying how sorry we were that Doctor Lamb felt that he had to carry on his work in London through the Jubilee, whatever that work is —"

Again the insinuations. Could Charles not be quiet? Mary found herself saying coldly, "They think my husband may be Jack the Ripper."

"No," Hamilton said. "That gentle man? Impossible."

"Indeed," May said quickly. "I am sure my husband doesn't mean —" She stared so hard at Charles that it was now he who was flushing.

"No," he mumbled. "No offence meant, ma'am." Yet he had offended, even if he had called Mary 'ma'am' as if she was the Queen Herself.

"Forget it then," Hamilton said. "A misunderstanding. But there is bad news. I suppose you have heard, the Queen — she is not well. She may not see in the next century."

"God forbid," Charles said. "I thought the problem was the Prince of Wales. His leg —"

"She receives daily bulletins about that at Osborne from his yacht. Signor Marconi's new invention — the ship-to-shore wireless, he calls it. He hangs up electric wires on kites and masts — and you may now communicate from vessel to vessel or to port."

"Another one of your damned inventions," Charles said. "Semaphore is good enough for me. What you can't say with flags shouldn't be said at all."

Hamilton finished his rum in a gulp and signalled the waiter for some more.

"I don't know," he said. "No more turning blind eyes or deaf ears like Nelson. The right orders will go straight through to every ship's captain —"

"And where's the initiative, sir? That is the tradition of the navy."

"Communications," Hamilton said, "are more important."

Mary intervened again. "There is something I have to tell you all," she said. "That is the real reason I came down here. I have heard from Katie in Vancouver — only what we expect. Hannah is sore ill — and Hamish grieves for her. I think he will follow her. We must be ready to go to Canada, as many as can, the next year. For they will not see the next century, even if the Queen does."

"They will," May said. "They will always be with us."

"No," Mary said. And now other tears were falling from her eyes. But this was the weeping of pure grief, not of anger. "They were always with us, even though they took us away or left us. We would not be here if they were not always here. But soon —" She gave a sob. "We must go to them."

"We cannot go," May said quickly. "Even to see grandfather and grandmother. Charles has his duty, and I have the children."

"And your life here," Mary said. "But I will go."

"Perhaps your husband can spare you," Charles said.

"He will come with me," Mary said, "if his duty allows him."

"I will move heaven and earth to be with them," Hamilton said, "but I may be transferred. They say there's trouble at the Cape. They have need for ship's engineers to carry our troops to South Africa."

"I wish there was trouble in Canada," Mary said. "Then you could carry me there." Then she caught herself at her own words. "Of course, I do not wish that. Thank God, Canada is at peace. But we must be with them." She dabbed at her eyes with her handkerchief, then blew her nose to clear it in her forthright way. "Let us get there. All of us. However far we are scattered over the earth."

24

ALL THE CORNERS OF THE EARTH

"Lord, Thou has been our refuge: from one generation to another. Before the mountains were brought forth, or ever the earth and the world were made."

Mary stood by the open grave in the churchyard, looking down at the coffin, in which her father was hidden. The pit was dug by another grave, covered with roses, the grave of his wife, Hannah. He had not lived a week after her death. Something was broken in him. Mary had sat with him as he lingered, and now he was laid to rest, with the clergyman reading over his body from the Order for the Burial of the Dead.

"For a thousand years in Thy sight are but as yesterday: seeing that is past as a watch in the night. As soon as Thou scatterest them, they are even as a sleep: and fade away suddenly like the grass. In the morning it is green, and groweth up: but in the evening it is cut down, dried up and withered."

It was so. How long since they had moved from the glen to the shore and the kelping, how long since they came over the oceans to the shipwreck and the fever island and the forest and the great plains and on to the western shore of Canada? And she – how long a dairy maid in the Castle at Dunrobin, how long a parlour maid in the mansion at London, how long a nurse in the *zenanas* and in the famine in the Punjab? How had she lost both the men she had loved, Erskine Montgomery and Harry Lamb? They had never loved her back. Her yearning for them, her passion and desperation for their touch – they had withheld themselves from her. Erskine because of his mad wife, and Harry because he was like that, fearful of women, something killed within him in his fearsome trade, and now dead of a broken faith inside him, ripped open by the knives and scalpels of the tongues of London, accusing him of crimes he never had done and never could do. Yes, he had not loved to touch women, but he loved one woman – herself. Mary Sinclair, the widow Lamb, knew that. Not even his death would take the love of him away from her.

"Man that is born of a woman hath but a short time to live, and is full of misery. He cometh up, and is cut down, like a flower; he fleeth as it were a shadow, and never continueth in one stay. In the midst of life we are in death."

It was true, it was so true. All that nursing of the dying. Mary had spent her life by the beds of sufferers, and yet – *Man that is born of a woman hath but a short time to live.* No man was born of this woman Mary, but of Hannah, how many had been born and how many were still living, how few were cut down, like a flower. And she had no child, not a one. It was her right, and she had given it away in serving others all her life. A useless sacrifice for a barren womb. What was it for? Who was grateful? Not the sick. When they were well again. Who remembered? Not the married brothers and sisters, nieces and nephews, who looked at their old aunt and pitied her, the widow who had never had a proper man and never a child, condemned to be single now and an old woman. Even her father Hamish, who had been given so little from his long life had his Hannah until his last few days. And she had been given nothing but a bleak age. She was not pitying herself, she was telling herself the truth, and it was making her angry. And at her father's funeral, too.

It was the time to cast the earth down on the coffin. Mary picked up some loose clods and dropped them over the grave's edge. They thudded on the wooden lid. So did the lumps of soil thrown down by Angus and Isabella, by Bain and his wife that had been Julia Mackenzie. None of their children had been able to make the journey – indeed, Angus's eldest son was already in South Africa, serving in the Seaforths with his uncle. But Katie was at the grave side, sobbing below her black veil and clinging onto Marie, who only wore a small black cap like a pennant of death flying on her mass of red hair, her blazing beauty as shocking as lightning at this scene of grief.

When the rattle of earth on the coffin had ended like a volley of shots at a military funeral, Mary heard the voice of the priest read on from the service: "We therefore commit his body to the ground; earth to earth, ashes to ashes, dust to dust; in sure and certain hope of the Resurrection to eternal life, through Our Lord Jesus Christ; Who shall change our vile body."

Tears prickled in Mary's eyes, so that she could no longer see. A roaring was in her ears, and she swayed and felt Angus's hand under her elbow to keep her steady. She was blind, she was deaf to the end of the service. But when it was over, Angus took her away to the carriage covered with *crêpe* which would pull her behind black horses to the house by Vancouver Sound.

"They had nothing to leave us," Angus told the rest of the family, assembled over tea and cakes, which nobody ate. "Their old Bible in Gaelic – which none of us can read now – and a few trinkets. This house is in my name, as I built it for them. It was theirs as long as they lived ..."

"And now?" Mary said.

"If any of you should wish to bide here still. Mary, you have been here since Harry's death, helping to look after them. Will you stay on?"

"For a while," Mary said. "Then I must get my courage back, and go to the work in London. At St Thomas's Hospital, where Harry was and did so much. Miss Nightingale still expects, though God knows why she should." Her resentment suddenly spilled out of her. "What have I got from it all? She always expected too much."

"Too much," Angus said. "Isabella and I and the family will not be needing the house while my railroad work is still in South America. But we may retire here yet. And you, Katie, and Marie ..."

"I am going to London," Marie said. "The theatre there –"

"It is rubbish," Mary said. "Gaiety Girls. And the actresses who are not at the Empire –"

"The theatre there," Marie said, "is excellent. Mr Wilde and Mr Shaw and Mrs Campbell. Here, I can only sing and dance. There is no acting."

"How can you speak of that?" Bain was flushed with anger. "Your wickedness – it drove them to their graves! Flaunting yourself in the theatre – the music-hall!"

"She is the toast of Vancouver," Katie said. "I know mother disapproved – but if you are as beautiful as my daughter –"

"Vanity saith the preacher." Bain's wife Julia had little to be vain about, except for her strength. She was built like a plough. "There is some as have no time to prettify –"

"Or reason," Katie said.

"Julia helps me on the farm," Bain said. "And the boys, young as they are, Rob and Gillon. You're never too young to get eggs or muck out. You would not know the place, Mary. It is the barbed wire. It keeps out the beasts and the Indians."

"Your trouble always was," Mary said to Bain, "keeping people out. You have always kept the family out of the land you got from father."

"I have made it," Bain said. "There is wheat now, as far as the eye can see."

"It will blow away," Angus said, "the soil. Unless you engineer the ground – plant it with trees."

"Build your bridges," Bain said. "And your railroads. Leave farming to the likes of us. You left us – all of you left us – even Hamish and Hannah – you left me alone till Julia came, and now, the land is mine – ours, I mean." He put an arm round the shoulder of his wife. They looked hewn together.

"You would keep out my grandmother, Uncle Bain," Marie said. "She was a Crow, and I am so proud of her. My father Henri was. He always said I got my looks from my Indian grandmother and my brains from Katie."

Certainly, that was Marie's special beauty, the upflung cheek-bones under her green eyes, the bronze tint to her skin under her flaming hair, the spring to her taut body. To Katie, she was lovelier than sin or even the memory of her husband.

"If you have my brains," she said, "you will bide here and not gallivant off to London to try your luck on the stage."

"You will help me, Aunt Mary," Marie pleaded. "You will –"

"Acting is not my profession," Mary said. "Nursing is." Marie was too striking for her own good – or anybody else's. She would have everything that Mary had never had. Men would give it to her, and they had given Mary nothing. A stab of jealousy pierced the side of the older woman, and then she was ashamed of it. Marie was her kin. Marie was asking for her help. "I will see what I can do if you come to London. But I promise nothing. You should heed your mother and stay."

"Oh, thank you." Marie impetuously threw herself on her aunt and hugged her and kissed her, not on the cheek, but on the mouth.

"Get away with you, girl," Mary said and pushed her niece away, but she was smiling as she shook her head. Ach, the energy of the young. But it was good to be needed. "I dinna promise, but I will try to help you."

"My mother says you can do anything and everything," Marie said, "if you only want to."

"That I cannot, Katie," Mary said, but she was smiling now at the recognition. "Everything I canna do. But when I put my mind to it –"

"Angus says the same," Isabella said. "Now it is you who will hold the family together. In a family, there must be one –"

"But Iain," Bain said.

"Is he here?"

"And Hamish Jamie."

"Is he here? No." Isabella smiled at Mary. "It is you, Mary, who will be our Hamish and our Hannah."

A kind of peace began to steal over Mary. Yes, Hamish and Harry Lamb were laid to rest. But she would go on. Childless she might be, but there were all her parents' children, and their children's children to new generations. If Isabella was right, they would come to her. Because she was single, she would be fair or try to be. She would give her love equally, although her special Seaforth ... Mary smiled at her weakness for him, but she would be the judge and jury and court of appeal of them all.

Now she was given her rôle, she would use it. She walked over to the table and took up the tea-pot to go round the room in the ritual pouring that was the quiet wake at this funeral. None of the Gaelic fiddling and the drinking. This was the sober ceremony of a family that had gone a long way, and still had a long way to go.

"Thank you all for coming to this burying," Mary said. "It was a sore journey to come here – but not so sore as it was for Hannah and Hamish. But they are at last at rest. They have found peace."

She began to pour from the pot into Julia's cup. "More tea?"

In London, another aged woman was fulfilling her role after sixty years of doing it. From Her wheel-chair, Queen Victoria pressed an electric button in Buckingham Palace before She rode in Her open landau pulled now by eight cream horses to St Paul's for her Diamond Jubilee. The night had been hot. The Queen Empress was restless. She was not sure that She could support the occasion, driving six miles through the cheering crowds and listening to a short service from the steps of the cathedral. "No," one of Her German friends had complained, "after sixty years reign, to thank God in the Street!" Yet she was too lame to climb stairs, and Her people wanted to thank God for Her reign in the streets. And so She would go. Already the beacons had blazed all across the Highlands of Scotland from Ben Nevis to Her beloved Balmoral. And the signal on the button was using the telephone to send a message to every last corner of Her empire. "From my heart I thank my beloved people, May God bless them!"

The noon was the Queen's weather, as at the Golden Jubilee. When the first salvo of guns in Hyde Park announced that She had left the Palace, the sun burst out from the grey skies and blazed down all day. Triumphal arches spanned the route, picked out in tributes: OUR HEARTS THY THRONE or SHE WROUGHT HER PEOPLE LASTING GOOD. Tiny gas-jets flared and the new electric-light bulbs glistened like constellations fallen from the heavens. And with the Queen in the carriage sat Alix, Princess of Wales, in lilac, and a favourite daughter Lenchen. Her two elder sons rode on either side of the landau, Her youngest Arthur to the rear. The Commander-in-Chief, Lord Garnet Wolseley, rode in front, while the tallest man in the British Army, Captain Ames of the Life Guards, headed the whole procession. All the imperial forces which were not guarding Her domains marched or rode past, Bengal Lancers and Ghurkas, the West African Rifles and the Black Watch from Canada. The shouting and the hurrahs from millions of throats quite deafened Her Majesty who was already hard of hearing.

"No one ever, I believe, has met with such an ovation," She recorded that night. "The crowds were quite indescribable, and their enthusiasm truly marvellous and deeply touching."

Hamish Jamie thought it was stupid from the beginning. Advancing into the jaws of a dragon. Hills to the left of them, kopjes to the right of them, and a strong scarp to the front. You couldn't see the Boers, of course, they were too sly for that, hidden under their slouch hats with their repeating Mausers that gave out more rapid fire than the Lee-Metfords, and even better artillery: Creusot Long Toms and Krupp field-pieces and Vickers-Maxim pom-poms lobbing their little one-pound shells in bursts of twenty and blowing up gun crews and crowded infantry in clusters of explosions. The Boers had been clever. They had used their gold to arm in good time. They had better weapons than the British, and they fought from the ground like ferrets or wildcats. Hamish Jamie did not like the Highland Brigade going at dawn into the jaws of death in four massed columns, soaked to the skin after the deluge of the night. And he did not like going in himself. The quartermaster led from the rear.

Yet if General Wauchope was himself leading the Black Watch, with the Seaforths along with the Argyll and Sutherland Highlanders on the flank backed by the Highland Light Infantry in reserve, Hamish Jamie felt he would have to join the action, even if it were his last action. Also Angus's son Hamish Charles was in the regiment. The young fool had volunteered fresh from Harrow, following the footsteps of that other young fool at Omdurman, Winston Churchill, who had also come to beat the Boers. Hamish Jamie felt he had to keep an eye on another nephew. He had already lost one in South Africa.

Nobody knew the Boer trenches were at the foot of the ridges instead of on the top of them, where they should have been. Having no military experience, the Boers did better than those who knew how things should be done. For they did the unexpected, and it worked. They sprang their trap and surprise that dawn at Magersfontein from their bolt-holes behind barbed-wire fences hung with tin cans. The night advance of the Highland Brigade in its columns, linked with ropes to keep their masses perfectly aligned so they might suffer the worst from the Boer Mausers, blundered into the trip-wires. A hailstorm of bullets and pom-poms killed five hundred men in ten minutes.

"Fix bayonets! Charge!" Hamish Jamie heard the hopeless orders yelled in the gloom. Then at the back, another shout, "Retire!" And round him men in kilts stumbling forward, standing still, retreating – and all the time dropping and bending and falling, hurled down by the relentless fusillade to their front. He saw a few men reach the barbed wire and collapse, spread-eagled, on that final metal barrier, sieved with blood and bullet-holes. Ahead of him, General Wauchope was hit, a red spray gushing from his mouth. And Hamish Jamie found himself cradling his dying commander in his arms, hearing the cough and froth of the last words, "Goodbye, men. Fight for yourselves. It's man to man now."

It was not. It was repeating rifles and barbed wire that stopped any man to man. As Hamish Jamie laid down the body of Wauchope and rose to stagger forward at the impossible charge, he saw for the first time the broken Highlanders retreat or take cover behind the ant-hills from the murdering storm of the Boer volleys. He knew he was as good as dead. Where his nephew and namesake, Hamish Charles, was in this massacre at dawn, Hamish Jamie did not know. But he knew he must move forward. And when the bullet hit him in the chest and knocked him to the ground, it was almost a relief. The blow was like a pardon. He had done his duty. He could not go on. He could only lie on his back, watching the sun rise over the kopjes, and feeling his life gasp away from his shattered ribs and pierced lung. He sensed a dry smile on his face, then his lips moved to say, "After all that – and you will not have to pay my pension the now."

The rest of the Highlanders were staked out on the dry plain without food or water for the whole broiling day to follow, unable to raise their heads or move, stranded and sweating and beaten down before the enemy, overseeing their humiliation. Hamish Charles's dreams of glory were lowered to the red dust he inhaled from the ant-heap that was his only cover. The insects were active in the full sun, crawling over his bare knees and stinging him into movement, which unleashed a whirr of bullets worse than swarming bees. All around him were the cries and moans of the wounded, the dreadful sing-song of defeat. His own throat was too parched to cry, and by the afternoon, there was stillness except for the Lyddite shells of the British guns and the running explosions of the Boer pom-poms in their intermittent arguments.

War shouldn't be like this, Hamish Charles thought. We always charge. We always win. We're fighting a bunch of Dutch dirt farmers. What bloody fool sent us into this death-trap? Someone had blundered. And then someone else was singing, "Over the Sea to Skye." And a lad from the Seaforths had gone mad in the sun and was wandering towards the barbed-wire and the hidden Mausers, singing the old lament for the Stuart kings:

> "Speed, bonny boat, like a bird on the wing,
>   Onward the sailors cry,
>   Speed for the man who was born to be king
>   Over the sea —"

A crackle and a thudding and a scream stopped the song, and Hamish Charles kept his head down until evening, until he could stumble back to the rear, over the corpses of the Highlanders who made wounds of flesh and tartan across the plain. He did not find the body of his uncle, who had died towards noon, and glad of it, in the end.

The news of the defeat at Magersfontein and the death of Hamish Jamie and the survival of his cousin reached Hamilton at Simonstown in the lee of the wild tableland of the Cape of Good Hope itself. He immediately sent a runner to find Seaforth and bring him to the naval base to tell him of his father's death. While he was waiting for him, Hamilton supervised the coaling of his new frigate, for the power of the British navy now depended on pyramids of best Welsh coal and coke, shipping out to dozens of dockyards and bases and stations across the world. Simonstown itself was like a home base with its pretty cottages and villas and whitewashed sailors' barracks and naval stores and a church with a steeple and the Admiral's House with its rose-gardens leading to a quay, where the flagship and the squadron lay. Wherever the empire went, Hamilton had observed, the British took their surroundings with them. Even at the tip of Africa, he stood on a piece of England.

Seaforth was not moved by the news of his father's death at Magersfontein. "He was too old for it," he told Hamilton. "He should never have joined the attack. His job was getting the supplies up, not getting killed. That is for fools like Hamish Charles – and he survived."

"Stopping a bullet has nothing to do with justice," Hamilton said. He signalled the mess waiter for another drink of lemonade for Seaforth, whose frock coat and black bow-tie made him look like a visiting ambassador to the all-white officers of the Fleet.

"Stopping bullets has a lot to do with medicine," Seaforth replied. "I am dealing with your casualties all the time. Horrible wounds – dum-dums, explosive bullets, lacerations from barbed wire. Although the Army medical corps is better now, they can't cope with all your wounded – and they have to call on me. I must say, you are taking a beating from the Boers."

"And which side are you on?" Hamilton said, all too conscious of a senior captain cocking an ear from the next armchair. He might be hanged from the yard-arm for treason.

"Not the Boers. I find their attitude to people they called Coloured even more extreme than yours."

"Whose, Seaforth?"

"Not you personally, Hamilton. But you see, my father –"

"Your dead father –"

"Dying with the Seaforths at the hands of other white men – not Indians, because he survived the Mutiny. Killed by the latest techniques of western war. Myself, patching up the badly wounded – their lives in these hands –" Turning up the pale palms of his dark hands to Hamilton – "Begging me to save their lives... You must see, Hamilton, it is quite a reversal."

"I do see," Hamilton said. "But Aunt Mary, she saw you trained as a doctor."

"Yes. A wonderful woman. And now Peg is a fully-qualified woman doctor in Bombay. It is remarkable what British women have done for the Empire. But as for the men, I am not so sure."

"Are you staying on here, Seaforth?"

"I am doing well. But if the Boers win their independence ..."

"They will not."

"I will go back to India and see what I may do about ours."

"We will never let India go. It is the jewel – the Koh-i-noor."

"I know that. It just makes our independence more difficult. I always wonder why the Scots are taking so long to ask for their independence back."

"We are a United Kingdom."

"Really? Ireland too?"

"You go for the sore spots, Seaforth."

Seaforth smiled his thin black smile.

"That is why I am a doctor." He rose. "I must go back to your wounded, Hamilton. Thank you for telling me about my father's death."

"You seem to have his independence," Hamilton said drily.

"Fair enough. My regards to that idiot Hamish Charles and tell him to stay out of the line of fire. The Boers are very good shots. And if you do see Aunt Mary when you go back to England —"

"Yes, I will."

"Tell her, I love her still. She kept her promise to my mother about Peg and me. And she will be proud of us yet."

"She is to head the nurses' school at St Thomas's ..."

"If you have the gift of self-sacrifice," Seaforth said, "I am afraid you will lose yourself and only be left with the sacrifice. Who is Mary herself? She is all given to us."

A thousand wax candles made a flickering firmament under the high arches and vaultings and aisles of the abbey. On this matins of the new century, the great and the good, or at least the famous and the invited, were giving their thanks in Westminster Abbey to the Lord of Hosts. The Almighty had led the nation to become almighty upon the waters He had made, and upon a quarter of the dry lands He had also made to push back the waters. Standing beneath the marble images of previous rulers, so Roman and imperial in their still statues and busts over her, Mary Sinclair was moved to join in this paean of praise which appeared to be for the glory of God. Yet given the fervour of the singing, it might be in praise of the British people themselves. Strange it was, that the small population of two inconsiderable islands off Europe had spread themselves so thin and wide across the globe and had webbed and netted the seven seas. There might be a divine purpose in it, there must be a heavenly intervention. For the achievement was against all the odds. As it had been for the daughters and sons of Hamish and Hannah Sinclair, a scattering and a fulfilling.

And now the massed congregation were singing the *Venite*, "Come and Let Us Sing Unto the Lord." And the strains swept up past the stone images and the monuments with their swords and crowns and emblems to the roof of ancient England, Norman and Tudor and

Stuart and Hanoverian, and the Britain of the aged Queen Victoria at the apogee of Her empire.

"For the Lord is a great God," they sang, "and a great king above gods. In His hands are all the corners of the earth."

Yes, they were, and in the hands of the British. And the Scots and the Sinclairs were flung to the corners to hold them.

"And the strength of the hills is His also."

For the Scots and the Sinclairs would endure where they were posted. The strength of the hills was theirs, that was the gift of the Lord.

"The sea is His, and He made it: and His hands prepared the dry land."

Hamilton was on the steam ships, and the ships held together the seas and the seas brought them from one far land to another shore.

"For He is the Lord our God: and we are the people of His pasture, and the sheep of His land."

There would be a homecoming for all of them hurled to the far corners of the earth. If not for their children, then for the children of their children. And the sheep which had made their clearing would now be cleared as all beasts were cleared. And the humans who were the true sheep of His land would be restored to His pasture of the Highlands.

"Forty years long was I grieved with this generation, and said: It is a people that do err in their hearts, for they have not known My ways."

What were His ways? What were their errors? They had been banished for forty years and more to the edges of the earth. But they were already coming home. Perhaps they had loved their high places too much, perhaps they had been cast down and cast away for their pride. There was no answer in it, but there seemed a kind of forgiveness, for the new generations at the least, at last.

And now Mary sang in full voice with the choirs and the believers in the Abbey of Westminster.

"As it was in the beginning, is now and ever shall be. World without end. Amen."

THE STRENGTH OF THE HILLS

1

BLACK WEEK

1899

Even in Black Week, the starch on the nurses' bonnets had to be whiter than white. Mary Sinclair saw to that, just as Miss Nightingale had seen to that. A snow peak on the nurses' hair as pure and stiff as one of those Alps. "If you dinna show clean," Mary used to say to the novices, "you canna be clean. If the patient, he looks at you and sees a dirty sister, will he not think he will end in a dirty grave? I will not say, Cleanliness is next Godliness, but I will say, Keep your aprons proper, wash your hands, and thank God for the carbolic."

The first of the wounded from the Boer War had begun to reach St Thomas's Hospital after the long voyage home on the hospital ships. Mary had seen it all before in India and the African campaigns, the men without a leg or an arm, still thinking they had one and saying, "Move the blanket, it's hurting my foot," when the foot was not there at all. The soldiers bandaged round their head with their jaw or cheek shot away, and they had to eat through a funnel or suck through a straw. And the lying bodies that were alive, but had the shrapnel or a bullet in the spinal column, and so they could not move, but the young nurses had to shift them on the hour to stop the bedsores and to use the bedpan. Ach, a man was a man for all that, and there was not a bit of a man that her nurses did not know.

Yet she could not bide here, in the office that had been Harry Lamb's before he died, her poor husband. She stroked the oak desk with her fingers, his desk where she had sat all afraid on the other side on their first meeting, the wood so smooth it put the wrinkles on her ageing hands to shame. Poor Harry! He would have had his work cut out, trying to repair the damage done by the field surgeons out in the veldt after all the disasters of trying to fight the Boers. But now she might be sent out herself on a last mission, the only matron they could trust with the experience to run a floating ambulance. Lady Randolph Churchill and her rich American friends were equipping a hospital ship, the *Maine* was its name. And there was nobody to manage the nurses, nobody but her old self that the War Office would trust. For had not Miss Nightingale put her trust in Mary Sinclair, who had never let her down.

Mary rose to take her cloak and call a hansom cab. She had never liked the rich ladies. She had never forgotten her first days as a parlour maid in London, after the clearing of her family from the Highlands and its scattering to the far corners of the earth. All those airs and graces the duchess had used to put her down, all the dirty linen below the frills and the flowers. But Lady Churchill was better, being an American, though sometimes those not born to it were the worse for it. For when they took on their new high position, they went too far, fearing they would be found out to be not what their lifted noses said they were. What had Harry told her? "Some are born noble, some achieve nobility, and some have it thrust upon them. Those are the true scum, the guttersnipes in coronets."

The crowds in Westminster and Mayfair were hushed and draggity, with only the watercress-girls and the muffin-men crying their wares. "Cress, cress, penny a bunch!" and "Who'll buy my lovely hot crumpets?" The illness of Queen Victoria, nearly ninety now, and the three defeats in a week in South Africa, they had cast a dark veil over the end of the year. You would have thought in the weeks before Christmas and the turn of the year into a new century in 1900, there would be singing in the streets and bright colours on the pavements, not only the red tunics of the bandsmen still not turned to khaki as the new uniforms were now, but the players blowing the brass and the pipes in the gay tunes of war. Yet no music sounded in this late afternoon of Black Week, only the rattle of the carriage wheels and the crack of the coachman's whip on the hindquarters of his stumbling horses.

Lady Churchill was waiting with her committee of ladies to receive Mary Sinclair in Grosvenor Square, and she was welcomed as if she were a poor relation who owed more service.

"I do not know if you have family there," Lady Churchill said. "My young son Jack is out there with the South African Light Horse, and, as you know, Winston is a war correspondent for the *Morning Post*. He was captured on an armoured train, but he is alive, thank God. And knowing Winston, I very much doubt if the Boers can keep him for long. We could never keep him at home. Always breaking out. You know what young men are, to be sure."

"I do that," Mary Sinclair said, "though I have none of my own. But I have two nephews, Hamilton with the ships – he looks for the engines – and Hamish Charles with the Seaforths like my poor brother was – he was killit at Magersfontein." Mary could not stop her Scots tongue breaking out, faced with the high condescension of the English voice. "And I hear another is coming from Canada – Robert, my brother Bain's boy – all the way from his farm on the prairie. It is not his war, but he will come, for he is a cowboy, you could think he had hoofs, not two feet. And this Lord – Strathcona, you ken? – he asked for the Mounties and the cowboys to ride for him over the water and teach the Boers there were other hard men on ponies as good as they were."

"My son is in the Hussars," a lady in a green shroud spoke now. "And I have a nephew in the Lancers. I am sure we do not have any need of this colonial cavalry."

"My brother Iain did say, when he was with the Highlanders in the Crimea and the Mutiny, that devil a bit the regular cavalry did, on their fancy gee-gees riding into the guns. Horsemeat with ribbons on."

Lady Churchill coughed discreetly. "Strategy is not our province. Let us leave it to the men."

"And look what a fair mess they have made of it," Mary said. "Losing to the Dutchmen three times in a week."

"You have the best reputation in London, Matron Lamb, for managing a hospital. Lord Robert himself has heard of your services in past campaigns. Through the generosity of these ladies present –" a slow sweep of Lady Churchill's mauve silk arm indicated the other members of the committee with their pinched waists and swelling corsages, "– the *Maine* has been fitted with the very latest in medical equipment. There is even something called an X-Ray, I believe, that can actually see through the body and detect a broken bone. Splendid, is it not?"

"If it is only a bone broken," Mary said, "a soldier will thank his luck for it."

"And we have plate glass on our operating table. And we have room for more than two hundred patients in four large wards and an isolation ward for dangerous cases."

"Typhoid," Mary said. "Cholera and malaria. Enteric and black-water fever. They'll carry off more than the bullets ever will."

"There are also splendid quarters for the nurses and the doctors and the medical orderlies. We see no reason that they should suffer as well as our soldiers."

"Most considerate," Mary said. "In my experience it is not many that think a nurse may suffer too."

"American women know it," Lady Churchill said. "We know it is our function to foster and nourish the suffering. And we are more adept at it, we believe, than any others."

"Will any of your ladies," Mary asked drily, "be coming with us the now to do what you are adept at? Or are you sending us to do it for you?"

There was a silence in the drawing-room, then a woman in a long cerise skirt and red bodice said with severity, "We have our duties here. Our husbands, our commitments. We would all welcome the opportunity to do what you will do. Do not think that because a woman's place is in the home, that she does not nurse the sick and the dying there. I have lost three children, matron, in my time. Very slowly with many tears. Have you?"

"Not personally," Mary said. "But I have watched die the hundreds of children of other mothers. You are right, I ken that. Every home is a hospital. We have not enough of them. And a big home like this –" her eyes moved up a marble pillar to the lofty ceiling with its frieze of fleur-de-lys and stucco roses below the chandeliers "– what a lot of dying there must have been in here. All those people, all those rooms, and it nearly the size of St Thomas's. Where there's high living, there's a high dying too. Now, Lady Churchill, if we can get to the detail. The how, when and where. And as for the why, as you say, it is the province of the men. I dinna ken why we are fighting some dirt farmers in slouch hats for a piece of dry veldt. But I ken that there's never a good enough why to fight any war, but if there is a war, why we must go in and patch up the poor men that are fighting. Or if they do not ken the why, the order is good enough for them, as it is good enough for me."

"You do not sound very patriotic," Lady Churchill said.

"And you Americans are so?" Mary smiled at the circle of ladies around her. "For our Empire? Is that not a strange thing?"

"I have sons there as I said." Lady Churchill rose. "I would not fall behind in my duty." She reached out her hand to Mary. "They said you were most direct, Matron Lamb. And as you are, I will direct you to the how, when and wherefore of this hospital ship. For arguing the whys will not cure a single soldier."

"That it will not," Mary said, taking Lady Churchill's hand. "But bless you all for doing all you can do for them."

The Dutchmen had put barbed wire under the Tugela River. It was a damnable trick. It hooked your puttees and dragged you down. If the Mausers and the pom-poms didn't get you, the waters choked you. A fire storm above, a snare below. When a bullet or shrapnel didn't stop you, drowning did. Why, he could make the Irish Brigade charge over

mountains and deserts and marshes, Colonel Thackeray knew that.
But running into a loop of sandbanks opposite the Boers in their
trenches the other side of the river, that was sticking your nose into a
noose. So the survivors of the Dublins and Connaughts and Borderers
and Inniskillings were trapped on a skillet, grilling in the glare of the
sun. And if they poked their head up to fire back, *ker-phut* the bullets
were a whiplash in the sand or a hole in the brain-pan. All to save
those damn-fool navy guns that had gone too far forward, and now
the Dutchmen were swimming the river and hauling them away. And
the Irish had to stay put and lie low like badgers in the earth, only this
was powder. Dust to dust and ashes to ashes, Thackeray thought, into
the tomb the colonel dashes. His laugh at his jingle turned into a
cough. And the moaning of his wounded men and the neighing and
rattle of the shattered horses in their harnesses were the winds of
dying.

Funny that the Red Cross should save them from surrender. The
Irish never surrendered, but even so, behind the stretcher-bearers
coming up with their white flag and the bloody crucifix set on it, there
was a cordon of Dutchmen tightening the hangman's knot. But
Thackeray wasn't having any of that. It was as sneaky as the wires
under the water. The bearded burgher in the slouch hat might shout
out, "Surrender, *kakies*, or we will kill you, by God." But Thackeray
was ready for him. He jumped up and gave the Dutchman a dressing-
down. "That's not sporting," he said. "Coming up behind the Red
Cross. That's not a fair fight."

Now the Dutchman laughed. "Dom fools," he said. "We shoot you
like *diuker* – stembuck –"

"Not behind a white flag," Thackeray said. "The devil you don't.
You go back where you came from. And we'll begin the battle over
again."

Again the Dutchman laughed. "Well," he said, "I won't look at you
while you take your men away." And he turned his back on Thackeray
to face his own cordon of men. "We don't want prisoners," he said.
"Let the *kakies* go. Dom fools – but brave fools."

And so Colonel Thackeray called up his men from the sandpits
they had made with their prone bodies, and each soldier who could
stand and even the walking wounded, they were the crutches for those
who had stopped one in the leg or the body, while the stretcher-
bearers took up the maimed and the mutilated who still breathed and
could not hobble. And as Colonel Thackeray walked among them, he
saw that the carriers of his shattered brigades were Indians, *char-
wallahs* and coolies. Had this war against bush farmers and small town

burghers brought the Empire down to that? Brown hands strapping the bloody khaki with white bandages, brown arms and brown legs bearing the heavy bodies of the Irish to the field hospitals, brown heads wearing old helmets and bowlers and tam o' shanters. It couldn't happen in Connaught.

Now they reached the ambulance waggons, which would take the wounded back to the field hospitals and the operating tents. The stretchers were shipped aboard, the non-walking wounded hoisted on. And the mules pulled the vehicles over the rocky ground, pitching and tossing like drunken ships on a choppy sea. The walking soldiers and the bearers running behind heard groans and shrieks and curses, a barrage of pain. Blue flies hovered over the canvas flaps in clouds that buzzed. And when the soldiers reached the three operating tents to the rear, it was a factory. The victims were laid out in rows on straw, waiting their turn under the knives of the teams of surgeons. Every man who could drink was given a mug of hot Bovril from boiling cans outside. And Dr Seaforth Sinclair, taking a break after three hours of hacking and stitching at the operating tables, saw a drummer boy no more than fourteen years old, as he sat against a wall by the boiling Bovril with his left arm a mangled mess. With his right hand, he was eating a biscuit. And one of those staff officers, who never saw enough of a fight to ruffle a side-whisker, he took half-a-crown from his pocket and gave it to the drummer boy. The lad said, "Thank you, but would you mind putting it in my pocket. I mustn't let go of the biscuit."

Fury at the boy's taking of the condescending gift sent Seaforth into the field hospital. Dr Treves, Surgeon to Queen Victoria Herself, was already there before him. He was kneeling beside a small young man, lying almost like a baby in the womb, strapped round the groin with a bright red loincloth. This infant had to be important for Treves to be there, giving him chloroform to dull his agony. Seaforth knelt too, not in mercy, but in curiosity.

"May I help, Mr Treves?"

"Hold the pad over his mouth." Treves offered Seaforth the soaked gauze, and Seaforth slipped it between the face and the knees of the shape, doubled in a ball on the straw. With his palm, he smothered the breathing of the dying youth, forcing him to inhale, choking and sneezing.

"That will ease him," Treves said.

The two doctors knelt and waited for the gasping to die to a low grunting. Then Treves stood up, followed by Seaforth.

"That's Freddy Roberts," he said. "Lord Bobs's son. If we could only get him out here. Instead of that butcher Buller."

"I agree," Seaforth said. "Another frontal attack at Colenso. It was as bad as Magersfontein." He paused and gave the thin smile that always warned the British of a surprise. "My father was killed there."

"Father?" Treves was surprised. "I thought you were an —" Treves stopped himself in time. "Of course, your name is Sinclair."

"You thought I was an Indian," Seaforth said. "My mother was. My father was in the Seaforths. That explains my name."

"You're a fine surgeon," Treves said diplomatically. "Where did you train?"

"St Thomas's in London. Do you know my Aunt Mary? She was married to Harry Lamb. He was a doctor there."

"Of course. The best, Harry was. Simply the best. And your aunt, too — all that work she did for Miss Nightingale in India. Now we must get back to work."

He looked down at the unconscious Freddy Roberts, then he led the way towards the door of the field hospital. Already rain was tapping on the roof, and it was nearly dark. "We must get tarpaulins over the men out there," Treves said, then heard a voice at his feet, "Doctor, I can't move them." And Treves dropped on his knees again, where a wounded gunner with a blistered red face was sitting against a bale of straw, looking at his legs laid out in two logs in front of him.

"Where were you hit, man?" Treves asked.

"In the back. In the spine. I must walk again. Man the guns."

"We will try. I pray that you do." Treves stood up again and walked away, and as Seaforth followed him out into the wet he heard the gunner say to himself, "So I was in time for the fun."

The stretcher-bearers were already covering the soldiers waiting for their operations with canvas and tarpaulins. They were themselves drenched, their tattered khaki tunics sticking to their thin backs. And as Seaforth came up to Treves, he heard him say to the Indian bearers, "Good work. Keep it up. We'll operate on them all and get them ready for you to put on the hospital train as soon as we can."

"Perhaps you think I should be among them." As Seaforth said the words, he wished he had not said them. "As an Indian I should know my place." He could have bitten his tongue out.

Treves looked down at the lying soldiers spitting out the rain that fell in their open mouths. "Perhaps you think I should be among them," he said.

Seaforth was shocked into a straight answer. "Of course not."

"Your place is curing them with me, Mr Sinclair."

And so they went back to the operating tent, where the sound of the fusillades of heaven on the canvas was louder than the pom-poms and the Mausers, and the amputation of limbs was worse than the scything of human bodies by shrapnel, and the dropping of human arms and legs into the waste buckets thumped on the zinc like mortar shells. Seaforth took his own skills for granted, but now he marvelled at the steadiness of the surgeons and the silence of the soldiers under the saw and scalpel. Chloroform helped, but courage had much to do with it.

The eight hundred men in need of immediate surgery were not all treated until dawn, when the rain at last had stopped. Some fifty of them died, the rest were to be shifted by train to convalesce down at the Cape. Going outside red-handed and red-eyed, Seaforth saw the Indian bearers waiting patiently on the grass, wrapped in drenched cloaks they had improvised from tent flaps. He went over to the nearest of them and squatted beside him.

"They are treating you like dogs," he said. "Why are you fighting their war?"

"Why are you?"

"I am a doctor. I must."

"Gandhi tell us —"

"Gandhi?"

"Mohandas Gandhi. We are from Natal. He is barrister. He says, if we show loyal to the Empire, then — then they give India back to us."

"When's that?" Seaforth was incredulous.

"When the war over."

"Your Gandhi's a fool." Seaforth stood up. "We will have to take India ourselves." He saw Treves walking towards him from the operating tent. "These men have been out all night. They are being treated like animals."

"War turns us all into animals," Treves said. "Dogs in the rain. There is no shelter for them. We do what we can."

"It is because they are Indians. Volunteers for the Empire."

"You do not pity them, Mr Sinclair." For the first time, Treves's voice was as sharp as a blade. "You pity yourself too much. You really shouldn't. I had a patient once — now he had every reason to pity himself — but he never did. He even met the Royal Family —"

"Oh, your freak!" Seaforth grimaced with his black lips. "The Elephant Man! All his patrons, his noble patrons. They went to see him for his deformity —"

"For his dignity, actually." Treves looked at two bearers putting a soldier with two legs gone onto a stretcher as delicately as a baby into a cot. The only sound was their feet slushing on the wet grass. "Does anyone complain here? Only you, I think. We help one another. Or we will become animals, like elephants and not men – even when the war is over."

Seaforth was ashamed, but he was also bitter that he was ashamed. That damned conscience his Aunt Mary had implanted in him. That hook the British could always tweak to make their subjects feel small. And he felt even lower, when Treves put an arm round his shoulder and said, "I'm whacked. Help me in, Sinclair. We need a hot drink. And thank you for all your help."

If you could give the Strand and Piccadilly the name of London, then London had never seen anyone like Marie Sinclair, and she had never seen a city like London. Her proud Crow beauty, the bronze flush in her cheek under the slant of the bone, the green eyes that slit in laughter and blazed in song, the body that quivered as a knife flung into wood, the stride as lithe as a Greek runner, the whip of her step and the leap of her dance and the shake of her loose red hair. She was the first woman to wear Indian buckskin leggings on stage and off in the street without being a male impersonator. With her slipper, she could kick a champagne glass raised to toast her out of a swell's hand, and she could do hand-springs and back-flips all across the Domino Room of the Café Royal. Then her body was reflected a hundred times in the opposing mirrors, brighter than the infinite vista of exuberant gilding and crimson velvet, a caryatid of grace fallen down from the wall to somersault through the blue cigar smoke. And she never made even one domino fall on the marble tables of the artists and gamblers. Monsieur Gérard should have escorted her away, but how could he exclude such talent and beauty any more than he could throw out that outrageous faun Augustus John with his gold earrings and red shirt, almond eyes and quicksilver lust?

When she had come to London from Vancouver, Marie had made her way straight to Charles Morton and his Theatre of Varieties. He looked like a fat cherub of a banker or a solicitor, yet Morton knew his Music Hall. In fact, he had invented it at the Canterbury over the river and had saved the Alhambra and the Tivoli on the Strand with his shows. Of course, Richard D'Oyly Carte had built the terracotta Palace on Cambridge Circus as The Royal English Opera House, but to tell the truth, only Queen Victoria had liked Sir Arthur Sullivan's opera *Ivanhoe* when it was put on there. After a time, the shares cost

pennies, until Morton came along with his motto, "One Quality Only
– the Best." Of course, it did mean what you meant by the best.

The trouble with Music Hall was, the ladies could not go to it, and
places like the Empire with its Lounge were really knocking-shops for
the chorus girls and the young blades about town. But the Palace was
a palace of the variety show, and anyone could take a grandmother to
tickle her fancy, if she could still remember she had one. Marie was a
natural. She had faced down the frost-bitten miners coming back from
the Klondike in Vancouver halls, she had none of that shy holding
back that was the curse of the English artistes except for Marie Lloyd,
she was all brass and sauce.

And the horses! She could gentle a gee-gee and giddy-up a stallion
till they were hot wax to her act. The audiences went wild at her
mastery of the beast, which they loved better than a wife or a husband
or even a child. She would ride bare-back on her white pony onto the
boards, then chant as she circled its body, first round its belly and back
astride, then over its hind quarters and up under its tail, never
touching the ground while every man Jack thought a hoof would kick
her head in. Then round the neck of the brute with its straining
muscles swelling to the sex of her, and her song rising to its high note:

"Pony of the prairie,
Come for me –
Indian Kathleen
In my teepee.
Pony of the prairie,
Take me where
The wind is wanton
In my hair.
Take me, take me –"

The white pony bucking and pawing now, sweating under the
sinuous body, encircling and embracing its hot hide, not daring to
bolt; the energy as electric as the new house lights that blazed instead
of the old spluttering candles; and Marie ending her enticement of the
beast and the thousand spectators just a jot and tittle short of how far
the Lord Chamberlain and his blue pencil would tolerate her show:

"Take me true
Over the prairie –
I am you –"

Then Marie would catapult onto tiptoe on the pony's back, and cry, "Take me!", and the white horse would rear now, with Marie only steadying herself with one hand on its mane and her feet still on its spine. Then it would kick away off-stage into a stall full of bales of straw with Marie shouting, "Take me! Take me!" and the house thundering with clapping hands and hurrahs, the men's faces red with passion and the women's pink with jealousy and envy.

Going down Shaftesbury Avenue to the Trocadero, Marie could not stop the urchins yelling, "Take me! Take me!" and the mashers sidling up with their propositions, "Take you – I'd take you anywhere." But nobody dared molest her, the pride of the Palace, the toast of the Strand.

It took a while for Marie to persuade her Aunt Mary to meet her at the Café Royal for dinner after the show, to be held not in the Domino Room – shades of Oscar Wilde and Bosie Douglas, scandal and ruin – but in the restaurant upstairs, where the best cellar in the world was lifted to accompany some of the better grub.

Mary found the way to that culinary heaven quite stimulating, but as she lifted the skirts of her long bombazine dress, she wondered if it was the right thing to wear. At least, black did not show the dirt if the hem dragged on the red carpet on the stairs. She did not know what the allegories meant on the walls with their swirls and symbols, but the gilt railings and little grove of shrubs and flowers in the waiting-room at the top of the stairs were bonny.

The big dining-rooms beyond were partitioned by screens of mirrors, but Mary did not dare sit down in one of the easy-chairs, scooped out by the weight of many a large man. She would never have got out of it again. Instead, she sat on a small cane chair and looked up at the domed glass roofing that gave the great room the look of a greenhouse at Kew. So tight was her dress that Mary felt like a potted plant, her feet crammed like roots into her button shoes. She needed some care from a gardener. And she was glad that Marie came bounding up the stairs, her wide ochre skirt flailing round the skip and hop of her legs, her red hair burning in a comet's tail behind her.

"Aunt Mary," she cried, "I got you here – into the house of sin!"

Never was Mary better treated or fed. She was appreciated without flattery, heard without yawns. The two young men, whom Marie introduced familiarly as Bill and Algie, almost revered her as much as they fawned on Marie. There was no patronizing or condescending, although Mary had rarely seen a pair of such precious young fops. Algie's hair was as red as Marie's and carefully curled: his pallor was unhealthy beside her tan. But he wanted to know every detail of the

Maine and how our brave boys would be treated after they had been wounded by the beastly Boers. And Bill, who was a skeleton of drawling emaciation, wanted to listen to everything about her life, the looking after the Indian women in the closed *zenanas*, the marriage to Harry Lamb, and particularly how Marie had found her in London before setting up on her own as the belle of Cambridge Circus. "I must confess," Mary said, "I have never seen Marie ride her pony —"

"Take me," Algie giggled, "take me now."

"Theatre," Mary went on, "is not my line. I did see the ballad singers in the Seven Dials —"

"Darling," Marie said, "that does date you. But you never age —"

"And the Vic once. And the opera. But a Theatre of Varieties, even though it's a Palace. But I ken Marie. She'll take the house by storm."

"More than we can do," Bill said, "against those boring Boers. Now, Mrs Lamb, try the terrine. I know the geese of Strasburg stuffed their livers and parted with them nobly for this, but we do give them a fond farewell. Those blocks of truffles look just like mourning hats."

Mary took the liver paste, but she did not like the talk. Dying was not funny, at least not in her trade. And Marie intervened with that quick sympathy that stopped her from being impossible about her beauty.

"La-di-dah, Bill. Food's food. Give my aunt some of that Cliquot *rosé*. It's better than Canada. What we got there was bear's blood and gunpowder with a dash of iron filings. But Robert's coming over, have you heard?"

"Yes," Mary said. "With Strathcona's horse —"

"Can he ride like you can?" Algie laughed shrill again. "Take him *anywhere*."

"His grandmother wasn't a Crow," Marie said. "And *père* Bain is no French trapper like my father. He's a dirt farmer in the prairies. But Robert, I must say, he always loved a horse. Born to the saddle, not plodding behind a plough."

"He should not be fighting," Mary said. "It is not his war."

"It's not mine either," Algie said. "I do think fighting's for those who are fit for it."

"And dying?" Mary said.

"That's for others. I don't mind a *beating*, a good whacking —" here Algie's eyes glittered with amusement — "but death is going too far."

"Shut up, Algie," Marie said. "You can't shock Aunt Mary. She's nursed more dying people than you've had forty whacks."

"Yes, do shut up, Algie," Bill drawled. "We should support our soldiers. I didn't tell you, Marie, I did try and volunteer. Lovat's Horse, a family thing. But they said I was too skinny. The nag would bolt away with me."

"You Scots?" Mary said. "You dinna give the impression –"

"Been down South rather too long, really, Mrs Lamb. But the old heather has its pull. I mean, Marie says she's never seen Scotland, so I said I'll take her back to Sinclair country."

"Little of that is Sinclair now," Mary said. "Our own folk, there's no muckle in the crofts."

"All the same," Bill said, "we still have an acre or two. And one cannot change a moor or a mountain or a loch, whoever claims to have it. But one can choose a menu. *Caille cocotte*, I recommend, to melt in the mouth before we freeze our palates with a *pôle nord*."

"Ach, it's too rich for me," Mary said, only to give way to her niece's laugh.

"Mary, Mary, quite contrary – you deserve all the riches in the world." And she held up her glass of pink bursting bubbles. "To Mary – who has given more and taken less – the only generous spirit in all the world."

The two young men lifted their glasses and drank too, saying, "The only generous spirit in all the world."

Mary felt a prickle at the back of her lids. She groped in her little evening bag and found a handkerchief and dabbed at her eyes. She did not like Marie's young men – flimsy-whimsies and namby-pambies, not worth a curl of Marie's red hair – but they oozed charm enough to float the royal yacht *Britannia*. And they did want to hear about her life. And at her age, appreciation was pretty well all.

"Thank you," she said. "I try. And what do you do?"

And when it turned out that Bill was a painter and designer, for houses rather than the stage, she was more impressed. Particularly as he was also the Earl of Dunesk, and Mary never expected a nobleman to lift a finger to do anything. He did, though, lift his glass in one more toast, and rose with it.

"The Queen," he said. "May She live and prosper."

Algie remained seated with the two women, although he drank the toast with them.

"The Queen. But She is ninety."

"Yes," Bill said as he sat down. "But when she dies, it will be a new age – and not surely for the better."

With brass buttons gleaming like mint golden guineas, his braid shining and a rose in his buttonhole, his hunter chain across his belly button and his silver whistle in his waistcoat pocket, his flag furled for the last stop at Vancouver, Bob McDowell rode the Canadian Pacific Railway like a king, not a guard. But he was out of sorts, puffing and snorting through the heavy breathing that he said was asthma, but his wife Kate said was overweight. He had not liked the sly look in Charlie Mackinnon's eyes, when the steward had handed him the *Illustrated London News* which some vacationer had left in his dining-car.

"Looks like your Marie, showing a leg," Charlie had said and smacked his lips. Yes, he had positively popped his lips in a wet kiss.

"Offensive noises," Bob had to reprimand him, "are not permitted in these premises."

"But girls' legs are," Charlie had said and scampered off. The young wouldn't know a manner from a water closet, not these days.

And the drawing in the magazine did show his step-daughter riding a rearing pony bare-back and half-bare herself. Naked limbs almost up to the thigh as her loose leggings were rucked high. That was the Indian in her. It had to come out. Blood always told. And his own blood was drumming high in his ears as Bob McDowell fought to control his temper. He wanted to bellow like a bull moose. But he clenched his hands on the tails of his frock coat and pulled it down. He would maintain his dignity, however much Marie tried to drag him down.

The huge locomotive came into the station in a storm of steam and a rolling grindstone of great wheels. The black face of the engine loomed like a meteorite, the funnel blew fumes high as a twister to the sky. The waiting Kate could only feel awe and a kind of worship for these iron behemoths which her man rode and commanded. She did not love him as she had Henri, the gentle frontier savage of her dream days, but Bob was steady, for sure, and he had fought for forty years to be where he was, nobody to help him, but only her now. And there he was, riding the end carriage on the steps down, hanging on and blowing his whistle, then jumping heavily down – plump – plump – to unroll his flag and shake it over his head. He called, "End of the line – the Pacific!" He always did that, as if announcing a victory. And it was a victory of sorts, the crossing of a whole continent on a metal road, the spanning of the two great oceans of the world.

Kate ran to him and saw his red face and his fury. He pushed a rolled paper at her. "Marie – *your* daughter – shameful – shaming us." He turned away to his duty, seeing the passengers off the train. And Kate ruffled the pages to find the drawing of Marie performing on her pony at the Palace. Her heart swelled. She could have sung with joy. Marie successful, Marie loose, Marie free. Henri would have loved that wild liberty in his daughter. But how to tell Bob? How to explain that women now – and maybe women always – needed to break out, if only for a time? There was no putting up with a man's world if a woman had never known how to ride fast and dance a fling and run her own wild way. But Kate knew the diplomacy between the two of them, Bob and herself, in the marriage bond. So she hid the delight in her heart, and she said gloomily to her husband, "She's doing terrible, terrible things –" and then she could not stop herself from adding – "thank God."

2

A BARE TABLE

Spion Kop had a flat top. Some giant seemed to have sliced its head off its shoulders like an executioner with his axe. For once the Lancashires and the Engineers and the Rangers were above the Boers after a night attack. But with the coming of the light, snipers and sharpshooters edging round the crust of the kop peppered the British, lying uneasily between the flat rocks. And the Krupp and Hotchkiss and Maxim-Nordenfeldt guns of the enemy artillery had made a target of the tableland on the height of the mountain. They deluged it with fire. From a distance well out of range, Captain Charles Seymour-Scudabright, on detachment from his battleship with his battery of naval guns, saw the bombardment from nearby Spearman's Hill. There was nothing to do but watch. And finish his letter home to his wife May in purple prose that would prove that he had himself been in the heat of the action. And it was hellish hot. So he wrote in pencil on the ruled pad on his knee:

> Ping! ping! rang the rifles in chorus. Bong! bong! go the guns, with a *basso profundo* that reverberates in the hollows of these hills. What an awe-striking revelly! Shrapnel from Teutonic guns sprays hither and thither. Lyddite opens out umbrellas of earth far and wide. The roar and the roll of fiends in fury rend the clear air, scented with mimosa. Even the bosom of the placid silvery river shudders and quakes as it winds round Potgieter's Drift. Hour after hour, the tornado pursues its deadly course...

Stumped for his next lush patch of words, Charles looked up at the top of the kop. He could see reinforcements creeping as big as lice up the near steep slope past the dressing station, set up for the wounded below the ruin. They would hold the mountain, turn the flank of the Boers and use his naval guns to break through to besieged Ladysmith. He was there all night, in the thick of it, at risk. So he wrote on, the sweat from his fingers smudging the letters:

Death – mutilation – agony – thirst – these mean more here than the word glory – and you know, my dear May, what glory means to me. Other than you, it is dearest to my heart. Officers and men alike can scarce lift a head lest they meet the doom that hangs over every creature in this murderous arena. We crouch and take cover and wait. And the Boers see the dance of death among us and sneak up and are upon us. But we do not flinch. We will not be able to hold much longer. The trenches that we are grandly defending are becoming our graves. The number of the slain is appalling to see. The dead lie literally in stacks at our Thermopylae, and they are the sole protection of we few who survive...

One couldn't beat a classical education at Eton, where Gordon and Graham already were, growing up like their father to serve in the army or navy. Greek gave one all the right adjectives. And the army gave him the right borrowed batman Higgins, who produced from nowhere biscuits and scrambled eggs in a mess-tin. He was smart, even though the egg was orange-yellow, perhaps from one of the ostriches Charles had bagged on his way up from his battleship *Terrible*. He had the tail-feathers in his bag for May's hats.

The British were certainly not going to show the white feather here. But there was precious little to view on Spion Kop until the evening came. And only then did his naval gunners receive the orders to drag their battery to the top of the mountain, just as the last of the heroes were retreating back down the last scarp. But he still had time to end his letter home:

We reel from loss of blood – not mine, personally – but this is Victoria Cross time. Dozens of heroes have earned it all about me, and I do not boast about what I have done. A thousand are dead, hundreds live – yet I have come through to the other side. Fear not for me, for I will live to drub the Dutch. The next time is the time for the pounding of the guns until they beg for the mercy which they never grant to us. I will keep you all safe.

A kiss from Daddy to little Ruth

Charles

What was damnable about watching the battle was that he was actually wounded at it. While they were limbering up the guns, some dozy idiot dropped an iron spike and crippled Charles's foot. He felt he had five broken toes through his boot. Ingrams it had to be, and Charles was not so sure it was not deliberate, for he had had Ingrams tied to a gun-wheel every night for a month for falling asleep on picket, as an act of mercy. He could have had Ingrams shot for dereliction of duty in the face of the enemy. And now the cretin breaks his Captain's bones. And all he says with a smirk is, "Sorry, Sir, must a' slipped outa me 'and," like a skivvy dropping a Dresden plate. Watch it, Ingrams. When I am back in harness, I'll have my eye on you.

The naval guns never reached Spion Kop, for its defenders had abandoned it already. Yet on his Calvary in the ambulance cart back to the field hospital, Charles wondered if he could get a medal for being wounded in the course of duty. He might have to settle for a mere campaign ribbon – but that would be rotten luck. The pain in his foot was just as excruciating as it was for the other wounded soldiers lying bloody and cursing about him in language that gentlemen only used between each other. All who were harmed – however they were harmed – should be rewarded equally for their service to their country. If only he could find a friend in a high place who would write him a recommendation for his derring-do at Spion Kop. His letter to his wife May would be proof of his presence of mind.

So it was that Charles Seymour-Scudabright arrived at the field hospital, where he was not pleased to meet his wife's cousin, Seaforth Sinclair, that little mistake on the other side of the blanket by her uncle Hamish James in India. And Seaforth was in no hurry to treat Charles, who had to wait his turn in the lying line of sufferers, soldiers and commissioned ranks treated in the order of arrival. And what was worse, Charles saw Seaforth take his time off from sewing and strapping up the sick to jaw with a jumped-up Indian in a black suit, who seemed to be in command of the coolie body-snatchers that had assumed the title of the South African Indian Ambulance Corps. Charles could not hear what Seaforth was saying, but it was bad enough that he was saying it to one of his kind instead of saving British lives.

"You are doing a good job, Mr Gandhi," Seaforth was saying to the small Indian who was wiping mist off his spectacles, "you and your volunteers are doing a splendid job – but I fail to understand why you are doing it at all."

The voice that answered Seaforth was so compelling and reasonable that he was almost seduced into assent.

"We are showing our loyalty to the Empire," Gandhi said. "And then it will show its gratitude to us."

"We want liberty, not gifts."

"Like the Afrikaners," Gandhi asked, "you want to take liberty with guns? Like the Afrikaners, you want to discriminate between the races? The British, at least, claim we are one Empire and we are all British subjects. They give their domination over us all to some free Dominions – Canada, Australia ..."

"Free white Dominions. Not to India."

"In the end, to India too."

"I cannot wait that long. Free India now."

"And have this?" Gandhi looked along the rows of shattered and bleeding men, as they groaned on the ground, with only the Indian bearers to give them water and comfort. "Which would you rather be, doctor? A live negotiator or a dying soldier?"

"I would rather be free."

"But we are. We are free of dying. We are excluded while white man fights white man. We merely bear the Empire as it kills itself. It kills itself by fighting itself. That is not the way. Sit down." The words were said as a quiet order, not as an invitation. So Seaforth sat awkwardly on his hams in the British fashion, while Gandhi sat cross-legged and easily, as he went on talking. "If I say, 'Sit down', to all my ambulance corps, and they all sit down, what will happen to the British soldiers? They will die more quickly. If you stay on sitting here and do not go back to your operating tent with Doctor Treves, more British soldiers will die. Fighting does not win wars. It only piles up bodies. Sitting makes for changes. Doing nothing can be a big action. Refusing is resistance. How would this Empire work, if the people who worked for it sat back and said, 'Work it yourself without us, until you set us free!'?"

Seaforth paused before replying to the persuasive force of the argument.

"We would be made to get up and work," he said. "Flogged into hard labour."

"I doubt it," Gandhi said. "The British have laws. I practise them as a barrister. They know what they do – and what they say they will do – and do not do. And when they behave badly, when they are guilty, I can play on that guilt. That is the way to make India free. We must make them depend on us. We must make them guilty. Then we must sit down, when they really need us. As they now need you, Dr Sinclair, and you are sitting down."

Treves had, indeed, appeared at the entrance to the nearest operating tent and was looking round, searching with his eyes.

Seaforth found himself getting to his feet against his will, answering an unspoken call to duty.

"Have to stretch my legs," he heard himself mumbling as an excuse. But he was all too conscious of Gandhi, still sitting cross-legged on the ground and smiling at his going.

Just as Treves saw him coming and said, "Ah, good man, we need you —", Seaforth heard a shout from a familiar voice behind him, "Seaforth! When are you going to treat my bloody foot! I am a captain on the *Terrible*, you know, in the Royal Navy!" Seaforth was relieved from his embarrassment in front of Gandhi by turning and shouting at the intolerable Charles Seymour-Scudabright, "Wait your turn, captain! Being family won't do you any good." He found Treves laughing as he pushed his way past the Queen's Surgeon into the operating tent, then he heard Treves giggle as he spoke, "I must say, Sinclair, you do seem to have family everywhere!"

And Charles had to put up with his foot aching worse than an attack of gout until past midnight, before he reached the head of the queue and was strapped up and given to the Indian body-snatchers to ship off on the train to a hospital ship, where the proper due would be paid to his superior rank. From his train compartment, he saw a face he knew, pug-nosed and pugnacious under the Boer hat and cockolibird feather of the South African Horse. He was Winston, Lady Randolph Churchill's son. He must have escaped from his prison camp and wriggled his way into a cavalry post as well as war correspondent for the *Morning Post*. But he could write up Charles's role at Spion Kop.

"Hey, Churchill," Charles called. "Over here! Churchill, I say."

The young man sauntered over and looked through the open compartment window at Charles lying along the seat. He did not recognize the captain, who had to add his name, "Charles Seymour-Scudabright. With the naval guns at Spion Kop."

"You didn't see much action," Churchill said.

"Oh, I saw it all right."

"They peppered you."

"Only my leg."

"I got up and down the kop twice," Churchill said. "One hell of a mess."

"Was it not."

"You were up there? We must have missed each other."

Charles swallowed. The lie had to be by omission, but he must be mentioned in Churchill's dispatch.

"I was wounded with the others. I have written all about it in a letter to my wife. Would you like to see?" Charles held forward his ruled pad. "I think I have captured the pluck and the glory."

"Thank you." Churchill did not move to take the pad. "We lost, you know. We did not win. I have my own view and style. Get well man, soon."

Then he turned and walked away. Quite a puzzle how the captain had been wounded – the naval guns had never been in action. And he had seen no glory, nor would he match the style of Charles's letter home. In his own manner, Churchill wrote the next morning of his first pilgrimage to the summit of the bare table mountain.

Streams of wounded met us and obstructed our path. Men were staggering along alone, or supported by comrades, or crawling on hands and knees, or carried on stretchers. Corpses lay here and there. The splinters and fragments of shell had torn and mutilated in the most ghastly manner. I passed about two hundred while I was climbing up. There was, moreover, a small but steady leakage of unwounded men of all corps. Some of these cursed and swore. Others were utterly exhausted and fell on the hillside in stupor. Others again seemed drunk, though they had had no liquor. Scores were sleeping heavily. Fighting was still proceeding.

Churchill put down his pen. It had been not much like glory, really. War was anything but.

A letter had come from home – or what the British in India called home, whatever that was. For Peg Sinclair at her hospital desk at Lucknow, home was wherever the few people she loved were. With a Scots soldier father and Hindu mother, she had no real country and no home, no more than her brother Seaforth had in spite of his identification with India. Her Aunt Mary had been more of a mother to her than anyone else, putting her through her training at St Thomas's in London. But a 'home' in England also meant a place where they put unwanted children to teach them to be good. Yes, Mary's letter to her was a letter from a home.

Dearest Peg,

I must ask you to come home. They have asked me to go out to South Africa on a hospital ship called *Maine*. It has an X-ray machine that can see through bodies and tell us what went wrong.

But there is no X- ray machine to see through this terrible war and tell us what went wrong, why there is more of this senseless killing, worse than Glencoe.

We need you here at St Thomas's. There will be many wounded from the war. I want my best lassies back here. You will have a ward to run. The poor soldiers – it is not their fault they are shot by Dutchmen holding onto their land.

My dearest Seaforth, as you know, is working with the wounded at the front line. He is with Doctor Treves, one of our best surgeons. He serves the Queen, though she is poorly they say. I think Seaforth serves in the war because he loved his soldier father who died in South Africa. You love him, I know. Of course, Seaforth will never say it. No Sinclair can ever say he loves another Sinclair. Though some of the Sinclair women can. You and I, Peg, we can say it.

As I prepare to sail, it is all rich women and committees. You would hate it. This big city is empty without you. I miss you sorely. But your cousin Marie is the toast of London. She does something wicked on a horse, but she will not allow me to see it. Not for you, Auntie, she says. Cows and a milk pail are more your line. What does that mean? She has all kinds of friends, Earls and such. But never a man like your father or your Uncle Iain. You must tell me of the news from Annandale.

But you must come *home*. The India Office and your cousin Margaret's husband Douglas will be looking to it. Do not say you will not come, even if we miss each other in London, for I may have sailed by the time you reach me. I do not ask you to come for the war or the Empire, but for me. I need you. Your hospital needs you. And don't forget to bring back that green chutney I muckle like. But not Bombay Duck. It is everything hygiene is not.

All my love

Mary

They were so unconscious about their orders, the people you loved, the British. They told you they needed you, they arranged for you to come 'home', and then they said, "Of course, it is only if you want to." In fact, their command was your wish. To tell the truth, Peg knew that she wanted to go. Lucknow was all right, her position was good, almost an assistant matron to the whole hospital. But these were sad times with the Boer War, a rebellion in a colony. The Indian regiments were marching away under their British officers to fight in an alien conflict. And there were whispers of another Mutiny in India in aid of the Boers. Her brother Seaforth would be working for that, for Indian independence. He was obsessed about it. But she – a soldier's daughter – she would move with the soldiers, as she always had, to take care of them.

Outside her window there was the sound of the neighing of horses, the jingle and clanking of the guns. Peg rose from her desk to stand by the open window and peer round the edge of the canvas screen. A squadron of horse artillery was passing the hospital wall. She could see the heads of the horses, the plumes and banners of the mounted gunners, and the covered barrels of the guns on their wheeled carriages. They moved in a cloud of dust as if they were already firing the earth. Their going was a quiet explosion. They were heading for the sea on a dictate from London, as she would be. And yet they were not unwilling. The horses' heads jerked and pranced, the gunners shouted and tossed their helmets. They were going somewhere, if not home. And she would also soon be at sea, going to do what she knew how to do. But the why of it, Peg knew no more than her Aunt Mary.

Robert Sinclair hated being a Mountie on a transport ship. Even sailors had an easier life. Revelly was half past four, a trumpet tooting at the dawn. He was sleeping on deck, and he had to roll up his blanket and carry it down to the store-room. At five in the morning, he had a mess-tin of dish-water tea, and half an hour later, there was roll-call in case a Canadian cowboy had gone for a swim off Africa. Then the worst, mucking out the stalls below decks, and feeding and watering the horses. It had to be done to drilltime. If one bronco was fed before the next bronco in line, there were ructions, and the whole herd of horses was fighting and kicking. The din of the hoofs on the buckboards was deafening. The order, "Stables!" meant swabbing out the alleyways between and behind the nags. Robert was enough of a farm boy to know anything you put into a horse came out worse at the back end. And he laughed to see the gentlemen volunteers, the friends of Lord Strathcona himself, grubbing after manure to put in buckets, then banging their oily heads against stanchions and beams as they carted the dung away.

Slopping out was never done, but somewhere towards eternity, the bugle always called breakfast. The scrum in the wash-house wasn't for washing yourself. You needed a curry-comb and a frayed rope's end to get the muck off you. And as for a meal, you had ship's biscuits and a

scrape of jam and tepid bilgewater with a trace of tea. And pickles –
always pretty pickles! One day, there was a treat, a tin of sardines
among thirteen men. If there was a bit of bully beef, the bully got it –
and it was not Robert. All he got was a suck at the tin-opener. The
man behind him had a look at the tin and the label for hereafters. Such
was life on the ocean wave, but then there was the call of "Buckets!",
and some bronco had kicked it, and they all started up stamping and
squealing, and woke up the sleeping Tommies, and Stripes leant over
the hatchway and wanted to know what that son of swivel-eyed sea-
cook was playing at. And you were down to the horses again, which is
why you were there, although you didn't know where you were, just in
the middle of the godforsaken sea.

Washing-up was worse. You doubled over two pints of tepid water,
trying to clean up forty greasy tin plates and mugs, and you were
jamming rusty fork points into your fingers, while your tea towel was
an old dirty jersey and your brush was the straw cover off a beer
bottle. That was the time you blessed your wife, if you were old
enough to have an old woman, or your mother, god bless her, how did
she put up with it all! Men looking after men, it was the sorriest sight
in all the world, except for men looking after horses, which was
bloody murder.

The mess room was just under the main deck-houses and measured
about forty feet square. There were thirteen long tables with a
hundred and forty men seated at them. It was always noisy, but that
was silence compared to the noise when the beer didn't arrive on time.
The din then beat feeding time at the zoo into a cocked hat, every man
Jack hitting the back of his tin plate and mug till the sparks flew and
the plates and mugs looked like the order of the boot. And when the
music started, it was "Swanee River" and "Beer, beer, glorious beer"
and "We are not working now" and "Oh, listen to the band" until
everybody choked and the tinware was bashed into smithereens.

The other sport was boxing. The Britishers reckoned it was kind of
like war. Down in the stuffy hold, a ring of sorts, and a couple of
idiots smashing their noses flat and thinking they were bashing
Johnnie Boer, old Uncle Kruger and Botha and all. But that was all
fossicks. Sport wasn't war. Play wasn't war. And this ship never got
where it was going.

Fire and boat drill, that was a laugh. Three hundred men with four
boats and two dozen life-belts five hundred miles from shore. If they
had a fire or hit a reef, they'd see their Maker sooner than their
saviour. They knew that. This bloody ocean, it went on too long.
Where was Johnnie Boer? Here's luck and blue blazes to his good old

sjambok, but when he saw the Canadian cowboys coming, he'd go hell for lather for home.

Funny, wasn't it, but however big the world was, and wherever you went, you could never get away from the good old kith and kin. When Robert was a kid, Cousin Marie couldn't say "kith." So she said "kiss and kin." It was nice for him, he got kisses from Marie if he was kin. Which was something to say, now she was the belle of Piccadilly, the darling of the Strand. But who could reckon this chap would come up from the engine-room with the long Sinclair face and the mournful chops and say, "I saw you on the roster, Robert Sinclair. You must be Bain's son. I'm Hamilton, your cousin from India. We'll have a chat over the games."

The British navy didn't run on engines, whatever Hamilton said. It ran on three games which passed the time of day, if the horses didn't. Otherwise everybody would be overboard – sharkmeat – nothing else to do better. They played Under and Over, Crown and Anchor, and 'Ouse About, as 'Arry called it. Under and Over was a dead loss. A piece of canvas marked in three squares, Under Seven and Over. You put on sixpence, and if it was a seven on the dice, you got eighteen pence. If not, the game was over and you were under the odds, you couldn't beat them. Crown and Anchor had six squares, the crown, ace of spades, hearts, clubs, diamonds, and the ship's hook, the anchor. You had three dice, which meant you lost three times quicker. But at 'Ouse About or 'Ousey 'Ousey, you got an 'Arry for your money, because he was a riot, though you still lost. Talking to Hamilton while 'Arry was on the blarney, Robert didn't know which ear to use.

"How could you leave the farm, Robert? Didn't your father go wild? And your mother – I would have thought she would have chained you to your bed."

"'Ouse about," 'Arry was calling. "Come away, my lucky lads. 'Ouse correct. Oo'll 'ave a card? Sixty-nine, eighty-four, seventy-two. Oo's the lucky man? Twenty-nine, thirteen, unlucky for some – but top of the 'ouse."

"You got away," Robert said. "That farm of yours in the Himalayas. Iain couldn't keep you. You love them, your engines. You're a mad mechanic."

"'Ouse correct, gentlemen," 'Arry was calling. "'Oo says another card. Come on then! All of you ready?"

"It's not the same," Hamilton said. "My father wanted me to go. He wanted me to be an engineer. Ship's engines. Do something useful. He builds canals himself in the Punjab. He didn't want me to die like

my brother Hamish – and my uncle – fighting for Africa, which we
didn't want. It isn't any use, anyway."

"Three to one on the lucky seven! Now then, gents, you pays your
money and you takes your chance. Now's your time to seize the brass
bull hopportunity by its silver-plated 'orns – nifty fifty ..."

"Pardon me," Robert said and put his coin on thirty-three. "You
never ploughed a field behind an ox. You never cut corn or fixed
barbed wire. I tell you, you can break your back on the land. I love
horses. Christ, Ham, a horse – being on a horse – a gallop on the
plains – it was the only way out. And when Lord Strathcona said,
volunteers, anyone who could ride, shoot straight – and I've shot
grizzlies – well, you would be here, wouldn't you? And not *there*."

"As you were, gentlemen," 'Arry was calling. "Number eleven, get
to 'eaven. Ninety-nine, end of the line. Sixty-four, knock on the door,
and no 'ouse yet."

"There's no need for cavalry in this war," Hamilton said. "It's all
twelve-pounders and machine-guns. The poor bloody horses are all
riddled with bullets before they get near the trenches. There are no
lancers now."

"We don't have lances," Robert said. "We have six-shooters. We're
cowboys. You've never seen anything like it."

"You've never seen anything like Johnnie Boer," Hamilton said.
"He rides like the wind when you're after him. Then he'll suddenly sit
in a donga or a spruit bed and knock you off with his Mauser like
quails for breakfast. Don't count your chickens, Robert. You hang up
your saddles to dry."

"Sixty-six, pick up sticks," 'Arry was calling. "An' no 'ouse yet. Oh,
is it you, sergeant? 'Ave a tanner on a number. What? Game's over,
and there ain't a winner? Strewth, what a bummer. Sorry, lads, and so
long. Two pound five in the kitty, and I'll 'old it till next time. Cross
me 'eart and 'ope to die. But if you care to join me, I'll get a jar out of
Pills."

"What?" Hamilton asked. "A drink out of the doctor?"

"Stout," Robert said. "For rheumatism. We can get it for the
broncos, when their withers don't work so good."

"And we can get it too? I mean, we are humans – or are we?"

"'Arry can," Robert said. "'Arry can get anything, including the
fingers off your hand. I don't know, Ham, but 'Arry's taught me one
thing about the Mother Country."

"What's that, Robert?"

"Sharp, they are. You must count your blessings. Because if you don't count them, the Queen – God bless Her – will lift them off you."

"I don't know," Hamilton said. "I thought what you learned was to play the game – whatever it was – whatever the rules were."

3

POUND THEM DOWN

Kitchener was a butcher, as the Duke of Cumberland had been when he cleared the clans at Culloden. The problem was, he seemed to like killing his own men. Coming to South Africa late with Lord Bobs, he had to make the same mistakes all over again at Paardeberg, and make them worse. As though they hadn't before tried to charge across the chocolate-brown Modder River and make it redder. It was just like Magersfontein – Hamish Charles knew that – and there he had lost his uncle. Yesterday the Highland Brigade had marched more than thirty miles after the relief of Kimberley and then the Scotsmen were thrown straight at the huge snail of the Boer position in the morning. The Dutchmen had hidden sharpshooters in the willows and mimosa and brushwood and dongas along the river bank, but the laager of their waggons and trenches bulged out in a fortified shell on the north bank of the river. As usual, the Highlanders had to charge across open ground at Mauser rifles firing from dug-outs, and as usual, they were pinned down and staked out among the ant-heaps, the backs of their necks and their bare knees below their kilts blistering in the sun, their throats drier than sand dunes with the dun river-waters mocking their thirst a hundred yards ahead. Hamish Charles did not even dare brush away the horse-fly that bit into his leg. If he had, likely as not a dum-dum or a pom-pom bullet would have taken away his relieving arm.

Yet this time, the Highlanders did not break and run. They knew they were not in a trap now, the Boers were. Old Cronje with his burghers and women and children, he had stopped trekking and was trying to fight it out behind the river. But he was being surrounded. And now the twelve-pounder naval guns and the howitzers were on the kopjes, and they were pounding the laager with lyddite and shrapnel. Waggons were blazing or else charred to black scrap. Explosions blew up eddies of earth and plumes of soil. Already the tempting beige waters had begun to smell, as the bodies of horses and men floated down and stuck on the banks to putrefy in the shallows. Vultures waited as gravely as undertakers to profit from death. But this time the Dutch were being peppered and they could not trek away.

Lord Bobs arrived that night after a tummy upset, and he would have none of death and glory. Dapper and tiny, not a pip on him to show his rank, he decided to win by shot and shell as the Boers had always done. There was one charge more for Hamish Charles across the river. The Seaforths and the Cornwalls went in with the bayonet into the brushwood and drove the snipers from their cover by the drift. One fat farmer was the first man that Hamish Charles had ever killed with the steel, driving it into his back as he tripped over a root, then putting a boot in the ribs of the lying and squirming Boer Johnnie so that the point could be pulled out. Then the corpse turned over like a porpoise and looked up at him, red froth coming from his mouth. "Why?" he said, and died in a spasm of crimson bubbles. And Hamish Charles found himself retching and swearing never to stick a human being again. He did not have the blood lust in him.

De Wet and his commandos took a kopje nearby, but Cronje would not budge to join them. So they rode away, and the Old Man surrendered. It was chalk and cheese to see. The huge and portly Cronje slouching down suspiciously, his small eyes sly and darting between the brim of his grey slouch hat and his bush of a black beard, his pantaloons rolled up from his tan boots to the bottom of his bottle-green overcoat and his *sjambok* in his hand. Confronting him, the imperial whippet, Lord Bobs with his picquet cap straight along the parting of his white hair, a glossy strap slicing down his erect back to his swordbelt, and the sheath of his sabre arching forward to the gleaming toe-caps of his riding-boots. Lord Bobs held out his hand. "I am glad to see you," he said. "You have made a gallant defence, sir." Cronje engulfed the hand of peace in his large one as a dog might grab a bone. He did not speak, but stared in hate and shame. His little wife stood behind him, a thin and toothless woman in a rough straw hat and a dirty black dress, rather like a gypsy who had her fortune told wrong.

The beaten Boers themselves appeared to be refugees. In shapeless and muddy clothes, they carried pots and pans and parasols and Bibles as well as rifles. From the rolled blankets in their knapsacks, teapots and bottles and galoshes were hanging. Hamish Charles could not believe such a bunch of derelicts could have thrashed the British armies so often and so bloodily. There were about fifty women shrouded in reach-me-downs, some carrying babies on their hips. A tall Australian went among them, insisting on kissing every infant. And the Dutch women held up their children to be blessed by those foreign lips.

This was not yet the time of the concentration camps. The women and children were let go under safe-conduct, the men taken off to prison on the island of St Helena. And wandering into the remains of the stinking laager, Hamish Charles could not imagine how the enemy had endured the pounding for so many days. The whole camp was a dark chaos, slashed with zig-zags of green and yellow from the lyddite. Waggons were mere smashed struts and wheels or twists of black metal. The whole area was a rubbish heap of saddles and leather panniers, tin trunks and brass cartridges. And everything reeked, an open slaughter-house in the stench of the sun. Shrapnel had scattered the bodies of the oxen, and the horses were turned inside out as wet gloves are. Flies were heaving blue cloaks on the entrails of the poor beasts and unburied men. The very river stank like a sewer, and typhoid and enteric infused its waters with more deadliness than Maxim bullets. Hamish Charles was too sickened to pursue his hunt for souvenirs to send home, but he did poke under the flap of one upturned waggon, only to start back, his heart in his throat. For a dead man moved.

He was no threat. The Afrikaner lay back, his leg caught under an axle-tree. His thin face was striped with ochre and soot from the lyddite shells, his breath was sharp as vinegar. But he smiled up at Hamish Charles and said, "Oy, *rooinek*, can you get me out?"

So Hamish Charles put down his rifle and tugged at the axle-tree and managed to heave it high enough for the Boer Johnnie to pull his limb free with his hands. He had grit all right. He pulled himself upright on the struts of the waggon and tested his weight on his injured leg. "Oy yoy, I can't – but it's better than your shells on our *schanses* – I must. Find me a stick, man." So Hamish Charles found a broken spar and gave it to the young Boer, who put it under his armpit and hopped out of the waggon. "Let's trek."

"You're my prisoner," Hamish Charles said.

"*Vrede*," the Afrikaner said, "Peace. Not *vlug*. How can I run, man?"

So Hamish Jamie gave the Boer Johnnie his shoulder and supported him along the Modder bank towards the drift, where they could ford the river to the grouping area for the other prisoners. But in a clump of willow that the shells from the far *berg* had spared, the hobbling man asked for a rest and sat on a stump. His name was Piet Krug, he said. And he came from the Orange Free State, that would not be free much longer after Cronje's surrender. With his crushed leg, he could not fight any more. For him *huis-toe*, the war was over. He would go back to his farm. Hamish Charles should try it, dry farming with cattle and mealies, it was a good life. The Kaffirs round there were not bad, if you could make them work. Nothing was like the bushveldt. It was better than choking on lyddite fumes or the shrapnel they called hell-scrapers. Could Hamish Charles use Krug's slouch hat to get some river water and wash the muck off his face from the *klein kafferkies*, the lyddite shells. He looked a *swart* sight, he knew he did.

So Hamish Charles swabbed off the face of his enemy with dirty water, and then performed an act that amazed himself. Piet Krug said, "Hell, man, that drift, I don't know if I can make it across the Modder. Leave me here. Forget me. And if the other *rooineks* forget me, I go back to my farm, not to your prison camp. Look at the leg – I won't shoot you again." And Hamish Charles found himself consenting to the possible escape of Krug and even the thought of visiting him on his farm near Bechuanaland after the war was over. "I must be crazy," Hamish Charles said, "to trust you, Piet Krug." But he knew he could. For he had forgotten his Metford rifle when he had gone to the river for the water to wash Krug's face, and Krug had not turned the weapon on his helper. When it came to it, and if there was mutual respect, you could trust Johnnie Boer.

Hamish Charles did not have mutual respect for all of his own side. The Scots had never got on that well with the English, nor the Seaforths and the Highland Brigade with the cavalry. Yet now there were the volunteer colonials, come to help their mother country in a far corner of Empire. They were good scrappers, the Australians and the Canadians – Hamish Charles had even heard from Aunt Mary in London that his cousin Robert might be coming out with Strathcona's Horse. But these colonial cavalrymen, the planters from Assam with their Hindustani words and their pony ambulance tongas with two wheels and their total contempt for the natives, they set Hamish Charles on edge. A joke was a joke, but not the joke that Hamish Charles heard round the campfire that night, when the pickets gathered for their scalding Bovril in tin mugs, before they relieved each other. Then a gangling planter told of the best laugh he had ever had, and that in the battle, too.

"I saw some Kaffirs right out to the side of us, watching the show. There was a man and his wife, two girls, and a collie dog. I let drive a couple of bullets right behind them. Spout! Spout! went the nickels in the dust close behind them – pretty fair for a sighting at eleven hundred yards. Even a Dutch parson would have laughed! Up went civilisation waist high, in the shape of three gaudy petticoats. And did those Kaffirs run!"

"So would I," Hamish Charles said, but he could not stop the planter's flow.

"Run! Why you couldn't see their heels for dust. Away they went, hard as they could go, down the donga, up a spruit to the other side like so many black snipe. Then helter-skelter into their hut, banging the door against the white devils. Laugh! Laugh!" The planter laughed, but none of his hearers did. So he went on more hurriedly. "To see those black feminine limbs with nothing on but their big boots – while rolled up around their waists were those lovely Liberty Pattern skirts – I could have cried laughing. I could have died."

"Many did die," Hamish Charles said. "Or didn't you notice?"

The planter's face grew red with anger. And incredibly, tears ran from his eyes as if by order.

"What do you mean, Jock? My friend Eric, he was killed. Only a few hours ago, he was telling us what he was going to do when the show was over – and when he went home to the Old Country." The ruddy cheeks of the speaker were as wet as puppies after rain. "Aye, he's gone home now, if ever a good sort of chap went home. And his sister and the mother he was so proud of, they'll only see him in our Eternal Home. Poor Eric, he's gone home."

"Get on with you," a sergeant said. "Change pickets." And as Hamish Charles walked away, he knew he would never understand it – the terrible mixture in them all of cruelty and sentimentality, crassness and feeling. He really did feel a sympathy for the Boers now – they did not know how to deal with what they were facing, these soft hearts and these harsh acts, these schoolboy japes and this careless violence. The Dutchmen knew what they were doing, as their President thundered his telegrams at them: *Officers and burghers, place all your faith in the Lord. He is our highest General, and the final victory is in His hand. You must not think that all who fight against us belong to the Beast. There are certainly hundreds of the children of God among them, who are forced to act as they do from fear of the Beast. But God knows all hearts. We did not seek that the blood that lies on the ground should be shed. But when they wished to murder us, we rose up against the Beast.*

The Boers knew they were fighting the Beast, and Hamish Charles did not believe that he was fighting the Beast, nor that he was the Beast. All had seemed simple at Harrow. He would join his uncle's regiment and come out for the show. But now he did not know the face of the enemy. For the enemy sometimes wore his face or even the faces of his own side. What he did begin to feel was the power of this strange land of trial and woe with its terrible beauty and bleak choice.

4

PAST IT

"I never thought I would see you here." Charles Seymour-Scudabright said. "I mean, aren't you a bit ..." His words died in his mouth. It was not only Mary Lamb's dour look, it was the fact that he was a gentleman, and no gentleman referred to the age of a lady, even if she was a hospital matron.

"A bit past it. That is what you were about to say." Mary was examining the plaster cast over Charles's injured foot. She tweaked at his protruding toes, which he had not expected.

"Ouch."

"Ach, you do feel something," Mary said. "I never thought you could feel anything. That means we can knock this cast off and get you back on deck."

"The answer to my prayers," Charles said.

"You do pray?"

"Of course I do."

"I am not past prayer myself," Mary said, then she turned to the orderly Maxwell. "You saw this cast off. Do not trouble Doctor Sinclair. He has more important things to do."

As Maxwell left for the companionway of the *Maine*, Charles protested.

"You permit an orderly to take off my cast –"

"Seaforth has vital operations to perform. They may save lives – I think yours is safe."

"Your darling Seaforth – you sent for him to serve on this ship – you had him seconded here."

"He is the best surgeon there is. I know from St Thomas's –"

"He is your darling," Charles sneered. "And if you think I would look forward to him getting his hands on me –"

"Those coloured hands –" Mary smiled and shook her head. "You know, his sister Peg – she's a doctor now, too – she's coming from India to London to help to take my place, while I am over here looking for you."

"You sound like a family recruiting sergeant," Charles said. "The wrong side of the Sinclair family, may I say." And he said it.

"That's what families are for," Mary said. "To help each other. And I am the head of what is left of our bit of the clan. Ach, Maxwell —" the orderly had returned with a huge pair of scissors and a small handsaw. "Please cut off that cast. Not the foot, if you can help it. Captain Seymour-Scudabright does not want to hop between his broadsides from H.M.S. *Terrible*." And as Charles spluttered from the bed, Mary left on the words. "My regards to my niece May Sinclair. She always said I had bad taste in men — poor Harry Lamb — but meeting you again, Charles, I wonder ... your wife or me ... who chose well?"

In the narrow companionway outside, Mary found her age beginning to tell. Her legs hurt, too. There were blue veins in them, varicose they were called. She had to wind bandages round them to keep herself on her pins and in her duty. But her skirt was long enough to hide her body down to her boots, and nobody now would even care to see her ankle. Not like those ladies in Piccadilly descending from their coaches outside the Café Royal in a foam of white lace petticoats, and the men writing sonnets about the swish of one foot. Ach, you're a daft old lady, Mary Sinclair, and you had better look to the leg of Jack Churchill. And his mother, she's a witch. How did she see he would be first on the *Maine*?

"There's no wrong with your leg, Mr Churchill," Mary said, looking at a flesh wound in the calf. "I will be writing to your mother, who was giving us this ship."

"Mother gave this?" Jack Churchill was surprised. "She never gave much except to the widows of the tenants. I never knew she cared about shows like this."

"I dinna ken she does," Mary said. "But she cares about you and Winston. Let me tell you, lad —" And she stared down at the bulging Churchill eyes — "there's no a woman cares for a country more than her own. And I dinna have sons — nephews only. But you can take all of Westminster and call it Pretoria, for all I care, as long as my own flesh and blood keep their own flesh and blood. And there's no woman in the world would not say the same as me."

She had finished the changing of his dressing, and she clipped shut the last safety pin. "You will live," she said, "and ride again."

"But we are meant to be fighting," Jack Churchill said, "for a woman, Queen Victoria, and our country, which She rules."

"Ach, that woman," Mary said, standing up. "More a mother than a Queen. Look at Her, trying to stop all those wars with Germany, because She canna have a grandson fighting another grandson like the Kaiser. I tell you, Mr Churchill, if we are ever to have peace in our time, it will be while She lives. There's not a drop of Royal Blood to be spilled – although perhaps some of ours."

"But her grandson Prince Victor of Schleswig-Holstein, he's on the staff of Lord Bobs –"

"Well back from the front line. The staff always are."

"And the Kaiser, he's sent out German officers to fight for the Boers."

"As long as he won't come – his royal selfishness – it will be no grandson against grandson."

"I mean, we'll soon be in Pretoria, and that will be that."

"I'm not so sure, Mr Churchill. You may be riding again. It's a big country, I hear tell, and they have horses, and it will be not so easy to track them all down." She rose and asked for her report, "Any complaints?"

"The ladies," Jack Churchill said.

"Ach, not the nurses –"

"The ladies also come in to wash our faces and gossip. I had my face washed five times yesterday. And I know much more about Piccadilly than the Transvaal. There's a girl rides a white pony called Marie Sinclair ..."

"I have heard tell of her," Mary said severely. "But I canna stop the ladies – the visiting ladies from London. They paid for this hospital ship. I dinna approve, but they say, since all the men are here, they must come too – to mop your faces and chatter away. And what you need is rest and the carbolic."

So she left Jack Churchill thinking that Mary Sinclair was as direct a woman as his mother had written to him that she was. But she was thinking that the awful Charles was right. She was trying to make the *Maine* into a floating family hospital. Hamish Charles might be carried in from the front, and Robert was riding out there with the cowboys, Lord Strathcona's Horse. She had Seaforth ready to treat them, if they were brought in – and even Hamilton was waiting to ferry them home on his wonderful ship's engines. There was no harm in running the war like your own business, if you were called into it at all. Favouring your own, that was to be expected. And if the Queen lost her grandson, that would be the end of the war, to be sure it would.

Hamilton caught her between rounds before she had time even to visit Seaforth. He told her of shipping Robert across with his horses along with munitions and supplies and some of the visiting ladies from London. "Except for you, Mary, ladies are a pain in the neck in a war."

"I'm a mere wee working woman, laddie."

"They take ten times more looking after than a soldier, and three times more than a horse. Some of them even brought their maids. And they told the stewards what to do, until one of them dumped a stewpot over a Lizzie and said, 'You want it all your way. Now you have it all your way'."

"What do you think, Hamilton? The ladies – they never ken what war is. Nobody will ever ken, so nobody will ever stop it."

"The ladies are all off to Bloemfontein, now it's ours and the field hospitals are there. Lady Roberts went up with her daughter and a whole special trainload of personal supplies – and we're not so sure that Lord Bobs wants it. The Queen doesn't like it, perhaps because She is too old to go Herself –"

"I am not," Mary said.

"You deny time," Hamilton said gallantly. "And you make eternity blush."

"Where did you learn those fine words, Hamilton? Are you courting?"

Now Hamilton did blush.

"And where would I meet a lady in the engine-room of a transport ship?"

"You said they were all ladies on board with the horses and Robert."

"*Married* ladies. Now, Aunt Mary, I said the Queen did not approve of them. Mr Chamberlain sent out a dispatch, which I know of. The Queen regrets the large number of ladies visiting South Africa and the hysterical spirit which has influenced them to go where they are not wanted."

"Good for Her," Mary observed. "She only came out here on a chocolate tin."

"Ah, you heard of that. That Lancaster private saved by the Queen's Christmas chocolate tin. The Boer bullet hit slap in the middle of J S Fry's best indigestibles and was squashed flat. Fudge beat lead. I had to bring him out another tin, wrapped in red, white and blue ribbons. You know, the tins are selling for a fiver in Christie's – souvenirs of the war."

Seaforth now came in to Mary's cabin, the small centre of the hospital ship. His eyes were circled in soot, yet there was pallor under his brown cheeks. "Hell," he said, "it's hell here. Hello, Hamilton, you've brought in more of the pom-pom fodder?"

"Only Cousin Robert and the Canadian cowboys. And some of the chit-chat ladies from Hades. Sometimes I wonder if we have a war on

or a side-show. The Mauser Music Hall or Oom Paul Kruger's Palace
of Varieties."

"Seaforth," Mary said, "You look dog tired. Have a rest in my
bunk."

"I can't, Aunt Mary. The show goes on. We're still getting the Irish
in from Hart's Hill. They were left lying out there between the lines
for two nights and a day in the rain. Murder, sheer murder. But that's
what you do to them in Ireland anyway, isn't it? Murder them in the
rain. It solves the population problem. Fewer of the rebels to deal
with."

Hamilton laughed.

"The same old Seaforth," he said. "Never a good word when a bad
one will do. And never a cruel act when a kind one will do better."

"Ach, Seaforth's got the hands of a saint," Mary said. "With that
needle and scalpel of his, he could raise the dead – God forgive me for
saying it. And he does not care whether it's Boer or Tommy or Kaffir
or Jew, he'll put them back on their feet, he will."

Seaforth smiled his thin smile.

"But I might care more, Mary, if I was operating on an Indian,
don't you think? But we're not allowed to fight for you. Only patch
you up."

"You are a doctor, Seaforth Sinclair, and you know it. Here, some
Camp coffee. Put on the primus, Hamilton. That cousin of yours, he
does more good with his bag of tricks –"

"Than I do with all my engines." Hamilton turned up the wick of
the primus stove and struck a Lucifer match and started the little blue
flame. Then he picked up the bottle of liquid coffee and looked at the
label of the Highland soldier standing in his kilt with his tent and his
sirdar and the Himalayas behind him. "When I see this," he said, "I
think of my father Iain and the Mutiny, where we all began fighting
for the British, in India, after we were cleared."

"You left your little legacy from there," Seaforth said. "My sister
and I."

"And lucky we are for it," Mary said. "Look what you are doing for
us."

Marie had been lassoed. The rope had caught her, and she was hog-
tied. It was not so much the convention – she could buck that – it was
the competition. Those lovely ladies sweeping from their coaches, the
A La Girls. She had to admit, Sir George Davies's little number was
even better than her own 'Take Me':

> "Oh, the A La Girl is an English girl,
>   With lots of A La talk,
>   And when she goes down Regent Street,
>   She has an A La walk.
>   She's an A La twinkle in her eye,
>   She wears an A La curl,
>   And she cuts a dash,
>   With an A La mash,
>   Does the A La English girl."

And what a splash of a dash the A La girl cut. As she frothed down in her cascades of lace fringes on her countless petticoats, she swung her padded curves below her tight long skirts like two foxes curled in a bag. The men liked 'a fine woman', and that meant adding to bosom and behind rather than taking them in with corsets and stays. The whole mystery of woman – or so the swells said – lay in the undressing. You never did know what might be revealed: the Venus de Milo or a skeleton from the closet. As each layer came off, the excitement grew, the shape of Aphrodite was shown. Marie found out that she showed too much. Of course, her body was perfection, but the men knew too much about it. What was suggested was more tempting than what was seen. So Marie bought herself a Directoire dress, as soon as it was worn by the Lady Dandies. It was tobacco brown with no belt and a bolero. Marie could not resist having a slash in the long skirt, which did show rather too much of one leg – and much too much for most of the London ladies.

The changing fashions demonstrated that Queen Victoria was dying, and that her voluptuary of a sixty-year-old son, Edward, the Prince of Wales, would not have to wait in the wings much longer before reigning over an easier style of British life. The question was whether the aged Queen would last out the Boer War. Now it seemed won, with Piccadilly a huge street party on Mafeking night, when the besieged town was at last relieved. Bill Dunesk escorted Marie through the mob and the Union Jacks and the squirts and the peacock-feather ticklers – only a penny a plume. He looked rather like Banquo's ghost, a thin and tall spectre at the feast. Then he invited her to Scotland for the two weeks when the Palace was closed, changing its variety acts. Marie accepted. "Back to my roots," she said. "And I've never even seen them."

"There's a Sinclair castle and chapel down the glen," Bill said. "The old Sinclair places."

So Marie came to Dunesk Castle without even a chaperone. She would manage herself. The castle was near the paper mills of Penicuik and the coal mines, where the green glen of the Esk ran down through red-orange gorges past two other castles, Rosslyn and Hawthornden, down to the Firth of Forth by Edinburgh. The castle was elementary and magical, a fortified tower with rounded turrets under pointed slate hats rearing from the pink rock walls. Inside, the stairs were bare stone, but carpets covered the guard-room and great hall now, while huge log-fires warmed the chillness, and there was even hot water from an old boiler in the sole bathroom with its enamelled iron tub on four clawed feet. "Designer I may be," Bill said, "but my old castle defeats me. Basic it was, and basic it remains."

Yet he had designed the new paper-mill at Penicuik, which Marie discovered was making him rich along with his mineral rights from the coal mines on his land. Green tiles embellished with pale lilies and water-nymphs decorated the square brick factory, but the stream running from it was livid with red and yellow chemicals, and frothing with caustic soda. Inside, swatches of esparto grass were treated with lye before they were mangled into rolls of thick paper, which were then sliced into pages. Village women shuffled the pages into reams, riffling the papers with fingers as fast as the flutter of the wings of larks. "They are never wrong," Bill explained to Marie. "They do not count, they feel one hundred and fifty sheets to the ream, and they are always right."

"What are their wages?" Marie asked.

"A living," Bill said. "Before this it was starvation except for the Midlothian mines. The work at the paper has saved them."

"But not the river," Marie said.

Marie was right. The lye and the caustic and the bleach ran down to the Esk and painted the brown waters. And as she walked with Bill down through the ash and oak and thorn that lined the gorge, Marie could see trout floating white belly-up in the dark rock pools. But past the rose-red walls and ruined tower and causeway bridge of Rosslyn Castle, down in the zig-zag orange gorge across the rapids called The Dreepers, she saw the blue flash of a kingfisher and even the ochre swirl of an otter in the stream. All of nature had not been killed by the spills of man.

"William Wallace lived here with his rebels," Bill said. "In caves the ancient Picts made. Then the English caught him and they hanged him – they drew and quartered him – all for Scots freedom. You know the Burns poem, do you?" And his English drawl suddenly became a Scottish rant, his passion changing his voice from a trickle to a torrent.

"Scots, wha ha'e wi' Wallace bled!
Scots, wham Bruce has often led;
Welcome to your gory bed,
Or to victory."

"Robert the Bruce did fight here, and the Sinclairs, and my people the Frasers. There's a place I will take you riding – the Shin-bones or Stinking Rig – where the Frasers and the Sinclairs beat three English armies in the same day – and we're still digging up their bones, for they litter the field there."

"My grandmother Hannah told me," Marie said, "when we were being cleared from the Highlands, the Sinclairs and the Frasers, we were at school together. My uncles were always fighting your uncles ..."

"Sometimes we fought on the same side – at least against the English." Bill gave one of his rare smiles to Marie, which gave life to his pale skull of a face, where the bone almost seemed to push through the skin. "The Frasers and the Sinclairs – we can agree, you know. And look, there at the end of the gorge, there is Hawthornden." Another castle rose from the top of a cliff. "It is not a Fraser or a Sinclair castle – the Drummonds have it. Of course, William Drummond, he was the first traitor – or a diplomat, as you might say. The first good Scots poet to write in English, Drummond of Hawthornden."

The third of the castles along the Esk was the most dramatic. Although only a fortified manor house now, it stood on the far bank a thousand feet sheer above the tumbling river. It brooded over the rushing water, evoking the fierce and free streak in Marie – the child of the wilderness that would not be tamed. Yet as she looked at these strongholds of the centuries above the glen, she felt the love and the security that their owners must feel in them, and that the people of their clans must feel about them. And as if answering her unspoken thought, Bill said to her, "This was raiding country. The English over the Border, the steel bonnets of the other clans."

"We were a raiding nation," Marie said. "My other grandmother's people, the Crows. But when the raids came, we had nowhere to keep us safe. We had to pack camp, ride away with our keepers, begin again. I love it here."

"You know that they wrote of ancient Petra in Transjordan as a rose-red city half as old as time." Bill's hand swept towards

Hawthornden as a bird in flight. "I think of our fortresses in the glen as a rose-red castle twice as old as time."

On the walk back up the glen, Marie was taken up the hill to see Rosslyn Chapel, where Sir Walter Scott had confirmed that twenty Sinclair knights were buried in the vaults in full armour. Inside was the Third Day of Creation with every variety of fruit and leaf and plant carved over every pillar and arch and wall. A jungle of stone. The faces of green men shouted in dumb show or leered from the garlands and friezes. Marie was entranced.

"A Sinclair built this?" she asked. "It's as fierce as a forest."

And Bill nodded and said, "I do not think your ferocity comes only from the Crows. The Scots, you know, are a ferocious people ..."

"Not you, Bill. You're so soft ..."

"Try me," Bill said. "You might be quite surprised."

And Marie was surprised, when she went riding with him over the Pentland Hills in the afternoons. Although he looked like the Grim Reaper on a horse, he stuck on a saddle as if he were a spear in the back of his mount. When she galloped like the prairie wind on her pony, he went with her neck and neck over the moor, and when she leapt the rough stone walls, he soared beside her. She threw back her head and cried her Indian cry, "Wah-heeee," and her red hair flew in a banner behind. And when they reined up in a bog and turned, panting and laughing to each other, Marie saw another man, the colour high in his cheeks and whipcord in his lanky frame. And when he said to her, drawling again, "You will be my Countess – actually – will you?", she was unsure whether it was a proposal, and anyway, she certainly did not know what to answer. So she turned her pony and walked him off the soft ground, then she drummed her heels into his flanks and shouted over her shoulder, "Catch me first." And he did not catch her before she reached Dunesk Castle again.

When Peg Sinclair reached London on the P & O steamer from India to help to replace Mary at St Thomas's Hospital, her first wish was to meet her cousin Marie. The fame of the Canadian actress had reached Bombay. The *Illustrated London News* stretched to the ends of the Empire. Not an officers' mess or club missed the long white magazine, in which the drawings had given way to photographs, and the tidings of the metropolis had become the chat of the globe since the city was now an imperial hub, where the new god of love, Eros, stood erect with his aluminium bow and arrows above a fountain in the dead centre of the planet, Piccadilly Circus.

In fact, Peg met Marie under Eros. When they saw each other, they knew each other at once by their brown faces and prominent Sinclair bones. Marie bought Peg a posy of violets from one of the motherly flower girls who sat round the fountain in bonnet and boots, shawl and voluminous skirts. "I'd take you to the Cri," Marie said, "but it's men only, dirty rotters, and I have to be wearing my leggings to pass for male. So what do you want to try? The Troc or the Café Monico? But if you want to be really English –" giggling and looking at somebody who also said she was an Indian, Marie went on – "we should go to Snow's Chop House and have two poached eggs on finnan haddie and sit on oak pews. Or Scott's, of course, and have oysters and sole till we burst."

"Scott's," Peg said – "because we are not really."

So they left Eros and the painted façade of Swan and Edgar's towering over the horse-buses pulling round the circus, and they walked to Scott's with only two swooning swells coming up and muttering, "I say – take me, take me anywhere." When they reached the restaurant, the doorman swung the glass panels open as for royalty, "Miss Sinclair, how are you?" and Marie ushered Peg inside before her and said, "Nice to be known. If I wasn't, we'd be put out like two ladies of the street. It's just that now I am treated like a man." And the *maître d'hôtel* did indeed defer to Marie as to a gentleman, taking her over to the best table, offering her the wine list, and bending over her every wish with fond attention.

Looking round the other dining tables in the expanses of white linen and polished wood, Peg saw that she and Marie were the only two women dining with each other. The few other ladies there all had male escorts. Marie was privileged, that she was.

"Sauterne," Marie said. "Whitstables and Sole Walewska. What do you think?"

"Choose for me," Peg said, and Marie gave the order.

"It will be normal soon," Marie said. "Women dining together or even alone. When we have the vote."

"The vote," Peg said. "You are not serious."

"Oh, I have friends," Marie said. "Through Bill Dunesk – he is a friend of mine. They are serious. After the war they are going to fight for female suffrage. Suffragists – that's what they say they are."

"But men don't have the vote in India," Peg said. "So how can women? Many of us still wear the veil."

"You're just a colony still," Marie said. "But I am going to vote before I die. You will see. Things change. Look at you – a qualified woman doctor. It was not possible, even for Aunt Mary."

"I know. She made me do it. And Seaforth, my brother. Marie –"
Peg gave a mischievous smile which suddenly splintered her solemn
face – "it is so comic to me. In your acting, you call yourself an Indian.
And I really am an Indian. I know we're both Scots, too, but Indians
– how can you believe that?"

The opened oysters were set before the young women on beds of
cracked ice and vast silver platters with lemon slices in gauze to
squeeze over them and Tabasco sauce to sprinkle on them and fingers
of brown bread and butter to help them down.

"Some people say you can hear an oyster scream when you swallow
it," Marie said nonchalantly. "Others say they are good for making
love."

Peg smiled.

"We hear that in Bombay too. Although ginseng and powdered
rhinoceros horn – not medical prescriptions, I assure you."

Marie laughed.

"Buffalo horn for the Crows," she said. "We were called Indians
only because that fool Columbus thought he had reached India, when
he discovered America. Discovered? Actually, we discovered America
rather before Columbus, and when we discovered Columbus had
come, we let him overstay his welcome. Indians, I don't think we are.
But the name has stuck." Marie swallowed an oyster in one gulp and
then sipped the juice from the shell. Peg was closely watching her to
follow her example exactly.

"But meeting you, Peg, I tell you, I don't mind being called an
Indian, as long as I can be like you."

"Don't compliment me," Peg said. "You are the toast of London."

"I would rather be a doctor. Somebody useful."

"Not if you were one. The hours are terrible. And the human body
– if you see too many, you even are disgusted by your own."

"Nonsense. A beauty like you." Marie considered Peg's severe, but
handsome face with lines of judgement already etched deep by her
eyes and nose and only a full mouth to suggest any weakness. "It's
only your hair, you know. You mustn't waste it and coil it up like that
with that bonnet on. I reckon, when you undo it, you can sit on it.
That's what all the ladies want to do in London – sit on their hair."

"I am *not* a beauty –"

"You are."

"You're acting, telling me what is untrue."

"You are a beauty. And you can sit on your hair. Which is more
than I can. I have a mane like a red pony."

"It is beautiful. All London says so."

"Well, I will not wear a hat. I know all London wears hats because the Queen does. But I will not. I think hats are only for people who don't care for their hair, so they hide it. Don't you?"

"I have to wear a hat," Peg said. "In my position."

"Do you operate with your bonnet? Diagnose through your hat?"

"Oh, Marie, you know what I mean."

Marie swallowed another oyster, then she drained the salt juice.

"What other people do," she said, "you should never do. I never do. Except –"

"What?"

"Except – shall I tell you first?"

"Do, please."

"Only because we don't know each other. I believe in confiding in strangers."

"We are cousins."

"We live a world apart. Until now. Peg, what do you think? Shall I – shall I –" Marie prodded with her small silver oyster-fork at the flesh of the nearest shrinking mollusc. "Shall I go home to Sinclair country – Scotland – marry a Fraser and be a countess?"

"A countess. Marie, not really –"

"He is a good man. A fine man. I won't do better. And the influence I would have – the power. And I might be able to fight for the vote. But Peg, a *man* – to be bound to a man. I am free."

"The only free woman, Mary wrote to me, in all the world."

"Well," Marie said and drove the prongs of the silver fork into the raw oyster, "I reckon we're free to give our freedom away, if we want to. The Countess of Dunesk. That is something to crow about."

5

BURNING TIME

Hannah had told him how it was before she died. Only these were farms on the veldt, not crofts in the glen. But it was the clearances all over again. The worst moment was riding up to the house. The Boer women went to fetch a cup of milk. And the troopers had to say they came to burn the place down. They gave them ten minutes to evacuate, the women and the children. Some of the mounted men also gave the Boers a hand with the beds and the chairs – they took out their Bibles and the blankets themselves. Then the horsemen piled up the bales of straw round the walls and set them on fire. The women did not shout, they did not complain. They only opened their eyes until the troopers saw the flames dancing in them. And the men said, "How long will your men go on fighting? We only do this because you give the commandos food and supplies." And the women answered, "How long? Till you have gone away. We will still be here. We will be here longer than you."

So the mounted men rode on after the Orange Free Staters and the last of their armies. And they saw the mountains. They were blue and purple and bigger than the mountains of Scotland. With the Seaforths and the Highland Brigade were Lord Lovat's Scouts. They all felt that giddiness in the head to see the mountains, which is almost like the sea-sickness of a sailor, to see the strength of the hills ahead. Some of the Wittenbergen and the Roodebergen, the White Mountains and the Red Mountains, were smooth and round like the braes; but the most of them were bleak and bony ridges of crimson and bleached rock with stripes of snow in the gullies. Good lurking places for the Boer snipers, unless they could be cornered against the scarps and the steeps. And whoever heard of hemming in Brother Boer and certainly not de Wet, unless he made another bad mistake and decided to fight it out?

The Boers' weakness was their waggons. They would not leave their oxen and their carts. They were farmers. They had these travelling homes. However, they were boxed in now in the horse-shoe of the Brandwater Basin with enemies commanding three of the four passes out and Basutoland behind them. And the troopers had told

Chief Jonathan to stop them doubling back to the east. The Basutos hated the Boers, anyway. But trust de Wet: he did not stay in the trap, but rolled out over the open Slabbert's Nek with fifteen hundred men and four hundred waggons, rolling too fast even for the British cavalry. Yet the rest of the Dutchmen stayed put in their laagers. It was a hard fight carrying Rietef's Nek, but nothing that the Seaforths and the Black Watch could not do. When Hamish Charles heard the first challenge, *"Wie gaat daar?"*, he knew it was to be the bullet storm and the murderous jets spouting disaster from the barrels of the Mausers. But the five-pounder cow-guns were in the rear, and they hammered the Boer trenches. Then it was the charge and the bayonet as usual, but Hamish Charles would not use his pig-sticker, and he swung his rifle as a club to knock the Dutch skittles down.

Now Brother Boer had his neck in the noose. While he dithered about his surrender, Hamilton Charles rode over to see his cousin Robert in Strathcona's Horse. As he was not fighting now, he put off his khaki helmet and put on his full Lieutenant's uniform: his white cockade over his bearskin bonnet, his red sash over his scarlet coat and pipeclay bandolier, the white and red criss-cross of tartan lines griddling his green kilt that fell as far as the top of his black riding-boots. He seemed quite a sight to the shaggy Canadian cowboys with their unclipped broncos, the only colour in their camp a guidon presented by the ladies of Ottawa – crimson silk with a broad white stripe through the centre, bearing embroidered letters, *Strathcona's Horse*, and the noble lord's motto *Perseverance* below a Baron's coronet, a green maple leaf and a brown beaver.

"Very neat," Hamish Charles said to Robert, when they encountered each other in immediate recognition, the long Norse features being as they were.

Robert was shy, although that was hardly his nature. His cousin was an officer, and he was a trooper. And the Tommies were meant to care about rank. But he did not salute, and Hamish Charles did not dress him down for it, but shook his hand and said, "Far cry from the prairie."

"It's good country," Robert said. "You could make a go of it here."

"I met a Dutchman at Paaderburg," Hamish Charles said. "He said farming was good round Ficksburg. We might see him again."

"He got away?"

"Not far. He had a broken leg. But, yes, I hope he got away. It's better than being in a prison camp, and caged like a fly in a beer-bottle. St. Helena's full up of Boer prisoners. I hear they're sending them to Happy Valley in Ceylon."

"It's better than fighting."

"Is it? Not if you're a farmer. You want to go back to your land."

"I don't," Robert said. "My father Bain, mum and brother Gillon, they're stuck on the soil. All they think of is crop yields and barbed wire. The sky's big here. And the mountains. You can kind of breathe."

Hamish Charles looked over to the livid knuckles of the bergs in Basutoland, the cruel blue heaven stretching away, infinite to the end of sight.

"You can stop breathing here, too," he said. "Brother Boer – will he throw his slouch hat in the ring again? Or throw in the towel?"

"He's had it." Robert spat. "I don't know why he gave you such a hard time of it. Till we came and did it right for you."

"We had to learn," Hamish said. "We're still learning. We don't know how to fight a war like this. And even if this lot give in, there is still de Wet and the commandos. Don't think the war will be over here."

And it was not, even when Prinsloo threw in the towel. The finale at Fouriesburg was almost worthy of the Palace of Varieties. All the generals and their staffs were mounted, while the Highland Brigade and Strathcona's Horse and the rest of the contingents stood in two lines on the hills overlooking the basin. Prinsloo rode in between the ranks and handed his rifle to General MacDonald. After him, the Dutch farmers slouched along on their little ponies, throwing down their Mausers and bandoliers with a swagger into a weapons' pile. Then came the carts, dragged by the oxen and looking more like Romany caravans, bulging with cook-pots and blankets. And on the back-board of one of them, swinging his good leg, Piet Krug sat sucking at a pipe and lean as starvation. Hamish Charles broke ranks to greet him.

"Krug, you devil," he said. "You did get away."

"Sinclair, man," Krug said, "my farm's here. You are burning the farms now. A man has to fight for his *huis*."

"They'll send you to Ceylon now."

"If they can keep me," Krug laughed as his cart rolled on. "I see you in Ficksburg."

Hamish Charles resumed his post. He admired Krug for going back to the battle with a gammy leg. That was the trouble with a brave enemy. Soon you valued them almost as much as your own. And Krug was right. It was a dirty business, the burning of farms. He hoped it would not become worse, if the war went on against the commandos. Lord Bobs had mercy in him, but he was going home, now Pretoria was ours and Oom Paul Kruger was fled. If Kitchener took over, the K in his name did not stand for Knut, like the man in the music-hall song, Gilbert the Filbert, the pride of Piccadilly and the Kernel of the Knuts. It stood for Killer, for that is what Kitchener was.

Hamilton had succeeded in getting the permission of the Padre's Wife to take her daughter Ellen Maeve to a concert at the hospital. It might not have been quite the thing for a young lady, but there were more officers in Bloemfontein than there were in Aldershot, and if many of them were wounded, they would recover soon and be matchwood for marriage. And as for Naval Lieutenant Hamilton Sinclair, he was all in one piece, although inland. He had come to recuperate the naval guns, he said, although on the voyage over on the transport, the Padre's Wife had seen him often enough staring at Ellen Maeve, too shy to speak – or so she had thought. But they must have spoken in secret, impossible as privacy was on a troopship. Or Ellen Maeve would not have insisted with her quiet whim of steel in going to the concert with him. The Padre's Wife thought Ellen Maeve could do better, but she also knew better than to try to change her daughter's mind when it was set. Ellen Maeve might look like a buttercup with her forget-me-not eyes and body no bigger than a child; but she was as stubborn as an Afrikander ox, and when she said pretty please, it was a royal command. And if she had Hamilton in her sights when he thought he had her in his – well, he would be holed below the waterline and sunk without trace before he could bring a gun to bear on this gillyflower.

The skits in the smoker were uproarious, if one judged by the uproar. Yet Hamilton never even smiled at *Punch* and his feeble and occasional laughs were followed by Ellen Maeve, lifting her eyebrows and tut-tutting into her elbow-long gloves. She was, after all, a lady who visited the hospitals, and the humour was directed at her. And as for the fat old sergeant-major dressed up in a check table-cloth as a skirt and a frying-pan with paper roses as a hat, she did not think it was amusing that he sported a placard over his false bosom – OLD MAIDEN VISITOR – and spoke half in bass and half in falsetto, while a wounded Tommy with both legs in plaster reclined on an iron bed on stage.

OLD MAIDEN VISITOR: "Well, my dear man, and how are you today?"

WOUNDED TOMMY: "Me? I'm topping. How's yourself?"

OLD MAIDEN VISITOR: "Is there anything, but anything, I can do for you?"

WOUNDED TOMMY: (*Softly*) "Go away." (*Louder*) "No thanks, mum, I'll have a sleep."

OLD MAIDEN VISITOR: "Oh, very well, but are you sure I can't do anything for you?"

WOUNDED TOMMY: "Evaporate – I'll have a sleep."

OLD MAIDEN VISITOR: "But are you *sure* I can't do anything for you, my man. I can wash your face and hands. *Do* let me give you a nice little wash up."

WOUNDED TOMMY: "All right, mum, take my bally hands and wash away. If it ain't the seventh bally time I've had my hands washed today."

OLD MAIDEN VISITOR: "Then I shall read you to sleep. *Little Women*. It is very suitable – Louisa May Alcott and *Little Women*."

WOUNDED TOMMY: "Perhaps you would read, mum, to my friend Mac in the next bed. He'd appreciate it."

OLD MAIDEN VISITOR: (*Offended*) "Then I will read to your friend Mac in the next bed. It is so nice to be appreciated." (*She turns her back and opens the book.*)

WOUNDED TOMMY: (*Settling down*) "Mac's been dead since morning."

As Hamilton took Ellen Maeve away from the concert, he felt his cheeks burning at the mess that he had made of the entertainment. But she was all sweetness and light, hanging on his arm no heavier than a dandelion puff or thistledown. He had no idea of the mischief in her.

"I don't think soldiers are ever very funny," she said. "Plod, plod, plod – that is all they do. Boots, boots, boots, boots, marching up and down again – it does not sharpen the wits. But a sailor on the ocean wave – springing up and down, all that rum and hornpipes – it must be most stimulating."

"Routine, miss, routine." Hamilton racked his brains to think of one nautical joke, and could not come up with any. His brain was like a pea-soup fog on the Solent. "My brother-in-law Charles serves on the battleship *Terrible*. He's just had a good time, picking up some Germans sneaking in by Delagoa Bay to fight for Johnnie Boer. Dirty trick, that. And the Kaiser's our own Queen's grandson."

"Wagner," Ellen Maeve said. "And Goethe. The Germans do have music. And a great deal of soul, especially soul."

"And big guns," Hamilton said. "And ships as good as ours. I wonder, in a scrap, if they'd fire Wagner at us. Pepper us with Mozart or sink us with Goethe."

Ellen Maeve laughed. Men liked to have their little jokes laughed at, and it was easy if one liked the man.

"I would rather be battered by Beethoven," she said. "And sunk by Nietzsche."

"Who?" Hamilton said.

"A philosopher," Ellen Maeve said. "He believes in the Superman. And I must say, I think I see one around."

Now Hamilton's cheeks burned again. Never in his life had a young woman complimented him. He had long believed he was irredeemably ugly and born to be a bachelor. And now, this wisp of a thing, this sprite of mere ether, she was saying, Superman.

"Oh, I don't know – really."

"Modesty," Ellen Maeve said, "is not an attribute that Nietzsche gives to a Superman. But you must break the rule." She smiled and added, "And you must take me home now. Mother will be worried. And if we are late, Father will denounce you from the pulpit."

"Yes," Hamilton said in ecstasy. "But when – when will I see you again?"

"How long is your leave?" Ellen Maeve said. "Or your mission."

"Nothing will take me away," Hamilton said, "if I have to spike the Admiral."

"Then the day after tomorrow," Ellen Maeve said, knowing that waiting always increased the mettle of a man. No young woman should ever be too available. "I will look forward to my Superman."

6

A MATTER OF
CONCENTRATION

Peg Sinclair was standing with the crowd on Trinity Pier at East
Cowes, when Lord Roberts came home. The noise was deafening, all
the ships at anchor blowing their whistles as shrill as shrikes, and the
horse artillery bombarding their ears with a nineteen-gun salute. The
little polished hero seemed too tiny for such a large welcome. But off
he went from the gangplank to Osborne to see the ailing Queen
Victoria, who had put the Victoria Cross on his tunic forty years
before and now made him an earl and a Knight of the Garter. The
honours were for giving Johnnie Boer a bloody nose, and they were
almost the last honours that the Queen and Empress would give. For
she herself would be needing the last rites in twenty days, dying with
Her grandson the Kaiser of Germany at attention at Her left bedpost
and her eldest son, the new King Edward the Seventh, at Her right
bedpost. As the King had to leave for London to attend the Accession
Council, the Kaiser would make the arrangements for the lying-in-
state. He would order Union Jacks to be draped around the walls of
the room where his grandmother's coffin lay, covered with flowered
wreaths. He would even stay in England for Her funeral and be made
a British Field Marshal for his devotion, although he was on the other
side.

Peg's concern was not with this royal display of care. Her job was
with the wounded, who had come back with the new Earl Roberts on
the ship from South Africa. They were to be taken to St Thomas's
Hospital for further operations or to convalescent homes in Hastings
and Hove. She supervised their transfer from their sea-borne wards to
railway train seats, where the compartments had been converted to
ambulances for the journey. Of course, the new upholstery with its
bulging curves and scarlet and yellow dragon patterns was protected
from any contact with the bleeding by linen sheets. And the sharp
smell in the air was of varnish, not of ether or carbolic. Yet the
soldiers found their berths comfortable after the sea voyage, and the
jolting at the points on the tracks better than the pitching of the vessel

in the Bay of Biscay. It was nice looking up at the nets of the luggage racks rather than at swaying hammocks. They were home on the land where they had longed to be.

This was a heroes' homecoming, too, in the last popular war. Peg met another trainload of disabled men, when Earl Roberts reached Paddington Station, and the new Prince and Princess of Wales were there to greet him – and a fine crowd that nearly shattered the glass roof of the steam terminus with its hoorays and huzzas. While the earl and the countess – Bobs's wife had always wanted to be that – went off to Buckingham Palace with fifteen thousand troops lining the route, Peg again oversaw the shipping of the men from the train seats to the horse-drawn ambulances waiting outside the station. The stretcher-bearers were too rough with them. One trooper with an amputated leg was dropped onto the platform and swore like his rank. "Pig-dogs," was the best word he found for them. The rest was unprintable, and was not printed.

Yet Peg found that she could support these ceremonies at what was meant to be the end of the war more easily than she could deal with Marie's wedding in St. Mary's Undercroft in the consecrated vaults below the House of Lords, with their painted arches and ceilings which showed saints and martyrs being boiled alive in scalding cauldrons. She had so looked forward to it. This would be the best occasion in her life – except for her own wedding. She had spent three months' pay on a pink silk dress, long and tight, but flowering at the bosom into the opulent petals of spring. Her white hat was wide and grew glass cherries; her white gloves made an eighth skin as far as her elbows and buttoned over her wrists with small pearls. But the condescension of the other guests killed her, the terrible talking down their noses and the cutting inflections of their voices that the English used to demean lesser breeds by the social death of a thousand slights. Her own family was the worst, her cousin May and the snobbish Charles Seymour-Scudabright with their mincing daughter Ruth; but she had to say that Murdo, allowed the day off from Harrow, was sweet to her, perhaps because his childhood in Peru had taught him that brown people could also be human.

The reception at the Café Royal after the marriage ceremony was in the wrong place and at the wrong time, but that was what Bill Dunesk and Marie wanted, and that was what they had. Peg thought that Marie's wedding-dress was miraculous and outrageous: ten thousand pearls stitched over a clinging sheath of a gown with a head-dress of osprey feathers that made her look like an Indian princess on the peace path. But her husband loved it, stammering in the receiving line to his astounded family and friends: "Meet my wife – all oyster seeds and wings; mermaid and bird – Marie." And her bronze beauty and quicksilver laughter won them all, whatever they were saying behind her back.

"I am so glad, darling," Peg said. "If you are half as glad as I am, you will be happy for ever."

At the reception, Peg backed herself into a corner. It was so much easier that way. To be ostracized was nothing. She was used to it, far better than being patronized or having to explain why she was there or what sort of a cousin she was exactly to the bride. People would come to her, if that is what they wanted to do. But only one waiter did, to offer her a glass of champagne, which she did not drink. And Murdo came, all gangling and floppy-haired, and spoke to her about how topping it was to be a schoolboy at Harrow, all the fun and the games of it with a little work added. Latin was not for him, and Spanish, which he knew, was not on the curriculum. And then at last Marie reached her, ignoring the rest of the aristocratic guests as they had ignored her.

"Peg, my darling," she said. "Have I done the right thing?"

"You have done well for yourself," Peg said.

"That's just the sort of thing my mother Kate would say. I don't expect it, Peg, from you."

"His friends," Peg said. "You have to marry his friends and family too. And if these are they –" her right white glove swept in the stroke of a scythe to indicate the room – " then I don't know."

Marie laughed like a clash of cymbals.

"He won't have *them* long," she said. "If you think we will have the *same* kind of friends – but some of them I like. The poets and the painters and the architects and the designers."

"They're so decadent," Peg said. "And not very interested in women."

"I am."

"I know you are. The vote –"

"We'll get it now."

"*You* can do it?"

"I can do anything," Marie said. Then she laughed again, now in a descant of bells. "Didn't you know that?"

"But –" Peg was not quite convinced by her cousin's confidence. "Do you know you will be happy? With Bill? In *every* way?"

"What do you mean?"

"Oh –" Peg flushed. "I –" She looked for the right words. "You're so human – warm – strong. You are physical. He is so withdrawn – inward. That male world. Clubs and other men. That is England."

"He can kiss," Marie said. "I know. And soon I'll know more, I guess."

Peg smiled and stroked the pearls on Marie's gown. Her nail caught a strand and snapped the stitches and white granules fell onto the carpet.

"Oh, Marie, look what I've done!"

As Peg bent to scramble for the pearls on the carpet, Marie straightened her.

"Don't," she said. "We'll find them later."

"People with step on them, crush them."

"So what? They're only pearls. Not people. Peg, I must go. But keep in touch. When you can manage after patching up our stupid men back from the war. I am honoured – truly honoured – you found the time to come here for this –" she found the right word for it – "extraordinary occasion."

Peg smiled and looked round the room, crowded with morning coats and cravats, diamond sprays and mellifluous voices, broken by cackles of malice.

"Yes," Peg said. "An extraordinary occasion. For an extraordinary woman, too. You, Marie."

At eighty, Mary Sinclair was another extraordinary woman. She had met a bustling, dumpy lady from England, Emily Hobhouse, who burrowed like a mole after the truth in the hole where it had hid itself. "The concentration camps," Emily told her. "We are killing Boer women and children there. You must come and see them with me, Miss Sinclair. They will believe your word in London – as they would believe the word of Miss Nightingale, God rest her soul. Even if they will not believe my word. For I am a liberal, you see. And a busybody. And a woman. And I do not think General Kitchener likes any of the three. He only listens to his moustache."

So it was that Emily Hobhouse and Mary Sinclair saw the conditions beside the railway sidings, after one of the great drives against the Boer commandos still on their flight over the veldt. The bag of the game was women and children in open cattle trucks, sodden in the icy rain. And if they arrived alive after the rail journey, the camps were a shambles. Potchefstroom and Mafeking itself, these were a revenge. The Boer women thought so. This was genocide, the killing of a nation. Because you could not catch their men on their horses, you killed their women and children by herding them into camps to die of disease and bad weather and poor feed. But people were not cattle. Even the Boers loved their oxen, their Afrikanders, better than the *rooineks* loved the *vrous* and *kinders* in their forced care. This was the matter of the concentration of them in the camps.

The thinking of it was army thinking in the divisions that set humans apart. There were the *hensoppers*, who put their hands up and got double rations, and the *bittereinders*, whose men were still fighting in the commandos and who did not fare half so well. Not that the rations were so good, anyway: a pound of meal and half a pound of meat a day, a scrape of sugar and coffee if you were lucky, and no fruit juice or vegetable or jam or milk, even for a baby. It made a *vrou* think. If they were killing her and her *kinders*, what was the poison? There were the blue things in the sugar, that were said to be making it whiter. There was ground glass in the meal and fish-hooks in the bully beef. Not that anyone had found them, but they must be there, because of all of the sickness that was going on. Certainly, the women and the children were dying in the camps in their hundreds and their thousands. And if it was meant to be typhoid and enteric from the bad water, and measles and dysentery, pneumonia and influenza and scarlet fever, malaria and bronchitis and diphtheria and whooping cough, why, these were just the names of the illnesses that the *rooineks* used to excuse the killing of the Boers. At Potchefstroom, there were no tents to put them in, only reed huts. Even the oxen were treated better in their *kraals*. As Emily Hobhouse reported:

> I call this camp system wholesale cruelty. It can never be wiped out from the memories of the people. It presses hardest on the children ... Entire villages and districts rooted up and dumped in a bare strange place. To keep their camps going is murder for the children. Of course by judicious management they could be improved; but do what you will, you can't undo the thing itself.

Sweat dropped from Emily's forehead and blotted the ink on her writing. She put down her pen and wiped her brow and turned to Mary Sinclair, sitting like a still judge in a corner chair in their tent in the camp at Potchefstroom.

"Do you think they can be improved, Miss Sinclair?"

"Improvement?" Mary Sinclair sniffed. "Hell canna be improved. It willna stop the killing of the bairns. Thousands will die. Tens of thousands. I dinna ken how it was done, why it was done."

"Policy," Emily said. "It's the name men give for stupidity. Kitchener wants to win the war quickly. He does not mind how."

"Concentration camps," Mary said. "Now we have made them, they will be made again. It is a terrible invention. It will haunt us all our days, and the generations that will come."

"I cannot get Kitchener to close them."

"Then we must improve them, as you say." Mary tried to rise from her chair, but fell back. "Ach, my bones. They are set. Old bones set. Give me a hand, Miss Hobhouse." And Emily pulled Mary to her feet. "I am set in my ways like my bones are. But we must find new ways."

"In London, we have Miss Fawcett," Emily said. "Millicent Fawcett is formidable. She wants the vote for women. Then we shall change things."

"I dinna hold with that," Mary said. "It is not the time yet. But the women here – the Afrikaner women – I think they can change things. Women – all women – they can shame men into the changes. If there are children. Though they forget it, every man – he was a child with a mother."

"The incorrigible women, the women who protest, they lock them in a barbed wire *laager*. They call it the Hog's Paradise."

"We will see about that," Mary said grimly and hobbled to the entrance of the tent. "And as for the sickness, I have sent for my nephew Seaforth to come here and help us to report. It is the more important to look for these prisoners than to care even for our soldiers. And Seaforth is the best doctor in all Africa, although he is my nephew."

Even the sentry could not refuse Mary Sinclair admission to the Hog's Paradise, although he had orders to do so. He quailed in front of the bent figure in black, whose power of command had more force than a brigadier's. Inside the *laager*, a dozen women lay in the dirt, wrapped in their single brown blankets. One of them stood up to shout at the two visitors, howling in an Afrikaans that Mary barely understood. "*Ons mans ... kinders ... broers ... huis ...*" She cut the edge of her hand across her throat as if slicing with a knife blade. "*Wat sal van ons word?*"

"She means" – Mary explained to Emily Hobhouse – "I think she means, what will be for us? What the now?"

"She will be out of here," Emily said. "And *now*." She started forward and caught the young Boer woman as she tottered on her broken boots and began to sag to the ground. "Look." A dark stain was spreading over the sand from under the woman's draggled skirt. "She's bleeding to death. Help me."

The old Mary and the dumpy Emily stood either side of the young prisoner — two living crutches to assist her out of the *laager* of her rebellion. The protest of the sentry died on his lips. In fact, he bowed a little as they passed and grounded his rifle. And so it was that Seaforth, arriving, met his aunt returning with a victim of the war, that was now a total war against family and house, the shape of the new war to come.

Seaforth could not do much for the woman, who had suffered a massive haemorrhage. There was no stopping the blood coming from her. And Mary and Emily, kneeling beside her in their tent, they could hardly understand her broken words in Afrikaans. But they did discover her name before she passed away in the evening. Annie Krug from near Ficksburg and Basutoland. Her husband was Piet Krug.

"That is a name I know," Mary said, as Emily helped her to her feet. "My nephew Hamish Charles, who is fighting here, he told me of a Piet Krug. He may not be the same. But if it is, he has lost a wife."

"It is shameful," Emily said. "Shocking." She began to cry silently, the tears rolling in glass beads down her cheeks. "I never saw a sister die like that before."

"Hundreds I have seen," Mary said. "Having a baby. Or not having a baby, like that poor Annie. A miscarriage."

"A miscarriage of justice, I think," Seaforth said. "I'll bring in the grave-diggers. Do they have one of those dark *predikants* round here? To bury her in her misguided faith."

"Aye," Mary said. "There is one. Find him, Miss Hobhouse." And as Emily left, Mary put her hand on Seaforth's. "You do not like their faith?"

"It does not like me," Seaforth said. "I am the son of Ham, the devil, really. Why, this woman would not have let my coloured hands touch her — and certainly not intimately — only she was too sick to stop me."

"They are women," Mary said. "They suffer. We all suffer the same."

"I know, Aunt Mary. I took an oath, the Hippocratic oath. To care for all equally. But as you know, all do not care for me equally. And these women, many are *trekboers* — they do not know hygiene, they have never seen a latrine. And their remedies! Their cures kill them. Fever — they put tar on their feet. They drink dogs' blood to feel better. Cow dung ... horse dung ... smeared on or boiled and eaten ... that aids arthritis and enteric."

"I would it would aid my arthritis," Mary said, "if I could take the cure."

"A black chicken, cut open – its blood on the chest is the remedy for pneumonia. Shave a cat and its roasted fur will charm away bronchitis." Seaforth shook his head and smiled. "Witchcraft. And ignorance. Poor farm people still living in the Dark Ages."

"Poor people," Mary said, "who dinna deserve to be here."

"Right," Seaforth said. "Right as always. Indomitable and right." He looked down at the dead young woman, whose cheeks were bleached now in a sort of peace. "If I felt the pity I feel, I would not do my job."

"I know, Seaforth. You are a good doctor, a good man."

"But this sight, Aunt Mary, how can you go on believing the Empire after this?"

Mary now looked down at the young woman, who had bled to death. "Hold me," she said. And as Seaforth held her by the waist, she managed to bend and close the eyelids of Annie Krug and cross her hands, the one over the other. "There." Now she straightened herself as best she could, and she answered Seaforth's question. "You are right, Seaforth. I canna believe in the Empire. If it does this ... to the women and the children."

Seaforth did what he rarely did. He hugged his old aunt, who had been as much of a mother as any he had had in his life.

"You were always the fair one," he said. "The only one who could understand."

"Get away with you," Mary said, pushing at his chest. Then she rapped his ribs with her bony knuckles, quite paining him. "Find the facts. Write them for the report for the Distress Committee. We will stop the dying. We must. It is a wrong, a great wrong, that canna be forgot. But it will be a greater wrong if we dinna do something for it."

There were a few Commandos still loose on the borders of Basutoland, but Hamish Charles knew that the war was over. He had already applied to be released from his commission, when he took leave and rode from Ficksburg over the Karroo towards the blue mountains. They were drawing him towards them. They were an answer to what to do after the war. And he had to find Piet Krug. His aunt Mary had told him of the death of the wife of a Piet Krug in a concentration camp, that shameful way of winning the war. Of course, Piet might now be rotting in a prison camp himself in Ceylon, but Hamish Charles had his doubts. Piet would have escaped again and be back in his farm, if the British troops had not burned it when they took his wife away.

The sandy road across the Karroo was caked and cracked, although the hoofs of the horse kicked up pillars of powder. Here and there, a dust devil danced with ragged veils among the milk-bushes that poked out their dry leaves from the plain. Soon the coat of the horse and the khaki uniform and pith helmet of the rider were matted with a clinging reddish dust, while they plodded heavily towards the promise of the far bergs. A song that the Boers were singing kept on haunting Hamish Charles, as he licked his lips that tasted like old ropes. It was written by a young woman when her sweetheart had been trapped and sent to prison camp after the surrender at Brandwater Basin. Hamish Charles only knew the first line in Afrikaans, the rest in English. He mouthed the words dumbly, unable to croak a sound:

> "Zeit gy Ginds de Blaawe Bergen
> Did you see those Blue mountains,
> Who will us betray?
> Taken prisoner by the foemen
> And sent so far away."

That evening, he was singing the song loudly after slaking his thirst from his water bottle, when a bullet flicked off his pith helmet and flung it against the charred wall of the abandoned farmhouse. As he swung round, his hand reaching for the butt of his service revolver, he heard a familiar voice say, "Drop it! *Soe*, it is you! You are a *schelm*. You have your damfool head shot off."

And there was Piet, lankier and hairier than ever, dropping the barrel of his Mauser, as he stood in the ruined doorway, fit to scare a buzzard in his patched dirty overcoat and clobbered slouch hat.

"You missed," Hamish Charles said. He bent and picked up his helmet and stuck his forefinger in the hole in the top of it. "You'll cost me a guinea to get a new one. I have two saddlebags of supplies, man. And a pannier of water. You must be starving."

"You come to look for me?"

"Yes. I did."

Hamish Charles saw the change in the troubled gaze of the Afrikaner. His eyes pierced with sudden certainty.

"She is dead. You come to say Annie is dead."

"After supper, Piet. I tell you then."

"Tell me now. She is dead."

"My aunt Mary, she is a head nurse. She went to see one of those terrible camps, for the women."

"They take her from my farm," Piet said. He shook his head slowly. "They burn it. They kill her. And you say, this is a war of gentlemen."

"It was fever," Hamish Charles said. "My aunt Mary is writing a report to the Government. She says it is barbarous – immoral – the concentration camps. Making war on women and children. I think so. I am leaving the army. I will not fight like that."

"Your bloody generals," Piet said. "They lead you to our guns like waterbuck. Then with fire and barbed wire, they kill mother *vrou* ... *kinders*. Hyenas, *aasvogels, tijgers* –"

"I agree with you with all my heart," Hamish Charles said. "Kitchener is a butcher. The means don't worry him as long as he wins. But I came here, man, to find you and do you some good. There may be a way to build all this again – for you to start all over again." His hand swept quickly over the blackened bricks of the walls, then dropped to his side. "I love this country, I don't know why. I am damn sorry what we have done to it. And to you."

Piet looked keenly at Hamish Charles and believed him.

"You are here to say that," he said. "Eat. You are right. Eat. Then we talk."

They lit a campfire in the nearby *kopje*, where Piet was hiding until peace was officially declared. He had left the commandos, he said. Captured twice, he would not ride out again for a lost cause. He still had a limp from Paaderberg, he had no oxen or horses left, his home was in ruins. He lived on what he could kill with his rifle, but he was down to six rounds. The last two weeks he had lived on two ostriches and their nest of eggs – he had to kill both parent birds to break his immense scramble of yellow yolks. "Man, they can take your belly out with one claw. And that old cock, why, he sit on the eggs and hatch them like she sit. You can steal them not." He was even out of *biltong*, the salted and sun-dried antelope sticks of meat which kept the commandos going.

Hamish Charles's iron rations were a life-saver: biscuit and corn-beef and mealie meal and salt fish and dried apricots and coffee. He even had a hundred rounds for the Mauser, because he now carried one of the rifles himself. "Better than ours," he said. "German guns are."

Piet dribbled the brass cartridges through the long bones of his fingers, thick at the knuckles. A laugh like a death rattle made a hole in his beard, but the open mouth might have been a plea to put something in it. "God – it is not possible. An *rooinek* give me bullets. And we still fight."

"It's a stupid war," Hamish Charles said. "We don't need your land."

"The gold," Piet said. "The diamonds at Jo'burg. You want that. That Baas Rhodes of yours, he want everything. But the poor land ... I think you leave it me."

"Actually," Hamish Charles said, "I thought – after the war is over –I might come and help you farm it. I mean, nobody wants it, do they?"

"The land here, take what you want. But there is grass not. For each ox, five acres to feed. If there is *vlei* not, wet land, then the ox die. But plenty *vleis*, plenty ox. You can make *trek*, pull a hundred waggon."

"Are there *vleis* round here?"

Piet's eyes were shrewd now, even if he looked direct at his friend and enemy.

"There are *vleis*," he said. "I had two hundred Afrikanders. I can show you *vleis*. Depend the land you want."

"And what I can do for you –" Hamish Charles poked at the charcoal under the cooking-pot hanging from a tripod of branches above the campfire. "I have a proposition, Piet Krug. When it is peace-time –"

"Peace? Time? Too long time for peace, I think."

"Four years? Too long, true. When it is peace, we buy – I buy with my back pay – two teams of oxen. You choose them, you know the beasts."

"My old ox," Piet said sadly, "they had names. Biffel, Bonteman, Witbles, Vaalpens ... I know them. I say name, he do it. Not *sjambok*, whip not. He do it."

"We take the waggons to Delagoa Bay. We load up with supplies, what we need for building your farm again – and starting mine. Then we trek back here. And we pick up any surplus army stores on the way. When we win, you know, when we pull out of Africa, they'll sell all the army surplus stores for a song. War – it's a bloody wasteful business."

"That it is. Why you – you want to farm this dry country?"

"I don't know." Hamish Charles looked up at the black quilt of the night above, studded with Orion and Andromeda and the Plough and a myriad of stars, the Milky Way a bright scarf flung across the constellations. "It is so big, I suppose. And it's here, as they say."

"You are here," Piet said. "Let us eat."

Over their meal of stewed salt pork and beans, washed down with a pint of Cape brandy, Hamish Charles and Piet agreed their deal. When the war was over and the Seaforths had discharged Lieutenant Sinclair with his back pay, he and Piet would make the trek to Delagoa Bay and back again. Then they would set up on adjoining farms on the Karroo below the blue mountains of Basutoland. Then Piet learned that Hamish Charles had a cousin Robert from Canada who now wanted to join the Colonial Service and become an Assistant District Officer in Basutoland, for he also had fallen for the bergs and the *kopjes* and the riding wild. So Piet laughed and said, "Man, we have everything. Those Kaffirs over the border, they take ox, they no good. But if your cousin is the *baas*, the law, he hang them."

"I don't know, Piet," Hamish Charles said. "Robert never struck me as a hanging man. He's more of a cowboy, really. But he wants to be a Mountie now – in Africa. He was brought up on a prairie. Nothing as far as the eye can see. Worse than the Karroo. But when he saw these mountains, he went ape. All Scotsmen love the mountains. It's in the blood."

"Your cousin in Kaffir country," Piet said. "I like it. But you ask everything, but not the one thing. Wife. You farm not if wife not."

"But I thought – your Annie – you have just lost her."

"Lost?" Piet's voice was bitter. "You found Annie here. You killed her. But did I say, my wife? I say, your wife. Not wife, not farm."

Hamish Charles felt his cheeks redden, but he put it down to the smouldering charcoal.

"I haven't had the opportunity lately –"

"Marry our girls – they lose their young men. In the war, in prison camp. I know sisters – van der Merwes – family with three sisters. If you like one, maybe I like other sister. Then we brothers, no?"

"If I like one –" Hamish Charles was hesitant.

"She know ox, cow, sheep, mealies, butter. How you run farm, my friend, my brother – and farm wife not?"

7

ALWAYS NOWHERES

Bain was the last of the three old Sinclair brothers. The other two, Iain and Angus, had always thought him the slowest and the least. But he did not care for their opinion. He alone had endured in Canada. He lived by the wind and the sky. The earth did not move for him. But the blades and heads of his wheat rippled and shook and shimmied to the gusts. The heavy and bowing winter grain stalks moved in eddies, while the spring wheat with its young seed-rows danced in the breeze. Yet the wind seemed to blow the horizon away even beyond the reach of human sight, which could only scan the edge of the world in the semi-circle of the watching eye-ball.

The pure light was scoured by the rush of the air, which blew everything clean and sharp except in the dry fallow falls, when the dust storms huffed and puffed grit into every crack and corner and room and mouth. Some folks would call the Canadian prairie before the Rockies a kind of desolation. But not Bain. By fence and post and seed and stock, he had made the land his own. Or he believed he had, unable to see his tiny irrelevance on the gigantic shield of the red grass plain, where the buffalo were reduced to a few bleached bones.

He worked the land with his son Gillon, who had stayed home while his brother Robert rode off to the war in Africa and now studied to become an Assistant District Officer in London. Gillon was no talker, but he was a worker, and he would stay from dawn to dusk behind the plough, turning up the furrows after the horse-teams. The work had built up his shoulders which topped his strong body like a cross-beam. But the work was killing Julia, Bain's wife. Although she was born stocky and powerful, there was always something out of sorts with her. Women – always complaining about their innards, and too delicate to say exactly what the matter was. And all the dosing and sulphur and molasses to thin the blood didn't seem to do a tad of good. She was not fading away, but she was swelling up, as if there was an ill water in her, as in the creek at the end of summer, near dry and poisonous until the snow melted and flushed it bright in the spring.

"We're nowheres, pa," Gillon said around the kitchen table in the evening. "Ain't you never reckoned, this is no place, noville, nowheres, noworld, nix in the sticks."

"Where are we?" Bain said. "Right here. Right now. If you can't see it, you can't see it at all. Now your brother –"

"Pancakes," Julia said, bringing in three plates that looked like steaming dumplings. "And gravy." And that was a china sauceboat full of dark juice.

"What's in them?" Bain said.

"Don't you mind," Julia said. "Beef and stuff. I'm the cook."

"Sure are," Gillon said. He took his hot lump on his plate and cut into it with his knife. Vapours rose out, smelling of meat and herbs. He put a morsel on his fork, lifted it and breathed on it to cool it before he put it into his mouth. "Tasty," he said, not very well for his mouth was full with the savouring.

"Very tasty," Bain said. Julia had to be praised for her cooking.

"That old stove," Julia said, "we need a new one."

"It's cast-iron," Bain said. "It lasts for ever."

"I don't," Julia said. "I'm not cast iron. And I'll not be lasting without a new stove."

"All right," Bain said. "But the harvest this year – eighty cents a bushel, if we're lucky."

"Kill ourselves," Julia said, "working the land. What do we get for it?"

"Ma's got a point," Gillon said.

"It's my land," Bain said. "We was cleared from Scotland. Never had food. Now it's our land. Don't forget that. Our land. And we never had none."

"It's not the Highlands," Gillon said. "The mountains, I go for them. You remember that grizzly I shot, pa?"

"Yeah," Bain said. "I remember the grizzly."

"On the mountains," Gillon said. "Not on the prairies. All you have here is coyotes and gophers. Not grizzlies and mountain lions."

"You got wheat," Bain said. "And stock."

"And nowheres," Julia said. "Gillon is right. Give me the dishes, I'll wash them."

"Good, ma, good," Gillon said and handed back his plate, which he had cleaned out. "Kate, she's coming. We'll see her."

"Anyone –" Julia waddled to her feet. Her legs were so big now they almost stuck together – "any folks come here, it's a miracle."

"It's ours," Bain said. "What do you want? It's our land."

"I don't know." Julia stacked the plates and moved heavily towards the kitchen. "I want more folks. I don't want to live always nowheres."

When Kate did come along the dirt track from the faraway station where her husband Bob McDowell had dropped her off the Canadian Pacific Railway, she had not particularly wanted to come. Family – family – that was the word people in the family always talked about, because they were part of it. She felt she had to meet with the family in Canada from time to time; that proved there was a family there. But on the other hand, she knew she would only be walking into the censure of the family, because it had never approved of her marriage with a *métis* and half-breed, her daughter Marie being a quarter-Indian and a Crow. She was very defiant when she delivered the opening shot in the permanent family war.

"Now that Marie is the Countess of Dunesk –"

"The marriage," Bain said, knocking the bowl of his pipe on the table like drum taps. "The marriage – it is certain?"

"Like the railway timetable," Kate said. "You can catch a train to Scotland, and it will be there. Marie was married to the Earl of Dunesk. And a good Scots family it is, the Frasers."

Bain shook his head very deliberately. He was the master of his own land in Canada such as it was. Nobody could take away his soil and his creek. There was an absolute certainty in his manner, which weighed down the doubt in his mind. For all his air of conviction – and Kate knew that – Bain was a timid man. His caution and stability was actually a fear of moving and of risk.

"An actress," he said. "Your daughter."

"Sinful," Julia said. "Your daughter."

"And she married the Earl of Dunesk." Slowly Bain stuffed the head of his meerschaum pipe, stained brown with nicotine already, with a pinch of the stimulating brown weed. "That is why we left the old country. I reckon they are soft. They make the wrong choices."

"What?" Kate was indignant. "My Marie, she is not good enough for the Earl of Dunesk? She is better. She could be Queen. Mary, Queen of Scots, Marie, Queen of Scots. That's my Marie."

Bain stuffed his tobacco down into the bowl of his pipe as tight as an argument.

"She's part Indian," he said. "A Crow. I don't see a Crow sitting on the Stone of Scone."

"All I see," Kate said, "is a fool with a pipe sitting on dirt which blows away on the wind."

That started it. That is what family quarrels always were. Surely, there was a difference, but always about the same thing. One branch of the family disapproved of the other branch, not so much what they had done, but how it affected the family through the blood. Then it was nasty. But in the end, they had to make up. For they were family, were they not? Whatever they had done or had not done, blood would tell. They were related.

"Where's Gillon?" Kate finally had to talk about the son, who was missing that evening from the table. "Does he really not want to meet me?"

"He says he's sorry." Julia was adamant. "He cannot be here. He is – he is –"

"Courting," Bain said. "We do not approve."

"Good," Kate said. "I hope she's a Sioux or another Crow."

"Worse," Julia said. "A Russian. And still something too bad – a Christ-killer."

"A Jew?"

"A Jew."

Kate began laughing fit to burst. "I don't believe it," she said. "Gillon. The good boy who didn't run away like my Marie and your Robert. And now he's off with a Russian Jewess. You must be so proud – and pleased. What is her name?"

"Rachel." Julia's mouth closed in a tight ring. "Is that a name?"

"It's in the Bible," Kate said.

"What is the Bible?" Bain said, sucking on his pipe, which he had not yet lit. "The Scriptures, some of them are fitter than others. And their *names*! Nebuchadnezzar, Melchizedek, Zedekiah – you would not approve them all."

"There's nothing wrong with Rachel," Kate said.

"Nothing wrong." Bain tried to make his composure that of a Solomon at the judgement. "But all the same, Mary or Kathleen – and you are Kate – I think there are better names for the Sinclairs."

Kate rose to her feet. "I will not be resting here," she said. "I come in between trains, and it is a sore trial to reach you here on the carts before Bob and the CPR come back near here to collect me again. But I wish Gillon well with his Rachel. She will teach you a thing or two as my Marie has taught me. And I tell you, you can learn from a daughter – though never a mother can learn from her son." Now her glance was a dart in the heart of Julia. "Listen to your Gillon and your Robert. And listen to their women, wherever they may be. I have to go to Scotland the now, as you know. To the visit of my own daughter, the Indian – the Countess of Dunesk. And I will give her your love, Bain and Julia –what love I truly have of it, that is."

"What do you name a girl?" Marie looked accusingly at her husband. "I mean, boys are easy." And they were. He had dozens of names for boys: Andrew and Angus, Fergus and Malcolm, Stewart and Tralala, tralalee — but a girl. He had presumed it would be a he, it had to be a boy. Only it came out of her as the wrong gender. "So what shall we call her now?" Marie said. "In my language, I would call her Owl Feather."

"I do not think," Bill Dunesk said, "that we could have her baptized under that name." He hummed and hawed a little, as he did when he hardly knew what he was meaning to say. "There is a poem by Sir Walter Scott about a girl who lived down the glen."

"And what was she called?" Marie was holding her infant to her breast, as she sat by her four-poster bed in a lounge chair in their London house. The feel of the baby's lips sucking the milk out of her, the life out of her — that was the greatest giving, it was total love. "Is there a name for our child?"

"Rosabelle," her husband said. "Fair Rosabelle."

"Rosabelle," Marie repeated. The name had a lovely ring to it. She stroked the pink-brown crown of her baby's head, the hole in the top of the skull not closed yet, but breathing under the skin, the red wisps of hair upon it. "Rosabelle — tell me."

"There was a dance at Rosslyn Castle down the glen," Bill Dunesk said. "And fair Rosabelle wanted to go there to meet her lover. Only a wind blew up across the Firth of Forth –"

"And Rosabelle?"

"She was drowned. She never reached her lover. But he was a Sinclair like you are."

Marie looked down at the baby feeding at her breast, hurting her, but making her feel a woman at last.

"She was to be a Sinclair," she said. "If she had not gone down. Well, Bill, I am now a Fraser. I have lost my name to you, with the marrying of you. But I am still a Sinclair from my mother and a Chatillon. And I like the name of Rosabelle, *la rose si belle* and beautiful. Tell me the poem, if you know it."

"I know some of it," her husband said and looked to the white ceiling of their chamber which had wreaths and posies plastered onto it. And he recited:

> "Oh listen, listen, ladies gay!
>   No haughty feat of arms I tell.
>   Soft is the note, and sad the lay,
>   That mourns the lovely Rosabelle."

"Moor, moor the barge, you gallant men!
And gentle lady, deign to stay,
Rest thee in Castle Ravensheuch,
Nor tempt the stormy firth today."

Marie put her hand softly over her baby's head. "I don't like sailing," she said. "All that sea. I don't wonder Rosabelle was told not to go over the firth."

"O'er Rosslyn all that dreary night"

Bill Dunesk was in full flow now.

"A wondrous blaze was seen to gleam.
'Twas broader than the watch-fire's light,
And redder than the bright moon-beam.

"Blazed battlement and pinnet high,
Blazed every rose-carved buttress fair –
So still they blaze, when fate is nigh,
The lordly line of high Sinclair."

"Lordly, are we?" Marie laughed and took the baby from her breast. "You're a lucky one, Rosabelle," she said. "And you've had enough for now. Lordly on both sides, you are – or so we are hearing."

"There are twenty of Rosslyn's barons bold"

Bill Dunesk was intoning the poem like a psalm –

"Lie buried within that proud chapelle.
Each one the holy vault doth hold,
But the sea holds lovely Rosabelle."

Marie rocked the baby in her arms. "Mummy holds the lovely Rosabelle. Are there truly twenty Sinclair knights buried in Rosslyn chapel?"
"In full armour," her husband said.
"Why? Were their women getting at them?"

"It was the custom then. The Sinclairs were always half-Vikings. Normans and Norsemen as well as Scots. Their being buried in full armour – and blazing when there was a death in the family – that's really a memory of Viking chiefs being buried with all their war booty when they died."

Then Bill Dunesk finished the poem.

> "And each Sinclair was buried there
> With candle, with book and with knell.
> But the sea-caves rung, and the wild winds sung,
> The dirge of lovely Rosabelle."

Marie was rocking the child in her arms, crooning, "Rosabelle, Rosabelle, Rosabelle..." when her mother Kate came into the bedroom through the half-open door, saying, "I hope I'm not intruding," but Marie held up the baby towards her and said, "Meet Rosabelle, mother. Isn't it a lovely name for her?"

"We never had one in the family," Kate said. "Not a Rosabelle." She moved to take the infant from her daughter and look at the clenched face of the baby, all tight in sleep.

"Well, you will have a Rosabelle now," Bill Dunesk stood up. "A Lady Rosabelle Fraser. It trips off the tongue. Dinner at seven. With those weird women you wanted to meet."

"Millicent Fawcett?"

"That's the one. She met your aunt with Emily Hobhouse over those concentration camps. I don't know if she's very amusing."

"The camps weren't."

"But at dinner?" Bill yawned. "I do like a bit of spice with my soup. Not stodge and seriousness. Anyway, enough of being domestic. It's not a role to which I am accustomed. But for love of you, my dear ..."

"You will even put up with a baby girl," Marie said.

"Even that." Bill Dunesk smiled at Kate. "Marie must have been a baby girl once. Thank you for that. And seeing she grew."

"It was a pleasure," Kate said. "Having her, I mean. It still is."

"I have her," Bill said. "Or shall we say, she has me in thrall. Goodbye for now."

He left mother and daughter together to remind each other of what they had been before their long separation, and what the baby girl would be because of that past and that inheritance. "French, Indian and Scots," Kate said. "It's a lovely mixture. More than the auld alliance. It's the very old alliance. The civilized and the primitive and the savage – and the Scots are the savages."

Marie laughed.

"Rosabelle's father. He's Scots and very, very civilized. Too much so. And I bet she will be."

"Too much so? Your Earl? He's a perfect nobleman ..."

"So perfect," Marie said, "he hardly dares lay a finger on me. For fear it will hurt me."

"You mean –"

"Not since she was born," Marie said. "It was like that with the Crows. A woman was unclean after giving birth. For months. I think for Bill I'll always be unclean now. Now I am a mother, a woman. No longer a beautiful pony-rider like a young man, except for having this –" she patted her breast, where a stain was spreading from her milk on her muslin night-gown. "Maternity – it's not for our Bill. He liked me like Oscar Wilde liked Bosie ..."

"Who?" Kate asked.

"Lord Alfred Douglas," Marie said. "He's still a friend in spite of the scandal. You'll meet him at dinner, though many people won't ask him any more. Oscar called him a slim gilt soul. And when I was a slim bronze soul – that's when Bill loved me. And now, a mother –"

"He'll love you the more," Kate said. "You see. I am your mother, and mothers are always right."

"I am Rosabelle's mother now," Marie said. "And I tell you, I'm right about Bill and me."

The dinner party that night was a fearful mixture of family and friends and foes. Such a hotch-potch was bound to work or explode. Millicent Fawcett, the leader of the new women although she was getting on herself, was matched against the redoubtable Mrs Humphrey Ward, who believed that women were incapable of sound judgement, although her publishers did not think so when she screwed another extortionate advance out of them for her ornate prose. To partner this couple, Bill's idea of the incongruous was to invite Lord Alfred Douglas, who admired formidable women, if he admired women at all. And then there was Kate, and her nephew Hamilton, the ship's engineer with his new buttercup of an Ellen-Maeve, looking for a job for him so that they could settle in England. And Marie, of course, her bare shoulders burnished above her low long gown of crimson *crêpe* which seemed to dress her softly for the warpath.

This was a curious dinner of pheasant that had been hung too long with the women firing at each other across the plates of ripe birds at the men, who were forced into silence or giggles.

"I met your Aunt Mary, Lady Dunesk," Millicent Fawcett said. "Splendid work she did for the Distress Committee –"

"You love Boers," Mrs Ward put in. "Personally, I can't abide them. Traitors."

"She helped us save thousands of the lives of those wretched women and children —"

"Those camps were perfectly adequate. Better diet there than they had at home on the veldt. We *saved* them."

"Oh, do be sensible, Mrs Ward — if only for the novelty." So Millicent Fawcett silenced her opposition. "And can I count on you, Lady Dunesk, to help us gain the vote?"

"You surely can," Marie said.

"You already have mine," Bill said gallantly, seeing storm signals blow across the face of Mrs Ward.

"Why does treason — this support of the Boers and Home Rule for the Irish," Mrs Ward asked herself, "always go hand in hand with asking for the vote? If you had it, you new women, you would use it to betray our country. I'm afraid, our biological weakness does not lead to right conclusions."

"But you only speak for yourself," Marie said sweetly. "And if you are right, you can't be a woman."

"Mrs Ward's paradox is this," Bill said. "I am a woman. No woman is ever right. I am right to say this."

"Unless you are *not* a woman, Mrs Ward." Lord Alfred looked quizzically at the stern dowager beside him. "You could be in disguise."

"I believe I resemble my womanhood," Mrs Ward said. "While manhood is not a word to be confused with you, Lord Douglas."

Bill laughed and finished chewing a piece of pheasant. He picked some lead shot from his teeth and dropped it on his side-plate — ping — ping — ping.

"Careful, Bosie," he said. "She's holed you by the groin."

"Aeroplanes," Hamilton crashed in with another subject to save the day with magnificent irrelevance. "Aren't aeroplanes the most exciting things on earth?"

"I thought they flew," Lord Alfred said. "I mean, that is their point."

"They land again," Hamilton said. "They don't glide for long. It all depends on their getting engines. But if we can get an engine small enough — with enough thrust — we could fly over the Channel."

Everybody laughed. The idea was too absurd. Only Millicent Fawcett took him seriously, but then she took everything seriously.

"You're a ship's engineer," she said. "In the Royal Navy, aren't you? And you say it's feasible."

"It's feasible," Hamilton said. "I'm trying to arrange a transfer. A naval air arm. A fleet air arm."

"They'll land on water, will they?" Lord Alfred was amused. "Like ducks."

"Yes," Ellen-Maeve said, surprising herself. "Like ducks. And take off again. Like ducks."

"Sitting ducks," Lord Alfred said. "That's all they will be."

"The only sort you are able to shoot, I suppose," Mrs Ward said.

Bill Dunesk laughed at this.

"We will have to shoot your seaplanes, Hamilton," he said. "I can see it now. Flocks of seaplanes –"

"Squadrons. Like the cavalry."

"Bagging squadrons of seaplanes. An air machine shoot."

"They'll bag you," Hamilton said. "They'll drop bombs on you. They'll destroy whole cities."

"Don't be silly, Hamilton," Marie said. "All these scare stories. If we were made to fly, we'd have wings. But I do believe you. If we can't have wings, we'll put them on machines and fly in them." She put her foot on the bell on the floor to summon the servants for the next course. They had the new electricity in the house. Progress was not all bad.

"Exactly," Mrs Ward said. "We don't fly because we were born without wings. It is biologically impossible. Like women and the vote."

"Not technically impossible," Hamilton said. "That is the engine – the air engine – I mean to work on. And change the world." ·

"Nothing wrong in that," Lord Alfred said, "as long as you get it beautifully wrong."

"Like so many women do," Mrs Ward said. "They cannot think right."

"Except for you," Millicent Fawcett said. "You are the exception who proves the rule."

"Yes," Mrs Ward said. "Exactly that. I am."

He would never come. She did not know if she really wanted him to come. And if he ever came, she would not imagine how he would look. Men were often disappointing, particularly when they were not very old, and when they were very old, they should be put out to grass, where nobody could see them. Virginia Callow had heard that the new Assistant District Office was a horseman – you had to be in the job, there was so much country to cross, and young men usually cared more for their mounts than their wives. But he might not have a brain in his head or a mind bigger than a pimple. That was not necessary in the job, even if he had the power of life and death, or at least of flogging and taxing, over an area larger than Yorkshire.

As for his looks, Virginia told herself that she didn't care about that, although she did in those curious dreams of intruders which violated her sleep – a face as long and silver-white as the blade of a carving-knife approaching her. There were people in Vienna who said that dreams really mattered, but she had not read them yet. In case he did come, she put dabs of rouge on her pale cheeks, although it was a little fast, and it made her small school charges giggle and point and whisper, until she had to rap the desk with her ruler and say, "Children, the three times multiplication table. Three times one is three – and the three in one is God the Father, God the Son and God the Holy Ghost. And three times two is six – and you will get six of the best, Jonathan, if you don't stop that right now!"

When he did come to the Mission School at last, he was not what she expected. He was simply the only possible man around for fifty miles, she knew that. For she would not settle to be an old frump of a Boer farmer's wife, breaking mealies with a log and beating butter with a churn stick and grinding coffee between stones. She had a yellow Hottentot maid to do that at the school, but she could hardly pay for her servant. The wages were beggarly, twenty pounds a year, it did not buy her one decent dress. Sometimes she thought there was no sin in all the world save the sin of being poor, though there was the second sin which the Bible stressed – which was to be a woman like the original Eve and be cursed to labour for your bread if you were an orphan and there was nobody to look after you. Yet the man who would come to her would not care that she had nothing and was born nowhere. He was her only ticket out of oblivion, her passport back Home. In that way, he had to be a Galahad or a Young Lochinvar. And the man she saw entering her front room was not so wide of the mark. He was all wire and cord beneath his dusty riding-boots and jodhpurs and khaki jacket, while his face was as lean and sharp as in her dreams, but burnt to brick by the sun and the wind. His golden hair did not flow free, but was slicked to his skull so it looked like a shell for a field gun.

"Howdie, Miss Callow," he said, which was not much of a greeting, but had to do, she supposed.

"I am very pleased to meet you, Mr Sinclair," she said, then added, "at last" to blame him for his long delay in getting to her, as they had obviously already heard of each other at a distance.

Robert saw a tall thin woman with a pallid face under a cartwheel straw hat as big as a parasol to keep the glare from her milky cheeks, which blazed all the same with a red patch on either side. Her brown eyes were round and large and glistened as if they were washed, her thin lips were avid with desire and expression. There was certainly no woman like her for two days' ride anywhere, and if she was not the type of woman he had always admired, for these were of the soft and rounded sort, she was a lady and from England. And with that deference to the authority of a teacher or a mother, which had been drummed into him in the prairie, he said, "Duty kept me away, marm – duty." For he was the authority here even if he was only twenty-two.

"Well, I am very glad you came in the end," Virginia said. "And now you are here, pray do not rush away. Whatever your duty is, do let it wait."

"I don't know how it can," Robert said. "There's always a heap to do. It's crazy, but I am a sort of a father round here – a fixer for the Great White Mother."

"The Queen, you mean."

"The Indians called Her the Great White Mother where I hail from, and I don't see it as it may be different here. The tribes, they are all under Her blanket, aren't they? If there's room enough for them, which I reckon there is." Robert laughed at his own comment. "It sure is a big and beautiful country. These mountains, I could hug them."

"I consider it a bleak and barren land," Virginia said. "And it is a misfortune for those who have to live in it."

"But you came out –"

"No choice, Mr Sinclair. Needs must. Or should I call you District Officer?"

"Robert. Or Bob. We're not on parade. And you're Miss –?" His voice trailed away on the question.

"You are most informal," Virginia said coldly, but then relented. What was protocol in the wilderness? "Virginia is my name. But don't call me Ginny. Gin is a drink, I think."

"A pink drink. I never touch the rotgut. Scotch or beer."

"You do imbibe?"

"When I can track it down. I've a good nose for that spoor." Now he noticed two framed drawings on the wall, the rough outline in red and yellow crayon of a buck, but no buck looked like that, and some little black stick figures and a sort of serpent.

"Not bad, those paintings, for a Bushman."

"The Bushman is I," Virginia said and watched Robert scowl with shame. "Actually, I copied them off Bushmen drawings. I was shown in a cave by one of my children — the children I teach, that is. I think there is something wonderful in primitive art, don't you? It is the first art. Primal — and so —" She reached for the right word to come up with, "simple."

They were just daubs to Robert, no better than kids' pictures, but he said valiantly, "I reckon they're great," and he hurried on to ask, "Now tell me, where can I bunk down? I guess I can stay over a couple of days. And I've got all my trek kit on my pony."

"There is the chapel," Virginia said, surprising herself by suggesting it. "It is all there is, except the huts, and they are occupied. You obviously cannot stay with me. But I am sure that God will not mind. You will probably be good company. And the chapel is really not much."

And it was not much — mud walls painted white with a zinc roof and twenty crude chairs and stools facing a table, on which stood a cross, delicately covered in black wood as a flower with four petals. That was the only sign of Our Lord. In front of it, Robert unpacked the kit he had bought at Walters and Co, the Recognized Overseas Outfitters — the Improved Compactum Folding Bed with its best rotproof canvas and groundsheet and mosquito rods and net, his "X" Pattern Long Shape Folding Bath and Washstand and Tray and Latrine Seat and Collapsible Bucket with Rope Handle, items one of each, all contained in their special padlocked cover or Wolseley Valise in Waterproof Khaki Twill. It was all regulation gear, and now Robert Sinclair was living by the book, if not the Good Book. And he was looking for a regular woman, and there seemed to be one here. As he prepared to leave the chapel to send the Hottentot maid for some water for his ablutions, he saw the flowery black cross on the altar, and he fell on his knees. He should thank Somebody for striking it lucky, and that Somebody had to be God.

Virginia had done what she could over dinner for the two of them. The maid Tsutsie did not run to much more than corn mush and grilled deer, if you could call those tough antelopes and bush things anything to do with venison. But Virginia had hoarded a tin of Crosse & Blackwell vegetable soup, also of Christmas Pudding, which she had not been able to face alone for the last festivity, a particularly hot and trying one. She concocted a hot white sauce out of the mealie flour and rather rancid butter, but as for the main course, she could only provide a roast salted leg of what looked like buffalo, so huge and dark it was, and an excuse of a Yorkshire pudding, which was the same as the white sauce with more flour and salt in it. It would have to do. Even if the way to a man's heart was through his stomach, she could only do her best with what she had. Mrs Beeton herself would have been in despair.

Yet Robert liked the meal and ate hugely. He even praised the faint taste of lime in the boiled water. He seemed to appreciate the trimmings, the embroidered napkins and damask tablecloth she had brought out with her – yellowing now from scrubbing with lye soap – and the candles which she had concocted from animal fat. The niceties were so important. If you let yourself go in the bush, you went native. Manners were really the rules you could not break. And though they hid a woman's true character, the needs and the wants that drove her, they were her weapons against any violation. So when Robert took out his pipe and pouch after dinner and began to stuff the bowl with coarse-cut tobacco, Virginia did rebuke him, although she did not mean to offend him in any way, her only prospect of escape in any way.

"Would you mind if you *lit up* later? And perhaps outdoors. I really do find tobacco smoke a trial and not good for the disposition."

"Pardon," Robert said amicably and rolled up his pouch and put it in one of the side pockets of his drill khaki jacket and the filled pipe in the other pocket. "The bush does make you forget you're not alone. But that's what the ladies are for, I reckon. To tell you how to behave yourself in front of the ladies."

"There are more things than that in a relationship between the sexes." Again Virginia was surprised to find herself using so crude a term about human love. Yet she was hardly a sheltered woman. She was masquerading as a mission teacher. It was the only job she could find. And she had even read her Havelock Ellis. She knew what most women did not choose to admit yet – the desire of a woman for a man. "There is companionship and even a certain mystery." She rose from her chair and bent to fiddle with the brass knob, which adjusted the wick of the oil lamp. She knew its subtle light softened her face and suited her style. "I think when one meets somebody one *knows*. That is the loved one for life. It is immediate. It is there." She turned and fixed her huge and moist-bright eyes on Robert. "I have been waiting so long – and now –" She let her words hang in air as he might the smoke from his pipe.

Robert really did not know what to make of this. She seemed to have said a great deal, but nothing at all. She liked him, though. And she was a fine woman, no doubt of that.

"I'd have been here before," he said, "but I have all this work."

She sat near him and gazed into his eyes, until he had to look down. "Tell me about your work," she said. She knew that was the second way to a man's heart.

So he told her about how strange it was to be so young, and yet have such power over people old enough to be his grandparents. Whatever the missions were doing, the witchdoctors were still in control. If there was a palaver you could not solve, they could, and what they knew about herbs and plants beat quinine and boracic into a back pocket, if you got fever or the runs. But all these cases and squabbles you heard, you weren't Solomon at the judgement, you really didn't know who was right and who was wrong, the natives were all such liars in court, if you could call his little meetings a court. So he would say almost at random, "Ten shillings fine," which was a hell of a lot for them, they might have to trek to the mines to earn it, or maybe a few lashes. But he did not like that, the *sjambok* hurt like the devil, it was only meant for oxen. But he had to do it. Black people did not feel as much as white people. Their skins were simply not so sensitive. He had met a doctor and a preacher in the army, who had told him that.

"Tell me about London, your training there," Virginia said, beginning to dream of her escape as he was speaking. While he told her of classes and senior officers and learning the rulebook, she was seeing the spires of Whitehall and the red robes of the peers at the future coronation of the new King of England. Then she suddenly heard that very word in Robert's mouth, "Coronation – and my cousin's been asked." And at that moment, she knew that she might love him.

"Your cousin, who is she?"

"Marie? She's a countess now. Married somebody called Bill Dunesk, a nice enough fellow, but damp behind the ears. Still, she has to go to the Coronation with him. All the peers are summoned by the Earl Marshal. Quite a shindig, I imagine."

Although she would like to have heard more, there was time enough for that. So Virginia asked, not quite at cross-purposes, "What do you intend to do with your first leave?"

"Well, this tour is two years, then I get six months. But my mother's real sick in Canada, and I reckon I just might go along there."

"But by London, through London –"

Robert laughed.

"The good old Union Castle line, it does sail thataway."

"Oh, I should so like –" Virginia caught herself at being too forward. "I mean, don't you miss Home?"

"Home's a log house on the prairie for me."

"But Home – real Home – England. London. The real Home of all of us."

"It's a dirty great city," Robert said. "But it is fun. The Troc and the Long Bar at the Cri. But no ladies. I'm sorry."

"I just long for Home. I feel there, somehow complete. Whole. This life is a kind of exile, a trap." She gazed deeply at Robert until her eyes seemed to flood her face. "Anyone who would take me out of here, take me Home –"

"You needn't be looking far," Robert found himself saying. He certainly wouldn't round up anyone better here, and two years was a long time to wait for a woman. "A fine young lady like you, why, any man would be proud –"

"Any man will not do for me," Virginia snapped suddenly as if breaking the neck of her hope. "A particular man who will nurture – understand. I said there was a mystery in this." She rose to stand beside the oil lamp again, to adjust the flame, to look her best. The light flickered in little shades over her face. "I need a man who will engage all of me. And engage all of himself to me. For, you know, we women – if we are not held, captivated – we can be fickle. I promise you. I warn you. Fickle."

Now Robert was engaged by this threat of waywardness. His sense of possession was fired. He found himself on his feet and advancing on her at the lamp. His voice was thick. "I'd hold you," he said. "Tight rein. You'd never get away."

"Now, now," she said eluding him and moving away. "Don't charge. You are not in the cavalry now." She walked to the door and opened it. "You cannot drop me with a shot between the eyes. We do not know each other, but there is time. I cannot run away, you know." And as Robert passed her to leave the room, she did not back off, but let him brush against her. A brief softness seemed to burn him.

"Tomorrow morning, will you breakfast with me? At seven. We start at sun-up."

"Seven, then. Good-night, Virginia."

"Good-night, Robert."

And he would have no good night of it. Robert knew that as he walked away. He ached for her, all because she was elusive. He had to possess her. Women were damnation that way, teasing a man. Like the Boer commandos, as you advance, they retreat. As you retreat, they advance. Female tactics. But just to make sure, Robert found himself kneeling by his folding bed again in front of the flowery black cross and saying his prayers, remembering Virginia Callow this time, just as his mother had taught him to do, if he loved somebody or they were family.

8

RAJ AND TREK

In the sprawling house above the valley at Annandale, Angus was enthusing to his older brother Iain about the railway that had just been opened up the mountains to Simla.

"When I built those mining railways in the Andes," he said, "I never thought I'd see my work done better. Certainly not here, in India. And not just to serve a hill station."

"Simla is the seat of government in the summer," Iain said. "The Viceroy's here. And that American of his, Lady Curzon."

"But sixty miles of track – a continuous succession of reverse curves with a radius of one hundred and twenty feet – the steep gradients three in a hundred – rising to seven thousand feet. And a hundred and seven tunnels – in all five miles long – and fifty arched viaducts nearly two miles overall – and cuts and stone walls – all to spare the Viceroy the eight hours on a tonga cart up the hill road. Though that two-and-a-half foot narrow gauge, you sway so much, you're sea-sick."

"You're still an engineer," Iain said. "You'll never retire."

"No more than you will."

"Planters never retire," Iain said. "You have to mow us down. Like hay."

"For eighty," Angus said, "you look hearty."

"I'm near the last one as fought in the Mutiny," Iain said. "No one remembers it at all. Not Lord Curzon. Nor that office-wallah Margaret's married to, Douglas Jardine. They're visiting soon, by the way. He's come up to Simla to report to Curzon. You will meet them the now."

"Good," Angus said. "I have come a long way to see the family. And this time, it may be the last time, brother."

"Aye," Iain said. "But it's been a wee while since we played bools at the dominie's in the glen."

Angus looked through the window down the wooded slope of the Himalayan mountain to the race-course in the valley below.

"You've made a glen better than Scotland here," he said. "Your Annandale."

"But it's no the same," Iain said. "Ach, Anna."

A Gurkha servant wheeled Anna in her wickerwork chair into the living-room. She was handsome still, her face fine-drawn under the black lace cap that perched above the rest of her white hair.

"The world is coming to us," she said, "because I can not go to the world now. Peg also is coming – the doctor. She says your sister Mary wants her back in London. And she is your niece, Iain and Angus, in her way."

"But Seaforth," Angus said, "he will still be in South Africa?"

"Yes," Anna said. "It is best for him over there. It is very embarrassing if Douglas and Margaret visit when Peg is here. In his position – mixing –"

"No," Iain said drily. "Peg is not a Maharanee. Douglas would mix with her, if she was. But she's better – a doctor."

"Caste and class," Angus said. "The British were made for the Indians, and the Indians for the British. A perfect understanding of what keeps us all apart."

Peg was already at the house at Annandale, when Douglas Jardine and Margaret and their daughter Ruby were carried by *jampanees* on their evening visit from Simla. Douglas Jardine had had a trying day. Lord Curzon could not abide the architecture of Simla, where all the public buildings were crosses between ironworks and chalets, and the Viceregal Lodge had been decorated from Maple's: lincrusta and pomegranate and pineapple patterns on the walls – fit for a Minneapolis millionaire in the opinion of Lady Curzon. So Curzon had fled to The Retreat at Mashabra and even further to a mountain camp on Naldera. There he penned his devastating and ceaseless minutes, while signallers informed him of the news of India by heliograph in the day and by flashing lamps at night. What a devil of a journey there, Douglas thought, and just like a viceroy to put his staff to the greatest inconvenience. People did not come to Simla for the climbing, other than social climbing. Even if the Curzons found local society dull with the chief official sport 'hunt the slipper', not the tiger, it was filthy inconsiderate to drag a fellow over the Himalayas just to present a file no more important than a chit to the great panjandarum. Yet duty called, and Douglas always answered that call, however out of the way.

Duty had nothing to do with the sight of Peg at Annandale. Margaret's half-caste cousin was an official embarrassment to the Jardines. Just as bad as her being a woman doctor was her being partially Indian. She even came under Douglas Jardine's department. He had to approve some of her requisitions at the hospital. Yet the only approval he had given willingly was her coming transfer to London to look after a ward of wounded soldiers for her Aunt Mary. At least, she would be out of India. As she was a relative, and in the Indian Civil Service, one should never do a favour for a relation, and never accept a favour. Of course, it was different when the posies came round at Christmas from grateful recipients of impartial imperial bounty. Then if one found a hundred gold mohurs hidden in the bouquet, well, as long as the gift was anonymous, and one didn't exactly know who it was from.

"So glad you could come too, Miss Sinclair," Douglas said. "Margaret has not seen you for simply ages. And Ruby – our daughter – never."

Another galling fact was that Ruby and Peg were strikingly similar with raven hair and long oval faces and large dark eyes. They even looked like relations. And Peg made this worse by saying, "I am glad to meet you at last, Ruby. Your mother and I were brought up here together as children."

"In a way," Anna said from her wheel-chair. "Peg's mother kindly helped us with our children. But Peg is a doctor. That is something I always wanted to be – but I was born too early for that to be possible. I met your grandfather, Ruby, when I was nursing at Nainital after the Mutiny."

"I can still feel the sword-cut in me," Iain said, "when it's cold."

"He gave me the emerald ring," Anna said. She moved to shift the brilliant blaze of green light round her finger so it shone from her palm. "I have been thinking about it. I mean to pass it on."

"Not the emerald." Margaret could not keep the quiver from her voice. "If you do think, mother, it is time to pass it on –"

"I found it when we took the palace at Lucknow," Iain said. "Spoils of war."

"Then it is Indian," Peg said. She held out her hand to Anna, who had managed to pull the ring past the swollen joint of her finger. "Let me see." She took the jewel and rolled the ornamental gold hoop between forefinger and thumb, so that darts of gem flashes struck the eyes of the Jardines. "Are you giving it to this Indian?"

"Oh, Mother, you cannot –"

"Let me see it," Ruby said. She almost snatched it from Peg's hand. She examined the jewel closely.

"It's huge," she said. "But it's got a mark in it. A flaw."

"We all have a flaw in us," Iain said. "And yours is –" he held out a huge bent palm for the ring – "wanting something too much."

Reluctantly, Ruby dropped the ring into her grandfather's hand. He closed his fist about it and did a slow uppercut in the air.

"I won it hard," he said. "I killed for that."

"Indians fighting for their freedom," Peg said.

"We were not free neither," Iain said. "We were bound to the colours. Slaves to the regiment."

He opened his fist again to consider the ring, while Douglas Jardine said softly to Peg, "You're in favour of Indian independence, I believe. As is your brother, Doctor Seaforth Sinclair."

"You know that?" Peg was not surprised. "In your official capacity?"

"We have our intelligence. Your brother is not thinking of returning to India ..."

"Not immediately."

"We have head of a lawyer called Gandhi organizing something called passive resistance among Indian immigrants in the Transvaal, where we have rather decently allowed the Boers to have a say again. Now, we don't want him back here, trying to do the same thing. Agitators – they may seem to be harmless eccentrics – then, before you know it, suddenly they are national leaders."

"You know a great deal about us, Mr Jardine. In a country of more than a hundred million people, you know about the important few. Even when they are abroad. Will you know what I am doing when I go back to London?"

"You never know, do you?" Douglas knew he had revealed too much, which was unusual for him. "But then, it is better to know."

"Let us eat," Anna said.

"Tiffin time, Mother," Margaret said, but she could not resist adding, "but who *is* going to have the emerald?"

Iain lobbed the ring into the air and caught it falling and closed his fingers round it again.

"We'll keep it a wee while yet," he said. "And then it shall go to our favourite child."

Anna smiled.

"And who would that be?"

"All of you." Iain opened his arms wide to include them all. "All of you who are good enough to come here and visit with us in our lonely life – while we are still alive, that is."

"Coming here is nothing," Douglas Jardine said. "You should have seen the miles I had to climb to visit the Viceroy this morning. I know he likes to be inaccessible, but that was ridiculous."

"You should have marched across all India with the Highlanders," Iain said. "And then charged ten times over five miles in a day in full kit at one hundred and ten degrees. That was moving. But who wants to hear the tales of an old soldier, when life is so much harder on you young folk these days?"

Only Peg laughed, and then she put her hand on Iain's arm.

"You did put down the Mutiny," she said. "For the moment. You were brave to do that – so few against so many."

Iain opened his fist again and showed her the emerald ring, which now was dull green and shadowed.

"It was not worth it," he said. "Or was it?"

Piet was a wonder with the oxen. When the tiny black *voorloper* drove them up to the waggon, they took up their places in double-span in front of the vehicle as two rough ranks on the parade ground before dressing to the right. Then Piet would limp up and down the team, calling each ox by his name: "Bakir, oy" – the wise front ox with horns as long as elephant's tusks – "Bantom ... Rooiland ..." and then his running joke on his new partner, "Hammie boy", and finally the big after-oxen which carried the pole or dissel boom, "Zole and Zwaartland." And each ox moved on command exactly into position beside the trek chain. And the *voorloper* and the big Zulus fastened the necks of the span to the yokes by strops of rawhide, which were then tied to the wooden slats of the *yukskeis*. Piet would now climb into the driver's seat and give a last call to any beast which had edged out of true, and it would sidle back.

Out of the blue, Piet would crack his long whip like a Mauser shot and yell like a trooper. The oxen would all strain to the yoke in one mighty heave, and the overloaded waggon would jolt into motion. Piet was so tender with all the beasts that he hardly ever scored their hides with his *sjambok*, though he could flick a fly off their rumps with the lash at twenty paces. He had bought good wheelers, and these were so trained that they swung out or turned in to correct the bumpy roads or bring back in line any unsalted ox in the double-span to their rear. But Piet was not so gentle to the strapping Zulu drivers he called 'boys'. He preferred most beasts to most men.

In the waggon behind Piet, Hamish Charles took weeks to get the hang of driving the oxen. Piet had bought him a good span, the front ox was old and wily on the track, but he could not work the long whip or talk to the straining cattle as Piet could. He relied heavily on Din or Dingaan, a burly Zulu hired by Piet to teach Hamish Charles the way of the trek. But Din was savage with the *sjambok* and surly with his *baas*, flogging the beasts into their lurch forward and rolling on. And when one of them lay down in the middle of a path through a narrow kloof blocking the progress of the whole convoy, Hamish Charles had never seen crueller torments inflicted upon an unmovable object by Din and the furious Boer trekkers behind – giraffe-hide whips, blows from rocks on skull and spine, doubling the tail and biting it, stabbing the rump with clasp knives, even branding the beast again with hot irons. And then Piet woke up after a sleep on the forward waggon and asked the name of the brute and quietly went up to its dogged sprawl and spoke in its ear. And it rose at once unsteadily as oxen do, then leant into the chain. Some swore that Piet bit its ear in the secret place no ox can withstand, but Hamish Charles knew he had only talked to it, man to almost a man.

The whipping of Buldoo showed the other side of Piet. The sound of the lashes broke the rest of Hamish Charles. He started up to hear the slow slap of rawhide thong against flesh and came forward to see a black shape tied against a waggon-wheel as he had seen Tommies tied when they had slept on sentry duty during the war. Such flogging was banned in the British army now, but Hamish Charles had heard of men dying under a hundred stokes in the Indian Mutiny, when his uncle had been alive and fighting. But this was a cruel punishment, the *sjambok* cutting the back into red outlines of squares and diamonds as Piet inflicted a pattern of pain on his victim. Now the Zulu groaned and shuddered for the first time, and Hamish Charles caught Piet's wrist on the next back-stroke.

"Enough," he said.

Piet's look at his friend was bright with hate.

"Never," he said, "never come you between a *baas* and his boys. Or we will be dead all."

He shook his arm free and raised the *sjambok* again.

"I'll have him," Hamish Charles said. "He will work for me. He won't work for you after this. He's too proud."

"Have him." Piet lowered the whip. "You are hiring me also. You pay for us all. But he is useless, Buldoo. Always he ask for meat. Drunk on Kaffir beer. You have him."

"I will." Hamish Charles spoke to the watching Zulu drivers. "Set him free." He turned his back on Piet, who was rolling up the thong of his *sjambok*. "You do not whip him," he said. "When you use that lash, you whip yourself."

"You a *predikant?*" Piet sneered, but he mumbled in a sort of defence as he walked away. "You tell me, and you know nothing of the trek ..."

Now Hamish Charles went over to the wheel and helped to catch Buldoo as he sagged back. "I have some boracic for those cuts," Hamish Charles said. "Bring him to my waggon. We'll wash those wounds."

Then Buldoo stood on his own feet. "*Inkos,*" he said. "Chief. I work you. But this – nothing –"

Hamish Charles smiled. "All the same," he said, "you'll work better for me if we treat your back." And he did swab and dust with stinging powder the criss-cross of weals on Buldoo's back, in spite of the Zulu's protest that he did not need his back, for he would never lie down on his work.

Buldoo never seemed to rest until the trek had reached the blue mountains. He was the same as Piet, patient with working beasts, hard on men, harder on men who were not Zulus, and hardest on himself. After Din had flayed Rooiland for a stumble from a broken *nekstrop* that jolted the span aside and the waggon off the track, Buldoo took the whip to Din and made the *nekstrop* good and talked the ox back into its plod and toil. He tormented the little *voorloper*, however, because he was a Hottentot and fit only to be a slave. "You stop the Zulus," he told Hamish Charles. "Or we kill these boys, we have all Africa." He had fought at Isandhlwana, when the Zulu *impis* had wiped out a British regiment and killed the cousin of Hamish Charles. He had been wounded at Ulundi, when the Maxim guns had cut down the Zulu kingdom. He was fierce in his loyalty, when it was given; he was terrible to his enemies; but he was firm and fair in his use of nature. From instinct, Hamish Charles had never thought to trust such an alien figure in the new landscape. But he found in Buldoo an education and gave him a grudging respect.

Perhaps the time of conversion came when Buldoo saved the pianoforte and the fowl coop, while they were trekking over the berg. Piet had laughed at Hamish Charles buying the musical upright which weighed half a ton and unbalanced the load on the waggon, perching on the top of the zinc sheets and coffee sacks by the squawking hens like a rock overhang. Buldoo was negotiating the double-span of thirty heaving oxen on the edge of the precipice round the stuck lead waggon, which had lost a wheel on the narrow cliff track. The hoofs of the offside steers tore loose stones from the rim of the gorge,

which clattered down the berg in ricochets. The outer wheels stayed
on the level only inches from the plunge down. And then the load
began to sway behind Hamish Charles and Buldoo, who moved like a
lion to the kill. He sprung up and threw the whip to Hamish Charles,
swung round and pulled himself high on the sacks, then caught the
weight of the piano, tugging against its ropes and threatening to tip the
whole waggon sideways, over the drop. Man and object made a
triangle of force against force on the top of the load with the fowls in
their coop screeching at the struggle. The waggon lurched, the wheels
crumbled the rimrock, the oxen swung in to safety past the stranded
team, and Buldoo wrested the piano back to straight. Hamish Charles
could only swallow and clear his throat, useless in this time of danger.

Hamish Charles would see that Buldoo – with his craving for meat
– was fed from the hunter's pot that the white trekkers kept for themselves. The iron cauldron on its tripod legs was a study in perpetual
eating. It was always full like a horn of plenty. Something was put in as
fast as it was taken out, anything killed that day which passed for meat
– *dassie* or partridge, wild pig or *duiker*, ostrich or porcupine. The old
bones were removed and given to the dogs, and new ones put into the
stew. Any edible roots thickened the broth, but on the whole, it was
flesh and blood and marrow, and the brew set in a cold brawn for a
game pie breakfast without the crust at the start of the day. Hamish
Charles took a double portion and left half of his plate for Buldoo,
who could not abide the mealie porridge and mush for the rest of the
drivers. Piet caught Hamish Charles at the feeding of Buldoo and
warned him that he had no place in Africa, if he spoilt his servants.

"Soft you are on man and beast," he said. "And you will end
stropping them to death. And you were almost dead with that damfool
piano. You do not play it even."

"No home is a home without a piano," Hamish Charles said
stubbornly. "And you never know who will come to play it."

When Mary came to visit the farm of Hamish Charles by the blue
mountains, he was almost ready to receive her. The zinc roof was
raised on the joists above the stone walls, the pianoforte stood proudly
in the middle of the drawing room and its stool and two wooden
lounging-chairs with green canvas cushions and flat arm-rests for
perching drinks on. There was a working kitchen, too, with an iron
oven and china willow-pattern plates and sacks of all the basic foods
and a cold cupboard of stone slab and wire-mesh. There was a well in
the yard for drawing up water, and barns and pens for the cattle, and
kraals of piled boulders for the sheep. The chickens had the run of the
house and they even laid eggs in one of the two beds from time to

time. A dozen saplings of marula and mimosa were planted for a wind-break and for shade, when they were grown. Their bark was protected from the nibbling antelopes by wooden stakes, driven around their slim trunks and stems. Watering them every evening was the worst chore of all, but they would survive in no other way.

"You have well done," Mary said, settled too long on one of the arm-chairs, her joints set almost as hard as the wooden ones. She had the arthritis her mother had. "But I will see Piet Krug, for I must tell him of his wife. It will be hard. I have been telling of the dying of dear ones to the living for too long now."

"He comes this evening to see us," Hamish Charles said. He was uneasy about it. He had already been quarrelling with his Afrikaner friend about a *vlei*, where both of the herds went for water, and which both said was in their land, as if the open karroo could have any boundaries. "And there will be more people coming. I sent Buldoo over the border to fetch Robert. And he is bringing his new wife, Virginia. She taught at the mission school."

"A good woman," Mary said, and then added unexpectedly. "Good women are often the worst. They know they're good."

"That's very cynical of you, Aunt Mary. And I never thought you had any cynicism in you."

"Good works, that is all I have seen all my life. And I have worked too long with the women who say they do good works and don't at all. It is all in the saying and not in the doing."

A Hottentot boy came in with a teapot and two cups and saucers and a sugarbowl on a tray, which he set down on a low folding canvas table.

"Don't you move," Hamish Charles rose. "I will be mother." And he began pouring some green liquid into the cups. "I am afraid it's only bush tea. We've run out of Indian."

"First," Mary said, "I canna move. I am set. Second, if you are ever a mother, the Lord will have to change his creation. And as for bush tea, I drink everything that is hot, sweet and herbal."

Hamish Charles added two piled spoonfuls of sugar to the brew in the teacup, stirred it with a spoon and took it on its saucer to his aunt.

"I don't even know the bush it comes from. The locals pick and dry it for me. They know their plants."

"Now, is that Piet Krug coming over here before or after your cousin Robert and his bride? It is not a sociable thing to be telling him of the death of his wife in company."

"I hope so. But if not, I will take you aside, Aunt Mary. It is splendid to have you here."

And it was. Buldoo led Robert and Virginia on their ponies to the farm before evening. There was time for introductions and memories of the war against the Boers that was over now. The peace terms were generous enough. There were reparations, there was amnesty, as long as the Boers would give up their independence, which they could no longer defend. "There was conscience over those dreadful concentration camps even in the government," Mary said. "My report went to the War Office, very high they say. It would have gone to the old Queen, I dare say, but it was too late for that. Her Son the King – I hear he does not muckle fancy the reading. But the thing is, when the English are guilty, they can be generous. It is a generous peace. But some things can never be put right no more than broken china. I fear with Piet Krug –"

"He has forgiven us," Hamish Charles said. "He is a friend."

"I will see." Mary was not convinced.

Virginia's effect on the two Sinclairs at the farm was that of the opposite poles of a magnet. She attracted Hamish Charles immediately and repelled Mary less evidently. When Virginia laughed with joy to see the piano, and Hamish Charles led her over to it and she found it out of tune, yet still played Strauss and Chopin recognisably with the wrong notes, Hamish Charles thought a genius had ridden into the house. And watching her look up at her host with shy appraisal in her brimming eyes, Mary felt a stab of fear like a lancet to her heart. She called Robert over to her and spoke of Seaforth, now decorated for his medical services in the war and called to Johannesburg to help run a private hospital, endowed by the Apfelsteins with their vast mining interests in the Rand. "But he's coloured," Robert said and could have bitten off his tongue, when Mary snapped back. "So are you. You just happen to be a different shade of bleach from most of the people in this country." And Robert remembered that Seaforth was the apple of his aged aunt's eye, who was blind to any blemish in him.

When Piet came unwilling into the room, passing the brim of his old slouch hat round and round in his long knobbled fingers, and darting suspicious glances at everybody in the room, Hamish Charles helped his aunt to her feet and waited by her until her bones unlocked enough for her to walk, then he said simply to Piet, "So good of you to come. Aunt Mary wants to talk to you about Annie. Perhaps you could take her out under the *stoep*." And Piet took her by the elbow which felt as dry and bent as the crook of his walking-stick and supported her to the wooden seat outside and said, "Tell me of Annie. I must hear." And in her plain way Mary told him of the death of Annie and said that her last words were of her love of her husband, which was not true. But when Mary told a rare lie, it was always to the living about the dear dead, and she was always believed. And Piet wept silently, the drops and trickles from his eyes marking his beard as if with dew. Then he snorted and wiped his nose on the dusty sleeve of his jacket and said bitterly, "I hate all *Uitlanders*, then there is you. How hate you?" And Mary said, "You have good cause to hate us. But hate is useless. It destroys the hater. Thank you, Piet Krug, for loving. You have helped Hamish set up on his farm." And Piet said, "Ach, that is nothing. He help me." And Mary said, "You must go on helping him. He needs a wife." And Piet said, "And I need. We see sisters. Bunjie and Lizzie van der Merwe." And Mary said, "That is good. I do not like the way he looks at his cousin's wife, when she plays the piano." And Piet laughed and said, "Do not worry, Tant' Mary. Hamish is good, too good for a cousin's wife. Sometime I think – he is too good for this life – for this life here."

9

SOCIAL GAMES

At Lords, there were two games proceeding. On the cricket pitch in the middle, flannelled youths were playing the traditional game, with Eton in its Second Innings batting against the clock to make two hundred-odd runs to win, and Harrow bowling out the middle order like skittles, only the opener Plunkett-Drax looking like carrying his bat to defeat because nobody would stay in with him. Murdo Sinclair had taken three wickets for Harrow, but he was now fielding at long leg and keeping half an eye on the stands to see if he could find his father Angus and his sister Arabella, come over from Peru with his mother to meet the right sort of man, if she could.

For that was the second game being played in the stands and the promenade round the cricket ground back to the Pavilion. Few of the thousands of strollers were watching the cricket. This was hardly the purpose of the attendance. Matches were being made, not played. Young women aimed the points of their parasols at their marks and hunted them down through the introductions of their parents. Two circles, an inner and an outer one, slowly perambulated in opposite directions round the green oval, where the thwack of willow bat and leather ball on bare hand sounded like an irregular flogging. Black top hats and straw boaters, morning coats with carnation buttonholes and grey check spongebag trousers, these were the male costumes, while the ladies had plundered pastel chalks and watercolour boxes for their soft colours or their tight linen or floating chiffon and lace. Now that the sun was shining, it was time to make hay and a bright future.

Angus had been to the Crown Colony of Hong Kong after his visit to India to discuss an engineering scheme for Kowloon, the leased lands across the bay. He had returned to Peru to retrieve his wife Isabella and daughter Arabella to sail with them to visit their son in England and see to his career, as he was leaving Harrow at the end of the term. Outside some business interests, Angus knew little of the London social scene, and he was hoping that Murdo would do something for the family when he finally left the cricket pitch. It would be better if Eton were bowled out soon, and Angus liked to hear the cheers as the wickets went on falling quickly, with only

Plunkett-Drax soldiering on. There would be more time for the social game.

Brother Iain's daughter May was there with her husband, Charles Seymour-Scudabright, and their two sons, Gordon and Graham, although neither of the young men were good enough to play in the Eton team. The encounter between the cousins was almost like that of rival battle fleets, all evasion and suspicion under smoke screens of pleasure at the meeting.

"So good to see you *here*," Charles said, and then added, "and so unexpected."

"Our son is bowling you all out," Angus said. "Your sons don't represent their school."

"I am a wet bob," Gordon said.

"What is that?" Arabella asked. "You swim? You fell in?"

"I row."

"What is row?"

"A scull. With oars."

"A skull? You are a medical student?"

"Give it up," Angus said to his daughter, so like her mother when she was young that she seemed to her father an instant memory of a lasting love. "You will never understand public school games. At Eton, they even play a game with a wall."

"You cannot play with a wall," Arabella said. "It will hurt you."

"Beside a wall," Graham said. "But you get hurt all right. You can tread on the tugs, if you like, with your boots, as long as you don't kick them. And knuckle their faces. Like this." He switched the black top-hat he was holding from his right hand to his left, then made a fist and ground his knuckles against his brother's pink cheeks. "You knuckle them to force them away from the wall."

Gordon struck his brother's arm aside.

"You don't play the Wall Game at Lords," he said.

"I don't know if the battle of Waterloo was won in the playing-fields of Eton," Angus Sinclair said. "Perhaps it was lost there."

"What do you mean?" Charles Seymour-Scudabright was annoyed. "We have a tradition of service. Gordon will join the army, and Graham will follow me into the navy. Good God, there's Hamilton —"

And there was Hamilton, May's brother, joining in the skirmish of cousins with his tiny spouse Ellen-Maeve. He did not salute Charles, for all were off-duty from the navy in morning coats or black tails, the uniform of that day. But after the usual salvo of greetings, he did continue the provocation of the Seymour-Scudabrights.

"I am leaving the navy," he said. "Ships are finished."

"What?" Charles was outraged. "Britannia rules the waves. Where would we be without the Home Fleet?"

"Better off," Hamilton said. "The best thing to do is scuttle it."

"And you – a serving naval officer –"

"Not much longer," Hamilton said. "I am going to work on other kinds of engines –"

"Hamilton believes that these gliding aeroplanes they have in America and France –" Ellen-Maeve said.

"Balloons, do you mean?" Gordon said. "Those spotter balloons our troops used in South Africa? Winston Churchill flew in one when we were marching to Pretoria."

"No, gliders," Hamilton said. "They will soon be powered with engines. Then they will be able to fly long distances."

"You can't intend to use steam engines." Angus was interested. "A steam engine would be far too heavy for an aeroplane to support."

"An oil engine," Hamilton said. "A petrol engine. As in those new cars we have. An automobile engine."

"Stuff and nonsense," Charles said. "A flying machine. It's about as real as Pegasus."

"What is Pegasus?" Arabella asked.

"A flying horse," Charles said. "He carried the Greek gods around. Only he did not. He never existed."

"They will exist," Hamilton said. "Flying machines. They will fly over your Home Fleet and drop explosives on them and all our iron-clads will go straight to the bottom. If submarines under the water do not torpedo them and sink them first."

"Poppycock," Charles said. "Tommyrot and twaddle. You sound as if you had been reading that science peddler – what's his name? Wells."

"H.G. Wells," May said, always exact with other people's names.

"I have actually read Wells," Hamilton said. "You are right. He does believe in flying machines. So does Marie, or so she said."

"Is Marie coming here?" Isabella was now intrigued. "With the Earl of Dunesk?"

"We're meeting them by the Pavilion," Hamilton said. "I don't think cricket is quite their game. But they wanted to meet all of you."

"We're not much of a family for reunions," Angus said. "But that would be splendid."

"You could hardly call this a reunion," Hamilton said, looking round the fluttering and floating assembly. "More like a dress parade."

"For those who went to School," Charles said, "it is a reunion."

"One big happy family, your old school?" Hamilton laughed and turned to Gordon. "Is that really how it is?"

"It's not so bad," Gordon said. "As long as you don't get a Pop tanning."

"What do you get that for?"

"I don't know. Smoking. Not training. Side."

"I'd rather even be a sailor," Hamilton said and gave Ellen Maeve his arm again. "Shall we reunite ourselves with Marie?"

Arabella had always been proud of her own pallor and had fancied her chances of making a good marriage in England, but Marie was so bronze and bright and blazing in her clinging amber dress with her red hair piled beneath a golden hat like a sun, that Arabella could see why she had become a countess and the toast of London. In Peru, her family despised anyone with Indian blood; but in Marie's case, her ancestry had enhanced her beauty.

"I am so glad to meet you," Arabella said. "You are so beautiful."

"That from a young woman," Marie said, "and a cousin too ... that really is a compliment. Uncle Angus has taken too long to bring you over from South America."

"It is a long way to travel," Angus said, "until we have one of Hamilton's flying machines."

"Oh, Hamilton —" Marie laughed. "Not more of your weird and wonderful inventions."

"There is an inn in Wiltshire called the Flying Monk," Bill Dunesk said. "A monk made a pair of wings, thought he was an angel, and threw himself into the air from the top of the local church tower. He only broke both his legs. Luckily, he landed on the town pig. Lucky for him, I mean — not the pig. It made nice bacon, though."

Gordon and Graham laughed, and Marie admired as usual her husband's gift of easing the uneasy by his drawling stories, rather off the point. This was the most pleasant thing about her new society, its understatement and its anecdotes. It was something which could not be taught. That had to be lived in until it fitted like an old ulster. She could see Arabella's fascination and envy at her husband's charm and languid distinction.

"Bill doesn't like these grand occasions very much," Marie said. "He would rather be with just a friend or two, discussing nothing very much, but very well."

"But you are going to the Coronation." May and Charles had evidently discussed the unfairness of life that somebody as ill-born as Cousin Marie should go to the crowning of their new King.

"Without fail," Bill Dunesk said. "The King commands us to be there without fail. The trouble is, I failed pretty well everything at school, even when I was commanded by the beaks. Don't you, boys?"

Gordon nodded.

"Graham and I aren't swots," he said. "We don't have to be. We're going in the army and the navy."

"It's better to have nothing in your heads," Bill Dunesk said amiably, "if you're going to be cannon fodder. You make less of a target." He looked aside at the cricket ground, which all of them had quite forgotten, but now was echoing to ragged cheering. The batsmen and the fielders were walking back to the Pavilion. The last wicket had fallen, Plunkett-Drax had carried his bat for seventy, but Harrow had won by a hundred and two runs. "Another defeat for the old school," the Earl said to the young Etonians. "I hope it is not an augury for your military careers."

"We'll beat them next time," Charles said.

"That's what the British Army always says," the Earl said. "And rarely does."

Arabella found her cousins Gordon and Graham too young and shy. She felt almost old enough to be their mother, although she was their age. But when her brother Murdo appeared in his white flannels with another young man dressed in a pale blue blazer as soft as a spring sky, she did not find him too immature at eighteen. He was the celebrated Alexander Plunkett-Drax, who had stood at the crease like Horatius on the bridge, so that even the ranks of the enemy could scarce forbear to cheer. His lanky height made him stoop slightly to talk down to her, so that his compliments fell on her like guineas from heaven. He was certainly sure of his own attractions as well as hers.

"Where have you been hiding your beautiful cousin?" he accused Gordon and Graham. Then he turned to her. "In a dungeon, you're so pale. But now you've got out, we don't intend ever to let you out of our sight. Did you see me having my knock?"

"Knock?" Arabella said. "Don't you bat?" It was the only word of cricket that she knew except for one more, which she now used. "And ball?"

Plunkett-Drax began to laugh in a curious high-pitched way. Everybody laughed with him as the English always do at the unintended word of double meaning.

"Bowl," Bill Dunesk said. "You bowl a ball. Or if you are a beautiful young woman, you dance at it."

"I know no games," Arabella said. "I am hopeless at games."

"Then I shall teach you," said Plunkett-Drax. He turned to Arabella's mother. "Don't you play games in Peru? It must be very dull."

"Not young ladies," Isabella said. She did not know what more to say to the young man, but Bill Dunesk again came to the rescue.

"All young ladies play games, thank God," he said. He gave his hand to Marie. "Marie played with me and hooked me like a trout."

"I never fished you," Marie said, still getting the word for the sport as wrong as Arabella had. "But I rode you into the ground."

"Too true." Her husband opened his palms to include all her cousins and guests. "Shall we toddle off to tea? And celebrate such good company in strawberries and Veuve Clicquot?"

"Tea?" Arabella asked. "Veuve Clicquot is tea?"

Plunkett-Drax laughed again.

"You are as witty as you are fair."

"I am dark."

"There you go."

"Speaking the plain truth," Marie said, "is the funniest thing there is." She looked at the thousands of spectators who knew themselves to be the cream of the metropolis of the world. "Nobody here speaks the plain truth. That is why it is so funny." On impulse, she darted forward and kissed Arabella on the cheek.

"Come along," she said. "To tea with bubbles in it."

"Oh, Alexander," Bill Dunesk said to Plunkett-Drax. "Give my regards to your mother. I haven't seen Lily in an age."

"I never knew you knew each other," Murdo said.

"We're related," Plunkett-Drax said. "Vaguely."

"Everybody's related, aren't they?" Bill Dunesk shook his head at the little crowd around him walking towards their tea. "That's the trouble, isn't it? All these relations."

All had started with the invitation, which was signed *Edward R.* in the top right-hand corner. Marie could hardly believe the language, when Bill Dunesk gave it to her to read:

Right Trusty and Right Wellbeloved Cousin
We greet you well

Whereas the twenty-sixth day of June next is
appointed for the Solemnity of Our Royal Coronation

These are to Will and Command you and
your consort to make your personal attendance on Us
at the time above mentioned furnished and appointed
as to your Rank and Quality apportioneth so
to do and perform all such Services as shall be
required and belong unto you.
Whereof you are not to fail
And so We bid you most heartily Farewell

Given at Our Court at St. James
the first day of December in
the first year of Our Reign
By His Majesty's Command

"I am asked too?" Marie asked.

"Of course," her husband said.

"What do I wear?"

"You wear the same as the other peeresses."

"But I am not the same."

"I know Marie, but – red velvet robes trimmed with miniver. And lots of chocolates in the linings because the Ceremony is five hours in Westminster Abbey, plus the wait before and after and the chore of getting there and away. Never go to a long occasion without chockies in your socks."

"And hats?"

"Tiaras. You have to wear a tiara."

"Do you have one?"

"In the vaults. Two or three."

"Will they fit me?"

"We'll find one which will."

"And if it doesn't?"

"My grandfather – Queen Victoria's Coronation was so long ago – he told me the funniest moment was when She had the Crown put on, all the peers had to put their coronets on their heads. And sometimes their ancestors had bigger heads. I think heads shrink with too much inbred heredity. Anyway, when the peers put on their coronets, sometimes they slid down to the chin of a noble lord, wrapping his head up in the bag which is the velvet cap on top of the coronet. All those headless peers – it looked like the Wars of the Roses all over again."

Marie was worried.

"But if my tiara slips down when I put it on?"

"It won't. You have a beautiful big head and lots of lovely red hair."

"You could put a little coronet inside it. Then it couldn't slip down."

"We'll do that. Then a second Queen will be crowned. The Queen who reigns over me."

"You say the nicest things," Marie said.

"And I do not *do* them." Bill Dunesk bent forward and gave his wife a soft kiss on the forehead. "Well, I will this time. I swear you will be the prettiest peeress – the nonpareil – the goddess of the Abbey at this coronation."

It nearly never happened. The king was struck down with appendicitis. Sad crowds stood outside Buckingham Palace, waiting for the hourly bulletins about the royal recovery or decline. Sir Frederick Treves, back from the Boer War, was said to have been so overcome by his responsibility that his assistant had to complete the operation. But the news improved. The King mended. And a new date was set for August the ninth with a shortened ceremony to spare the royal health. "Fewer chockies," Bill Dunesk whispered. "We'll race through the show."

They did not. The crawl in the coach to the Abbey was slower than a slug's progress. Yet when the crowds lining the streets saw Marie through the glass windows, the cheering rose to a crescendo as well as the rhythmic chant,

> "TAKE me,
> TAKE me,
> TAKE me, anee – WHERE!"

"You are not forgotten," Bill Dunesk said to her. "Still the most famous woman in London."

"I don't want to be remembered," Marie said, "for that old number."

At the entrance to the Abbey, Marie saw the other guests ranged in tiers on either side of the long aisle. A page spread the velvet train of her robes, and she strode in with the lithe and bounding walk of her past, her back so straight and her head so high that it seemed to fly above her red robe. All looked at her in a sudden hush as she took her place in the transept among the massed scarlet and white fur and myriad diamonds of the peeresses. But they, too, looked only at her, whom they did not know, but now recognized as a rival, a solitary blaze among them.

Hours seemed to pass as Marie remained in her seat, rising only at the passage of minor dignitaries of the blood royal on their way to their due places. Then the comedy came, all the old lords coming in with their robes, tucking them under their arms or tripping over them, and holding their coronets in their hands like children with little hoops. Then the trumpets blew fanfares and the bells pealed and hundreds of choirboys sang hosannas and the organ intoned Parry's setting of:

> "I was glad when they said unto me,
> We will go into the House of the Lord."

And the Westminster schoolboys in their surplices shouted hurrays for the King who was to be crowned, and the anthem rose in its praise of harmony.

> "Jerusalem is built as a city,
> That is at unity in itself ...
> O pray for the peace of Jerusalem.
> They shall prosper that love Thee.
> Peace be within Thy walls,
> And plenteousness within Thy palaces."

And all ended on the glorious high B flat that only English choirboys and nightingales and thrushes can achieve.

Now the long procession was passing – the Court officials with their white rods, the Clergy with vestments of gold and green and blue, the bearers of the royal insignia, the crown on a red cushion held before, the tall cold Queen with Her train borne by eight ladies-in-waiting, then the rounded and bearded King, His pages holding His train. But as He passed the peeresses rising in their ranks of seats, He paused – perhaps He stumbled, although Kings cannot stumble even when They do. But He stood still for seconds and gazed at Marie, not at anyone else, directly at Marie, as though He had never seen such a woman before, as though she had an unspoken message for Him, as if there was already something between them. And all the other peeresses saw the new King looking at the new Countess, and they began to whisper behind their hands. Then the King stepped forward again to the sound of the choirs. And Marie knew she had been chosen by Someone whom she did not wish to choose her.

When the Queen was finally anointed by the ancient Archbishop of Canterbury, Marie was standing near Her, helping to hold the canopy above Her. She saw the Archbishop pour too much of the sacred oil from his spoon onto Her forehead so that a trickle ran down the Queen's nose in greasy tears. The Queen could do nothing but kneel and pray. She seemed to be weeping as a great cheering shook the abbey roof when the Crown was finally placed on the head of King Edward the Seventh. Marie wondered if the Queen were mourning the life of the sovereign that was to come. There would be no escape from it for Her. But as for Him ...

Within a week of the ceremony, a note was conveyed through Alice, Mrs George Keppel, an intimate of the King, that the Earl and Countess of Dunesk would be welcome at a small function at Court, where Her Majesty the Queen would not be present. This invitation was hardly as formal as the invitation to the Coronation had been, but it held the same implication – *Whereof you are not to fail.*

10

A LONG LABOUR

It was a long labour. A night and a day of it and now another night. Mary was too old for this, hobbling with her arthritis, always minding the birth of other women's babies, never her own, and in South Africa of all places. Of course, there was that story in the Bible of barren Sarah, ancient Abraham's wife, who brought forth well after her time of life because the Lord decreed it. But really, although the Good Book was always right because it was the Good Book, you could not believe everything you read in it. May God forgive me, Mary thought, for thinking so. Anyway, at eighty years old, she certainly couldn't hope for a blessed event, even if an angel had a hand in it. She could only hope to deliver Lizzie's third before the poor creature failed and her life ebbed away between the contractions she was almost too weak to have anymore. The baby's head was too big for such a little woman, although she was broad enough at the hips, and Hamish Gordon and Martha had slipped out as easily and regularly as lambs in spring. "It'll have to be the forceps," Mary said to herself and looked in her black bag for them and found them, then turned to Virginia, who was useless at this sort of thing, having none of her own and not likely to have one by Robert, who was always away on trek and went on his leaves to see his sick mother in Canada. There was not enough pay to take his wife along.

"Get some more boiling water and towels, Virginia," Mary said. "I have to use the forceps. I hope I willna crush the wee babe's head." And as Virginia left the room, Mary went over to Lizzie, soaked in sweat and moaning with pain, and she said, "Have a last try, girl. And I'll pull his head out with the forceps." And Lizzie said, "Let me die, Tant' Mary. Not him. Do not hurt him. Cut me and take him out and save him. You call him Paul. Like Oom Paul. You call him Paul." And Mary said, "We dinna ken even if he is a wee lad. But with a big head like that. Now pull, girl, pull –" And she gave Lizzie the sheet twisted into a rope and knotted to the bedpost. "Pull. For the last time. Pull!"

Outside in the drawing-room, Hamish Charles stood. He caught Virginia's arm as she carried the kettle of boiling water and a towel back into the room, where Lizzie was now screaming. "I can't bear you suffering," Hamish Charles said, but Virginia shook her arm free, spilling some scalding water onto the man's boots. "What do you mean? She is suffering – your wife – you have all these children by her." And Hamish Charles looked down at his steaming boot caps. "Yes, she is suffering," he said. "But you are too. And I ... can't you see I suffer? For you." Virginia kept her voice down, but there was anger in it. "How could you? At a time like this. But men are so selfish." And Hamish Charles found himself muttering, "But I care only for you – I live only for you ..." And then there was the sound of a smack as sharp as a shot from a rifle, and the thin reedy wail of an infant, its first breath a small protest at all the trouble of being born.

"Thank God," Hamish Charles said. "Thank God." And he slumped down in the wooden arm-chair, his head buried in the palms of his hands as in a sort of praying.

When Virginia went back into the bedroom with her kettle and towel, she found Mary holding a squealing red small shape and cutting the cord and life-line to its mother and tying it and saying, "Have you ever seen such hair? That's what saved you, my lad, your hair. Though I pinched your ears a bit." And as Virginia poured the boiling water into the enamel basin and carried it over to the bed with the towel, she heard Lizzie say weakly, "Is it Paul?" And Mary answered, "Yes, it is Paul. And he has golden curls all over his head like a ram."

In the morning, Mary sat at the breakfast table with Hamish Charles and the two bairns, Hamish Gordon, aged two, and Martha, one year old, in her high chair. "You'll not be having any more," Mary said firmly. "It would kill your Lizzie. And these wee ones need their mother. You canna be so selfish."

"Indeed, there will be no more," Hamish Charles said. "I can promise you that."

"This one near killed her. The great big head on him, and born that way round. It is lucky for you I could be visiting. Oh, Hamish!" The man flinched as if the rebuke was for him, but it was for the tiny boy, who had tipped over his bowl of milk and porridge. "Will you not mind your food?" But his father was already mopping up the mess with a napkin, and saying, "He's too small to know how to eat." And Mary replied, "Nobody is ever too small to know how to eat, if there is precious little to eat. But it is worrit I am. That Virginia – she is asleep now – I think the birthing wore her out more than Lizzie. How long is she stopping here, Hamish? When will your cousin Robert be back to fetch her?"

"She is a great help to Lizzie round the house," Hamish Charles said defensively, wiping the face of his small son with the wet napkin. "She looks after the children."

"She dinna ken a farthing about that."

"She taught a whole school of piccaninnies –"

"She has none of her own." Mary's judgement was final. "And in this house, with a fine man like you here –"

"She is my cousin's wife."

"I hope you mind it. And she does."

"Of course. You wouldn't suggest –" Hamish Charles looked out of the window as he went back to his seat. He had to hide his flushed cheeks. "Another scorcher," he said. "The drought will never end. The cattle will all be dead soon."

"So will I," Mary said. "And that is a matter that also makes me worrit. I am head of the family, if you can call our scatterings a family. And I must pass it on."

"There's still your youngest brother Bain in Canada."

"He's failing. He will not live beyond Julia muckle long."

"Well, how about Hamilton –"

"I like him well. But in fact, the best of all my nephews and nieces is Seaforth –"

"You would say that."

"He is doing very well at the hospital in Jo'burg. And he may ... yes, Seaforth may be marrying. And to Miriam Apfelstein, too. What do you think of that?"

"She couldn't." And Hamish Charles couldn't believe his ears. "One of the richest families and Seaforth –"

"Coloured." Mary gave a short laugh. "Born on the wrong side of the blanket, too. Everything that can be wrong about him is wrong about him. And yet he is the best of you Sinclairs. She will be lucky to have him. Though she is not all I would want for him. Very radical. A socialist, she calls herself. And about the Empire, she is worse than I am. And you know what I feel since the war."

"You call it Your War," Hamish Charles said. "Not the Boer War. And they did start it."

"Did they now? Your war it was, Hamish, and you fought in it. So did that good neighbour of yours, Piet Krug –"

"He's not such a good neighbour now. Oh, Martha!" The baby had thrown her feeding bottle onto the floor, where it smashed into smithereens. Then she began to howl at the noise.

"Leave it," Mary said and turned to the little girl and fixed her with her eyes. "Hush," she said. "Little miss – you hush, do you hear?" As if mesmerized, the infant stopped howling with her mouth open, then put in her thumb and sucked it. "That is better," Mary said and turned back to Hamish Charles. "You will not be falling out with Piet Krug. He has married Lizzie's sister."

"His cattle still drink the last of my water."

"They are beasts. They go where water is. Who can stop them? Has he children?"

"Two now. Sannie and Pieter."

"You were married at the same time?"

"In front of a *predikant*." Hamish Charles smiled. "A funny old fellow in a black frock coat. He spoke in Afrikaans. I didn't understand a word of it, except where I had to put on the ring, and then Lizzie dug me in the ribs."

"Your mother will not think you married at all," Mary said. "A Roman Catholic that she is."

"It doesn't matter, Aunt Mary." Hamish Charles was embarrassed. "At Harrow, I didn't really say I was a Catholic. I was C of E like everybody else."

"The Church of England," Mary said severely, "is much more soft than the Church of Scotland. Or the Presbyterian. Or the Wee Frees. They will let in anybody. Including you."

"As long as you believe in God –" Hamish Charles said. "And I certainly do." He rose. "I must go and see how Lizzie is. And the baby. Thank you for all you have done, Aunt Mary. Really, we can't get by without you. I hope you'll stay with us as long as you can."

"Help me up," Mary said, and Hamish Charles helped her to her feet and waited while her joints were loosening. "I must be going back to Jo'burg. You can spare Buldoo to drive me in the cart?"

"Yes. Of course. But you must stay –"

"As my father was saying, he would rather wear out than rust out. I ken I am past it, but Seaforth still asks my advice at his hospital. And there is the orphanage for the children of the war. We have to pay back, Hamish. We have to pay back."

Hamish Charles bent and kissed the thick white hair of the old woman.

"You have paid back what you have taken from us a thousand fold," he said. "If I was asked, what is a giving spirit – a good soul – I would say, Mary Sinclair."

Mary was secretly pleased at the compliment, but she was still anxious about leaving him in the house with Virginia, and his wife so sick in her bed. So she merely said, "You canna talk me round with that honey in your mouth. You watch what you do, Hamish. For if I canna keep my eye on you, God will – and not that soft English God you think is so easy on you."

The cave in the mountain had a fissure in the roof. A sun star sprayed light onto the sandy floor. "It must have been a natural altar," Virginia said to Buldoo. "A holy place for the Bushmen." But he stood contemptuous and silent as a boulder of granite, while she peered at the drawings on the walls and traced the outlines with her fingers. "Deer," she said. "Giraffe. A hippo. And, I wonder... It looks like a mammoth, but it is probably an elephant. Do elephants come this far south?"

Buldoo grunted. "Maybe sometime," he conceded. "Maybe old time. But why do you look for this Bushman trash?"

"It is not trash," Virginia said and began to take her crayons and her drawing-pad out of her satchel. "It is art. And I am going to set it down. I intend to become an expert, you see. Why don't you go and wait outside while I work?"

"The cattle, *baas* say I to take out ticks. And some they have *rinderpest*."

"*Baas* say," Virginia said, "you look after me, bring me home."

"You be long?" Buldoo growled.

"As long as it takes me, Buldoo."

So Virginia set to work to copy the Bushmen paintings, marvelling always at their exquisite simplicity, which seemed to catch the essence of a beast in a few strokes of red or brown pigment. In those early ages, the artist seemed to have lived in the animal, to be the antelope or the snake himself. It was not like that now. Even in her own body, there was a terrible distance between her nature and her spirit. Nothing was simple, all her desires were at odds. She had begun to hate her husband Robert – he abandoned her, he repelled her, he never took her to London, so far and so longed for. Yet she wanted the marriage to last, she could not bear scandal, she could not go off with his cousin, Hamish Charles, who wanted her and understood her as an artist and a free soul. But the dear fool had married a woman he did not love, just because he had to have a wife to run his farm, which he did not really want. He was no farmer, but something of a cavalier, that look of Quixote from his Peruvian mother – ascetic, melancholy, hollowed and chipped with eyes that could both yearn for a quest and look as humble as a whipped puppy dog. A man would get himself into an inextricable mess, and then expect the woman he loved to get him out of it. But free in thought as she was for her time, she could not take a man away from his wife and three babies. She had no family to blame her, that was so. And that Mary Sinclair. She shuddered to remember how the old biddy had glared at her.

There was a shout from the outside, then another raised voice yelling back. Virginia packed up her work and ran through the star of sunlight falling from the crack in the roof of the cave into the yellow wall of the blinding daylight. There she saw Buldoo leaping down the slope of the berg towards a horseman, who was driving some oxen before him with his whip. He was shouting at Buldoo in Afrikaans, and Buldoo was bellowing back. And as Buldoo came at him, the rider struck with his long lash. The rawhide thong caught round Buldoo's arm, and he held on to it, trying to drag the man out of the saddle. As Virginia ran down the hill, she could see the grotesque tug-o'war played out between the Zulu and Piet Krug, whom she now recognized on his brindled pony. The contest ended with the thong of the whip slipping out of Buldoo's hands. He fell over backwards, while the Afrikaner raised the *sjambok* again. But Virginia ran under it to protect the sprawling Buldoo with her own body.

"Get out you!" Piet shouted.

"I will not," Virginia said. "What are you doing on our land?"

"Our land? You have part, I suppose?" Piet's sneer gashed his beard below the shadow of his slouch hat. "My sister-in-law Lizzie, it is her land, maybe. And that fool Hamish. But now it is your land, your Hamish?"

"He take our cattle, miss." Buldoo now was standing behind her.

"They are my span. See the brand," Piet said. "They come over here. To the *vlei*."

"Our *vlei*," Virginia said.

"The water is for all to drink. It was a *vlei* for all. Until you come." Piet pointed his whip at Virginia, who did not flinch, but stared proudly up at him on his saddle. "Now there is bad blood. Bunjie and Lizzie, sisters – now you ... you take Lizzie's man."

"I am helping Lizzie with the children, as you know," Virginia said. "With the new baby, she cannot do much. They need me."

"They need you here?" Piet gave a laugh like a bark. "Drawing – it help Lizzie? You look for babies here? Go back to your home, woman. And your man. Or there will be blood here."

"Don't threaten me, Mister Krug. My husband is the law, over the border in Basutoland."

"Go, I tell you," Piet said. He cracked his whip towards his oxen. "Before there is blood, go!" He was denouncing her as if he was Ezekiel or some Old Testament prophet.

"Get thee gone too!" Virginia found herself shouting, as if she were casting out a devil. And as that was the last word and she had said it, she was quite proud at having stood up to the Boer so well.

Robert was due any day now to take her back to the quarters she would not call home over the border. Lizzie had not recovered from Paul's birth and still lay in the bed most of the day, leaving Virginia to supervise the Kaffir maids as they pounded the mealie grains with their wooden pestles and cracked and ground the coffee beans between two smooth stones. Virginia had bought Tsutsie with her, but the other African women would not listen to a Hottentot, so that Virginia had to give the orders herself. She was rarely alone with Hamish Charles. She took care not to be so, keeping the tiny Hamish Gordon and Martha near her skirts. But every evening when the children were put to bed, she would play the piano, which she had managed to tune herself. And her recitals of Liszt and Brahms and Chopin would plunge Hamish Charles into an ecstasy of gloom, sometimes filling his eyes with tears as he gazed at her. But this particular evening, when Lizzie and baby Paul were sound asleep and the door to the bedroom was closed, Virginia nodded towards Hamish Charles to come over to the piano while she played. As he approached, she said to him softly, "I know. We must talk. I know."

"I love you," Hamish Charles said. "I am desperate. What can we do?"

"Nothing, my dear. Your wife, your children, your farm. But if..." Her voice trailed away into the notes of the *étude*. "What would you propose?"

"I would leave all – risk all – for you." Hamish Charles's voice was broken. "I would take you away – start again – where nobody knows us."

"To London," Virginia heard herself saying. "Would you take me there?"

"Anywhere. If you would come away with me."

"You promise. To London."

"They would not know me there. You are right. I am not a farmer. My father Angus would help us. And you know, my mother does not even think I am married to Lizzie. It was not a Catholic wedding."

"But your children."

"Ah." Hamish Charles winced. "The children. Their mother would keep them."

"But you love them."

"I love you most. Wholly. Absolutely. If I must give up the children, I must."

Virginia's fingers ran up and down the keys. They were separate from her. She might have been playing in a dream. She was touching the ivories, the bones of dead things. She almost had forgotten why sweet sounds came from them.

"We met too late," she said. "Why didn't you wait for me?"

"You had already married Robert. You didn't wait for me."

"I hadn't met you. I had to get away. But you met me before Lizzie."

"Yes," Hamish Charles said. "I had to keep a wife to live here." Then he added bitterly, "Now I don't want to be here. I don't want to live."

"Don't say that." Virginia lifted her right hand and held it out to Hamish Charles. Her left hand still picked out Chopin's theme on the keys. Hamish Charles took her hand in both of his and chafed it between his palms.

"But could you – would you – leave Robert, if somehow ... I was free?"

Virginia withdrew her hand and looked down as she finished the study in music. She spoke so softly that Hamish Charles could hardly hear her speak.

"I should not say this. But we are modern –"

"Yes. Tell me."

"Robert and I – there are no children – there is a reason. I can't say more."

"And with me? Do you feel –"

"I feel ..." Virginia watched her fingers moving to the end of the piece. "I feel – far too much. And far too late."

"It is never too late. Not while we have life. Virginia –"

Virginia finished the Chopin. In the silence, she looked up at Hamish Charles. Her large brown eyes spilled over. They seemed to flood her face.

"My dear," she whispered.

As Hamish Charles bent to kiss her, there was a burst of coughing from behind the bedroom door. The man drew back and listened. Then the summons came. "I need you. Paul is –" The words were lost in a thin wailing from the baby that cut through to the heart of Hamish Charles, and his face puckered in despair as if he also would cry.

"There," he said. "You see. It is hopeless." And he moved towards the bedroom door.

Miriam Apfelstein came through Seaforth's bedroom door before their marriage. It was an act of defiance as much as love. She would show the world what she thought of convention. She would break the barriers between the castes and the classes. She was so open as she strode down the corridor into his quarters near the hospital that Seaforth thought she almost wanted the other doctors to see her going to bed with somebody they considered as Coloured – that was the official term for him. Neither black nor white, but ambiguous. Seaforth thought that Coloured rather suited him.

As he followed Miriam into his bedroom, Seaforth was glad she had not been seen, and also he was annoyed that she had not provoked a crisis with the law.

"You are too bold," he said, closing the door behind them, as she sat on his bed. "This may not be the right time to have us flung out of South Africa."

Miriam smiled at him, her lips spread and plum-red, her heavy eyelids masking the brilliance of her gaze.

"Don't you want me, Seaforth?"

Now Seaforth was kneeling in front of her, his head buried in her lap. His face was pressed against the warmth of her thighs, his hair against the small swell of her belly. He spoke thickly into the cloth of her skirt.

"You know I want you. My whole life – it is in you."

He felt her fingers combing the back of his head. Her voice sounded far away.

"Yes. My life too. In you."

He could feel the pulse of the beat of her blood against his cheeks, and after a silence, he laid his head sideways on the cushion of her seated body. His lips were muffled no more.

"I never thought," he said, "I could feel like this. Doctors, we are meant to be cold fish. No feeling. Or how could we operate and examine and cut people up?"

"You are warm, Seaforth."

"Even Aunt Mary ... you know, she loves me. But she was always worried I could not love. But then, you came along. Aunt Mary always laughs about it. The Scots and the Jews, she says – they always got on well. Both are tribal – clannish. Loyal and suspicious. But I am an Indian, I say – and she just laughs and says, Seaforth Sinclair by name, Seaforth Sinclair by nature."

Now Miriam's hand was stroking the head of the man who would be her lover and her husband.

"I love you being an Indian, too."

At this, Seaforth raised himself to look at this glorious woman, who would marry him.

"Not too much, I hope." The usual dryness returned to his voice. "I mean, I would rather you loved the man than the Indian in me."

"I do," Miriam said, "but —"

"I am not just forbidden meat, am I? Your proof that you want to end the class system? Your demonstration that you hate imperialism by going with an Indian?"

Now Miriam was stroking his cheeks with the palms of her hands. Then they caught his face and held it and made him look at the huge green stare of her eyes, glistening in her desire.

"You silly man. I want you. You, Seaforth. What you are. Yes, I hate the Empire, the class system, all this terrible exploitation —"

"As only the rich can ever hate it."

"Seaforth, shut up! I hate it. I can't help my family being rich off the gold-mines. They've given you your hospital —"

"I don't think they meant to give you to me too, Miriam."

"I do what I want. I'm a free woman. They brought me up to be."

Seaforth smiled his thin smile, although he dropped his eyes at the fierce blaze in hers.

"They wanted a good Bar Mitzvah boy for you."

"I am my own woman. I choose. I choose you."

"Yes," Seaforth said. He rose and stood over her, looking down at her. Her legs were spread open beneath her long skirt, her breasts were alive beneath the little embroidered waistcoat she was wearing. He ached with the want of her.

"You," he mumbled. "You. I want you. And you —"

"Yes," she said and fell back as he sank upon her.

11

A MINE

Marie never thought she would ever go down a mine, but Keir McBride had insisted on it. Her husband was away more and more in London with his amusing friends such as Lord Alfred Douglas. And she had to flee the capital after the King had pressed his attentions on her at a private dinner arranged by Alice Keppel. So she was left in charge at Dunesk with her Rosabelle, who was now four years old and would not be detached from her mother's left ankle. Marie loved her daughter's dependence on her, and through that absolute love, she worried over the future that her daughter would inherit. There were the coal mines between Dunesk and Rosslyn as well as the paper mills. And when there was trouble at the pits, and Keir McBride came to the castle to tell her husband of it, Marie took it upon herself to solve it. And as she could not decide without seeing for herself – for what was the use of a man's word unsupported? – she said she would go down a pit.

"Women," Keir McBride said, "they nae go down. Never."

"I will go down," Marie said. "You will take me."

"Aye, the Countess, down pit." McBride set his hawk's face into a hard mask of denial. "You will nae go down." He twisted his black cap in his hands as if he were strangling her in the cloth.

"I will," Marie said. And she did. There was no man who would dare to stop her. That Scots toast, "Here's to us, who's like us? Damn few and they're all dead." She drank to that, even though she was a woman.

She wore her Indian buckskin leggings again, trousers like a man, also a flat Roundhead helmet, which Cromwell's troopers had left behind when they had stormed the castle after the Battle of Dunbar. The pit cage was a slow descent to hell, while the grim galleries that spoked out to the coal-faces from the shaft were so low and dark in the patches of light from the oil-lamps that she had to stoop and stumble over the rails for the coal-tubs, which the pit-ponies were dragging between their limbers. Ahead, the flickers from the lamps of the miners hacking at the face. Behind, a pitch darkness and a burial in the deep earth. Then they went through a door worked by a trapper-boy no more than fourteen years old, his job the opening and closing the barrier for the putters with their ponies and coal-tubs. And one time of danger, with Keir McBride's arm crashing her against the side of the gallery as a set of sixty empty coal tubs came hurtling back down the slope to be filled again. And the shouting of the overmen to keep the miners working, the echoes of their screams to hurry the lumps of the black diamonds to the surface. And the water dripping from the cracking shives of stone on the roof down the props, the threat that Keir McBride had brought her see, a catastrophe waiting to happen.

"When it breaks," he said, "there will be the flood. And we will drown all."

"So what is to do?" she said.

"Close the gallery. With explosive."

"Close the whole mine. It would be safer."

"And your husband's fees? His royalties? He willnae." McBride's twist of a smile gashed his sooted face.

"The Earl," Marie said, and was surprised to hear herself use his title, "the Earl cares for human lives more than profits."

"Nae Earl dinnae."

"I will ask him. And answer for him."

"But the wages," McBride said. "The families will starve wi'out the wages."

"So you don't want the mines closed."

"A piece of them. This wet piece." McBride put his dark hand on a soaking side-prop, a trunk of oak. "You could be in a wee boat. 'Half o'er, half o'er to Aberdour is fifty fathom deep. There lies the guid Earl and Countess wi' the Scots lairds at their feet.'"

Marie laughed.

"I've heard that poem from my husband," she said. "It should be Sir Patrick Spens, not he and I. But you're right. We are under water. And he'll never come down to see it."

"And you ... never you should."

"I am here," Marie smiled and put her hand lightly on McBride's sopping shirt. "And I am safe with you. And we will have this piece closed, I swear it."

And she did persuade her husband to close it, although he had one of his rare fits of anger, when he heard that she had been down one of his coal mines. "It's that pernicious McBride," he said. "He says he is *organizing*, as if he could organize a game of marbles. He talks of a union, when the only time a group of Scotsmen come together ends in stabbing and bloody noses. Does he say he is a socialist?"

"You do," Marie said sweetly. "Like your old friend Oscar Wilde did."

"Oscar's socialism was purely aesthetic," Bill Dunesk said. "And he was right. Men should not be slaves to their work. Machines must do that work. And the machines should be the new slaves. Unfortunately, civilisation needs slaves so that artists can be artists."

"You can be an artist now," Marie said. "Only because your miners are slaves."

"Yes," the Earl said. "I cannot change the system. But I do try to understand it."

"But the point is to change it."

"What?" For once, Bill Dunesk was sneering. "You come from nowhere – you are now a Countess – and you want a change of the system? Or perhaps you would like to be Cinderella in reverse. Back to the bareback riding and the Music Hall, which you have so successfully risen above."

"Bill," Marie now rose above her husband as he sprawled back on the Empire sofa in the drawing-room of the castle. "You know I am not ungrateful."

"Two negatives do not make a positive, Marie. Simply, you are not grateful. Gratitude is not part of your wild nature."

"I married you ... part of it ..." Marie tried to pick her words carefully. Anything she said would be wrong. "I thought, if I was your wife, we could change things. We could have the power –"

"Ah, yes – being a Countess, you would have the power –"

Marie went off at a tangent, seeing herself in a trap.

"Rosabelle is there. Don't you think ... isn't that the best thing about our marriage – Rosabelle."

"She is not a boy – an heir."

"In Scotland, women can be heirs. Mary, Queen of Scots –"

"We could still have a boy."

"If you were more interested."

"Or if you appreciated me more. My particular ways." Bill Dunesk stretched up his arms from the sofa towards the hovering Marie. "Descend on me, Marie, from heaven like a shower of gold. For that is what you are."

"That was Jupiter. A male God, descending on a girl."

"Well, let us reverse roles," he said. "If you will not be Cinderella backwards, then let me be your Minnehaha, and you be my Hiawatha, my Indian brave."

Marie stooped and kissed her husband, then broke free from his arms and walked away to look out of the keep window down to the glen with the brown Esk river curling below.

"We could change so many things," she said. "And make a better world for Rosabelle."

Bill Dunesk sat up on the sofa to consider his wife by the window. "You really are quite an upsetter."

"And you're a spectator, like your friend Oscar Wilde. You do know what to do, but you won't do it. It would upset you if you did. You merely want to be free to pursue your art ... and your fellow artists. But you're not a socialist. You just say you are selfish."

"Aren't we all?" Bill yawned. "Of course, we're all sorry for the poor and needy. But it's word-deep. We say it to soothe ourselves."

"Then don't!" Marie swung round on her husband. "It's wrong. Don't say you're with your miners. You can't be, you're the Earl. That's what Keir McBride says."

"Adieu to dear Keir. I do not need to take my words from him. But I am closing the wet part of the pit."

"Yes. To stop a tragedy."

"To save lives."

"Yes, but oh, Bill, can't you see?" She ran towards him as he rose to hold her. "Don't just stand back. Don't make your little jokes. Engage. You must commit."

Gently, the Earl put her away from him and gently he shook his head.

"Perish the thought," he said. "Always retire and stand back. Always have a little joke. One only engages servants. One commits perjury – or commits people to prison. Engage – commit – you really don't know what they mean, dear – and they are not words for people like us."

"Really, to have to be selected," Charles Seymour-Scudabright said. "It is lucky for them that I choose to represent them." The former naval Captain from HMS *Terrible* spoke as if he were issuing a command, not having an opinion.

"I agree," May said. "But it should not be too embarrassing."

"To question me about my private affairs? And my beliefs, which are between me and my God? It is degrading – blasphemous, you might say."

"It is only a selection committee for a seat you will certainly get. It is a formality."

"Then they need not go through the process. They could merely select me as their next Member of Parliament."

"They are often nice people," May said. "Very nice."

"That is their trouble," her husband said. "Nice people are often very nasty. I cannot abide nice people."

"I am sure there will be no impertinent questions," May said to soothe him. "They will be too scared of you to ask about any horrors."

"There are no horrors in my career. As someone who was a captain in the Home Fleet – a defender of the realm – as well as having a family connection with North Mimsbury for generations, I would have thought that examining me before selecting me –"

"Charles, you will toddle it."

"May, to tell you the truth, I don't approve of all those Reform Bills. My great-grandfather served North Mimsbury for decades when it was a rotten borough. And he served it well, as I will. But none of this fuss about selection."

"I wouldn't say that to the committee," May said. "Not if I were you. You know what a collection of nonentities is – they think they really do matter."

"Then I will not speak more than I must. I will say nothing very much – but very well."

"You usually do," May said.

Charles Seymour Scudabright gave his wife a sharp look. Sometimes he suspected her tongue was a little on the tart side, but she smiled sweeter than a syllabub, so he always forgave her.

"I will follow your advice, my dear," he consented graciously. "My service in the Royal Navy, my wife an angel, a son at Cambridge before he joins the Army, another at Dartmouth Naval College, what could be better for a county constituency?"

"Ruth," May said. "Our daughter is your problem."

"But she has not caused any trouble yet."

"She will. Her ideas –" May threw up her hands and said no more, as if Ruth's thoughts were too shocking to express.

"We can pack her off," Charles said. "She can visit relations. Or we can marry her off. That will shut her up. Marriage always does."

"No suitable man is presently on tap," May said. "But she has had an invitation to Ireland. To stay with my cousin Arabella, who married that Alex Plunkett-Drax."

"He's a bit of a devil, isn't he? Didn't he marry her for her money?"

"Yes. Uncle Angus married rich himself. A Peruvian nob's only daughter. So Arabella went with a dowry – too, too Spanish South American, but that's how they are out there."

"What do you think? Shall we pack Ruth off there to hunt and fish a bit?"

"Do her the world of good, don't you think?"

"And no bloody books. That's one good thing about the Irish, brains isn't their line."

"No – they have bogs there, not libraries." May contemplated the florid bluff face of her husband that had once seemed so masterful, and now appeared overdone. "Brains isn't a line that ever does a man any good. Or a single girl."

The selection committee was, indeed, a walk-over. All the Tories were male solicitors and tradesmen with two brace of squires and landowners. Presenting himself as a hero of the Boer War – the naval guns at Spion Kop – as a commander of battleships and an opponent of votes for women and any radical change, Charles Seymour-Scudabright seemed to have inherited the seat for which he was being chosen. When he added that he believed in protection for English corn and English beef against cheap imports and free trade, he turned a certainty into a sanctuary. He was the right man in the right place at the right time doing the right thing. He had always known he was. It was only that, when he had been asked to take early retirement from the Royal Navy because of his inability to concentrate or navigate, other people had not appreciated his true qualities. Yet he knew what a good man he was. And the electors would certainly know. After all, it was a seat which had always sent a Tory to parliament, and always would. Particularly if he was top-notch, as Charles indubitably felt he was.

At first, Ruth thought that Normanton was worse than the Slough of Despond, where the poor Pilgrim fell in and stopped his Progress. The grey stones, the draughts as keen as slivers of ice, the wet grass sopping through her boots, it was a cold store for human beings. And isolated in glowing patches amid the general darkness, a few peat fires and one of wood in the hall, as lonely as light-buoys in a sea channel in a storm. There was no question of living in an Irish winter, there was a matter of surviving. And Ruth did not see how she could keep on until spring, when her exile would be over and her father elected.

There was another bright spot, to be sure. And that was Alexander Plunkett-Drax himself.

"I am rather beyond the Pale," he used to repeat to her, in his favourite joke and explanation. "But we live inside it. The Pale, of course, explains the name of this friendly mausoleum. Normanton. The family estate, God help us. I wish Father had lived a little longer, he might have spared me this at least, until I was too gaga to mind about it. Normanton. The Normans took this part of Ireland and put a pale –a fence – around it to keep out the savage Irish. But personally, I wish we had let them in. Then we wouldn't have to live here. Like them, we too would be beyond the Pale."

For all his pretences, Alexander seemed to love his land. His complaints were really an appreciation of his possessions. For fear of seeming to value his inheritance too much, he ran it down in the way that the English often did. They mocked what they held most dear. There was no other reason, Ruth thought, for him to have married her cousin Arabella, except for having her money to pay for all the repairs to the house and for the draining of the fields. Arabella really was sinking fast, both personally and literally. The juices were running from her into the ground. Yet it was easier to drown than walk in County Kildare. The big house itself might disappear like the House of Usher into the dark tarn, swallowed up by the swamp of the land.

Arabella had retired upstairs with one of her migraines, the smart French word which had taken over from the vapours or fits of melancholy. Now her husband went beyond the pale. He pounced on Ruth, who had long expected it, as had all the servants and Arabella. He did it under cover of helping Ruth, as he did everything. Such was never his intent, she must be positively begging for it. Ruth was sure that the embroidered low stool which she stumbled over had been laid in her way as a trap by Alexander, so that he could catch her as she fell into his waiting arms, and not onto the carpet. Before she could resist, his grip of concern had changed to the claws of desire, one hard arm locking her against him, his other hand pulling her head back by the hair so that he could bite her neck and ears with hurting kisses.

She could hardly breathe, she could not say no, her protest was smothered by his mouth, which clamped on her lips as in the jaws of a vice. When he freed her to crush her face against his throat so that she could still not speak, matting her hair with the pressing of his mouth, she had to twist her head to the side to utter a word.

"No – Arabella –"

"Don't speak," she heard. "It spoils everything. Bloody words."

She was forced back against the sofa, her dress ripped and hoisted high, a thrust into her was a fierce pain. She did not scream, her throat was locked.

"Virgins," she heard. "Always such a mess, virgins." Then he did not speak, but lunged and panted, then shook and trembled, then lay heavy on her for a moment, then sprang back from her, recoiling. She closed her eyes, lying spent on the sofa, waiting for him to say one word of want or of love. But all she heard was, "It's awful first time. Much nicer next time." Then a caress of her cheek as if it were the light flick of a whip. "You'd better do something about that blood. It'll stain the sofa. Before the servants come in."

He presumed correctly. She should have told Arabella, and she said nothing, for shame and fear of scandal. She should have left Normanton that night, but she had nowhere to go – her father was in the middle of his election campaign – and she had no money. She should have resisted his next attack on her two nights later, when his wife was sedated with opium, but his assault was too sudden, and she would not shout in case the butler heard. And this time, she did feel a certain response to his driving need. Something in her answered to his cruelty and his anger at his desire for her. She almost revelled in the knowledge he would reject her. She knew that she did not want to be a martyr, but she did want to be a rebel. And this rape of her, it severed her scruples at cutting off from her family and its pompous decency.

"I can't stay now," she said to Alexander Plunkett-Drax, as he lay against her side, still tensed in an arched bow of lean flesh.

"You've nowhere to go."

"Marie Dunesk, she'll take me in. She's wild too."

"A savage. An Indian. Very alluring."

"She'll take me in. I want to be free."

"With your father and mother?" Alexander laughed in his shrill way. "They are so conventional. And they get a wild one. One never can tell what sort of a brat one will get." He paused in order to make everything worse. "I didn't tell you. Why Arabella is so under the weather. She's expecting something – he, she or it."

"And you –"

"Exactly. She won't exactly be in service for quite a while."

"You're a pig, Alexander."

"That's what you like." Alexander rolled himself onto one elbow to look down at her in the moonlight that shone through her bedroom window past the open shutters. "I knew it when I first saw you. Like a good filly, you like to be broken. A touch of the spur and the quirt."

"I do not." Ruth beat against his bare chest with her right fist, until he caught her wrist, nearly crushing her thin bones. "Women aren't horses," she sobbed.

"No," Alexander said, releasing her. "A better ride." He lay back beside her, and then did the unspeakable, making it her fault. "I knew what you wanted. I gave it to you. If you think I enjoy being a bit of a bastard, I don't. I'd much rather play Young Lochinvar. But you wanted a pirate lover. A Blackbeard. A Captain Blood. So I had to oblige –"

"I'm to blame?" Ruth could not believe her ears. "You can't think –"

"It's the truth," Alexander yawned, then sat up in her bed, rising as a pale spear from the shadow of the canopy over the four-poster. "I must get back to Arabella. She may wake from her druggy dreams and want me. Oh God," he drawled, "the wants of women. How can we ever satisfy them?"

12

TO SHOOT A DUCK

The news of the death of his mother Julia had recalled Robert back to Canada. Again there was not enough pay to take Virginia with him; the Colonial Office was mean with the servants of the Empire. So Virginia was once more staying with Hamish Charles to help with the three children. Lizzie did not want her there, but Hamish Charles had insisted in the name of charity and mercy and the fine words used by men to get their own way. Only the little ones, now two and three and four years old, kept the brew from boiling over. Looking after their love absorbed most of the emotions of those who were now grown, but unable to cope with their hearts.

Affairs had to begin one day. The star cave with the Bushmen paintings in the foothills had become Virginia's refuge. In the recesses and cracks branching from the entrance cavern, she found with her oil-lamp amazing drawings, which suggested a primitive religion. There was a complicated pattern of geometry something like a maze. Out of its wavy lines stuck the heads of buck and giraffes. The pattern even ended inside the neck of an ostrich. The wandering paths were a labyrinth that led her to the inwardness of living things – long ways winding within to the animal in her.

Buldoo no longer guarded her at her paintings, but he told Hamish Charles where to find the star cave. And when a shadow fell across her closed eyelids as she lay back in the blaze of light falling from the hole in the roof, Virginia knew who had come to see her. She only blinked to check the outline of the dark head above set against the glare, then she closed her vision again. She did not speak or recognize that he was there. She knew what he would do, if there was enough of a man in him. Any word from her would foil his will. And he was so hesitant, so controlled, so good – she could not stand it.

She felt his weight on her, his dry lips fierce on her cheek, her eyes, her mouth. She heard him mumbling and rasping sounds that might have been his desire or her name. She felt his hands tearing at her skirt, lifting it. She knew a dry piercing of her that became a soft entrapment. Then she heard his cry and howl, and she found herself crying out as well in answer or from her own need. She could hardly hold him to her within her arms, he trembled so violently in a spasm of shivering. Then the burden of him pressed her down into the sand until she was the earth itself. And then he spoke at last, his lips against her ear.

"I am sorry, Virginia."

"Don't be."

"I did not mean —"

"I hope you did."

She was laughing now. The silly man with all his apologies. She would have to make him bolder than that, if he was going to do what he said he would do for her.

"Move over," she said. "You're crushing me."

"I'm sorry," he said again, rolling across her to lie at her side.

"No, don't say that. I might like being crushed."

"I never thought of that. Virginia ..." He sounded almost frightened. "You didn't mind that I ..." His voice trailed away.

Virginia was laughing again. She sat up and smoothed her skirt down on her bare legs.

"Hamish, you know what I minded about — why did you take so long to come and find me?"

Now he began to laugh, almost uncontrollably. Their mirth reverberated within the rock. There was a sudden clatter, a ricochet of wings, a squeaking and a screeching. Thick bullets whirled through the air. Virginia flung her head onto the man's chest and hugged him.

"Bats," he said. "Only bats."

"I hate bats."

"I won't let them get in your hair." He kissed the long black waves that hid her head. "They eat insects. Bats are good for us."

"That doesn't stop me hating them."

The clatter in the air had died away. The sun in its falling had foregone the hole. It was growing dim inside the cave.

"I'll take you home," he said. "How did the painting go today?"

"I must show you something," she said. She sat up and found her oil-lamp, its flame still guttering.

"Here, on the wall. Look." Two long flat shapes seemed to crawl towards each other on splayed legs. "The Bushmen drew these lovers like two lizards. Just like us. How long we took to approach each other."

"I do see," Hamish Charles said. "You're quite right. These primitive things — they can be relevant, I suppose."

"Better than that," Virginia said. "Stimulating. Look at this one I drew. It's in a crevice a long way in." She pulled her sketch-pad out of her satchel and opened it and held the picture out for the man to see. The mixed bag of crocodiles and wild dogs and zebras and wildebeeste and hunters and snakes and scorpions was clear in its meaning to her. Yet Hamish Charles did not seem to understand, but shook his head, puzzling.

"Don't you see," she said, almost exasperated. "It's all one for them. Creation. They're part of all of it. That's what's wrong with us. We divide things. This good, that bad. This spirit, that flesh. This do, that don't. We don't need this and that. We should just say, I want. I do it."

Hamish Charles smiled and put his arms round her waist and grabbed her so tight that she thought a rib or her spine might crack.

"I wanted – and I did," he said. Then he let her go.

She breathed in deeply and breathed out again with a sigh.

"So I noticed," she said drily, and then she said, "darling" for the first time to him.

The cattle lay dead or dying about the *vlei* – not from the drought, for there was still water in the muddy dip. Piet Krug scooped up some of the brown liquid in the hollow of his hand and put his tongue in it. Then he spat out, his face contorting. As he looked up past the lying beasts, their horns sunk into the land, he thought he saw a movement among the stones of the nearby *kopje*. One figure – two? Or was it the heat-haze making a couple of rock points dance? He would have known in the Boer War. He would have picked them off both with his Mauser. Two single shots and both of them dead.

"Keep down," Hamish Charles was saying to Virginia. They had dismounted behind a boulder, and the man was peering round the obstacle down towards the plain. "I think it's Piet Krug. I don't know whether he's seen us. Most likely he has. He's got eyes like a hawk."

"What if he has?" Virginia said. "We were out on an innocent ride."

"It won't work. I'll ride down, brazen it out. I'll say I'm alone. Give me five minutes. Then you ride back and round to the farm. Then nobody will know for certain."

Virginia stroked the hanging head of her pony. "Lizzie already knows for certain."

"I haven't told her. I've always denied it."

"She knows." Virginia knew the wife knew. "Women always know."

This was no time to argue. So Hamish Charles said, "I am going down." And he led his horse round the boulder and mounted it and rode towards the *vlei*.

Piet Krug took his rifle from its sling by the saddle of his horse. He was shaking too much to control his hands, but he willed himself to be still as his brother-in-law rode towards him. Hamish Charles was not carrying a weapon. He had not ridden to the star cave to shoot, but to make love. He dismounted near his Boer neighbour and walked towards him, ignoring the rifle in the hands of the other man.

"Where is she?" Piet asked.

"She? I don't know who you mean." Hamish Charles tried to sound puzzled, but his worry made his voice quaver. "I have been riding alone."

"She was riding. You were riding her."

"Piet!" Hamish Charles was shocked. "Don't be so crude —"

"I see two people on the *kopje*. You and she."

"I am alone. I swear it."

Piet moved the barrel of his rifle forward. He tapped the end of the muzzle on his brother-in-law's knee.

"Now you are alone. And you lie. Bunjie say, you sleep with her. Lizzie say, you sleep with her. In there." Piet now jerked the gun-barrel towards the mountains. "Where the whore, she paints."

"She is not a whore." Hamish Charles rocked on his feet, waiting to strike at Piet, but fearful of the rifle. "Never say that. She is the governess of my children. My cousin's wife."

"That? It stop you?" Piet gave a dry, short laugh. "You poison Lizzie, your *vrou*. She is sick. She die slow with your bad heart. Now you poison the ox. My ox. I taste the *vlei* with my tongue. Arsenic. Are you crazy, Sinclair? You want for we all are dead?"

"Arsenic?" Hamish Charles was shocked. "I saw the cattle. I thought they were resting."

"Dead. Dying."

"Arsenic. I can't believe it. I couldn't do it. Some of the cattle are mine. Why should I poison my own stock? This is my water."

"Your water. My water. If it is not you —" Now Piet was raising the muzzle of his Mauser to aim casually at the other man's chest. "Then it is your *dom* miners. You let them on your land."

"I cannot stop them. They come anyway. You can't keep off a wildcat prospector."

"Chase them. I do. Chase them like we chase you in the war."

"They're looking for gold. If they strike it rich, so do we. Mineral rights — ever heard of them?"

"They start the *dom* war. Gold on the Rand. And now, they put poison in the *vlei*. To wash the ore down. For shiny metal, they kill – they kill." Now Piet was tapping at the chest of his brother-in-law with the gun barrel. The blows were as quick and hard as the beak of a pecking vulture. "I kill you not, Hamish, in the war. In my sights, you were. I kill not. Now you are in my sights. And I kill, I think."

"I have no gun," Hamish Charles said. "You can't shoot me. I can't defend myself."

"Get on your horse," Piet said. "Go home. Send the whore away. I give you one week. If the whore is there, I kill you."

"She is not a whore. She is innocent."

"She is arsenic in the *vlei*. She kill us. Now get on your horse." Suddenly Piet hit Hamish Charles on the chest with the metal barrel, bruising his ribcage and knocking him two paces back. "One week, man. Or I hunt you. I kill you like a buck."

Hamish Charles walked back to his horse. With one foot in the stirrup, he turned towards Piet, who was still aiming the Mauser at him.

"You'll never get a Dutchman to recognize the truth."

"Lie," Piet said. "But true – you kill Annie, my first *vrou*. Now you kill Lizzie, the sister of my second *vrou*. I do not think. I think you die first."

In face of such unreason, this lack of thought and logic, Hamish Charles had to ride silent away. The trouble was, the Dutchman was right about the main points. There was poison in the home and out here in the open.

On the fatal day, Hamish Charles never knew, or believed that he never knew, what made him pick up the wrong gun. Or if he had picked up the right gun, he never knew why he said he was shooting the wrong thing. That was the case against him. Why did he say he was going to shoot duck with a rifle? Unless it was a sitting duck, as his wife was. He should have taken a shotgun or said that he was hunting buck, not duck. But then Lizzie would not have gone with him. She would not let Virginia go, she was too jealous. Their guest and governess had to remain behind with the three small children. And Buldoo could not leave the poisoned cattle, which had survived the dose of arsenic in their dip. So Lizzie went out with Hamish Charles, to shoot duck with a rifle.

They had driven out to the marshland in the light cart, pulled by a single pony. Lizzie seemed almost happy, her broad face breaking into smiles or appeals for sympathy, her yellow curls almost golden in the setting sun. "We will have roast duck," she said. "Then soup from the bones. Then a brawn and a paste. There is four thing to do with duck. I know them. You are lucky, Hamish, you marry a wife know how to do."

Yes, Hamish Charles thought, he had married a wife who knew how to do. And she knew how to do when they came to shoot the duck on the marshland just over the border. Piet had made and given him the two decoys, when matters had been better between them. He set the wooden and painted toy ducks in the marsh and sent Lizzie a little way off to hide in the reeds. She had an unexpected gift, which she used to amuse the infants. She could reproduce bird-calls – the screech of the black stork or *groot-swart sprinkanvoël*, the hoot of the spotted eagle-owl she called *steen-uil*, the croak of the pied crow, the *bont-kraai*. The quacks of the ducks were child's play to her. So she sent up her coarse siren calls to the skies in the evenings, when the birds were settling down.

Later, Hamish Charles was to point out one factor in his favour. If it were he who was intended to be the victim of the bullet, it could have been the mistake of a marksman – a Piet Krug or a Robert Sinclair, for the border had been crossed into the district of his authority. A straight line could be drawn from the peak of the rise behind the marshland through the back of Hamish Charles, where he was standing to shoot, and on to the place where Lizzie was squatting in the reeds, calling down the ducks. A bullet aimed from the high ground at his head could have missed him and hit Lizzie instead. This was an explanation. Only there was nothing to prove it. And nothing to show why he had taken his Mauser to hunt fowl. He would have needed birdshot for that feathered prey.

As it was, when the teal and the pochard and the dwarf geese, the *rooibek-eendjies* and the *bruin-eends* and the *dwerg-ganses*, came skidding down the twilight, Hamish Charles discovered what a fool he was to bring the wrong gun. His mind must have been elsewhere. It had obviously been on Virginia and the impossible situation at home. Still, he thought he would risk a shot with the rifle, and he fired once at a fluttering shape descending down the air. The shot seemed to echo in his ears, as if he had shot twice, a left and a right. Then there was a cry, a human cry. Then silence. Even the wings of the birds ceased their beating. And the false calls of Lizzie in the reeds were hushed. She would never call again. A bullet had hit her head.

"Lizzie," Hamish Charles shouted. "Lizzie!" Then he began to blunder across the wet ground towards the reeds. He could only hear the squelching of his boots in the muddy soil. "Lizzie!" His fear grew with her silence. "Lizzie!" Parting the reeds with his hands, he looked down. His wife lay on her back as if she were asleep. A small red spot, no bigger than a wedding ring, was in the centre of her forehead. But the moss behind her was a red cushion to the scarlet curls on the back of her head.

Hamish Charles did not remember what then he had done. Virginia was his witness. An hour after he had driven from the farm with Lizzie, she had discovered that he had left his shotgun and taken his rifle to shoot duck. Some premonition, or perhaps a touch of guilt, had made her turn over the care of the children to her maid Tsutsie and ride on her pony towards the marsh in Basutoland, where her husband Robert was already overdue on his return from his leave. The darkening sky had made her ride full of terrors. Her pony had stumbled on an ant-heap and she thought it had broken its leg. But no, it was slightly lamed, and she could go slowly on. As she reached the rise before the wetland, she heard two shots. She was adamant about that. The second sound was not an echo. There were two shots, fired close together. She rode round the rise to the marsh and she heard Hamish Charles's voice, as he was calling out, "Lizzie!" When she reached the reeds on her pony in the gathering dark, she could just see the shape of the man standing by the body of his wife. He was putting the barrel of his rifle in his mouth. "No!" she shouted and fell off her pony and picked herself up from the mud and ran towards him, screaming, "No, no, no!" And he did not pull the trigger before she came to him and took the rifle in her hands and led him away behind her.

Virginia kept him from killing himself. She told Buldoo to remove all the guns from the house and hide them. She concealed the sharp knives and even the hanging ropes. He was inconsolable and guilty. He said he hadn't done it in one breath. Then in the next breath, he said he had and he could not forgive himself. He had to die, too. The infants asking where Mama was sent him into tears and despair. And this was the witness, and perhaps this was the murderer, whom Robert found when he arrived at the farm early in the morning after the shooting to collect Virginia. She thought that his arrival was so timely he might have known of the killing. He might also have followed them home from the marsh.

"Robert," she said. "Thank God you've come. I'll take you to the body. It's just over the border, in your territory. It's your case."

So she rode with her husband to the marsh in the morning. They had so much to say to each other, to confess to each other. But there was nothing to say but the unsaid and the understood. The silence between them was fused with meaning. And in the end, Virginia said, "Whatever I've done, Robert, don't let him suffer. It was an accident. You judge. You try it. It's in your jurisdiction. Don't let the Boers judge it. They'll hang him. It'll be the Boer War all over again."

"Why do they hate him?"

"Because of me," Virginia said flatly. "They think he and I ..."

"Is it true?"

"It's a lie." Virginia had to save her lover. "I swear it's a lie. We like each other –"

"Natural, I reckon. We are kin." Robert's voice was dry with disbelief. "But it's bad, real bad, he's a Sinclair, she was an Afrikaner, you're an Englander. And her sister married to Piet Krug. I can see – Black Week all over again."

"You'll save him?"

"I'll do my duty," Robert said, and he thought he would try to do it, whatever he felt.

Robert spent a while examining the body, which was still lying undisturbed in the reeds. He heard Virginia's story of the two shots. "But you say Hamish only fired one – we can check that." He made Virginia sketch the body, its position in the reeds, relative to the geography of the place. She shuddered as she drew, the lines of the pencil wavering on the paper. Then he picked up the dead woman, putting her over his shoulder. And he walked heavily back to the position of the hide, where the huntsman had concealed himself. He laid down the body and searched the wet ground. After a time, he found one cartridge ejected from a Mauser rifle. He did not find another.

"Two shots, you reckon?" he asked his wife. And when she nodded, he looked at the line between the rise and the hide and the place of Lizzie's death. "So he could have shot at the duck," he said, "and somebody shot at him. Only they missed and shot her." Virginia nodded again. "If there were two shots," he said, "it doesn't say who the second gun was. Though there were folks with a reason to hate him. Piet Krug, you say. A threat to kill him, if he didn't throw you out. It's possible." But then Robert paused and shook his head. "But one thing I don't get. A man, he won't take a rifle to hunt duck. It's not natural. However much he had on his mind."

They brought Lizzie's body back slung over the saddle of Robert's horse, her bloodied yellow curls trailing down. She would have to be buried on the farm. Already the news had reached the neighbours, and Buldoo came in to say that twenty Boer farmers were riding in with their rifles, for they did not trust the justice of the *rooineks*. So Robert gave Buldoo the concealed shotgun and put him in the barn in front of the porch and told him to fire to wound, not to kill, if he lifted his hand. And he told the rest of the farm hands and the maids and Virginia and Hamish Charles and the children to stay inside out of harm's way. He would deal with it. So he waited on the wooden bench of the *stoep* with his American carbine and the Mauser of Hamish Charles and the cartridge belt. He had checked the magazine. It was true, only one shot had been fired. Unless Hamish Charles had fired twice and reloaded with one cartridge. But that was unlikely. Even so, Robert reckoned he might need some evidence, if only to save his wife and his cousin from the vengeance of the Afrikaners. So he fired the Mauser once in the air and put the spent case in his pocket with the first case he had found in the hide. And he reloaded the rifle with a single cartridge, so that he could say it had only been fired once.

An hour later, Piet Krug and twenty Boer farmers came riding in with their rifles. Only Krug dismounted and limped towards Robert, sitting on the porch.

"Don't get in the way, *rooinek*," Piet said. "This war you lose."

"There will be a trial," Robert said. "The tragedy took place in my district. I will try it. I swear I will."

"*You* try him? A cousin?" Piet's savage smile gashed his beard. "That is justice?"

"It will be a fair trial. And Piet Krug, you will come to it."

"I will?"

"You may be tried, too. For your mistake."

"What? *Rooinek*, you want I should kill you –"

"Here." Robert took a risk and tossed the Mauser of Hamish Charles over to Piet, who caught it in surprise. All the time Robert kept his carbine trained loosely on the Afrikaner. "Check it. One shot fired." Piet broke open the magazine and checked that one cartridge was missing, spilling the others on the ground.

"So? One shot, that kill Lizzie."

"There were two shots, Krug. My wife heard them. So did Hamish Sinclair."

"They lie."

"They do?" Robert fished in his pocket and brought out the two cartridge cases, rolling them together in his fingers. "I found one of them in the hide – Hamish was there. The other one – on the rise behind Hamish. Squashed grass, too. Somebody was there. You, Krug? You fired at Hamish. You missed. You killed your sister-in-law."

"You lie. Three times you lie." Piet's face was blotched tan and scarlet above his beard. "Your cousin kill Lizzie. Your wife lie. You lie. And maybe – it is you, not me. You jealous of your wife. And that devil. So you shoot him. And you miss. And you kill, Lizzie. So?"

"I go for your evidence," Robert said. "It will sound great in court. But there is a hitch –" Again he rolled the brass cases against each other. "These are both Mauser cartridge cases. I use a carbine. Made in the US of A."

"Then you make the two cases. You lie. You *Uitlanders*, you always lie."

Piet raised the barrel of his rifle, but Robert was too quick for him. He flicked up his carbine, shooting from his chair as if from the saddle. The bullet struck Piet's Mauser and sent the gun spinning away and left Piet crying out and wringing his bruised fingers. And as the outriders – the new Boer commando – as they raised their weapons on their horses, the blast of Buldoo's buckshot behind them sent their guns falling back on their saddles or to the ground.

"You're surrounded!" Robert shouted. "I'm not crazy!"

He could see Buldoo, grinning from his revenge on the Boers as he emerged from the barn with his smoking shotgun, which he reloaded. But the Boers did not know if Robert had twenty Zulus waiting in the barns with rifles trained on them. He had the advantage, so he shouted, "Go home! We bury her here tomorrow! I swear! And there will be justice, I swear. No more blood now! No more blood!"

Piet turned back towards the outriders. He had clenched his hands and now he raised them into the air in a great fist.

"We will go," he commanded in Afrikaans. "We will come back. We will bury Lizzie. We kill him and her. This is our land." And all the outriders answered him. "This is our land." And then they rode away.

Virginia was proud of Robert for what he had done, and her guilt pricked her heart at what she had done to him. Hamish Charles could only mumble his thanks in an incoherence that made him sound drunk. Nobody could resist Robert's suggestions, which were really orders.

"Pack all you can," he said. "They will be back in the morning to kill you. We take the children and Tsutsie and Buldoo with us over the border into my territory. They will not follow there."

"But what about burying her?" Virginia asked.

"They will do that," Robert said. "With a *predikant* – their faith. If you stayed for the funeral, they would lynch you. We go tonight. Tomorrow – it's too late."

At last, Hamish Charles managed to speak, for all the shame and guilt clogging his tongue.

"Why Robert ... why are you ... why ... all this for me ... and Virginia?"

"She is my wife."

"Yes, but —"

"You are my cousin? I think you are."

"Yes."

"Well, then." Robert patted Hamish Charles on the shoulder. He was clamping his feelings, keeping his anger to himself. "Blood is thicker than water. Bain always said that. Fathers are always right." He paused. He could see that his cousin and his wife could not judge his mood or his intent. "Now there's blood in this," he said, "we have to be thick. Thick as thieves. Thicker than water, I think."

So that night, there was a trek over the border to British colonial law in Basutoland, as administered by its District Officer, Robert Sinclair. And Lizzie's body was left washed and groomed lying on her bed in her best nightgown, her hands folded together in silent prayer, but the dark ring of death still in her forehead.

13

NOT PROVEN

Not proven is a Scots verdict, and it has no value in English law. But Robert Sinclair was a Scotsman before he was a Canadian, although he now served the British Empire and carried its passport. He knew of the old country's judgement. Not proven in a murder trial did not mean the accused was not guilty. It meant that his guilt was not proven, so that he might stand trial again, if there were new evidence or if he admitted the offence. In a way, not proven was the worst of sentences, for it lasted life-long. The noose was always hanging over the head of the one who was charged with the crime. If he were guilty, daily he feared discovery of his conscience pressing him to confess. And even if he were innocent, the world might get to know that his innocence was not proven, just as his guilt was not. Such a permanent torment only ended in death, natural or legal.

At the inquest, however, Robert could not give that verdict. The great fortune of Hamish Charles was that the killing of Lizzie had taken place over the border in Robert's district, and that he had fled with Virginia and the children to stay with his cousin, who was also his coroner and his judge, before the court met and the trial took place. His great misfortune was the same. For Robert knew that his wife loved Hamish Charles, and that his cousin loved her to the point of folly, and perhaps murder. But of course, that was not proven.

And there was the outcry from over the border, and the press. The Boers wanted blood for blood. They were furious that the accident of a frontier had placed the inquest and trial in Basutoland. The neighbours had ridden back the next day to find the farm deserted except for the hands they called Kaffirs – and the dead body of Lizzie, lying decently on her marriage bed. They had called in the *predikant* and buried her in their Old Testament way, refusing to say, "Vengeance is Mine, saith the Lord." They wanted the vengeance to be theirs. They threatened raids over the border to kidnap their quarry and execute him. And they could easily have done it – they were trained commandos, after all. And the newspapers in Ficksburg, their reports of the case reached Cape Town. And when they reached Cape Town, they reached the Colonial Office in London. And it was a scandal. And scandal was the one thing which the Colonial Office abhorred, particularly if it had to do with a District Officer in a sensitive colony. And that District Officer was Robert Sinclair.

"You're riding me into the ground," Robert said to Hamish Charles on the night before the inquest. "Yeah, a life's gone, and maybe you had something you done with it. But now it's my life."

"I'm sorry." Hamish Charles was stooped in front of his cousin. "I didn't mean to ..." His shoulders slumped even more.

"Never say that," Virginia snapped at him. "Never *say* that. You did nothing."

"Sure," Robert said. "He did nothing. But I still need to know a thing or two before the inquest tomorrow. That is, if the brothers don't ride over the hills and make a Magersfontein out of us again."

"Oh, yes," Hamish Charles said bitterly. "Your cowboys weren't there. That's why we lost. That's why our uncle was killed."

"Right," Robert said. "Right for once, Hamish. But the cowboy's here now and he wants to know a thing or two. Tell me – come on – the truth. Did you shoot Lizzie? Did you?"

Hamish Charles looked at the straw mat on the floor. Then he looked up. "I don't know," he said. "Truly, I don't. But I swear I shot at a duck. Not at her."

"With a rifle?"

"With a rifle."

"And the second shot?"

"I heard it."

"And I heard it." Virginia spoke a sort of hatred. "I told you. Don't you believe your wife?"

"Yes – on this," Robert said. "But not, I reckon, when her feelings are in question." He swung back on the accused. "So there was no intent? It was an accident?" Then he said, as if almost to convince himself. "It had to be."

"It was an accident," Virginia said.

"Let him say," Robert said.

Hamish Charles tried to remember what had been said, then groped for the right phrase.

"It had to be," he repeated. Then he paused in the silence, and he added, "An accident. That's all it was."

"That won't get you off," Robert said.

Virginia could not stand her husband being an inquisitor over them. She had too much guilt to hide.

"You dare question him? He's innocent."

"I am trying to teach him the questions he will be asked," Robert said.

"By you?"

"By me."

"Why?"

"Because I am the law. If I don't ask them, they will kill him – the Boers. And they will fire me – the Colonial Office."

"Ah." Virginia was silent. She never knew Robert could be so discriminating. "So how do you, as you say, get him off?"

"I go for your evidence," Robert said. "I say there were two shots. I say I found two cartridge cases – both of them from a Mauser. I produce those cases. Just as I did to Piet Krug on the porch in the farm, when you were hiding inside. Two shots – only one from you, Hamish. Another killer – aiming at you – hitting Lizzie. You get off. Accidental death. Or death by persons unknown."

"Christ," Hamish Charles said. "I should thank you. Why are you doing it for me?"

"I don't know," Robert said. He searched in the pocket of his khaki jacket and took out the two brass cartridge cases.

"They trouble is, it's wrong. It's phoney-baloney. I shot off your rifle on the porch. I made the second cartridge case. As you fellows say, I manufactured the evidence."

There was a silence longer than a memorial service.

"So we're at your mercy," Virginia said. "And you are giving it to us. Why?"

Robert rose from his low canvas chair with the flat wooden arms, where the servants set the sundowners. He walked over to the thin mesh that covered the window from the mosquitos. He looked out into nothing.

"I hate you, Virginia," he said in a small voice. "And you, Hamish. You were made for each other. You met in Hell. But you were always there. You are damned for each other. And it's nothing to do with me. I was in the way." He kept his back turned on the shocked faces behind him. Then he said, "So you met. So she died, the woman in your way. So she had to die. It doesn't mean you killed her, Hamish. You didn't mean to kill her. And if it wasn't you, somebody else killed her. Somebody did. From that rise behind the marsh. Shooting at you and hitting Lizzie, because she was in line behind you. I reckon somebody did that."

There was a hush that extended time. Then Virginia with that quickness of hers seized upon the implication.

"It was you, Robert. You shot at Hamish. You hit Lizzie. That's why – why you give us your mercy."

Robert turned back from the wire mesh of the window. He was smiling, almost debonair. Lightness played on his face, almost a joy at being found out.

"You're crazy, Virginia," he said. "But if I let you go – not proven, I mean – you'll never forget it, will you? You'll never forget me – how I let you go. For all you did to me – you bastards – *I* let you go."

Then Virginia learned, and later she was to know for certain, that the Sinclairs might seem to forget, but they never did forgive. A mercy from them was a sentence for life. No one could ever repay.

Mary knew that it was the last visit of her life. She could not endure the chaise as it jolted and bounced over the karroo towards Basutoland. Each shake stabbed at her locked muscles and bones. It had been the same for her mother. Arthritis had crippled her at the end. Mary had even had to retire from her consultancy at the Apfelstein Hospital in Johannesburg and live with Seaforth and his new wife, Miriam. Most of that family had hated the marriage, but Seaforth was working at the hospital which they had endowed, and nobody could deny his brilliance. Too many people owed their lives to him to talk against him. Poor Seaforth, Mary thought, always bitter just because of his colour, yet with the best hands on a surgeon she had ever seen. But Miriam loved him, even if she saw him through pink spectacles, a victim of discrimination, an exploited colonial, a slave of the Empire. She would grow out of it. Or so Mary hoped. Most people did.

But the killing of Lizzie. Mary knew Hamish Charles, or she thought she did. Even if he were head over heels in love with that foxy Virginia, he would never murder his wife. It had to be an accident. But Robert, the wronged husband, being the judge and the jury. This was a wicked thing. And then there was the farm. What would happen to that? And the children? What a mess as well as a tragedy. But Mary had spent her long life cleaning up messes. She was the effective head of the family, and this was the last, the very last thing she could do.

She was too late for the inquest when she reached the District Officer's bungalow, the verdict had already been given. Accidental death. Two people shooting at the marsh, one of them unknown. Hamish Charles given the benefit of the doubt. No evidence of his relationship with Virginia or of his falling out with his wife was submitted to the coroner or allowed to be heard. As the chief witness, Virginia was cool and composed, even distant from Hamish Charles. She was merely a governess on the farm, helping out the family while her husband was away on leave. There was no need to refer the case to trial, whatever the scandal might be. Accidental death. That was Robert's verdict.

Helping the bent old lady in dusty black from the chaise, Hamish Charles trembled. If there ever was a true judge, it was his Aunt Mary. Her verdict was inescapable. But she kissed him as he stooped down to her and said, "Dinna worry, Hamish. It is the future the now for you. What will be." And she leaned on his arm as he led her into the bungalow, where she took up her position on the only wooden chair as if on a throne or a chief's stool. "I want to talk to you one by one," she said. "Or we will never get anywhere at all."

Virginia was most frightened of Mary's judgement. She knew the old woman disliked her. She had meant to be scornful, refusing to admit Mary's right to make a second trial of the accident or of her love for Hamish Charles. But the blue stare of Mary's eyes from her lined face, as crushed as a crumpled towel, broke Virginia's resolve, and she found herself weeping and kneeling, her face buried in Mary's lap, and saying between sobs, "We never – I did not mean – I don't want to hurt Robert – we met too late – it was an accident, too. But love – it's so strong –"

"Sit up, girl," Mary said. "You may not think it, an old one like me, but I ken love. I ken what love is."

"You do?" And Virginia straightened herself and looked at Mary, but stayed kneeling beside the ancient woman on her chair.

"Ach, yes. Robert tells me, he will let you go. It is over. Hamish tells me, he loves you. He will never leave you. But that is a terrible thing. Divorce. It is a terrible thing."

"Yes," Virginia said. "But I will stand it, if I must."

"Not here," Mary said. "Where will you go?"

"London," Virginia said. "Hamish says London. And I want –"

"Ach, I see." Mary shook her head. "Why every fool girl in the bush wants to go to London is a mystification to me. But there you are. And what will you live on? Hamish only has the farm. And who will sell it?"

"I don't know," Virginia said. "The Boers will kill us if we go back. That Piet Krug, he's married to Lizzie's sister –"

"I will do it," Mary said. "I know Piet Krug. He will not kill an old woman. I had to tell him how his first wife Annie died. In our camp. Now I will tell him – his sister-in-law – an accident."

"He hated Hamish Charles. There was a quarrel. Arsenic in the water. Miners."

"I will give Piet Krug what he wants. Water, land, whatever. A reparation, if you can ever repair a death. The rest, I will sell and send you the money. But, Virginia, tell me true – one thing – you will care for the wee ones."

"I will. I swear I will."

"As if they were your own folk?"

"I swear."

"And if you and Hamish Charles, you have a bairn? It is a terrible thing to be a step-mother. To try and not love your own more. And not to see the other mother in the step-family."

"They are Hamish Charles's children. I will love them, because I love him."

"You will try, I think." Mary put her hand on the shoulder of the kneeling young woman. "I wish you luck. Hamish will have written to his father Angus in Peru about this and about you. His mother's folk are a wealthy family. They will help. And he has a brother Murdo in London, he has kin there. And there is the house in Vancouver in Canada, which Angus bought for my old mother and father. They are buried there, and Kate is still there. You will have help, if you truly love Hamish and the three wee ones."

"Thank you, Aunt Mary," Virginia said. She rose to her feet and looked down at the shrunken figure in black who had been sitting over her. "Then – I have your blessing."

"For what it's worth," Mary said in her dry way. "And for what you are worth."

When she reached the farm, Mary had expected it to be burned. But it was not. So she sent for Piet Krug, and he was not long in coming to her. In fact, he came to see her so quickly that she hardly remembered that she had sent the message. But when he entered, gangling and lanky, the long beard and sprouting whiskers covering the face under the shadow of the slouch hat, Mary felt a pity for him that almost obscured what she had to say.

"Nice," she said. "Very nice. You come to see me, Piet Krug. And you did not burn the farm."

"It is also Lizzie's farm," Piet said. He stood in front of the seated Mary. Now he took his hat off and rolled it between his hands. "They come not." His voice was as bitter as an aloe. "They send you."

"You would kill them." Mary smiled up at the scarecrow with the beard. "But you canna kill me. I know you, Piet Krug."

"And I know you." Piet bit his lip. "The dirty tricks, the *Uitlanders*. They know us. They send in old ladies."

"You send in commandos," Mary said. "Dirty tricks, you Boers, you did them all. But then, the English they did dirty tricks to my folk, the Scots. So we ken you – and we ken the English."

Piet laughed. "You are worse than the *predikants*. You tell me. The *Uitlanders* are so clever. Their soldiers, they hate the *Uitlanders*. But they fight for the *Uitlanders*. Then they come to us, they say. We hate the *Uitlanders*, too." Piet laughed again. "Now, Mary Sinclair –"

"It is true," she said. "Yes, it *is* true. Now, Piet Krug, I will say what we must do."

"I listen," he said. "But only to you."

"I have to sell this farm," Mary said. "The folks here, they canna come back again." And Piet nodded, wagging his head. "I have said, they will all go away. Robert, he is to be transferred to West Africa, because of all the talk and the feeling. He willna rule your border no more." And Piet nodded again in satisfaction. "My nephew Hamish Charles – and *that* Virginia –" Piet smiled at the emphasis Mary put on the woman – "they are going to London. But with the children, I am afraid."

"I want the children here."

"I know," Mary said. "But as Lizzie is dead, they must stay with their father. Now, Piet, if you are right, and you may be –"

"I am."

"They will come back to you. Believe me, Piet. The bairns are your bairns too. I am still a Scotswoman, against the English. They will come back to you, if you are right. But now, the law is they stay with their father. Lizzie is dead."

"They will come to me," Piet said. "They are Afrikaners. They must be here."

"No," Mary said. "I bring you peace. Hear me."

"I hear." But Piet was moving his teeth against each other, splitting them.

"You have the *vlei*, the water. You have the land you want. It is your land, as you say. You give some to me to sell, as the law says. You get rid of the prospectors – the miners. You are right. They are greed. They kill us – they kill all of us. For metal."

Piet laughed at the old woman.

"You are the enemy. You are the friend. You come to confuse."

"No," Mary said. "I will be dead, Piet, before you see me again."

Piet laughed once more.

"You never die. You live for ever. You bury us all."

"I am dying," Mary said. "And I am like the people you call Kaffirs. You are wrong. I know the day I die. They know. They could teach you."

"A Kaffir teach me?" Piet laughed for the last time. "Tell me, Mary Sinclair, why? I take all the farm."

"Tell me, Piet, will you break the law? I know this is your land. But not all of it. Some must go to the bairns. The rest I give to you."

"You cannot give for a death."

"I agree," Mary said. "You canna give for a death. But this is no blood money, Piet. This is an answer. This is an end. This is peace. This is your land. This I give to you." Piet shook his head, swaying from side to side. He said nothing, so Mary went on. "Ach, dinna you ken. You win a war, you lose a war. But you lose a war, you win a peace. You have won, Piet Krug. And you have lost. And we are winning, too, the Scots, who lost to England. We are winning the peace."

"Wicked," Piet said. "Wicked, it is you."

"The war is over," Mary said. "It is peace the now. I am dying. An I am dead, it will be peace. I saw your Annie die. I will give you peace, Piet Krug. And you will have it. You are as proud – as terrible – as all the Sinclairs are. You will have peace from me, Piet Krug."

At this command from the little woman in black, Piet shook his head, but smiled and asked himself, "Who shall say no to you, Mary Sinclair?"

"No very many," Mary said. "But I want your peace with me, Piet Krug."

"Two killings I have," he said. "Annie and Lizzie."

"Then it is two pardons you have to give," Mary said. "Annie and Lizzie. But now you have the land you want and the water, your land."

"Devil," Piet said and walked away and returned. "No," he said. "Devil you are."

"Now then," Mary said, "my lad, I need an end of it. I am to die. I will live to sign the damned lawyers' paper – to give you the land – to sell the rest of the land. Then I die. I know. I am a Scots Kaffir, a Scots Indian. I know when I die. That is why, Piet Krug, you will believe me. You will end the war."

"*Soe*, you," Piet said. He walked to the old woman and bent and kissed her hand. He had never done this in his life. Then he said, "You."

"When you are near dead," Mary said, "it dinna matter. All you wish for, it is all in order. You canna meet your Maker ... he willna let you in through the Pearly Gates ... if you canna say – The Ledger, it is in order. I did what I could. It is in order. There is no sin, you see – and I was told all is sin. You live in sin for ever. But there is no sin. I have lived so long – too long – and I ken, Piet, I ken – there is no sin. There is only peace to be found. We must forgive, even if we canna. There are no judges. Listen, Piet. In your thinking, God knows. He says – forgive. I am an old woman. I know folks. Let them be. And wait for Heaven, till God is your judge, your only judge."

"Oh, Mary." Piet said her first name at last. "Mary – it is the name of the Mother of Christ."

"And of the Magdalene," Mary said. "The sinner."

"Mary," Piet said. "I wish for vengeance."

"Too late," Mary said. "Peace the now."

"But we will have our land."

"Yes. The peace is good to you."

"And if we have children –"

"If –"

"It will be our land. We will be the most in it."

"There might be the blacks," Mary said. "Your Kaffirs, you know."

"This is our land," Piet said. "And you will give it back to us."

"Aye," Mary said. "But not I. If you have a majority –"

"We will have many children – *kinders.*"

"Then the land is yours. Or the Kaffirs."

"Our land." Piet smiled at Mary Sinclair. "I will stop the commando. We will not go over the border. Your Robert, your Hamish, they will be gone?"

"Yes," Mary said. "They will go."

"I show you something?"

Piet took out of the pocket of his jacket a brass cartridge case. He put it in Mary's hand. And he said, "I find this yesterday only. On the *kopje* down where Lizzie is killed. And the inquest say, somebody aim at Hamish and kill Lizzie. Two shots. Look, Mary – American cartridge. Remington cartridge. I know. The bullet is Robert Sinclair. That is why he let Hamish go. He kill Lizzie. A mistake. He mean to kill Hamish. For his wife."

Mary rolled the cartridge in her old fingers, which would hardly close, the arthritis had clamped her bones. Then she took this brass bit and tucked it down the black bosom of her dress.

"Piet," she said, "it is too late. You were my enemy. You are my friend. You have the land. And as for this –" patting her bosom – "it is over. We have peace." Then she sighed and said, "There is no truth in the peace. But we must have it."

She was set solid. She could not move. She knew it would happen. The stiffening of the bones, an absolute paralysis. But it did not reach her mind. Her thoughts were flowing free. Ach, just in time. The signing of the papers done. The sale of the rest of the farm done. And her lying in the old iron bed, where dead Lizzie had lain with Hamish Charles, now in London with his Virginia. All tidy now, that was the way to go. All in order, the last things done for the living, who must go on. Poor wee ones, what a world for them.

God had now locked her in the cage of her joints and her bones. She would never shift for herself again. But she was alone. She would die alone. That was good. She was never the one to look for others to look for her. She had always looked for others, never for herself. And surely, never for her old bones. She had had her time. It had come to an end. And she had done well, or well enough. When she passed those Pearly Gates — and pearl they were not, old oak at the best of it — and she came to the final Accountant, sitting by his Book of Lives, and he would say, "Mary, you didna do this, you didna do that," why, she would draw herself up on her bones and say, "Wee angel, but I did this, I did that, I did, I did, I did so. And muckle more." And so she had done. It was more the doing of it than the not doing of it. That was what the Sinclairs were about, at the end of it all. The doing of it. And so some of the clan might slip into Heaven ...

14

TEA, GRIT AND CARBOLIC

The meal was highly coloured and they ate their way through the rainbow with their fingers. Saffron rice, red peppers, brown curry, green chutney, and even fine silver paper over the top of the sweet rice pudding, which gave it a bitter aftertaste. Rather like the Empire, Seaforth thought – then he caught himself thinking that sour thought and smiled at himself. Marriage must be softening him. And he looked at his wife Miriam, who was still embarrassed at eating with her hands, and he said, "Darling, use a piece of the *chapatti* like a shovel, and scoop the food in. It's like digging a ditch."

"Thank you," his sister Peg said. "My cooking – like a ditch?"

Seaforth laughed, and Miriam said, "If all ditches were like this food we'd have them instead of restaurants. This is *grande cuisine*."

"I don't think so," Peg said. "A humble Indian meal. Would you like some Bombay duck?"

"Please." Then Miriam looked at the proffered blackish hard slices of dried fish, and she said, "Duck, this?"

"Fish. They salt it and squash it and dry it on the pavements."

"No, thank you. Not the sort of process of curing food I care for."

"You prefer tins."

"Well, they're cleaner."

"Natural foods," Peg said. "That's what I always recommend." She ate her last piece of filled *chapatti* and licked her fingers as delicately as a cat licks her paws. "Anyway, if you do get to like India –"

"I do already."

"Then you will find us very natural. Almost too near to nature."

"Not in our religion," Seaforth said. "I have warned Miriam – sacred cows, corpses in the Ganges, even *suttee*, the burning of widows, although it is forbidden by the British. And caste – how I hate caste."

"Only because we are outcasts," Peg said. "Literally, born out of caste. Eurasians. Neither one thing nor the other. We are worse, really, than the untouchables."

"Touching Seaforth," Miriam said, "is quite a pleasure."

Seaforth laughed and stroked the back of his wife's hand.

"Miriam likes men who are tall, dark and brilliant."

"You, of course."

"Of course." Now Seaforth was suddenly melancholy. "I have to tell you, Peg, now we're home in India at last –"

"I know," Peg said. "We can't put it off. I must know."

"She died peacefully – and alone. That neighbour of hers, Piet Krug, he found Aunt Mary. He was fond of her, though he is a bastard of a Boer. He hated us coming to the funeral. And as for me being married to Miriam – why, he treated me as if I was contagious while Miriam was a walking mortal sin. I tell you, I would rather be out of caste here than a Coloured over there. Anyway, Robert came over the border, and we buried Aunt Mary in a cave in the mountains – in a place where the sun shines on the grass every afternoon. There was bad blood between Krug and Robert – it was over the shooting of Hamish Charles's wife. But they didn't have a fight – they were burying Mary. We all disliked each other, but ... I can't explain, but you know how Aunt Mary always was with us. She always made the family get on with each other and get on with the job, even if we refused to do it. She may have been dead, but her spirit – I don't believe in spirits, so let us say, her memory – her memory kept us all at our prayers, those of us who had prayers to say – and being civil to each other. Peace – that was her message from below the ground."

"Yes," Miriam said. "That funeral out in the veldt, it was so tense and strained – just the four of us and a Zulu Buldoo as a grave-digger – yet there was a strange calm in the air, a truce in nature."

"I loved Mary," Peg said. "She was the only one of the Sinclairs who ever did a thing for my brother and me."

"I wasn't what she did," Seaforth said, "it was what she was. And I never thought I'd say that old chestnut about anyone, particularly not a member of our Scots family. But Mary – there's not a truce in nature now, Miriam. There's a gap in nature. You know, Peg, I can't believe she's gone. It's like an amputation. I feel I've lost a leg."

"Her work at the hospital in Jo'burg was miraculous," Miriam said. "At her age, too. I once asked her, 'What keeps you going, Aunt Mary?' And she said, 'Tea, grit and carbolic'."

Seaforth laughed and shook his head.

"One of a kind, Mary was. You couldn't help but like her. Even that damn race-hater Krug did. And Cousin Robert, colonial copper Robert, he was sentimental about his old aunt. He read a poem over her grave, which was the worst thing ever written, but somehow it seemed right at the time. Absolute tosh, but it expressed all the loving that the Roberts of the world feel about running the Empire. And Mary, in her way, would have felt the same too. It was written by a Scotsman called Murray – Robert met him in the Boer War. He pressed a copy of the dreadful verses on me when we left Mary's grave, and here they are –" Seaforth handed over a folded paper to his sister. "Scotland our Mither – it's the only memorial service you will ever receive for our dear Aunt Mary."

Reading the verses, Peg did not know whether to laugh or cry, but the last line blurred with her tears for her dead beloved aunt. Her lips moved as she read silently:

"Scotland our Mither – this from your sons abroad,
Leavin' tracks on virgin veldt that never kent a road.
Trekkin' on wi' weary feet, an' faces turned fae hame,
But lovin' aye the auld wife across the seas the same.

Scotland our Mither – we've bairns you've never seen –
Wee things that turn them northwards when they kneel
                                        down at e'en;
They plead in childish whispers the Lord on high will be
A comfort to the auld wife – their granny o'er the sea.

Scotland our Mither – since first we left your side,
From Quilimane to Cape Town we've wandered far an' wide;
Yet aye from mining camp an' to wn, from koppie an' karoo,
Your sons right kindly, auld wife, send hame their love to you."

Peg wiped her eyes.

"It's impossible," she said. "Even the messages on Christmas cards make me cry. And Scotland is not even our Mother. India is."

"And Scotland," Miriam said. "Your father's home."

"Not really. He was always fighting for England here and all over the Empire. If we have a Scots home, it's at Simla in the Himalayas. It is even called Annandale. Uncle Iain's house."

"A sort of baronial bungalow," Seaforth said, "where our uncle lives in some state with his wife, entertaining the Viceroy in summer. He's come a long way since he was a Highlander in the Mutiny."

"Will we go there?" Miriam said.

"In time. There's no hurry. I must take up my job first. At Lahore."

"A military hospital?" Peg said. "That's unlike you."

"Oh, some soldiers are humans," her brother said. "In fact they are all humans and only too human. I found that out in the Boer War. Unfortunately, it was the best post I could get, once Miriam and I decided to come back to India. I have these wonderful military recommendations from the King's Surgeon himself, old Treves. Even the man who married our cousin Margaret, Douglas Jardine, couldn't block my appointment."

"I wrote to you in South Africa, didn't I?" Peg said. "About how suspicious he was of you and your politics. He hates the idea of independence."

"You wrote to me. But, as I said, he couldn't stop me getting the post at Lahore."

"Perhaps he wants you under his eye. To see that you don't get into mischief."

"I think I can outwit Douglas Jardine."

"He's in Intelligence, more than the Civil Service –"

"The Great Game? Really?" Seaforth explained to Miriam. "We call Intelligence here the Great Game, because that is what our imperial bard Kipling called it. And it is so British to call intelligence a game. That is because they think independence a play – child's play for silly little Indian boys like me."

"People in Intelligence," Miriam said, "are rarely intelligent. They use the name to disguise their mental deficiency."

"Douglas Jardine is brighter than he seems," Peg said. "Never underestimate him."

"I have no need to," Seaforth said. "Because he is bound to under-estimate me. A *shi-shi*, that's what they call the half-and-halfs."

"*Chi-chi*?" Miriam smiled. "That means very smart in France."

"Miriam," Peg said, "you must get Seaforth to take you to Annan-dale soon. Anna's on her last legs – I didn't mean to say that. She is in a wheel-chair, but she's dying. It's cancer, like our mother."

"Something in common at last." Seaforth could have bitten off his tongue at his tart comment, when he saw the look of shock on his wife's face. "I mean, the same sad disease. How long will Anna last?"

"A week – a month – you should go. I don't think Uncle Iain will survive without her, any more than grandfather did our granny's death in Canada."

Miriam put out her hands to cradle Seaforth's left hand in her palms.

"I made Seaforth promise that we would die together. Not just leave one of us behind. Isn't that silly? It will have to be on the barricades."

"No," Peg said. "It's right to try and die together, even if it does not always work that way. You know, Seaforth, if Iain goes, that's the end of a generation in India. The men who won the Mutiny. It might be the time for a change, a great change."

"It is." Seaforth stood. "Thank you, Peg. Miriam and I must go. To make that great change in India."

"That soon?" Peg laughed. "Only you, brother dear, would be confident of throwing out the Raj by tomorrow breakfast."

"I only give them till midnight," Seaforth said.

"You're always asleep at midnight," Miriam said. "That's no way to run a revolution."

"No man can change the world," Peg said, "without his beauty sleep. That's what Mary would have said."

"And carbolic," Seaforth said. "No revolution without carbolic."

Douglas Jardine found that being in Intelligence made him more of an office-*wallah* than ever. This was no Kim's game, the fairy-tale that Kipling had recently published, all disguises and boyish ambles along the Great Trunk Road. More a permanent sentry-duty against going to sleep. Goodness, it was so soporific in the hot season, the creak or crackle or chortle of the revolving *punkah*, the rustle and flutter of flimsies under the paperweights, the pens of the *babus* scratching as though they were irritated by an incurable itch, and the padding of the bare feet of the *chaprassis* as soft as floor-rags as they moved files from one desk to another or brought another cup of sweet and milky tea. The temptation was to do nothing except what Lord Curzon had done, to write a minute answering another minute and to file it away to be unread until the hereafter. If there was work to be done, the clerks or the subordinates would always do it for one, and if they did it wrong, one could disclaim them. A velvet tongue and a sharp ear were the only qualifications necessary for keeping the position. Intelligence was a desk-bound affair.

So it was with anticipation rather than disdain that Douglas Jardine waited for Seaforth to come and see him. Bloody cheek, it was. The Eurasian doctor wanted to survey his surveyor. Rather the case of the goat hunting the tiger. But arrogance was written all over the file which was already being kept on Seaforth. And the file was not wrong. The bounce in Seaforth's walk into the intelligence officer's room was almost impertinent. Yet courtesy was always the best concealment. Douglas Jardine rose from his office chair to greet his wife's cousin.

"Dr Sinclair," he said. "It is good of you to want to come and see me. Do be seated."

"Thank you." Seaforth sat. His skin had been burned dark in the sun, which framed the intensity of his eyes as sparks glow in anthracite. "Better come and see you, Mr Jardine, than wait for you to come and see me."

"How is the Hospital at Lahore? It is near one of our largest cantonments. Do military manoeuvres really interest you?"

"Oh, I am not a spy." Seaforth smiled. "I leave that to British Intelligence, whoever they may be." So Seaforth showed his knowledge to Jardine, who knew that the doctor knew he was not just in the Indian Civil Service. "I cure the sick. I am not interested in boots, boots, boots, boots, marching up and down again. Or where they are marching."

"Knowing you were coming, Dr Sinclair, I hoped you might return with me to see the family. My wife Margaret and daughter are with me, although my son Wallace has left us to go to Cambridge – much brighter than his father, I can tell you." Jardine gave a self-deprecating smile of total pride. "You did come back to India to see the family again, did you not?"

"It was one of my intentions. I will bring my wife, if I may?"

"The famous Miriam Apfelstein. What do they call her? The Red Rand Robin."

"No, no." Seaforth smiled again. "The Boer Bolshevik. Only my wife's family, as you know, is Jewish."

"They would hardly approve of your marriage..." Jardine's words were both a statement and a question, for this was a meeting and not an interrogation. "But you might have converted ..."

Again Seaforth smiled.

"Convert from what? I am not a good Hindu. And I would be a worse Jew. We are both, you may say, free-thinkers."

"Socialists and anarchists and free-thinkers ..."

"To be short – yes, no, yes. There's not a law against it."

"No, not if you are not against the law."

"Your law?"

"Our law."

"Shall we say," Seaforth said, "how highly I regard your code of medical practice."

"And our law?"

"Your law for the rich? Or your law for the poor?"

"There is only one law."

"Two," Seaforth said. "Ask the rich, ask the poor. You will have different answers."

"Don't you think, Dr Sinclair, that doctors are best as doctors. Your *medical* opinion I would value ..."

"And I your intelligence?" Seaforth shook his head, then stared at Jardine. "Let's get down to it. You don't want me back in India. I may be a trouble-maker. What are you going to do about it? If you try to intern my wife or me – like those vile concentration camps I saw in South Africa –"

"Why should we? For what cause?" Jardine was almost honeyed in his tone. The doctor seemed frightened. He might break easily. "We do not intern people here. Unless they threaten the state."

"You know – we make no secret of it – we hate imperialism. We want Home Rule for India, like you are giving the poor Irish at last."

"Freedom of speech –" Jardine swung his swivel chair to one side and slowly crossed his legs, fastidiously pulling the crease of his trousers to one side. "It is a principle of the law here. You may say what you wish and you may think what you like. But do not say it so as to cause a disturbance."

"Or incite a Mutiny."

"No, not another Mutiny." Jardine gave his broad fatherly smile to Seaforth. "You know the law. You are intelligent – and almost one of the family. You are a cousin of my wife. I do not have to tell you. You know – and I am sure that your wife knows – even with her rich and radical connections –"

"Don't spy on us," Seaforth said. "Don't bother us. I am telling you. My wife does have rich and radical connections."

"Oh, yes, the Jews – they *are* meant to run the world." Jardine yawned and hardly bothered to hide his pretence of boredom with his hand. "But I simply don't believe it. The Jews are really quite an insignificant and dispersed people with only a minor talent for making money."

"Christ was hardly a financier."

"Not that, please. How odd of God to choose the Jews. And odder far that Christians choose a Jewish God and abuse the Jews. One has heard that before."

"You have heard it all before." Seaforth rose from his chair. "We will not come and meet your family just yet. We must do our work."

"I am sorry." Jardine also rose. "Margaret will be desolated not to see you. She longs to meet Mrs Sinclair. But what work is it exactly that you must get on with?"

"The hospital. Medical work."

"And your wife?"

"As you say, her politics are her own affair. Unless you interfere with her."

"As a gentleman, could I?" Jardine walked round the desk to usher Seaforth out. The *punkah* now swished as regularly as the strokes of a cane on flesh. "It was good of you to bother to come and see me. We shall meet again..."

"In different circumstances," Seaforth said.

"I have no doubt."

The way the Great Game ended was hardly great and not a game. Fearing that the Russians were taking over Tibet and threatening India across the Himalayas – if trying to traverse those celestial mountains could be called a threat rather than a folly on ice – Colonel Francis Younghusband led a thousand Gurkhas and Sikhs, four thousand yaks, seven thousand mules and ten thousand porters into the snows of the uplands. The Dalai Lama decided to resist. From Lhasa, he sent a band of warrior monks in orange robes and fifteen hundred troops with matchlock guns and sacred charms, each one sealed by His Holiness Himself to make the wearers bullet-proof. Quite kindly, the brigadier in command of the Indian Forces, James Macdonald, surrounded the Tibetans with his men. And shortly, the only person who spoke their language, Captain O'Connor, told the monks and the local warriors to lay down their museum pieces. But the head monk had a revolver, which he drew from his robes and used to shoot off the jaw of a Sikh. Four minutes later, seven hundred Tibetans were dead or dying.

"A terrible and ghastly business," Younghusband told Iain Sinclair on his way home through Simla. "We shot down monks with machine-guns as they were walking away. And there was a Tibetan who lost both legs and laughed with our doctors and said, 'Next time I will have to be a hero, because I can no longer run away'."

"And did you find the Russians in Lhasa?" Iain asked. Then he had to catch his breath before he could continue. He was very short of wind now. "Were they there?"

"No," Younghusband said. "They are all being killed by the Japs in Manchuria. Who would have thought it? Europeans being beaten by yellow-bellies."

"The Ivans are bonny fighters," Iain said. "Dinna I know it? That Crimea – they gave us a hard time of it."

"I had forgotten, Mr Sinclair – you were there."

"I am that old," Iain said and laughed. "But the Ivans, they had the worst generals in all the world. Did I no hear their navy shelled our fishing boats in the English Channel, thinking it was the Japs come all the way from Japan with their torpedo boats?"

"I have heard that," Younghusband said. "But as you know, I have been away from home over the Himalayas. I was sorry to hear about Anna."

"We must all come to an end," Iain said. "Hers was merciful. But I canna do without her." He felt tears prickle at the corners of his eyes and blinked furiously. No self-pity now. "I willna be aye here myself at Annandale."

"You must," Younghusband said. "You and your Gurkhas, you have been our eyes and ears for forty years and more on what is happening over the Himalayas."

"Old soldiers never die, they say," Iain said. "But they do, and they do not fade away." He wheezed and had to suck air into his lungs in order to continue. "They run out of steam."

"You're not an old engine –"

"I am. I need coal to stoke me up."

"As coal goes," Younghusband said, contemplating the brown spirit that trapped the candle-flames like yellow lilies in his clear glass, "it's good stuff. How do you get good malt here?"

"Whisky travels," Iain drained his own glass. "Whisky and Scotsmen, they travel well."

"And age well. But there are very few of you left in your own country. Thank you, I'll help myself. And you." Younghusband leaned forward and found the decanter and filled both of their glasses again. "Here's to you and Scotland and all you've done for us."

Iain did not drink again. Something was worrying him.

"You said it was a Macdonald, the one that had those poor Tibetan folk killit. You canna trust a Macdonald."

"Now the clans are talking. If you had ever got together against the English – instead of killing each other – you would have beaten us, instead of fighting yourselves and then having to fight for us."

"Aye, that's a fact." Iain did drink to that, and then he said, "Younghusband, will there be no more fighting here? Will we be having peace with the Ivans?"

"Yes," Younghusband said. "The Japs will beat them, and then they will make peace with us. In Persia, in the Himalayas, in China. In the end, you know, it will be Europe – the white races – fighting Asia, the Yellow Peril. And there are many more of them – India and China,

hundreds of millions of them – they can swamp us. Now the Japs
have won and proved they can beat us."

"We shall lose this? Annandale?" Again Iain paused to breathe as
rackety as a cog-wheel missing some teeth. "Aye, the Indians shall
have it back one day. My niece Peg, she said that. So she shall have the
emerald. As a pledge."

"What emerald?"

"Anna's. I had it of the siege of Lucknow. When we buried her –"
Now Iain was fighting for breath, for his throat was thick with feeling.
"Only my daughter Margaret came. And her daughter Ruby. The
others were busy. They askit me, Iain, the emerald ring, can we have it
the now?" Iain coughed and coughed into his hand. The spasm
seemed to ease his lungs. "Not yet, I said. Not till I am gone."

"You will be with us," Younghusband said, "always. India needs
you."

"Ach, get away with you." Iain laughed. "India dinna need us.
Those mountains –" He nodded at the window panes. Beyond them,
the crags of the white and indigo Himalayas were piebald in the night.
"They were there for aye. They will be there for aye. When we are
come and when we are gone." He breathed in, the slow pistons of his
lungs still just in trim. "This talk – this Home Rule – this
independence for India –" Again the slow chug of his search for
breath. "My brother's boy and girl – wrong side of the blanket – their
country, they will have it of us –" A gasp and a sigh and a slow filling
with air. "But they – they are more than we were –" A long pause, a
silence. Then Iain said in a loud voice. "Stronger than us – and them –
the strength of the hills."

Younghusband put down his glass and rose and went over to the
window to look out into the night and the striped slopes of snow
crevasse and pitchblende rock.

"I do not know how we passed those mountains in winter, Sinclair.
We killed poor people, we reached Lhasa, we found little, we achieved
nothing, we returned. And Tibet is independent again under the Dalai
Lama. And he will persist, for there is always another Dalai Lama.
Almost as eternal as the Himalayas."

"We do nothing," the old man's voice said behind Younghusband.
"And we are right proud of what we do."

Younghusband turned his back on the ambiguous barrier to the
north, where nothing was ever done by man.

"We do what we can do," he said. "And we are not the judge of
what we did. Another ..."

His voice trailed away into the deeps of the night.

15

A VOICE WITHIN

Bain found himself talking to Julia's grave. There was never an answer, but he talked to comfort himself. "Three years of the drought," he said to the tombstone. "Like the plagues of Egypt. But it canna be a judgement. Look, there's no flowers to your grave – and it is the first time I have put no flowers to your grave. But there is not a one here the now, they are withered with the grass. You ken, Julia, the bones – they are showing through the dust before it blows away. The bones of all the buffalos we killed when we first come here. A prairie of bones all the way to the mountains, and the dust blowing through the wire..."

So Bain would talk to himself, squatting by the headstone to his wife. He told her of Robert, so far away in Africa and transferring to the West Coast and the jungles, he would not like it there, the malaria and the blackwater fever would have him. And his wife running off with Hamish Charles, who might have murdered his own wife. Blood was blood and kin was kin, but if his brother Angus had to marry a woman from Peru, he could not count on all his bairns being right, they would have the Spanish and perhaps the Indian in them, which Hamish Charles did, and that was why he was what he was. And as for their son Gillon, well, he had stayed on the farm, but there was no living in the dry land any more. Gillon got three bairns quick from his wife Rachel. She had the hips for it, but there again, perhaps not the blood for it, her family coming from Russia, Jewish peasants driven out by a *pogrom*, the Cossacks beating them with whips and firing their houses. But Leah and Fiona and Colin, they were fine wee ones, and the family would go on. That was surely the point of it. But they could not all go on here. The land would not stand it.

Bain never thought that Julia would answer him. And when he heard her voice, he knew it was inside his own head. But the voice was so real, it was herself speaking. He was not speaking to himself, it was the wife he had lost who was talking to him and saying, "Bear up, Bain. The drought will end. The rain will come, because the Lord God will not forget you. Only bear up. It is your land and the only land that will ever be your land. Do you not run away over the Rocky Mountains."

Hearing her with his eyes closed and her repeating to him so close and clearly, Bain almost expected to see her dear self when he opened his lids, but all he saw was the tomb with her name, JULIA SINCLAIR – BELOVED – REST IN PEACE. Even then, at her dying, the farm could not pay good dollars for more letters from the mason to be writ on her stone.

"Gillon himself says we canna bide here. The land will not feed us. The mortgage for the machines and the wire is not paid. The bank will foreclose. He says we must away over that McDowell's Canadian Pacific Railway to the house in Vancouver, where Kate is, and where we have room. And we must sell the land and start again. But I canna start again. It is the end for me, Julia. With Iain gone the now in India, I am near the last of the brothers and sisters of our father and our mother – the last of them, but for Angus and Kate. And the last of our land, it will be going with the last of me."

A wind blew up over the dry plain and dust beat at the stubble on Bain's face, peppering his unshaven cheeks with the buckshot of the dirt. And he could no longer hear his wife's voice inside his head for all the noise of the powdered earth blowing into his face. So he cupped his palms over his nose and waited to hear Julia speak her final words to him. For he had to know what he must do.

"Go, if you must," she said within his mind. "Go, but do not sell all of the land. Our son will come back, or our son's son. For God will provide – if not for us, then He will provide for them. And they will return. Our land, Bain, my beloved. Our land."

The wind had been banging at the shutters on the farmhouse, crick – crack – crash, and Rachel was looking from the door to see that her father-in-law was coming home from his wife's grave before the hot blast which would surely follow that day. And she saw him bent against the force of the air, but smiling as he walked towards her. And he said to her surprise and her relief, as he passed her to join the children in the farmhouse, "We will be going to Vancouver, Rachel. But Julia says, we will keep the land." And Rachel knew that his old wife was long dead, but if she still gave such good advice from beyond the grave, long let her live in him.

They had hardly been in London. Virginia could not believe it. She had spent most of her life and her feelings on getting back to the artists in Piccadilly and Chelsea, and she had no sooner arrived back in England, when they were shipped off again to Vancouver. They had no money, that was the secret of existence. If you had no money, you had to do what your paymaster said. And her rich father-in-law Angus had insisted that they go to the family home in Vancouver to wait, until a post was arranged for Hamish Charles in the Far East. Angus now had his connections there. Yet however grand the connections of Angus were, they always seemed to be in the most godforsaken places. If Angus was your bankroll, you were rolled out of the way, as far as he could send you.

"There's nothing wrong with Vancouver," Virginia told Kate. "But you have lived so long here, only you know what is right."

Kate laughed and said, "Even if mother and father died here, it is not our house. As far as I reckon it, it's a stopover between Bob's trains."

And Bob McDowell did come and go according to the timetables on the Canadian Pacific Railway. So assiduous was he in his duties, he might almost have had a timepiece ticking in his head. But he was approaching retirement. And there was no way that he would give the Company any excuse to lay him off before his pension. He did more than live from the Rule Book, he breathed it, he ate and drank it, and he would only quit on the due observance of it.

"We are putting you out," Virginia said. "We must be most unwelcome guests. All five of us – and –" She looked down with horror at the swelling beneath her own loose blouse. "Another one on the way." That had been the consequence of her marriage to Hamish Charles in London, after her divorce. She would never admit it was the cause. "I am sure it will be a girl and if she is – as she will be – I shall call her Clio. After the Muse."

"That's not a Sinclair name," Kate said. "Italian, is it?"

"Ancient Greek. Classical."

"It is not right for a girl," Kate said. "But if you and Hamish wish it–"

"I do. So he does."

"You rule the roost."

"No," Virginia said. "I do not. Do you think I would choose to roost here?"

"You're very welcome," Kate said. "It's good to have children round the house."

"Step-children."

"Children, for all that. They are good little ones. But how will you manage them, now you will have one of your own?"

"Not very well," Virginia said. "To tell you the truth, I am not domestic. Primitive – I favour the primitive. More Lapsang Suchong, if you please." She held out her porcelain teacup with the blue dragons on it towards Kate. "You are so kind to get me China tea. It must be difficult."

Kate filled the cup.

"Not at all. We face the Orient. Two lumps?" At Virginia's nod, she dropped the sugar cubes with silver tongs. "And will you really be going to that plantation in the cannibal islands? My nephew knows nothing about it. Growing copra – it sounds like a snake-farm."

"Cobra, you mean," Virginia said. "And needs must. For it is Angus who insists. He says there is no other job available for his son. Well, Hamish did not know how to farm in Africa. So it will be no handicap that he does not know how to farm in the Pacific."

"Some say it is paradise in the South Seas. Do you read our Scotsman – Robert Louis Stevenson?"

"Paradise for me," Virginia said, "is not a coconut palm on a deserted beach. It is a street lamp in Regent's Street. I look for London, and I am in exile."

"You will find work to do there," Kate said, "helping your man."

Virginia stirred her cup of tea, dissolving the last residues of the sugar-lumps with her silver spoon.

"Men help themselves," she said. "Very rarely do they help women."

"You sound like my daughter Marie," Kate said. "She is quite for the women now. Votes – and she will not let the men stop her."

"I did not meet her in the brief time I was allowed in London. I regretted it. But when my penance in paradise is over ..."

"Ach, stay here," Kate said. "And I will show you Vancouver is a finer city than your old London. That is in the future, that is."

And Kate might have showed Virginia just that, only she did not have the chance. For her brother Bain arrived, and Gillon and Rachel and three more little children, so that the old house was bursting at the seams, and the sound of half-a-dozen tots squealing and squalling together fair drove everybody to distraction. Kate loved it. An old woman now, and suddenly to be mother to these six wee things, thinking she was the be-all and end-all of everything, because their mother and their stepmother could not really cope – that was a satisfaction, and Kate had waited long for the moment, while pretending it was too much for her, too. And, of course, it was also the future of the family.

The men in their usual silly way thought that they were providing for the future of the family. As if their talk raised a single child or solved a single problem. But Gillon was set on never going back to the plough and the bad soil, while Bain his father was too sick and ailing

to leave his room and answer back. So there was only her husband
Bob to speak for the railways, when the timetables let him rest – and
handsome Hamish Charles, who knew a very great deal about
everything and nothing worth saying about anything at all. The three
of them had retired to the parlour with a bottle of malt whisky, which
men said was a medicine as well as a stimulant, and women knew to
be a blaze of foolishness as well as a black tongue.

"You do reckon, Mr McDowell," Gillon said, for Bob was a
stickler for the right title, "your trains wouldn't run on time bar the
Morse Code. It runs a sight faster than your locomotives and
waggons."

"There is a use in it," Bob said, playing with the chain on his hunter
that spread over his dark waistcoat like the Milky Way over the
bulge of the night sky. "But it is for buying tickets, meeting goods.
The trains ran before the Morse Code, and they will run after it."

"But I saw a cinematograph –" Hamish Charles said.

Bob McDowell glared at him.

"You do not attend those penny arcades –"

"It is a wonderful invention, the cinematograph –"

"Dumb illusions. What is the film of a train running into a station
compared with a train running into a station? The first – trumpery.
The second – majesty."

"The film was called *The Great Train Robbery*. And the Morse Code
... the operator at the station, he gave away the robbers. They were
caught because of him."

"So, your cinematograph, it is the tinkle of a warning bell. A
policeman's whistle. Child's play – and I would not bother to see it."

"Maybe," Gillon said. "But I guess there's a future in it. That
wireless. What do you think, Hamish? You were in London. What do
they say over there?"

"There's a Mr Marconi –"

"Sells spaghetti, does he?" Bob McDowell laughed. "Pasta vendor."

"Radio waves, that's what he calls them. He has them on the ships.
They may talk to the shores from the seas. Now they want the radio
waves all over the British Empire. It's one of the biggest things in
London. Cousin Hamilton, he's in it."

"He's in the navy," Gillon said.

"He has left it," Hamish Charles said. "He is not interested in
ship's engines. He talks of air engines. And wireless. He has met two
brothers called Short. There is something – seaplanes for the navy.
Seaplanes that will fly the Channel. There is a Frenchie called Blériot.
He says he will fly across on his wood struts and canvas wings."

Bob McDowell could not contain his laughter. His breaths made the top of his malt whisky seethe and bubble.

"They'll run like trains, will they?" he said. "In air? Seaplanes. Only a bloody gull can do that."

"I believe you, thousands wouldn't," Gillon said. "Do you have Hamilton's address?"

"Of course. I'll find it."

"Will he help? A cousin? A Canadian cousin?"

"Yes, I'll see he does." Hamish Charles was embarrassed. "After you have been so decent – I mean about me and your brother's wife ... I mean, you could have taken his side –"

"I don't reckon I know what happened. That's between you and Robert. And Virginia. Well, lucky for some ..."

"What do you mean?"

"Lucky for you," Gillon said, smiling. "You're some man."

And Hamish Charles did not quite know how to take the remark, but he had never understood the local idiom. And it was as well that they were going off to Polynesia soon, where this damned plantation might be. For Virginia was getting sick and tetchy with her baby on the way, and he could not stand the racket of all the toddlers in the old house, his own three and cousin Gillon's brood. It was touch and go, really, whether Virginia gave birth or Uncle Bain expired or he himself went mad from the stupidity of trying to be a family man, which he was not cut out to be – or the clipper came in on time. Fortunately it did, and it carried him away with his second wife and four children including an infant called Clio, while he left an uncle breathing his very last behind on the Canadian shore, never to be seen again.

If there was a civilizing mission to clean up the world, copra was certainly a means to do it. Sending the coolies or the blackbirds up the thin trunks of the palm-trees like monkeys on sticks, dodging the fall of the clumps of coconuts crashing down in green cannonballs after their hacking on high, cutting them open to extract the kernel, drying it in the sun, then grinding out the oil to use in soap for million on million of pale skins. Whale blubber and animal fat had been used, but vegetable oil was better to soften and make supple the fairest of the fair. Naturally, working conditions were hard, and Hamish Charles could never have exploited his imported Indians and Chinese and his kidnapped Solomon Islanders as Bulberry did, a sweating hulk of an overseer, who drove on the work gangs in between hangovers and bouts of fever. When he heard the screams of the workers after

Bulberry's assaults with truncheon and cat-o'-nine-tails made from strips of sting-ray skin, Hamish Charles always walked the other way, preferring to ignore what he could not stomach. He knew there was no other way to treat the labourers and get the work done. Yet it was not a way he chose to see.

Virginia kept to the house by the sea, except for long expeditions into the interior, when Hamish Charles sent four armed house-boys with her. She was making a collection of devil-masks and totems and carved sacred paddles and prows. To her husband, it was all primitive junk, but it was art to her. And one evening she returned with carved and painted doorposts, rather like the gargoyles on medieval cathedrals. Indeed, they were made by a European, she said, who called himself an artist, and who had gone native. Gauguin was the name. But his woodwork and daubing seemed to Hamish Charles even inferior to the products of the pagan natives. Art was the opposite of the savage and the wild. If it was not, there was no point in being in this hell of a paradise. All the soap from all the copra in the world would not scrub out one more cruelty of the white race to lesser breeds.

Virginia was on another collecting expedition, when Chung killed Bulberry. Hamish Charles had not noticed the Chinaman among the others. Not that all yellow faces were the same to him, but he flinched from their looks at him, their passive resentment and loathing. So he had not noticed Chung's long and hangdog look or his stooped height. But when the guards brought the man to the big house, his body red with his victim's blood, also flayed and bruised by terrible beatings, and his hands bound behind his back, Hamish Charles saw a fierce and haughty culprit, who stared at him in judgement and contempt.

"He killed Bulberry?" Hamish Charles asked. "How?"

"Boss Bulberry beat him many time," the head guard said. "Look. No skin Chung. Then Chung catch whip. He kick Boss here." The guard kicked up one leg high and tapped a weal on the side of Chung's neck. "Bone break. Boss fall. He dead. Chung here."

"Did you do it, Chung?" Hamish Charles could hardly bear to look at the prisoner, who was staring so intensely at him. "Translate. Ask him if he confesses he killed Bulberry."

The head guard spoke in Chinese to Chung, who nodded. Then he answered rapidly, darting sidelong glances at Hamish Charles, as if he were referring to his master. The head guard shook his head, refusing to translate what he had heard. But Chung's voice became angry. He pointed at Hamish Charles, accusing him and forcing him to insist to the guard, "Tell me what Chung is saying. Tell me. Translate."

The head guard hung his head.

"Is no good. He say name Chung Sin Chu. He say same name you. He say Sin Chu him *maman* Peking by and by. No good."

Hamish Charles looked at the long face of the Chinaman, pale with loss of blood and fear. Yes, it was possible. Certainly, he had the large nose and frame, the drawn features of the Sinclairs, but with narrow Chinese eyes. And Uncle Hamish Jamie had been at the sack of Peking. And he had had two children by an Indian woman. Why not by a Chinese woman, too? But it was impossible, because it was intolerable. To admit to a relationship with a coolie, who had just killed the overseer, merely on a delusion that a name was somewhat the same. As if he had not had enough scandal with his marriage to Virginia. He could not condemn her and the four children to more shame on a claim on the family guilt.

"No good," Hamish Charles said to the head guard. "He lies. He lies to get off. Take him to prison. Tell him if he repeats his lie or his false name, Sin Chu, to the judge, he will certainly be executed. Tell him, he lies. I know he lies."

When Chung heard what Hamish Charles had said, he crouched as if to spring, but was caught by his bleeding arms by the guards and dragged away. The last that Hamish Charles saw of him was a grimace of such bitterness and despair that it wrenched his master's conscience. Hamish Charles wanted to absolve himself and tell Virginia, but he did not. He could not confess to her another cause for dirt to be flung at them. They had hidden the news of the killing of Lizzie and the divorce of Robert from the other Europeans on the island; but they lived in daily worry of being identified by some sea captain, sailing round from South Africa and knowing their story.

"Truth will out." Hamish Charles had learned the phrase from his Aunt Mary before she had died. He had denied it, but he believed it secretly. Everything was always known in the end. But for the moment, to admit to a false kinship with the Chinese murderer of a white man... They would have to flee again. No island would be remote enough to take them in.

So all that he said to Virginia on her return was, "A terrible thing. Bulberry was killed by a coolie. He is mad. Raving. He does not know what he is saying."

"Anyway, you wouldn't understand it," Virginia said. "You do not speak Chinese."

"I do not understand him," her husband said, "killing Bulberry."

"I would kill him. If he beat me like he does them. But look —" She unrolled a canvas and held up the picture for Hamish Charles to see.

Two yellow women in red and purple skirts lay in front of green mangoes and yellow gourds. "Another Gauguin. A painting this time. Do you like it?"

"It's ghastly," her husband said. "How can he paint such subjects ... so sloppily?"

"I'll keep it," Virginia said. "You see, it will make us rich."

"That's rich." Hamish Charles laughed at the absurdity. "Only copra will. And that is a rotten way to make money."

16

WITH WINGS

"We are Official Aeronautic Engineers to the Royal Aero Club," Oswald Short said in 1913 to Hamilton, "but we started in balloons. We used to supply them to the Balloon Company of the Royal Engineers for observation work. But then with the Green engine and the Sunbeam and the Rolls – all those automobile engines – why, air ships did not seem the big thing, but aeroplanes."

"And seaplanes," Hamilton said. "I am sure you will go to that."

"Yes, yes." The stocky businessman smiled at his new recruit. "I see you are still a naval engineer at heart. You want flying boats. But the fact is, the navy is far more interested in our aeroplanes than the army is. Ever since we won that *Daily Mail* prize for an all-British flying machine that could cover a closed circuit."

"That is what brought me to you," Hamilton said. "I am sure the future of the navy lies in the air."

The aircraft manufacturer laughed.

"That's a contradiction in terms," he said. "Navies are for seas. But you are right – the seaplane will be their salvation. Spotting enemy fleets –"

"Bombing," Hamilton said. "And why not aerial torpedoes?"

"Steady on. We don't even have seaplanes yet."

And Hamilton was soon set to work on the design of them. They were based on the Short biplane with a Gnome engine, basically a training machine with tandem seats, the pilot in front. Hamilton put two long pontoons into water-tight compartments under the wings with subsidiary floats at the tips, and he added a small float on the tail with a rudder to steer by while taking off from water. At first, there was not enough power to lift off the seaplane, so a 12-cylinder 275 hp Sunbeam-Coatalen 'Maori' engine had to be installed. But if there was a swell running, let alone a choppy sea or small waves, the seaplane would tip up before taking off. A dead calm was necessary for success, and that was rare enough at Calshot on the Solent, where Hamilton supervised the trials for the first pilots of the Naval Wing of the Royal Flying Corps.

There it was that Hamilton had the first of his two revolutionary ideas. And they were so simple. "Wheels and floats," he told Oswald Short. "Then it can fly off a ship and land in the sea."

"Fly off a ship?" Short was amused. "What do you think the navy's coming to? A sort of aircraft carrier?"

"Exactly," Hamilton said. "That's the right word. An aircraft carrier. They have your old balloons on board some ships already – blimps for spotting. Why not seaplanes or flying-boats? If you had a ship with a flat top – the funnels projecting out of the side or an elevated top deck – then your aeroplane with wheels and floats could take off the deck and land in the sea."

"Can you really see the admiralty slicing the superstructure off a battleship and making it into an iron airstrip?"

"Seaplanes could even land on deck, if there was a net to catch them in."

"Steady on, Hamilton. That's going too far. First, think how long your aircraft carrier would have to be to allow for a take off –"

"Catapult them, if necessary. Or steam into the wind."

Oswald Short laughed again.

"Now, really. So you shoot the aircraft off and catch them in a net to get them back. Why the floats?"

"Because you could use a crane to lower them into the sea and retrieve them after they landed in the sea."

"Wings. What are you going to do about the wings? They are far too long for lowering and storage."

And here Hamilton had his second inspiration, which came to him out of the blue.

"Fold them," he said. "Like a bird or a butterfly. Fold the wings."

"I don't believe it. Wings on hinges? They have to be fixed. You can't have folding wings and a stable aeroplane."

"Let me try," Hamilton said. "And then there will really be a Royal Naval Flying Corps."

He was living with Ellen-Maeve and their two children, Hamish Henry and Titania, in a curious edifice known as Luttrell's Tower, only a mile away from the base at Calshot, where hangars in dazzle camouflage now surrounded the castle, built by King Henry the Eighth as a defence against the French. The tower was six storeys high and had smugglers' caves beneath for the storage of illicit brandy and silks tax-free from over the Channel. It was a children's paradise, a pebble beach beneath the sea-gate, and gardens leading to the big house inland. It was also nearly grand enough for Ellen-Maeve, whose social aspirations were as lofty as the folly she lived in. When

Hamilton joked that he was in the right profession now, his seaplanes would take them higher and higher, his wife failed to see the point.

"On your pay," she said, "we will always remain at the bottom of the heap. And this place, those winding stone stairs – it is not even a country house, and certainly not a stately home."

"But think of the man who had it before us –" Hamilton looked out of the window of the high octagonal drawing-room across the dark Solent towards the lamp-lights of Ryde on the Isle of Wight. "Marconi himself. He did his wireless experiments from here, flying his wires from kites."

"Marconi? Isn't there some big government contract with his company? Are they not going to base telegraph stations all across the Empire?"

Hamilton had to admit Ellen-Maeve was always very well informed, although he never knew where she got the information, as she was at home most of the time with the children. But he said, "Yes, you are right, naval communications will be very important. But do you know, Ellen-Maeve, Marconi could communicate with old Queen Victoria Herself at Osborne in the Isle of Wight from this tower? And his family saw from this window the *Titanic* sail out. Look –" And, indeed, through the window he could see the lighted floating palace of another transatlantic liner – "And when the *Titanic* hit the iceberg, it was his wireless on board tapping SOS which saved some of the passengers. He would have been on the *Titanic*, only he decided to leave by an earlier ship so that he could greet the *Titanic* on her arrival in New York. Only, she didn't sail in. She sank. You know, stewards on liners, they always give the toast, 'Bottoms up', every time a ship passes over where the *Titanic* went down last year."

"Don't be morbid," Ellen-Maeve said. "And don't say *Titanic* so often. It's unlucky. It's so like the name of our darling little Titania. And I don't want her to go down with anything else."

Both of the children had chicken-pox. And that was after mumps and measles and whooping-cough with scarlet fever still to come.

"Childhood," Hamilton said to his wife, "does seem to be one disease after another."

"They have to have them," Ellen-Maeve said. "It makes them immune later. Anyway, nanny's had them all, and you have, and I have. So we won't get it. And their being sick, it is sickening! We never go to London, even when Marie asks us."

"I thought she was in Scotland. Did she not have to avoid the previous King's attentions? But he's dead and gone now, I agree."

"Oh, that's all over." Ellen-Maeve came to stand beside her husband, her yellow curls no higher than her husband's shoulder. "She is very active now. Votes for women. And socialism, I hear. And the new labour unions. I do not think that is very feminine."

"But you are." Hamilton put his hand on top of his wife's head. He gently felt her hair with his fingers, and she did not protest. "But some of the family are coming down here. Murdo, Uncle Angus's boy – the one we met at Lords, playing cricket. He wants to be a pilot. And so I've pulled a few strings with Murray Sueter, the airship man at the admiralty. Murdo will be one of the first air seamen."

"He was a nice boy," Ellen-Maeve said. "But please stop messing my hair." She put her hand up to take away her husband's fingers from her curls. The lights of the liner were distant now on the dark channel. "But he introduced us to Alex Plunkett-Drax. Who is being beastly to Murdo's sister. And didn't Ruth Seymour-Scudabright have to come back very suddenly from staying with them in Ireland? The talk –"

"There is always talk," Hamilton said, "when two women get together. And more talk, if the subject is another young woman."

"You used to like to talk to me. Now all I hear about is your beastly engines and flaps and floats."

"I will take you up in a seaplane one fine day, Ellen-Maeve. And then you will see that it is all worth it."

"You will never do that. I will never fly."

"You will." Hamilton put his arm round his wife's shoulder as she was too tiny for him to encircle her waist. "Flying – it will soon be as natural as breathing. Mark my words."

"Gamma minus. Bottom of the class."

"Flying. We will all have wings."

The extremes of the different lives which she lived in London stretched Marie to the brink of breakdown. Other women seemed to cope with the abyss between what they said and how well they lived. Perhaps Society was immutable and could not be avoided. So it was better to accept and not resist, to live in luxury and think like a seamstress in a sweatshop. As a girl, Marie had been poor. As an actress, she had worked hard. Even now, she paced her appetite and kept her body lean. But there were other actresses among the aristocrats – and other North Americans. The waspish and chinless pecking parrot, Maud Cunard, the willowy and witty Consuelo Marlborough, the devastating Nancy Astor. But with their socialist friends like George Bernard Shaw or the leaders of the rising Labour Party, Keir Hardie and Ramsay MacDonald, they would praise Marx and pass round the port. Their lip service to the poor did not affect the banquets made by their servants. They digested more treats than social change.

Yet Marie did agree to go with her husband to the most terrifying dinner party of her life. They were estranged now, almost separated. She went her way and had her flings with the vital people she knew like Keir McBride, the miners' leader at Dunesk. And her husband Bill certainly went his own way with his male friends, who claimed to be making a new world by reviving the gothic and the flamboyant, a sort of pretty gloss on the slums and the black truth of the time. Where Marie saw squalor and degradation, Bill saw a beautiful veil drawn over the harsh facts. They stayed together, opposed in mind, divorced in body, for the sake of Rosabelle and what was called Society.

Yet they had come together for a dinner. "It is better than with the Asquiths in Downing Street," Marie's husband had quietly informed her. "There you have nothing but the Souls – and their repartee is greater than their aesthetic gifts. And you may walk through a green baize door directly into the Chancellor of the Exchequer in the next house, who is more rewarding, but less witty. So let us toddle along to Consuelo's in Belgravia. She was a supporter of your sainted Aunt Mary, you know, in the Boer War. She does good – and what is worse, she loves your votes for women."

The intimate dinner party seemed to Marie more like a show trial. Round the long table with oval ends, twelve people were ranged on their isolated hard chairs like witnesses in the box. Their role was to testify to their reputations and their intentions. The great hostesses were there and the *literati*, Shaw and Barrie, who alone looked wistful, as if Peter Pan had just flown out of the room. The butler moved round between the conversations, which died like shot birds between the serving of the seven courses and the four wines.

"Those who can, do," Shaw said, "and those who can't, eat." His red beard wagged as he masticated another forkful of game brawn.

"I thought you only ate greens," Maud Cunard said. "Peck, peck, peck, like an Irish hen."

"I eat what is put in front of me," Shaw said. "It is called hospitality. The Irish are good at it. The English often fail."

"Please don't think you are being force-fed," Consuelo Marlborough said. "Like our poor Emmeline in that dreadful gaol."

That started the real discussion, the feeding by force of the imprisoned suffragettes on hunger strike led by Mrs Pankhurst. Such a dreadful business, the forcing of the rubber tube down the throat, the pouring of the gruel down the aperture, the saving of life by violence. Must anyone be made to stay alive, must women be denied their power to protest?

"You can go too far." With horror Marie heard her husband's provocative drawl at the end of the table. "That deluded girl, who threw herself in front of the King's horse at the Derby – he might have won the race."

"She died, damn it," Nancy Astor said.

"He lost, bless her," Bill Dunesk said and smiled. "Only the bookies were happy. And as for chaining oneself to iron railings to make a protest to Parliament. I don't think the fair sex has been worse off since that lady who was rescued by St George from the dragon was chained to the rock."

"And what do you reckon you mean by that?"

"Only that we men will give you dear ladies the vote, which you richly deserve, as long as you don't bully us into it. My dear Marie, for instance, has never picked up a tomahawk –" And seeing Marie's look of fury, her husband changed his words – "I mean, picked up an axe to defend her rights. She has them, anyway. She is free of me."

"She does not want her rights from you," Shaw said. "She wants them as her rights. For herself."

"Right." Bill Dunesk smiled to himself, appreciating his point. "Precisely right. But we do live in odd times, don't you think? Right's not quite the word for what's happening now. Your lady friend, Dr Stopes, and all this contraception –"

"Personally," Marie intervened, looking hard at her husband, "I believe nature should take its course. Or not – if not."

The others laughed. Her estrangement from her husband, his style of life with his male friends, these were known in the small circle of metropolitan society, so small it often seemed like a hangman's noose.

"Nature," Barrie said softly, "is something we are given to rise above. If anyone says nature, I run out and mow the lawn."

"Darling Peter Pan," Bill Dunesk said. "And you never grew up, either."

"Who wants to?"

"Nobody."

The two men looked at each other in silent agreement.

"Women are rather more practical," Consuelo Marlborough said. "We do want our male babies to grow up. They become men, and they sometimes listen to their mothers – even Winston. And they may listen enough to give us the vote." She rang the bells. "We are eating duck and truffles, if you can stand it. English truffles. Somebody has trained a pig in the New Forest to find truffles, and these are they. Wonderful noses, pigs have. They're more use than just pork."

Over the main course, the conversation turned to falling standards. This was something which Marie had always noted. Things were always worse than they had been before. The older the guests and the speakers were, the better it had been in years gone by. Now the worry was not Russia, but the rise of Germany. The new King George the Fifth was a sailor and almost as stupid as the Danish Queen Mother, who still concentrated on keeping one of the smallest waists in London. Yet the fact of a blockhead on the throne need not be a disaster, if the Liberal government under Asquith could put through old age pensions and Irish Home Rule and income tax, some of the acts which might drag Britain into the twentieth century.

"We want the future," Marie said. "But you all look at the past and regret it. Why, why, why?"

"Because we were born into it," her husband said. "Or some of us were. We did not just *arrive*."

There was a silence after his remark. Few men cut down their wives in public, and Dunesk was usually known for his subtle tongue. But Marie was writhing. She would have no more of it. She would not.

"When I arrived here," Nancy Astor said – "and I'm sure it goes for you, Consuelo – we didn't feel we were joining the old – other than our spouses, I mean." The women at the table smiled, the men looked down. "We were bringing in the new. Only it's taking a hell of a long time to arrive."

"We will retire," Consuelo Marlborough said. "And leave the gentlemen. As my husband is never here himself – he rarely arrives except to depart to his club – we are rather separate now – will you, Mr Barrie, preside and ask the other gentlemen to join the ladies in due course – if that is what they want to do?"

With the other women in the old bedrooms and bathrooms of the Belgravia mansion, Marie found another scene, a new world that was overcoming her life. She loved men, she was rejected by her husband, she even had the occasional dangerous moment with her miner in Lothian. But women were her friends. They would change society. Only they had the power to do it.

"I thought I was free," she told Consuelo Marlborough, "when I was a girl, riding an Indian pony on the prairie. And when I was an actress, I was free. But ... I guess I didn't know. No woman was free. She had nothing for herself. But I didn't know. And now I do."

"Sweated women, Marie. Will you join me in that? Women working for nothing in factories. Prostituted labour. You will join me to end that?" The intensity of the duchess's face, her belief in her cause, almost made Marie feel that the other woman was a Keir Hardie, a social evangelist for her truth. But she was as much the man whom she had married as Marie was – the peeress in a silk gown, cosseted by servants. "You will help me?"

"But we live like this," Marie said. Her hands spread and drooped. "We are ..."

"Hypocrites? I don't think so. If I was a Poor Clare, I could do little. Feed a few miserable people and pray for them. But we have the power to change the lives of millions of women –"

"That's why I married Bill Dunesk," Marie said. "I thought ... with the power to change ..."

"And what went wrong?"

"Living like we do – that changed me while I wanted to change things for others –"

"Look, my dear." Consuelo Marlborough put her hand under Marie's chin, tilting her face into her blinding gaze. "You said, you did not know you were unfree. Your marriage, your life with us, it has educated you. Without riches, we do not have the time to learn. Without power, we can do nothing. Having this position, I mean to do rather well." She smiled and released Marie's cheeks from between her hands. "Privilege – it's only an opportunity to do better for other people."

"If I didn't feel so guilty about it," Marie said.

"Don't. Guilty is a word people use to do nothing, because they can excuse themselves." The duchess rose from where she was sitting on her great quilt of silk roses with the question, "Shall we join the gentlemen? They need us to tell them what to do."

"I am leaving Bill," Marie said abruptly. "I can't stand it. Even at dinner, he says things about me ..."

"Stick it," the duchess said. "Like I do with my intolerable man. So we keep a bit of power to do what we want."

Marie Dunesk joined the Duchess of Marlborough's campaign for sweated women in the East End garment factories. She also went to Calshot to fly with her cousins Murdo and Hamilton in one of the new Short seaplanes. "You are the first human duck which ever took off the waters," Hamilton told her. "Nobody will ever shoot you down. You have wings."

"Maybe," Marie said. "But there's a man who still reckons I am tied down."

"You?" Hamilton laughed. "You're a bird. You have always been free to fly away."

17

SWEATED WOMEN

She believed in it, but it had hardly ever happened to her. When Ruth intruded on her life, Marie had expected to be distant to her little cousin. Yet there was an immediate recognition between them. The girl was both defenceless and reckless, shy and fierce, stammering and pouring our her heart. She told Marie about her time with Alex Plunkett-Drax, her shame at his rape of her and also of his repulsive attraction. She had to leave Ireland and return to her home, but some gossip had reached her father, the member of parliament, Charles Seymour-Scudabright, or it had got to Alex's wife, her cousin Arabella, who had hinted at something in a letter. Anyway, the affair was now a common suspicion, if not knowledge. She had to run away. Could Marie house her and find her something to do?

Marie could and would, feeling in Ruth's need that she had found a sister soul in the crusade for exploited women. She had become fiercer in the struggle, raising money for the militants, visiting those who were put in gaol for disturbances of the peace. Yet she did not wish to compromise her husband. She was now separated from him as Consuelo Marlborough was from her husband, the duke. But the parting of the ways and Bill Dunesk's coldness towards his wife had fuelled her fight for women. She was also involved through the pits in Lothian with the cause of the miners, who were striking at long last for higher pay and better conditions. There again, it was a personal involvement, this time with a man, the union leader Keir McBride. Their closeness in Scotland had turned her own daughter of thirteen, Rosabelle, back towards her father, especially as the child now looked like a pre-Raphaelite dream, her long red hair curling down to her waist from a pale oval face with heavy lids that drooped over green jade eyes. This fey beauty was the toast of her father and his friends, enthralled by the swirling designs from France and a new style. Rosabelle was also no sexual threat, as she was on the far verge of childhood and wanting never to grow up.

Ruth became a secretary to Consuelo Marlborough, who was organizing a conference on sweated women, working seventy-hour weeks to earn a few shillings. If she could set a social trap, the Liberal government might do something about it. Lloyd George had forced through a National Insurance Act, and the Conservative House of Lords, fearful of the creation of hundreds of new peers, had not thrown it out. Yet the anger on the Tory side ran high, and in no one higher than in Charles Seymour-Scudabright, who stormed in one day to her office in Sunderland House, where the conference was to be held.

"You will come with me at once," he said. He was more corpulent now and seemed to carry a cushion under his waistband, while his cheeks were two red balloons, waiting to burst.

Ruth remained sitting. Her heart trembled, but her voice was firm.

"I shall stay here, father, where I am."

"You are a disgrace to the family."

"Not to all of it."

"The Dunesks, if you mean them. They're in trouble."

"If you mean Marie — women's suffrage, sweated labour — the disgrace is that you do nothing about it."

"We are for England," her father said. "Its proper values. None of these seedy share dealings, the corruption of the nation."

"Oh, the Marconi business. That is mere slander."

"The attorney-general — the postmaster-general — buying shares in a company which is awarded a government contract. It's disgraceful. And the head of the company is an Isaacs too, the attorney-general's brother."

"Just because they are Jews, father, you suspect foul play for money. Like Mr Belloc. If they were good Catholics or Protestants —"

"They are degrading the ethics of the nation —"

"Which God sent the Conservatives to protect."

"You will wash your mouth out with mustard, young woman."

"I am too old for that. Calm down, father. Anyway, what has it to do with Marie?"

"Her husband, Dunesk, he has been involved in the Marconi share dealings. Through another of your disreputable cousins, Wallace — Margaret's child from India — the one who left Cambridge to go into the City. University, it never does anyone any good."

"Oh, brother Gordon survived it before the Grenadiers got him. And brother Graham didn't need it before he started messing about in boats."

"Hold your tongue, young lady. Both of your brothers are serving their country. And the way the Kaiser is behaving, they may be most necessary sooner than we think. But I don't know if we are worth saving. With a corrupt government ..."

"It is not corrupt. Just because it cares for the poor and working people –"

"Its Ministers buy shares in firms which profit from government contracts."

"But we need those wireless stations, don't we? For your blessed navy. In Egypt, East and South Africa, India and Singapore. Graham will be able to sail anywhere, and you will always know exactly where he is sinking."

"I warn you, Ruth, to show some respect. I shall cut your allowance –"

"You haven't paid it in months."

"You may expect to inherit nothing."

"Good. If I inherited your politics –"

"You will give up working here immediately. I have just found you a job in a law firm."

"Do you think working for the Duchess of Marlborough is not respectable?"

"Her views are insupportable."

"But her character?"

"If a woman has wrong thoughts, her character is affected."

"But you will come to our grand occasion, father. Look." Ruth added her father's name to the list on her desk. "I have put your name down with only the most distinguished people – bishops and law lords, half the peerage and you, the most influential of all the members of parliament. You are to come to Sunderland House –"

Her father paused. He was never one to refuse a glittering social occasion, which might advance him.

"For your sake, I may not say no. But what it is for?"

"Sweated women."

"Then I will not come. People who work for low wages choose to do so. It is what the market will bear." Her father smiled sourly down at his daughter. "And what does the duchess pay you? Enough for stockings?"

"A living wage," Ruth said. "So I don't have to depend on a man."

"You call your father a man?"

"No," Ruth said. "If he is not man enough to help sweated women."

Her father did not come to the conference, although most of the high and mighty did, believing it to be yet another charity event with strawberries and champagne at the fag-end of the Season. Instead, Consuelo Marlborough and Marie Dunesk produced twelve old women on a platform. Each told of decades of working for nothing, not the song of a shirt, but its requiem mass. One of them did unfold a real shirt she had made as if it were a white flag.

"A dozen of them, and I get ninepence. Last week me and my old man, we sat from five-thirty in the morning till eleven at night – fourteen dozen shirts. And we got ten shillings less ten pence for cotton. A penny, that's the price of our dinner. Never more than a penny for twenty years."

There would be a trade board on the matter, a cabinet minister promised Consuelo, but Marie did not believe anything would happen because of that. "Sweated women," she said. "That's all we ever are, unless we marry out of it."

On the top of the stone tower that stood as a marker in the paddy-field, a brother and a sister were looking across the green rice-blades towards the blue ridges of the Himalayas. Seaforth had taken Peg out to the country to show her what he called the only triumph of the Raj, the great survey of India by Captain Everest.

"Triangles," he said. "He mapped our continent out in huge triangles. He started down at the tip in Cape Comorin, and then in base lines of seven-and-a-half miles, he plotted this continent all the way up to the north. And when the distance was too great to calculate on the ground, he built these stone towers we are sitting on. Just to get the measurements right to one inch in a mile. The thing is, Peg, what was he doing? Was it worth it?"

"*You* think so."

"I do. I don't know why. It is not there to see, but it is enduring."

"These stone towers are. We sit on them."

"Yes," Seaforth sighed. He stretched out an arm towards the mountains. "A grand illusion – like the British in India, which is ours and always will be. But it is a fiction like Mr Rudyard Kipling writes, even if these are monuments. Most of them will become target practice in time. But this one – absolutely useless – a tower in a paddy-field, it marks something marvellous. A madman with his instruments who correctly plotted the true length and breadth of India in giant triangles all the way to the Himalayas. You know, Peg, when he was paralysed by malaria, Everest had himself hoisted to the top of these towers, just to be sure his measurements were right. He was a fanatic for the numbers and the rules. That is why the British will lose India to us. It is not the way of this country."

"But you admire it. Their method."

"I do. Old Uncle Angus did it, you know, when he was a young man. He surveyed what he called the Medicine Line, the frontier between Canada and the United States of America. It was an artificial line, but it mattered. Canada is still there and fairly independent. It took him years. Surveys are a kind of truth, Peg. You cannot see them, even if you sit on their towers. But they define your land for ever, even if it does not belong to you." Then he added, "Yet."

"Angus is dying. I heard that from cousin Margaret, over at Annandale. She has it now."

"They all have to go. Like our father in that silly Boer War. And Iain's gone and dear Mary. Angus now and Kate soon enough. A generation passes, and they leave us. The future." Seaforth showed his thin and bitter grin to his sister. "Do you feel like the future, Peg?"

"Not much," she said. "But I will survive it. As long as they need doctors."

"And pay you." Seaforth smiled again. "They will need doctors and pay you. They have wars to come. Imperial wars."

"You are a doctor, too, Seaforth. You treat anyone. Soldiers. Anyone."

"Yes, I do. Peg, there will be a great war, a world war. I know it. And when it comes, we will serve again, as we did in the Boer War. But this time, we will ask our price. We serve you, you give us our freedom."

"They will say yes. Then they will not do it."

"They might. If we send for Mister Gandhi."

"Your Mister Gandhi. You think he walks on water."

"No. He sits down and does nothing. So he moves mountains. Talking of that, you see *that* mountain." Such a clear day shone that the eye seemed to travel through infinity. At that range, one peak looked as another, even to the discerning eye. "There is Everest."

"How do you know?"

"Because I do. The great surveyor died before he finished the survey. So the team went on, and when they first came to the Himalayas, they used his methods, theodolites and triangles, and they worked out the height of the peaks from the plain. And when they came to Peak Fifteen, a young surveyor did his sums and said, 'It's the highest mountain in the world. It is twenty-nine thousand and two feet precisely'. And perhaps it is and perhaps it is not, but it is the highest mountain in the world. And it was called Everest."

"Is that a good story or a bad story?" Peg looked away from her brother towards the blue ruffle that broke the horizon.

"Both good and bad. The great surveyor Everest, who had never seen it, had the highest mountain called after him. But nobody would have known it was the highest mountain without the great surveyor."

Peg smiled now. She liked her brother best when he was ambiguous, and not too fanatical.

"I think you admire them, really," she said, "for doing and building what we could not do." Then she was malicious. "At least, the *Sinclair* in you does."

She touched a nerve. He was still too raw at his age to take gentle teasing. Even Miriam had not taught him to laugh at himself.

"Don't say that," he said. "You heard of that case in Polynesia. That Chinaman convicted of murder on Hamish Charles's copra plantation. He was a Sinclair, he said. Our half-brother. When our father was in Peking."

"You don't believe it."

"I don't know. I can't prove it." Seaforth began to bite his thumb-nail, a bad habit of his middle age. "What if he is?"

"They did not hang him?"

"No, a life sentence. Extenuating circumstances, they said." Seaforth gave a short laugh. "As if life is not a sentence, anyway. With no extenuating circumstances."

"If you could hear yourself talk, Seaforth, *you* would not believe what you say."

"That is what sisters are for – to tell their brothers what bloody fools they are."

Seaforth hugged Peg, drawing her into his arms.

"Look," he said, "you should get married, I recommend it."

"Some have asked me," Peg said. "But I take after Aunt Mary. There's a while yet. And Seaforth, I would lose my independence."

"Independence?" Seaforth smiled. "We have not got it for a whole country. Why should you worry? One Indian woman."

"I'd rather be a free spinster," Peg said. "And walk my road to the river. And as for you, brother, you should not be with your old sister up here. You should have brought your wife."

"Miriam has to look after the children. She's not English. She won't leave Shankar and Solomon alone with the *ayah*."

"Our mother did."

"She was the *ayah* to our cousins at Annandale. But you, Peg – if a man is lucky enough ..."

"I take after Aunt Mary, I told you so. A doctor has to remain alone."

"Mary did marry, in the end."

"It isn't the end. Thank you for bringing me up here, brother." Again the sweep of the eye seemed to comprehend all India, green and growing by the Ganges, the garden of the world in the right season. "We have time to talk and think. There's nothing of that down there."

"Serving the Raj," Seaforth said. "They don't give you time to talk and think. It's part of their policy. Oh, can you come to Bombay some time?"

"Why?"

"Communications. They're setting up a Marconi station there. We will be able to talk to South Africa directly – and Gandhi."

"And our family."

"One of them is coming. I heard it from Margaret. Gillon, a cousin from Canada. He is mad about the wireless. The farm there is a desert. Like this, before they put in the irrigation."

They looked down over the green paddy-fields. The sight was hard to credit. Such fertility, it must have been there always.

"The British put in the irrigation," Peg said. "I remember, Uncle Iain worked on it."

"More mouths to feed," Seaforth said. "More colonial mouths till we have independence."

"More rebels." Peg smiled at her brother. She knew how to switch his words. "More supporters for you. More people to throw bombs at the viceroy."

"The bomb missed," Seaforth said. "It only blew up the viceroy's howdah and hurt his elephant. But it made the Durbar in Delhi go with a bang." Peg smiled. "But, you see, the power of the new communications. All the world heard immediately of the bomb under the seat of the Raj."

"And saw it. The cinema."

"I have seen that. In Bombay." Seaforth looked down across the pattern of the paddy-fields, which was not a survey, but the skein of irrigation canals which made rice grow on the earth. "In Bombay, too, there is the P & O coming in. Hamish Charles cabled Margaret that his wife was on it. That Virginia, the one he killed his first wife for."

"Aunt Mary said, 'No, he did not'."

"Aunt Mary was wrong. I think she is leaving him. Like she left cousin Robert. A fickle Virginia. She is on the way back to what they call home."

"Home." Peg looked over the verdant quilt below. "They use that word too much. Home is here." She thought that now. She had not thought that before.

"The only way I excuse our father — and our cousins that call our India a kind of home." Seaforth's left leg seemed to have gone out of control, as it was tip-tapping the stone. He had to hold his calf with his hands to stop it. "They were forced to wander. They were driven like cattle from their lands. Their own Scotland."

"They can go home now."

"Cousin Margaret is going. She may be on the boat with her darling daughter Ruby. But she will return to Annandale. She loves Annandale. She waited long enough to get her hands on it."

"It would never have come to us. It was Uncle Iain's."

"He gave you the ring."

Peg twisted the emerald on its gold band till its green stone caught the light and blazed round the flaw in it, filling her sight.

"Yes, he did. Conscience — they do have conscience. Something makes them give it back, the Scots, give back what they took. In the end."

"In the end? We may not be here to see the end."

"We will be," Peg said. She rose on the top of the tower like the statue of a dark victory. "You have just shown me all India, brother. In the end, it must be our land."

18

FIGUREHEADS

However much she might dislike Virginia, Margaret had to admit a certain splendour in her pose by the rails in the bows of the P & O liner, the *Viceroy of India*. The hard, rakish lines of her face made her seem a fierce figurehead. Both of the Sinclair wives were travelling POSH, of course, on the starboard side of the ship to avoid the worst of the sun. The women passengers outnumbered the men. There was a giggle of Returned Empties, those young hopefuls who had come out in the autumn under the name of the Fishing Fleet and were being shipped in the spring without a catch in the Indian Civil Service back to a spinster future in Dear Old Blighty. Margaret was bringing her daughter Ruby in the opposite direction, looking for a match in England. And Virginia, although evidently running away from her husband Hamish Charles and her step-children on their copra plantation, was taking her child Clio, even if she was only seven and rather a distant prospect in the marriage stakes. But calculation, Margaret knew, was something that Virginia was never without.

"My dear Virginia," she said, "who would have ever thought we would be on the same boat?"

"We aren't," Virginia said. "You export India with you. And your little castes and classes. Here sit the Civil Servants —"

"The heaven-born."

Virginia smiled at Margaret, sensing a sister in malice. "The heaven-born. And there are the military, all *pukka sahib*. And they don't speak to the planters or to each other. And then there are the rich unmarried girls going home, and the poor governesses, equally segregated. Then the real pariahs like me, who come from somewhere far too far east. So we don't count at all."

"You do pretty well, Virginia — not being counted, I mean. You always stand out in a crowd."

"But do I add up? That's what I ask myself. And the answer is nought. I add up to nought. A mother with a seven-year-old. Hardly a desirable proposition. And I don't even know how to dress for dinner. There's the Punjab Club wearing white jackets and black trousers, and the Calcutta Club wearing black jackets and white trousers, and the Lahore Club wearing blue shortie jackets and pink trousers –"

"Bumfreezers and cherrypickers," Margaret said.

"My God," Virginia said. "I didn't know you could speak like that."

"Oh, you can't avoid the army in India. You have to listen to troop talk till the bitter end."

"So what is a woman to wear? I feel I should come on in a chessboard back and front with a geranium hat."

"You do all right," Margaret said.

And Virginia did look good, the wind blowing her long white dress flat against her leanness, showing the small curves of her body.

"In fact," Margaret added, "you do better than all right."

"Your Ruby is simply beautiful," Virginia said, lying through her teeth about the young miss with her sausage curls and milksop face with huge eyes bright as new pennies.

"And so is Clio," Margaret said, talking of the little monster, who tore around always in a temper and had even bitten the purser in the leg. The way to ingratiate oneself with another mother was by praise of her child. Both Virginia and Margaret knew that, and they also knew that the other knew it, and discounted the compliments.

"I'm glad to be taking Clio home," Virginia said. "She has never seen it. Never seen home."

"Ruby has. And to tell you the truth, if we can find the right situation, she may even remain there. Her brother Wallace is doing so well in the City ..."

"Really?"

"He is a financier, interested in scientific advance. Wireless telegraphy. Curiously, not a British invention. An Italian called Mr Marconi, I believe, did it first."

"Oh, they've had a few bright ones outside the ice cream parlour," Virginia said. "Leonardo da Vinci and the rest. But that was a time ago. But tell me, do you think there's anyone really interesting on board? I mean, who will pass the time of day until the gully-gully men come on ship at Suez and find chickens in your bosoms?"

Margaret smiled. "If there was someone special, you would have seen him."

Virginia smiled back.

"No, you would have seen him. For Ruby."

Both women then smiled at each other and left the deck. For both had seen the most intriguing, and perhaps eligible, man of them all. Always dressed in a spotless white suit – he must have worn three pairs a day in the heat – Maurice Walter exuded the quiet arrogance of wealth and the secret knowledge of power. His manners impeccable, his behaviour imperturbable, his only faults the chain-smoking of thin black cheroots and the using of violet *cachous* to scent his breath, Walter gave no hint of his trade or his reason to travel back from the East on the *Viceroy of India*. Before she engineered her introduction, Virginia noticed one of the cavalry captains, the beanpole Alistair Abercrombie, keeping watch on Walter in a nonchalant way. There was something mysterious about the man, and she would find out. And she would use none of the usual methods which Margaret might use, dropping a glove or pretending to stumble near him. He was too sophisticated for such an approach. She would brazen her way to him.

She walked straight up to Walter as he lay in his steamer chair, smoke trailing from his cheroot in a miniature parody of the liner's funnel.

"You look the only sort of man on board who would know what I am talking about," she said, leaning down to look at him directly under the brim of his white panama hat with its scarlet-and-black band. "What do you think the value of primitive Polynesian art will be? And a painter called Gauguin?"

Walter climbed slowly to his feet and took off his hat.

"May I have the pleasure of knowing who –?"

"Virginia Sinclair. You are Maurice Walter."

"You can read the ship's list. And perhaps there are some aboard who know me."

"I feel you know about the primitive."

"Dear *madame*, a little. My interest is, indeed, the import and export of things from the Far East. *Les choses qui puissent frotter l'avenir* –shake the future."

"That's very well put, *Monsieur* Walter."

"If I may see your primitive works, *madame*. I should be honoured. But, in general, you are correct, if you wish to enter that trade. There is already an appreciation of the violent and the primitive in Europe – *l'homme sauvage* is the new man in Paris and Milan. Ferocity is quite in fashion. And as for Paul Gauguin, if you have any of his works and held onto them for a while, you have your fortune."

Walter appreciated the ceremonial masks and carved clubs and paddles, which Virginia was bringing from Polynesia. He was ecstatic over the Gauguin paintings, though reserved over that artist's carvings. "The brush," he said, "is mightier than the chisel." He even showed an interest in Clio, who was fascinated by his elegance and his cheroots and displayed a tendency to flirt, which almost made her mother jealous though her daughter was only seven. When she apologized for Clio's innocent forwardness, Walter merely smiled and said, "Girls mature early in the tropics. And if she matures into half the woman her mother is ..." His compliment trailed away into a silent suggestion of some complicity between them. And that night, they danced together to the ship's orchestra, twined so tightly together that they seemed like a single reed swaying. They were the scandal of the ship, and Margaret told Virginia so in the morning.

"You were being simply shocking."

"I hope so," Virginia said.

"Everybody knows you're married."

"So to say, and you say it."

"Well, you are married to my cousin – or cousins – and your name is Sinclair. I can hardly avoid informing –"

"On me. You wanted him for Ruby."

"I did not. But to see you making such a spectacle of yourself. As if you had not already had enough scandal in your life. That dreadful murder of Hamish Charles's first wife ..."

"It was an accident." Virginia pricked Margaret with a look like a hatpin. "If you say murder to anyone, it is slander. The verdict was an accident."

"Robert's verdict. Your *husband*."

"Then. Not now. And didn't he have every reason to call it a murder, if it really was? But he told the truth. An unhappy accident. And if you tell a lie on this ship, I shall know. And Margaret, if you do, I shall sue you. Or scratch your eyes out, whichever you prefer."

Margaret quailed before Virginia's fierceness. Of course, she had already spoken about the murder, for that is what it surely had been, to Alistair Abercrombie, when she had been to him to find out all about Maurice Walter. Anyone would have. Why should she lie to hide the shameless Virginia's past? But she did lie now, to save herself from Virginia's menaces.

"Of course, I haven't said a thing. You know I wouldn't. One always stands by one's relations. But it is very difficult, with you stuck to that man in front of everybody. Alistair Abercrombie said you might have been glued – welded like the ship is."

"Why don't you weld Alistair Abercrombie to Ruby? Then he would stop spying on us."

"If you think I have my eye on Abercrombie –"

"Ruby has. She shone her eyes on him like a lighthouse."

"You are merely trying to change the subject. To accuse Ruby of the designs you have on Maurice Walter."

Virginia laughed and said, "Well, I am a designer, but I assure you, Maurice Walter may have his own plans, and perhaps I may not fit in with them."

"You *fitted in* very well last night on the floor."

"Dancing together does not mean sleeping together," Virginia said coolly, watching the shock freeze Margaret's face. "It only implies it. And frankly, one's chances on a ship as crowded as this beggar probability."

"You are shameless," Margaret said.

"Because I say what you think?"

"All the same, I must warn you. Abercrombie says he's dangerous. He's under surveillance." Margaret's voice dropped to a whisper as though somebody was listening, hidden in a lifeboat on the empty deck. "He may be a foreign agent."

"I do hope so," Virginia said. "Anyway, we have a lot of time to find out about one another, Maurice and I – and simply nowhere else to go, unless we jump overboard in a lovers' leap. Actually, I think the sharks' jaws would be kinder than the local comments."

So Virginia continued to flaunt her relationship with Maurice Walter, which always stopped just short of going with him to his luxurious cabin in the First Class (she was travelling Second with Clio sleeping in the bunk below her). But as they approached the Red Sea and the Suez Canal, the weather became so sultry that Maurice must have been changing his white suits six times a day to look so serene and uncreased, while the *dhobi-wallah* on board was on permanent duty, washing and ironing and starching in his hell-hole of an oven below decks. The *Viceroy of India* had not yet been equipped with the new electric fans in the cabins, so the passengers began to sleep on deck, which was sweltering enough.

The sexes were segregated, but Maurice Walter bribed a steward to erect for him almost a caliph's tent on the foredeck. And there he seduced Virginia, his lovemaking so sensitive and assured that she was confounded and destroyed, clinging to him and bursting into tears and sobbing, "Never, never ... how can you? I never knew ..." And he soothed her and stroked her into silence, then gently made love to her again until her pleasure became intolerable, and he had to hold his hand over her mouth to stop her cries waking the other passengers asleep. She bit into the side of his hand like a panther.

Now she was even more a pariah than she had ever been, shunned by the servants of the Raj returning from India and the English women who had not found a husband out there. Her affair with Walter made her an outcast worse than a murderer, for she was sinning almost in public, and she had her small daughter with her. She was an affront to every standard of morality. But Walter himself became more amused and immobile, saying to her, "When everybody disapproves of you, you know you are right."

"I am right," Virginia said. "For the first time, I follow my heart. And I do not care."

"You are reckless," Walter said. "And that is what I love in you – beside your obvious charms. And now, because your dear Wilde said, nothing is more repulsive than the British in their occasional fits of morality, I shall give you this, to wave in their faces and shock them more."

And so he gave his first of many gifts to Virginia, a pearl-handled small revolver, inlaid with gold. "It was for a maharanee," he said, "but I kept it. The deal with her husband – *kaput*."

Virginia looked at the revolver, which fitted as snugly in her hand as a toy.

"Thank you," she said. "Curiously, I have always wanted one. You deal – in arms?"

"Didn't you know?"

"No. I had not suspected."

"How else can one become rich? Or be so suspicious?" Walter drew on his black cheroot until the tip blazed like a gun muzzle. "Weapons are the one thing everybody always wants. I supply them. A commodity like any other. And these days there are more and more buyers, especially in the east."

"They may be used against us –"

"Us?" Walter shrugged. "Who is Us? You and I? The people in this boat? A so-called nation? The human race? All of these are Us. And we all want weapons to defend ourselves against Us."

Virginia shook her head and smiled.

"You are very convincing, Maurice, and corrupting."

"Inspiring, Virginia. I inspire you to know the woman you really are."

"The woman who loves you."

"Yes. She."

For Robert, arriving on the Elder-Dempster or the Union Castle steamers to Nigeria was rather like trying out the attractions on a fairground. The heavy seas made him find his way down to the surf-boats in a mammy-chair, a wooden box hanging on a chain from the ship's derrick, which also lowered all his bags and baggage. The surf-boats took him to a tender, which dumped him and his possessions on the Customs wharf. And even though he was a district officer, he was searched as if he were a smuggler instead of an importer of regulation kit and chop boxes, full of food for his eighteen-month tour of duty, all packed by the Army and Navy Stores for getting by in the bush. His prize and joy was his Lord's lamp, which indeed appeared to be a gift from the Almighty. Its kerosene flame on its four legs scared off everything from crocodiles to mosquitos like God hurling fire against Sodom and Gomorrah. And the sternwheeler up the Niger to his district was a journey through humid swamp and mangrove to a protracted hell. In a box slightly bigger than the mammy's chair, he sweated on the top deck, while an African village spread itself over the lower deck with chickens and goats and mounds of yams, floating to nowhere very much.

Life on his station in the three larger boxes of his bungalow was ruled by quinine and calling-cards. When his boy brought in his pink gin on a tray, a bottle of quinine stood by the glass. Not taking five grains a day was held to be a sort of suicide and worthy of a reprimand. Not sleeping under the drooping aisle of his mosquito net was self-mutilation. If malaria did not strike, blackwater fever would. The only thing that kept a man from falling victim to alcohol or infectious bites was the strict observance of convention. At every new station, Robert had to leave cards, even before he unpacked. No matter that the extent of his calls was a dozen bungalows much the same as his own and a ramshackle club, where one was likely to be knocked legless after an hour at the bar, but protocol demanded the dropping off of tiny pasteboards with one's name at every door where a European might be malingering. Two cards were the rule, if somebody had a wife, but wives were a rare commodity and severely discouraged. Few of the few wives survived more than a tour or two.

Patience Silvers was the special case, the matron in charge of the infirmary which bore the good name of the Lugard Hospital, the only one for a thousand miles around. She had survived seven tours and was reckoned to be a walking pharmacy. Scratch her skin, the story went, and anti-fever bark would come off. Her pale blue eyes were yellowed with medicines, her body thickened by endurance. Yet she was a handsome woman, and even if she was formidable, she could mock herself and drink among the men at the club as if she were one of them. Their forgetting of her sex was a compliment in her eyes.

Only Robert saw her differently. It began with her getting rid of the worms which afflicted all the men. The usual way of getting rid of the jiggers that came from flies was to wait until their tunnelling under the skin reached a hole and then to wind the tail of the parasite round a straw and slowly draw it out over the succeeding days. But Robert had an attack of sudden blindness in one eye, and he went to Patience Silvers and told her. And she said, "That's the *filaria* fly and you're very lucky, we can get rid of it." And she produced a needle, as if truly to blind him, but instead she took away with the point the tiny thing working its way across his eyeball. Her delicacy was extraordinary, her touch exquisite. Robert felt nothing but relief. And as he blinked and wept involuntarily, she said kindly, "You're not crying for the jigger, I hope."

"No," Robert said. "And thank you, Miss Silvers. I sure am happy you took him off."

They became friends at the club, and the other members noticed with disbelief a little lipstick on Patience when she knew she would meet him, even a hint of scent. Yet Robert was as they were, a confirmed bachelor during his job in the White Man's Grave, and hoping to survive enough tours to earn his pension. Both because he trusted the matron and wished to discourage her, he told her the story of his divorce.

"It isn't I hate Virginia," he said. "I just don't trust women. Not you, of course," he added. "But it was the accident, the shooting of my cousin's wife."

"You gave the verdict," Patience said. "An accident."

"Yes. I think it was."

"Weren't you being ... merciful?"

"Right, I guess." And here Robert made an admission that surprised even himself. "I had a carbine up above the *vlei* myself. I guess I must have thought ... an accident ... it might have been me."

"But it wasn't?"

"No. No for sure."

"Then you are a good man. And you do not want to admit it." Patience looked severely at Robert, as though to blame him for that quality. Then she suddenly broke into one of her rare smiles which illuminated her set face. "I like that you are better than you want to seem."

"Worse," Robert said. "You don't know me."

There was a nightmare he could never escape in his sleep. He would wake under his mosquito net in a pool of sweat, shuddering and shouting incoherently, knowing that he had done a crime, knowing that he would be judged for it, hanged for it. The nightmare was the truth, the waking was the dream. Everybody on the station knew the verdict. Living through each day was waiting for the just sentence to be carried out. He had fired at Hamish Charles, intending to kill him. His bullet had hit the Boer wife in the reeds by mistake. He was guilty of murder, and yet he was set in Nigeria to administer the law. The killer was the saviour, the condemned was the magistrate.

Only Patience knew – without knowing the cause – that Robert had lost the will to live and dragged through his days. This was an explanation of his recklessness in the riot. He wanted to go down for ever. When he heard that his fellow officer Sanderson was surrounded by the mob and was being beaten to death, he did not wait for his Ibo policemen, but ran to the compound without his pith helmet or his boots. He was carrying only his special hand-made truncheon in his hand, black leather hiding the lead weight at the end of the rattan cane with its wrist thong. Reports said that he beat the backs of the crowd, shouting, "Get out! Sinclair! It's Sinclair!" And the howling rioters parted for him. He charged through and found men beating Sanderson's head with stones. The brains of the man were spilling out of his smashed skull. Robert pointed his truncheon at random at five of the screaming attackers in their white robes. "You - you - you - you - you! You hang if this man dies!"

There was a sudden silence in the front of the crowd. At the back, the yells became muttering. The five men who had been singled out began to edge away, but the press behind them was too great for them to escape. They watched Robert kneel and rip off the shirt from his back. Then he rolled up the cotton into a rough bandage and wound it round Sanderson's head below the jaw and tied it in a tight knot. This held the brains in place and stopped Sanderson from moaning.

"Now - you five - lift him up! Just his body - I'll hold his head. And if you drop him, by God –" forgetting he had left his revolver behind – "I'll shoot you!"

And so the five chosen men picked up Sanderson's body between them and staggered through the crowd, carrying it, with Robert cradling the victim's head in its bloody bandage. And nobody held up a hand against the District Officer. Later, Robert never knew why. Was it fear of retribution? The myth of the invincible white man? A belief that he had some secret power that made him do such a foolhardy thing? He had never thought about it. He had done it. But Patience Silvers knew that he had done it because he did not care enough for his life not to risk that.

Incredibly, Sanderson lived. He broke every medical rule and survived. The five men did not hang, but were sent to labour gangs to build roads for twenty years. Patience would find a shape standing at the end of Sanderson's bed every midnight for two hours, keeping a silent vigil when the rest of the bungalow boys, as she called them, were drinking at the club.

"There's no need to do that, Robert," she said. "He can't talk, you know. We have to feed him through a straw. There may be damage to the brain. We don't know."

"If he sees me, he'll know I'm there. When he needs me."

"You were there when he needed you."

"He didn't know that. He was unconscious."

"And you, my dear, will be unconscious if you don't get some sleep. Don't you trust me to look after him?"

"I do trust you."

"Then go home. I'll call you when he needs you."

"What in hell is the point of going home? You've seen it. Nothing there but my camp kit. And bottles of gin."

"You need somebody to look after you, too."

"No takers."

"You might find a wild card."

"You play poker, Patience?"

"I do. And I play hard. Haven't the bungalow boys told you?"

"They don't know a darn thing about you."

"And you do? I order you, Robert – go to bed. Doctor's orders."

"I don't like sleeping. I get ... bad dreams."

"Take this." She put a bottle of dark brown fluid in his hand. "If this doesn't knock you out, Jack Johnson wouldn't."

"You know about boxing too. The first black heavyweight champion."

"It won't be the last. But it will be the last of you, my lad, if you don't go home and knock yourself out."

The brown drug was an uppercut, as Patience had promised, and Robert had his first straight and guiltless sleep in months. And as his head began to mend, so did Sanderson's. And three months later, Robert found himself giving a dinner party for three in his bungalow with a borrowed canteen of cutlery and the club's cook, who knew how to add game and tasteless river fish to the tins of bully beef and peas from home. For the patient's sake, drink was banned. It might go to his head.

"You can't be here," Patience said, raising her glass of lime juice. "But here's to you being here when you're an impossibility."

Sanderson raised his glass. His wounds still showed in black ridges through his cropped hair. He spoke slowly, but he made sense.

"Here's to ... being here ..."

"Hear, hear." Robert smiled. "Though being here isn't plumb the here where I'd go for being in."

"And thank you ... for –" Sanderson winced at some sudden pain – "saving ... my life ..."

"I didn't," Robert said. "She did."

"He did," Patience said. "He wrapped his shirt round your brains and held them in. You're still all there."

"Here." Sanderson smiled. "Anyway – thanks."

"I thank you," Robert said. "You did something for us." He smiled at Patience, and Sanderson noticed she was wearing a red ring, a ruby or a garnet. She had never worn one before. "I guess you brought us together."

"You knew ... Patience ... before."

"In a way."

"Not at all," Patience said. "I didn't know him. Now, he's quite a hero, you know."

"I am not," Robert said. "A damn fool."

"That, too."

"You're not," Robert said. "There's nobody like you in the whole world. Except my Aunt Mary –"

"Your old Aunt Mary, the one who died?" As Patience spoke almost dourly, Robert could see his error. She was older than him, it did not matter to him. Yet the comparison had made her think it did. "She was a matron, too."

Patience gave Robert a quick, thin smile. "Perhaps you love only people who can be an aunt to you?"

"No. You know that."

"Who can look after you."

Sanderson intervened.

"We all ... want ... to be looked after." He was pleased to manage four words in a row. "And by you – that is best."

Now Patience shocked them, for it was the last thing the men expected her to say.

"Can you conceive," she said, "that I might want to be looked after? All this time caring for others – and who cares for me?"

"I do," Robert said.

"How much?"

"Enough to marry you." Robert looked at Sanderson. "I want you to be the witness. Patience and I, we will marry."

"Congratu –" Sanderson had to draw breath. "Congratulations."

"They are premature," Patience said, "like a baby can be. We are not married yet."

"But we will be," Robert said.

"Not here," Patience said. "Perhaps on our next leave. It is true, you do need looking after." She turned towards Sanderson and showed him her red ring. "Ruby for the heart, ruby for remembrance. Robert got it off a Syrian trader. Probably illegal, but – he took a risk. He likes taking risks."

"No longer," Robert said. "Unless you want me to –"

"I don't," Patience said. "I want you here with me."

"I am ... his last risk," Sanderson said.

"We'll drink to that," Robert said. "Lime juice – dash of bitters."

So they drank to that, and Patience thought how vulnerable Robert was despite his hard good looks. She would have to run him to the top, for he would never make anything of himself. She was tired of running a bush hospital now, she was weary to death, all the sap dried out of her. But running a man in his career, catering for his comfort and her own, that would be a challenge. She doubted if they would have children, she had only a couple of years when that might be possible. But he would be her child, and he would think himself the man about the house, as men always did, when a woman arranged it.

Peg also thought of marrying. Her wish was out of focus, no particular man to marry. She wanted to have a child. Her blood stirred her, her womb gripped her. In the nights, a fist clenched inside her that doubled her up and demanded a baby to be born to her. Yet all the suitors seemed impossible, mostly other doctors and an occasional civil servant, men withered with duty or plump with self-satisfaction. But there was Shilendra Menon, who had distinction and had even studied at Cambridge University. He was too small and too plausible, but he was gentle and persistent. And there was a glance and a gleam in his eyes that made his courtship appear more as a need than an arrangement.

"Peg, you must give up," he was saying to her. "You hold out longer than the Statue of Liberty. You have not seen that. I have, I tell you. And her torch – it only has the electric light in. You, you need flesh and blood in you."

Peg considered the smiling, little man in his white suit. He could have been at a first communion, which she had once seen in England.

"Shilendra, I would accept you – but you are too good to be true. You have a good family, you have money. You are in the government of our India. You are a Brahmin – even your caste is right. How can I refuse you?"

"Indeed."

Shilendra's eyes glittered at the prospect of this improbable denial.

"But that is why I do refuse you." Now Peg laughed at him. "Can't you understand? I am a doctor. I deal with bodies breaking down. Nobody is perfect. You come to me, perfect Shilendra. All I know is the imperfect. Human people, full of flaws. So how can I refuse you, Shilendra? I hate the perfect. I want life – raw and beastly. Like that Darwin says, nature red in tooth and claw."

"A tiger hunt," Shilendra said, "Perhaps that is more your style."

"Oh, come on, Shilendra – I am not being totally serious!"

Shilendra laughed now, but he was watching her too closely, almost cruelly.

"You like to tease. You learn that in England. When I was there, the ladies did tease me. I learned to call it amusing – fun – but –" Shilendra paused and looked for his words. "Pride, it hurt me. There can be insult to a man, you know."

"You would not want me to think you perfect?" Now Peg was smiling at Shilendra. "The perfect husband. What every Indian male person wants his wife to believe that he is. You know, drink my bathwater when I am away."

Shilendra shook his head. His mouth was a purse drawn tight.

"No," he lied. "Not that."

"You want it."

Shilendra broke out of his embarrassment. His smile would have won over the world, but perhaps not Peg.

"That is why I come to you. A woman, educated in England. A woman who know who she is. A woman who is a doctor. A woman to share my life."

"You don't mean it."

"I do."

"You do not. Even my brother Seaforth –"

"Ah, the famous doctor. The radical. The man who want our independence now –"

"My brother Seaforth is married to a white woman from South Africa. She is very independent – more of a radical than he is. Yet, he thinks she should stay at home with the children. But then, even my darling brother is an Indian man."

"*Achta*," Shilendra said. "You do not make it easy for a man who loves you."

Peg fixed him with the intense search of her eyes.

"Would you let me go on being a doctor? Swear it."

Shilendra looked directly back at her with his arrogance and his need to believe what he was saying.

"I swear it."

"And a child. I want a child. Or it may be too late."

"A son. I want a son."

"A daughter. A child."

"Yes. A child."

"And you will always stay. Always stay with that child?"

"Yes."

"Swear it?"

"I swear it."

The stares at each other had never wavered. Now both looked down at their own ground at the same time. Finally Shilendra looked up.

"So you say yes, Peg."

Now Peg looked past him, almost shyly.

"I did not say that."

"But I may hope."

"Next Wednesday," Peg said. "You visit at the same time next Wednesday." And she took his arm and almost pushed him out of the door. But as he left, she brushed her hand against his cheek. And then she was ashamed of herself. He might think she was encouraging him.

19

MEAT CLEAVER

Perhaps because she was the daughter of a Member of Parliament, Ruth Seymour-Scudabright was not the hatchet woman. Yet she took the meat cleaver into the National Gallery in a carpet-bag. Something about her look of innocence stopped the guards from searching her. They did investigate the handbag of the real avenger, who was to take the axe to male lust and the degradation of women. But they found nothing – no orders from the militant suffragettes, no Pankhurst proclamation to destroy the art treasures of the nation. So Mary Richardson passed through to her rendezvous under the *Madonna of the Rocks*, so remote from the concerns of modern women. There Marie was waiting with Ruth and the weapon, rolled up like Cleopatra in its rug covering, to be revealed for a different effect.

"Ruth and I will be at either end of the gallery," she said softly. "We will give you the go-ahead. Then you are on your own."

"Yes," Mary said. She took the carpet-bag. "They are now destroying the most beautiful woman in history in gaol. The Cat-and-Mouse Act of that horrible man Asquith. Bringing Sylvia Pankhurst in and out of Holloway Gaol at the government's beck and call, just because of a false bomb charge."

"Well," Ruth said, "we did blow up Lloyd George's villa. It quite spoilt his golf. And there was that arson at Kew, which did not help the gardens."

"There is something else I can spoil," Mary Richardson said.

Watching from the door of the gallery where the Rokeby Venus was hanging, Marie felt a vicious excitement. Perhaps it was the Crow Indian blood in her, the thrill of anticipation before the charge. Yet there the picture was, the naked woman admiring herself in a mirror, the inverted vanity of her sex that allowed the domination of men. And the painter was a man, a genius they said, but still a man, who lingered over female flesh like a voluptuary, enjoying the self-satisfaction of a beauty in her own form. Now it would be violated, chopped open. And not violated by a man, but a woman with a chopper, fighting for the rights of women with a butcher's blade. Even the languid Asquith would take note of that. But Marie had to take note of where the guards were as well as the spectators. She looked to the next gallery. Only two dawdlers were nodding over a masterpiece.

She flicked her hand towards Ruth at the far entrance. Ruth waved her hand back. "Now!" Marie called. Standing in front of the naked lying Venus, Mary Richardson put a hand into her carpet-bag and came out holding the meat cleaver. She dropped the bag and set about the canvas, stroke after stroke. Cut breast, cut waist, cut thigh, cut and cut and cut again at slavery and lechery, hack at the male use of female self-abuse. See, the canvas curls back like skin from open wounds. Venus is dead.

The noise of the blows of the chopper hitting the gallery wall alerted the guards. Men in blue uniforms ran past Marie and Ruth at the entrances and rushed towards the suffragette with the axe. Mary Richardson had only time for one more blow at the revealing mirror on the painting, when she was dragged down to the ground by three men. Marie's blood boiled to help her sister in distress, but she had her orders. She and Ruth must get away to report the reasons for the attack, which would be called an outrage when it was a legitimate protest. The truth must out.

"Don't you think you were going a mite too far," Bill Dunesk said to his wife. "It is a dreadful picture, all that expanse of too, too solid flesh. But to take a chopper to Venus. Couldn't you have used a cut-throat razor?"

"It wouldn't make the same point," Marie said.

"It rather reminded me of that surgical husband of your favourite Aunt Mary, Harry Lamb, who was meant to be Jack the Ripper. Only it was a woman doing the disembowelling this time. And it might have been you."

"It was not me," Marie said. "Anyway, how do you know it had anything to do with me?"

"It always does, Marie, these days. But thank you for keeping my name out of it. It would not have done."

"I was the cover," Marie said. "I managed to get Ruth away with me. Who would believe the Countess of Dunesk had anything to do with a lunatic lady with a meat cleaver?"

"Respectability is the best disguise," Bill Dunesk smiled. "I always use it myself."

"Oh yes," Marie said. "Congratulations. You and the government over the Marconi share scandal. Cleared at the libel trial. Not a stain on your character."

"But a few thousand pounds more in our pockets. Money, my dear, is such a messy business. I wish I had more of it so I could ignore it."

"I wish you would spend it on your miners and your pits. They're still a disgrace."

"The disgrace is what you do with them. And him, their leader, Keir McBride. I do know, my dear. I do keep my ear to the ground."

"You should keep it down the mine."

"*Touché.* But I would point out that all your radical activities are financed by my money – immoral earnings though they may be."

Marie could not answer that, for it was too hurting and too true. She must counter-attack.

"But I turn a blind eye on your artistic activities. With Douglas and your friends."

Her husband shook his head and smiled again, looking down.

"Blackmail," he said. "I never thought you would stoop to that."

"I would never betray you. You know that."

"Yes, I do. But reminding me – pointing out the truth – that is a personal betrayal."

"You point that out to me."

"True. But that is why we will not divorce. My finance for your discretion."

"And for the sake of Rosabelle."

"Her, too. She is simply the most divinely beautiful creature in London." Bill Dunesk rose from this rare visit to his wife, and, as usual, his gallantry got the better of him. He bent and kissed Marie's head. "Except for her mother, of course, who is even more divinely beautiful."

"If I could believe a word you said –"

"The trouble is," Bill Dunesk spoke as he left the door, "that you always do."

Discretion did not stop Marie's activities for her cause. Soon she found herself advancing on Downing Street with unlikely allies from her own family. For reasons of boredom and snobbery, since so many duchesses and countesses had now joined the suffragettes including Marie, Ellen-Maeve had thrown her caution aside to aid her social progress in London. And Virginia, newly arrived from Polynesia to set up her art business, had also swelled the ranks of the marching women, although she was rather more credible in her beliefs. Marie took to her cool ambivalence, while Ruth was bowled over by her flaunted independence. So the four Sinclair women marched on the home of the Prime Minister, escorting the released Sylvia Pankhurst as an honour guard. She was frail and emaciated after her forced feeding.

She had to be released or she would have starved to death. For Asquith and the opponents of votes for women could not stand another martyr after the sacrifice of the suffragette who had died under the hoofs of the new King's horse on Derby Day. Better an on-and-off imprisonment of the militant leaders than a dead heroine to inspire more rebels against the rule of men.

The police were waiting for them, blocking off the dead end into the hidden corridors of power. Their charge into the double line of bluebottles was a foredoomed affair. Hack and kick and scratch as they could, knock off a helmet and pull a copper's hair, the women were hustled off to the police-waggons or were routed down the Mall. Ruth broke through and reached the black iron railings. There she handcuffed herself to the metal uprights before the police could handcuff her. They broke her poster – DON'T FEED SYLVIA – GELD THE LIBERAL CAT – but it took three hours and two blacksmiths to cut her loose and take her to gaol, where Sylvia Pankhurst had also been returned for breaking the conditions of her brief parole.

The worst of the ordeal for Ruth was a visit she could not avoid from her outraged father – the furious Tory Member of Parliament had had his name dragged through the mud and Fleet Street. Any more jokes in the Members' Tea Room of the Commons –"I say, I say, I say, who's got a daughter behind bars today?"– and he would have had apoplexy as well as having to forget preferment. He raged at Ruth across the table in the visiting room at Holloway, the wardress behind her scarcely able to contain her sniggering.

"You damned peahen!" Charles Seymour-Scudabright shouted. "How dare you?"

Ruth had meant to reply, "Very easily," but she found herself hanging her head and saying meekly, "I really am sorry." This was hardly what she had meant to say. But that is what a father's anger did.

"You have ruined my career. I shall lose my seat – what will I say to the Association in my constituency? Did you think of that?"

"No."

"Of course, you didn't. You don't think of me. Only of yourself. I suppose you are under an evil influence. That is the only possible explanation. If you would say so to the authorities – how Marie Dunesk or Sylvia Pankhurst have misled you. If you would testify –"

So that was it. The law of betrayal. Sneak and escape scot-free. Exactly the same at school, but then her father had never grown up from his old school disloyalties. Ruth found her nerve again.

"What I do is entirely my own fault," she said. "You have always told me to be responsible."

"Not when you are led astray."

"I believe in what I do."

"Handcuffing yourself to the railings before Ten Downing Street—"

"It showed how I felt."

"Do you realize, Ruth, you are a traitor to your country?"

"I am trying to save it."

"Don't you answer back, my girl. We are going to be at war with the Kaiser soon. All that fleet he is building, as though the seas weren't ours as they always have been. We have had to bring back the Home Fleet from the Mediterranean. And even I had to cross the House to vote for that pipsqueak Winston Churchill's navy budget – forty-five million pounds for four more dreadnoughts, eight cruisers, twenty destroyers and some of those new-fangled submarines I don't hold with. Though I must say, the Prince of Wales went on one and it didn't sink him. But you are sinking us, you and your bloody women friends. You are trying to sink the whole country. Thank God you are not representative of your sex. Your mother says she will have nothing to do with you."

"Send her my love," Ruth said sweetly.

"She doesn't want it. And she told me, on no account to appeal on your behalf, to engage my lawyers –"

"You are too mean for that. And merciless."

"What!" Still more blood pumped into Seymour-Scudabright's purple face. "I who have reared you, paid for you, I who have forgiven you outrage after outrage –"

"I would not be grateful to any man now," Ruth said. "Even to you, father."

"Well, I do not mean to do anything for you anyway."

"Then you will not."

"You will serve your full sentence, as you deserve."

"Oh, I shall go on hunger strike. Then they will force-feed me and Sylvia again and let us out under the Cat-and-Mouse Act on our good behaviour. And then we won't behave. And then we will be here again."

"You revel in your infamy! And you bear my name!"

"I did not choose to." Ruth smiled at her choleric father, who did seem on the point of breaking a brace of blood-vessels. "You gave me my name."

"I wish I had not. You are not my daughter!"

"But I am. You told me so. If I am not –"

"You are not."

"Why did you sign my birth certificate, if my mother is a whore?"

This was the first time Ruth had succeeded in rendering her father speechless. He rose on the other side of the table and raised a fist to strike her. Then he gasped and straightened up, breathing heavily. Then he glared at her and walked out of the visiting room, never looking back.

Ruth also rose and slouched back towards her cell and managed a smile at the wardress with the words, "Happy families."

Above them at Brooklands, the Blériot monoplane was doing the impossible. The Sinclair cousins had talked to the French pilot before, and he swore that he would loop the loop, a somersault in air. He had boasted that flying upside down was as easy as sitting at home in an armchair. There was no rush of blood to the head, merely *élan* and *esprit*, those wonderful words the French used to excuse their daring. And he rolled his aeroplane over in a circle as easily as a child spins a hoop.

"That's something," Murdo said to Hamilton. "We can't do it in your Short Folderwing."

"Ah, but you can fly from ships, Murdo. And that fancy Blériot with all its tricks, it can only go one way. Even if it takes off on a platform slung between the big guns of a battleship, it will have to ditch in the sea at the end of its mission. I'd rather get back than do cartwheels in space."

As they started to leave the air display and return to the Short works at Rochester, a gentleman in a white suit was waiting to meet them. He introduced himself to them as if he had known them all their lives.

"You must be Hamilton Sinclair," he said. "And you, Murdo Sinclair, the test pilot. Your relation Virginia, she described you to me so accurately that I felt I was meeting old acquaintances who should never be forgot, as your 'Auld Lang Syne' says. Maurice Walter, at your service."

"You know Virginia?" Hamilton said.

"I had the fortune to be on a ship with her from India. She told me so many interesting things, particularly about your seaplane with the folding wings. A stroke of genius, and —" He smiled at Hamilton — "your genius, I believe."

"I did have the idea," Hamilton said. "You say you are at our service. But what service may we do for you?"

"No," Walter said. "I insist I am at your service. I believe that your company is a commercial enterprise."

"It is, indeed. Although the Navy is buying some of our seaplanes."

"Then I shall be your second navy. I wish to buy some of your seaplanes."

"That's good," Murdo said. "Good for business."

"And good for who?" Hamilton asked. "Who would they go to?"

"Those who wanted them. Please —" Walter extended a flat platinum case towards the two Sinclairs. It snapped open to reveal slim black cheroots packed as tidily as bullets in a magazine. "Would you join me in a smoke? No?" He took out a cheroot himself and lit it from a Lucifer match. "You will excuse me. It is my only vice." He drew on his smoke. "I should say, my only obvious vice."

"You deal in armaments?" Hamilton said.

"Exactly."

"It must be profitable. All the great powers arming for the war to come."

"And the little powers. The thing about the arms race is everybody has to catch up."

"Ireland," Murdo said, thinking of a letter he had just had from his sister Arabella, married to the Irish estate of Alex Plunkett-Drax. "You don't dabble in Ireland?"

"I do, naturally. An admirable situation." Walter blew a white puff that hung briefly in the air. "Ulster needs rifles and machine-guns for its volunteers. They will not tolerate Home Rule from Dublin. And the Irish also court independence for their island, so they also want rifles and machine-guns. There is prospect of civil war — and most uncivil it will be. But for me, it is an opportunity. And most civil the Irish are, north and south, to give the opportunity to me to supply their needs."

"You don't care where you sell?" Murdo was shocked. "What if our own weapons are used against us?"

"I am a businessman," Walter said. "I am not a moralist. I leave that to your bishops who will say it is a just war, when you go to war against Germany, as you soon will. But then, the German bishops, they will say exactly the same. Do two just wars make for peace?"

"We may go to war." Hamilton considered Walter. "You know, Jerry has Zeppelins. We are afraid they may bomb London and our fleet."

"I would supply you with the plans for the Zeppelin," Walter said, "if you would sell me six of your seaplanes with the folding wings. I hear one of the models can even carry a torpedo."

"We hope for that. But tell me, Mr Walter, would you sell our seaplanes to the Germans?"

"The highest bidder is always my best client. And –" Walter smiled at his own statement – "I always pay the highest price for the best."

"I am not sure that the Short brothers would accept your offer. If we did not know where the seaplanes are going."

"Money talks, as you say. And its message is this. If I buy your seaplane, you will have more money to develop the next model. The aeroplane which carries the torpedo. Money talks, don't you think?"

"You are very persuasive," Hamilton said. "But I am not sure if I like –"

"I did not ask you to like," Walter said. "I ask you to accept a large sum of money. Of course there will be a commission for you two gentlemen in it. Shall we say, five per cent?"

"We do not do business that way here," Hamilton said rather stiffly.

"Pity. It makes things so much easier. Wheels are made to be greased. I hope your other cousin, what is his name? A Canadian, I think Gillon. I hope he will be more amenable."

"He's working on the new Marconi telegraph system. Across the Empire. You're not seeing him too?"

"Virginia has been most lavish with her introductions. Would you say, Mr Sinclair, that communications – in the air and in the air waves –will win the next war and the wars to come?"

"Yes," Hamilton said. "The next war and the wars to come."

"It will take millions of troops on the ground," Murdo said. "These are early days."

"But the early bird, as you say," Walter said, "does he not catch the worm? You are not at war, Mr Sinclair. You are a commercial company. You are obliged to sell your early products to a fair bidder, who is not at war with your country. If I wish for your seaplanes or for your telegraph systems – and Marconi is so commercial a company that it can buy and sell governments, including your own, apparently – you will sell them to me. And I will resell them where they are most prized."

"In Ireland, I suppose," Murdo said. "I have just heard from my sister. You are right. There will be a civil war there. And you may be arming both sides. And you don't care."

"I care like God for each single sparrow," Walter said. "Each human life is as precious to me as a diamond ring is to a *fiancée*. I only supply the weapons. And some men are stupid enough to use them.

That is not my affair. For I do not pull the trigger. I do not drop the bomb."

Then Hamilton remembered that he had heard of Maurice Walter before. Cousin Margaret had told him of the arms dealer's affair with Virginia on the liner from India and what Intelligence knew on him.

"We may be commercial, Mr Walter," he said, "but we do draw the line. And that line is between you and the Shorts. The seaplanes are not for sale."

"Have you told that to your chairman? And to your shareholders?"

"They will follow my recommendation."

"Pity." Walter dropped the stub of his cheroot onto the tarmac at Brooklands and ground out the spark with the sole of his black patent leather boot. "I will have your seaplanes, Mr Sinclair. But by other means."

They were only wearing cloth shooting caps and jerseys and riding britches and boots, but they were an army, no doubt of it. And they were a hundred thousand men, all against Home Rule and dedicated to keeping northern Ireland free for Protestants to rule, as God had decreed since the Battle of the Boyne. As an ex-officer, Alexander Plunkett-Drax was high in the chain of command under Sir George Richardson in the Ulster Volunteer Force. It was he who had brought in the smuggled shipment of five thousand .303 Mark 3 Lee-Enfield rifles with a million smokeless cordite cartridges and six Vickers machine-guns. With this firepower, they could put paid to any Catholic plot to make the Pope reign in Belfast, where Old Red Socks would certainly be murdered if he tried to say a Mass there.

He had also been the bagman who had carried two hundred thousand pounds in used Bank of England notes to the depository in advance. Yet how could an obscure cousin of his wife Arabella have been an intermediary? He had never had anything from Arabella's family, which seemed to dislike him. The women were radical, the men so stiff they might have been wearing corsets. But Gillon, fresh arrived from Canada on his Marconi training course, was desperate for money to buy a house for his wife and three children, Leah and Fiona and Colin. The mysterious Maurice Walter had found an ally in him and a go-between. So Alexander went to London with the price for the weapons plus another thousand pounds for Gillon himself.

"I am a good Protestant, I guess," Gillon said as he counted the white five-pound notes which Alexander gave to him. "Otherwise, I couldn't take the cash. I'm for your cause all the way."

"When money and morals mix," Alexander said, "it is very convenient. Where is Mr Walter?"

"In the next room, buddy."

And so Mr Walter was, waiting for his price. He did not even count the notes in the two suitcases. "If they are short," he said, "you will have short guns."

"How do we know we can trust you?" Alexander asked.

"You must. Necessity means belief."

"You have a bad reputation."

"Except in delivering the goods I am paid for."

"You do that." Alexander looked at the arms dealer, so imperturbable in his white suit, even with a fortune in his grip. "Tell me, how do you get modern British Army supplies?"

"A trade secret."

"I suppose British civil servants in the War Ministry are underpaid."

"That helps."

"You have thought you will be depriving our army of these weapons, if they are suddenly called upon to fight?"

"More will be manufactured. It is good for trade."

"If you do not deliver," Alexander said in a flat voice, "we will kill you, you know."

"That is normally said, Captain Plunkett-Drax. But it is unnecessary. I always deliver. I value my life."

"But not the lives of those killed by your guns."

"Naturally not. My own life is the one I care about. Other lives are the concern of others, who value their own."

"How did you get to my wife's cousin? The Marconi man."

"We are expected," Walter said, "by a beautiful lady, who is also related to you. Virginia Sinclair, who has married two of your wife's cousins – although not at the same time."

At Virginia's house, Alexander Plunkett-Drax was astounded at the decorations. He had never seen the like – weird coloured squares and oblongs called Cubism from Paris, devil-masks and tribal gods from the South Seas and Africa, crude oil paintings of native women or peasant life or French landscapes. He bridled his scorn, knowing that it might appear to be ignorance. For he found Virginia fascinating, and the way she looked at him with frank appraisal was a signal of a future meeting of bodies, if not minds. She was older than him, but she had the lean grace of a whippet. Only Maurice Walter seemed to dislike the mutual attraction between the two of them. Was it possible that the serene and assured merchant of weapons would be jealous? Well, if that was the case, Alexander Plunkett-Drax would give him cause. Only he would have to be careful, for once in his life. He had threatened to have Walter killed if he did not deliver the weapons to Ulster. But Walter was equally capable of having him killed. He was sure of it.

"I hope you will both remain very happy." Alexander Plunkett-Drax raised his glass of pink champagne in a toast to Virginia and her lover. "I am sure you will. Unless there *is* a great war. But that will only mean more business for you, Mr Walter. And, I should think, your absence from London."

The skies over the Summer Isles spoke of conflict. They were a madness of changing light. No day was ever the same for an hour, no pattern in the sky or on the water. They had a fitful beauty in glower or in shine. In her retirement from Canada, Kate McDowell could not count on heaven, wayward and dangerous as it was. The clouds might graze like sheep in a blue meadow, then a high wind would shear their rumps and the bright fields above would grow dark. Then the falling of the day would put armoured scales on the sky and sea, leaving the isles as black dreadnoughts, striped in camouflage by the broken and bright ribs of their superstructures. And when the sun slouched in its long setting below the horizon, red and orange flakes spilled onto the water from the bleeding of the last light. Night killed the day so slowly that it made the evening retreat insidiously, not with the sudden ambush of the tropics. Even then, the spume of the waves made bright wounds on the stricken Atlantic loch. With the bad news from Europe in her ears, Kate saw a battlefield where there had been a peace on earth.

"Ach, the war will not come," she told her husband Bob, slumped and heavy in his armchair before the peat fire that smouldered daily in the hearth, for he always felt the chill in every season now. "It will not come," she insisted, trying to convince herself against her fears. "Folks canna be so daft."

"Because you say so?" Bob was rarely ironical. "People are crazy. Now that they have killed that prince in Sarajevo."

"What's that to do with us?"

"Nothing. But people fight for nothing. It is the armaments. Men never pile up weapons unless to use them."

She and her husband in their decline were sitting in their converted crofts at Achiltibuie opposite the Western Isles. Kate had wanted to return to her Scots homeland from Vancouver for her dying, and there was Fraser land near where she remembered as a child her melancholy leaving for Canada on the ship that foundered. Two adjoining crofts had been converted into one cottage home for them, but all around stood the ruins of other abandoned crofts like Pictish barrow graves, the wrecked stones of a lost race. And their invaders and destroyers, the Cheviot sheep, cropped the land barren up to their walls. Bleat – bleat – bleat like the hiccups of a slow-firing gun, this was their requiem to the folk who had gone before.

"Now Angus is gone," Kate said, "I am the last, you know, of the sons and daughters of Hamish and Hannah Sinclair, who left this land so near to here."

"Enough children," Bob McDowell said, "there are enough children from all your dead brothers and sisters to people this Scotland all over again. Breed like rabbits, you do."

"I only have Marie, and she Rosabelle. I wish she would spend more time with her girl, instead of leaving her to her father. But she will have her votes for women."

"I am grateful to the father," Bob said. "For he gave us this house."

"He could well afford it." Kate rose stiffly from her chair. Her old bones ached. "I will prepare the pheasant, for it is the first that I have ever eaten. When I was a bairn, we couldna eat a pheasant. It was the laird's. You were hangit for the taking of it, or sent to Australia."

"There's laws to save the crofters now."

"Ach, too late for us."

Kate hobbled into the kitchen. She had plucked the bird that morning. She picked up a sharp knife with its bone handle in her right hand and held the claws of the fowl in her left. She would do as she was told. A pheasant was no chicken. She must take out the croup, or it would poison her. She slit the cold puckered skin of the bird below the neck and put down the knife and scooped out a small pale dumpling with her fingers. Now the innards, that was the next thing to do. And she plunged her hand into the stomach of the pheasant, feeling for the heart and the lights to pull out. And on the sudden, she thought of the chill of death on her father's cheek, when she had kissed it at his laying-out before his burial. And she thought of the drawing down of her days and those of her husband, that they might not last until the coming of the great war, which would as surely come as the conflict of the sea and sky each night over the Summer Isles.

20

POT SHOT

He went out for the flight.

The pigeon came in at dusk. Waiting under the oak and ash canopy, Bill Fraser, the Earl of Dunesk, could hear the whisper of the woods. As in a protest against the fading of the day, the trees were murmuring. The rustle of the branches, the twitches of the twigs, the flutter of the leaves were answering the little breeze. Even the early birds were not asleep. From the chaffinches and the robins, a cheep or three were staccato against the long stroked strings of the evening. Like a naughty child, the copse would not settle down in its green cot. Bill almost thought that the noises were scaring off his game.

Then the squadron swooped down in a swish of wings. From his sentry's post, Bill could swing the wood butt of his shotgun beside his cheek and onto his shoulder, and point the double metal barrel at the grey smudges diving low. Sweet the pull on the trigger, a blast as a loud sigh, a swerve on an arc to the next bird checked and rising, another huff and puff of cordite, and the smack of feathers falling. That was that for the night. The flight would seek another base. Without his dogs, he would have to find his own prey. Only two in the bag, but worth it for that slow standing in the spinney at the dying of the light.

Walking back past Dunesk Castle over the meadows, Bill had to pass the moat under the pink granite walls. Dry now, the big ditch would hardly keep out the invading English, if they bothered to come. In fact, the Germans now were supposed to be intruding. They were the jokers to be kept off the premises. He and Marie, when she was there, no longer lived in the ancestral keep with its rounded turrets and single bathroom, but at the nearby manor house of Ermondhaugh, where they could entertain house parties in something approaching comfort. Although, as far as Bill was concerned, guests were usually more trouble than they were worth.

He came in by the back door. On the hooks in the passage hung the coats and the scarves and the tweeds. On the racks, the heavy boots stood to attention in their rows on the racks. He sat on the elephant stool some uncle had brought back from the Ashanti wars, and he unlaced his brogues. His velvet slippers had been laid out by Arthur, and when Bill walked past the larder into the great kitchen with its iron range as large as a ship's engine, he saw his valet spitting into a champagne glass. What might have been the beginning of a class war was merely a case of rinse and shine. Arthur began rubbing the thin surface with a leather duster, then held it in front of him, where it sparkled even in the wan gleam of the new electric bulbs.

"Spit and polish," Bill said, "are for boots." He put the brace of pigeon on the deal table almost as long as a cricket pitch. "Nobody knows what's in your spit."

As he spoke, Bill was sorry for what he was saying. The dogs licked everybody here right in the face. Nobody could say Arthur's saliva was worse.

"Sugar and spice and all that's nice," Arthur said. "And brilliantine. Look at those then."

Eleven more fluted glasses glittered on a silver tray. Arthur always seemed to have an answer and a special ingredient for everything.

"As long as the guests don't know," Bill said. "Tell the cook Martha to pluck and hang these." He prodded one of the dead birds in its plump breast, reddened by shot. "I'll bag some more tomorrow. Has everyone arrived? I hope we're not thirteen for dinner."

"I think as they's all here. Marm says you've got to step on it, sir."

"Not in those words, quite."

"Your dress suit's all laid out on the bed. And the tub's boiling hot. Like a stewpot."

"Oh, dear. Cannibals now, are we?"

Bill almost scuttled up the broad and carved wooden staircase. He did not care so much about the bad luck of passing somebody on the way up, but he could not stand the bore of showing concern about a relative stranger's welcome before the first drink of the evening. He hated having people to stay, but that was the form. They almost put him out of his own home. And certainly his temper.

Ill fortune frowned on him. He met an upright weasel on the stairs. Bill knew the type with their hair slick against their tall skulls and their mouths too wide and thin, so that a forked tongue could slither out. They were always civil servants.

"Hello," Bill said. "You must be –"

"The gamekeeper," the vermin replied.

"You don't look like a gamekeeper. And you're not one of mine."

"You do," was the answer. "Dressed like that." Bill remembered his baggy plus-fours and weathered jacket. But dammit, even poachers didn't wear velvet slippers. "You wouldn't happen to be mine host?"

"I am. And who might you be?"

"Ernest Overman. Marie asked me down."

Another of her friends from Whitehall. All those charity balls, and those *salon* politics, all that billiards game of influence and powers to be. Bill had no time for his wife's London intrigues. On his estate, he measured out his life in cartridges and bottles and a few male friends, not in chitchat and backbite.

"Pleased to meet you," Bill mumbled, almost shouldering Overman aside. "Got to run. Have a bath." He lumbered onto the landing, knowing he should have said more, knowing he would be reproached when he was reported to Marie. Graciousness, as she often pointed out, was hardly in his game book.

The tub had cooled enough for him not to boil alive in it. He couldn't see the point of very hot baths. They added to the sweat instead of taking it off. You got out perspiring and put puddles on your white shirt. Bill liked his water tepid, so that he could emerge relaxed, not overdone.

Arthur had laid out Bill's evening dress on the four-poster bed, where he usually slept alone except on the Friday nights when Marie might let him in. The black-and-white attire looked like a tailor's cut-out of a suit which wasn't there yet. Clothes might make a man, and manners did, but clothes without a man were rags and illusions. If they were not worn, they only fitted scarecrows.

As he was putting the last pearl stud in his starched shirt front, Bill heard a soft knock on the door. Marie always pretended that she hardly dared to intrude, though she would glide in unannounced when she felt like it. "Enter," Bill said, knowing that he could not put her off. And in she came, two pendants of white lace, one balancing on the other at her gold belt. Still only twenty-two inches within her stays, she defied time and the law of gravity. Her magnificent breasts did not topple to her knees. She had never had her two Adam's ribs removed, just to keep so little around the middle. And she had provided her husband with a daughter, before she became a martyr to her waist.

"You must come down to dinner, Bill. You simply cannot keep us waiting."

"I'm coming, my dear, coming." Why wouldn't that stud go in? Was he getting senile? Or arthritic?

"And do powder your nose. Your veins are showing." She reached in her beaded bag. "And go easy on the gout. You don't want to have an attack of port, do you?"

Marie had little sense of humour, but when she got her words in the wrong place, she was called a wit. She made people laugh unintentionally, but that was better than not making people laugh at all.

Bill coughed as his wife's powderpuff sent some white dust down his throat.

"That's enough," he managed to wheeze. "I'd rather blaze away from my *nez* than choke."

"Bill, my dear, don't worry. You are a beacon to us all, when we are on the rocks. Without the guiding light of your nose, we'd all be sunk. But *do* come down to dinner. Not that you would be particularly missed, but it would be polite."

"How's Martha, incidentally?"

"Oh, the kitchen's tolerable, but not too clean."

"I don't know if servants are the problem, Marie. Sometimes it's the masters, too. In spite of all your worker friends."

"You're so feeble, Bill. You can't even deal with your revolting miners who deserve much more from you. But dinner! Descend. I am."

Marie cruised from the room. No feet seemed to move under her long skirt, only an even keel. Her hair was ruddy smoke, her train a foamy wake. As Bill watched her leave, his stud popped out again. He sometimes wondered why he had to marry a woman. A motor car might have been a better choice. She said that of him, too. His new love was the new machines, but as for feeling for his wife, that emotion had long been in the gear box.

Five minutes later, Bill stepped into the drawing-room. The guests were assembled in front of the oak bookcases, where the volumes were ranged in their spines of darkling gold and green and red leather. They gathered dust on their tops but it did not rise, for few books were ever removed. The shelves were for viewing, not for perusing. The inheritance of four hundred years was not a library, but an antiquity which needed excavation rather than reading. And nobody in the house had the time to bother with that.

As far as Bill could see, nobody in the house was up to much. There were the usual suspects, who would go anywhere for a free week-end. There were Samuel and Mary Bindon, something in the City, which meant nothing elsewhere. There was Sir Tristram Ozone, rather pink and indeterminate, said to have been a friend of the late king, when he was Prince of Wales. Asked as his partner was Candida Hautemain, whose existence on the fringes of society meant she often snagged her appearances. There was the Embassy Man Carthew, who was on every ambassador's guest list because he courted the protocol secretaries, and hardly had any other invitations. Lady Amanda Heliotrope was there in her jacket and split skirt and monocle; the two Wetherby Janes, who were as inescapable as winter; the Mowbray Moultons with their tiresome talk of pedigree in fish and fur, horse and human; his cousin

Laetitia, separated from her husband because divorce was unthinkable, but said to be expecting; and the abominable Ernest Overman, the stoat from the stairs and the government.

"Everybody fixed up?" Bill announced himself with a question, although he knew the answer. Stilton would have given the guests the drink they wanted. He turned to the tall and stooping figure of his butler, who looked like an elongated query himself. "The usual, please." Bill liked the usual. Whisky and soda. Champagne got in his nostrils, gin and it was for colonials, while sherry was for clergymen and aunts.

"Out hunting?" the male Mowbray Moulton said. "Any luck?"

"Sport can wait," Marie intervened. "We were talking about dissection."

"Selection," Overman said. "Natural selection, actually. Though if you dissect it, people do divide into the fit and the unfit, the superior and the inferior, races and classes."

"The better and the worse."

"Gentlemen and players."

"Eton and Harrow."

"Odds and sods."

"Speak for yourself," Lady Heliotrope told Sir Tristram Ozone.

In the chatter about the categories of humanity, Bill slouched back on the sofa, displacing Badger, actually a King Charles's spaniel, ending his days in comfort on the couch. All this fashionable talk of breeds, Bill thought, was fine for dogs, but he didn't know really if it worked for humanity. He scratched the knob of bone beneath the skin and between the ears of his hound, too aged to hunt.

"Less fit every year, old chap," he whispered. "I hope they let us toddle on a bit."

When Stilton came in with a tumbler of whisky, he also announced that dinner was served. Without so much as a sip, Bill had to march to his fate by *placement*. Which of the harpies had Marie set him between? It was worse than the tumbrils going to the guillotine, with the knitting women commenting on when his head would fall into the bloody basket.

He was flanked by Cousin Laetitia, which wasn't so bad, and Candida Hautemain, which was. Luckily, there was so much silver and china stacked on the linen cloth that the spacing between the seats was quite an abyss, and Bill at the head of the table felt as if he'd been sent to sit in the corner. The point was that the two women said to sit beside him could talk across the candles to each other. And they did, praising their hostess and ignoring their host.

"You never know she'd had a daughter," Candida said.

"No, you wouldn't," Laetitia said. "And she wouldn't, either."

"It doesn't do to spoil children. Being too much with their mother."

"Oh, I don't know," Bill found himself intervening to his surprise. "It's nice for a child to know she has a mother."

The two women looked at him accusingly.

"How much do you see of Rosabelle?" Candida asked.

"You've always got your head stuck in a car engine," Laetitia said. "Or down a gun-barrel with your pull-through. Not like the old days."

"When I used to racket round London myself," Bill said, "I saw a lot of Rosabelle. But she won't come down here much, now I've become a countryman."

"Oh, fathers!" Candida did not hide her scorn. "Sometimes I think mothers and offspring would be better off without them."

Leaving the field to the Amazons, he retired into sipping at his soup spoon. With the new women, it wasn't as it used to be. But then, it never had been. All these feminists now. He was for giving them the vote, but not the clubs to whack him around the ears. From then on, he rarely butted into the conversation, until the end of dinner and the moment for the ladies to leave to order their toilette and talk to each other. High time too, after four courses.

When the men gathered round him for the port and brandy and cigars, Overman led the languid pack, as Bill knew he would. His self-importance strained at his waistcoat. Bill feared its buttons might be rounds from a machine-gun, and hit him in the eye.

"War," he said, "Dunesk. What do you think about the war?"

"What war?" Bill was puzzled. "The Boer War? Or those Balkans things."

"The next war. With Germany. They've mobilized, you know. Against Russia."

"The Balkans have nothing to do with us," Carthew said. "The Serbian ambassador chap, he told me killing that Austrian Archduke was nothing to do with them either. So what's the point?"

"There will be war," Overman insisted. "France and us with Russia against Austria and Germany. It cannot be avoided."

"Not this time of year, old boy," Bill said. "It's the wrong season. Summer. Anyway, not at a week-end. Nobody goes to war on a week-end."

"Sir Edward Grey is away at his country house," Overman said. "And I am sure our Foreign Secretary has traditional manners. But it does not stop the Kaiser declaring war on the Czar."

"They're cousins," Wetherby Janes said. "Queen Victoria's lot. Won't fight. Settle it in the family. Blood will tell."

"Blood will tell." Overman smiled his thin grin. "And spill."

Rather a gloomy dinner, Bill thought. Politics and port didn't mix, but then the Overmans of the world liked a splash of Westminster with everything. He left the men in the billiards and gun room, with the cues in their racks as long as lances, and the gleaming gunmetal of the shotguns ranged in their glass cases in his country armoury. He had to retire early, for he wanted to meet the dawn flight in the spinney over the hill towards the paper mills at Penicuik and the mines and his royalties. He had to keep his eye on them, too.

Noises in the corridors woke him in the middle of the night. At first, he had believed they were rats and had brought in the terriers. Yet the sounds turned out to be slippers, slopping between the bedrooms. Asking people away for the week-end appeared to be a sort of sexual chairs. Those who didn't get their bottom on the right spot when the music stopped were bumped off for a night alone. Not that he cared any more. He was sure – or he hoped – that Marie would have nothing to do with all those comings and goings in her separate place. Although when he dropped off, a cry followed by a moaning seemed to wake him again from the bedroom next door. A nightmare, poor thing, perhaps he should console her. Then all was quiet on the Ermondhaugh front, and he drifted off to slumber again until Arthur woke him with coffee and scones at first light.

When he took up his position under the dawn trees, he was not in a hide. The birds flying in had a fair shot at life. He was not tucked away as for wild duck on a marsh, he was merely lurking under the boughs. Beyond the branches, almost bowed by the heavy leaves, he could see the great spoked wheels of the cages above the mines. The night shift was coming up, the day shift would be going down soon. Cranked and dropped to the bowels of the earth, these retrievers of coal were his income. Mineral rights, they were called, because they happened to be on his property. A largesse from Hell or from Heaven, Bill had never worked it out. But there was nothing bad about inheritance. Hardly his fault that the miners were striking, wasn't that the new word for it? With his wife's friend Keir McBride egging them on.

Ignoring the turmoil below, the flight dropped down. Again the twin blasts of the shotgun, again the two weights spiralling down in a scatter of greenery. Walking forward, Bill found each dead bird. He picked them up by the claws and opened the flap of his game bag and dropped them in. The black smoke over the colliery had not spread yet over the moist air, so that he could gulp it down, glad at the rising of the day.

He had to sit down on the walk home. There was a little hammer tip-tapping at his heart, or nearby. He rested on a cut stump until the sun inched over the fields on his way. They were already out and mustered, the summer people. Against the hay and the poppies and the thistles, the line of men were scything. He could see the weaving hump of their shoulders, the strong sweep to the left, the falling of the slain stalks. On they came, remorseless, nothing to check them, really. Behind the women for the gathering and the binding, and further against the hedges, the shire horses steaming with the carts for the taking in.

The scent of cut grasses was so strong that Bill coughed upon it. The rank sweetness started him up. He lurched to his feet and set off for the stables. Not so many horses now, but room enough for the motor-cars. He knew Albert would be at the Dion-Bouton well before he had arrived. Blacksmiths were all very well in their day, but pistons were better for real tinkering. To shoe a horse with hot nails was nothing to making a machine fire and move. Horse-power, they called it. And sure as wheels were wheels, motor cars would take over from hoofs on the roads to come. Given the potholes.

Albert was already ducked down in the engine under the bonnet. Streaks of black grease covered his tweed jacket so that he looked like a Scotch zebra. "Something wrong with the tappets, mun," he told Bill, who wished he knew what tappets were, as long as they were not what he thought they might be.

"I'm sure you can fix it, Albert," Bill said. "Have you heard about this war coming on?"

What Arthur didn't know, Albert did. Between them, they were a sort of *Encyclopedia Britannica* in words that made sense.

"Well, I've heard as --," Albert brought his oily face out of the crankshafts. "The Kaiser wants to sink all our ships. Rule the ruddy waves."

"But it's a land war."

Albert put his left forefinger on the side of his nose, leaving a dark edge to it.

"Just for the kick off. Then it's the briny. Knock out the Home Fleet. And Blackpool is Potsdam. A Hun lake."

Bill hadn't thought of it that way. But he did trust Albert to fix his engine.

"She'll start now, will she?"

"Yes, sir. Like a filly with a hot poker up her backside."

"Quite so. I've got to go in for breakfast." Bill paused. "Tell me, Albert, this next show – saddles or shifting gear?"

Albert laughed with brown teeth wide.

"Don't go for the horseflesh. Go for the controls. Morning."

Bill went for the breakfast table, where he did not wish to go. Most of the August mob were having it in their room – or another's – so that Bill was faced with the kedgeree alone. And the kidneys and the bacon and the scrambled eggs. Rather a full and bloody meal to start the day, but that was how it was in Lothian.

Two guests came to join him, because they were evidently not welcome elsewhere at this hour, Ernest Overman and Amanda Heliotrope, looking even more severe in britches.

"Ernest tells me," she said, sitting down briskly with a plate of kidneys and bacon, "that the war is definitely on. Where will you enlist?"

"Hadn't thought of it yet," Bill said. "But I will. People like me do."

"If there's room for you," Ernest said, folding his napkin over his Adam's apple to keep off the splash of the marmalade, when spread on his toast. "Fit for the slaughter, are you?"

"You're front line stuff, too," Amanda said. "Where will you be?"

"In the Ministry," Ernest answered. "We are rather necessary, you know. We are not cannon fodder. And you, Dunesk?"

"Something mechanical," Bill said. "I always fall off horses. And I am not very good on brain fodder."

"You used to be. Didn't you know Oscar Wilde and Bosie?"

"Yes, yes. The point is, sons always become their fathers. I'm like old Queensberry now, and I like my rules."

Amanda laughed at that.

"What I like about war is the cleansing. First, only stupid men get into it. And then they eliminate each other. So there are fewer stupid men left. And second, when those men are gone, the women can do something about things. So you fight, and we manage. I think it's rather a good idea, a great war now."

"So do I," Ernest said. "A purifying process. Only there is a snag. We're fighting the wrong people."

Amanda laughed again.

"You mean you care. I thought men never minded who they fought, as long as it was a good scrap."

"We should be with the Germans. Against the French and the Russians. All that blood and kin, you know. It does matter."

"Does it?" Bill sighed. "I wish we could just have a quiet week-end."

21

WAR AND CHRISTMAS
1914

Cold, cold, cold, with no protection from the whiplash of the high air. Tears formed under the goggles, making a mist on the glass. Murdo Sinclair, on the run in to the Zeppelin sheds at Düsseldorf, felt like an icicle in pursuit of the improbable. Guns were firing at him, useless stuff whizzing past, random bullets in space. Attack from the air was a new tactic, and there was no answer to it yet. Yet a stray piece of lead could put an end to the whole enterprise, so Murdo jinked the wings of his Short seaplane and stayed on target. Then he came in slowly over the sheds where the Zeppelins were hidden like queen ants hatching within the hive of London's future destruction.

Behind him, his observer and bomber sat. An elementary raid. He released the bombs like a hen laying eggs. And down they went onto the sheds, all three of them. One hit, one missed, and one failed to explode. But the huge detonations and the twin puffs of black smoke, that was a success. One Zeppelin perhaps was destroyed in its hangar, so Murdo banked and turned. He could land in the sea off the Heligoland Bight, and then he would be winched onto the Dreadnought. Then he would fold his wings, as a bat did after its hunt at night. And he would report to his cousin Hamilton that the sea battle had taken to the air, the era of the battleship was numbered.

On the Marconi telegraph, another cousin, Gillon, reported the success of the mission to Hamilton before Murdo had returned with the Home Fleet. "A-one OK," he said. "Mission accomplished. Out." And Hamilton, sitting on the threshold of a new age of war, did not know what to believe. They had accomplished so little. One Zeppelin was destroyed, when millions of men were massing on the western and eastern fronts in Germany. This prelude might be an overture to what was to come, but how long, O Lord, how long before the curtain went up?

Fighting at Mons was a pleasant shock. Captain Gordon Seymour-Scudabright with his battalion of Grenadier Guards watched the execution of the hordes of Huns on the barbed wire. His trained riflemen fired their Lee-Enfields with their rugged greasy bolts until the barrels grew red-hot and the linseed oil boiled from the wooden stocks and burned their palms. The worst marksman could not miss, there was hardly need to aim. He had only to shoot into the grey figures, now charging in mass into the concentrated fire of trained guns. So great was the point-blank murder that the Germans thought that they were being mowed down by the Vickers machine-guns, when there were only two of these issued to a regiment. But the steady stutter of the Lee-Enfields at their rapid fire was a fusillade without mercy or end. Thousands fell and screamed and writhed as the German advance came on to sicken Gordon and exhilarate him. Slaughter was just so, and a joy.

The British Expeditionary Force was broken by the Boche artillery. At first it had been a game, the salvos passing overhead and crashing in the rear like cymbals at a pantomime. Gordon's Guardsmen had poked their heads over the shallow pits, which they had dug with their entrenching tools. "Look," they had shouted, "a black bastard – four whities – a washout – another miss – lower your sights, blind-eyes!" Then the enemy gunners had adjusted their range, and the lyddite and the shrapnel began maiming and carving open their ranks. And when the order for the retreat came, they were glad to fall back. Of course, the Brigade of Guards never retreated, everybody knew that. They were merely taking up new positions. Yet this time, they were regrouping rather near Paris and not on the Belgian border, where the Germans had sliced through.

Day after night, and night after day, they slogged back along the dusty roads under the plane trees. Lurching about himself with fatigue, Gordon had to wave his revolver and curse his men awake at dawn. "Damn you, I'll shoot you if you don't get up! What do you want? Spend the war in a Boche concentration camp?" So he swore and threatened, and all his Guardsmen fell in and slouched on towards the Marne and the Aisne, sleep-walking in a nightmare of retreat. And their sergeants made them polish the toe-caps of their boots every night, even when the soles had worn away and they were walking on bare feet. And on their flanks, the cavalry hovered as angels of death.

One evening, Gordon saw someone he knew, Alexander Plunkett-Drax, as he dismounted to report. He was attached to the Fourth Dragoon Guards, which were screening them from the German First Army. Ridiculously, these mounted troopers were intended to deter the shot and shell of the concentrated firepower of the Huns. It must be the last grand illusion. Some folk memory of Mongol hordes on horseback or crusading knights stopped the German corps from annihilating the routed British forces. Or perhaps the Boches were as tired as they were. They had advanced too far and too fast. They had run out of steam.

"Alex," Gordon said, "what the hell are you doing here?"

"Not running away like you."

"They'll shoot your nags to smithereens."

"They'll put you in the bag."

"What you need is armoured cars. The Belgians had some. Better than a bloody horse."

"Says you. I can ride off, while you plod on."

And so Alexander Plunkett-Drax did, when he had delivered his message to regimental HQ. But the retreat became harder, because the soldiers were now mixed up with the refugees. On farm carts and on hand carts, on prams and wheelbarrows, the French of the northern villages were taking to the road. The Guardsmen broke ranks to help out the old men and women pushing their grandchildren and few goods towards Paris. The British Expeditionary Force became a fleeing rabble, khaki tunic and blue blouse mixed in a straggle of disorder. Sleeplessness led to a form of mass insanity. After ten days and nights of stumbling along, the soldiers began to dream as they walked, to talk nonsense or to their distant mothers and wives over the Channel. A fearful babble filled the dusty air with jabberings, while foot dragged after foot to the safety of the south.

Somewhere near the Seine, they could eat and sleep. There were stocks piled there and bedding. After twelve hours of unconsciousness, an Orderly Room was held, and some sort of discipline was remembered and enforced. "You're a bloody lot of cripples," the sergeant-major shouted. "A disgrace to the British Army." But reinforcements arrived, all plump and clean and tidy from Blighty, and raring to have a go at the enemy. They had good boots, while the mob in retreat had rags wrapped round their toes. And the order came to regroup and counter-attack as far as the River Marne and over it. Paris was saved, and the war ground to a halt in the trenches and below the earth along the banks of the Aisne.

One day they brought the aeroplane down which had also brought the Guardsmen back together again. Yesterday and the day before, the maniac Hun in his Spad Albatross came screaming along the lines of troops, firing a scatter of bullets and sprinkling a bomb or two, which exploded nowhere in a puff of dust. The third day, every man had fifteen rounds ready and the belts were on the Vickers and the Lewis guns. As the shrieking machine came down, the machine-guns and the rifles poured their iron tracery into the sky. The din was terrific. A ragged wall of steel and lead darts stood up before the flying engine which could not pass, although its charge on high carried it past its holocaust, trailing black smoke to its crash two miles away. The cheer that split the sky was the noise that Gordon had been waiting to hear. His men had recovered – in the bond of the death of their lone foe.

"Aeroplanes," he told his sergeant. "They will never win this war."

Although Marie wanted her all the time for the hospital work which now engrossed nearly all the suffragettes, Ruth found Virginia's modern art gallery more exciting. She had collected the work of the Futurists, our allies from Italy, who exalted speed and machines, violent action, and even war. "Burn the museums!" they cried in their riots. "Drain the canals of Venice! Kill the moonlight!" The aeroplane and the racing car were their Madonna and Angel Gabriel. The swirling motion and raw colours of cyclists by Boccioni, the expansion of lights by Severini, and the flight of swifts by Balla, these hung with the Gauguin primitives of the savage state on Virginia's walls. Maurice Walter had brought them over from Milan on the eve of war, before his disappearance. As he said, "It is good for trade, that Futurist leader Marinetti. When he said war was the only true hygiene of the world, business went up two hundred per centum."

Yet Ruth did not expect the violence in her own feelings on the evening she let herself into the Bloomsbury gallery and went up the stairs to the maisonette above. There was nobody in the living-room decorated with the brown blocks of Cubist paintings from Paris, by artists with names like Picasso, who were unknown and would always be. There was a noise from behind the closed door of the bedroom, and soon Virginia came down the treads, her hair a black tangle, but her flowing wrap of spring flowers painted on chiffon making her float above the steps in a picture of fresh innocence.

"Oh you, Ruth, I wasn't expecting you."

"I hope I am not inconvenient."

"Oh, you could never be. You are always welcome here." She enfolded Ruth in her arms, crushing her face against her breasts, so that Ruth could sense the scent of sex on her. "You might as well know."

The man who followed Virginia, buckling the copper mirror of his Sam Browne belt, was the man Ruth loathed. How could Virginia have fallen to Alexander Plunkett-Drax? She swung round on her friend, who was saying, "I believe you know each other –," with an accusation, "I told you about him! What an utter swine he was!" And all she heard was him mocking her through his nose. "I told you, Ruth, some girls love swine. They make us what we are."

Ruth found herself blocking Alexander with her body from the approaching Virginia.

"You are a swine because you always were. What are you doing here? You should be getting killed in France."

"Leave, and I earned it. And some tommyrot. They want us to move from horses into tin toys and I have to check out some contraption with tracks and armour on."

Virginia now held Ruth round the waist from the back, stopping her from attacking her tormentor. She answered for both of them.

"I heard about these armoured things from cousin Wallace. He's joined the Yeomanry. And you know how interested he is in backing new inventions."

"If Maurice finds you here," Ruth said, "he'll kill you."

"Oh, Maurice Walter won't get back here." Alexander Plunkett-Drax walked over to a decanter shaped like a shell-case and poured himself a brandy. "He's had to hotfoot it to points east. British Intelligence got onto him. Gun-running to Ireland."

"To you, I bet."

"Those were the old days. Ulster, who cares? The Paddies have joined us in fighting the Huns. So have the Springboks, our old Boer friends. All those things are post-war problems now. When we've won."

Virginia released Ruth, who was shivering from a turmoil of loathing. Now the girl would not attack her past lover.

"War is a great solution," Virginia said. "All our troubles – strikes, votes for women, Ireland – all postponed till the next truce. Perhaps our dear Marinetti is quite right. War may not be hygiene, but it bandages our old wounds. And we can't take off the plaster till the peace."

"It's disgusting to hear you talk like that," Ruth said. "I always thought, Virginia, you're so sensitive – your fine feelings –"

"She likes the real thing," Alexander said complacently. "A real man. Like you do too, Ruth. Don't tell me there's not a streak of violence in you. And you want it satisfied. You know the only thing better than having a woman?" The two women looked at him, knowing and fearing what he would say. "Killing a Hun. Sticking him with a lance. I got an Uhlan right between the shoulder-blades as he was getting away. Going in ... ah –"

Whether the story was true or not, Alexander smiled at the shock of it on his audience. Virginia spoke first.

"You like killing?"

"Who doesn't?"

"I hate it," Ruth said.

"You don't admit you like it."

"We spend much of our time at hospitals, trying to patch men up. What they have done to each other."

"Don't you want to kill them, really?"

"If it was you," Ruth said, "I would."

"There you are. Women are so perverse. They always want to kill the men they want."

Virginia laughed.

"Don't think we only want you, Alex, because you are so intolerable. Even you can go too far."

"I doubt it." He finished his brandy. "I must amble off and win the war. Till next leave, Virginia."

"*Au revoir,*" Virginia said. "Or rather, *adieu.*"

"Break your neck," Ruth said.

When the impossible man was gone, Ruth fell into a storm of accusation of her friend, which ended in a fit of weeping and consolation with camomile tea. Virginia did say she was sorry, but what could she do? Maurice Walter had vanished for ever, Alexander wanted her, the average life of an officer in France was now six weeks only, how could she deny his need? "For me," Ruth cried, "for my sake!" But even she knew that however strong the bonds were between women, when they wanted the same man, they slipped the knot. In fact, the more she confessed how terrible Alexander was and had been, the more attractive he became. He traded on that, the conspiracy among women which made him the demon lover. He was not as great as all that in bed or on the carpet, but his reputation made him so.

"I do love you, Ruth," Virginia said, "and we won't let that Casanova *manqué* come between us. With any luck, he'll stop a bullet before he bothers us again."

As she said it, Virginia knew that both of them did not really want that. They still wanted him, alive and kicking.

Another war was being fought in India, but only a family row. Peg was dandling her baby in her arms – another Shilendra, the father had insisted on that – when Seaforth and Miriam had burst in upon her. Seaforth was quivering with rage. He shook as an arrow fixed into a tree, trembling with the impact.

"I can't bear it," he said. "Orders from England. Back there to patch up the victims of another of their bloody wars. And you, Peg – you with your baby."

Peg put her baby down on the divan behind her, holding the back of his head as if it were an eggshell.

"I don't mind," she said. "But Shilendra's not coming with me. His father's got a wet nurse who is a cousin. Anyway, I cannot risk him." She smiled at Miriam, who smiled back at her. "I don't mean to shock you, brother, I will miss Shilendra awfully, but ... to be a doctor again, in England again, I will feel I am doing what I was meant to do."

Seaforth stood still, as if she had struck him into the face. He was shocked into silence. Miriam spoke for him.

"But working for British soldiers," she said. "In an imperialist war. German Empire against British Empire."

"O, just men," Peg said. "They do expect us to look after them when they are dying for their eternal stupidity."

Now Shilendra came into their drawing-room, hung with Moghul rugs and bright with brass jars and hanging lights. He shrugged and spread his hands.

"She's your sister, Seaforth. I am only her husband. What can I do with her?"

"Tell her to be a mother!"

"I do tell her. And she tells me, when she married me, I said she could be a doctor. Always. I said it – and now she tells me."

Seaforth walked across to his sister. His eyes were hot embers.

"Stay with your son. Don't go!"

She taunted him back.

"*You* are going, aren't you? They ordered you to go back. They ordered me. And you, Miriam –" Now she swung on her sister-in-law. "You have agreed, haven't you? You will stay with the children in India. You will see the work through here. While Seaforth is away – patching up the agents of British imperialism because he has to, he's a doctor – you will keep the cells going here, the flames burning for a free India – that free India we all want."

Seaforth was silent, and Miriam, too. They had no answer to what Peg had said. Yet Miriam had to say, "I will be going with Seaforth. I will have to leave the children here, Shankar and Solomon. But we have excellent *ayahs* –"

Peg's look at her was as a steel blade. Now the baby on the divan began to wail in a voice as thin as one note on a reed pipe. His mother picked up the infant and challenged her husband.

"Do you think I don't love him? I gave him your name, Shilendra."

Shilendra could not look at her. He dropped his eyes and said softly, "If you did love him and me, you would stay here in India. It is not for you, my dear Peg, it is not for you to bandage our oppressors. Your brother is right. This is not your war. It is, in fact, our opportunity."

Seaforth smiled at Shilendra. They did not like each other, but in families, even opponents might say the right thing.

"Peg darling," he said, "your husband is correct. It is not your war. It is our opportunity to make India free."

Ah, the hypocrisy of men! Peg could not stand it, even with her baby in her arms.

"You are going, Seaforth. Why not me?"

"I have to. I have orders."

"So have I."

"But as a mother with a baby. You know the British. On compassionate grounds, you can get away with murder –"

"Or birth, apparently."

Again there was a silence. Even Seaforth did not know his sister could be so formidable. So he said weakly, "You do not have to go."

"And if I feel I should. It is my job. Even if I must leave the child I love."

Miriam was torn. She had to love the woman in Peg, who had to do what she must do. She hated the war for the Empire, which she hated more than all the past. But she was leaving her children in India to go with her husband. So she said, "Peg, do what you have to do. But this is murder – exploitation – shame. Do not go to help these murderers."

"Ah," Peg said. She put her baby in her husband's arms, and he received the child gently, loving him. Then she walked over to Miriam. "My dear," she said, "You know and I know, we must do what we have to do. And perhaps be mothers after."

Miriam hung her head and mumbled, "Perhaps ... what you have to do... it's all wrong." Yet she knew in her heart that Peg was right.

"God knows," Peg said and challenged her brother Seaforth with her stare. "Doctors have only one thing to do. They save lives. There's nothing else. They cannot choose. That is it. What, Seaforth?"

And Seaforth looked gloomily at the tile floor.

"Women," he said. "Sisters. What else do we have?"

Marie's war efforts were directed at the Women's Emergency Corps and the Wandsworth General Hospital. When Virginia and Ruth were not involved with their art dealing, they were starched into service, as was Ellen-Maeve, up from the country at last, and Ruby, dead set on picking up an officer too wounded to run away from her. Her grandfather Iain, after all, had picked up his wife that way in a Himalayan hospital after the Indian Mutiny, when he had been hamstrung and fancy-free. For the wounded, wards were another way of meeting women. Many a match was the result of an accident in the field.

Most importantly, Marie had her friend Peg recalled by the War Office from India for service at home, and with her came her brother Seaforth and his wife Miriam. Again, there was an understanding of women, rather to the exclusion of men. Miriam had already become a firm supporter of Peg in India in her battles for higher appropriations for her hospital. She found in Marie another fighter for her favourite causes, although Marie's wealth and title stuck in her craw, and the Countess of Dunesk had to disarm her suspicions.

"You're quite right," she said. "I am a filthy capitalist and class enemy. But you come from very wealthy parents, Miriam."

"They don't help me any more," Miriam said. "They know I want to destroy them and their mines in Jo'burg."

"But you still love them, in their way, which you cannot alter."

Miriam was silent and scowled.

"Yes," she said.

"Well, I was born poor – and the American Indian in me hated the British aristocrats. And now I am married to one – in a kind of a way – I love what I have the power to do. Surely, the thing is to change things –"

"That's what Marx said."

"And you cannot change things without the power to change them."

"We should not use your sort of power. Workers' power is right."

"Not with our sort of workers," Marie said. "Not yet. You don't know them. They have no idea of their own power."

Seaforth reorganized the Wandsworth General Hospital. He insisted that soldiers only understood rules. The problem was that army rules were not the same as hospital rules, although there were coincidences. So he drew up a wounded warrior's guide and order book, which ran:

– NEVER DESERT YOUR BED WITHOUT PERMISSION

– STOP TALKING WHEN SISTER SAYS SO

– NO DODGING OF TAKING MEDICINE

– IF YOUR TEMPERATURE CHANGES, SAY SO

– SISTER IS ALWAYS RIGHT AND DOCTORS ARE RIGHTER

– DON'T DISCUSS YOUR CASE – ACCEPT IT

– DON'T FLIRT WITH THE NURSE. YOU ARE HER PROBLEM, NOT HER OBJECT

Come home to catch her officer, Ruby Jardine from India was one of the volunteer nurses who disobeyed the last rule. She was very popular in the Senior Ranks ward. They always asked for Ruby to bathe them. At first, she had been delicate about too much contact with male anatomy. But she warmed to the work and caused considerable jealousy when she seemed to prefer treating a stricken lieutenant rather than a maimed major.

"Seniority," the older officers would say. "That's what the army's all about."

"Hospitals aren't," Ruby would reply demurely. "I'll get round to you when my rota says I do."

Yet Ruby's rota was a moveable feast. And when Alistair Ogilvie was brought in with his shattered leg and shrapnel in his left cheek, Ruby tended to him as if he were a relative. Certainly, his right profile made him appear the best-looking man in Britain, and once the bandage was removed from his wounds, his whole aspect would prove it, and as for his character, Ruby loved the mordant streak in him that made her laugh, although he always implored her not to be amused in case he followed suit.

"You know, Miss Jardine," he would say, "it hurts me to laugh, but it does tell me I still have a face."

Alistair had no hope of leaving his bed before he was engaged to Ruby. She then allowed him to limp with her round the garden. And before he was returned to the front, they were married in the absence of her parents, who were in India, but her brother Wallace came to the short ceremony, dressed in his new Yeomanry uniform. He was being kept back in Britain to attend trials of a new armoured fighting weapon.

"It won't be in good enough time to save me," Alistair Ogilvie said. "I'd love some steel plate between me and the Hun machine-guns."

The honeymoon was only forty-eight hours. Exhausted and wounded herself in body and soul, Ruby could not see her husband for the storm of her tears at Victoria Station, where she had to suffer his leaving for France.

"No, no, no," she was shouting. "Don't go!"

She provoked shock on the faces of the other deserted women. "They must go," an old dowager said to her severely. "You must let them go to fight, and not make such a fuss about it."

But Ruby could not stop crying out, "He won't come back. I know it!"

And she was right. On Christmas Eve, 1914, Alistair Ogilvie was killed in action on the Western Front.

On Christmas Day, Gordon Seymour Scudabright heard the Germans singing from their trenches. He knew the tune, *Stille Nacht, heilige Nacht*. And then a lone violin sent out its sad sweet notes – Handel's *Largo*. By God, who would believe it? Better, though, than the explosions of the *Minenwerfer*, the Minnies. And then his own Guardsmen gave three cheers and began to sing, 'Home, Sweet Home'. As if this were home, this foul morass of muddy shell-holes and tangles of wire. And the firing stopped. No sniper bullet flew. He could hear a blackbird sing, too.

Yet he could not stop his men dropping their rifles, leaving their trenches, and wandering into No Man's Land. The Germans brought over wine and *schnapps*, the English took bully beef and Christmas cake. Hoarfrost glittered on the soggy ground, a million million brilliants of light as if the Milky Way had fallen down to carpet the bog of death. And there was a football game of sorts, if you could call kicking an old German bucket helmet through a pair of splintered stakes a kind of soccer. Down where the Gordons were, the ball was a hare, and the beast jinked and swerved between the two roaring teams of captors, until a German bagged it from the kilted Scots for the stewpot that night.

Alexander Plunkett-Drax was savage about the voluntary truce of Christmas. He threatened to shoot any of his dragoons who went out to make a private peace. "They're bloody Huns," he shouted. "Baby-killers! They spit children on their bayonets. They burn cathedrals. Look at Arras!" And his rage was only exceeded by that of Charles Seymour-Scudabright doing his war duty from the Ministry of Information at home, keeping up the morale, which the troops were letting down so badly at the front.

No newspaper was allowed to carry the story of the Christmas peace in northern France. The Hun had to be labelled as he truly was, a butcher and a rapist and a fire-lighter. Even apostate daughters like Ruth had to be told to toe the line. Being a radical might mean being a traitor to one's country. So her father studied the proof of the poster before him:

TO THE
YOUNG WOMEN
OF LONDON

Is your "Best Boy" wearing Khaki?
If not don't YOU THINK he should be?
If he does not think that you
and your country are worth
fighting for – do you think he
is WORTHY of you?
Don't pity the girl who is
alone – her young man is
probably a soldier, fighting
for her and her country –
and for YOU.

If your young man neglects his duty to his
King and Country, the time may come when
he will NEGLECT YOU.
Think it over – then ask him to

JOIN THE ARMY – TODAY

"Myrtle," Charles shouted. "Myrtle!"

He approved of secretaries with the names of trees or flowers. A Violet or a Lily, an Iris or a Petunia, these names reassured. They reminded him of the English Roses which the Tommies out there were defending, and who would wait by their window boxes until the men came home.

When Myrtle entered, she was enthusiastic over the poster, her smile opening in petals to a patriotic glow.

"Oh, yes," she said, "we should all be worthy of the sacrifice. And then they will not neglect us."

Charles Seymour-Scudabright gave her the address of a certain gallery in Bloomsbury, where his daughter Ruth was said to be living with a cousin's wife, Virginia Sinclair. His strict instructions were to plaster the neighbourhood with this particular poster, to recall the women to their senses and their duty. He did not know that it would remind them both of Alexander Plunkett-Drax, who was not worthy of either of them and neglected them both. Yet he did loathe the brief Christmas peace of the Great War as much as Charles did. And in hatred of the enemy, both men were able to come to terms with their own selves.

22

MY ENEMY, MY FRIEND

Below the Short seaplane, the mangrove swamp spread out its claws and crooked legs as ten thousand thousand crabs scuttling towards the grey Pacific Ocean. At the controls, Murdo Sinclair peered down as best he could through his steaming goggles. His observer and wireless operator, Boggis, was also on the look-out when he was not tinkering with his set. And there, suddenly, in a channel of the Rufiji River, were two different sorts of trees, straight with crosses upon their trunks, the masts of the missing German cruiser *Königsberg*. Murdo put the seaplane into a dive, then levelled out to follow the twists and turns of the tributary to where the warship was lying, concealed off the swampy river. The sound of a machine-gun firing from the cruiser's deck putt-putted in his ears, and the crackle of the rifle shots. Holes were punched in the fuselage and the upper wing as they flew past the grey side of the warship, its 4.1-inch gun pointing uselessly at the empty sky. Then Murdo banked and nosed, turning in a lazy half-circle to report.

"We're like a ruddy sieve," Boggis shouted to him.

"Good for lettuce," Murdo shouted back.

"Where are we?"

"Down the drain. Camera ready!"

He brought the seaplane down over the superstructure of the *Königsberg*, ignoring the bullets whizzing as useless as hornets past the floats of the biplane. Boggis was hanging over the edge of the cockpit with his rosewood camera. "Got her!" he shouted. "Head for home!" And Murdo did just that, clearing the mangrove trees and flying over the forest to the sea creek, where the monitor *Mersey* was lying, its one vast Howitzer pointing up from its iron platform. He put his aircraft down bumpily on the muddy waters and waited for a cutter to take him and his observer aboard.

Hamilton Sinclair was quite impressed by the quality of the aerial photograph, while the captain of the *Mersey* thought it near to magic. "It's clear enough," he said. "We'll fire over the trees. She's a sitting duck." Then he turned to Hamilton. "Your seaplane, it can observe and report. Where our shells land."

"Of course," Hamilton said, then verified with his cousin. "That will not be a problem?"

"A tea party," Murdo said. "As long as the wireless works. And the wings don't fold up on us."

Hamilton laughed. The voyage had been long round the Cape for the seaplane to East Africa, where Von Lettow and his black *askaris* were leading the British armies a dance through the bush in Tanganyika, and the German fleet still had a major warship on hand to sink the troop convoys from India. The Royal Naval Air Service was slowly proving that flying was an answer to the big guns of the battleships, even if Nelson was turning in his grave.

"We can have them now," Hamilton said. "After we have refuelled."

As he took off, Murdo could see the vast antique cannon on the monitor elevating to lob its shells one by one in an arc onto its target. It would be curious if a haphazard coincidence put a steel projectile from his own side through his wings. But there was a lot of room in space. And the Short seaplane had not reached the moorings of the *Königsberg* again before the British bombardment was detonating mangrove trees in flying umbrellas beyond the enemy cruiser.

"Four hundred yards long!" Boggis was shouting into the wireless. "Two hundred right. Over. Roger. Out."

Now the *Königsberg*'s cannon were replying to the heavens, hurling their reply over the swamp at their hidden enemy. Yet the explosives were closer now, fountains and plumes of river water spraying the hostile deck. And then, a direct hit, the funnel of the German cruiser cartwheeling in flocks of metal birds from the force of the black strike. And as he saw, Murdo was struck himself. A fragment hit him in the shoulder. And looking behind, he glanced at Boggis sprawling forward, his flying scarf crimson from his blood. The joystick would not pull back. He could not gain height. He dropped to fifty feet above the brown channel and headed for the sea, following the course of the Rufiji.

Cousin Robert Sinclair was also aboard on the *Mersey* to watch Murdo bring down his crippled aircraft by the ironclad monitor. The seaplane stalled on landing, tipped forward and began to list, half of one of its wing-floats shot away. But it could be salvaged. It had other missions to do.

"You have destroyed the *Königsberg*?" Robert asked.

"We have crippled her. She will not sail again."

"But her guns, her naval guns?"

"They'll rust with her hulk."

"Von Lettow will have them off her. They're better than our guns."

"That's your problem," Hamilton said. "You're on the ground with your West African Rifles. You stop Von Lettow. We have, from sea and air."

"It's so bloody frustrating," Robert said. "It's our stupid generals. There's only one good officer, a bullyboy called Meinertzhagen. The rest are so dumb they wouldn't qualify as animals. And Von Lettow's real smart. He's like the Scarlet Pimpernel, I guess. We seek him here, we seek him there – and he's always got a march on us. We've transferred troops from all over the Empire – India, Africa –"

"How's the wife? Patience?"

"Had to leave her behind."

"She's older than you, isn't she? A matron?"

"You shouldn't ask that. Yes, she is. It doesn't matter. I'm happy now." Robert looked at his cousin. "And Virginia – do you ever see her in London?"

"She's doing all right," Hamilton said, not knowing what to say exactly to his cousin. "But Hamish Charles isn't happy, and nor are his children. They're all dumped at boarding schools. She's pretty well left them. I suppose that might give you some satisfaction."

"It doesn't." Robert looked over the sails of the *Mersey* to the cutter heading for the stricken seaplane. "I haven't got anything against Hamish Charles."

"But he did kill his first wife. And ran off with yours."

"Did he now?" Robert turned on his cousin, his face both set and desperate. "How do *you* know?"

"I don't, I just heard –"

"Don't hear. *Know.*"

"You said, it was an accident. We – the family – we've always though how good you were ... how generous."

Out by the sinking sea-plane, sailors were lifting free the body of Boggis, crimson with blood even at that distance.

"Don't be too sure." Robert's voice was bitter. "I don't know why I gave that verdict. I would say who killed her was a matter of doubt."

Over the swell, the sailors dropped the corpse. It fell into the creek. There was a thrash of water. The sailors beat at some creature with their oars. The body was dragged away. A sailor in the bow of the cutter picked up a rifle and began to fire aimlessly at a crocodile heading towards Africa.

"We are killing so many now," Robert said. "And it doesn't matter who kills who any more. Why should one little death matter? So long ago? Why one?" He looked towards Hamilton for an answer, but

Hamilton could give him none. So he had to add, "But it does matter. To me."

As the gas casualties came into the station, Hamish Charles was also thinking about the death of his first wife. He remembered her thick hair red with blood as she sprawled in the reeds by the *vlei*. The soldiers on the cattle-trucks were dead or dying, too. No one was breathing. Those who were living were coughing and retching. Thick green and yellow phlegm came out of their mouths. They twisted and arched from some internal agony. They cursed and groaned, their blankets drenched in their sweat. They were on the racks of hell. No inferno could be worse.

Hamish Charles, the transport officer at Rheims, moved away the men in torment. He directed the stretcher bearers to some, the gravediggers to others. They had been conveyed back day after night, and night after day. Hamish Charles had lost count. Another stupid push over the top into the machine-guns. But this time, the breeze had been blowing in their faces, and the Germans had added mustard and chlorine gas to the wind. Chemical warfare, it was worse than poisoning the wells with arsenic to kill the African cattle. These men were slaughtered like vermin and worse than vermin. No rat should die this way.

Hamish Charles dreaded to find a face he knew among the myriad of the wounded. But on the third sleepless night in the railway sidings, drinking cognac openly from the silver hip-flask covered with crocodile skin which he always carried and used too much, he came across the aged death-mask of a young man he had met recently and long ago. The Grenadier uniform was streaked with sulphurous stains, the worn young-old face was stubbled and grey with dying. The voice gagged at the sight of Hamish Charles.

"I'm Gordon," the soldier croaked. "Save me."

Hamish Charles knelt by his cousin and opened his hip-flask. Drop by drop, he tilted the brandy into the open mouth of the Grenadier. Gordon Seymour-Scudabright coughed, but mercifully held down the poison in his lungs.

"Save me."

"I will try, Gordon."

There must have been some reassurance in his voice, for Gordon closed his eyes. Then a spasm shook him, a fit of twisting and screaming that added to the cacophony of pain in the carriage. And when he arched up, he choked and fell back. And he did not breathe again.

Hamish Charles closed the lids of the dead man's eyes with his forefinger. He tried to cross his cousin's hands in a prayer for such a release, but a sort of stiffness had already set in. He looked in Gordon's breast pocket and found a wallet and some creased letters from England. He would send them home.

He rose to his feet. The stretcher-bearers were hovering.

"Take him to the hospital."

"But he is dead, sir."

"To the hospital. Tell Dr Seaforth Sinclair it is his cousin Gordon. I want the body shipped home with the wounded. He'll be buried in England. Understand?"

"Yes, sir."

Hamish Charles jumped from the charnel house of the railway waggon onto the gravel by the tracks. He took a pull from his flask again. He had worn the scaly skin of the river beast to chestnut and smooth with the palm of his hand. Again he took a swig of brandy. It did not help much. The pleasant haze in his head had become a lump of lead. Why had they not killed him, too? Why make him a Charon, a ferryman of the dead? He was the one who should have died. He had killed a woman once, an accident, but he wanted her to die. And the woman he had married, Virginia, she was a tart by all accounts, whoring with a French arms dealer, and too damned clever for him. He did have four children, Hamish Gordon and Martha and little Paul – and one by the tart, sweet Clio – but boarding schools had engulfed them, as they swallowed up all colonial children in their harsh regime so like the British army.

There was money enough to pay for that, since his father had died. There was no need ever to return to the slavery of copra in the South Seas. But why survive? Who needed him, a failure all his born days? Perhaps the children did. But it was a wise child who knew his own father, and a bad father he had been. He still loved little Clio, but Virginia would not let him see her, even on his leave, which never seemed to come. Altogether, for everyone's sake, he was better off dead. But he was living, and the moans and screams of the dying were all about him. Even in war, being killed was so bloody random.

He finished off the brandy in his flask and staggered towards the bar in the station to fill up. As he lurched along, he felt in his pocket for his talisman. Under a light on the platform, he studied it – a white fleur-de-lys set in red glass surrounded by a lead border – a fragment of the stained glass windows of the torched cathedral. The three petals on their stem were a flowering cross.

"Thank You for Your mercy," Hamish Charles mumbled to God. "I don't deserve it."

The *Ben My Chree* had been a passenger ferry between Liverpool and the Isle of Man. It had been refitted for the seaplanes with a hangar on the upper deck and a testing and repair workshop. It had reached the Dardanelles to reinforce the *Ark Royal*, which could only winch up its ten aircraft on steam-driven hoists from their hangar in the hold. Transferred from East Africa because of their expertise, Murdo and Hamilton Sinclair had sailed through the Suez Canal up to the Aegean Sea. For Lawrence of Arabia was already beginning to assault the Turks in the southern deserts, and soon there would be a fresh crusade to recapture Jerusalem.

"I don't know," Murdo said. "Do you think it will work?"

He was looking down from the deck of the aircraft carrier to the Short "Shirl" seaplane bobbing at the side, heavy in the water, for an eighteen-inch torpedo was slung beneath it.

"You know the specifications," Hamilton said. "Rolls Eagle 8 engine, 400 horse-power. That's enough thrust to get your tub airborne. And you've got six and a half hours' flying time at a top speed of a hundred miles an hour. Think where we were only five years ago. We got a prize at Shorts for flying round one closed circuit on an airfield!"

"If I didn't trust the engineers," Murdo said, "I'd never bloody fly."

"And I'd never send you up, Murdo, if I didn't know you would stay up till you came down."

So Murdo set off in his single-seater biplane on his epic journey towards his Troy across the Dardanelles. The entrance to the straits was heavy with the hulls of British and French battleships, their names a register of an ancestry which Homer might have written himself – the *Majestic* and the *Agamemnon*, the *Vengeance* and the *Albion*, the *Triumph* and the *Indefatigable*, the *Charlemagne* and the *Queen Elizabeth*, with the *Lord Nelson* and the *Swiftsure* and the *Prince of Wales* in reserve. With their lineage and nobility, how could the Allies lose?

Heartened by the evidence of the grey invaders beneath, Murdo found his target in a harbour on the near side of Asia. The old Turkish transport was low on the waterline, almost beached. He took a straight run into the ship, as direct as a cavalry charge. He dropped to fifteen feet above the swell and released his explosive cargo. The mechanism worked. He jumped another twenty feet in the air from the loss of weight. The aircraft skipped with joy. The propeller still whirred round and about in a blue blur. He rose and banked and swerved and looked back and underneath. An explosion rent the ship, a tiara of smoke blazoned the horizon. Smack dab in the middle, the torpedo had gone home – and that is where Murdo flew back.

"It is history, naval history," Hamilton told him that night in the mess of the *Ben My Chree*. "The first ship torpedoed by an aeroplane."

"I've hit a submarine, I think," Murdo said. "In the North Sea. With a hand-bomb."

"But if that U-boat had been under the sea – its proper habitat – instead of recharging its batteries." Hamilton was smiling. "You could never have hit it. While a ship, its place is top of the water. Not under it, until you send it there."

"True. So?"

"The war is ours. In the future, all will be air wars. Including the sea battles. All the guns of the ships won't be pointing at other fleets. They will be watching the clouds."

Certainly, Hamilton proved right in the evacuation of Gallipoli. All the heroics, all the courage, all the sudden deaths to gain inches of beaches, these were as useless as the ten years the Greek Allies had spent assaulting the walls of Troy, before they took it with their feigned retreat and the deceit of the Trojan Horse. But this Allied withdrawal was for real. And it was by sea. The great poet was futile on a brief visit writing about the beauty of the slaughter of the troops from the far dominions:

> With all the fury and the crying of the shells, and the shouts and cries and cursing on the beach, the rattle of the small arms and the cheers and defiance up the hill, and the roar of the great guns far away, at sea, or in the olive-groves, the night seemed in travail of a new age. All the blackness was shot with little spurts of fire, and streaks of fire, and malignant bursts of fire, and arcs and glows and crawling snakes of fire, and the moon rose, and looked down upon it all. In the fiercer hours of that night shells fell in that contested mile of ground and on the beach beyond it at the rate of one a second, and the air whimpered with passing bullets, or fluttered with the rush of the big shells, or struck the head of the passer like a moving wall with the shock of explosion. All through the night the Turks attacked, and in the early hours their fire of shrapnel became so hellish that the Australians soon had not men enough left to hold the line.

So all departed by sea, with the great poet well in the lead. Yet it was not the great departure that it might have been. For the British Army – except from Afghanistan – had almost always been perfect in its retreats, which were never admitted, rather than in its advances, which rarely succeeded. The fleet had to take them off in old steamers brought over from the English Channel, the peacetime notices in French and English still painted on the gangways: PRENEZ GARDE – MIND THE STAIRS.

As the last of the soldiers strolled softly from Suvla and Anzac at night over the hulk of the *River Clyde*, beached as a jetty, they found that the rearguard had to wait for the final lighter to safety and the battleship *Prince George*. The problem was that General Maude had lost his valise. And only as dawn was breaking did he find his missing bag. He just made it to the ultimate barge from Gallipoli rather as King Arthur did on his terminal voyage to Avalon, before the first of the ammunition dumps was blown up, the signal to the sleeping Turks that this was another failed crusade.

Like Ichabod, the glory of the Allies had departed. But one of them, Naval Lieutenant Graham Seymour-Scudabright, had not. In charge of the Marines who were igniting the abandoned heaps of explosives and stores, he had stood for a moment between the rising light and the phosphoros waters of the Aegean, used by the ancient Greeks to sail on their *Iliad*. A Turkish sniper had a clean shot. And Gordon's brother died on land as he had done, but with a pain so quick that it was gone as it was felt, in a classical land that bred the myth of heroes. Only he would rather have been alive, as all heroes would.

May Seymour-Scudabright had never seen her husband Charles cry. Yet now he wept for hours on end. He would not come to terms with his grief. To lose one son and then both sons, he who had done all that was right in this world. There was no justice in it.

"Gordon and Graham," he blubbed to her like the schoolboy he was under his bluster. "Taking them. They could have left me one." He did not think of her. She was only their mother. "One boy to go on with my life. Just one boy. It would be enough."

"You are always saying," May said, dry-eyed because she only wept in the silence of her bedroom, "what a just war it is."

"It may be a just war. It is. But it doesn't mean they should take both my boys."

"They. Who are they?"

"I don't know. The people who killed them."

"Gas. A sniper. Just another target."

"Gordon. And Graham."

"I know. Our boys."

They fell into silence, and May looked across at the man she had thought she had loved once for more than his wealth and air of command. Now he was a sad fat man nobody could love. Except her. For he was at his depths. And there was the past between them, two boys were dead. She rose and walked over to him sitting in his plaid chair and took his head out of his hands and pressed his face into her soft middle through the cloth of her dressing-gown.

"There," she said. "There. I'm here. And we do have Ruth."

Muffled the voice she heard below her.

"Don't talk of her."

"I must. She is the last one left to us. And just because she is rebelling now – that modern art with that awful Virginia – it doesn't mean that one day –" May had to be positive. "She is nursing. She is out of gaol. No more of those dreadful votes for women. No more Cat-and-Mouse Act. She is helping to heal our soldiers. She may meet somebody. You never know."

Charles Seymour-Scudabright brought up his tear-streaked face from the security of his wife's dragon silk material.

"I know about Ruth. She will never –"

"Never say never, as they say, if you are a parent."

"She will never love us. Or respect us."

"Those are very different words. Charles –" May looked down on her obese, crouched, dependent husband with some affection. "She still loves us. We are her mother and father. But respect us? That is too much to ask in wartime."

"But here I am, running the war with my propaganda – that's the new word for it." Charles was almost pleading for reassurance. "I mean, morale is very high, is it not?"

"When the Zeppelins don't bomb us. Or the Gothas."

"Very high on the whole. And something to do with me."

"Very much to do with you, Charles. We simply don't know what to think until we read your posters. Britain's New Million Army – Complete the Second Million – Men wishing to join – Fall in and follow the band. Come and help us – For Honour and Freedom." May paused for effect. "If I was a man, I'd join up at once. As I am a woman –" She paused again. "I vote for you to keep us enlisting."

"Oh May, what would I do without you?"

This was the first time Charles had expressed any need of her since the war had begun. It had taken the death of two sons to make him admit the truth. Then May repressed the thought as too cheap. She had not had the time to mourn herself, to lament the void of this double loss of the flesh which had been born of her. But she had to console him first, her biggest baby as he had always been.

"I am here," she said. "I always will be. England has to do without our sons. But she does not yet have to do without you."

And in his look of surprise and gratitude and sudden hope, she had her sort of reward. She had helped the man who lived.

23

MURDER BY MACHINE

The tank was an armoured boat, really, born out of the Admiralty Landships Committee. Clambering inside one was like entering the gun turret of a battlecruiser or the steel lozenge of a submarine. But this was the flat ground before Cambrai, not the North Sea off Jutland. Four men were needed to steer the Mark IV tracked monster with its Daimler six-cylinder engine working a worm differential and the pressed steel plate revolving tracks, which only lasted twenty miles at the full speed of four miles an hour. Inside the groaning and clanking tin of claustrophobia was worse than being processed into bully beef. But three hundred of them did break through the first time they were used properly. They cleared the German machine-gun nests with their Lewis guns and 57mm cannon. They bridged the trenches with rolls of firewood dropped off their bows, and they cleared the barbed wire for the following infantry with grapnels and pulling power. They changed the face of future war as much as the armoured knight had in the ages of the Crusades.

Before he climbed for the last time into his greasy, noisy and smelly turret, Bill Dunesk was thinking of his one flight above the lines as an observer above Cambrai. In the biplane BE2 surrounded by humming wires, he had looked down at the triple trenches of the Hindenburg Line. These huge wormcasts stretched from one horizon to another, fronting a morass of craters, a mixture of fen and rabbit warren gouged out by the bombardments. The dug-outs and bunkers in their interminable crawl were the burrows of the Great War; but like digging the fox or the badger out of its earth, this was a sweaty and killing business. To hump over that slough of despond into barbed wire and machine-gun fire was intractable. A dead man's land, what ho! That is why Bill was inserting himself like a piston above the six-cylinder engine of the male Mark IV tank.

He was with Alan and Jock and Barny. Just like the blokes at home, no class in it, the machine took all out of them. In front, it carried a bundle of fascines of stakes and brushwood to drop into shell-holes or trenches so that it might lumber over. Cannon stuck out from bulges on the armoured sides. Ahead, the artillery was already dropping shells and gas and shrapnel for the assault of the mass of three hundred of these

scaly dragons, sneaked up by the night railway to cluster for a
breakthrough on the western front.

Crouched and coughing, Bill wrestled with the levers and wheels of
his Bedlam of clank and oil. He was in an iron coffin with the nails in the
lid hammering into his ears. The tanks and the backing infantry were
meant to clear the way for the cavalry, forty thousand fancy horsemen,
who would then charge all the way back through Belgium to Berlin. A
rotten plan, using an antiquated arm. Rather like asking a cripple to run a
marathon. Still, bad plans were what this Great War was all about. Or
the army would not have been bogged down for three years and millions
of casualties.

The machine was thumping on. Rolling and rumbling, the twin tracks
churned the debris of the soil. They yawed at one shell-hole and
straddled another, just grinding across the gap. The barbed wire was
weeds in their progress, the bullets were midges pinging off the armour.
Halting on the sandbags at the lip of the leading trench, Bill pulled down
the stick to drop the bundles of faggots so that they might cross the
abyss. They sank and rose again the far side. Objective accomplished.
They groaned to the left towards Flesquières. "We simply came here to
die, my greasy darlings," Bill Dunesk said to himself, but he did not
speak aloud.

Through the slit in the turret, Bill could view the bodies. Sheaves of
sodden black wheat asprawl. Then the scrapheap of a tank on its side,
one track trailing in broken steel stairs. Another tank was stuck in a bog,
only its top cannon turret showing and firing at some Hun gun. As black
smoke belched up from his engine to obscure his vision, Bill saw a rent
driven into the swamped armour in front, then tongues of fire leaping
out of the wound gouged in the metal.

"Gunner ahead," Bill yelled, but nobody could hear him in the din
and the stench. He did not cry out again.

Unter-Officer Kruger of the 8th Field Battery killed Bill Dunesk and
his crew in the third bag of his day. Working his 77mm field gun single-
handed after the death of his men, he knocked out seven tanks before
his own end. There would be no Allied gain at Cambrai because of
dogged German resistance, as the communiqués would later state.

Watching the assault with his dragoons, Alexander Plunkett-Drax had
to admire the ingenuity of these rolling iron elephants. They were
camouflaged like chameleons and lurched from side to side, but never
turned over. They would plunge down a shell-crater and come up from
drowning on the far side. They belched out petrol fumes that he could
smell a mile away. This black smoke was their own screen against the
enemy. Their caterpillar wheels crunched barbed wire as if it were

spaghetti. And the sound of bullets ricocheting off their scaly sides was as ineffective as the buzz of a distant swarm of bees. They would cut a swathe in the Hindenburg Line for the cavalry to charge through and roll back the Huns to the Rhine.

As the horsemen moved forward behind the foot soldiers, who were consolidating the ground overrun by the armour, Alexander saw the first disaster. A tank was lying on its side, its wheels still revolving, its tracks askew. It looked like a gigantic beetle on its back, flailing at nothing. The rent in its blackened flank showed where the German shell had punctured it and incinerated the humans in its metal belly. Another giant tin lump straddled a stream, bogged down in mud, showing only its top gun-turret as a crocodile would poke out its snout in a swamp. And then a third tank waited, immobile, a wireless aerial betraying it as one of the new command centres of modern war, relaying signals back to headquarters, which would not know how to respond, or if they could, how to respond in time. Bill Dunesk was burned to death, but nobody yet knew.

The dragoons never had their charge. The forty thousand cavalrymen behind the mechanical attack were stopped by a few German gunners in a village on the flank that the tanks had forgotten to take. The Highland Division never stormed its way into the strong point. All the kilted Jocks did was get into a muddle with the mounted men. Ahead was a canal, and nobody had a pontoon bridge to cross it. Yes, horses could swim, but who was going to start a water charge of the Light Brigade into the machine-guns? That sort of glory and folly had gone out with the Crimea.

Then some of the tanks came waddling home. They had run out of steam and spare tracks. And Alexander Plunkett-Drax and his forty thousand horsemen who had ridden in their heads through and beyond the impregnable line, now rode back again. Over their heads flew the Sopwith Camels, which had cleared the air of enemy spotter planes and enabled the assault to be a surprise. There was some talk of them fighting duels in the air, of jousts and tournaments as if they were knights on wings. Even the Baron von Richthofen had left the saddle for the cockpit, and his battles in his red triplane were examples of chivalry in space. The Lewis gun was the lance now, the propellers were the hoofs of the charger. Alexander Plunkett-Drax felt demeaned by the machine.

A later meeting with a wireless operator at headquarters did not improve the mood of the dragoon officer. The man, who had the rank of captain, bore the name of Gillon Sinclair and turned out to be a Canadian cousin of his wife Arabella, whose relations were legion and usually unspeakable. Gillon enthused to Alexander about communications and war. The messages received back from the spotter planes and balloons and tanks and infantry wireless sets with their long cables rolled back behind the advance had altered the planning of battles. Instant information was the secret of success. The enemy would be beaten in the air waves, not in the trenches.

"Tommyrot," Alexander said. "In the end, there's only the bayonet and the lance, the bullet and cold steel."

"I reckon not," Gillon said. "The right info and you won't know what hit you. You won't even see it. Bombs and gas from the air, mines and long-range guns, tanks and submarines – they'll win wars in secret."

"Men win wars. Weapons don't." Suddenly Alexander remembered something his mistress Virginia had told him about this Canadian cousin. "Didn't you deal with Maurice Walter? Sell him some of our secret weapons."

Gillon flushed. He had almost forgotten that early episode, when he had come to England to work for Marconi. But how could this cavalry captain know anything about it?

"You know Walter?"

"Yes. I dealt with him. Over Ulster. We bought rifles, machine-guns. But I never supplied him. Like you did."

"I did not." The lie direct came easily to Gillon. "Your info is plumb wrong."

"It's right. It's the best. You always get the truth between the sheets."

"Someone I know?"

"She knows you. What happened to Walter I would like to know. You with all your information."

"I last heard of him in the Balkans. Supplying the Turks. He wasn't very popular here, when the war broke out."

"I'll say." Alexander Plunkett-Drax smiled at Gillon and stared him down. "Mum's the word over Walter. I bet you'd like him dead."

"Yeah. I guess I would."

"Snap. So would I. For reasons of my own."

Maurice Walter was facing a firing-squad. On the Salonika front, he had been captured in the advance on Bulgaria. He had stood out in his white suit in this dirty war, the only immaculate being on the whole front line, even though he was found hiding in the wine-cellar of an old taverna. "I am merely a trader in curios," he had told his captors, who had then told him that he was a merchant of death, the fashionable phrase those days for the international arms dealers like Nobel in Sweden, who were supplying every side in the Great World War and would institute peace prizes when the conflict was over for the cripples who survived. What Walter did not know was that on the Salonika front was a man who might wish him dead, the husband of his London mistress.

Hamish Charles had another problem on his mind. As a transport officer seconded to Greece, he had to deal with mules and donkeys as well as the rare railway train, and now an aeroplane had landed on a strip which had been cleared in the mountains, and the local peasants were frightened. They had never seen a flying machine before. Greek they might be, but Ancient Greek they were not. They were hardly soothed by folk memories of Pegasus, the airborne horse of the Gods, or Icarus, who had flown too near the sun on his feathery wings until the wax had melted and he had crashed to his death in the sea. They took the bomber from the sky as a visitation like the plague, and only Hamish Charles having his photograph taken with the village chief beside the Handley Page with its hundred-foot double wingspan persuaded the locals that this omen might be a blessing from Heaven and not a curse.

The photograph was to be his memento of the war, and he would send it home to show that he also was helping to win the struggle and not only drinking himself to death on *ouzo* now, a local liquorice drink that looked like milk and burnt like blazes. He got on well with the bomber pilot, who had trained with Murdo in the fledgling Royal Naval Air Service before the start of the fighting.

"If you had told me," the pilot said, "that five years on I'd be flying a bloody big boat to bomb Constantinople, I'd have said you were barmy."

"Constantinople?" Hamish Charles was impressed. "We lost at the Dardanelles, but we can bomb Constantinople?"

"Yes. Like another Crusade, isn't it?"

"Like another Crusade."

And it was now. The Christian armies and navies and airforces were defeating the Turks. Hamish Charles had heard from his cousin Robert, his enemy and his friend, that he had been transferred with a man called Meinertzhagen from East Africa to Allenby's army, advancing upon Jerusalem. Again, Crusaders would take the Holy City. Onward, Christian soldiers, marching as to war...

"I don't know," Hamish Charles said, passing his flask of *ouzo* to the pilot. "I suppose this war, when we win it, will be good for us."

"Thanks," the pilot said and took a swig from the flask. "Cor, bloody awful! Is this the local petrol? We lose the peace, I bet. Even if we win the war."

"Right," Hamish Charles said.

And right he was, Hamish Charles thought, watching the Handley Page fly off after its refit. Against the savage mountain range, its size diminished to a speck, its engine roar to a drone and silence. Its passing was evanescent against the northern peaks, which still blocked the British advance. Nothing that was hurled against them, aeroplanes and armoured cars and artillery, made the least difference to that barrier of stone and gorge and ravine. "You shall not pass," was the unspoken message of the crags, and they did not pass. That was the strength of the hills, that was the irrelevance of all this military effort, of human existence.

Hamish Charles kept his thinking to himself. He knew that he might be projecting the failure of his own life onto the failure of all lives and all endeavours. He had killed his first wife, or he believed he had. He had lost his second wife. He had abandoned his children, for the war had taken him away from them. There was nothing left for him to do. Except that evening, when he returned to brigade headquarters, he was told of the capture of Maurice Walter, the merchant of death, condemned to be executed in the morning as a spy and a traitor, whatever the legal niceties might be.

"I know the man," Hamish Charles told his brigadier. "I mean, I know of the man. He kn-kn-knows my wife." He betrayed what this Biblical knowledge was by a slight stammer, which he corrected. "Knew her before the war."

"You think you could get some intelligence out of him before he gets the chop?"

"I'll try."

Walking into the cell and seeing Walter for the first time, Hamish Charles felt the satisfaction of revenge. He was not jealous. How could he be of this haggard figure, his face blotched with bruises and stubble, his white suit fitting no better than a canvas sack?

"Maurice Walter," he said. "You don't know me. I know you. I am Hamish Sinclair, the husband of Virginia."

To his credit, Walter drew himself upright and even essayed a little irony.

"Destiny, to think it could be so shabby," he said. "What a fate to meet *you* here? I am hardly at my best, you are my executioner."

"Not exactly. The firing squad will be twelve men. I shall ask, however, to be the officer in command."

"And if they miss —"

"They will not."

"You will finally execute me. With your revolver."

"Did you supply it?"

"In the back of the head. Will you do me a favour?"

"Why should I?"

"To prove your generosity to your enemy. That will make you feel better about yourself. Virginia told me –"

"Do I want to listen?"

"You do. All men like hearing about themselves. Virginia told me that you are uneasy with yourself. You cannot forgive yourself. You killed your first wife, took Virginia from your cousin. You suffer from that idiocy called guilt. *Ce n'est pas la logique*. But what Anglo-Saxon was ever rational?"

As he talked, Walter seemed to recover his confidence and his dignity. He might have been judging Hamish Charles, who was his judge.

"You feel no guilt for all the killing from the weapons you were selling?"

"One death. That is all that matters to you. One particular death rather than the ten million who will die in this war. The wife you killed, Sinclair. Your wife. And now you will kill me. For no crime –"

"For killing thousands of our men."

"I do not kill. You do. You use my weapons. But – the favour I ask–"

"What is it?"

"If you will not let me escape –"

"Don't be absurd."

"No, you are too limited – too military – for mere magnanimity. Then kill me yourself. Cleanly, quickly, and now! One bullet to the back of my head. With your service revolver. So I do not have another night of anticipation before my execution."

"It would be against regulations."

"I attacked you. You were defending yourself."

"A bullet in the back of the head? It would not look like a defence."

"Think of the satisfaction. True revenge –"

"You will die, anyway."

"Not by your hand. And it will not be murder. As killing your first wife was."

"It was an accident, Walter –" Hamish Charles heard his voice rising at the taunt. He must control himself. "An accident."

"Not as I heard it. *Voilà*, a *crime passionelle*. You wanted Virginia. And now the killing of me, because you are jealous of me and Virginia, that will also be a *crime passionelle*, but a legal one. It will lay the first illegal act to rest. Kill me with the blessing of your military law. And you will satisfy your honour – and save the name of your wife."

The mockery in Walter's voice influenced Hamish Charles. His hand dropped to his holster. He undid the flap and drew out his weapon and thumbed loose the safety catch. There seemed to be an obstruction in his throat. He spoke thickly.

"Have you thought you may get what you want?"

"I hope so."

"Well, you won't. I wouldn't give you the satisfaction."

Walter shook his head as if in regret for what he was forced to say.

"Virginia, she is a courtesan. Of all the *poules de luxe* I have ever had, she excels in the arts of love. Breasts like a nymph, thighs like a leopard –" The barrel of Hamish Charles's revolver hit Walter across the mouth, splitting his lips on his provocation. "Ach." He fell to the floor.

"You will be executed in the morning," Hamish Charles said.

Walter looked up at him, wiping at his lips, which were streaming with scarlet.

"You fool. You will never live her murder down. Or mine. You will never live us down."

The disappearing trick was too much. Hamilton was reported Missing in Action off Scapa Flow. There was no knowing whether he was alive or dead. There was no trace of her husband, and little chance of ever finding his body or even the wreckage of his seaplane. Ellen-Maeve had lost her Hamilton, just as the nation had lost Lord Kitchener. They had both gone down near the same stretch of sea off Orkney. The Field-Marshal and Minister of War had been on his way to confer with the Tsar and plan a pincer campaign against the Kaiser and Hindenburg and the German armies, when H.M.S. *Hampshire* had struck a mine off Marwick Head on the island of Birsay. His huge handlebar moustache had not buoyed him up, and he had fed the fishes, and his bones were fifty fathoms deep.

Hamilton had flown out on a recce from the naval base at Scapa Flow, where most of the Home Fleet was anchored, waiting for another crack at Jerry like the Battle of Jutland, which had sent their battleships and cruisers scurrying back to their German ports, hardly to put out again. Yet Hamilton had gone scouting for them on a fine day, the visibility was top notch, and nothing was ever to be seen or heard of him again.

Ellen-Maeve had been to Scapa Flow, and she tried to tell her little ones, Hamish Henry and Titania, how the naval base was. "There are all these green islands in the far far north sea. They are very old. Five thousand years ago, people lived there. They have rings of tall stones that tell the hour of the day." The children looked at their mother with eyes as round as hunter time-pieces. "The shadows of the stones fall on the ground, and it's like a huge sun-dial. Like the hands on a watch-face. And these islands are all around a deep lake. It's called a loch up there, or a Flow. Scapa Flow. And they put all our big ships in there so that they can be safe."

"I know," Hamish Henry said. "Safe from the mines. And the submarines."

"The U-boats. And then there are the big ships of the Germans."

"But we beat them."

"They can come back again. And Daddy in his seaplane."

"It goes *vroom*," Titania said. "And it lands on the water."

"Just like the ducks in the park," Ellen-Maeve said. "Only you feed it with petrol, not bread crumbs. Daddy went out over the sea, looking for the German Fleet, in case it was coming in. And..." Ellen-Maeve put her arms round both her children. They were warm props under her worry. "And, my darlings, so far..."

There was a ring at the door-bell. Whenever you had something you had to say, somebody always interrupted you. She could only be her impossible cousin May Seymour-Scudabright. And surely it was, for the maid Phyllis ushered May into the room, a black pillar with her swaying walk. She must have little rollers on her shoes under the long sweep of her dress.

"My dears," May said, removing the hatpin from the flywheel of her hat, "I am so sorry to burst in on you —"

"We were not doing anything," Ellen-Maeve said. She rose from holding her little ones to offer a hand to May, who touched her fingers and dropped them like a hot scone.

"Charles told me about Hamilton. These new things they have. Crystal sets and morse transmitters, as well as telephones. You can talk over thousands of miles. Get all the news."

"Or not talk," Ellen-Maeve said. "Or not know. Children, go away and play in your rooms. I must talk to Auntie May."

"But you're telling us about Daddy," Titania said.

"Off you go. Go and play Nurses. Or Soldiers and Sailors."

"I'll be a sailor," Hamish Henry said, and off they went.

"I am so sorry," May said, when the door was closed. There was a glitter in her eye which was not a tear. Almost a look of triumph or of recognition. "He is missing, I hear."

"Yes," Ellen-Maeve said. "And there's not much hope."

"My two boys..." Now May did begin to weep. "I heard so soon after they went..."

Ellen-Maeve put an arm round the stiff shoulder of her cousin, rough under her ruched dress.

"It was very hard, May, losing both of your sons. But you still have Ruth."

"In a way."

"Please sit down. I'll send for tea."

"Thank you."

The two women arranged themselves side by side on the velvet embroidered sofa with little tassels over its wooden legs. Propriety was so important, even for furniture. Ellen-Maeve rang the bell, and when Phyllis came, tea was ordered with cakes. Yes, ma'am.

"There is still hope for Hamilton," Ellen-Maeve declared, feeling no hope at all.

"Well, it is best to be brave about it."

"The men have to be. Why not us?"

"Even Bill Dunesk went down. And what a soft lot he was."

Ellen-Maeve was wondering why May had come to see her. She was not the compassionate sort. Nor was she cruel enough to gloat at a cousin's misfortune. Perhaps she was reaching out to a fellow sufferer. Or was there something more?

"All these deaths, you know," May was saying. "We are all so worried about who is going to get what we have. That ghastly little squirt Lloyd George. Putting in Death Duties, just before we had the Great War on. He must have known it was coming. Sons dying, and then the fathers. All in weeks in the trenches. He wanted to take all we have away. I mean, who's going to get what we keep on trust?"

"It rather depends how much you have," Ellen-Maeve said. "And these London houses —" She looked at the frieze of scallop-shells that fringed the ceiling of her Georgian living-room. "Haven't you ever wondered how many other people lived here before us? We didn't know them. And they certainly didn't know who they were leaving their houses to."

"I know, I know." May sounded like a school mistress to a dull pupil. "That's my point. The heirs had to sell it on to people like you. Strangers. But the whole point of having a family is — you must *pass* it on. What you have — all that's precious to you — you must be able to give it to your children."

"But you only have Ruth. And she is —"

"Don't tell me, Ellen. It's the principle. And just because Ruth hasn't married yet —"

"Is she still living with Virginia? All that artistic thing."

"Yes. And that's my other point about this bloody war — excuse my French. By the time we've won, there won't be any young men left. Or suitable ones. I mean, they are all dead or wounded. Some places in the country, there's not a young man alive for twenty miles round. What are the girls going to do, I ask you?"

"Perhaps being a spinster may be popular."

"Oh, none of that. It never was." The maid Phyllis came in with the silver tray and the Japanese porcelain tea-set and the fruit cake. She put it down on the onyx small table with the gilt legs. "We are here to have families. To keep the British race going." Ellen-Maeve began to pour the green tea into the cups that were so transparent under their peony pattern that the flowers seemed to be watered into a quick life. "That is our duty. But, my dear, what are you going to do, if Hamilton is truly gone?"

Ellen-Maeve was still wondering what May really wanted from her, so she only replied, "Go on. We'll just have to muddle on."

"But you can't afford..."

"Tea, May. Here's your tea." Ellen-Maeve looked up again The ceiling was no white sky. It was a large trap door. "He may come home, you know. That's all I want. Here – how can we know there's a war on? What it's like out there. The cold, the mud, the rats, the wounds. We're snug as bugs in a rug. And Hamilton –"

May's smile was as false and bright as a Very rocket before an artillery salvo.

"He'll be flying home. I am sure of it."

"He won't. I pray he will."

Far to the north, the basking shark swam to the surface, longer than a cricket pitch under water. Searching for tiny sea creatures and weed with its toothy grin it lipped the white body of a pilot, dragging below the waves with the weight of his flying boots and blue uniform. The shark grazed around him, but left him alone to the harsh mercies of the North Sea. He had come to rest in an element even colder than the air he had tried to make his own.

For some, who knew from their families what it was like to be prairie farmers starting from a sod hut, the trenches were not too much of a shock. The wet sludge at the bottom, the dribbling walls, the smears of earth all over khaki sleeves, the soaked beams holding up a soggy collapse, these were nothing new. But when a slide revealed the bones of an arm with a charcoal-green brass wedding ring on its finger, or a Moaning Minnie blast loosed a scurry of rats as big as gophers, then the soldiers of the Black Watch knew they were in the wrong territory. This was not Canada in the thaw, this was near the Somme in winter.

When they had marched out to the quay in Maine in their kilts, the bagpipes were playing the charge and the dance, though Colin knew well that the only other Scottish tunes were the dirge and the lament. The troopships over the Atlantic had treated the soldiers on an equal with cattle, but Colin had a better journey than his great-grandfather's scumboat to Canada after the Highland Clearances. Yet France was a put down. Maybe it was crazy to expect a Gay Paree in every town from Rouen to Rheims, but the *cafés* and the *estaminets* were more like cellars and bunkers than places you went to have a good time, and the reek of the army bodies was like a graveyard you hadn't met yet. Only the skies were not like the West, heavy with gloom and dark, then all of a sudden pierced with spokes of bright light.

"Ye'll nae hear the birds," Jock said. "They dinna sing. They dinna want a bullet for their dram."

Jock MacNye had a vein of black humour out of a corpse, but then he was the great survivor. He told Colin never to put his tin hat over the parapet, but use the periscope. Not to volunteer for a sortie or a recce, but stay out of the way of the sergeant. To watch the tell-tale trails for a buried mine, and use the shell-holes as a hide, not a grave. "Ye'll never kill a Hun, if you canna live to kill him."

Jock was tough and gentle. He would bite the heads off rats and bleed them and skin them and gut them and steam them into a billycan stew with vinegar and whisky. "Jock's grouse," he called them. "Poor folk's deer. How d'ye like the stew?" He'd smile at the sodden sandbags around them and say, "Fit for a laird." And the taste was not half bad, sour and sweet with a flavour that stayed in the gum. But when there was a wounded man, Jock would tend to him like a cobweb before hoisting him back to the field hospital as light as carrying a spring lamb. "He'll live to see another day. Nae good, if it's this day."

As they waited to die, they hated the generals. A quiet loathing they had of it. Hardly voiced it was. If they had said what was in their hearts and minds, it was a mutiny. For all would have stopped obeying the orders, which were madhouse. Only when a swaggering major came to inspect them in his white cavalry britches and a bonnet with a cockade, and said to them, "We are all fellow Britons and proud to be. Carry on, men, carry on." Only then did Colin hear Jock growl behind him, "Carry on, carry on. And will ye carry me off, then?" And Colin put his hand back over Jock's mouth to hush him. The dumbell was a sort of a sod of a Sinclair cousin through some place in Ireland, and he must not become the judge and executioner of a friend.

Jock was condemned by a recce that they could not avoid. They had to bring in a prisoner, a live prisoner, to find out what the enemy was doing, although they both had been stuck in the trenches for so long that they might have been potatos. But when the five in the party went into No Man's Land and slithered among the watery pits, the lead man hit a trip-wire and all hell broke loose. Pitter-patter, not tiny feet, the drizzle of the machine-guns, while they squashed themselves into the soft muck. And then they had the good luck, before it went to bad. There was a leftover half-dead Jerry in there, worse for wear, but 'Kamerad' it was, surrender. He couldn't walk, so Jock had to lug him back, soft as a quilt in his arms. But as they squelched out of cover when the barrage lifted, the Jerry was a hero or touched in the head, and he sang out something in Boche, and the rain of the guns came on again, and Jock went down in front of Colin, rolling the Jerry loose. Colin lay over his back, trying to save him from any more pain. He could feel the pumping of that great heart through the wet cloth over the chest. And then stop, and Colin was running with warm blood and he crawled over to the shouting Jerry and dragged his head back and slit his throat with his sharpened bayonet like Bain did a pig on the farm.

"Hush," he said. "That'll hush you." And later, when he had dragged Jock's body into the trenches near first light, and when the officer asked him at the debriefing why they had lost the prisoner, Colin said, "We lost Jock." And he would say no more. And the other three with him, they would not tell on him. A terrible thing it is to kill an unarmed man, but a more terrible thing is to lose your friend.

Before they went over the top on orders from the back-bench beserkers who could only charge on their mess bill their next b and s — brandy and soda for them, blood and shit for the Black Watch in their mess — Colin had a letter from home. His mother Rachel wrote from Vancouver that his grandfather Bain had passed away at last in dignity in their clapboard house, not on the clapped-out land. And his father Gillon was stuck as her son was, in a place unknown in the wide war, when communications were already breaking down the oceans between the continents. And his sisters Leah and Fiona were well, "so pretty and bonny, you would hardly know them."

That was the truth. And they would hardly know him. He had meant to write them a last letter, but the orders came too soon. They were going over the top before dawn, to catch the Germans by surprise. Some surprise, as the heavy artillery had been pounding the trenches and the barbed wire in front for twenty-four hours, so that even the crashes and the whizz-bangs became a sort of dull symphony, out of tune, but as regular as a muffled beat. As they crouched in the dark below the ladders to the sandbags above, Colin was prepared to die. If Jock could not make it, how could he? He was ready to slog into the guns, bleating baa-

baa-baa like a sheep. That is what the French had done at Verdun, or so they said. Only he would howl like a wolf, a long shrieking and keening, all the anger and sorrow for the loss of the man who had kept him alive.

On that dark dawn assault, 5,371 was the official casualty figure. The one was Colin, who died as he reached Doctor Seaforth Sinclair in the field hospital. His distant Indian cousin only recognized him by his name-tag. The bullet which had blown away the side of his skull had left a piece of his naked brain pulsing. Only his incredible strength had kept him alive on the stretcher back. Seaforth had been working on the wounded for fourteen hours, and he cracked. He had not collapsed before on duty, but now he fell on his knees and banged his head against the side of the iron bedstead, and he wiped the tears off his eye-lids with his fist.

"Never," he shouted, "never, never, never, never again."

A nurse raised him, but he fell over the end of the bloody sheets and Colin's white stiff feet.

"Again," he slurred. "I know. Always again."

24

THE STUTTER OF
THE GUNS

Wallace Jardine never quite knew why Winston Churchill had plucked him out of a tank turret and put him into an office in Whitehall. His father Douglas had something to do with it, for Churchill was always interested in the Empire, and Douglas must have fed information from India to the First Lord of the Admiralty as well as a recommendation for his son to be taken from the killing grounds of France to the security of London. Yet as Wallace soon found out, the squat aggressive pug Churchill also had an interest in science and technology. "Machinery wins wars," he once said to Wallace, "although men often lose them."

Wallace was officially in the section of the War Office dealing with propaganda, not procurement. He helped to put out all the information fit to print. Anything which helped morale was good, yet any truth that smacked of defeat was treason. Now that the United States were in the war and the doughboys were coming over, American methods swept all reason under the carpet. Spies were in every dustbin, Hun agents plotted to blow up Big Ben, pigeons flew in with plague germs. Fear was fed by fantasy. No conspiracy was too absurd. Vague terrors were loosed in the daily news. The people could only sustain the war effort by living in the certain terror of gang rape and burning churches, if the Kaiser's armies reached these shores.

Meeting Chaim Weizmann on the chemical deal was altogether more satisfactory. The bearded biochemist had renounced Germany to become a British citizen, yet he did not fall under the cloud of mass suspicion. He was too valuable. He could put together groups of scientists to make acetone for making explosives. He could also put together Jewish battalions to fight against Turkey in his impossible dream of creating Israel again from the wreck of the Ottoman Empire. The Welsh terrier Lloyd George was now the Minister of Munitions, and he fell in with the plans for better shells and bombs combined with the return of the Jews to the Promised Land. "Blow up the old," Wallace once heard him say. "And bring on the new."

Churchill needed thirty thousand tons of acetone to blow up the Boches on the Western Front and the Turks in Palestine. Weizmann was glad to provide the big bangs, and Wallace was an assistant, travelling with him among the laboratories at Birmingham and in the North.

"Do you read your Bible, then?" Weizmann asked Wallace, who did not read it as much as he should.

"Yes. From time to time."

"Samson. Do you like the story of Samson?"

"Yes. Smiting people with the jawbone of an ass. Blinded, and pulling down the heathen temple."

"Not the point, young man. I see you wondering at what I do. All this stuff for killing people. Even though they are Germans and Turks, they are fellow human beings."

"I know. But there's a war on."

"The melancholy excuse for everything bad we do. No, in the Samson story, it says, 'Out of the strong came forth sweetness'. There is honey in destruction. In the Torah – your Old Testament – there is no Israel without a struggle first."

"We believe that, too."

"Too much." Weizmann sighed. "You have your land. Why do you need an Empire, then?"

Wallace hardly knew the answer, but he managed to say, "We spread the light. Something like that."

"Spread the light?" Weizmann smiled. "What spread? What light? I hope you can spread it so far that your God and our God can return to Israel."

"We have taken Jerusalem."

"We? Who?"

"My cousin Robert was there. He's with General Allenby and the cavalry. They're advancing on Syria."

"We," said Weizmann and gripped Wallace quickly by the arm. "I hope so."

Wallace read the communiqués of the war correspondents, when he came back from the north of England to report that all the volatile chemicals were flowing through the retorts and vats to detonate the Axis powers into submission. The journalists in Palestine seemed to have been swept away into a biblical fervour:

> We fought on the fields which had been the battlegrounds of Egyptian and Assyrian armies, where Hittites, Ethiopians, Parthians, and Mongols poured out their blood in times when kingdoms were strong by the sword alone. The Ptolemies invaded Syria by this way,

and here the Greeks put their colonizing hands on the country. Alexander the Great made his route to Egypt, Pompey marched over the Maritime Plain and inaugurated that Roman rule which lasted for centuries; till Islam made its wide irresistible sweep in the seventh century. Then the Crusaders fought and won and lost, and Napoleon's ambitions in the East were wrecked just beyond the plains.

When the Commander-in-Chief had to decide how to take Jerusalem, we saw the British force move along precisely the same route that has been taken by armies since the time when Joshua overcame the Amorites and the day was lengthened by the sun and moon standing still till the battle was won. Geography had its influence on the strategy of today as completely as it did when armies were not cumbered with guns and mechanical transport.

Fair enough, Wallace thought. And then he had a family chore to do. Virginia and Ruth had invited him round to one of their *soirées*. That was the word they used for the occasion, if it wasn't *salon*, which occurred during the day. There seemed something immoral in all their dressing-up in the war, but women always did. And the only time that he had protested, Virginia had laughed and said, "We simply have to keep up with all your gold braid and ribbons and cocked hats."

The walls of the studio were covered with bright zig-zags and whirls of colour. They looked like patterns of searchlights on the sky or exhaust trails of Sopwith Camels in a dogfight. They were a madness of streaks and motion.

"What do you call them?" Wallace asked Virginia, who herself looked like a rainbow in a sieve, so many little blobs of the spectrum were floating round her hanging chiffons.

"Futurism, darling. They're what you're going to look like. When you can see properly. And you know, the Italians are our allies."

Now Ruth came up, her beautiful oval face crowned no longer with a coil of long tresses, but with a bob. She might have been wearing a bronze helmet.

"You've lost your hair, Ruth."

Sometimes Wallace was shocked into saying the obvious.

"Better than losing my mind, sweetie. Have you met everybody?"

Everybody did not look like anybody very much to Wallace. Many were dressed as hospital orderlies, some in the suits of civil servants, only a few in uniform like him.

"Not many people serving here."

"Serving?" Virginia laughed, then winked at Ruth. "What you call serving, they're all over there, aren't they? In the trenches. Cannon fodder."

"You mean, the people here are mainly conchies?"

"What did that old hymn say?" Ruth was smiling. "Who sweeps a room as for thy cause, Makes that and the action fine. Here we've got artists. Philosophers. People sweeping out the muck of the war. Binding the wounds. Conscientious, yes, they are. They object to being murdered for nothing."

Now a fat youngish man with soot around his eyes and a pout on his mouth came up to them. He was wearing khaki, and it clung to him in a rough skin.

"Virginia, darling," he said. "Could you whistle up a brandy?"

"For you, Cecil, ambrosia."

As Virginia moved away, Ruth introduced the plump soldier.

"Mister Chesterton," she said. "Another Mister Sinclair. Cecil is Gilbert's brother, you know, the writer. He's serving, in your sense, though I'm sure he doesn't know quite why."

"Doing my duty," Cecil shrilled. "For God and country. Like taking on Marconi."

Now Wallace remembered. The scandal over the Marconi trial, the libel suit when the Attorney General was accused by the Chestertons of buying an interest in the communications company, just before the government signed a world-wide deal with it. A chain of wireless stations was to be set up to keep the whole Empire talking. Only cabinet ministers had traded on the stock exchange, and the shares had risen to their profit.

"We do need those global links," Wallace said diplomatically. "The Germans have them. Their bulletins to their ships as far away as Africa before the war broke out are meant to have saved half the German navy. And because the government broke off the Marconi deal, we've only got two half-built stations at Leafield here and in Egypt. And they don't work. And the Post Office has the contract, and it can't even deliver the letters on time." He paused. "We could lose the sea war because of it."

Cecil's balloon cheeks were changing from pink to puce.

"Are you telling me," he said, "when I expose corruption in high places – risk everything to print the truth – bear witness – that the stench will go away, just because we are caught in a conflict which will ruin us all? I am fighting, you know, for things I believe in."

Wallace only nodded.

"I cannot fight for politicians with their hands in the till and greed and stealing from the people. How can you? But you're a desk chap."

"I have served in a tank," Wallace said.

"Just like you. Very safe."

Wallace turned his back and walked away. If the war had taught him anything, it was not to respond, but to leave. There was no use in talking to people who would never be convinced. Why waste breath?

Wallace did not believe in fate any more than in spiritualism or table tapping or the hidden hand. Yet two days after his encounter with Cecil Chesterton, another cousin Gillon turned up in his office. Of course, this was no chance, for Gillon would have had to pass all the checks and guards. Yet the fact that Gillon had found him out so soon made Wallace wonder about his sources of information. Certainly, he was well-connected with what he did. He was wearing a black arm-band over his army tunic.

"I was so sorry to hear about Colin," Wallace said. "Hamilton was lost, too. I wrote to you. It is so unfair. Just when it is the final push."

"My son," Gillon said. He looked at the lined long face of his cousin, which was so like his own a decade or two ago. The family seemed to be born to be in mourning and even their jokes were sad. "It's hard to forgive the death of a son, an only son. I must. I will never forget it."

"How could you? We're all so sorry."

Gillon walked to the window and looked out over Horseguards Parade. There were no scarlet uniforms now. Everything was changed to dun and green. How could you Troop a Colour in front of His Majesty, the thin red lines wheeling and marching, in this long slaughter of millions in the mud? His Colin, too.

"We may all die out, you know. Families expand and shrink. Like concertinas. Look how many of us came out of Hamish and Hannah when they had to leave the Highlands. And we are going down like flies. All of us in this grinding business that never seems to end."

Gillon looked in silence over the empty gravel of the parade ground. No one there now. Too many little white crosses in Flanders.

"How can I help you?" Wallace asked.

"If we want to win this war," Gillon said, "and I suppose we do, we have got to be able to talk to each other. Over great distances. And after the war, too. This is one planet. One globe. Or the fabric will crumble. It already has. We can't communicate."

"You have come to me over Marconi."

"You know Churchill. He knows. He would forgive anything to win a war."

"Is it the only system which works?"

"The only one. Marconi invented it. The Germans stole from him. They have it, we are giving it away. Like we give away all our inventions.

If God gave anything to the English, it was not an Empire. It was thinking of something new."

"Marconi wasn't exactly English."

"He came here. He'll go again, if he has to."

"He wasn't exactly wise about business."

"No genius is. They leave that to businessmen."

"Like Isaacs. Who made the company and got the contracts and paid off ..."

"Your friend Winston," Gillon interrupted, "would tell you that was irrelevant. All is not fair in love and business. But what is essential in war is to communicate. To stop another disaster happening like the last one. Do you think we'd go on with all this stupid slaughter in the trenches – or have a Gallipoli – if our commanders knew quickly what was happening? Instant news. Change the plans. Don't persist in failures. Don't repeat the mistakes. Talk."

"I'll see what I can do," Wallace said. "But that Marconi business, it hurt Lloyd George and the rest of them. They won't forget easily."

"They would prefer to win the war. And the peace, perhaps."

"And the peace, perhaps. If we ever get there. I am so sorry about Colin."

Gillon held out his hand in farewell.

"You were good to see me, Wallace. Do all you can. We must start talking. In the end."

Robert had been at most of the cavalry battles of the Palestine war. He had seen the Australian Light Horse galloping into the Turkish ranks with their sabres, shouting, "Allah, you bastards, we will give you Allah." At Huj, he rode with the Warwickshire and Worcestershire Yeomanry up the mountain into the machine guns, hacking the Turkish loaders into a bloody silence with a carnage of kicking and falling horses around him. On the Mughar-Katrah Ridge, there had been the same suicidal charge, as if they were as berserk as the Templars charging against Saladin. This was a Holy War still, Robert supposed. When they took Jerusalem, General Allenby had walked on foot through the Jaffa gate, as humble as a pilgrim, and promised that all religions would be respected, Muslim and Jew as well as Christian. He had to do that because Colonel Lawrence was with him, and his Arab legions had become the finest mounted guerrillas of the war.

On the advance to Damascus before they reached Megiddo, Robert once had the chance to talk to Lawrence. The colonel now wore khaki drill, although he still sported his Bedouin head-dress against the sun.

Robert had ridden out on a patrol to probe the Turkish defences of the ruins of the old site of Armageddon, the final battle between good and evil in the Bible. Lawrence was waiting for him on his return, wanting to hear his report first, although there was nothing much to report except the usual forward positions of the enemy among the wadis and outcrops of stone.

"So there will be a charge," Lawrence said. "Fairly open ground. Our speed will make us moving targets." His lean flanks and the austerity of his face made him appear bone dry. "That is the theory. And we don't even have chariots like the Israelites. Another unnecessary massacre tomorrow."

"That's what cavalry are for."

"No, they are not. They are raiders. Frontal assault is for tanks, which we don't have and infantry protected by cross-fire. We will have an Armageddon all right."

"The last great cavalry battle of the war," Robert said.

"Of any war, I hope." Lawrence moved away to stand between Robert and the setting sun, its usual blazing ball turning to an orange saucer and then a red ember as it sank over the bleak land. "I'd rather ride a camel than a motor-cycle, but if you're sending dispatches, it is the machine. You can't avoid it. The horse is obsolete."

"Never," Robert said. "Horses and mules, they can go places tanks and motors will never be able to go."

The last light stretched Lawrence's shadow a hundred feet along the ground until the head of his black long line was broken by the wheel of a truck.

"This is a desert war," Lawrence said, "not a mountain one. And this is Armageddon. You know your Book of Revelation. Where the armies of Satan will battle the armies of Christ at the millennium. The only question is, which is which."

Robert was shocked at the remark.

"But us – we're Christians."

"Don't worry," Lawrence said. "We will win. But my Arab friends are also with us, King Feisal and his men. They have already won the war for us. And will they win now?"

"Of course. They'll beat the Turks, too."

"But freedom. Independence Will they win that?" Lawrence paused against the red strip of the horizon that showed in a long wound. "We are an empire, you know. If we gain ground, we tend to want to keep it and rule it. Thank you for your report. On to Armageddon."

In the morning of the battle, Robert rode out past the Jewish Legion, three battalions of volunteers who were fighting for their ancient land, now promised again by the British government. These soldiers suited the ground as if it were already their own, blending into the sand and the rocks, while the British Yeomanry appeared absurd on high horses with lances and sabres. And when the charge came in the dust and the cannonades and the stutter of the guns, Robert felt the shiver of fear before the spurt of thrill, and he rose in his saddle to hurl himself into the thick cloud, and the dum-dum which exploded his head into a crimson rose was so quick that it was a shattering mercy and a final judgement.

On the day that Wallace heard in Whitehall of Robert's fall, he had to go to see Weizmann about the acetone for the explosives. And when he told the Zionist about his cousin's death at Megiddo, Weizmann nodded gravely and said that it was a good place to die, if death had to come. "I thank you for my people," he said. "He died for our return. If we can return. And when we can, we will."

25

FIRE FROM HEAVEN

The new searchlights stitched the night sky over London with their seams of light. They criss-crossed in moving patterns, searching for the pale coughdrops of the Zeppelins and the vultures of the Gotha bombers, coming to void their high venom on the city. The anti-aircraft guns hiccuped at the armada above, sailing the dark sky, suddenly trapped as targets in the shifting beams of brightness. This was no night for a reunion, and yet it was. For it was to celebrate a death that was the herald to a new generation. Kate was dead in the third year of the Great War, nine months after her husband Bob the Railwayman had passed away. And her daughter Marie had called the clan together in memory of their forebears, who had begat them. If there was a war in the heavens, it would not stop their memorial feast. All was apt, in a way. The death of Kate was marked by fireworks over their gathering.

The arrival that morning of the postcard from Hamish Charles in Greece had also suited that night. He must have bought it after it had been imported to the canteen there. It showed young lions walking towards an old lion, lying on his stone hill and tagged ENGLAND. The other lions were tagged by the names of the dominions: CANADA, AUSTRALIA, SOUTH AFRICA, NEW ZEALAND and a distant yellow cat called INDIA. This was the true gathering of the Empire in defence of the mother lair. A pride of lions walking across a dry plain under a sun that flew the Union Jack above its rays. The caption of the whole postcard – THE LIONS COME HOME.

The message on the back was curt, but it confirmed that Hamish Charles was still alive. Addressed to the Countess of Dunesk, it read:

Dear Marie,

I am in the pink. Here's hoping you all are. Murdo is fine and flying high. Tell Virginia a fellow called Walter met a sticky end. And a good show too.

Best
Hamish

All a bloody game to the men, Marie thought. Death and retribution, envy and emotion, the men played it as cricket. Play on, and play the game. She could not tell how Virginia would react to the news of the death of her lover and financier, but probably not too badly. After all, she had the ghastly Alex Plunkett-Drax in her life, and Walter's end would solve a problem for her. She was lucky or unlucky with Alex, because he was never exposed to any danger in France. The cavalry were kept firmly far behind the lines. Civilians were more likely to catch a bomb unloaded on their bonnets from a Zeppelin than the fancy horsemen were to see action over the Channel.

They could have been sitting in the basement of Sunderland House, which Consuelo Marlborough had kindly opened as a shelter for the duration of the air raids. But this was not the night to duck for cover. They were meeting in the Pall Mall, now called the Haymarket. If places had been where they were named to be, German spies or bombs might have dropped in there. The old biddies were presiding over the theatre bar as they always did, Bunnie and Mac – Helen Macdonald, the *doyenne* of the trade. And there talking to her sat a little man in a khaki tunic with a vast sunflower stuck between his brass buttons. "Roses and chocolate creams," he was saying, "nectar and ambrosia. The world has no greater pleasures." Except for his uniform, Marie thought, nobody would ever know there was a war on.

Her daughter Rosabelle was there, tall and angular with her wild red hair long enough to sit upon; and Ellen-Maeve, more like a daisy than ever with her yellow head and white flounces, but wearing a dark bonnet now for her drowned Hamilton; and another widow Ruby in black with black ribbons in her ringlets, and her hard mother Margaret from India, where husband Douglas still connived with the Civil Service to keep the Raj in order; and Ruth and Virginia, still bosom friends in spite of their shared lover; and her own friend Peg from India, hating where the war brought her and what it made her do. But Arabella would not come over from Ireland with her son Peregrine, what with all the troubles there after the Easter Rebellion: somebody had to guard the house while Alex Plunkett-Drax defended the whole British Isles from his stables near Rouen. Nor had her husband come, Bill Dunesk. His death had ended their living separation.

Marie called the table to order. She was used to public speaking and living as well.

"We are met to remember my mother Kate," she said. "She is buried now in the Scotland she left and always loved. She has come at last to her home. I know you could not be there. The war calls us all to serve. But she lies at rest, where she would be, looking over the sea to the Western Isles. Do not cry for her. She had a full life. And she lived her span and is done. For never any rest she had in all her long life. She is at peace now – and we are not. To my mother Kate."

Here Marie picked up her glass of pink champagne, and made the others drink with her, shocked as some were at this kind of a memorial service in a theatre bar. Then Marie got her words wrong.

"She asked me to give this tribute to her going. She never stood on cemetery. She was proud of me, of what I have become. But she never understood what I was doing – working for women and for miners, for the rights we shall have when the war is over. She was the old school. We are the new. When I remember, how I came to London – a music-hall turn on my pony – that's why they know me here at the old Pall Mall."

"Take me, take me –" Virginia said. "Even I have heard of *that* number of yours."

"And now – a war to win – a peace after which women will be free – and puberty over with fair wages for all. India and Ireland given Home Rule –"

"Steady on," Margaret Jardine said. "You sound just like Seaforth."

"My brother," Peg Menon said. "Saving your boys."

"And all that tosh you talk about independence. Douglas says you are positively *dangerous*. As bad as those Irish rebels."

"At the moment," Peg said, "we Indians are mainly in France, saving you on the Western Front."

"Darling Peg," Marie said, "more about your family, less about saving the world. No politics in the mess, you know that golden rule. Nor in the Pall Mall." She rose for another toast.

"The Sinclairs, God bless them, may they always meet again wherever they may roam."

"The Sinclairs."

The clinking of the glasses in tiny chimes made Ruby begin to cry for her brief lost husband. Already a baby kicked in her belly, and there was no father for it. Her mother Margaret put an arm round her daughter. "Hush, it'll be all right. We can cope back in India. We'll go back to Annandale." And Ruth thought of the dead, not of her Aunt Kate, but of her two brothers killed within the week, and now of her coming together with her mother and even her father Charles again, vain and censorious though he was and always would be.

"Isn't it a terrible thing," she said to Virginia, "that dying brings us together, and living never does?"

Virginia had already heard of the sticky end of Maurice Walter, and that her husband Hamish might have had a hand in it. She hardly regretted her loss. She had, indeed, met Alex Plunkett-Drax through Walter and his arms dealing.

"People introduce you before they die," she said. "What do they say? You pass away. But before you pass away, you pass on – you pass on to your friends, your lovers, to people who are still living."

She now rose to her feet, her glass held high.

"To Kate," she said, "and to the others who serve or have gone in this war –" to Ruby – "to your Alistair –" to Ruth – "to your Gordon and Graham –" to Peg – "to your Seaforth and Miriam –" to herself – "to a friend and helper of mine –" and raising her glass – "to all those who have passed on so that we may know each other better and be together now."

All drank to that. Outside, a siren wailed over the night streets. Marie put her arms round the thin shoulders of Rosabelle. "Come on out," she said. "You'll be able to say, I was in the Pall Mall the night they bombed London."

"And out of it," Rosabelle said. "I'll go out with you."

Mother and daughter went out into the Haymarket, where no hay was sold now, for the horse-buses had given way to petrol buses and electric trains on rails above and underground. And in the darkness, a ragged comet was falling, a sign of the beginning and the end. An English fighter-plane had soared above a Zeppelin and had dropped on it bombs and flechettes sharper than the arrows of Eros's bow in Piccadilly. The great gas bag had burst into flames and was descending slowly on the great city, trailing rags of fire in a burning scatter. Around it the searchlights crossed their beams, drawing a blaze of peaks and crags, making outlines of ranges and hills against the dark nothing of the night, sending up bright pillars to hold up the heavens from London. And Rosabelle spoke softly to her mother the opening lines of her favourite poem from William Blake:

> "The fields from Islington to Marybone,
> To Primrose Hill and St John's Wood,
> Were builded over with pillars of gold;
> And there Jerusalem's pillars stood."

Marie watched the dancing buttresses of light as the fiery debris of the airship floated down the dark.

"Robert was in the real Jerusalem," she said. "He helped to take it before he was taken." She paused and said, "Our holy city now."

"It always was," Rosabelle said. "It is here. Can't you see?"

"I can see."

The burning tapestry against the night sky sketched towers and walls, summits and spires. And Marie stroked the red fall of her daughter's hair that streamed down while the last embers of the Zeppelin were buried in the far roofs of London.

"I can see." Marie said, "why we survive."

This was the war to end all wars, they were saying. Yet wars were never ending. Peace was the dove that did not reach their clan. And so many of them were already dead. Marie trembled. She would have to take Hannah and Kate's place now, and keep them all together. And she feared she had not the strength. Yet she must. For only through the women could the children and the men go on.

THE SEAS ARE HIS

1

PEACE, WHAT!

1918

Banners and bunting, bunting and banners were flying from all the lamp-posts and the ladies' hats, ribbons of the red and the white and the blue, the green and the yellow and the black, the colours of the Allies, their flashes and flags. And the stars and the stripes burst out against the heavens in fireworks and rocket trails. The singing and the shouting were so loud that the air seemed to vibrate as the strings of a harp. And there was no way to squeeze through the crush of the tommies and the Yankees, the jocks and the khaki without being kissed twenty times over through your veil and under the brim of your hat, if you could manage to keep it on with the hand which wasn't defending your bosom.

Crushed and torn at the hems, Marie Dunesk reached the doors of the Café Royal off Piccadilly. She had called an emergency meeting for the family in this lapse into decadence, the dining-room of the Emperor Napoleon the Third, all decked with red plush and gilt chairs and mirrors and imperial monograms. He had been ruined by going to war, and that was happening to what was left of the Sinclair men. Too many had died, leaving the problems of the peace to the women and the children. If it was a peace, that is, and not just another long armistice before the next world war to come.

When Marie reached the large table spread with white damask and a platoon of silver things, her least favourite members of the clan were already sitting there, Virginia and her daughter Clio of thirteen, and her leech and imitator, Ruth Seymour-Scudabright, who had been sucked into the rebel world of modern art to put a chasm between herself and her conventional parents. But nobody was buying the Cubists and the Fauves any more, because there was no money left to buy anything with now. And they had worked with her at Wandsworth in the Women's Emergency Corps, along with Ellen Maeve, probably the worst trio of nurses in history after the Three Witches in *Macbeth*.

"Double, double, toil and trouble," Marie found herself saying as she sat down. "What a lot of trouble getting here. A hell of a brouhaha outside. How did you darlings reach it?"

"I was kissed by a black man in baggy trousers," Clio said, smiling with her curling green eyes. Shy she was not, even at her age.

"A Zouave, actually," Virginia said. "But I doubt if my daughter will be swept away to a sheikh's harem in Morocco. Though I must say, recruiting troops from all over the world to win the war has made London at last cosmopolitan."

"I could have done without some of them," Ruth said. "Especially the Canadians. They can't tell a Picasso from a picture postcard of Bognor Beach."

"Much the same for me, too," Marie said. "But they did save our skins. How is the gallery doing, incidentally?"

"I thought you knew," Virginia said. "Closed for the duration."

"Are you opening again?"

"I doubt it."

"No buyers, and you're all cleaned out?"

"Absolutely."

"Well then, back to the wards. Ah, Ellen-Maeve. We are so glad you could come and find somebody to look after your two children."

Marie rose to meet the young widow, whose curls seemed even more blonde with grief.

"It is difficult getting servants now," Ellen-Maeve said. "They are all in the munitions factories."

"Making shells, not babies. How are Hamish Henry and Titania? They haven't got this awful influenza we are hearing of?"

"No, thank God," Ellen-Maeve said, as she sat, spreading out her frilled skirt. "Only mumps, which may be worse."

"Isn't it contagious?" Clio drew away from her cousin.

"Quite right," Virginia said. "Go sit in that other chair, and you won't catch it."

"It is wonderful for you to have us to dinner here," Ellen-Maeve said. "Especially when there is so much to celebrate. Or is there?"

"This is more an emergency planning session," Marie said. "But let's just chat until all the others come."

And the other women all did come, battling their ways through the jumble and the seething and the shouting in the streets outside. Patience came, although she was hated by Virginia for having been the second wife of her first dead husband Robert. She did, at least, wear a matronly black gown, while Virginia and Clio wore striped outfits that might have come from beach tents. Then another widow Ruby appeared in a deep purple robe of mourning. She had met her dead mate at the Wandsworth General Hospital and had left her baby Ian at home. And last of them, in strode Rosabelle, as magnificent at eighteen as her mother Marie had always been, her high Crow cheekbones and blackcherry lips and red horsetail of hair sweeping above the short slight split in her long skirt above her white chamois leather boots with stick heels.

"Now we're all here," Marie said after kissing her daughter, "let's see how we are going to go on."

The lasting problems of the world have to do with land and water, because nobody can escape death. Marie knew as much, but the lethal urgency of the World War was that too many fathers and sons had died too soon for the survival of their property.

"It's that Lloyd George," Marie said. "His new death duties. They have risen to forty per cent. That might be fair if an owner had lived out his natural span and passed on parcels of his estate to his nearest and dearest before he passed on. But when you have all the gentry rushing into the army at the first sound of the trumpet – and swatted like flies – then you've got a revolution. They say more land will be forced to change hands after our Great War than after Cromwell's Civil War. You can lose nearly all the men in the family in months, and the government will grab nearly all they have. We're five widows here –"

"I still have my second husband," Virginia said. "Hamish Charles. But he's a nervous wreck, what's left of him."

"There is no money coming in," Marie went on. "If you get a disability pension, Virginia, it will be a joke. So are widows' pensions. And War Bonds are a fraud. And there's a huge slump coming. You know what I think? The government declared the war and then decided that it would make the people it killed pay for the damage. The ministers put in huge death duties to pay back the War Loans with the blood of those they have sacrificed."

"Marie, Marie," Patience protested, "we had to fight, save our empire."

"We did not have to fight, and our empire cannot be saved. It will wither away from its own natural causes."

"Such as?"

"People wanting to be free and govern themselves."

"Not so well as us."

"Perhaps. But then, you see, liberty has always been the enemy of good government. We want to mismanage things our own way and run our own finances. Which is why we are all here. I have a way out of death duties, so we can keep most of what we have now. We just do privately what we have been doing for free at Wandsworth. Charity doesn't begin at home. No more charity means we keep our homes."

So Marie set out her strategy of salvation. Ermondhaugh, surrounded by its coal mines, would become a private convalescent home for the long-term war wounded. They had all worked at the General Hospital in London as volunteer nurses, while Patience had the experience of running a whole hospital in Africa. Many of them did not get on with each other, but in their care of the sick, they could forget their differences. And the ill might also be from the family, Hamish Charles and Doctor Seaforth, who had also collapsed from the strain of tending too many victims of the catastrophe, now called a victory. There was also Edinburgh University nearby for Rosabelle, and a good school for Clio and nursery schools for the three smaller ones, Ian and Hamish Henry and Titania. Scots primary education was far better than English, as everyone knew.

"Scots weather isn't," Virginia said tartly. "We'd spend all our time up there knitting wool jumpers to keep the ice out."

"You'll find other things to do," Marie said. "Edinburgh was called the Athens of the North. Very artistic and intellectual."

"About as much as a haggis and a bagpipe," Ellen-Maeve said. "I went up to Scapa Flow, to see Hamilton. There's nothing there at all –" she began to weep. "Not him, not him now –"

"There." Rosabelle put her arm round her cousin. "Our home, it's a soft country. Not like Orkney. Your children will love it. I'll teach them to ride and fish and run like the deer. They'll love it. It was their lost home, you know."

Marie knew she had to win, for there was little alternative. Everyone was ruined. The Penicuik paper-mills were sold already to pay the taxes. There was no other plan. Children had to be raised, even the impossible Clio. The family was the only place to go, when you had to keep your head above water. What did the down-and-outs say over the ocean about where they came from? A home was the only house where, when you went, they couldn't slam the door in your face.

At the end of a meal of pheasant and brussel sprouts and meringues and claret, paid for by Marie, Virginia rose. All her objections had been damp flares.

"Needs must," she said. "Thank you as always, Marie, for very little."

Looking at the mirror behind Virginia, Marie could see that beaky painted face reflected again and again in the facing glasses, almost to infinity. That was having relations, she supposed. You had to go on seeing them, time after time.

There was no long daylight now, only moment after moment, worry after worry, errand after errand, and slow woe. Marie's thoughts flicked round her mind like a cloud of midges. These men we look after, I don't know why they are here in my house, I mean they do not have to fight these silly wars, and they never tell us the reason why, they just ride out in front of the guns and expect us to pick up the pieces, but we can't always do that if all we get is a bit of a body, a patchwork of stitches, particularly in the mind, they seem to lose their marbles and forget themselves in their dressing-gowns, they call it shell-shock or something, but it is merely a good old attack of the nerves and nothing like having a child or losing the husband who is meant to be around looking after me, only he went away to fight as if it was just another shooting party.

There is no coming back, they say, and it is no good crying over spilt sherry, but I cannot stand the smell in my bedrooms now, the carbolic and the unmentionables, we used to have roses and dahlias from the walled garden, and the floorboards were polished and not scrubbed, and as for the rules, they were understood between ladies and gentleman, even if all of them were not quite, but we all had calling cards and we knew where we sat at dinner, not in this appalling free-for-all, and mess, mess, mess.

I know I shouldn't feel like this. I am all for the miners who are coming out on strike again under my old lover Keir, and so they should with those starvation wages, and there is this dreadful influenza everywhere with more people dying than in the whole Great War, and we have no more room for them, try as we may, but finding my own home overrun although it is a castle – I know every Englishman's home is his castle, but it's not a hospital, is it? – now this here is completely different, although I said I would do it to save the family. But I didn't think I would lose all my privacy, all my peace, and I'd have to watch the slow destroying of our place by people who don't care where they are, but only want to get well again.

Sickness makes us so selfish. The ill ones don't care who we are or where they are. They don't care if we break down or they break it up. They just want to be well and out of here. We can't blame them. We're just a sort of terminus on the life line to nowhere very much, because this certainly isn't the home for heroes it was meant to be.

As for my nearest and dearest, that is a nightmare. I must have been off my rocker to let in Hamish Charles with Virginia and his daughter Clio here. They gang up on him, making him even sicker in his head than he is. He saw too many horrors in the war and now he is as bitter and stinging as a bunch of nettles, and he takes to the bottle, whenever he can sneak a gin in. Seaforth is not so bad, although he suffered more, curing the tommies of an imperial system he does not believe in. He's pining to get back to India and make it independent of us, a jolly good idea, and we'll be short of him soon for the good of his own country, only he is rather gaga, I must say.

As for Ellen-Maeve and her two, and Ruby and her little one, I somehow feel that they are worming their way into here as if they will never leave. Rosabelle is sweet with the tinies, I would never have suspected her of having a maternal streak with all that natural wildness, but she'll make a better mother than I ever was to her. Patience, a matron without a son, tried to turn the nursery into a dispensary, but I put my foot down. I am sorry, I said, but this is my home, and while I am doing everything to help win the peace, I want to know who I am winning it for. I am more concerned with the children than the cripples, and even you have to put the living before the dying, these little ones, Ian and Hamish Henry and Titania, they are the future, like it or not, they will inherit the rubbish left behind after the last war, which will not be the last war whatever you may say, so you had better lump it, and so she did.

I think Ruby moved in with her little boy to help me, she said, but actually to bring up Ian with Hamish Henry and Clio, a clever move given what might happen. If I had known then, of course I would never have let that slyboots insinuate herself into my home. But who knows what will be until too late. Just about then, the influenza really reached us, and Titania caught it, and the poor little soul was all cough and fever, and we couldn't save her, and she died. And I couldn't think badly of her mother or any mother ever again. That is the worst thing, the very worst, the loss of a child, so young.

There was a medieval church built like a cross at Ermondhaugh, and the Earl of Dunesk had the living of it, and Marie had it now, so she had Titania buried there. The grave was as small as a paddling pool, while the coffin could have held a large doll. Tears ran as dew for that lost life. And nothing could have been saved from that saddest of days but the coming of cousin Peregrine and his mother Arabella Plunkett-Drax, sent away from Ireland because of the troubles there.

Even at eighteen, Peregrine looked as fallen as Lucifer. His quick-silver eyes promised more experience than he ever could have had. A helmet of bronze curls curdled round his high forehead, while his mouth moved as coral snake. His whipcord body danced on strange small brown boots.

"Hello," he said. "Come at the wrong time, I see." He leapt to pick up a sod and cast it on the coffin-lid. "Bye, bye, dear. I love you, whoever you are."

Impossible and forgivable, Marie could see that he was the most dangerous one. Clio was looking at him, her mouth open soft, as if Dr Mesmer had her in his care.

"I am sorry we're so late," Arabella was saying. "If I had known. But there you are. That packet from Dublin and the porters. They nearly left my best tin trunk behind. And do you know, we weren't even at the Captain's Table. I do not think he knew who we were although it was perfectly clear on the passengers' list..."

And so the trivia of travel took over from the tears of grief. It had always been so, Marie thought, except for the mother, who had lost the child who had come out of her body. Ellen-Maeve seemed to have a limb cut off. She was hobbling and staggering under her bee-keeper's black veil, and Marie had to hold onto her to keep her upright.

"There is nothing I can say," Marie said. "But I do know. Titania will always be with you and in you. But it's the might-have-been, what she might be, who would be her children. But you still have Hamish Henry, and he is the bonniest boy of them all."

He was toddling in the wake of Peregrine, who had already charmed Clio to his side with an invisible thong. What he was talking of, Marie could not hear; but she could see Clio's face upturned to his as a sea anemone drinking in light. With a sudden dart in her womb, she remembered how she had wanted young men before she knew that she did. Sexuality came too early. Too hard to thwart it, even in this country of attempted prohibitions.

At dinner, Arabella explained why they had come over the Irish Sea. Her husband Alexander had sent them away from Normanton. After the Easter Rebellion during the war, the whole country had been in uproar, with the Irish Republican Army growing in daring and gunpower. They were fighting out of the hills and the bogs, they were hard to find and impossible to eliminate. They slid into the local people like salmon into fish paste.

"You know," Arabella said, "you can't even trust the servants. We had a raid on the Big House, and if it hadn't been for Alexander and his trip-wires, they would have slit our throats in our beds, for sure.

But they fell over, and the alarm went off, and we found one of our guards followed them over the wire. Could you credit it? We had paid him to have us killed."

Then the Black-and-Tans had come, the militia of the unemployed old soldiers from England, and atrocity had met violence, and burned police stations and cottages soon were reeking across the land. All was ambushes and arson, shots in the back and cinders. Nothing was to be trusted, the password was treason.

"But the Irish should be free, shouldn't they?" Marie suggested, very softly.

"Not if they're killing and burning the people who have helped them for centuries. We've taken them from the bog into the university. We've taught – they butcher us –"

Arabella was whining under the strain, wanting to be believed. Marie gave up. Sympathy came before principles any day.

"I am sure you are right for you," she said. "And I do hope Alexander is safe."

She also knew that when a topic became impossible at dinner, for any reason, she had to change the subject. So rather too brightly, she asked: "And what do you think of votes for women? Now we have our first Member of Parliament. Nancy Astor."

Peregrine intervened.

"Horrid idea," he said. "Women voting. They weren't born for that. Many other things, like..." He laughed and left his sentence unfinished. "But Nancy Astor. She's a bit of all right. She's lovely, she's funny, and she's rich. If she wasn't married to that newspaper chap, I might run after her myself."

"Wouldn't there be rather an age gap?" Marie asked.

"I don't think that matters," Peregrine said. He stared coolly at Marie, his mercury eyes now frozen on hers, ignoring Rosabelle. "Sometimes it is good to skip a generation."

There was a silence round the table. Was this insolence or adolescence? Anyway, it was certainly too much.

"Pudding," Marie said. "Let's have pudding." Her voice was too high. But then, calling for pudding did silence this uppity youth.

Two pieces of news were the mustard gas of the next day. The surrendered German fleet was scuttled in Scapa Flow. And Alexander Plunkett-Drax had been executed by the Irish rebels, and Normanton was burned down. Arabella and Peregrine had no return.

"I wish they had been on their ships," Ellen-Maeve said. "Then all those bloody Huns would have been drowned on their own bloody cruisers. Forgive my French, but those bastards need to go down with their bloody battleships. I know it won't bring Hamilton back, but he was looking for them on his aeroplane. And it is a bit rich. He drowns, trying to spot them and sink them. And now they sink themselves, while they all get ashore for another pint of schnapps."

She burst out in another storm of weeping, and Marie had to take her to her room and give a lemonade with some morphine in it. She carried the infant Hamish Henry down with her to the garden table, only to find both Arabella and Virginia sobbing and shouting at each other over the news of the death of Alexander, while Ruth watched them with a smile of sly triumph. Her rape at his hands was paid for.

"You damn dragon," Arabella was spitting. "You're glad he's dead. Because I can't have him now."

"You never did." Virginia's voice cut like a thin knife. "He wanted a country wife. You weren't too bad at that."

"I wasn't a slagheap of art tarts, like you two."

"Better an art tart," Ruth said, "than a bog hag."

Peregrine began to howl now, with laughter. "I can't believe it – Mummy and the two lesbe lizzies – and all about daddy –"

Now Hamish Henry started to wail in Marie's arms, and she lost her temper.

"Do shut up, the lot of you. Your husband's dead, your father's dead, you Plunkett-Draxes, and all you do is settle old scores with a couple of women who should know better. For God's sake, let's have some manners in my house. If you can't mourn, behave."

"That from somebody whose mother was a Crow Indian," Virginia said, "is quite a lesson in etiquette."

"From a South African tramp," Marie said coolly, "whose husband killed his wife for her, I don't think I can be taught the social graces."

The two women stared at each other, until Virginia looked low.

"We'll have to be going," she said. "We cannot stay here any more."

"It would be advisable. When you find somewhere else to go. Until then, my home is yours."

"Come, Ruth." Virginia rose. "We'd better go and feel sorry for Alexander somewhere else. We're a bit out of key here."

The two women walked away towards the countryhouse hospital, holding hands, with Peregrine cackling after them. But as Clio went to follow her mother, he caught her by the arm.

"Don't go," he said. "I must talk to you. About daddy's death. I must tell you. You're the only one I can talk to. Nobody understands."

"But your mother –" Clio protested.

"We're running away."

Peregrine was up and gone with Clio, hurdling over the lawn towards the river glen. The two young ones seemed like spirits of the trees or the sunlight, and they were gone.

"We should be going too," Ruby said. "We're a burden to you, Marie, not a help. Patience does all the work, but she's a proper matron. She's the only one working now, while we mess about in the garden. We are bringing up our babies on your back."

"Stay, stay, stay," Marie said. "I love having you here, and the little ones."

"There's no future in it," Ruby said. "Look, we're young, and –"

"There are no men, are there? Well, here, what have we got? The mad and the maimed, and they're not good prospects. And I know, because of the war, there's hardly an eligible male in all the county. There's nobody for a pretty young widow to marry. Except in Edinburgh, and we never seem to get there. Rosabelle comes back down here, only when she can, and that's not often."

"You're very candid," Ruby said.

"Too much so, I am told."

"But true. Too true. We must go back to London. And meet people."

"When you can afford to."

"That'll be the postwar story. When we can afford to. Money, money, money. And Alistair dead –"

The weeping began again, and Marie had to take Ruby to her room now, and her baby. She could not hear what Peregrine was telling Clio by the rock pool on the Esk, where the brown trout wavered upstream, shadows and speckles in the eddies of the water. What he was telling her would bind them together for ever.

For he was talking of his fear and his loneliness, and she hoped that he would always need her to listen, and he would trust only her to speak to. There were sandbags and barbed wire and sentries round the Big House, there were shots and bonfires in the night, there were burned bodies crucified on the iron gates, there were snouted armoured cars and hooded men, there was shivering and flushing and messing his trousers, there was the stink and fright of growing up in a Civil War.

"I hate rebels," Peregrine was telling Clio. "I want order. I want to be strong. They think they will get away, the lice who killed my father. But I will find them, destroy them. We will be strong."

As Clio turned her face to his, Peregrine crushed his lips on hers. Marie could only suspect what happened down by the Esk, but nobody ever spoke of it, and even Clio did not blab to her mother.

2

THE MUSIC OF THE SPHERES

As Murdo dropped the bomb by hand over the side of his aeroplane on the palace in Kabul, he ended the third Afghan War, although he hardly knew that, as yet. The rebels, if they were so, had never seen an explosion from wings in the sky. This was a new terror. There was no answer to an indifferent force from the blue. Murdo had been reading a potted book on Alexander the Great, who had taken Afghanistan two and a half thousand years ago with his Greeks in their brief Empire there. When Alexander had beaten the Celts on the steppes, he had asked them who was the person they feared most. Their reply was meant to be himself, but was not. The Celts said that they were afraid a chunk would fall on them out of the roof of heaven. They would all be brained. Just what Murdo had done on Kabul, drop down an explosive brick from the roof of the clouds.

He banked and turned back towards Peshawar, as the pillar of dust and smoke climbed into the air behind his tail. Below him lay the wrinkles of the dry earth. Crack and crevice, gully and gorge, fissure and valley, the ancient hide of arid land was creased and crumpled. Water had once gouged out those deep marks, as had earthquakes from time to past time. Now there were no rivers beneath, only the sinuous streams of pebbles and mud beds. The surface of the moon was like that, Murdo supposed, but no one would ever walk there. The shadow of his biplane made four straight pinions stretch out in black from the sun. He was flying home, if he could call the Raj that, rather than just another posting.

His engine coughed and cut out. This happened in the thin air. Behind the ear-flaps of his helmet and through his goggles, all he could hear was the twanging of the wire and the plucking of the struts in the wind. He was not too worried in his noisy glide, for he was over the worst of the peaks. The sound was as a strum of violins or a drum beat against the music of the spheres. Somewhere up there, he could hear that celestial melody, especially when he was quiet on the ground, looking up at the orchestra of the stars, stuck against the back of the night in their clusters of bright notes. That was the song of the universe, so deep and long and mute, and only those who flew could hear its tune. So they were put in time with the flow of the air, when they soared on high.

There had once been a terrible retreat from Kabul to Kandahar in the first of the Afghan Wars. Everybody had died or been mutilated, except for one doctor, who had survived to struggle through. Or so the story was. The Afghans were the best mountain fighters in the world with their long-barrelled inlaid rifles, the ivory patterns in the stock and the lead murder in the breech. His bomb was useless, Murdo knew. For the British could never hold that proud and jagged land and people. Yet he supposed that to deter was as important as to conquer. There might be a truce on the North-western Frontier now.

He was tugging at the throttle. The engine barked and caught. He lifted his craft over the next range and sighted his way towards the airstrip. He did not relish the welcome committee of his cousins, who were bound to be there. Even the Great War did not seem to have winnowed his family enough, certainly not in India. He had always wondered how his grandfather and grandmother had reared so many children, who had spread to the far corners of the earth. The result was that when he landed, he would trip over some kith and kin. Only in the clouds was there any escape from all those relations. Perhaps it would be as chilly down there, as it was cold up here.

Douglas Jardine had bothered to take the train all the way to Peshawar. This mighty condescension was a recognition at last that his family was slightly important, even outside him. He could gain some credit from their actions, particularly as his own uniform was only the white and ribbons and feathers of the Civil Service. He had served Intelligence for so long that he had watched the Great Game between Britain and the Tsar of Russia for control of the Himalayas before the Bolshevik Revolution of machines and steel. What Red horde on armoured trains and planes would now threaten the greying of the Empire? If a cousin on wings could now end a conflict by lobbing explosives over the side from on high, this was far cheaper and more effective than sending Bengal Lancers on horses to Kabul to be picked off by Afghan marksmen. Hateful though the new inventions were, they helped the budget.

"Murdo," Douglas Jardine greeted the pilot, stiff and frozen from his flight in the muggy air of the hangar. "You did a wonderful job."

"Whisky." Murdo undid his flying helmet with rigid fingers. "I'm bloody freezing."

"On a night like this?"

"Try it up there."

"We're running with sweat."

"Thanks." Murdo took the silver flask offered by his cousin and took a swig and spluttered. Then he shivered like a cat when it wakes up. "Wah. You should try a cockpit to keep you cool, Douglas."

"What puzzles me, Murdo, is how you got there."

"By guess and by God." Murdo walked beside the aged intelligence officer back towards the mud brick building by the strip. "I can read ground maps, and they're good, but you have to have sharp eyes."

"You got back, too."

"They don't have much artillery. But those rifles. I think I had a couple of bullets through the wings."

"You didn't see anything on the ground?"

"What? The Red Army? Or the Whites? Just the bloody mountains."

"Well done, Murdo. We're proud of you."

If there was one phrase which Murdo hated, that was the patronizing "Well done." Captains of cricket, ministers of state, even royalty, they gave you a pat on the back and sometimes a ribbon, and those two words of praise that meant you had done something which they could not do, but suited them, if you did it.

"I don't know," Murdo said. "At least, I got there and back. How's it up at Annandale?"

"I haven't been there lately," Douglas said. "Are you going?"

"Yes," Murdo said. "By train." A prickly heat was pushing pins into his flying suit. "Thanks for coming over, Douglas."

"What you did was important."

"Ours not to reason why. Just to do and fly."

Douglas surveyed the yellow dry strip towards the mountains and the North-western Frontier. Looking at his lined and dried face under his topee, Murdo seemed to be seeing a mummy, all the life bled out this erect corpse into the wasteland, which he was meant to protect.

"I'll put you in for Dispatches," Douglas said. "That was quite a flight."

"And Seaforth," Murdo added. "Did he get back? I heard he was in a hell of a mess at Marie's hospital. Had a breakdown, but he had to come home here."

"He's always been a bit of a lunatic," Douglas said.

"And a damned good doctor."

"Physician, heal thyself. That's what the ancient Greeks used to say." Douglas smiled. "I think you'll find him at Annandale."

The hill plantation was as cold as his high cockpit. The morning mist hid the tea plants as clouds hid the land below his wings. It was all a matter of distance, Murdo thought, how near you were to things. And he felt far from Annandale, which he only knew from his father's tales of the old Indian home. They had put in potatos and indigo then, before they switched to the failing tea on the mountain slopes, to pay for the old place.

Welcome was not the word he would have used for his arrival. Yet there was acceptance. The cousin nobody mentioned, Hamish Macmahon, seemed to be lost in a fog of his own. A sort of hulk beached on a Himalayan hill, he did not know or want to know who Murdo was. He was the relation that time had forgot and the family wished to forget. "Not quite there," everybody said of him. Yet he was here, evidently.

That is why Annandale had gone to the dominant Margaret, the wife of Douglas Jardine. She knew how to run things and run the servants and the leaf-pickers off their bare feet. The other heirs, her sisters Ellen-Maeve and May, had taken a powder on a POSH boat to Blighty before the last war. Their childhood was lost in London etiquette. And perhaps, that was for the best in Murdo's eyes, as he caught Margaret's appraising look at him, while she wondered what he had come all this way to get out of her.

"Did you have a good journey?" she asked. "You couldn't fly, could you?"

"As good as could be expected," Murdo said, "in Indian trains."

"You did arrive, though. I had a message from Douglas. You don't miss your mark. Hamish, this is Cousin Murdo." Her voice was too bright, as if speaking to a child or an idiot. "You know, Uncle Angus's son."

The older man shook his head, not saying no, but as if he wanted to clear his wits. His mouth dropped open, but he did not speak.

In a whisper loud enough for Hamish to hear, Margaret said, "We're very good to him for father's sake. We've never had anything like him before. Good stock, that's what we are."

Down along the verandah, a frail dark figure in a white suit slowly approached them. He leaned on his cane, which bent even on the weight of his thin arm.

"I am Seaforth," he said. Then a wry smile was an eel on his lips. "Just some more of your bad stock, Margaret?"

"You're not well, Seaforth," Margaret said briskly. "You don't know what you're saying. You and your bad jokes. Where's Miriam?"

"Coming, coming. But I'm the Peg in the round hole." A squat woman dressed in a gold-and-purple sari drifted towards them. "Has my brother put his foot in his mouth again?"

A large emerald ring on her finger snared the light. It seemed to mesmerize Margaret, as the charmer does the cobra.

"Ah, the heirloom," Margaret said.

"Ah, the heiress," Peg replied.

After all, Murdo knew that both the splendid jewel and the tea plantation were the spoils of the Indian Mutiny, taken by his uncle Iain from the plunder. When he had died, Peg got the emerald, Margaret the lion's share of the land. One legacy was a restitution, the other was still an occupation. Avoiding ground fire, Murdo decided to change his flight path.

"Are you feeling better, doctor?" he asked Seaforth. "Marie told me you had a rough time on the Western Front. And you didn't get on much better in her convalescent home with all the relations playing at nurses."

"It was an amateur performance," Seaforth said, "although Marie has a good heart and good hands. She is not a *grande dame* of the Empire, playing proprietor."

Peg grinned as Margaret replied, "You cannot mean me."

Seaforth sighed. "Mean? What do I mean? I don't know. Meaning? There's no meaning in living. I mean ..." He straightened from his bent cane and tapped its end on the tiled floor as he spoke. "I have saved ... thousands of lives ... in a war ... I did not believe in ... I have given ... my own life ... to that cause ... It has ... no meaning for me." He paused to breathe. Nobody dared to interrupt. "And India ... what does it mean? ... I am a half-breed ... words you like, Margaret ... Neither one thing ... nor the other ... Neither the Raj ... nor the nationalists ... Not white, not brown ... No class, no caste ... just a trade, a doctor ... I save lives ... but there's no meaning ... in what they die for..."

Now he lifted his cane and pointed it at Hamish Macmahon, who shifted his bulk from its end as if from a threat.

"He over there ... who is he? ... Oppressor or patient? ... Supremo or sick in the head? ... Blood brother or stranger? ... Master or silly billy? ... He is all of us ... He is none of us ... Some luck of birth, Margaret ... His sister ... That made you boss ... Hamish your slave ... Same mother, same father ... Same India, same Raj ... Same power, same hate ... Same Hindu, same Muslim ... Same rule, same divide ... Except for those split in the middle ... We're the half-and-halfs. Me."

Seaforth started to cough like a repeating gun. Hack-hack-hack-hack-hack. Puffs of arid breath. Peg slapped him on the spine. And he hawked and hawed and cleared his throat.

"Is the lecture over?" Margaret asked.

"No, because ... the question isn't over ... Nor the problem ... for us ... We are split down the middle ... We have no identity ... How do we exist? Who are we?"

"As you said, *doctor*..." Margaret's final word was heavy with irony. "You have a job, which involves saving lives. Why not just do it? We all have our jobs. We just don't puzzle about it as much as you do."

"I wish you would." An intense and bony woman now joined them, awkward in her green sari, which did not seem to fit her body, although another skin to Peg. "If your sort ever asked yourselves why you should rule here, you might be like the cockroach on its back. Waving all your little sceptres in the air and wondering how you could ever get up again."

"I suppose, Miriam," Margaret said, "any little wife has to defend her husband."

"Little isn't the word for me, dear." Miriam took Seaforth by the arm. "You'd better come and rest. We're not staying, as you know."

"I haven't finished," Seaforth said.

"I'm your cousin Murdo," the visitor said as an introduction. "What the doctor's saying is damn interesting."

"To continue," Seaforth said. "As none of us mean anything ... I mean, you rule and we Indians don't accept it ... How does anything work?" He waved his cane round the verandah with its low teak tables and canvas chairs with wide arms and white-clad servants standing still and playing statues in the background. "India works because of manners. You have a social code ... which we do accept. Fairness, tolerance ... a sort of justice and decency ... not much corruption ... Even your clubs and schools ... some of us can join."

"Like your sons," Margaret said.

"Like our sons, Shankar and Solomon," Miriam said. "St Columba's, where east is west, and sometimes the twain shall meet. Of course, Seaforth being a British Army Officer, that helped the boys' admission. They couldn't be refused, could they? After their father saved all those lives at the front."

"There's no reason to be so nasty about it," Margaret said. "It just proves we do let a few in."

"A few of what?"

"I mean ..."

"Just what do you mean?"

"The be ... best." Margaret was forced to stutter. "The best children of some British officers."

"I know your husband is a diplomat," Miriam said. "A very little of it seems to have rubbed off on you. Though very unlikely."

"Anyway," Murdo came in, "if they go to a British boarding school, perhaps some of our values will rub off on them. They will come to like India as it is."

"Not them, knowing my boys. They'll probable knot their old school tie round your throats and hang you with it."

Murdo laughed.

"I don't know," he said. "We're all empire children, one way and another. We were all cleared from Scotland long ago, we served for British pay all over the world, we're rootless and roll around the globe..."

"Speak for yourself," Margaret said. "You never married. You're the dandelion puffball."

"Who'd marry now? What for? I agree with the doctor. Is our job to refill the ranks of the dead after a meaningless Great War? Perhaps if there were fewer of us, we wouldn't fight so much."

"Oh, I am all for not breeding too much," Margaret said. "As long as those of us who should have more children, do."

"Including the Sinclairs," Peg said.

"Of course."

"Well," Seaforth said, "we've no more indistinct sons to offer. You'll have to do ... with the two we have already ... If you can tolerate them ... Good stock, did you say? I'm sure you think so."

As Margaret shut her lips in a mousetrap, Murdo intervened again.

"It's good to see you all," he said. "You may not believe it, but I came here to meet the family. My life is knocking around from one hangar to another. At my age, too. I don't mind if you all bicker and pick at each other. That's what family is all about. At least, you all know each other, and I'd like you to know me a little bit, not too much of it, as the old song goes. Too many bloody strangers in my life. Too many flying messes – and I don't mean the stuff which hits the fan – when the other mates don't come back or get transferred. What a relief to find some sort of place which is always there. You know what we really all of us are. Wild colonial boys and girls."

Seaforth snorted a hiccup, while Peg said, "That certainly isn't me."

"Oh, I don't know," Murdo said. "There's a time for knocking about, and a time to stay put. And actually we've taken quite a knocking in this last war. I saw an old man playing a squeezebox in Piccadilly. One leg. Veteran. I gave him a few bob. His concertina reminded me of our family. It gets stretched out over the whole wide world. Then it gets

squeezed in. You know, we lost nearly a whole young generation in the
trenches. Half-a-dozen young widows in the family now. More even. I
hope that damn music box goes out again. And we who are left know
each other."

Hamish Macmahon spoke at last in a voice with a burr in it.

"How good of ye comin' t'Annandale."

Shankar always did that. Solomon shook his head as his brother strolled
back from the crease. He would throw his wicket away in the 90s. All
that brilliant batting, and he never reached his century. He would slash a
long-hop to slip, or heave-ho to long leg, or even make a hopeless call,
so he was run out. He did not want a celebration, only the mild clapping
of the rest of the St. Columba boys as he came back to the pavilion.

"Nearly, nearly," Solomon said to him. "It's never quite enough."

Shankar sat on the bench beside his brother, leaned his bat on a slat,
took off his gloves with his teeth, and began to unbutton his pads. All
was whiter than white. You could trust Blanco for that. Like the school,
really.

"Have a go," he said, "when they don't expect you to have a go.
That's the way to beat the system."

A vulture dropped down towards a fielder, and he took off his
tangerine cap. He shoo'd the carrion bird away. There was a Parsee *ghat*
near the grounds. The vulture was better off eating dead meat than live
cricketers.

"You and your working from inside, Shankar. The sudden coup. The
riot, when nobody's aware of it. Look at Amritsar. Even with that
massacre, nothing happened. And here you are, a cadet in the army
corps, going to serve in the bloody forces, which gunned us down."

There was much applause as the last man walked to the wicket. But
then he was the son of a Major-General in the Lancers. So he was the
School Captain.

"You see," Solomon was passing judgement. "If you'd carried your
bat and made a century, they'd know you were the best, as you are."

"Don't pretend to me, little brother." Shankar yawned. "I do well
enough here to get what I want. Good at games, that's the ticket to the
Delhi express. Who wants brains?" He lifted his bat and swished it
through the air. "Swat, swat, swat it away. And you, brother. Swot, swot,
swot."

"There's nothing wrong in joining the Civil Service."

"You'll just be a jumped-up babu with a ring in his nose."

"Better than being a brass-wallah with a ramrod up his arse."

Shankar knocked Solomon's school cap over his eyes. There was a shout, an appeal. They were all out for 147 runs. Shankar had made two-thirds of the total.

"Dammit," he said. "We've got to go and field."

"The rest of the team is pathetic."

"What? St. Columba's? Our motto, please."

"Nil Nisi Victor."

"Nothing If Not Vermin."

Shankar rose in his flannels, a black marker against the sun, which shut off the dazzle from his brother's glasses.

"We who are about to be whopped don't salute you. I'll keep that for the military."

"You know what Marx said."

"That menace to our India?"

"Don't moan. Organize."

"Nonsense, little brother. Don't moan. Command."

"Wrong again. Don't moan. Infiltrate."

"I'll buy that, for a Woodbine."

3

ESCAPE FROM BLEWSBURG

As the duiker deer jumped, the bullet hit its ribs and split its heart. Thrown sideways, it lay jerking on a thorn bush. Paul Sinclair put down his rifle and smiled in his hide. That was a good shot, perhaps the best of his life. There was something for the pot tonight. And the horns were undamaged. He would get the boy to boil the head and flay the skull. He didn't have that specimen in his trophy collection yet.

The sound of the shot was a signal for Tshamba to come running from the camp. His old khaki shorts were threadbare, but stiff creases made the seams stand out. Paul insisted on appearances. Even on tour, the flat-iron and the board were toted on the heads of the bearers. His mother Lizzie had always had his shorts and underwear ironed daily, and his sister Martha had told him why. When your day was up and God came to get you, He wanted to find you in pressed pants. It wasn't so much that cleanliness was next to godliness, but that the chaos of Africa would take you over if you didn't insist on the rules.

"Master," Tshamba said. His wide-mouthed glee reminded Paul of a split coconut. "Master, damn fine shot."

"Cut its head off and boil it, Shambles. The rest is for the pot. Get the boys to take it in. And get hot water for my bucket. Dress Number One. We're in court tomorrow. I want to check it out and the stores before we get to Blewsburg."

If you didn't have an inventory as you went along, all would get lifted or lost. A spoon here, a packet of salt there, and soon there was nothing. You had to have lists or you forgot what you had. That was what had kept Robinson Crusoe going when he was a castaway. He had lists of things so he could exist in his solitude. Accounts were the secret of survival. And nothing was more alone than being in the bush in Bechuanaland. There were the boys, naturally, but nature also meant you couldn't really talk to the natives, and they would never understand you if you tried. Anyway, that would let your side down.

All you had was fifty thousand square miles of vast indifference to administer, your district. And you were only twenty-two, and you did not really know how to do it.

Walking back to his tent, Paul wondered about the daring of having colonies at all. Agreed, this one was pretty much a desert except for the Okavango swamp in the south, and nobody had found enough minerals to make it worth mining like in Joburg, and you only met the tribes in handfuls on tour except in the baking tin roof shacks of misbegotten places like Blewsburg, which didn't live up to the name of a town. But why did the natives put up with him with his one rifle and medicine kit and the flogging power over them?

Punishment. If they touched him, dozens of their skins would hurt. The same at that vile petty boarding school in the English shires, where his weak father Hamish Charles had consigned him and his brother Gordon to the belt and the ruler and the rod. Why did they call the beatings they gave you 'six of the best'? Did it make a better man of you, my son? Or did it mean it was the hardest that they could lay into your backside? Still, the colonial children had to be trained somehow to continue the empire. And they could be guaranteed to pass to lesser breeds the codes and the batterings of their young manhood for the princely salary of two hundred pounds per annum plus allowances, and not much was ever allowed. Regulations also saw to that.

The bucket of brackish water was ready for his return, and his Number Ones laid out on his camp bed. Stripping off his jacket and his vest, he dangled his wrists in the warm goo. They were so scrawny now. They used to be quite thick, when they had fed him on porridge and mash at school and had forced him to box. Yet Africa sweated it out of you all right. Or all wrong. Not that right or wrong mattered much in this blasted wilderness. But he was meant to be the judge of it in Blewsburg.

When he had put on his best khaki Drill with the brass pips and the bits of braid and his blue forage cap, he found his folding table set out by his canvas seat. The silver from the baize inside the mahogany canteen hadn't tarnished too much. As for the duiker steak, it was tough, tough, tough. But the boys seemed to be grinding the meat down, though his molars could hardly munch through. What had his Boer mother said before she died and left him? "Those kaffirs have a better bite than you. Don't let them." He wasn't hungry, so he just had another spoon of the mealie mush on the side plate and another tot of whisky. And then he turned in.

Saturday night at the end of the month. Another Church Social Dance. All those sandpaper hands of the poor Boer dirt farmers and storekeepers handling me like a sack of mealies. Treading on my toes like spoor. They never heard of the foxtrot or the waltz, only the commando charge. And the records were so scratched on the wind-up gramophone, a two-step sounded like an electrical storm. No thank you, very kindly.

Yet Bridget O'Connor had heard there was a new Assistant District Officer in town. She had been in her hot smelly school stinking of untraceable horrors, when he had been in court, handing out his hundred shilling fines and few whippings. Prison was too far away for small crimes. The big cases had to go up to the boss. Mrs Meinertzhagen, the old frump at the Post Office, had said he was a string bean, but she was so anti the British military, her remarks were dum-dum bullets. Bridget would see for herself.

She had to get to England or give up and become some Dutchman's workhorse and housevrouw. The stranger was her only ticket to that mystical homeland, where she had never been. Those young men in their uniforms might not earn a lot, but they did get paid leave, and they could take a wife, too, on the Union Castle line. And once she was there...

She checked her looks in the flecked mirror of her hotel room. She hadn't found a decent place to rent yet, if there was one. Perhaps her face was a bit round, but that halo of blonde curls, those bluepenny eyes and rosepetal lips, the little dimple which peeked out when she laughed, nobody had ever resisted them, particularly round here, where there was no competition. She was small and her figure could be better, but if Helen had her Troy, Bridget had her Blewsburg.

The ADO had to be staying in the hotel. There wasn't another fleapit in town. With much ado about everything, Bridget went down to the desk, where Pederson was fast asleep in his chair. His fly-whisk had dropped on his cherryripe nose; its hairs were waving in time to his snores. Bridget leant over the counter and batted his face with his insect-swiper. He lurched awake with a groan.

"Mister Pederson," Bridget said, "I wish to write a note to the visiting District Officer. What is his name?"

"Sinclair. Ja, Sinclair."

"I want him to come to the Church Social Dance on Rhodes Street. Are you coming?"

"No, Miss O'Connor. On bloody duty."

Bridget scribbled and folded the note.

"See that he gets it, mind."

"Ja." And seeing her blue eyes glaring at him, Pederson weakly added, "Ja, ja."

Job done, Bridget returned to her room. The evening heat had brought out the odours of the previous occupants. What were these? The smell of cattle dung, the stink of dog piss, the stench of the secretions of innumerable bodies passing through and leaving their traces imbued in the planking. Nausea rose in her throat. She wouldn't vomit. She wouldn't. She choked down the acrid lump in her throat. She would go out tonight, and she would get out. She would never give up.

She only had one good dress left. The long one which hid her ankles. She held it up against her so she could see herself in the glass. On the beige silk, cornflowers were scattered, bouquets and posies on a wasteland. She twirled, so she could see the hem swing free in the glass.

"I'll get out," she said out loud. "You all just see if I don't."

He was too long in coming. She was almost in tears after enduring the clopping and the hoofing round the floor in the paws of the dishonest burghers of Blewsburg. But when he did appear in his dress clothes, her mouth dropped, her heart tripped a beat. He was like one of those photographs in the *London Illustrated News*. The aide-de-camp to the Duke of Gloucester at the Royal Garden Party. So cool, so tall, and his blue peaked cap set off his bony face with its long lines from nose to jaw. That was the cat's whiskers. He was good-looking, so what a bonus.

Bridget wrestled out of her partner's clammy grip with an "Excuse me. Must shifty to the powder room." As if she would go to such a bog of horrors. Then she marched across the hall before Mrs Meinertzhagen could exterminate her man.

"So glad you could come," she said. "Mister Sinclair, sir, welcome."

She turned her full blue eyes up to his face and held them there. He took off his military hat and bowed slightly towards her, almost as if he wanted absurdly to kiss her. But he was blushing and could hardly speak. "Miss ... er ... Miss ..."

"Bridget O'Connor. I am the local teacher here. For my sins."

He could not switch his eyes away from her gaze. His look was tied fast.

"I find ... Blewsburg ... pleasant enough."

"You don't really. Come on. It's a dump."

Paul laughed.

"Thank God I've found someone with the courage to say it."

"I think I'd marry Frankenstein to get out of here."

As she blurted out what she hadn't meant to say, Bridget blushed. O my Lord, how could I? How will he take it? I didn't mean it. Forgive me.

But he only roared with laughter.

"Thank God again for somebody with a sense of humour. The only funny people I've met for months are hyenas in the bush. And I don't find their giggles that amusing."

Bridget laughed with relief, releasing her dimple.

"The dancers here aren't much fun, either. All you get is mashed toes. You can even break an ankle, if a boot hits you during the hopscotch. You wouldn't dance with me, would you?"

"I'm not very good."

"Better than the rest, I'm sure."

She was soon clinging to him on the floor. In the slow waltzes, they were hardly turning, but swaying together, pressed against each other. Her hair was under his chin, her ear against the breast pocket over his heart, which was beating too fast, a pulse in a race. She felt a hardness from his groin thrusting against her tummy. She did not squirm to the side to pass it by at her waist, but she rubbed her middle against the thrust. She had him now, an officer and a gentleman. He would not get away, and she would with him.

The dance had ended at ten o'clock sharp with the playing of 'God Save the King'. They had walked back to the hotel and shaken hands in the lobby, a tight long squeeze, before going back to their separate rooms. They were having early breakfast together, before she went off to teach at her school. He was meant to continue on his tour, but he claimed other business in Blewsburg, where nothing ever went on.

She had always hated the first meal of the day, feeling low and sorry for herself before her first cigarette, the smell to go with her mouthwash, so nobody would know her vice. This time, though, she rattled on, telling him the whole story of her life, as if she were seeing it all in an instant before drowning for the third and last time. Her father had sailed over from Ireland – Protestant, of course – to fight in the Boer War. He had stayed on to become a rancher in the occupied Orange Free State. She was brought up with her brother and sister a couple of hundred miles from Blewsburg. There was hardly a place between there and here, nothing but the veldt. It was Eden, then. A black village round the farm, kill an ox a week for them and a sheep for us, all go to school together with Mother the teacher and nurse, you wouldn't know it now after Smuts took over. Then Mother died and Da married again and stepmother Boetsie had three more children and there was a drought and all the cattle died and things were tough and Boetsie gave her children all there was and we were eating turnips we found in the barn and Da wouldn't even give me fifty pounds a year when I got a scholarship to Rhodes University and I had to go to work and so I ended up teaching in this dump having breakfast with you.

When she had finished telling her tale of woe, they had to order another jug of coffee. Bridget knew she had blown it again. She had left out the hook, her interest in him.

"How about *you*?" she asked at last.

"Nothing much to tell," Paul said. "Except it's the reverse. My mother was a Boer, and when she died, my stepmother was our nanny and she was English."

"Sinclair." If possible, Bridget's eyes grew rounder. "Not the Sinclair case."

"What Sinclair case?"

"The one they still talk about all over the Free State. There were three children, then the father killed the mother. He was out shooting duck with a rifle." Bridget did not notice Paul's face draining from pink to bleach. "Who'd shoot duck with a rifle? He was lucky to get off. Then he married the nanny, and they all took off. They couldn't stay round these parts."

Now Bridget forgot her gossip to take Paul in.

"Oh no," she whispered. "Not you."

"Is that what they say here?"

"It can't be you."

"My mother's name was Lizzie van der Merwe. My father's was Hamish Charles."

Bridget looked down at her cup. She could not speak. Tears came to her eyes. This was the third and worst blunder she had made with him. He would never forgive her. She managed to look up.

"Didn't you know?"

"How could I? We went to the South Seas, a copra plantation. Then England. Nobody told us. They wouldn't, would they?"

"I'm so sorry. I shouldn't have."

"It's not your fault." Paul looked past her shoulder and said, "I am glad to know."

"You don't mean that."

"I do. Thank you for telling me."

"I'm a silly bitch. Ratting like that."

"You're someone who tells the truth. Nothing wrong in that."

Again, this incredible tolerance. Bridget could hardly credit her luck.

"So you're Lizzie van der Merwe's poor son, come back to Africa. It must seem strange. Like a dream or a nightmare. You're not like the Boers round here. You're so English. Do you remember anything? The country, does it mean anything to you?"

"I was so little. The one thing I remember, it's so silly. A thunderstorm drumming on a tin roof. Flashes of lightning outside. And my father trying to fix the electric lights, which had gone out. We had a sort of petrol genny engine then. The bulb smashed in his hand and cut him and there was blood and he got a shock, just as there was a big flash and thunder outside. I howled. I thought They, whoever They were, had got him for sure."

"Perhaps he deserved it," Bridget said. "And what happened to him and the nanny?"

"They parted. Virginia runs an art gallery in London. He fell apart during the War and is a bit barmy. He'll drink himself to death soon, I'm afraid. Which may be a blessing."

"Happy families." Bridget raised her cold coffee cup.

"Happy families."

They clinked china.

"You know," Paul said, "we might ..."

"*We* might?"

At Bridget's smile, Paul laughed and reached out for her hand.

"We might not let ourselves be victims of the past. Like father. What's really killing him was his killing Lizzie. And all the victims of the war. What killed them was old wars. They didn't need to fight the one they did. It was for lost causes."

"Tell me. In another country, does this one fade away?"

"Absolutely."

"For us too."

"We might escape. Be forgotten. Go somewhere where the past can't catch up with us."

"Escape from here," Bridget said. "That's all I dream about."

"You wouldn't go alone?"

"Not if somebody asked me."

"Anybody?"

She looked round the deserted hotel caff with its empty chairs, only full with stale air. Then she heard herself say something right at last.

"I can see only one body in this room."
"Meet me tonight here after school."
"I can't wait," she said and rose and fled.

Some say history always repeats itself. Some say history never does. All is hazard and chance. Paul never knew whether his memory sparked the storm which had nearly killed off his father for him as a small child, and now brought him Biddy. That is what she asked him to call her. Biddy, his Biddy, she had made him bid for her, she had a better hand, she won the game.

They had gone walking in Blewsburg, where there was nowhere to walk, nowhere nice, anyway. The squall grew out of the evening sky in a giant indigo toadstool, which blew apart above them in fibres of lightning. Slivers of rain drove down on them in assegais. Then, with the barrage of the thunder guns, volleys of hailstones big as musket balls shattered on the crowns of their heads. This was the battle of Blood River fought from the heavens again.

They might have died in the shock attack if they hadn't seen the lean-to by the curing shed. Paul dragged Biddy inside into the smell of dead game and hide and leather The flensing table was dark with gore. The hanging skins reeked in their coats of salt. The hammers of the ice pebbles pounded the metal roof, splitting the eardrums.

Biddy clutched Paul in a fierce grip. Their soaked bodies strained together. Their hearts and veins throbbed with the banging of the hail on their shelter. Paul forced her back over the bloody table. She looked up at the quivering rusty membrane of their cover in its battering above. He lowered over her.

– Paul is the storm, the hail, the thunder.
– I am the blood, the land lying.
– Rip, pierce, cry ,cry.
– Bleeding and dying.
– Crushed and free.
– The tempest within.
– Rage into peace.
– I hold all in me.

They were married three weeks later, but Biddy had to endure a camp life in Bechuanaland for six months until Paul was due for his home leave with her. She was pregnant with their first child before she reached the deck of her dream steamer, H.M.S. *Queen Adelaide*, docked in Cape Town. At the polished railings, she took Paul's hand and stroked his palm across the swell of her belly.

"He'll be born at home," she said.

"You've never seen what you call home," he said.

"It's home all right for him and me."

"And how do you know it's a he?"

"With a father like you..." Now Biddy was kissing the palm of Paul's hand. "He has to be a he, doesn't he?"

With her hopes of life in England flying higher than a buzzard, Biddy was bound to be disappointed over there. Money was the problem. There was hardly enough to be counted. They could only afford to rent two rooms in North Oxford near Summertown, where it was always cold, and was a suburb. Paul's family was not much help. His father Hamish Charles was being dried out in another home, and all his income was paying for that from an annuity: there would be nothing left. His brother Hamish Gordon was a ship's engineer and was far away, sailing the seven seas. And his sister Martha had reverted to the Highlands, marrying a poor teacher up in Caithness.

Only Paul's stepmother Virginia remained, and that would be an encounter. After the baby was born and named Kelso, one of the old places the Sinclairs had come from, the three of them went to London to greet the green mamba of the family. Yet whatever Paul had told Biddy could not prepare her for the meeting. Swathed in a silk *peignoir* under an emerald turban, with the head of a hawk, the pale skin drawn back tight from the lips and the beak of a nose, Virginia ushered them inside her flat, where all was beige and off-white except for the bright daubs and shrieking distortions of paintings, hanging on the walls.

"Oh, hello," Virginia said. "Back from Africa, Paul. Is it still in one piece? And are you?"

Biddy thrust the pink blob of the baby's face with the white shawl wrapped round the rest of it towards Virginia. From the smell, she could tell that Kelso had done something. She was speechless, and he started to wail.

"That's the little dear," Virginia said, "doing what little dears do. I am afraid I am not in the baby mood today. But then I never was. You must be Bridget. How do. Luckily my daughter Clio is old enough to need cocktails rather than nappies, and doubtless she will help you with the tot."

She called out, "Clio! Clio!", and a young woman came into the living-room, dressed in a short pink skirt, willowy with bobbed brown hair and legs to covet and a face off a Chanel advertisement.

"There is an infant in distress in the house. Please help his mother to change him – for a better baby, perhaps."

"He might spoil my dress."

"You have to learn, Clio. It might happen to you in the future. You never know your bad luck."

While Clio was taking Biddy and baby out to the bathroom, another woman came in, softer, fluffier, a creature all chiffon and scarves.

"This is my companion Ruth," Virginia said to Paul. "You know about her. She's your cousin Margaret's daughter. From the Indian side of the Sinclairs. I don't mean she's Indian, of course, though many of you are. I mean, she's born in India and educated there, or rather not." Then, after a pause, she added, "And how's your father?"

"I've only been to see him a couple of times."

"In his *home* from home."

"I don't think he recognised me. His mind, it's not quite – now – "

"His mind? If he had one, he couldn't put it to any use. He was a good shot though."

"How can you say that. Mother's death – "

"Well, it's the truth, Paul. He was a good shot. It was the only thing he was good at."

"We are glad *you* came round, Paul," Ruth intervened. "Though we cannot say that for your brother and sister."

"Why not?"

"Don't you keep in touch with them?"

"In the veldt? Now North Oxford? They're so far away."

"Even you must be able to afford a stamp or two," Virginia said.

"We don't write much," Paul said, a little pink in the face. "I never know where Gordon is, what port he's at. And he might as well be in the secret service, he never says what he's doing."

Virginia gave a quick smile to Ruth, who nodded back in complicity, while Paul went on talking.

"And Martha, she writes occasionally from Scotland, but I'm afraid I am a very bad correspondent. Biddy does write to her about the baby, although they've never met."

"You know why you don't hear from them." Virginia was triumphant. "They're reds. And Gordon, he's a real scarlet pimpernel."

"What do you mean?"

"He works for the Kremlin. He's Stalin's little stooge."

"How do you know?"

"We have *friends*," Virginia was both supercilious and smug, but then, she was a paradoxical woman. "Friends in high places. Not only here, either."

"Italy, Germany," Ruth said. "They love us when we go."

"Oh, do shut up," Virginia said. "Paul's not someone to talk shop with. We're just warning him about his brother and sister. He is in our police forces. Guarding our empire, as long as he's allowed to."

"You mean," Paul said, "Gordon and Martha, they're bolshies, or something."

"Labels, labels," Virginia said. "Anyway, now you know, be careful. Don't tell them anything they might tattle about in the wrong ears. Strategy, defence, that sort of thing. Just whisper it to us and we'll see it goes to the right places. There may be promotion in it for you, Paul. What are you now?"

"An Assistant District Nobody," Paul said. "But I've got a transfer. Biddy doesn't want to go back to South Africa. So they've given me the Gold Coast. The problem is, too much malaria and blackwater fever in the jungle. They don't allow children out there, because they die."

"So Bridget will have to stay here, unless you park the baby?"

"Yes. Bloody, isn't it?"

"Clever girl. Like us all, England is a better place to be in."

A scowling Clio brought Biddy and the baby, now scented with Paris perfumes, back into the room. And Biddy, trying to please, blurted out her usual howlers again. Those things on the walls, do they come from an asylum? Or from a kindergarten? Isn't Matisse a French pastry? And Cubism something you do in a factory? Abstract art? I thought you had to understand it. And Picasso, never heard of him.

"Well, Pablo is a dear friend," Virginia said, "though the wrong side of the political spectrum. But artists can't think. They can only paint. And he can't even draw. That's why the pictures look so quaint to you, Biddy. Anyway, he hates his mistresses like some men learn to hate their wives. Not you, Paul, of course, ever. But Pablo, he loves making his women look ugly. As men do, while women only love women to look their best."

4

BACK TO BACKS

Lying on the grass on the Backs in the noon and summer sun, Ian Hamish Ogilvie felt far from class and civil wars. The flannelled fools in their punts lifted their poles and ducked under the low stone bridges to push their craft down the Cam to Grantchester, where the clock had stopped at ten to three, when Rupert Brooke died in the Great War along with Ian's own father. The fretwork pincushion of King's Chapel punctured the long quad colonnades, while the far chant of choirboys was a dulcimer in air. Never was learning so easeful, never was struggle so like inertia. How could he ever move again?

Something was tickling his ear. He shook his head and squinted sideways to see his cousin Hamish Henry scratching a lobe with a stalk of hay.

"Comrade, arouse. This is no time to laze and lie. What did they shout when they heard the sound of the pipes at the siege of Lucknow? 'The Sinclairs are coming, hurrah! Hurrah'!"

"It was the Campbells, you idiot."

"What do the clans matter the now? But the Sinclairs are coming to Cambridge to roost. All the exotic ones we never see. Gordon the rover. And Shilendra, our long-lost eastern relation. And Rosabelle."

"Not her. She never comes. She is always acting or striking or something outrageous."

"She's coming too. And they all want to see you."

Ian couldn't work it out. He was reading languages, true, and mathematics, pushing himself in two disciplines. And he was in the Air Corps. Yet he was out of touch with everybody in the family except Hamish Henry, and even then, they saw little of each other, the divide between King's College and Trinity being deeper than the Wooky Hole.

"Why do they want to see me? I really don't know any of them."

"I do. And they all want to see you. It's a three-line whip. I'd be expelled from the Party if I didn't obey."

"What Party?"

"Oh, the Christmas Party. What do you think? Gordon's had a lot to do with Spain. Perhaps he'll tell us something. Isn't that super?"

"Jolly super."

Hamish Henry always played the schoolboy when anything looked like becoming serious, and he didn't want to discuss it then.

"Thursday, tea-time, about four. In my rooms in Nevile's Court. And no tea and scones. Vodka and crisps. Ta-ta for now."

Walking away, Hamish Henry thought how difficult recruitment was. He never knew how far to go. Particularly with family. You never knew which relation would tip somebody off about you. Of course, the kith and kin who were already in were dropping by to see him. And it wasn't only them who wanted Ian Ogilvie in the cadre. The Comrade Professor wanted him in, too. Even Marx didn't know why.

At his supervision that afternoon on thermodynamics and particles, Hamish Henry dared to broach the subject with the Comrade Professor, who squashed him.

"All you can know is your own cell, my dear young man. You are a groupuscule in the Party smaller than an electron in a cloud chamber. You mustn't even want to know the why of things. Your job is the what to do. And also, the less you know, the fewer you can betray – if they ever get to you."

"I never will."

"That's what they all say. Before the Gestapo get them, or our SS."

"Secret Service?"

"The same breed, the same methods. So recruit your cousin, but don't let on to anyone else who is with us."

"He'll know about our relatives after they come."

"He won't be sure. Only of you. But wasn't it splendid, my dear, the Senate vote today?"

"What?"

"They agreed to send the whole of our Peter Kapitsa's laboratory to Russia, now he has decided to return there for good."

"But it's atomic physics. How could they? The government will stop it."

"First, they can't. Cambridge is a free institution, run by its dons. Second, they're so stupid and unscientific, they don't even know its significance. The principle of the free exchange of information in theoretical physics world-wide is wholly liberal, absolutely democratic, don't you think?" The Comrade Professor was smiling as if opening a blade from a pen-knife. "How the bourgeois do destroy themselves and save us the bother."

When Ian Ogilvie arrived for his vodka tea in the gabled room of Nevile's Court, which overlooked the weighty rose-and-yellow stone blocks of the Wren Library, he did not expect to find all the trio of special guests there. Yet Gordon and Shilendra were squatting on the floor, while in the only spare chair sat Rosabelle, her legendary red-gold hair in a waterfall to her waist. Whippet and lean with a small moustache, Gordon jerked to his feet in his corduroys followed by Shilendra, so intense in his white dungarees that his skin seemed to smoulder as an oil fire.

"Gordon ... Shilendra ... Rosabelle," Hamish Henry said, also rising. "Meet comrade-to-be cousin Ian."

"I should have met you before," Rosabelle said, her mouth so mobile and her voice so warm that they seemed to suck Ian into her convictions. "But your auntie Ruth and Gordon's mother Virginia –"

"Those old queers and bosom pals," Gordon said.

"I didn't say that. Let's just say, Ian, that nobody in this room sees eye-to-eye with those relatives of yours. Do you?"

"No, not on everything."

"On anything?"

"Not much, actually."

"Hunger marches. The miners' strike. Aid to the Spanish Republic. Where do you stand? We know where they do."

And so the interrogation began. It was blatant, but irresistible. Rosabelle was so persuasive, almost insidious. Ian could not counter the mysteries of her moving lips. And he was no dissembler. He had nothing to hide, only the callowness of some of his opinions, which stood only to be corrected.

So he revealed himself, at odds with his mother and even his grandmother Margaret at Annandale. Like most of his fellow undergraduates, he was on the left side, blaming the Great War on donkey generals and drunken politicians, thinking the depression the fault of plutocrats and capitalists, believing the Empire should devolve itself quicker from dominions into independent countries within a Commonwealth, and backing the Republicans in Spain because they had been elected, while Franco and his Fascists had not. Communism and the class struggle, however, were not his satchel.

"But when the showdown comes after Spain, as it must," Rosabelle asked, "it will be Communism against Fascism. Germany and Italy against Russia. Which side would you choose?"

"There is a third way," Ian said. "Not to choose."

"But if you had to?"

"Russia, of course. It's not my kind of socialism, but if I had to choose..."

"A fellow-traveller, then?"

"I would travel anywhere with you, cousin Rosabelle, as your fellow."

At last, laughter. Shilendra gossiped about Annandale, where his mother had been for the funeral of Doctor Seaforth. Curiously, he had wished to be buried there, and Ian's grandmother Margaret Jardine had been unable to refuse. He was family, after all.

"Do you ever hear from your mother Ruby," Shilendra asked casually, "what her father Douglas is up to? He must be retiring soon from intelligence, still playing the Great Game against the Russians in Afghanistan."

"He's still at it," Ian said. "But he doesn't tell mother much, and she doesn't go out to Annandale now. Though she did say something about cousin Murdo being there, setting up airline links, and Gillon with his Marconi stations. When did you last go back, Shilendra?"

Ian found it no good trying to turn the questions. Shilendra was airy-fairy, but hardly a diary.

"I come and go all the time over the East."

"And West, I see."

"Rarely."

"And what do you do?"

"Consultant. An educational consultant."

"And who consults you? And what do you teach?"

Shilendra laughed and shrugged.

"I teach that most education is mere propaganda. And people consult me in how to get together. So I organize congresses. Happy now?"

Gordon took over the inquisition, apparently fascinated by Ian's education.

"Languages, French and German, and mathematics. Hamish Henry tells me your tutor is a chap called Turing."

"I'm lucky to have him," Ian said. "He's into theories of chance, statistics, computers. You have heard of them."

"We've heard of them. IBM is sending them over to Germany to help the Nazis to be more efficient. But we do ask, Efficient for what? And your Turing, what's he making those computers do? What do you think?"

"I really don't know," Ian said. He was uncomfortable. He couldn't spy on his tutor. "Something to do with aircraft."

"That's why he's teaching you," Hamish Henry said. "You're in the Air Squadron. I bet he doesn't want you to fall out of the sky."

"Nor do I," Gordon said. "But I have seen a few things fall out of the sky before. At a place called Guernica."

And he told of the dive-bombing of the Spanish town, the Stukas raining down their lethal loads from heaven, the horror of a *blitz* that now threatened every city in Europe. And he did admit that, as a ship's engineer, he was often in Bilbao, tinkering with the engines of the Russian convoys, when they got through with the munitions for the Republicans. Then he knew he had said enough, so he switched to films, saying that, in his trade, *The Battleship Potemkin* had to be the best movie ever made, but then it was Charlie Chaplin caught among the cogwheels before being spat out in *Modern Times*, and then Fred Astaire in *Shall We Dance?*

"Fred Astaire?" Rosabelle couldn't stop laughing. "You?"

"That dancing scene in the engine-room of the liner. The way he glided by and through the machines. That tap-tap-tap of his feet, prettier than pistons. I know the scrubbed black stokers playing in a cast-off jazz band were ridiculous as the slaves in a liner, but who cares? If you've ever served in the greasy infernos down there, this was the flight of an angel – genius – grace in motion. And Fred was pretending to be a Russian ballet star – the great con. And he was right. All Got Rhythm." Now Gordon was trying to tap-dance without falling over his toes. "Zoom, zoom, zoom." He was clicking his fingers. "Hiss, hiss, hiss, hup. Perthump, ump, clickety, click."

"My," Rosabelle was still laughing. "My word."

"Put on the Red Army choir," Gordon said. "Or Gershwin will do." He pulled Rosabelle to her feet. "Shall we dance? Will you be the Ginger on my Fred?"

"That's the worst pun –" But Rosabelle was laughing again as the gramophone scratched out a wild mazurka, and Gordon began a kicking and springing display like a mad March hare, then suddenly swooped on Rosabelle and swished her round the little room, leaping over the bodies of the guests, dancing up onto a table and down again with her, a cross between Astaire and the Gay Hussar. And when the exhibition of levitation was done, they collapsed into a tangle in the corner.

"I never knew you had that in you, Gordon," Rosabelle said. And he said wistfully, "Didn't you know? I always really wanted to be a ballet dancer."

Ian remembered his mother Ruby asking him what the family needed, breeding so many cousins like rabbits. He had replied, "Myxamatosis." After three more unknown cousins had turned Hamish Henry's rooms in Trinity into a warren, Ian hardly expected a fourth one to be sitting in his rooms at Kings. This bird was a different breed though – dressed in a black leather flying suit with soft top boots below his britches. Under his cropped bronze curly hair his eyes darted and his red mouth slithered even more than Rosabelle's at her inquisition, as he introduced his presence.

"I'm Peregrine Plunkett-Drax, your Irish relation. Naturally nobody wants relations in Ireland any more, who would in that bogland? They killed my father, as you may know, though I got away with my mother Arabella, and we never went back. Uncle Murdo flew the coop before on his ruddy sea-planes. Wise chap. I took a wee while to take flight myself, but here I am, Ian, if I may call you that. I hear you're in the flying game, too."

Why everybody in the family knew so much about him, Ian didn't have the faintest idea. And why an avalanche of the clan was landing on his head was still a mystery. So he asked this new stranger:

"Have you seen the other cousins who have just come to Cambridge?"

"No, no. Who can they be?"

"Rosabelle. Gordon. And the Indian one, Shilendra."

"What a surprise. I hardly know them. Gorgeous to meet them."

"They've all just left."

"Where?"

"I don't know. They're the sort of people who never tell you where they are going."

"Or coming from." Peregrine grinned, his lips two red leeches. "Just like me. Leaves in the wind. Blowing hither and thither. But more hither just now, as we seem all to come to see you."

"I can't imagine why."

"I thought I'd drop by because I was passing through. My uncle got me in the aeroplane business, too."

"Who do you work for?"

"Various clients here and there. I'm just a dogsbody.   A consultant."

That is what Shilendra had said, disguising what he really did and who paid him. But Ian decided not to tackle Peregrine on that score. All his cousins seemed so cagey about their business.

"My mother told me your uncle Murdo is setting up these sea-plane links to Africa and India, perhaps even Australia. London to Cairo to

Capetown – to Bombay – who knows, Melbourne. Are you helping him?"

"You could say that. He certainly is helping me with these imperial links. Very impressive. And Canadian cousin Gillon with his Marconi stations. Faster than Puck, they can girdle the earth in less than eighty minutes. Wireless, that's the thing. You know wherever you are that something's up even before it's started."

The energy in Peregrine's voice was infectious. It sparked off an admission from Ian.

"That's what my tutor says. Alan Turing. I've got a supervision this afternoon. We'll be able to see the enemy planes before they come in. New forms of radio. At night, too."

Peregrine's eyes were narrow and still for once.

"Very interesting. Do go on."

"The thing is to know when the enemy planes take off, where they're heading. Then our fighters can knock them down. Turing wants me to take up navigation. Don't be a pilot, he says. Be a plotter."

"Excellent advice." Peregrine pouted with amusement. "But I'd rather be in the pilot's seat. Plotting is so boring, all those graphs and equations. I'd rather leave figures and intrigues to others. And let my own number come up, when it does."

Peregrine stayed on another hour, charming Ian against his will. The new cousin was both elusive and seductive. He drew people to him, then he slipped away. As a child, Ian had once broken a thermometer, and some of the mercury had spilled out of the fine glass tube. He had pursued the rolling metallic blobs round the bottom of a cardboard box with his fingers. They would meld together or split, roll their wobbly ways and squirt off from his touch. Peregrine was like that, fascinating, but out of reach.

When they parted, Peregrine embraced Ian and kissed him on both cheeks in the French manner. His last words were, "We have to be continental these days. Or they'll blow us to bits. If you can't bomb them, join them."

Odder still was the conversation which Ian had with his tutor at the end of the supervision. In his spare way, both dry and shy, Turing seemed to be reaching out for confidences. Yet as the horns of a snail, he recoiled from any approach. This time, however, when he had suggested solutions to the problems of probability and even encrypted words, he surprised Ian by talking about the Cambridge cousin, Hamish Henry.

"I wonder if you could tell me," he said, diffident as usual. "Went to a party at Trinity last night. Met this charming young man. Said he was a relation of yours. Henry?"

"Hamish Henry. Yes. He's in the family."

"Very charming. Said he was very interested in what we are doing. I don't know. He's a physicist. Not that it's so far from mathematics. But the sciences should get together, don't you think?" Turing's mouth twitched in what might have been a slight grin. "And scientists."

"Get together?"

"Get together. Scientists. Cross disciplines. Cross fertilization." Again the little twitch of the mouth. "Anyway, I've agreed to give him extra supervision. Do you think that's all right?"

Ian did not know what to say, but in the end, he stammered, "I don't know... Er, he's fine. Good bloke... I suppose."

There was a glint now in Turing's eyes which hinted he was enjoying himself.

"Ian, Ian, you're so maidenly. You really are. But then, you're not one of us, are you?"

"How could I be? I'm not a don."

"No, of course not." Turing was smiling now. "And you're not one of them. Merely unconverted."

"If you mean I'm not a Communist like most of my cousins. Or a Fascist like some of the rest of them —"

"Politics has nothing to do with it, Ian. Let's say, it's a matter of persuasion." Again a sort of snicker. "A persuasion. As G.E. Moore might have said. Persuasion. Persuasions. A persuasion. All with different meanings, but it comes to the same question. Are you one of us? Can you be persuaded to be?"

So Turing dismissed Ian to take to the clouds that late afternoon, so he might escape the fog of trying to understand what was happening all around him.

In the Gladiator high above the aerodrome, Ian could look between the wings of the bi-plane, which framed the shire below. The fields were a skein on the land, oblongs of yellow and terracotta and green, with the dark patches of the spinneys spoiling the design, and the rivers writhing towards the Wash and the north sea. The canals and the drains of the Fens tried to stamp a griddle on this natural haphazard, etched and brush-stroked by the wind and the rain. But nothing men could do might shift the earth a jot or a tittle from its mazy patterns. Their noises were as jangling as the struts and wires that held the upper and lower wings of his aircraft together. As if one could bolt the atmosphere together, or channel the Ouse, or fashion events. Ian brought to mind his hero, Antoine de Saint-Exupéry, uplifted above gale and sand and storm in the liberty of the upper air. He screamed into the veined transparent prison around him: "Take me! I'm here. I don't want to know. Down there."

5

CROSSED LINES

In West Africa, Paul didn't think he would find a colony with three old castles. Yet the Gold Coast had Elmina, which the Portuguese had left behind them from their discovery and slave-trading days, its round watchtower still brooding over the palm trees and the waters. Then there was Christianborg Castle in Accra, straddling the sea and a Danish legacy to Paul's ultimate superior, the Governor. And there was Cape Coast Castle with its old ships' cannon pointing out to the beaches and to South Africa, the tombstones of the buried British settlers behind the guns, proving that this territory was truly a white man's graveyard.

Nobody could escape the malaria. However much he and Biddy were cocooned in their mosquito nets from nightfall to dawn, the whining biters always got through and took their blood and left their red landing marks. The quinine helped, but it did not prevent the sudden sweating and the shakes. Worse was the blackwater fever, and that could kill along with snake-bite and driver ants in an assault. But there was always the M & B against the rise of the fever, when the quicksilver almost climbed out of the thermometer at 107°, and the boiling skin broke out in a deathly sweat.

Pretty Biddy, so brave and small that she used to carry around a stool to stand on and talk to him on the level, she hated the drop from the side of the Elder-Dempster steamer to the surf boats off Cape Coast, following the tin trunks slung down into the open string of the big canoes towed by a tug and paddled by eight boat boys to the pier through the cold froth of the breakers on the shallow shore. And she could not bear leaving the little one Kelso back in England or in South Africa with relations, who didn't really want him, but knew that for a small child, an eighteen-month tour in West Africa was a ticket to the cemetery. If a wife went with the husband, it meant no children, except for the six months' leave back at home every two years. That was the burden and the heartache, that was the price for the miserable pay. But in a depression, any sacrifice was worth a job.

Biddy nearly made them rich, that time they visited the Tarkwa gold mine. Seeing the slight blonde with her cornflower eyes, the manager had said that if she could pick up a gold bar and carry it away, it was hers. He had no idea of Biddy's ambition and determination. Straight-spined as a weight-lifter, she went into a crouch and heaved up the ingot in both hands and carried it out of the door. The manager's mouth dropped, and he began to stutter.

"M-m-madam," he said, "I didn't really m-m-mean..." Biddy dropped the gold bar on the wooden verandah outside, where it broke a plank, and turned her wide gaze on him. "Are you saying, sir," she said, "that you are not a man of your word?" He was not. All she was given was a piece of gold-quartz to serve as a paperweight for her letters home.

Paul's posting to the Gold Coast Police meant serving out of their bungalow at Kumasi, where the railway ended in the Ashanti capital, on the northern loop from Takoradi to Accra. The passenger steam engines had a miner's lamp that drilled a bright shaft through the steamy coal darkness, while the cocoa trains smelled of sultry dormitory treats as their smoke hung in dense fog in the dripping stations. The bungalows sweated on their blocks, each movement like a dip in the river Volta, where nobody swam because of the crocodiles. "Paul, Paul," Biddy was always complaining. "I can never get the sheets dry. It's like sleeping in slime."

On parade, too, the creases never lasted on Paul's starched long shorts. They were as sharp as his ceremonial sword-blade when the boy Nana had pressed them with a hot iron; but after an hour's drill, they were limp flags of khaki, the colour of the Northern Territories that had little rain. Paul had his leather-covered cane truncheon specially loaded with a lump of lead at its head. Good for riots, especially with tough dockers at Takoradi, or the Ashanti miners, who would rather be warriors than hackers of manganese and gold. He also had a couple of fly-whisks, embroidered with beads, for keeping the buzzing insects off his forehead during the interminable palavers, when he had to go north and sort out the Escort police and the Muslim feuds of Tamale and Navrongo by the border of the Ivory Coast.

The upcountry tours took him away half the time, and Biddy did not know what she was doing in a sort of Surbiton, lost in a purgatory of the jungle. For the wives of the police and the colonial civil service, there were calling-cards and teas, there was teaching the black Girl Guides and the Brownies to do their duty to the Empire, also tennis and the monthly club dance, which was the only occasion for full dress and perhaps a folly. She attended alone when Paul was away in the bush, and there she saw the stranger in his Air Force uniform, surrounded by the other wives as wasps gather on a plum. Their fingernails were striking towards his white and blue outfit and his burnished curls, a helmet over the moving fascination of his everchanging face. His wings did not grow from his shoulders, but were stitched onto his sleeves. And he was asking after her.

"Peregrine," he said. "I am your cousin Peregrine." He shed the other wives as a gull shakes off drops of brine, and he looked down on her from his height. "Where's Paul?"

"In the bush. After the ID Buyers."

"I heard about that in Accra. Illicit Diamond Buying. They told me the Syrian women smuggle the stones out in their bodies – the places where the police can't search."

Biddy laughed and flushed. She knew Peregrine was an Irish landowner's son with a country estate and all that meant. He could say anything and get away with it. Risky comments were part of his charm.

"I don't think Paul would dare," she said. "Search them, I mean."

"Sounds like fun. I would. Where is your boy?"

"In South Africa, with his grandfather."

"It must be hard on you."

"I sometimes think," Biddy said, "that this whole empire is an excuse to separate young mothers from their sons."

"It's best not to marry if you're in the colonial service."

"He rises fastest..." Biddy's smile was acrid. "Who stays a bachelor."

"I didn't mean that, in your case." Peregrine's stare was too intense. "Anyone would want you along with him."

Biddy flushed again and hoped that nothing was showing through the white powder caulking her face.

"You've come on your own, I see. What does bring you to our dark corner of the world? Obviously an aeroplane."

"I'll tell you over a pink gin," Peregrine said. "You do?"

"I do. Gratefully."

He did tell her about his passion for flying, which began with a red kite over the fields of Armagh, and his own kestrel in his youth to bring down other birds, and the Cadet Corps and giving up university to join the Air Force, encouraged by Murdo with his ambitions to establish a world-wide seaplane service to stitch a patchwork quilt of red imperial pieces across the globe. These connections had caused Peregrine to be seconded to West Africa, where the French had their own strategy. Only Aeromaritime Française flew their aircraft into Takoradi harbour behind its breakwaters, and this was unacceptable with a war already brooding in Europe. There was a lake near Kumasi called Basumiwi, near the railway line. Did Biddy know it?

"Well," she said, "if you fell off your seaplane – if the crocs didn't get you, the mosquitos must."

"We land on the Zambesi just above the Victoria Falls. Crocs and hippos – and nobody has fallen over the edge yet." The intent in his eyes made her shiver. "Do people fall round here?" he said. "Just occasionally. I can't think what else there is to do."

The police band began to play a waltz with too much of a drum in it. But this was Africa. Beat, beat, beating at you. And when Peregrine took her on the floor, she felt absurd and tiny, her silver top on the level of his ribs, and her head in his grip against the hardness of his chest. His whirling steps made her giddy, and hot drops burst through her make-up, and she cried free. "I must go to the Ladies," she said. "Please excuse me."

She knew she was walking into a baited trap. She shook as she walked through the door and saw Molly and Pat looking at her, waiting to stick in the spikes. She knew that they had seen that instant recognition, which was the secret of love. Peregrine's fix on her eyes – she was startled, she meant to glance away, she could not, and she was caught too long. She was married, she should walk away, but her child was taken from her, her husband left her alone, what could she do? And all the other women wanted Peregrine, she could see that. He had picked her out.

Molly began the inquisition, in between drawing her lipstick for the tenth time round her severe pout.

"So he's your cousin."

"Only by marriage," Pat said.

"The rich one. From Ireland. He's very tall."

"You mean, for me," Biddy said. "Why don't you say I'm small?"

"How long is Paul on tour for?"

"Another week."

"So he is coming back?"

"Of course."

"Funny your cousin turning up when Paul was away. You must have known he was coming."

"Not actually. It was a surprise."

Molly looked at Pat, and Pat looked at Molly, with that wide stare of disbelief.

"Not here on business, then," Pat said.

"A flier," Biddy said. "You can see that."

"Kelso," Molly said. "How is your son?"

"The last I heard from the Cape," Biddy said, "Kelso had the mumps. But he was getting better." She dabbed her powder puff for the last time on her cheeks and rose. "If you don't mind, dears, I must be getting back to Peregrine. Before you all gobble him up."

In the week before Paul came back, she met Peregrine at the bungalow, after dark, when the hot streets were emptier, when not too many eyes were peeking by the muslin and the net on the windows. The first time he passed by, she had fretted too long, nervous and impatient, scolding Nana over and over about the drinks, saying the silver was dirty and the napkins were not straight, until he was pleading for Missus to have a gin on her own, but she could not. To drink alone on the Coast was the beginning of the end, especially for a woman. Yet she had to turn to the packet of Player's Navy Cut and smoke half-a-dozen cigarettes down to their butts and grind them out in the brass ash-tray with the embossed elephant's head, as if she were squashing time on the head. When the bell did finally ring, she jumped up to answer the door herself, then she remembered Nana and sat down on the leather sofa, brushing her long paisley skirt carefully over her knees.

Peregrine would not let her rise while Nana fixed the Haig whisky and sodas. In fact, he hardly said a word until they were left together, and then he was as abrupt and clipped as if he were commanding a fighter squadron.

"I shouldn't be here," he said. "You know that."

"It's all right," Biddy said. "You're family."

"Hardly."

"Anyway, Nana's here. He's a chaperone."

The Ashanti man with the soft manners in his white suit hardly looked like a dowager in a crinoline, but Peregrine only smiled and said, "He knows his place. Out of here."

"I hope so. Have you found your landing ground?"

Peregrine got to his feet and drained his cut-glass tumbler. He stood over the seated Biddy, putting his hands on the sofa back either side of her head, dropping his face towards her.

"Here," he said. "With you."

Biddy looked up at this order to her from above.

"You don't...I'm married...Paul..."

He fell on her, as he had said, and crushed her against the brown hide. She was given no chance, she wanted none. Her fate had dropped from the sky. There was nothing she could do, no escape. As she was torn apart, she heard a deep cry – hers, victim or desire, pain or delight. Nana will hear me, she thought, and then drowned.

After that, Peregrine came round on four more nights. They hardly spoke to each other, but explored and devoured their skins as animals. Biddy began by being enveloped under his power, but now she fought back with all her might, a mongoose against a python. She struck and struck again with her hips and her mouth against the thrust of Peregrine, who could have lifted her on one hand and thrown her against the ceiling above the tin roof. They had little hope now that their passion was secret, for in the small community of white Kumasi, even a fruit-bat could not screech at night without the whole world reporting it. The worst was when Paul rang in the middle of their love-making, and Biddy had to answer. That subtle betrayer, the voice over the telephone, gave her away, although she thought she was sounding perfectly normal. "Oh, Peregrine is here," she said breathlessly. "I saw him at the club dance. He's looking for a lake for his sea-planes." There was a silence to this piece of news, then a cold voice, "Is he staying long?" Biddy tried to be casual. "I don't know. I hope till after you're back. Is the tour going well?" And she only heard, "As usual. Touch of fever. Doesn't sound usual with you. Good night."

The two men missed each other by the length of the afternoon. Biddy was reckless enough to see Peregrine off on the Takoradi train. There were too many eyes inquiring there, but the hanging smoke gave her an excuse for her red eyes and her tears. She had to shake hands and wish him good luck, before he stepped into the carriage. They had discussed plans, but they could make none. She had a child and no money, he was in the Air Force and war was threatening. No love could break such a barrier, and a divorce would ruin Paul's career. To be together was unthinkable. And they could not even write to each other. Every letter that came to the bungalow was so precious that it had to be shared. The only hope was her leave in England, when that came, if it ever came, and Peregrine was posted there.

Paul had to know sooner or later. And given her good friends as Molly and Pat said they were, Biddy felt that Paul would know sooner. She was not wrong. At the next club dance, as she entered on Paul's arm, she met a cold fence. People talked across her to her husband or turned away or asked the same pointed question. "What's happened to that good-looking cousin, cousin, cousin..." Paul was taken aside, there was whispering behind the trembling of her back, nobody came up to speak to her except Molly, who said, "You really didn't think you would get away with it, Biddy dear. And you won't be seeing him again."

As Biddy was saying, "I don't know what you mean," she heard her voice dying in her throat, and she ran towards Paul and caught him to her and said, "Take me home."

"In a minute."

"Now."

"The bungalow can wait. Are you ill?"

"Home. Not here. I mean, really home."

"England?"

"Now. I have to stay there with our boy, when I get him back from South Africa."

Paul's face was set, as if he were passing sentence, not her.

"You won't come on tour with me again."

"No. Never again."

"This is rather sudden." He turned to the ring of avid faces, pecking at their few words. "Excuse us. My wife's a bit low."

"Home." That was all Biddy could say. "Home."

6

NO SIEGFRIED LINE

The greater advantage of the Great Depression was that maids were so cheap and replaceable. Unlike, indeed, the Great War, when not even a skivvy was available because she could get better wages in a munitions factory. The only boring thing was training the new staff, when the others had to be sacked for dropping a Dresden dish or letting a tea-cup handle come off in their hand. Virginia had so long sent down the plughole her early days as a nanny on a South Africa farm that she resented the five minutes to teach the new Mavis how to put pleats properly into a pukka short skirt.

"Either they're mischievous or stupid or plain pig-ignorant,"she was complaining to Ruth, as they sipped their mid-morning Earl Grey tea - no milk with a slice of lemon - and nibbled at a *petite madeleine* - so Proustian, although they forgot to remember time past and where they had come from.

"I don't know," Ruth said. "I think they're capable of couth. They're just not our kind, if you know what I mean."

"You're too kind to say that. There are people and people. And most people are not people we would like to know. Although it's not popular to say that any more in these times of the masses."

"Horrid word. Makes me think of cardinals chanting Latin in red red robes."

"Almost as bad a word as classes. Kept in for Fifth Form maths, when we'd rather be hacking the ball with our jolly hockey sticks."

"*W*e really are pig-ignorant," Ruth said slyly, "not to know a thing about what's happening in the big world outside. All those causes and nonsense."

Virginia laughed.

"My dear, wasn't it fascinating to hear what Peregrine said about Cambridge? All your cousin Ian told him. Isn't he coming to see you?"

"Soon, very soon. I told him we were off to Ivylinn. And you know what he said? He supposed it was cheaper than a ticket to Berlin."

"Oh well, at least he's got some of his aunt's wit. But wasn't Peregrine interesting about his last trip? He actually spent a day shooting with Goëring."

"Well, he is sort of touting for him. Not officially. Trying to get the Luftwaffe back to Tanganyika and South-West Africa. Via the Gold Coast, I hear. That's why he went out there and met Paul and that boring Biddy." Ruth showed her claws again, as it was that sort of a morning. "Doesn't she hail from that part of the veldt you were stuck in? When Paul's father shot his first missus?"

"Darkest Africa, dear, should remain darkest for ever. Will the last one there put out the lights. Peregrine also said that Goëring wasn't as fat as he looked - he was fatter. They were trying to build a bomber big enough to fit him in."

"Yes, wasn't that droll! And Himmler did have a good side. He had a yen for the Tibetans. They were the original Aryan Race. Through the Dalai Lama - or was it the yeti?"

The women laughed again, then Virginia leaned from her chair towards Ruth, lounging on the sofa.

"But what about Clio? We haven't seen her all morning."

"You know how she gets migraine every time Peregrine comes and hardly notices her."

"Love of her life. I do wish she would grow up and out of her childhood fling."

"And Peregrine's just as bad as his father. About women, I mean."

"We should know," she said. "Alexander Plunkett-Drax. What a bastard."

"Still," Ruth said. "He did bring us together. In a kind of a sort of a way."

"By being bloody beastly to both of us. I could have killed him."

"Luckily, the Irish did. Even they have taste."

Virginia smiled. "You know Peregrine said he met Unity Mitford out in the Reich. I hope he didn't have an affair with her, too."

"She's always running after Hitler, isn't she?"

"Without much success. I hear the Fuhrer prefers cream cakes."

Ruth shook her head.

"I think the Mitfords are even worse than our family. Half of them are Reds and rebels, half of them are duchesses and Fascists. And as for the Moseleys – that ghastly Oswald isn't going to be at Ivylinn for the weekend, is he?"

"No. He's marching in Stepney or somewhere. Though who'd take a stroll through the East End by choice, I can't imagine. But all men are such silly bastards, aren't they just? I'm lucky to have a daughter even if she is a little bitch. I really couldn't cope with those members of your family who don't *think* as we do."

"Ian's not so bad really," Ruth said. "I've got a soft spot for him. He's very influencible. He doesn't really know what to think until I've told him."

"He's quite old enough to think for himself."

"And then he can be quite adorable when that brown hair of his flops down into his blue eyes."

There was a ringing on the doorbell. The Mavis of the moment, who actually answered to Doris, went to let in the visitor.

"Speak of the devil," Virginia said.

"Angel," Ruth greeted her cousin as he came into the drawing-room. She stretched out a hand for him to take, still lying down on the sofa. "So kind of you to come and cheer up two lonely ladies."

"I wanted to see you before you went off to the country." There was a forced note in Ian's cheerfulness. "I see far too little of you, Ruth."

"Cambridge is light years away," Virginia said. "Although now and then a time traveller drops in to tell us of events in your galaxy."

"You're still seeing some of the family?"

"Those we can't avoid."

"That's Virginia's little joke," Ruth said. "Some of our nearest and dearest do come round occasionally to tell us what's going on with the rest of us."

"That's what has been happening to me," Ian said. "I really couldn't twig. All those cousins descending out of the deep blue yonder -"

"Deep red, more likely, dear," Ruth said.

"And asking me all those questions about flying and Alan Turing."

"Yes. Peregrine told us all about it."

"And him coming up after them. Don't tell me that was a coincidence. It was a conspiracy."

"The problem about the young," Virginia said, "is that they are all paranoid. They think the world is against them, which it may be. But it's not plotting against them. Ruth, what sinister plans do you have in store for Ian?"

"Nothing," Ruth said. "Except to say living is merely a series of accidents. Near misses. A few hits, but mainly off target. You don't get what you want."

"I did," Virginia said. "You. Didn't you?"

"I don't mean that," Ruth said, seeing Ian go pink. "I mean, it's all a roll of the dice. They may be loaded, but not for you."

"That's not what Turing says." Ian was insistent. "Or Einstein. God doesn't roll dice. And if there's no God, probability eliminates chance over any series of events."

"You don't believe in providence, child."

"If there is destiny - fate, whatever - then conspiracies would be part of it. And paranoia would merely be the misunderstanding of providence. You can see human skullduggery, but what if it's just part of a far greater plot and plan than we can ever know? A big design that takes faith to understand. And even revelation."

"Cripes," Virginia said. "What do they teach you in Fenland? Perhaps you should change your brand of professors. Or narcotics."

"My advice to you, my conspiratorial Ian," Ruth said, "is to lock your pockets, in case we steal anything from you. And empty your mind - then I can't pick your brains. There's only rubbish in your head now. Ah, Clio," as a young woman came into the room in a purple kimono sporting a spangled green dragon and split to the thigh, "meet my nephew Ian."

"He'll probably think," Virginia added, "that you are a Japanese agent on a mission to repeat the Rape of London *à la* Nanking. Aren't you a bit overdressed for going down to Ivylinn?"

"I thought I might provoke some interesting comments at last," Clio said. "Instead of, Isn't Hitler a darling. And is Mussolini coming for tea?" Then glaring at Ian. "He's not coming, is he? Peregrine's going to be there."

"No, I'm not coming," Ian said. "I saw him at Cambridge."

"He came to visit *you*?"

"Yes. Scout's honour."

"The plot thickens."

"Just what I've been saying."

"Shut up, you two." Virginia rose to her feet and flexed her shoulder blades. Under her robe, they looked like knives sharpening. "Packing, packing. The only thing worse than packing for country houses is staying in them a whole weekend. Are you saying bye-bye, Ian?"

"Bye, bye," Ian said and bent down to kiss Ruth on the cheek as she turned her face away from him. His lips tasted cold cream with a coat of powder. "Bye, bye, all," he repeated and left the room, hearing Ruth's "Fare thee well" behind him.

They played croquet for a fiver a hoop, which was more than Virginia could afford. Not that she had that British weakness of being a good loser. She had a killer instinct and would whack an enemy ball right across the lawn into the far dahlia beds. And swinging the mallet between the legs of her bell-bottomed white silk trousers, she could hit the mark at twenty paces. But that twerp von Ribbentrop with his clicking heels and jerking bow to her, he was unerring in smacking her away into the hollyhocks, while cannoning into line for his next shot. And he had only played twice before. Maddening.

"Beginner's luck," she tossed at him over her shoulder, as she stumped off after her ball, now dispatched into an ivy bush.

"Correct," the German diplomat said, taking aim and using his mallet like a pendulum to drive on. The ball didn't even touch the iron sides of the hoop in its passage through to the other side.

"Another fiver down the tube," Virginia muttered as she bent down to extricate her ball and pricked her fingertips on the spikes of the ivy leaves. Red drops bloomed on the ends of her long chammy leather gloves.

Altogether, the Nazi took thirty quid off Virginia, which was the wrong way round. The Axis should still be paying the Allies reparations for the last war! Of course, Hitler taking the Ruhr back off the French was a damn good thing, like his going into Austria. But surely that should give him enough to pay back his natural friends and blood-brothers, the British.

Her hosts, Lord and Lady Oliver Pinden, seemed to be skipping tea; but Ruth was there with Peregrine and some Permanent Secretary from the Home Office called Ernest Overman. He was instantly familiar, saying that he had known Bill Dunesk in Scotland before his death. Then with a wink and a shudder, he added, "Better not to mention what countess Marie and the fell Rosabelle are doing with the estate. Making it a Striking Miners' Rest Home, I should think."

"I was up there helping her when it was an officers' convalescent home after the war," Virginia found herself saying. "Marie and I never got on. An impossible woman. It must be the Crow in her. Or was it Sioux?"

"Sewer, did you say?" Overman asked.

"Sioux. Crow. Red Indian tribes. And the red rather stuck."

Everybody was failing to notice Clio in her kimono with that British gift for ignoring bad taste in public, so she soon left in a sulk to change. Now the men began to come in from their rough shoot. Not much luck, only a few hares and a partridge or two, but the dogs had a good run. Peregrine was chatting with the Marquess of Clydesdale, the heir of the Duke of Hamilton. They had met at the Berlin Olympic Games a couple of years ago.

"You've never seen anything like the staging," the Marquess said. "All that precision dancing and drilling of the youth movements. They make our Boy Scouts look pathetic. Puppies with their paws in the air."

"More like tadpoles, Your Grace," Peregrine said. "Or newts, to be really wriggly."

The weekend was an informal get-together of the Anglo-German Society. The perfect strategy for England was so obvious that even the Chamberlain government could not miss it. The universal enemy was Bolshevism in Russia, then the Yellow Peril from Asia. Although the Japanese were cancelling the Chinese threat in the Pacific, they would have to be eliminated finally in order to preserve the British Empire and control over India and Africa. If Germany and Italy dominated Europe, the United Kingdom could control the rest of the globe with its sea-power. The Americans were too far off to intervene. World peace would be assured for the thousand years of the Third Reich and the sister Royal Navy. As von Ribbentrop summed up the whole issue: "It only needs one act of will from your Prime Minister such as the Fuhrer shows daily to break the alliance with the decadent French and join us and Mussolini and General Franco in Spain."

Nobody in the stately home thought that democracy had much to do with a good government. Hitler's deal with the German barons such as King George the Sixth's cousins in Hesse had restored the aristocracy to real power. Much of the House of Lords, particularly the Dukes, wanted their authority back, particularly reducing the Other Place, the House of Commons, under their heel. Enough of elected ministers and tub-thumpers, who could please a crowd, only to scupper their country. Everybody at Ivylinn could agree on that.

At the general meeting in the evening over drinks, Virginia was surprised to find Ruth's aged father, Charles Seymour-Scudabright. He had been so long estranged from his daughter because of her. Virginia presumed he would not be in the same house, and Ruth had not warned her that he was coming. Yet there they were, chatting away perfectly amiably, before Ruth took him over to meet von Ribbentrop. Then she remembered. Charles had been in the Civil Service in the War Office. Before his recent retirement, he had been involved in procurement. What ships, what guns, what aeroplanes should our forces use? She moved across the room to hear the German diplomat lecturing as if to a student.

"It is no use putting your money into aircraft. The Luftwaffe is supreme. Look at Spain. Or spending on your army, except in India. Your defence is your sea. Yes. Put it all into ships. Rule the oceans.

The seas are yours. We will stop the Bolsheviks in the Himalayas as well as on the Volga."

Virginia could see Charles nodding at the advice. He had lost his two sons, Ruth's brothers, in the Great War, and he only had one great nephew, Ian Hamish, to lose in the looming World War. There was more chance of survival on the waves than in the trenches, and none in the air, if the German was correct.

"I agree," Charles said. "But you see, my nephew wants to be a pilot."

"Ground him," von Ribbentrop said. "It is better a live boy than another kill for a Messerschmitt."

At dinner, Virginia found herself quite well placed. She was to the left of her host, Oliver Pinden, although she had to tolerate Overman on her right. Fortunately, he spent most of the time trying to interest Clio on his other flank; twice Virginia caught her daughter yawning with desperation and disgust. She didn't know why Lord Pinden wanted her beside him, for he was running the whole elegant dinner for thirty people at a long table as if it were a works canteen. His younger wife Ermine at the far end had nothing to do with the affair. Pinden pressed the bell wired under the table; he whispered to the butler and four serving footmen in tail coats and breeches and white stockings; he even took notes with a gold pen on a small pad if anything was amiss in serving the quails' eggs and poached salmon, stuffed partridge and jugged hare, Chablis and Chateau Talbot, *meringues glacées* and blackberries and cream, Stilton and port - "simple country fare," as he put it.

"Simplicity is the greatest luxury," Virginia replied. "The dearest thing money can buy."

Pinden gave her a sharp look, which turned to a long one of appraisal. "They said you were very bright," he said. He had to peer up to her, although his chair had oak arms like a throne and was higher than hers. His bald head glistened slightly, even if his moustache was waxed into twin tiny horns. "Tell me – your Abstract Art -"

"Post-Impressionist."

"Whatever. They say you do very well with it. Is it a good long-term investment?"

Virginia looked along the dining-room walls with its portraits of the nobility by Gainsborough and Reynolds. She knew that Pinden had bought them along with his title, though that had cost him rather more than the pictures because of the greed of the peerage broker Lloyd-George, England's old Welsh leader.

"A much better investment than your family portraits, Lord Pinden." He did not deny her lie about his origins. "A Picasso or a Matisse will be worth twenty times those pictures of your ancestors in ten years from now."

"Really? Even after the war?"

"Especially after the war, when we win it."

"Splendid, my dear, simply splendid. I may take your advice."

"Visit me. I will show you some of the goods."

"I may well."

Pinden pressed the bell under the table, and a footman glided up on castors.

"Number Four guest, short of Evian water. I don't want to see it happen again."

As the footman slid off, Pinden turned back to Virginia.

"I am afraid I can't delegate these chores to Ermine. She really isn't up to them. Can't keep her mind on things, though a wonderful hostess in other ways."

"She was very lucky to meet you," Virginia said. "So I have heard."

"Well, four husbands at her age. And four children. You would never know, she still looks so young and beautiful."

"Four husbands? A bit of a bolter?"

"I wouldn't say that. A bad picker."

"Until she met you."

"Yes. And she cannot bolt, as you say, from me. She cannot afford to. Her father, the Viscount, is land rich, but mouse poor. In fact, he's rather become a tenant of mine, though we don't like saying it outside the family."

He was saying it to her, a stranger. He obviously liked parading his power and his wealth. Small men often did. Little Napoleons. Fed up with having to look up to other people until they had a crick in the neck.

"Rearmament," she said. "Don't you think that would put an end to unemployment, Lord Pinden?"

"Redundancy, my dear, is no bad thing for me."

"How is that?"

"I buy bankrupt or failing businesses. I reduce the workforce and then engage another one on better terms. The more out of work, the more eager my recruits. I like to call them my helping hands. But I am in iron and steel and chemicals."

"Then making new weapons can do you no harm."

"And the country good."

"And the country good."

So Virginia's dinner was most satisfactory. She was so pleased to attract a rich new client that she forgot to observe how her daughter was doing. And when she looked, she found that Clio had slipped the pen. And looking further, another empty place was where Peregrine had been. Both had bolted somehow before the coffee. They must have a tryst, or far worse.

In the gazebo in the rose garden, Peregrine was forcing himself on Clio. She had scratched his face at first, but he had only laughed. She sobbed, "You are always neglecting me," only to hear, "Not damn now." She screamed, "I hate you." His answer, "You've loved me since a kid."

"I do hate you."

"No, you don't, don't, don't."

All the time him grabbing her crotch, ripping down there.

"The other women -"

"None. Not *now*."

"You fool. Of course, not *now*."

She found herself laughing with hysteria.

"*Now*. There's only me."

"Of course. More fool you."

A bench sliced into her back. A thrust into her. Dry, hard. Never in. Sudden, sudden. Clutch his back. Pull him in, far, far. Ha! Again, ha! Break. Flow, flow -

Peregrine stood up, buttoning his trousers. One cheek was raked and bleeding.

"Clio, you've wet my flies. All over. What will they think when we go back in? They'll think I was caught short, I wet myself, you darling little tart."

There was even a grave of an *ISABELLA SINCLAIR, d. 26 years, 1900*, at the back of the only surviving arched window of the standing apse of the fallen round church of Ophir on Orkney, which had been built by a Viking Earl in the twelfth century, after he had been on a crusade and seen the Church of the Holy Sepulchre in Jerusalem. Beyond its fallen stones, a taggle of a hundred tombstones or so reached to the scratchy waters of Scapa Flow. Down towards Kirkwall, the battleships and cruisers of the Home Fleet were at anchor, riding out time on the eve of the war.

Wallace had been prospecting and assaying over the Highlands and Islands, but outside some aluminium deposits in Aberdeenshire, he had found few traces of the strategic materials, which the government was demanding. There was quartz, but the ores were spare and low grade. What he had not expected to discover was the desolation of the whole of Sutherland and Caithness. Nearly all the crofts had their roofs stove in, and many of the shops in the granite town were shuttered. When he bought stores in Wick, the shopkeeper seemed to be surprised at the sight of a white five pound note with its script promising to repay that sum from the Bank of England. "Ye dinna see muckle o' them in these parts. It is barter we live on here."

He found his cousin Martha's cottage outside the town, but the door was locked as well. She must be away with her husband Angus Mackenzie along with her two small children, but Wallace did not know where Angus taught, so they could not be told of the last time Wallace had seen Martha's father Hamish Charles before he passed bitterly away in his nursing home. But Wallace had more luck with his other relatives, as he drove his Morris down to Edinburgh and on to Ermondhaugh. He had stopped at Wick to see the great ruined Sinclair castle at Girnigoe, the spectacular sea-girt ruin on its crag and over its rock harbour, the monument to the Scots earls who had roved the northern ocean five centuries before. So much grand endeavour now brooding over the waves far below, the breakers so unrelenting and inevitable to all that anybody might do.

Marie had been expecting Wallace, and she was in the big house with her daughter Rosabelle and another cousin, the naval engineer Hamish Gordon. The rest of the house party was scattered about the gardens, men in shiny faded blue suits with belt and braces. They coughed and spat from bad lungs, and their wives sat with knees pinched tight and stared at Wallace as though he was a prison warder.

"Wallace," Marie said. "We are so glad to see you. We never hear anything of your sister Ruby and your parents in India. She's gone back to join them, hasn't she, leaving her son Ian here?"

"Well," Rosabelle said. "They certainly don't want to hear of us and what we are doing." She draped an arm over Hamish Gordon's shoulder and tickled the inside of his ear. "You haven't met cousin Gordon, though I've told him about your boat. If there's anything he loves, it's tinkering about with boats."

"Don't." Gordon brushed away Rosabelle's hand. "She's an irritating creature. Always tickling me."

"I thought," Wallace said, "what tickles your fancy does you good."

"I don't mind tickling her Sweet Fanny Adams," Gordon said, "but what she does back is lethal."

Another family affair, Wallace could see that, before Marie took him away to show him to his room. Times were bad everywhere, she said. The Dunesk coal mines she had inherited from her husband were losing money because of the low price of coal and the depth of the narrow seams. She had to struggle to keep them going and the remaining miners in some sort of a job. Those of them who developed silicosis or were crippled by arthritis hardly had a pension and no sick benefits. So she did what she could for their disabilities in the big house, helped by her old friend, the local union leader, Keir McBride. But he was on his last legs, too, and the miners couldn't even pay their subscriptions, so there were precious few funds from anywhere.

"You know the worst thing about this country, Wallace? The whole legal system. It's all based on property. So if we get a damned inheritance, we can't escape it."

"Most people wouldn't half mind inheriting a stately home and mineral rights."

"Sometimes I'd just rather be a Crow squaw on my pony, riding the prairie with the blast in my hair. I know, my old people are tucked away on an Indian reservation, but that's liberty compared with the fences the law puts round you here."

"I'll have a scout round," Wallace said. "See if you have anything else - make more money than coal."

"That's all you'll find, Wallace. Coal, coal, bloody coal."

"Don't worry. The price will go up soon. When the war comes, you'll have to keep the whole country warm on it."

"What about Chamberlain kow-towing to Hitler at Munich? Peace in our time. Didn't he say that?"

"Fatuous junk. And a smokescreen. To buy time for re-arming. I wouldn't give the outbreak of hostilities a year. Even less."

"Next summer. Thirty-nine?"

"Next summer. Like the last big bang. That kicked off in August. When the ground's hard and the German panzers can run on the flat all the way to the Channel or the Urals."

"What are you going to do?"

"Navy. Boats. I need to talk to Gordon about that."

And talk the two men did. A common interest in engines really brings two men together. By the time they had broken down the Fairey and the Rolls machines to the last piston, they found their political differences didn't matter. Gordon was off to the Glasgow shipyards, which were a hotbed of the revolution, with Willie Gallacher there. Wallace was down to the stockbroker South to sail his motor launch, *Croft Craft*, from Maidenhead to Cowes round the Isle of Wight. But no acrimony. Both men were grease monkeys at heart.

"You were up in Orkney," Marie commented later. "Did you see the Home Fleet? The *Royal Oak* and the battleships? That's where cousin Hamilton went down in the last war. And where our ancestor Prince Henry sailed from, when he got to America a hundred years before Columbus."

"What," Wallace said. "A Sinclair from Scotland pipped the man from Genoa to the great discovery?"

"Discovery?" Marie laughed. "We Indians discovered America."

"After the dinosaurs," Gordon said.

"After the dinosaurs were wiped out," Marie went on. "And then you genocidal Europeans nearly wiped us all out. Actually, the Vikings and Prince Henry didn't decimate us, the Crows. We were inlanders, not on the coast. They brought their diseases to the Micmacs and the Innuit, who did manage to drive them out of Greenland. Plus the Black Death, of course."

"Black Death," Gordon said. "Sounds like the next war against Hitler. That should lead to a population decrease, too."

"Talking of that," Marie said, "why are you a bachelor still, Wallace? Don't you like women?"

"I love women," Wallace said. "But I am against mothers these days. How can you have babies in a depression, when there aren't any jobs for the children? How can you produce cannon fodder for another war? I'm not for breeding more right now."

"We wouldn't be here talking," Marie said, "if our forefathers and mothers, Hamish and Hannah, shared your opinion. Wasn't it worse, the Clearances and steerage to Canada, in that Victorian shambles? And they had eight children, and that's our whole family. You can't calculate having children against bad times. It's been bloody so often for most of humanity over the centuries, we'd all be extinct if we thought about having babies, instead of just having them, because that's what a woman feels she was born to do, and wants to do, and has to do to feel a woman."

There was a silence before Gordon said, "Rosabelle wants a child before it's too late for her. I know I'm younger, but her biological clock is ticking towards midnight, when there's no more chance of having a brat."

"I want a grandchild," Marie said.

"But the revolution. We'll hardly see each other for years. I wouldn't do as a father."

"You'll do," Marie said and smiled. "*Faute de mieux.*"

Gordon shook his head.

"You women. You're bloody impossible. How can we compete?"

"When we're broody you're done for. Politics has nothing to do with it. We're gripped by the womb, not by Joe Stalin. And frankly, Gordon -" Marie's smile was wicked - "sometimes any man will do."

"Too much, Marie. Too far."

"Though I must admit, it's better to love a man, if he has to leave you."

In their rage of love-making that evening, Gordon was gripped between Rosabelle's thighs. Her heels drummed on his spine. Her lithe legs were a vice on his ribs. He could hardly breathe. His bones crackled. And he drove in so deep in his discharge that the tip of his cock was held against a throb of flesh, yearning, squeezing, insuck. He roared out loud, shuddered, slumped. The thunder in his ears was stilled so he could hear the old miners singing downstairs to the piano on their Saturday social night, which was the best Marie could organize.

"Roll out the barrel,
We'll have a barrel of fun..."

Gordon rolled off the body of his woman and lay like a flounder on the slab of the hard bed.

"Old soldiers never die," he said. "They simply sing away."

"Listen to this one," Rosabelle said. And now the miners were singing, 'We'll hang up our washing on the Siegfried line'.

"I like that, darling. That's where I'm going to hang those red panties you love so much. On the Siegfried line."

"But who's going to have a squint at them?"

"Our lot, when we get there."

7

UNPHONEY WAR
1940

From his balcony table in the main concourse of the Café Royal off Piccadilly, Ian Hamish looked down at the *literati* and the Soho limpets, who were coasting below and hanging onto every word dribbling from the bibulous lips of Louis MacNeice or young Dylan Thomas – DTs to his would-be intimate friends, while his enemies called him, toasted cheese. While waiting with his Pernod in his pretence of Parisian chic, Ian was self-consciously scribbling a poem on his paper napkin to prove that he was not out of his depth. He read over his inspiration, if these were the words for it. He had headed his verse: GREAT WAR?

> Too late regret
> For the boy, boy,
> Not of the world yet.
> Could he enjoy?
> Him a Focke got
> With a single shot
> This cockpit boy.
> He was, is not.
> O boy, O boy!

Ian was just about to crumple up the napkin and drop it under the table, when Peregrine arrived, piloting the iridescent Clio before him. She glittered in a diamanté bodice and snakeskin trousers and pixie boots, while he still sported his black leather flying jacket.

"Whatcha, chum," he said, sitting down before Clio, while Ian rose from his chair to pull out one for her. "We've all got to be so matey now." He grabbed the napkin and looked at the poem. "Bit pessimistic, old boy, aren't you? About our chances up there fluffing about in the air."

"It depends who's coming to get us," Ian said, putting Clio in her seat. "Your Hun friends. Or the Mussolini mob."

"They'd only fire spaghetti out of their guns with tomato sauce, perhaps. Of course, it might be *your* lot, too. The commissars in their Ilyushins, pelting us with Red Stars and icicles."

"Poor old Peregrine, he doesn't know what's what these days. Or who's who." Clio was waspish with mischief. "Since that Stalin-Hitler pact, and the war, and the Poles carved up between the two great dictators, he hasn't the foggiest which flag to fly, have you, darling? Or who to shoot in this show."

"Don't worry, tiger moth. I'll prang anything within my sights."

"Don't make it another Spitfire, darling, just because you'd like the enemy to win."

Ian was smiling now. The Nazi-Soviet deal had made things rather delicate in the family, to be sure, ever since the war had been declared.

"Luckily, I never took sides," he said, "like you all did at Cambridge. So it's easy for me. I'm just fighting anybody who's fighting Britain and France. To hell with the rest of them."

"So am I, sport," Peregrine said. "Are you still flying?"

"Hurricanes. Down in Kent."

"I thought they'd have grounded you. A boffin in the Ops Room, with all your maths. Running that radar." Peregrine winced as Clio put the toe of her boot into him under the table. "Oops, sorry, hush-hush. Though I don't think the Walls Have Ears here, as the slogan says. There's such a din from those slobs and yobs below."

"The *crème de la crème* puffs of the literary establishment," Ian said.

"You can hear them speak," Clio said. "Not yourself." And indeed, the voice of Cyril Connolly fluted upwards, saying, "Yes, my dear, he is a pouf and his fortune comes from margarine, but what other grease can we squeeze to oil the wheels of *Horizon*?"

"Anyway, Ian," Peregrine's darting eyes were now stiletto points. "They'll ground you for sure. Uncle Murdo will whisk you off to the Air Ministry to work on routes for his wallowing sea-planes. Or Uncle Gillon with his Marconi net of transmitters and cables across the Empire. Or your prof, Alan Turing, for his computers. Pranging people doesn't matter so much now. It's for numbskulls like me, sheer bone between the eyebrows. But for natural-born brainboxes like you, plotting's the strategy. Cracking codes, that sort of thing."

"Turing's gone down," Ian said. "I don't know where."

"Bletchley Junction. That's the place where you have to change trains between Oxford and Cambridge. All the dons do."

"You always miss your connection there." As she spoke, Clio hacked at Peregrine's leg again with her foot. "The loudspeaker doesn't work."

"Sorry, sorry." Peregrine grimaced. "Talking out of turn."

"Where did you learn about Bletchley?"

Ian was intrigued, but Peregrine had the answer as usual.

"From our cousin Hamish Henry. He's always taking the train from London there. Regular little commuter, is he."

"He's coming to join us. I'll ask him."

"Do. He's quite a chatterbox. Unlike me. Do you know, he's staying at a Rothschild flat in Bentinck Street. Very trendy and lefty. Half of the bent dons and the Foreign Office stooges seem to be kipping there. Ouch."

Clio bruised his shin for the third time, and complained.

"I'm dying for a *vino rosso*. Where are the bloody waiters? They're all born blind, though they can see a tip under the plate at thirty paces." She rose to her feet, stuck two of her fingers in a V in her mouth and blew a piercing whistle. The nearest waiter dropped his tray of canapés and stared at her. "You! Three red *vinos* pronto. Move it, Sancho. Clickety-click."

Clio slid back into her seat. "Don't look shocked, Ian. That's the only way to get service in dumps like this."

"Clio always did have a way with serfs." Peregrine was returning her compliments. "She is so gracious to the little people, as she calls them. You heard that wolf-whistle. That's her charming way of saying, "Hi, and ta kindly.""

Before Clio could answer in kind, Hamish Henry appeared, looking frail rather than natty in his grey suit from Jermyn Street and black Lobb lace-up shoes. Stooping, his shoulders seemed to be bearing the weight of the war, although nothing much had happened yet during the winter. Presently, a lull and inertia snoozed at the anti-aircraft guns, waiting to pop off at the raiders, who could come to blitz London. As lethargic as the silvery barrage balloons strung over Hyde Park to snag dive-bombers, the capital was drowsing in a faint expectation of catastrophe.

"Hello, all." Hamish Henry greeted them, snaffling a seat from another table. "Sorry, I'm late. Offices, you know, can keep you quite as busy as airfields."

"We pilots are rather adding to the figures on underemployment," Peregrine said. "All those training missions, and only sparrows to down. You must be having a much better time in the shires with the prof. Nuff said?"

"Nuff. But I must say, you should see the computers. We've got more bulbs there than a parade of Guards bearskins. Flashing lights. And keys tapping like a mob of woodpeckers. And the bumph. It comes creaming out with more numbers on than 101 squared to the nth degree. And a posse of secretaries carrying them off to the boffins to mull through. But for what, I ask myself."

"I ask you," Peregrine said. "What for?"

"How should I know?"

"You must know. We are friends now. I mean, Adolf and Joe... Blood brothers."

"I'm an errand boy."

"With big goo-goo eyes."

"Between friends, then?"

"Who else here?"

"Well, it is cryptography, of course. Surveillance. Trying to latch on to their systems. But I haven't the faintest if it's working. The Germans and the Russians are real code foxes. We've got a Pole, though, who got out, who seems to know something about their dodges."

"And Alan Turing," Ian said. "He knows all about probability. And series. If you can do zillions of calculations within seconds, you can convert the random into a near cert. Or that's what he tried to show me."

"Yup, that's what auntie Ruth's doing," Clio interrupted. "Or trying to do, and failing, as she will."

"What? Ruth in the war effort?" Hamish Henry smiled. "I can't see her... I mean, computers are hardly her handbag."

"Convoys, actually. Her father Charles got her the job."

"Did he now?" There was a sudden interest in Hamish Henry. "How did he fix that?"

"He's still got a lot of friends in the ministries. They had to recall him when the war came, he knew so much about munitions. And he told Ruth she should join up too, and he talked to Uncle Wallace, who's come back here to do something about minerals and mines." Clio giggled. "Sorry, silly me, wrong sort of mines. Mines and mine-sweepers. So he's in the Admiralty, and he got Ruth a post in the WRENS, and she was seconded to help the Atlantic convoys against the U-Boats, but she comes home all in a tizzy, and she says it's killing her, not them, she hasn't got a clue what she's meant to be doing, she's so tired she wishes she was dead."

"If she's not, other people will be." Hamish Henry rose. "I'm sorry I've got to blow. I could only drop by. I wouldn't have missed you all for the world."

The catatonic waiter weaved his way between the crowded tables, delicately balancing three glasses of red wine on a silver tray.

"You're sure you can't stay?" Peregrine said. "We're all blabbing so much. And here are the rations. Three glasses of wine. *In vino*, you know, there's so much more *veritas*."

"Pip pip," Hamish Henry said, bobbing and ducking round the waiter, who set down the drinks along with the bill. Ian looked after his cousin.

"What was that all about? Rather a hit-and-run raid, don't you think?" He picked up his glass and drained it and ordered the waiter, "Three more while you're here and stocks last."

"It's all coming out," Clio said. She put her crimson glass in front of her eyes to distort Peregrine's face into a fairground caricature. "Is that why we're such a happy family? We simply can't keep a secret between us. We *trust* each other so, so much."

"You know, Clio," Peregrine said, "when I turn my back on you, it positively itches. I never know when you're going to stab it."

"Then never turn your back on me again, Peregrine. And you'll be safe."

"A lifetime romance?"

"A lifetime penance. For me."

"Look." Ian was craning his head over the balcony rail. Below, the heads of the other guests at the Café Royal were sweaty or sleek, bald or Brylcreem'd, bushy or curly or crop-cut. The hubbub was groaning, like a behemoth from a cave. His eyes were blurring, and Ian found himself seeing a huge throat pulsating. Then he blinked and heard himself say, "If the bomb dropped here, bye, bye, arty farties and culturecamp."

Clio was beside him, peering down, when they heard Peregrine drawl behind them, "Why not?" A shower of sixpences and shillings and half-crowns came flying over their heads as a distant squadron of silver Dorniers before descending on the coiffures of their victims in the pit. "They'll think you did it." The metal manna from heaven fell and struck. A score of furious faces swung up at Clio and Ian. They heard Peregrine's chair scrape back.

"You'll cop it, darlings," he was saying. "Not very truly yours."

Our colonial masters took their Little England everywhere in their tin trunks. And they did a better job of transplanting it than any Count Frankenstein with their high white ceilings and chintz chairs and leather sofas and rosebud china and cut-glass port decanters. So Shankar was thinking, as he sipped his gin-and-It in the Imp in Singapore. He couldn't allow Shilendra to come and meet him in the

Mess. God knows how his cousin ever got a ticket here, and he was late. Not that the waiting and the rotting in the heat wasn't the only duty the Army had in this putrescent bastion of Britishness. And with General Percival too bloody idle to reach from his sundowner and drill the troops, what sort of a show would be put on, if the Japanese dawn on the road to Mandalay did roll up from China like thunder across the bay? Kipling was certainly far more aware than his sodding commander of the threat from the Rising Sun.

"Some one says he has come to see you, sir." The disdain in the doorman's voice under his tall turban grated like a nut in a cracker. Shankar looked round to a scruffy shambles in a greasy white suit. He could only be Shilendra, and he was.

"That's all right," Shankar muttered. "I'll vouch for him." He rose and embraced his cousin. "Thousands wouldn't," he whispered. "You look like something the cat brought in."

"Sampan, actually. I could use a sharpener."

Shankar clicked his fingers at a waiter, hovering as a ghost. "Double whisky and soda." Then to Shilendra, "That's your tipple, isn't it?"

"Yes." Shilendra cackled, shrill in his irony. "We talk just like *them*. Our masters."

"They taught us to. Lucky for us. So they think we are like them. And that we like them, too."

"But we'll never pass for them."

"Looking like that, Shilendra, are you surprised?"

His cousin slowly eyed Shankar up and down in his immaculate jacket and Sam Browne belt and creased shorts and puttees and brown boots.

"And looking like that," he said, "I am surprised."

"You knew I was an Army wallah."

"How did they let you in?"

"Cricket gets you everywhere. I open for the Asian division. My batting average is 123 point 4. I've been offered a contract with Surrey after the war."

"You never cease to astound me, cousin. What the hell has that to do with freeing India?"

As the waiter came up with Shilendra's toddy, Shankar looked round the rest of the lounge of the Imperial. Two old boys, reading newspapers; a salesman at the bar; the usual layabouts on a doldrum afternoon.

"Were you tailed here?"

"If I was..." Shilendra was savouring his drink as a loving cup. "I slipped them. I always double back, then again for luck. I've been too long in the game to be nabbed. Would it hurt you if they knew you saw me?"

"No. I don't know what you're doing, do I? You're just a relation, passing through. You can't be court-martialled for that."

"Just passing through. How's the family back home, by the way?"

"You probably know already. My father died in the end, and Miriam can't get over it. Aunt Ruby's out at Annandale, from England, trying to grab her slice of the inheritance. And your mother Peg has been drafted back to hospital duty. She rather loves it, though she swears she hates serving the Raj. And Solomon, well, the Civil Service was made for him. He's got a shifty to Info. He thinks he can slip in some stuff for Gandhi. He says independence is on the cards already. If they want to raise a dozen more divisions to fight their war, they would have to hand over. They've promised."

"Promises, promises." Shilendra blew into his whisky and soda, making the bubbles rise in a froth to the surface Then he took a long swallow. "They'll promise you anything to make you join up. They might as well fart at you. You should join the inevitable. Dialectical materialism. Nobody can stop the victory of the proletariat. All this..." A creased grubby sleeve waved round the crisp order of the hotel room. "Window-dressing."

"Yes, yes. But how, that is the question? So Solomon says. Wait. Co-operate. Then strike. And you?"

Shilendra looked round. There was nobody near enough to eavesdrop, and he did not suspect a hidden mike in the bowl of orchids between them. He leant forward and spoke softly.

"I was even up with Mao Tse-Tung in the caves in North China. He says he'll train an Indian Freedom Army, when he's dealt with Chiang, and then the Japanese."

"But Chiang beat him."

"Not at all. That Long March to Yunan from the South, that wasn't a defeat. He was regrouping so he would be supplied by Russia across Siberia. He's training his comrades in guerrilla war. He's making chili powder out of Chiang."

"And the Japanese."

"I met some of their commanders, coming back. They'd support an Indian Army, too. With Subhas Chandra Bose, you've heard of him. They're only waiting, you know. For the right time. The moment Hitler hammers France, they'll pick off Singapore. It'll fall like a rotten apple."

"You're too right, Shilendra. It is a rotten apple."

"But what will *you* do, if you're still here, and they take you prisoner? Sweat it out for a dead duck Empire?"

Before he could answer, Shankar's eyes were caught by a movement at the door. Bobby Putting was coming in, a lieutenant in the Bengal regiment. He hid his intelligence under a boyish charm, but he was nobody's fool. Shankar rose and spoke loudly.

"I don't want any of your shoddy goods. And I don't know how they let you in here in the first place."

Now Shilendra was on his feet, suddenly obsequious.

"Oh, sahib, I said there was an appointment. I am so sorry —"

Ignoring him, Shankar was turning to Bobby Putting.

"Have a short one with me, old chap. It's disgraceful how they let —"

"Going, sahib, going."

Bowing and grinning, Shilendra began backing out of the lounge, then turned and almost ran. The lieutenant threw back his head and laughed.

"I don't mind if I do. I must say, you put the fear of God into that greaser."

"Yes," Shankar said. "So I did."

The third unlikely encounter between the cousins in a world war which was hardly yet a war, took place in Jerusalem. Paul had been seconded to the Palestine Police, after Biddy's affair with Peregrine in the Gold Coast, and a second son Keiss being born nine months after the event. Neither of them could take it. They weren't exactly put to Coventry, but there were enough cold shoulders in steamy Takoradi to form a frigid fence of icy welcome. Anyway, with hostilities against Germany, there was no question of Biddy leaving the two boys and North Oxford. There was said to be a secret deal with Hitler. He would not bomb the university cities of Oxford and Cambridge, if we spared Heidelburg and Leipzig. We immediately surrounded both safe zones for dons with airfields, but there was also the Cowley car factory. So nobody was certain if the fix would not become a blitz one night.

Policing Jerusalem was an odd stroll through the Bible. The old city with its crusader walls and towers was no Sunday School lesson. Golgotha and Gethsemane lay behind the bus station. Petrol fumes belched over an arid rock desert where no grass grew. Standing there and thinking of the Gospels, Paul remembered Jesus first appearing to

Mary Magdalene, after He had burst from the Tomb. Paul had seen a picture once of the saint and sinner kneeling with her long red hair and a golden bucket or grail, which she used to catch the blood from His feet on the Cross. Jesus stood in the flowering garden, leaning on a golden spade. But that revelation was long gone now. With the covert conflict going on between Jew and Arab, the only grail tossed here would be a grenade with its wounds of shrapnel.

The Mount of Olives was no meditation area either, and certainly no picnic. Khaki patrols moved through the dusty dark trees with their black bitter fruit. The Arab Legion from Jordan was officially helping the British, but Paul could not be too sure. The Grand Mufti with his base in the resplendent Dome of the Rock, now crowning the ancient Temple Mount, inclined towards Berlin, and he could count on the support of most of the imams and mullahs to stop any more immigration. Too many Jews were fleeing to Palestine because of persecution in Europe. The Mediterranean Fleet couldn't stop all the old freighters, loaded over the Plimsoll line with refugees from the Balkan ghettos, as they lurched through the seas from Turkey towards Tel Aviv. Deter the Jews, so they would not want to enter, that was the policy of the Grand Mufti. Yet Islamic terror attacks provoked counter-terror by Jewish gangs, and the Palestinian Policemen were pigs in the middle, when pork was abhorred by both warring religions. Crackling, indeed, was their daily duty.

Below the golden cupola in its high place set above the holy city, the Western or Wailing Wall was the end of Paul's morning round. Little tables were set up under the huge blocks of the massive structure. Their backs to him, men in black Homburg hats or skull caps and ringlets above their thick black suits prayed to the stones, which could not hear them. They were praying against the loss of Jerusalem, for the mercy of God, that He might restore to them their Jerusalem.

Their God never would, Paul knew as much. Not that the British could continue their Mandate over the territory forever. There was no advantage in it, no resources, only a waste of money and manpower overseeing an insoluble problem. And the Arabs had to whip the Jews in the end. They outnumbered the Jews a hundred to one. Those were the odds on their eventual victory. And no takers among the bookmakers of history.

Back at headquarters, Paul found himself on a raid. There had been a tip-off. A Zionist group had an arms cache in a back street by the King David tower. The leader was a certain Avi Rabinowicz. He had come over as a child in the earlier waves of settlement in the 'twenties, when the *kibbutzin* were created to try to make the desert bloom, and had not made it. Avi was suspected of assassination and planting bombs in mosques. He would be quite a shine on the brass badge of the man who brought him in.

The squad operated in the usual fashion, surrounding the place, hammering at the squalid door, breaking-in and entering, revolvers at the ready. No Avi there, only a scrawny young woman with her hair tied back in a pigtail, wearing khaki fatigues, which might have fallen off the back of a military truck. While the rest of the police smashed into the wardrobes and ripped open the mattresses to look for explosives, Paul took the pale-faced woman into a corner to question her.

"Name," he said. "Don't lie. We'll get your papers."

"Leah," she said. "Leah Sinclair." Her accent was North American.

"Christ," Paul said, putting down his notebook. "Not Gillon's daughter."

"My father is called Gillon, yes."

"Used to work for Marconi? Back in London now in the War Office?"

"I saw him when I shipped out here."

"Why?"

"Why do you think?"

One of the police squad came in from the kitchen with an empty jam jar. In it, a detonator and few cartridges for a Browning pistol. Paul took the evidence.

"Not much of a haul," he said to Leah. "But something. You're in trouble, my girl."

"How do you know who I am?"

"I am your cousin, Paul Sinclair."

"No. Pig." Hatred puckered her face. "How could you serve in a load of shitkickers like this?"

"We're keeping you lot from cutting each other's throats. You're bloody lucky we're here. Or the Arabs would make non-kosher stew out of you."

"We can look after ourselves, Paul."

"Can you?" Paul looked into the jar. "Let's see. Six bullets, that's six months inside A detonator, say eighteen months. With good behaviour – though I shouldn't think we'll get it from you, Leah – a year in gaol. Where's Avi?"

"Never heard of him."

"Avi Rabinowicz. We know he's here."

"Then find him."

"You'll talk in the end."

"I will not." Leah scowled. "You can't make me."

"No, we can't. I know you think we're worse than the SS, torture, rape, that sort of thing. But actually we're just British bobbies abroad doing a lousy job by the rulebook. We can't make you speak. But Leah, tell us, and you're on the next destroyer back to Canada. I can promise that."

"You can't understand, can you?"

"No, I don't. I'm not a Zionist."

"Among you pigs, some of you were."

"Oh, Colonel Wingate. Orde Wingate. Yes, we know he helped train your little secret army, when he was here. But we've packed him off to the Far East. He's got to teach our men jungle war now. We may have to take on the Japs."

"Wingate, yes. A good man."

"A madman."

"You stop us coming here. You let the Nazis kill us, put us in their concentration camps..."

"They're not so bad, are they? That's our information. Work camps are always pretty awful."

"Death camps. And you won't let us in here. You won't save me. Just so you can lick the asses of the Arabs."

"We can't offend them, Leah. There is a world war on, not just your private one. We need the Arabs if we're going to lick the Nazis. Every Jew in Britain is fighting for us."

"Not here." Leah's face began to crumple. Her tears seemed to soften her cheeks. "You won't understand."

"You know, your Uncle Robert took Jerusalem from the Turks under Allenby. He died at Megiddo to help make an Israel. None of you Jews would be back here in Palestine unless the British had the Mandate. Unless we already allowed a hell of a lot of you back, in spite of the Arabs."

"Not enough, Paul. We need millions more."

"Then the Arabs will kick us out. And you out."

"Help us. For God's sake."

Looking at Leah's face, rounding now under the streaks of tears, Paul could see her father in her, and her mother Rachel. He began fishing the detonator and the cartridges one by one out of the jar and hiding them in the pockets of his drill uniform.

"I hope your mother and your sister Fiona aren't as demented as you. They're still safely in Canada?"

"They don't believe. Fiona's a real earth mother. Only she's a tad fat. Nobody will ask her. I think she'll marry a ram. Or a moose."

Paul smiled. He put the empty jar on the mother-of-pearl small table, the only thing of value left in the wrecked room. He spoke to his sergeant.

"Jenkins, back to HQ."

"Yessir. What about her?"

"Leave her."

"What about the —"

"The evidence? What about it?" Paul patted his pockets. "All safe. She doesn't know a thing. And you never know, perhaps Avi will come back for her. Post a man at the door."

As the sergeant turned to round up the rest of the squad, Paul hissed to Leah.

"Get out. And get out now."

As he walked off, he could not tell himself why he had done what he had done. He never broke the rules. He wanted promotion. This would be a black mark in the book. He hadn't liked anything about Leah. And he had let her go. Perhaps there was some sort of strange mercy in families, the gift of a guardian angel, which made the kin of others act against their will.

8

MESSING ABOUT IN BOATS

Most of the other captains of the riverboats massing at Maidenhead to fill up on rationed fuel hadn't the slightest notion why they had been called into port there. Wallace did, for he was one of the voices stressing the fantastic strategy to the Admiralty. The idea was absurd. How could anything which floated with a clapped-out engine be sent across the Channel to load aboard the débris of a defeated expeditionary force? The small fry would all be sunk by the Stukas or the German artillery, closing in on Dunkirk. Or the storm would send them to the bottom, as it had the Spanish Armada. A flotilla of hundreds of pleasure craft evacuating a mob of beaten soldiers was not folly, it was lunacy. Yet in a situation of catastrophe, what was the choice?

"Sail, boys, sail."

So sail they did, or rather they puttered along on their dodgy engines. One eight tried to make the trip in their scull, but they stopped when Wallace pointed out that there was no room on the row boat: an oarsman would have to stay on the French beaches for every runaway soldier who came aboard. Rather like in *Peter Pan*, most of the crewmen thought that this was to be a really great adventure, if not a lark. But if you'd served in the last world war as Wallace had, the whole show looked like a bad bet on a three-legged donkey to win the Derby.

The destroyers anchored way offshore the beaches could give the small ships some sort of cover with their ack-ack, but also they were looking after their own sweet Fanny Adams against the machine-guns of the diving Focke-Wulfs and Messerschmitts. The first fusillade which hit the *Croft Craft* stitched a hem of bullet holes from the foredeck through the cabin roof to the stern, missing Wallace at the wheel by inches. This wasn't enough to sink the old tub, so Wallace steered for a line of men, holding hands as they walked shoulder-deep into the water. He had heard that most of the squaddies couldn't swim, so he cut the power and drifted up beside the line, slung the rope ladder over the side, and leaned over the rail, his toes dug in under, his arms reaching down into the bloody and choking morass.

"Up, lads, up now."

He had to haul them aboard, some with their sodden packs still on their backs, two hundred and fifty pounds deadweight, their boots as buckets. His arms were bursting out of their shoulder sockets, his hands raw and bleeding, his chest bruised, and his feet broken as they were wedged against his heave high of the floundering men. Dark staining corpses floated by. Spouts from missiles threw up jets from the severed arteries of the sea. Wallace could not go on. He would die, too. He had to go on.

"Nineteen, twenty. That's all, lads. That's all. You'll sink the boat. We won't make it back to Dover."

At the bottom of the ladder, a young bloke was hanging on with one hand, floating on the water. His other arm was gone at the elbow, a tourniquet and a bandage keeping him alive.

"I can't get up, jock," he said. "But gi'us a lift."

"Tow you to Dover? You're crazy."

The bloke began sticking his head through the slats in the ladder, then twisting in the shoulder of his lost arm.

"Gi'us a ride."

"You'll die."

"I'm dead, fook it."

The bloke had now stuck the armpit of his stump under the ladder rope. He was secure.

"Take off, fook it, will ye?"

"Haul him aboard," Wallace said. He kicked at the nearest soldier, slumped and retching on the deck of the listing launch. "Help me, damn you. We've got to get this lunatic aboard."

The bloke didn't die as the *Croft Craft* chugged and wheezed the twenty miles back to Dover. They were hit twice more by tracer bullets, and two of the soldiers were wounded, but Wallace had the rest baling out with saucepans and buckets to keep his sluggish and sinking boat afloat. They were waterlogged by the time they were a sea-mile from the white cliffs and the castle, and the best that Wallace could do was run his ship aground on the pebbles of the shore. He could see the Rescue people and the Air Raid Wardens wading out to salvage what they could. Not the boat, of course. That had had it. He couldn't go back for more.

As the bloke with one arm was lifted off, Wallace put his last Player's fag in his mouth and lit it. "Thanks, jock, for the lift," the bloke said. They never met again, though Wallace often thought of him. If the bloke could hang on, anybody could. And perhaps the whole country, too.

The next assignment was a dirty business. Although he reckoned he had a conscience, Wallace did not approve of conscientious objectors. If they were fit, they could fight. But to make them man old yachts off Scotland to test the efficiency of the new magnetic mines was worse than the medieval pillory or the rack. They had to sail into the fields of death which the mine-layers had seeded on the approaches to the Firth of Forth. The question was how close they could steer to the lethal prickles before detonating an explosion, which could take them to Kingdom Come, except for the few who could be fished out of the water. The only worse experiment known to Wallace was inducing anthrax to the sheep of the Western Isles, in case Hitler opted for germ warfare and Winston Churchill felt he had to retaliate. The deadly spores would be more lasting than the broken crofts of the Clearances. Nobody would be able to live there for fifty years.

At least, there was the compensation of being able to dwell at Ermondhaugh. Marie Dunesk had turned the house back into a hospital again, this time for the survivors of the convoys, which the U-boats were sinking in the North Sea. There was a sudden inrush after the disaster in Norway, when the Nazis had brushed aside the British attempt to support the resistance there. Our fleet could not even control the fjords, where the German pocket battleships were now holed up, immune from attack.

There was one supreme consolation. Rosabelle had her baby girl and named her Rosa, after the German revolutionary Rosa Luxemburg. The estate would pass on to another woman, who would take it into the next millennium, whatever that might bring. And now with that milky howling pink-and-butter darling in her arms, Marie skipped back two score years to when Rosabelle was that size too, with the same streaky red mop on the wee head of her.

And Rosabelle was occasionally home from her ENSA tours, where she would sometimes perform her mother's old music-hall numbers for the Home Forces. And the father Hamish Gordon, back from the Clyde shipyards and the Atlantic convoys, was still talking tough about revolutions and no bairns, but he was melting at the wail of the bundle of nothing, then putting his forefinger in Rosa's mouth to hush her teething. The more men talked about being bad parents, the better they were, when they were near. Gordon hadn't married Rosabelle, neither of them believed in that with the war on. But with the peace, they would, Marie hoped so. Then the title would go on to Countess Rosa, not that it mattered, but it did in the end.

Gordon and Wallace grew close on more than marine engines. As well as his mine-layers, Wallace was still advising the Admiralty on seaplanes. The lumbering bi-plane Fairey Swordfish with its torpedo slung below its belly was a flying goose for the German naval ack-ack. If it dropped its missile at long range, the torpedo always missed with any evasive action from the Nazi boats. And the aircraft could never get close before being shot down into the drink. Aircraft carriers like the *Ark Royal* were the answer with the fighters and divebombers taking off from the deck and returning to land there.

"We used to have flying hotels from Southampton Water," Wallace said. "We thought we could connect the whole empire with our floating wings. The passenger ones even had a lounge and double-beds and a shower. You could fly a Commissioner anywhere in Africa with his wife, and they wouldn't know they had left Government House. But like that German airship Hindenburg, they were dodos, doomed, dead-weight. No speed, too big, defenceless."

"On the Atlantic convoys," Gordon said, "we could use air cover. But we don't have any, till we're offshore near Ireland. We could certainly use it in that U-boat highway off New Jersey. But the Yanks don't seem to want to come into the war."

"Until they've beggared us. Ancient Lend-Lease destroyers for all our foreign assets."

"Still, the destroyers are all we have." The lines in Gordon's face were sad and deep. "When the U-boats come in and sink the merchant ships, the destroyers buzz around with their ASDICs and bung their depth charges over the stern, and we get relief. But we can't stop for survivors, or we're sitting ducks. So we sail past all these drowning sailors, and they call up at us, and we must sail on. I remember one crying, 'Taxi! Taxi!'. We didn't stop. I suppose he wanted us to take him to Piccadilly."

There was something Wallace had always yearned to know, but had never dared to ask. But now that Gordon was actually fighting on the high seas, he found himself blurting out: "What if it was a Russian submarine, I mean, sinking you? Stalin and Hitler are allies. How would you feel?"

"You think I haven't thought of it?"

"It must be soul-destroying for a Marxist like you."

"It can only be a tactical pact. An alliance of convenience."

"But a Fascist and Communist alliance against the last democracy left fighting alone?"

"The last imperial power, too."

"The last democracy in Europe, Gordon. The Empire will finish after the war, we know that. We're broke. We can't afford to keep it up. But if all is what you call ideology, how come the two worst enemies are now bosom pals?"

"They are not."

"Nor is Poland. Divided between them."

"Communism will win. We know that. It is a scientific and historical fact. If there are difficulties on the way... Minor details..."

"Give me one man one vote," Wallace said, "warts and all."

Argument with a true believer or a fanatic was always useless. Better to talk about mechanics, how they worked, not why the workers did. Wallace was glad when Rosabelle breezed in after her ENSA tour for the troops. Motherhood had blunted the blade of her radicalism. She smothered Rosa with kisses and wouldn't listen to Gordon's tirades.

"There's a war on," she said. "And I won't have milk and rations for Rosa. Look what I lifted." She produced four chocolate bars, three packs of Players, half-a-pound of butter and a bottle of gin from a handbag as big as a haversack. "They won't miss them from the canteen. You should see how the other half lives – and I mean the army." Then she went on, "Oh mum, I got as far as the navy in Orkney. And they took me out to see where the *Royal Oak* went down. When that U-boat slipped through the defences. Must have had a plan from somewhere. And sunk the battleship."

"I remember," Wallace said. "I've been up there and seen the Home Fleet."

"Well, it's too sad. There are over a thousand men drowned in Scapa Flow. They were asleep. They're still in wet sheets in their bunks. And there's an oil leak. A spreading patch of oil over where the *Royal Oak* is gone."

"What are they doing about it?" Gordon asked.

"They're building a new barrier They call it the Churchill Barrier."

"Will it stop the U-boats?"

"It had better."

"It's only a *name*, my love. The Churchill Barrier."

"It's all we've got." Marie put a stop to the talk. "A name. Churchill. He will have to stop them. With us."

"It was like a game." Ruth was sobbing and quivering. "Moving all those ships with my pointer towards Liverpool. And the info coming in about where the packs of U-boats were. And trying to keep them apart. I was trying. I swear I was trying."

A storm of tears made her bury her head in the palms of her hands. The Man from the Ministry was waiting, and he went on waiting, until he insisted in that soft pointed voice of his:

"A game. You call it a game? We lose thirteen ships and three thousand lives. And it's a game to you?"

Ruth sniffled through her fingers.

"I don't mean a game. I said *like* a game."

"That children's game, *Battleships*, perhaps. Where you fill in the blank spaces, hoping to find the outline of an enemy submarine. Or *L'Attaque*. You move forwards hoping to find the German commander, but not knowing where he is. The point is, Miss Seymour-Scudabright, you did know where the U-boats were. You were told by our naval intelligence. Yet you moved our convoy straight into them in the Ops Room. Why?"

"I don't know. Please. Believe me I made a mistake."

Ruth turned up her swollen eyes towards the Man, but his voice was an oiled dagger.

"A mistake? An error that led to a disaster. You have been highly trained not to make errors. Of course, you may have been trained differently before you came to work for the Admiralty." He opened the file of papers on the deal table in front of him. "We have a fresh intelligence dossier on you. Strangely, the facts on evidence here were not disclosed when your father recommended you for your position."

"My father? Charles? He just thought I could help the War Effort..."

"Then, we did not know your father's background either. Anglo-German Society member, 1937. Visit with von Ribbentrop to Lord Pinden, summer, 1938. You were there as well with your, er, companion, Virginia Callow Sinclair. Correct?"

"It was only a country weekend."

"Country weekends may be one thing or a second or a Fifth Column. You have heard of internment, have you not? And Regulation 18-B? All Nazi sympathizers are to be interned or confined to a five mile radius from their homes – or in some cases, stately homes – for the duration of the war. The Prime Minister, being a Churchill, knew many of your aristocratic friends personally, and their politics. I think you will find some peers, including your host Lord Pinden, restricted in their movements already."

"But I haven't done anything." Ruth began to weep again. "I swear. Nothing."

"But you have, Miss Seymour-Scudabright. Three thousand men have been killed. You say it was a game, a mistake. Yet you were a Nazi sympathizer, as was your father. Incidentally, you will find him and his wife interned in a camp on the Isle of Man. I will supply you with their address at the end of this interview, should you wish to correspond with them, which in your present situation would hardly be advisable. The Censor, as you know, reads all the mail."

"O God, I didn't mean to... Please..."

"The question is intent. We have been through your bank balances, and you do not appear to have been paid for your services, whatever they may have been, to the Nazis. You had the motive to aid them in securing a victory over us. But it was not for financial gain. What do you actually believe? Are we in the right in this war?"

"Since Hitler joined up with Stalin, I haven't known what to believe."

"With many other deluded souls. Quite a quandary."

"But I do want Britain to win."

"Consciously?"

"Yes. I swear."

"But subconsciously? You may want Hitler to win without being aware of it. When you steered our convoy into the pack of U-boats, you might have been thinking you were doing your duty. But your mind wasn't on it, was it?"

"No, no. Or I wouldn't have made the mistake."

The Man gave a smile as thin as a Gillette blade.

"So your subconscious dictated the slip of your pointer, recorded alas by the captains of our ships, which were sunk. Subconsciously, you were and are still a Fascist sympathizer. When you are not thinking, your persuasion dictates your action."

"No, I..."

"If I thought you were a spy, I'd have you shot." The Man closed the file. "In fact, I find you a silly and over-privileged woman, too badly informed to know what you are thinking. You will be referred to a psychiatric hospital for extended evaluation. Your parents and colleagues will be informed of your nervous breakdown. This will spare your extended family, many of whom work faithfully for us, the shame of having a possible traitor among them. Consider yourself fortunate. Dismiss."

Ruth tried to rise from her chair, but she was trembling so much that she fell back onto its seat.

"But Virginia... what..."

"Miss Callow or Miss Sinclair will go through the same evaluation process as yourself. Neither you nor she, unlike your father, appear to have been actual members of the Anglo-German Society. She is a fortune-hunter and a frightful snob, but again not an enemy agent, in my opinion. Therefore you two may be reunited after a suitable period of treatment. Now go!"

This time Ruth did manage to stay on her feet and wobble towards the door. She opened it and fell on the floor outside. The guard on duty shouted: "Hup, hup, hup. Quick march!" And to her surprise, Ruth found herself obeying his command.

Five scrambles that day, and all of Peregrine's nerves were jazz piano wires, but Ace Hopkins had zoomed the squadron – what was left of it – above the Heinkels and the Messers and the Fockers, hovering below on blackfly wings. A clay pigeon shoot, though he was so bloody weary he felt needles in the pupils of his eyes. Now the dive, home in behind the tail of the Focker, let the cannon rip, splinters and smoke trail, a corkscrew fall, follow him down, give him one more burst, see him explode in a hayfield, the coup de grass. Seven kills. Peregrine's grin turned into a yawn big enough to swallow his flying helmet. No more gas in his tank nor in the Spitfire's. Head for Biggin Hill or he'd ditch, too.

As it was, Peregrine fell asleep over the controls as he was taxi-ing in on the runway of the aerodrome. The ground crew had to pull him out of the cockpit. "Are you hurt, sir?" Peregrine stirred. "Book me a bed at the Ritz, twenty-four hours leave, don't disturb on the door." He staggered over to Control to make his report, only to be told two people were waiting for him in the private office. "No peace for the wicked," he said. "No kip either."

He knew his cousin Ian, but the man with him was so nondescript he might have been anonymous. "Willoughby-Smythe," the stranger said. "You will answer my questions, Plunkett-Drax. Your cousin Ruth has been investigated, also your connections with the Anglo-German Society. And your cousin here, he tells me of visits to Germany before the war. Please elucidate."

So Ian had shopped him, and Ruth, too. Peregrine yawned mightily again.

"I'm done in," he said "Can't it wait till the morning?"

"Not if you don't want a transfer from Biggin Hill to Wormwood Scrubs instanter," Willoughby-Smythe said. Peregrine shrugged.

"You think I love dear old Adolf and his gang, do you? I've shot down seven focking Fockers, fock it. Do you call that Nazi love?"

"You must find it embarrassing to shoot down your old friends. Let me see." Another file was open on the desk in front of the Man from the Ministry. "We now know you also shot wild boar with Goëring in the summer of 1938. You were employed by him in an attempt by the Luftwaffe to set up an airline from Berlin to West and South Africa. You were also seeking information on our radar systems."

"Is that all your surveillance has come up with?" Another huge yawn from Peregrine. "Forgive me, but I may nod off with all this excitement. Thanks, Ian, for passing on the info to this bird. What do you get out of it?"

The Man from the Ministry answered.

"Mister Ogilvie is being transferred from flying operations to work in planning operations with another of your relatives, Gillon Sinclair. In the course of our clearance of his security, we came across your past activities. Will you explain them?"

"How can I explain what you already know?"

"You passed our military secrets on to Nazi Germany?"

"I did not, and you cannot prove it. I merely acted as a consultant to the Luftwaffe. Many people supported Mussolini and Hitler, you know, in the 'thirties. Even the Duke of Windsor, our not-quite monarch. It was perfectly respectable."

"I would say positively *chic*." Ian spoke for the first time "*Kitsch*, not *ertsatz*."

"Oh roll that log off your shoulder, Ian. Just because I like living better than you do." Then to the Man. "My cousin preferred the boring masses and the reds."

"Hardly in the same category as yourself," the Man said. "He was not involved or paid. You were."

"Not after I joined up," Peregrine said. "Britain's enemy is my enemy. This is my country. Anyway, I wanted to fight the Bolsheviks, and now Joe Stalin's joined Adolf, I might be pranging the old Red Star in the skies as well as the Swastika."

"I doubt if Russian bombers have the operational reach of German ones. So you claim to be a patriot since the outbreak of the war, not a traitor?"

"Seven kills. What more can I prove?"

"Seven kills. What it proves is that you are a killer, and it does not matter to you who you kill."

"Exactly. Isn't that what you need in a war? Somebody who loves the chase. Somebody born to kill."

"Unfortunately, yes. Your war record is the only thing in your favour. Your past is despicable and treasonable. But as you are already something of a war hero, mentioned in Dispatches, up for a medal..."

"A model for the nation." Peregrine was grinning. "How can you shoot me down?"

"We will have to rely on your old friends shooting you down. And personally, I hope they make a good job of it, very soon. You are most fortunate. Your present services are useful for our morale."

"So your propaganda has saved my neck."

"Your talent as a fighter pilot, too. You may dismiss, Plunkett-Drax. For the time being, you will carry on flying."

As he left the office, Peregrine glared at Ian, who dropped his head and looked down at his knees.

Talking things over with the ageing Colonel Gillon, now his boss, Ian spoke of his shame in betraying his cousin Peregrine. In a family, one does not rat on one another. But in a war, Gillon said, kith and kin are irrelevant. We all do what we can for our own, but if they step over the line, we cannot save them. He spoke of seeing his Zionist daughter Leah on her way to Palestine to stir up trouble.

"I couldn't stop her," he said.

"But you didn't stop her," Ian said.

"Children grow up." Gillon was non-committal. "They go their own ways. They won't listen. And your own family, as well. They become alienated."

"You never go back on leave to see them in Canada, Gillon. What do you expect?"

"Rachel is talking of divorce," Gillon said. "My fault. Travelling the world on communications, and I cannot even communicate with my wife. It's a paradox. The more we connect the globe together, the less we converse, the less we have to say."

"It's not your fault," Ian said. "Any more than it was Peregrine's. It's human error. We try to do our best in the circumstances, and then our good intentions become a balls-up. I hope I don't make a muck of our bombing raids on Germany like Ruth did with the Atlantic convoy. That was human error, I still believe."

"Wrong woman in the wrong job." Gillon patted Ian on the shoulder. "You're the right man in the right job. We'll have more

Halifaxes coming home, more Lancasters, because you plot the flight paths."

"I don't know." Ian put down a piece of white cardboard. "I wrote this out to pin over the ops desk. What do you think? The Wrong Ten Commandments."

"I hear you want to be a writer," Gillon said and read what lay in front of his eyes:

THE LAWS OF ERROR

1   Anything that can go wrong will go wrong.

2   The shortest distance between two points is sideways.

3   A lie is only tossing tails for the truth.

4   If you must make a mistake, make it a big one.

5   Existence is trial by error.

6   Disguise is putting another face on events beyond your control.

7   Failure is an opportunity to do it differently.

8   To retreat is to advance in a circle.

9   Deception can be kindness, while candour is cruelty.

10   Dodging is artful, commanding is brutal, and dying is total.

When he had finished the page, Gillon smiled and said to Ian: "Stick it up. You as a hack? In that, you won't err. You know what I once read on the subject? To err is divine, for God will hear you, as He has made you. To confess is human, but if you do, no one will forgive you."

Peregrine wished he had confessed to being a traitor, when the Junker pranged him over the Channel. Any gaol cell was better than a flaming cockpit of fire. The explosive shells from the enemy plane sparked in a crescendo of inferno under glass. He was roasting, crackling. Stink of burning flesh. Straps off. Hood back. Eject, bale out. Hands blistering.

Find the bloody rip-cord in plunge down. Yank it, fall, fall into shoulder jerk. And drift down into the scrawl of the waves of the sea. Cold on scalded skin. Scream, scream, till smother under parachute. Flail against wet silk cling. Yield. Drown...

The Airsea Rescue launch hauled Peregrine out two miles off Margate, and brought him moaning and mumbling to port. They had morphine with them, or he would have been yelling blue murder at the indifferent heavens. They knocked him cold in the ambulance, and when he came to the remnants of his senses, he was in a swathe of bandages. Two holes for eyes, two for his nostrils, one for his mouth. A zinc pipe stuck out from the cast over his groin, coupled to a rubber hose to get the shit out of him. The rest was the fleapit horror movie, The Mummy Still Lives. Or so the mirror showed, when he babbled to the nurse to hold it up to the openings for his sight.

He was mostly on the jungle juice because he couldn't bear the agony day and night. Christ was only on the Cross for three days, and He complained God had forsaken Him. Peregrine was on the rack for three months, and he had nobody to rail against except himself. In the haze of the morphia, he thought he saw Biddy from time to time. But he would float away on mists and fogs, only to know he was hallucinating. Yet he did remember the one time Clio came. Her flashy beauty was better than a pipe dream, a meteor across the dark, a nebula of hope. Then her lightning smile collapsed into an eclipse of the mouth, and fear and panic were thunderclouds over her eyes, and she fled, never to be seen again.

He should not be surviving, they said. Eighty per cent burns. Not enough skin left for grafting yet by the miracle man MacIndoe. He didn't think it could be worth the candle for the great surgeon to have a go at him. Even Count Frankenstein had a better chance at making his monster, and what was the result? Boris Karloff would look like a beauty queen compared to the final version of Peregrine Plunkett-Drax, who did not wish to live for the experiment.

All very well to want to die, but in his mummy case, he could not kill himself. Everything was done to sterilize him from a friendly germ and keep him ticking over. He was even wheeled out each day from his Oxford hospital into St Margaret's Road in a bath chair. He could view a cherry tree in bloom in front of the blacked-out windows of the houses opposite. And once, he saw a small boy with that Vera Lynn face of Biddy from the Gold Coast. The kid might be her child, or even his, too. One never knew, and even the mother didn't always.

9

WALLS HAVE EARS

Boy had to pass the place where the mummies were four times a day on his walk to school with his satchel. The nurses would roll the monsters out on chairs with wheels. They were bandaged all over with only a hole where the mouth was, and a dent under the nose, and sometimes the slits for the eyes. The air had to be let in so the mummies could breathe. Boy's mother Bridget told him they weren't zombies or the living dead, but Hurricane pilots or fire-fighters who got so badly burned that they had to be wrapped up from head to toe. And not too many of them lived too long. Bridget would go and sit with them and pray with them in the blackout. They couldn't always see, too.

Boy and his elder brother Kelso, who was all of ten, and Bridget lived in an old brick semi-detached house in Polstead Road, a mile north of the centre of Oxford, where the colleges were. The back garden, a few yards wide and a cricket pitch long, had a hen run behind the stumps, though if you hit a six over the wall, you could land on the roof of the shed, where Lawrence of Arabia used to write. Outside the rations, there were always eggs from Whitey or Brownie. These were pickled in great pitchers. On the shelves, hundreds of Kilner jars of bottled plums and apples and jams. And the treats – some salt-dried meat *biltong* from South African cousins and a tin or two of American Spam, and best of all, Marmite on fried bread.

The war made them all pioneers. Bridget made and preserved food from scraps and odds and ends, and she darned the clothes until jerseys and socks were joined patches. Kelso and Boy built battle fleets and tank armies out of pins and scraps of wood. They fought the Nazis on the living-room carpet. There was a Spitfire grounded in St. Giles, where you could sit in the cockpit and pull the joystick, if you could cadge a sixpence to help buy another Spitfire off the factory line. When Boy cut his thumb on a broken light-bulb, the doctor wouldn't give him anything against the pain because it had all gone to the wounded soldiers. Before stitching him up with something that looked as big as a carpet needle, the doctor ordered: "Don't cry, boy, there's a war on." So Boy bit his lip as the point and the thread went through his flesh, and he did not blub.

This was his war, and just because he was little didn't mean he couldn't do his bit.

Boy's best escape of all was down Polstead Road, across Walton Street and up a little track called Aristotle Lane. There he ran away every holiday to fish for silver roach with scarlet fins in the onyx canal under the humpback bridge. From time to time, a red and yellow and black barge was pulled past by a clopping Shire horse, on to London, on to London, down to the Thames, and as far as Rio, where did the canal end, how did he know? And further up Aristotle Lane was the higher bump of the railway bridge with its sides of corrugated iron, where he could stand in the middle while the steam trains shuddered the boards beneath his feet and sent up smoke on either side to make a church of cloud above him. And beyond was Port Meadow, where the horses and the cows grazed on the common land, rolling away and away to the bright river, with the swans so strong they could break a leg with their beaks or fly away to the end of the world.

Although the house was not very big, they had lodgers billeted on them, particularly the relatives of the badly wounded in the hospital. The strange men and mothers passed through. Boy was given gum, which stuck his teeth together, and once a banana, so black and foul he said he would never eat one again. His favourite thing was watching the sparks form patterns of stars on the soot at the back of the chimney of the coal grate. These would blaze and fade in little pin-pricks of red, a sort of changing heaven when the blinds were down and the sirens were sounding and the bombers might pass by.

A grand lady came to stay one day, calling herself Mrs Plunkett-Drax. No good it was his mother telling him that this was a sort of cousin called Arabella. She scared him more than even the PT Master at school, stripped down to his vest and shorts in the middle of winter, making all the shivering boys in the playground do flip-flaps and knee-bends against the cold. The lady's voice sounded like that gun Big Bertha, which they said could fire across the Channel. And the way she talked to mother – Boy thought it was a battery.

"I would not stay with you, Bridget," Arabella was saying, "if there were any alternative. I mean. You and Peregrine. Out in Africa. You?"

"Nothing," Bridget said. "Nothing at all."

"There's nothing much of him to see now, I'm told." The quaver in the lady's voice became harsh. "And this is hardly the Randolph."

"No hotel, I agree," Bridget said. "But all we have."

"I suppose it's full of those boring generals and admirals –"

"We are quite a way from the sea."

"Air-marshals, or whatever they are –"

Weren't grown-ups odd? Watching in silence from the stool in the corner, Boy suddenly saw the dragon woman begin to cry. He was always told not to. And here she was blubbing. Then she blew her nose.

"It didn't stop them with Peregrine. They should never have let him into the Air Force. His vision, you know, he couldn't really see."

"I thought," Bridget said, "they gave them carrots to eat. Then they could see at night."

"No, no. That's rubbish. They've got something called radar. Very hush-hush, but I know all about it."

"Walls have ears," Bridget said, looking round the room, but only Boy had ears, and he was eight.

"Peregrine flew so many sorties. Sometimes six a day. I mean, how could they do that to him?"

"I suppose...Battle of Britain..."

"When they wrote to me ... He was brought down ... burned ... sent here ... I ..."

The lady began crying again, and Bridget went over to sit beside her on the sofa and put an arm around her. It wasn't like that on the playground.

"I'm glad you came here," Boy's mother said. "I'll visit him every night when you have to go."

"It isn't fair. My only son."

All Bridget did was cuddle the dragon cousin and flip her head at Boy to tell him to creep out of the room. So he did, to play draughts with Kelso. He always lost to his elder brother, but at least he knew what the moves were. He lost all his toys, too, because Kelso made him bet on the winner, and Boy never won, so he never had any marbles to play.

When Arabella went, Bridget used to go out every evening to the hospital, where the mummies were. Boy and Kelso would get scared on their own, when the sirens went off, but their mother would tell them not to be cowardy-cats, there was a war on. That was true. There was always a war on, and that was all Boy could remember, the black-out and the coupons and passing the monsters in their wheel-chairs and the Latin lessons, which didn't seem much to do with what was going on, and the chilblains on his hands, because there wasn't any heating. He didn't complain, because he thought all children were living in the same way wherever they were in the world. The news on the wireless didn't tell him any better.

One night, his mother talked about cousin Peregrine, the reason she went to the hospital so often when she wasn't an Air Raid Warden in her blue trousers, which made her look like a man, but she wasn't, because she was his mother.

"It's very sad, you know," she told Boy and Kelso. "Peregrine was going to marry another cousin of yours called Clio. But when she saw the burns — and they are awful — she sort of went away. She didn't want to see him. So he's all alone, none of the family. It's very difficult for Arabella to get over from Ireland. I don't blame her. That's why I go so often to see him. I'm sorry I have to leave you two alone. But you're big boys now. You can cope."

"Daddy," Kelso said. "When's Daddy coming home?"

Boy saw his mother thin her lips. She might have swallowed something hot in her mouth.

"Soon," she said. "He's fighting."

"Where?"

"Kelso darling, I shouldn't tell you. It's a war secret. But — he's safe. He's in Palestine. And there are no Germans there."

"Who's there?"

"People called Jews. And Arabs. But there's no danger. He just has to keep them in order. That's his job. He's a policeman."

"But when will he be home?"

"It's difficult to come back. But he'll get leave, and he'll see you."

"Palestine," Boy said. "Wasn't that where Lawrence of Arabia was? The man who wrote in the shed next door."

"Yes," his mother said. "And that's where your cousin Robert passed away. At a battle called Armageddon. But it won't happen to Daddy." She suddenly put on her bright quick smile. "Friday. It's Friday. Marmite on toast."

And so the two boys reached paradise, as long as the taste lasted.

When Daddy did come home on leave with his kitbag slung over the shoulder of his uniform, he was another stranger. He smelt funny, stinks of tobacco and whisky and pong. While he was kissing Boy, sandpaper was on his cheeks. And funny, Mummy put him in the spare room where the lodgers were, when they came. There were few words between them, and silences. They hardly talked to each other, but to the boys, who didn't know what to make of their father. But one night after they had gone to bed, the sirens went woo-wah-woo in the night, and Boy was scared and wondered if they would have to go down to the cellar or the shelter, but Kelso was still asleep, so he crept down the stairs to squat outside the kitchen door, where he could hear the raised voices of his mother and father, who was saying, "I know you're still seeing him. You're always going to the hospital."

"There are dozens of others I see, Paul. And as you know, there's nothing much to see of him, poor boy. Eighty per cent burns."

"That will put you off."

"Don't count on it."

"I always believed I could count on you," Paul said. "But not, I see."

"I didn't ask for this to happen. I didn't ask to meet Peregrine when you were upcountry. How could I know he'd be shot down and end up here?" There was a silence, then Boy heard. "If you think I planned it... If you think I wanted him burned all over... Ending up in Oxford, where they sent him...nothing to do with me." There was a low sound, it was like weeping, but mothers don't cry. "Things happen, Paul. I didn't want to meet him again. We weren't seeing each other any more, even though you were posted to Palestine. And then he turned up here. In his state. He needs me."

"And I don't?"

"Not like he does."

"It's bloody in Palestine. You get shot at from all sides. Arabs and Jews, though you'd think they'd know we are helping them a bit against Hitler. You never know what you're at. Or why you're there. They don't want us, and we don't want them."

"The story of your life, Paul. And the rest of us. Colonials. They don't want us, and we don't want them."

Boy tried to hear more through the door, but no one was speaking for a time.

"I do need you," Daddy said.

"I can't go from here. There's a war on. You know that. Who'd look after the boys?"

"But... you and me..."

"The separation, Paul. You agreed to that. After Peregrine, in the Gold Coast. I didn't know..."

"What didn't you know? What didn't you know when Keiss was born?"

"You mean Boy."

"He was baptised Keiss," Paul said. "A family name. He's a Sinclair, is he not?"

Biddy had no answer, so she said: "And now...when Peregrine's like this, can't you see... I couldn't leave him."

"I heard that Clio – he was going to marry Clio –"

"You know, what he told me. He can speak. Or whisper. She took one look at him and said she loved him still and fled and never came back again."

"No guts," Paul said. "Her mother was always a rotten lot. There was that murder in South Africa. And she's a Fascist, really. On the other side. Hardly what you need in a crisis."

"But you're good in a crisis, aren't you, Paul?"

"So they say. I had a friend once, if I have any left, after you leaving me. He said the nicest thing to me. Wouldn't mind being in a trench with you, Paul. That was a nice thing to say."

"It was nice." Nothing for Boy to hear for a while, then his mother's voice. "We don't live in trenches. Not all of us. I'm not good enough for you."

"Oh yes, you are."

"I am not. I can't tell you about it. It's people really needing you. If you're not there, people will go. And you weren't there."

"Ah." Again nothing to hear. "I don't need you, then. And I have to go. Back to Palestine. And the boys?"

"I'll always be with the boys."

"I am their father. At least, the elder one."

"I'll always be with the boys. We don't have much to get by on, you know."

"I send back what I can."

"I know. But ... rations ... clothes ... you can't know how it is. Some of the soldiers who come here, they say war is a spree. No family, no responsibility, good grub and fags, a picnic."

"Until you get shot."

"Well, no responsibilities. But that's what we have. The wives at home."

"A wife. Is that what you are?"

"And a mother."

Again there was a break in the voices, then the scrape of a chair. So Boy crept upstairs on his hands and knees. He didn't know quite what he had heard. But he didn't think Daddy would stay too long, and he didn't. He left with his kitbag soon, and he never came back again. There was a war on, wasn't there?

Before the Man from the Ministry reached Hamish Henry at Bletchley, the expected divorce was announced by a *blitzkrieg*. Hitler's *panzers* rolled into Russia in a *Gotterdammerung* for Stalin, hidden in his Valhalla at the Kremlin. As the Tiger tanks blasted across the steppes towards Moscow and the Crimea, it was all change on the Eastern Front. Britain was the new ally and supplier of the Red Army: Tommy and Ivan stood together in the struggle against Fritz and Luigi. To sneak secrets to the Communists on how the Fascists wanted to clobber them was no longer treachery, but a helping hand. Winston Churchill might want to keep his code-breaking under wraps after the German Enigma had been cracked with a cypher log salvaged off a sinking U-boat; but it was now in England's interest to avert a Russian defeat and so draw off Hitler's forces, stacked across the Channel, ready for the invasion that never was.

Hamish Gordon had become part of the net that extended through Hamish Henry to the Bentinck Street cell of Cambridge dons and diplomats. He had wangled an assignment on the fresh convoys of munitions sailing round Norway to Murmansk. The Germans were pressing on Leningrad with the Finns. The commissars had to find from somewhere the tanks and explosives to continue the struggle, even if these came from a decadent imperialist bourgeois democracy. And they wanted to know what happened on the interminable icy voyages on the way.

"I would sing halleluiah," Henry said to Gordon, as they finished the last of the sherry in his small bedroom in a Nissen hut at Bletchley. "And I will. A miracle of a blunder by Hitler. Angels must have driven him bonkers."

"We've got to get the stuff out to Russia, me lad," Gordon said. "Or it'll be a bloody catastrophe."

"We will. Or rather you will. And keep us posted, comrade." Henry looked at the brownish glaze of his Tio Pepe, the dregs of the final bottle he would sip for ages. "Isn't it too delicious? All those old lines. His faith unfaithful made him falsely true. All for a handful of roubles he sold us, all for a red star to sew on his coat. You are the enemy I killed, my friend. Now it's all, all right. Perish the thought we were collaborators with the commissars. Having a red under your bed now is like having a house guest. You will stay the night, incidentally?"

As Henry smiled loosely and lopsided at him, the puritan streak in Gordon reacted.

"That's too narrow an iron bed you've got. And I don't fancy that folding chair. So I'll be off. I've got to be back at Scapa Flow by Thursday night. It is ironic. All those American Lend-Lease strategic materials sailing to Archangel, and on to Murmansk, where I'll report to the usual sources. Then I'll report back to the cell when we dock here. Tell me, did I hear Peregrine...?"

"Burned to a crisp by his own side. Irony goes even further than Uncle Sam supplying Uncle Joe with all the weapons he needs to screw capitalism. And now, we've even got Ruth and Virginia and the Scudabrights, singing 'Auld Lang Syne' and 'Auf Wiedersehen, Sweetheart' in the psycho wards or behind bars. While we, the gorgeous glorious Bolshies, are the toast of the town, the crumpets and butter for tea. Must you really really toddle?"

"I must," Gordon said. And by the time he had returned to Murmansk, the diplomatic game of lethal Musical Chairs was played again. The Japanese had bombed Pearl Harbor and Singapore. They had concluded an armistice with Russia, so they need not fight each other, only their pressing enemies. Hitler was insane enough to declare war on the United States, which now joined the British Empire in the Pacific and the Atlantic sea wars. All was a murderous muddle and mess, like the black ice rigging and breakaleg skidrow decks on his convoy to Russia. Gordon found himself mouthing the gibberish of the three witches from *Macbeth*, that unmentionable unlucky Scots play that ended so very badly. What were the spells?

> "Double, double, toil and trouble...
> When the hurlyburly's done,
> When the battle's lost or won...
> Fair is foul, and foul is fair.
> Hover through the fog and filthy air..."

Gordon could not remember any more, or see his way, that had been so clear. He had been so sure and now was not.

10

BLITZ FOR LOVERS

On the fifth day of the *blitz* on London, the East Enders stormed the underground stations. This was a great victory for the working classes, or whoever they thought themselves to be, if they did. They were kipping down in the tube, safe from harm. Soon a hundred thousand and fifty people were sheltering down in their hell from the bombs every night, or living there because they were homeless. They were lying anywhere, like haddock on slabs at the fishmongers. Women and suitcases, men and blankets, children and teddy bears, all in a mess and a mass. The trains roared round, the people woke and slept fitfully. A reeking monsoon swept through the platforms. A sort of litter of humanity coughed in this tepid and airless blast.

Up above, there were shelters under railway arches or warehouse cellars, in Tilbury and the Isle of Dogs. The seamen and the tarts dropped by, between tides and times. Soggy fried fish were on sale, expiring whelks and cockles. The stench retched in the nostrils, the fug encouraged the lice. A few candles, a few torches, if they had batteries, knifed a beam or flicker through the gloom. A handkerchief knotted over his mouth like a gasmask, Ian Hamish was scrabbling through this inferno to report on the conditions caused by bombing raids. He was told that the shelters in the Dorchester Hotel in Park Lane were better: in the Turkish baths there, cots with eiderdowns were marked for cabinet ministers and one was RESERVED FOR LORD HALIFAX. Ian was meeting Clio for breakfast, if he reached there, but it would take him three hours to pick his way to the West End through the rubble in the streets.

The sky was an exploding rainbow. The fires in the black buildings were copper and red, the incendiaries a violet-green, the coughing dust meandered in the yellow drift of a pea-soup fog. Detours formed by cordons prolonged the trek and the débris and the dying. Rabid cats shrieked through the streets. Gas tweaked at the smells of soot and burned flesh. Ian sneezed at the acrid foulness. And beneath his shoes, glass glittered in the flames like frost on bracken and broke underfoot in a strange grinding tinkle.

The dome of St Paul's Cathedral was the guideline from east to west, the surviving marker from the past. As a serene surgeon, it stood above the devastation of the streets. The anatomies of the blitzed houses were exposed, their ribs of rooms, the arteries of their plumbing, their rickety stairs falling into the cellars. Picking his way over the shards of a city he knew, Ian found himself in a dissection room of an urban morgue. The entrails of London were strewn about him, even in Mayfair. For each missile from the air, there was no distinction between rich and poor. The best thing about obliteration was that it had a lethal equality.

Clio's uniform seemed to trim her at her fuzzy edges. Her hit-and-miss emotions were clipped in by her creases. And incredibly, Ian had enough money to pay for the bin end of the champagne and orange squash to open another day, which might be their last. Yet he didn't even get to the bacon and eggs, before she broke down. Her tears made black rays of mascara down her cheeks.

"I'm a rat," she cried. "You know that. Running away from Peregrine. Jut because he was a mummy."

"We can only take what we can take. No more than that."

"Oh, blub, blub away." Clio blew her nose into her napkin. "What's that slogan? London can take it. But I can't."

"But you can, Clio. You're here, in a war job, taking it with the rest of us."

"German bombs. You know how I was. I loved them as long as they fell on the reds in Spain. So did my other Mummy."

"Yes. But changing sides when you're under fire from your last one is called wisdom."

"But I really have, you know."

"I know, darling Clio. Otherwise, we wouldn't be here."

"You know I'm a rat."

"The most beautiful rat I ever met. And my rat."

"Rats can't be beautiful."

"When they are, they're called right. What you believed once was nothing to do with who you are now. God, if you couldn't change, we wouldn't need God to help us change. Being wrong is merely part of the plan, so we get it right in the end."

"You're very consoling, Ian."

"But not exciting"

"I didn't say that."

"No, but it's not quite the adjective... I mean, for love."

Clio put her hand across the table and squeezed Ian's fingers.

"You make me feel better. Not quite such a louse. Can we walk and talk about it? I'm not due back in the office till eleven."

"Anything up?"

"I shouldn't tell you."

"No shop in the mess." Ian smiled. "Though you'll find outside, much mess and no shops."

"I can't talk to you," Clio said. "About work. I may betray somebody again."

"You won't. Ever."

"And you can't talk to me about what you're doing."

"Oh, mother Ruby's out in India, helping to run Annandale, so we can have enough tea to win the war with yet another cuppa. Top secret."

"You're a fool, telling me that. It means you still don't trust me."

"No. Just the rules of war."

"War has no rules."

"Yes, it does. Thou shalt not care for anyone except thyself."

"No human feelings then?"

"So I'm told. Orders is orders. Let's walk, Clio, in the ruins. And we'll try and see if we still can feel and do anything."

"We could run away inside us."

"The only escape now." Ian took Clio's hand as they left the table and walked towards the bill and the revolving doors of the Dorchester. "And if we do get away, who knows where it goes? We might get to the heart of us, if we still have one."

They played a game outside, called 'Bombsites'. As they rounded the corners of the streets, they guessed how many craters or holes in the ground there would be before the next crossroads or square. There were never more than four, though Ian claimed he had totted up six in the Mile End Road. Of course, there were no nightingales singing in Berkeley Square, nor had there been for ages. But the sirens went off again, woo-wah-woo, and they were too blasé to run for cover, it would be a false alarm with the clear skies overhead. And it was, so they reached the Embankment and their way to work. The only block was a big cordon round a UXB, an unexploded bomb which might be a dud or a delayed action device.

"There was one near St Paul's," Ian said. "They got it on a lorry and exploded it on Hackney Marshes. It made a crater a hundred foot wide. Like that big one the double-decker bus fell in."

"Late as usual," Clio said. "Buses always are. But do you think there's a bomb coming with our number on it?"

"You've been hit already, Clio. Bombs never hit the same target twice."

"That's what they say. But they also say there's a bomb now can chase you round corners."

"Only your fears can. That's absolute bilge. Like that new thing from the Ministry of Food and the Radio Doctor. Eat carrots and you'll see better in the black-out."

"And that's why our night fighter pilots can see the Luftwaffe in the dark. They eat carrots, don't they?"

"Yes, radar is unnecessary, with our vegetable-sharp eyes. But look at that –" The pair of them were edging their way round the cordon towards a row of houses, sliced sideways into an exposure of shoddy partitions and tangled pipes.

"The Jerry bombers do us a service, showing us our jerry building."

"And look at that, too." Clio was pointing at a dull metal canister. "It looks like a bottle of hock."

"Incendiary," Ian said. "Let's toddle. Leave it to the Heavy Rescue."

And so they went on to their occupations, past a blasted pub with its saloon bar windows a grey silver of glass daggers in the street, but sporting the slogan: MORE OPEN THAN USUAL, then by a Horlicks advertisement promising a DEEP HEALING SLEEP. Everybody wanted that in this bruising time. The *blitz* was no cure for insomnia. Yet living dangerously was also for Ian an incitement for pursuing Clio.

"The Café de Paris tonight," he said. "At nine."

"You can't afford it," she said.

"I'll become a looter. The streets of London may not be paved with gold, but after an air raid, you can pick up a fortune."

"As long as you're not ruining yourself."

"I can't count any more," Ian said. "Anyway, the next bomb may hit my bank." They kissed and parted. "Cheery-bye."

"Pip, pip."

Winston Churchill was demanding retaliation. If the Dorniers and the Focke-Wulfs and the Heinkels and the Junkers and the Stukas were plastering London and Coventry, then he would send back the Blenheims and the Wellingtons over Berlin. Ian knew that our bombers were inadequate, and the new four-engined Lancasters were having teething problems, while the American Flying Fortresses were still on their flights over here. But what the Prime Minister wanted, the Prime Minister got. And so he was huddled over his charts, when Gillon came up to cast an eye on his war effort.

"Very good," Gillon said. "We should be able to strafe Hitler in his bunker. Or somewhere close by."

"Yes," Ian said. "But how many of our boys fly home?"

"Our losses are acceptable."

"In men, or material?"

"Not in men. We can't train pilots fast enough. But you know who is winning the Battle of Britain? Not the famous few. The many in the aircraft factories. God knows how that old rogue from my Canadian country has done it, but that bloody Beaverbrook has kicked so much ass that we're turning out hundreds of Spitfires and Hurricanes every week. And we're speeding up on our new bombers. We'll be able to do a Coventry on Hamburg bloody soon. Blast them back to the Nibelungs, and their forest existence."

There was a brilliance in Gillon's eyes which Ian put down to hatred, not alcohol.

"It hasn't worked for Hitler," he said. "Bombing civilians is bad policy. It doesn't shatter their morale here. Why should it there? Now bombing airfields, factories, that might wash, if we can."

"That's not what Harris says, our Air Chief. Bomb the bastards everywhere. And if they don't crack soon, bomb them again, until they break."

"Aren't we becoming as they are? We don't care how many losses of lives, who they are, as long as we win."

"Look, Ian, if we bomb only the armaments factories, who do we kill? Our own people. The slave labour – Jews like my wife – prisoners – us, the French, the Russians. They're manning the Nazi war programme. They have to work there, or die. So what do we do? Kill our own and spare the German people –"

"Who don't all believe in Hitler."

"And if they don't, what the hell? Bombs are like showers. They don't discriminate. They fall on the just and the unjust guy."

"But the strategy can be different. We choose the targets."

"But not where the bombs actually fall. We can only do our best. The missiles can't think. They blast what they land on."

"We're trying to do better over that," Ian said. "Gees. They're OK. But they're short-range like the Oboes. They can't curve round the surface of the earth, which isn't flat, as I have come to know. And our poor bloody bombers have to fly in a straight line into a locked target, so they're sitting ducks. But –"

"But what?"

"Your new thingamajig. H_2S. With ultra-short waves. You can be sitting in your cockpit and see the target on a screen by the bomb button. That means we can bomb blind, through clouds, and land at least within a mile of the victims."

"It's in development. It will work."

"It must. Cut the casualties. A few thousand-pounders might hit the right object."

"Don't be smart. Work. And hope."

"OK," Ian said. "I can't preach. Now these targets in Berlin –"

So he went on plotting an ineffectual revenge raid on the capital of Prussia, but he was actually thinking about Clio and cursing himself for falling in love with her. Yes, she said she loved him, but she did not, sexually. Whatever Peregrine had done to her, Ian could not do. To be loved for being gentle, kind, considerate, that was gall and wormwood. He wanted her. He wanted her to want him. But that was an animal instinct, an irresistible grip on the groin. As he plotted the air paths towards the Reichstag, Ian could not see his own way into her.

Walking late towards the Café de Paris, Ian found himself in another alert. The skies were a palette of ochre and madder, crossed with the yellow diagrams of the searchlights. He would have to note these words in his mind of what he was seeing. John Lehmann and *New Writing* had taken his first piece. Parachute flares were drifting down with their amber and serpentine lights. Ack-ack batteries were screaming with their shells exploding in the night and sending down the patter-patter of steel rain. On the roofs, the silhouettes were standing against the lurid dark, the Jim Crows of the look-out men. He should have stayed in the cellars at the Ministry, but Clio might be waiting for him, and he could not wait to see her.

Off Leicester Square, Ian went down the stairs to one of the bigger craters in London. This was man-made, however, for entertainment, and was not the entrance to Dante's Inferno. Ian did not abandon hope because he entered there. Listening and hearing Snakehips Johnson and his jazz band sounded more like the way into the portals of pleasure. And Clio, incredibly, was there before him at a table on the balcony, where the oleaginous Charles led him, always the smooth introducer to fate.

"Ibyssinia," Ian said. But as he began to sit, his tummy flipped over in a pancake. Those spread cheek bones, the glitter in those wide eyes, those breasts crawling in the trap of her bodice. Christ, he had to sit down to hide his lust. "You're looking gorgeous."

"Well, it isn't down there," Clio said.

Peering down into the pit of the dance floor, Ian could view what she meant. Canadians and Yanks dancing boogie-woogie turned the place into a frantic machine, arms and legs whizzing off in broken pistons, a chaos of a jamboree of a fiesta. Some of the alien horde affected with St Vitus or other fits were wearing kilts, as if these shenanigans would have passed muster in Tobermory or Tralee.

"Those were the clansmen who got away," Ian said. "It's been a century since the Clearances and they seem to have forgot how to do the Highland fling."

Snakehips was playing *Oh, Johnny*, when the two bombs hit them at quarter to ten. It was the second chorus of the ditty, and there was a blue flash, a blast of dust, a knockdown, a big blow, the dark, the black-out for some. A moron lit his cigarette lighter, only to hear a call: "Silly bugger. There's gas about." A naked girl in the rubble below was screaming, "Help me," stripped by the blast, but with blood all over her body in a carmine dress. The band did not play on, as Snakehips was gone with his drummer.

Ian found Clio lying on the deck. He felt her face with numbed figures, as he couldn't see her wounds. A wetness soaked her forehead, but thanks be, at the next table there was a bottle of champagne, still upright in its bucket by the miracle of drink. He lifted it to pour over Clio's gash, which he wiped with a napkin.

"Bubbly, darling," he heard himself managing to say, "is the best antiseptic."

She was moving, she was moaning, she would make it, if they could get out. Something rolled and splashed against Ian's trouser leg. He reached to find a high-heeled buttoned shoe. The foot only went as far as the ankle, which was bleeding on him. He chucked it away.

"We've been rather lucky, Clio," he said. "Don't move. The Rescue will find us."

And so they did, and carted them off. In the ambulance, Ian insisted on sitting by Clio, in shock yes, but only with the single cut under her golden hair. He had not prayed for a long time, but words were tolling in the back of his head. *Thank you, God, thank you. Thank you for sparing her. We don't deserve. Thank you.* And he was babbling to her, as if she was hearing, "You know, you were all right. The bomb did have our number on it. But it missed, you see. That can happen. You can still squeak out of it, when your number's up. With a bit of grace. With a bit of mercy from up there." And looking up at the jolting ceiling of the ambulance, Ian added, "You can't see it always, or hardly at all, but up there, you never know, some one may be looking after you."

The rolls of bumph from the codebreakers were longer than loo paper, unravelled from end to end. Filled with more holes than a pincushion, they were meant to crack the German Enigma code. Until then, Hamish Henry had thought Enigma a musical variation. New he could hardly get to his old tutor Alan Turing to talk about it at Bletchley. He was too junior in the hierarchy of cryptography. All he could find out was that an American madman from MIT called Sutton was sharing cipher secrets, while riding his unicycle round the corridors of Washington. That was until Henry began dating Muriel, a secretary from the Russian front desk. As she was a big blonde who was squeezed like toothpaste into her uniform, he hated her attributes, but liked her gossip.

"We know what's going on out there, you know," she told Ian. "All them U-boats and pocket battleships hitting our convoys to Russia. And them Jerry planes hitting Moscow and places. We know it, we do. The thing is, we can't tell 'em, can we?"

"No, my dear," Henry said, patting her arm and working out ways to get some of the details back to the Red Army. What he did not yet know was to drown Hamish Gordon, who had reported back to him from a final Arctic convoy with all the contact details for the coven in Bentinck Street. Henry was only a whisker in that global cat-and-mouse game. The important thing was to save comrade Russia, not his cousins or his friends, if he had any. Family had nothing to do with war policy.

Gillon was the first to hear of Gordon's death on the perilous route to Archangel. As Scapa Flow had become with Iceland the hub of the war supplies from America to Russia, Gillon had flown there in a failing Blenheim to improve the Orkney Wireless Station at Netherbutton. Long-range fighters could protect the convoys as far as Bear Island off Norway, although Murdo's old sea-planes, the Swordfish with their slung torpedos, were useless – six of them had been lost when the battlecruisers *Gneisenau* and *Scharnhorst* had broken out of Brest and sailed through the Channel, hoping to join in the fjords the other Germany heavy ships, the *Tirpitz* and the *Scheer* and the *Hipper*. Actually, Murdo's new device, sea-mines dropped from the air, had crippled the two escaping Nazi gunboats. So they had to hole up in home ports and could not add to the menace against the Allied convoys to the Far North.

The threat rather than the reality of the *Tirpitz* had destroyed the PQ17 with its thirty-four merchantmen. Admiral Hamilton was ordered to withdraw his supporting cruisers because they would be mangled by the heavy guns of the battle-cruiser. What was not known was that the Germans had taken their heavy ships back to Altafjord, in case they suffered the fate of the mighty *Bismarck*, sunk the previous year. The convoy was told to scatter off Nova Zembla and left to the scant mercy of the packs of U-boats and flights of Junkers and Dorniers with their long-range fuel tanks. Twenty-three merchant ships were sunk; fourteen were American; one cargo boat was the brine coffin of Gordon, who died glug-glugging on his bunk in a sunken tomb.

Gillon's job was to see such a disaster could never happen again. He had to go to the Wireless Station to supervise the fresh transmitters. Some of them would translate Range Speech to fighters, trying to protect those doomsday voyages to Russia, also any bombing attack on the Home Fleet in Scapa Flow. The other machines were primitive, transmitting Morse Code to our punitive bombers. To Gillon, knowing something of what was going on at Bletchley, this seemed like sending Sanskrit out to modern scavengers. Yet he was told that the No. 19 'tank set' navy communications receiver worked in a way, even in heavy seas.

He was shown the Scapa Flow boom defence chart and told to review it for any penetration. Of course, it had nothing to do with an airborne attack, but that was unlikely, with the Luftwaffe pulling back from France to cope with the Russian front. He asked to go out to the Flow to survey the situation. His naval guide pointed out to him a dark patch, still bubbling and spreading over the waters, where the *Royal Oak* had gone down. Beyond it, the grey silhouettes of the *King George V* and the *Queen Elizabeth* and the *Prince of Wales*, a dynasty of majestic battleships. Beyond them, a silk screen of evening cruisers and destroyers.

"A hell of a lot of ships," Gillon said, "as long as they are safe."

"We've built the new boom barriers," the flunkey in blue said. "And the Churchill Barrier. The U-Boats will never get through again."

Gillon looked at the dark stain on the waters. "That's what they always say. Never again. Then it's again and again. You know, there are a thousand men drowned down there. They didn't know any better, did they? And there is only an oil slick to be their memorial. My cousin died out there." He pointed vaguely towards the North Star. "In a ship. And another cousin in a plane in the last great show." He gripped the pale guy by the lapels of his blue jacket. "Never say never again. Until you *know* it's the *last* world war. Then you say, never again. And then I will kiss you."

Which Gillon did not.

11

BYE, BYE, SINGAPORE

That January, Shankar knew they were doomed by the slow Malaysian rotting away, even before they had heard the bad news. The torpid atmosphere seemed to jab sloth into their veins, the sluggish wireless could scarcely dribble out the disasters. The two capital ships, sent out to rescue them, *HMS Repulse* and *Prince of Wales* had been sunk offshore by Zeros and Tojos. Winston Churchill had put his boot in his mouth again as in Norway; sea-power without aeroplanes on deck was a wreck. Even if we ruled the oceans, we had lost the air, and the jungle too, where we would not even send in the Gurkhas to ambush the strike from General Yamashita and roll a few heads into their swamp camps. He had taken Kuala Lumpur and was advancing with his 25th Army Division down the north-south road. On bicycles, so our poor Intelligence said. But every time we tried to stop them on their pedals, they swung a right or a left hook and came in behind us. And we waited festering in Singapore under a tired command with the big fifteen-inch naval guns pointing out to sea, where the enemy were not sailing from.

The bombs announced their arrival as Gog and Magog had once announced the coming of the Apocalypse. Hardly an order fluttered from above, few people were dug in, and the missiles from the heavens fell in exploding hail, as intolerable as a thirteenth uninvited guest for dinner. Shankar was trying to do something to rally his bewildered Indian company. If they had any spirit left in them, they were nearly fighting the Aussies next door and the pallid industrial Midlands riff-raff, sea-sick and bewildered on the other flank. Racial jibes were flying like shrapnel, every soldier was turning his personal misery on any stranger of a different stripe he could see. Nobody wanted to be there. Everyone wanted to shifty. And all of them knew they were going to lose.

The next morning, a sort of control was cast over the apathy. Something had to be done to protect the Johore Straits, where the front was collapsing. A few of the naval guns were pointed inland, but their armour-piercing shells could not do much to blow up troops, infiltrating in landing-craft through the mangrove swamps. Two

Australian and one British-Indian Brigades were sent up to protect the Causeway and Tengah Aerodrome, but these were beaten and their leftovers retreated in front of the Japanese Imperial Guards. The overall commander General Wavell fell off the quay in the dark, while being evacuated, and he broke bones in his back. After him went the top Air Vice-Marshal and Rear-Admiral in a fleet of eighty little ships, straight into slaughter by enemy destroyers. In many ways, it seemed better to stay than run.

Shankar was ordered with his men to blow up the supplies. They sweated all day to fix their explosives and detonators to the guns and munitions they were not allowed to use against the attackers. The reservoirs had been taken. Nobody had thought to fill the baths and the buckets of the city, so the defenders might last out for weeks in house-to-house fighting. That should have broken the Japanese, who were out of supplies themselves. Yet as Shankar knew, nobody wanted to resist. The Japs looked bloody invincible. So he was hardly surprised when he saw General Percival walk towards the enemy lines in his topee hat and starched uniform to accept an unconditional surrender.

Shankar spat.

"I will not," he muttered, but he did. He threw down his arms with the rest of his men, he was beaten into line, he stood in sweat and misery in the boiling sun, he was herded into a compound, no food or water for a night or a day, he pulled down his shorts where he stood when he had to evacuate himself, a beast among other stricken beasts.

When he was suddenly selected and hauled in by the guards, Shankar thought any humiliation might be inflicted on him, like Bobby Putting being buggered in front of his Indian troops. He got a rifle-butt in the back to send him stumbling into the old office with its fan still slowly stirring the soupy air. And who was sitting at the desk there but the seedy Shilendra, now as crisp as a ginger biscuit in a uniform of a Japanese colonel, while Shankar's own outfit was a sweatbag.

"I thought you might be here," Shilendra said. "So I asked to see you."

"Very thoughtful of you," Shankar said. "You look pretty pukka."

Shilendra poured a large Haig scotch into a cut-glass tumbler and pushed it across the desk towards his cousin.

"I must say, British war supplies are good stuff. Just as good as in the mess, don't you think? Why not have a *chota-peg*?"

Shankar took the glass and rolled its cool edge against his bottom lip, sniffing at the peat musk. Then he swallowed half the tumbler and coughed. And so he spoke.

"I should have said Cheers. But I can't see much to say Cheers about."

"You should sing Hallelujah like they taught us. Your time has come. You can fight to free India."

"What? Give it to the Japanese? They'd be worse than the Brits."

"We'll have independence. The Japanese have sworn it, if we help them."

"So have the Brits, if we help them."

"You can't trust their word."

"And you trust the Japanese?"

"Did you hear what Chandra Bose said from Berlin?" Shilendra read from a telegram in front of him. "The fall of Singapore means the collapse of the British Empire, the end of the iniquitous regime which it has symbolized and the dawn of a new era in Indian history." He looked up. "That is you, Shankar. You, too."

Shankar swallowed the rest of his whisky. His last glass for years.

"Your masters haven't won yet."

"We'll roll up the rest of Malaya and Burma. Their Free Army is already fighting for us. That gives us half the world's supply of tin and rubber and enough oil for all our ships and tanks. Your pathetic troops. They weren't even fit to fight."

"True."

"Do you know, you outnumbered us two to one. And you collapsed. Bourgeois imperialist lackeys."

"Don't count your chickens."

"Bose is coming over to lead us. We have already five thousand recruits for an Indian National Army. We need you."

"Not on your life."

Shilendra grinned and shook his head.

"You mean, not on *your* life. And what is that? A POW camp building a Singapore-Rangoon railway. Rations nearly nil. Life expectancy, say a year, if you don't get *beri-beri*. No tiffin. Nasty exit. And you have a cause you believe in. Do you really have a choice?"

"I don't believe in your lot playing Madame Butterfly to the Free India movement."

"What else have we got?"

"They are Fascists. Like the Nazis."

"Ah, but we will win. We will use Fascism to destroy imperialism. Then we destroy Fascism."

"And if they destroy us?"

"They cannot. No Japanese army could possibly control India. Too big and too far for them."

"They're doing a big job in China, which is rather bigger than us."

Shilendra sucked in his breath, but still he answered.

"Another lot of capitalist lackeys. I prefer the Japanese. They obey orders. Fight like devils. Put you all to shame."

"True again."

"And they give us a window of opportunity. Which will never come again. The British Empire is finished. *We* must be the ones to pick up the pieces."

"You can't mean you and me, Shilendra."

"I do."

Shankar looked at his cousin, that odd burning quality he had, a skin almost on fire.

"You're that ambitious?"

"I am a vehicle for the revolution."

"How could I be? A major in the British Army. I am not the vanguard of the proletariat."

"Join us. And all is forgiven."

"Never forgotten. With you lot, there is always a purge around the corner."

Shilendra was suddenly brusque.

"No shit from you. You're just a bloody sepoy. And I'm giving you a hand-out. Take it or leave it. Or you're dead."

Shankar did not take it then. But after two months in the POW camp, he had lost twenty pounds and had festering ulcers on his legs. So he took it and left his hell-hole for the Indian National Army on the jungle road home.

"Shankar's in the bag at Singapore."

His brother Solomon had got a chit for a week's leave to go back to Annandale to tell his family. He was not sure if he was taunting them or consoling himself. Certainly, there was accusation on his tongue.

"No guts." Margaret Jardine's words were acid drops. "Surrender? To those pathetic little yellow-bellies. It's unthinkable."

"If you don't want to think about it," Solomon said, "that is your privilege. But it is a fact. The Japanese are already into Burma, and nobody is stopping them. I always told Shankar he was a fool to join the British Army. But he would not listen. He always wanted to score another hundred for the regiment. He played up and played the game. And look where he is now."

Crippled with arthritis, Margaret was sitting in a wooden chair with a high back, her bent and swollen fingers gripping the arms as claws. Behind her, her daughter Ruby was standing, her trip to India now for the duration of the war. She was swollen, too, inside her black dress, but it was her diet, too much of it.

"And where is Shankar exactly now?"

"In a prison camp. That is the best we can hope for."

"What about this Indian National Army? The Japanese say they have recruited whole divisions of our Indian troops."

"Shankar wouldn't do that. He knows that is not the way to independence."

"Nor is your friend Mr Gandhi's Passive Resistance. Sitting down in front of machine-guns. That is no way to stop the Japs."

"I agree," Shankar said. "I came to tell you that I am being seconded to the eastern frontier. Assam. We have to take Burma back."

"But you're not a soldier. You're a desk-wallah."

"Supplies, that sort of thing. We also serve who only push a pen. And Aunt Ruby, I have some rather hush-hush news for you. Your son's coming out, Ian Hamish."

"Why didn't he tell me?" Ruby was startled. "I mean, his mother —"

"He would if he could. He can't. Top Secret. I only knew because they were doing a check on him. They wanted to know if he still had anything to do with cousin Shilendra."

"That rat. That traitor." Margaret spat out the words. "I did not know Ian had ever met him."

"At Cambridge, apparently. Anyway, I reassured them. And I'll get him to come up here, when he arrives."

"I haven't seen Ian for years," Ruby said. "This damn war. And the Empire. Sometimes I think the whole thing only exists to separate mothers from their sons."

"Well," Solomon said, "you invented the boarding school to create a colonial class of motherless young men."

"And you are one of them. Do you see much of your mother Peg?"

"Too little now. She's helping out, as you know, in the rehabilitation centres. Our troops, those who do get back from Burma, are scarecrows. Maggots in their wounds. A dreadful mess."

"You're a defeatist," Margaret said. "You sound you want them to win."

"Oh no," Solomon said. "Wars win nothing. Who wins the peace is he who has arranged to, before the war is over."

"You think we'll really give you independence?"

"You will have to because you need millions of us to fight for you. We will want our due."

"And this?"

Margaret brought up the open fist of her hand and clawed at the scented air coming through the window slats from the tea bushes outside.

"All we have worked for. All we built. And bloody impossible to run, now that my husband's gone. All that effort. Useless, was it?"

"Not useless for all who have worked for you. You pay them hardly anything, but just enough to scrape by, which is better than nothing. I've always wondered, all those tens of millions of cups of tea drunk At Home, a penny a cup, so cheap, so necessary for the morale of the nation, do any of the ladies ever think that bent picker in her sari and bare feet, she won't even get a farthing, perhaps one penny from a hundred cups of tea." Solomon bent his head in judgement. "No, nobody thinks of that."

"Market forces," Margaret snapped. "With prices so low. They are jolly lucky to get an anna at all."

"Market forces. That is the excuse for all the injustice in the world."

"Armed forces are," Ruby interrupted. "They take the sons from their homes. Earning a living or not, that's one thing. But forced separation. That's cruel."

Solomon rose.

"I will get Ian back to you, aunt Ruby. I promise."

"Thank you for coming all this way to tell me, Solomon. It was good of you."

"Only natural. We are still some sort of a family, are we not?"

A bleak grin split Margaret's sunken cheeks.

"Until you get your independence. And we know what you'll do with it. You'll push us out. You're bound to. Then you will have Annandale, won't you, Solomon?"

"And you both," Solomon said as he left, "will always be my most welcome guests."

There was no sense in it. Bridget knew that, and she had two small boys to care for. Peregrine was a brute, a bully, a liar. He was fickle and could behave like a swine. And now he was a monster, flayed and scoured and oozing. He was more bitter than quinine. His words in his despair lashed like the birch. And yet his power over her was so devouring that she had to love him. Decent men like Paul would never understand. To be wanted so much, once in desire and now in necessity, overwhelmed her. And there was Boy.

She used to scrutinize her younger son's face morning after morning. He still looked exactly as she was in the mirror, blond curls and cornflower eyes as big as sixpences in his serious moon of a face. His chin was going to drop, his cheeks grow hollow, into the lean Paul or the sly Peregrine. Yet nothing was clear yet, whose child he was. And as for Paul's certain son Kelso, he would never forgive her for dumping him in South Africa when he was little more than a baby, and she was trying to solve her affair with Peregrine on the Gold Coast. Of course, Kelso had also needed her, then. And now, he wouldn't keep his food down. She had to spoon-feed him until his cheeks bulged, and it was no good, he would spit it out on the carpet. And she was guilty, as all mothers are always guilty about their children, whatever they have done all right.

Yet Peregrine was overriding as he had always been. This was no longer physical strength and beauty. This was the demand of deformity as mercy. She could not let him down. One never did, particularly not a war hero. That was what we were fighting for. And there was Boy.

The spare bedroom was Peregrine's now. She could get him to the hospital three times a week to check on his skin grafts. MacIndoe had to do another dozen operations to bring him up to scratch. And then he wanted to go flying again. He had nothing else to live for, he said. Or to die for.

He might have said he wanted to live for her, but he never did, as she lit and put in his mouth the packets of Players, which she begged and borrowed and stole to keep him somewhat sane. Lying in an old lounging chair in the bedroom with the wallpaper of poppies – "I would rather have died quickly in Flanders," he said – he would drone on between puffs and coughs, as if he blamed all his ills upon her. Occasionally, her eyebrows would rise and she would mutter to herself, "What I have to put up with," and go on putting up with it. This was her catch phrase, her version of Mrs Mopp on the Tommy Handley wireless show, "Can I do you now, sir?"

She could never do for Peregrine and his flailing at her and the void in him.

"You can't amuse me, woman," he shouted at her. "For fuck's sake, a laugh."

"Thin walls," she would say. "Boy's in the house. And Kelso."

"And whose boy is he?"

"Shut up. He might hear."

"I want him to hear. I want him to know." He shouted. "Whose boy is he?"

Bridget took the flannel in her hand which she was using to wipe up after him, and she gagged him with it.

"Do shut up."

He spat out the wet cloth.

"Don't you dare do that to me."

"Don't you speak like that."

"You tart. You mince tart. Fit to be a mother? I doubt it."

She would have slapped him, only his raw and shiny cheeks stopped her. So she burst into tears, instead. And weeping, she heard him say:

"Oh, for god's sake, Biddy, don't blub on me. I know what you're doing. I know how bloody hard it is on you. But roll on, roll on. Roll on the day, when I'm off your hands, and bloody well up in the air and flying again."

Yet rolling on was not that easy, the lifting of him, the cleaning of him, the wheeling of him to the hospital, the whole sad business of trying to get a burnt man well. There was little question of making love again, though she did what she could with her mouth for him, when he became too angry and desperate to deny. She hated it, not her way, even though she knew it was her fault, her puritan ignorance from the bush country. But she would do anything to give him a brief spurt of release, although he always swore at her afterwards, as if she were a whore.

When Tobruk fell, he really came back at her. The South Africans were there, and evidently, they would rather surrender to the Germans than fight them. Her cousin Piet was among the Allied Forces, who gave up without a fight, although the Coldstream Guards did not obey orders and picked up a few abandoned tanks on their way back towards Cairo, still trying to hold Rommel back.

"Nice ones in your family." Peregrine's grin in his seamy face was a corkscrew. "They would rather cop a plea with Jerry than fight the bastard. Mind you, I still think they are right. Who is the enemy, my friend? Really, who? The black or the red? Frankly, I'll still put all my stake on the *noir* in the old roulette of life. The *rouge* is a bad bet, even if it's an ally at the moment. It'll be a Zero Minus for us in the end."

Loyalty and wars, choosing sides if there was a choice, that had precious little to do with a mother who had two little boys. Surviving through rationing was her business. The coupons at the queues at Oliver and Gurden's for a slice of Madeira cake, the ogling of the butcher for a piece of old offal, the whole business was exhausting and degrading. Yet the worst moment was the gas-mask drill, when she forced the ghastly rubber head-piece with its metal snout over Boy's face, and she could feel his ribs gasping with fright and lack of breath, and the glass shield over his eyes misted up, and she ripped off the bestial rubber mask to stop him suffocating, and he coughed and coughed, then he lay quiet in her arms, and he said: "Do we have to...wear this?"

"If when the bombs come, there are gas bombs. Poison gas bombs. Then you will be safe."

"I can't breathe in that."

"You'll learn. I'll show you."

"I can't breathe in that."

So she had to put on the gas-mask, and even through the foggy eye-shield, she could see the fear on Boy's face at his banshee of a mother with her monster lover, terrifying and hiding all truth from the innocent and the small.

12

OPS ROOMS

Before his posting to the Burma front, Ian Hamish was given his final technical lesson by the Duty Controller in the ops room of the Royal Observer Corps at Post Easy 4 at Watford. He watched on the Long Range Board the Sea Plotter pushing a magnetic arrow in the direction of the air assault. Then a red-black-blue plaque was added, to show how many bombers this time, followed by a red disc, giving their height and speed. If our ack-ack or Spitfires downed a Nazi plane, the numbers changed on the position markers. Then when the missiles fell in their deadly rain, the grid reference of the attack was given to the Warning Officer for telephoning to the threatened Air Raid wardens and factory workers, not yet in their shelters. "Flash 83 cut!" That was a shout to alert the target.

The whole system still seemed to Ian something between playing tiddlywinks and victory. We were still using counters and stickers and billiard cues, when there should be radar screens and computer symbols. Surely, sighting the enemy while they were flying had won the Battle of Britain, but to treat the aerial bombardment as Francis Drake had dealt with the arrival of the Spanish Armada by playing bowls on Plymouth Hoe seemed a trifle out of date. Yet Gillon had also briefed him to wander over to Danesfield where the Photographic Interpretation Unit was based between Henley and Marlow. Perhaps they would be more removed from the playground. Anyway, Clio had booked them both in a hotel in Bray for a last night out, perhaps in years.

The view of the mock-Tudor greystone mansion confirmed Ian's worst fears of a false front overshadowing a new technology. But he was in error, as Gillon soon showed him. A blonde bombshell, Flight Officer Babington Smith, brought out photographs of German bunkers and hidden airstrips on the French sea coast. She even knew of his far-flung family, as a former Private Secretary to the Viceroy of India. Her trenchant analyses were derived from the Mosquito PR4s of 140 Squadron, also the camera-equipped Spitfire 11s of 400 Squadron. And now there was the new low-level-oblique photo reconnaissance, pioneered by the Americans in their Mustangs and

Lockheed Lightnings and Northrop P-61 Black Widows. And there was somebody whom Ian had to meet, so that he might take the developments out to the Army Photography Intelligence Units in Asia.

A squat balding man in a leather jacket with an American military cap was belching black smoke out of a pipe, as Ian saluted him. US Navy Commander John Ford lifted up a black patch over one eye to see Ian better.

"You off to Burma, kid?" he said.

"Yes, sir."

"Just been there. Left behind one of my best men. Carl Eifler and a camera crew. Find out where the Japs are, then bust 'em. Then we drop behind the lines with that crazy sonovabitch of yours. Wingate and his Crapshots. Or were they Bullshits?"

"Yes, sir."

"We done good here with the Field Photo Branch. Connie B-S, she showed you the Normandy takes?"

"Yes, sir."

"They're getting so good, I'll get them in the cinemas."

Ian Hamish dared to interrupt.

"As good as that shot under the horses and the axles in *Stagecoach*?"

Ford grinned.

"Aw, this is the best kind of movies. Like that Battle of Midway. You saw me there. That was for real. Not like that sonovabitch Roosevelt's son. I had to cut him in when he was the other side of the Pacific. Just to get billions more for the Navy from the President. It worked." Ford pointed at Ian. "Now you. Before you go, report to my man in the studios, Mark Armistead at Denham. He'll give you the latest mount to take out to Assam. Then we can even photo-shoot the height of a Jap bunker. If they don't shoot us, kid, that is."

Gillon tried to explain.

"We cannot open a Second Front in France without this detailed aerial photography. Do you know, the best we have on the Normandy beaches is pre-war postcards. Till Commander Ford came."

"Do you a deal," Ford said. "We save your asses in Europe again, like first time round. And you get out of Ireland."

"Good idea," Gillon said. "We'll leave the old sod to you and John Wayne, and never have a rainy day again."

Ian bummed a ride in a Jeep over to Bray, claiming a priority pass to Denham, which was not too far away. How Clio had got there first, he did not want to guess. But there she was in the dim light behind the black-out in the lounge, her beauty as a galaxy. Nobody would ever refuse her a lift, even to Hades. Particularly when she was in that electric mood of hers, nerves snapping and crackles and sparks seeming to leap from her skin.

"I don't know what I'm doing here, Ian. You said it was an emergency."

"I can tell you now. I'm posted to India. Night flight tomorrow, after I pick up something on the way."

"Why tell me so late? You still don't trust me."

"Commandos are dropped to help the Maquis in France. And they don't even tell their wives. Gone, gone. Nobody knows when they will be back."

"Don't you ever desert me without telling me. Or I'll be gone, gone. And I won't be back when and if you're back."

"Darling Clio," Ian said, "I am always surprised to see you ever again whenever I leave you. Now what's for our last supper?"

It was excellent. Somebody had shot or snared a wild plover duck off ration. And there was an old bottle of burgundy, dredged up at a price which would have gone a long way to pay off the National Debt. Ian had heard that the MTBs on their sorties to France brought back more claret than information, but then Winston Churchill needed his supplies of cognac, too. His going on, he said, was half due to brandy, the other half to his doctors.

There was one advantage in Ian's posting overseas. He could give over his bed-sit in Pimlico to Clio, and she could get out of the ornate flat with her mother Virginia and Ruth, who were becoming more and more impossible, as the war dragged on. They were threatened with requisitioning if they did not take in lodgers, and their old spirit of resistance was weakening due to the bombloads shoved from above.

"But I did see Rosabelle's show," Clio said. "She did something for ENSA out in a munitions factory in Cricklewood. I never knew she could strut her stuff so. You remember Snakehips Johnson and the blast – well, she could have fronted his band, belting it out. I saw her after. We get on now like a house on fire, since we began working with Joe Stalin."

"And the baby Rosa."

"Marie's dotty over her in the Scots castle. But Rosabelle can't get over Gordon's death on that Arctic convoy. There was one thing odd, though. Rudolf Hess, flying over."

"The whole thing was too bizarre. Hitler's Number Two, grabbing a Messerschmitt, to offer us peace."

"He was counting on that Marquess who Mummy and I used to know – he's now the Duke of Hamilton, and he was pally with Hitler. Hess thought that the Duke and those old pro-German friends of ours, they had enough clout to tell Churchill to make peace, so Adolf could clobber the Russians. And there's an even weirder story. Hess was looking for the Grail down the Esk at Rosslyn."

"I don't know," Ian said. "He was certainly off his head. I think the war is making us all insane."

Yet in the double bedroom, there was not enough madness. Ian did not rip off Clio's clothes in a frenzy of lust. She undressed in the bathroom with its 5-inch red line painted round the tub to show the limit permitted for the hot water. Their desire was equally tepid and low. Ian climbed on her and performed the act, as it was called. And she rolled to one side, and he held her small bottom in the lap of his stomach and his thighs. He could not hear her silent weeping, but only felt the tear drops on the palm of his hand lying under her cheek.

"Are you sorry I am going?"

"Yes... No... yes."

"Crying for me?"

"No. Me."

"Don't. I love you. I'll be back."

"I'm hopeless, Ian. I want to love you. But..."

"You can't."

"I do. But not..."

"Not like I love you." Ian sighed. "Is it still Peregrine?"

"No, no. But..."

Ian felt pain in his fingers. Clio was biting them, grinding them, tearing them with her teeth.

"Christ."

He pulled back his hand from under her cheek. He licked the blood off his thumb and the joints and the knuckles.

"What did you do that for, Clio?"

"I don't know." She rolled over and leaned on her elbow and looked down at him, her face a pale blur in the dark. "I do know. Pain. Can't you understand? You have to hurt to love. You can't do it. You're too bloody considerate. Who wants a sodding gentleman?"

Shankar had found it odd when they took Rangoon. He found no pleasure in walking into time past when he was meant to be leading the future. Behind the broken windows of the stores, there were the little firs of Christmas trees coated with talcum powder, because snow did not travel this far south, and anyway, why into a Buddhist country? In the looted bungalows, tatters of floral prints flew as regimental flags with the battle honours of buttercup and daisy, pansy and rose.

Broken rolled black umbrellas from elephant-foot stands and smashed mock-Delft china littered these Dunroamins-from-home. The British seemed to have carried more of their baggage with them than the Romans. And yet, the broken pieces smacked less of grandeur than gentility. The Coliseum was reduced to the suburbs of Aldershot.

Yet what was retaken from what was left behind? On his way to the dominant Shwe Dagun temple complex, which the British had used as a barracks, Shankar bought a wicked great cheroot of dried powdered tobacco wood, mixed with brown sugar and tamarind juice, and wrapped in a maize leaf. On the steps up to the golden pagoda, Shankar could not keep the vast cigar alight: it went out time after time. Aloft at last in the sunset, he saw pink mackerel clouds making friendly wind dragons in the sky and bathing the top of the pointed rising rings of the stupa in soft beaten gold. Bayonets had scraped the shining leaf in stripes off the Buddhas, which clustered round him. Yet one orange-robed monk was still selling fragile squares of the precious metal. Shankar purchased one to stick on a slash in a golden god of peace. It hardly showed on the dark wood. How would he patch up a foul war? So he bought a sparrow in a bamboo cage from another monk. The door was opened, the bird flickered off. For the price of a copper coin, he had deserved a long life, though he had little hope of that.

On the march north to Assam, Shankar's Indian National Army regiment fed mainly on the dumps which the Raj had abandoned on its retreat. These were tin mountains of bully beef, distilleries of Camp coffee bottles, sacks of dried peas. They did not rot in this heat like the corpses along the way, horses and mules, men and women and children, sprawling in a stench of carrion for the birds. To the fetid jungle odour of palm-tree toddy was added the sweet-sour smell of putrescent meat. Shankar choked and gagged a hundred times a day, and he did not know where to look if he were to keep his faith in some sort of divinity up there looking after the horrors of human nature.

They captured the oil-fields to fuel their own 95-type tanks, and the British could not pull out their silly Lees and Valentines and Stuarts, only one of which survived the battle on the Chindwin river, 'The Curse of Scotland'. Their Bren-gun carriers were still good and their 75 anti-tank guns, and in the air, Shankar could see more Spitfires against the Tojos and the Zeros. They would make a stand on the Imphal plain before the hills on the borders of India, but General Mutagushi had called up three divisions, and after starting the war against China in the Marco Polo incident and taking Singapore and

Burma, doubtless he would supersede the Mughal emperors and push his Indian ten thousand deserters and recruits all the way back to Delhi.

They had to grab the airfield at Palel first, if they were to get their supplies through. Shankar was covering with the Gandhi Brigade his Major Pritam Singh and his striking force. Stupidly, they had left behind their machine-guns and grenades for a forty-mile hike and a midnight attack. When they charged with bayonets, they found fellow Indians opposing them and surrendering. This was what should happen all over their country. But when another Captain Singh yelled out that he wanted to kill the British officers, he was gunned down and the raiders were forced to retire. The next day, artillery pounded the National Army positions, and they were forced to pull back. They had lost two hundred and fifty men. All they had proved was that their comrades were still obeying the orders of the Raj.

The next morning, Shankar was summoned to the HQ of his commander, Subhas Chandra Bose, by the Logtak Lake and swampland. Around him were the peepul and peach trees, teak and wild bananas and bamboos bending under their high plums. Lilac creepers clung to the branches above the purple of the iris and the white jasmine. Wagtail and snipe, duck and pigeon, navigated the reeds, while by the command tent, a krait slithered in its snaky iridescence away from his boots. Such luxury of nature in such a muddy war. Shankar could never understand how we loused up such a wondrous planet, or for what.

Bose had all the brittle arrogance of those who think they have power before they achieve it. Yes, he had been President of the Congress Party, Mayor of Calcutta, the leader of the Forward Bloc, the friend of Hitler and Mussolini. There was a fissure in his authority. He was not there yet.

"Colonel Shankar," he said. "We did not achieve our objective. Why?"

"Your plan, sir. We had no back-up. Our comrades did not join us. You said that they would."

"Our message has not reached them. We must destroy the enemy propaganda. Is not your brother — ?"

"Indeed, sir. He works for the Indian Civil Service. Have you been in contact?"

"I have my sources." Bose looked away towards the map of north-east India and Arakan on the wall. "I hear he may be at Imphal. With a certain Colonel Wingate. Do you know of him?"

"A little, sir. He is an expert in guerrilla warfare."

"Our information is that they plan operations behind our lines. They will not use Indian troops. Three divisions oppose us at Imphal, where the British artillery may shoot them, if they change sides. As in the Mutiny. The British shoot their friends, who change their minds."

"Did my brother tell you this?"

Bose did not answer.

"Redeploy your forces. Prepare to advance."

"They are dug in, sir. The rains are coming. All will be a swamp soon. Our supplies are inadequate. And our comrades are not deserting to us."

"You will not dare speak to me in that manner, colonel. I will reduce you to the ranks." Bose's eyes blazed in his corpulent face. "Our mentor Gandhi shook the Raj in his 'Quit India' campaign last year. Now we shall force them out. Dismiss."

Shankar saluted and left, without thinking that Bose was another Napoleon.

Before Imphal, the Seaforth Highlanders had been the first to stop the rot of the retreat from Burma. Dug in on the Shenam Saddle by the defending hills which they called after the African campaign, Gibraltar and Malta, Crete West and East, Cyprus, then Scraggy and Nippon Hill, their trenches were already little canals. Their first refugees had been the Rangoon Fire Brigade, a bunch of Tamils in pith helmets and soaked dignity. Then the Japanese recce parties had finally come, and the enemy had not proved too scary, retiring after a few rounds from the 3-inch mortar bombs. The Seaforths could not be outflanked this time. Like Wellington at Waterloo, they were in a square, defended on all sides, the Kohima Box. They would be supplied by Dakotas and big Commandos C-47s from the air. So they could fight to the last bunker, and sod the foe.

Ian Hamish had taken the new aerial camera mount out to Colonel Eifler, who approved it, and it did fit in. "Good boy," he said. "How did you like Jack Ford?" When Ian said he hardly knew him, Eifler laughed. "Jack's got two hollow legs," he said, "and he's made out of that hickory you soak bourbon through and he scares Washington even more than he scares the Japs, but he does a good job. He thinks an Oscar is a fifth of scotch with a pickle in it."

Eifler was using the photographic Mustangs and Mosquitos more to cover General Stilwell's Chinese army over the Hump, but he was also preparing the drops with Ian for the Strategic Service units and the Chindits behind the Japanese advance. Ian had to agree that the

British troops were hardly suited to the terrible work. The 13th King's Liverpool Regiment were garrison bods, and even a vicious three months' training under Calvert's Bush Warfare School had only turned them from knapsack porters into adequate riflemen. But there were the Gurkhas, too, and they and their *kukris* had a lot to avenge from Singapore. Going in with mules to carry their Vickers machine-guns and ammo, they were meant to reach their jungle outposts, if they could. Any sick or wounded must be dumped on the way. Their chief ops commander was a monocled Etonian Scots laird, Bernard Fergusson, whose lengthy drawl and height were as steely as a ramrod. Yet if any force could disconcert the Japanese, these misfits might.

When Solomon came to check with Ian the material needed for the drops, he found a shambling shabby figure there, his long arms slouching from his shoulders as an orang-outang. A sprouting black beard seemed to hang from his flap ears below his glaring eyes.

"Of course," the simian general was saying, "I don't bloody know where the bloody parachutes will land. I think we do. We've got W/T sets. The thing is, blanket the bloody ground. It doesn't matter a hoot if the Japs get them. Our men must."

So Solomon met Orde Wingate, and learned of the Chindit campaign to come.

"We're going in with bloody gliders next time, and then we'll catch them on the hop. We'll cut 'em off when we bash 'em back from Imphal. But supplies, supplies, that's the key. The Nips don't have any, they'll be beat. And we'll slosh the bastards, we'll cream 'em. You, whoever you are, you're the supply-wallah. I want to know what, when, how, precisely. Every list, every chit, everything, down to the last nut and bolt. And anything wrong, you're for the firing squad. Because a dozen of my men will be dead because of you."

Solomon saluted, and Wingate lurched away. He would be dead soon, when, in turbulence, his plane hit a hill. And nobody would ever know if his Chindits were any bloody good, though they certainly put the fear of God up the Japanese backside. The problem was, would the Indian divisions hold Kohima and Imphal, or would they break and defect?

"What do you think, Ian?" Solomon asked.

"They will hold. There is no alternative."

"They could join the other side. Free India."

"Once you know what the Japanese do to their prisoners, there is no alternative."

Solomon changed the subject.

"I had another letter from your mother. She is desperate to see you at Annandale."

"I am defending her here. No leave possible. You know what war is."

"She told me it was a device to keep mothers from their sons."

"Did she now?" Ian gave Solomon a bleak look. "And a device to keep a brother from a brother?"

"What do you mean?"

"You don't know. I think you do, Solomon. Where is Shankar?"

"I don't know."

"You do not?"

"I tell you, I don't know."

"Our intelligence says he's in the Indian National Army." Ian waved towards the tent wall. "Out there somewhere. Our people are coming to see you, Solomon. Be prepared."

"Ah." Solomon kept a blank face, but his lip twitched. "I am loyal, you know, to the –"

"Not to the Empire," Ian said. "Only to India. There is a difference."

"Yes," Solomon said. "Yes."

When Shankar and his men attacked Jail Hill and took Kohima's water supply, the prelude to the fall of Singapore, they had to fall back before the West Kents and take shelter from the artillery and vengeance and Hurribombers in the brick ovens of an old bakery. Then they were blown out of these by grenades and slabs of guncotton tied to the end of bamboo poles. Only twelve of the company survived with their officer. And the retreat began. Shankar was in the last stand on the greasy slopes of the heights of Modbung. Winched up the hills by Indian engineers, Shankar saw the British black iron juggernauts coming to squash him in his sodden pothole. He had been given the ultimate weapon, the German tich-bomb, a thick glass ball with prussic acid inside.

He squelched upright and slid down towards the armour spitting fire above him. The turning caterpillar tracks were rotors of death. "Ha!" he shouted and flung his poison capsule at the open turret, where the officer was standing, silly as a scarecrow. The missile burst in a white cloud, but Shankar caught a tracer bullet in the guts. His entrails exploded in another choking death, as he and the tank crew fell into darkness. Last words? Some ruddy Valentine.

13

MINEFIELDS

1944

Perhaps he was chosen to die. The *Firebug* was a doomed assignment. The technology dated from the days of the Classics and Drake and Nelson. Once the ancients launched Greek fire to burn the enemy or the Elizabethans sent out blazing ships to cast loose the Armada from its Flemish moorings, or Jack Tars lit Congreve rockets to ignite the wooden enemy. Now was worse. On planking boats, elementary mortars were set in ranks. They threw seven hundred and fifty one-ton bricks over a hellish half-acre, which would incinerate anything living within its circle of murder. The problem was that a single spark on the *Firebug* would send them all sky-high to smithereens and beyond. This was a stacked deck, as Wallace might say at poker.

Captain of his rocket-ship on D-Day on his terminal posting, Wallace was weary. At night, he had sailed with seven thousand ships, far more than had left to burn Troy, for the Normandy beaches. Blobs of cruisers and landing craft oozed over the oily darkness. Then the wind began to rise. He had not slept for forty-eight hours, and his eye-lids were trap doors. He handed over the wheel to his first mate Howell. The course was clear, a hinge round the minefields towards Honfleur with a monster fleet as a guide. Even a moron could not miss out. Wallace hit the sack in his cabin.

Four hours later, he was ambushed from his drugged doze by Howell in a panic. "We've lost the whole lot sir. There must be something wrong with the W/T." Wallace could hardly move or see. His thoughts were lead sinkers in his skull. He dragged his boots up to the bridge. "Christ," he said. They were all alone in the middle of the Channel. They had mislaid the largest sea invasion force in history. "Sod you, Howell," he said. "This is impossible." Yet it had been done and he had to do something about it.

He had special charts, which his cousin Murdo had made available. There was a minefield between him and the beaches, named Magdalene. That was where all sinners blew up, Wallace thought, before they went to heaven or hell. The question was simple. Did he

risk the mines to save his honour and his command and get to the
shore on time, to squirt off his bricks? Or did he skirt the killing waves
like the rest of the assault ships and so not endanger the fourteen
members of the crew aboard? As for himself, his life wasn't worth a
damn. But how answer for those other souls in his care?

"I'll take over, Howell. You sod off to your bunk. It'll probably be
your grave."

He steered through the Magdalene. He was putting his pride before
the flesh and blood on board. Or did he put his fear first, his terror of
ridicule? No time for motives now, just the navigation. Overhead, a
swarm of red stars had overcome the galaxies, the lights of bombers
and gliders flying towards the south. The sparks on the bows from the
black breakers were phosphorescence, not the crackling of the horns
on the end of a magnetic mine.

At dawn, the *Firebug* was on station at the end of the line. The first
salvo the ship lobbed inland towards Caen hit a Mosquito diving down
into the fatal parabola. That was the bright incandescence in the air
before the huffing and detonating tent of smoke and flame rising on
the shore. Around him, the seven other floating battle-waggons were
sending off their curtains of fireworks. They were as much in danger
from our tracer bullets from above as from the few Messerschmitts
diving in and out before they were shot down.

Wallace was too tired to imagine much. Yet seeing the vast
spreadeagle of the ships and troops and bunkers and artillery flashes, a
great operation to reconquer a continent, he still could think of the
enemy as well as his own sad self, a pompous prick, who had really
put his ship in hazard to kill *en masse*. One hit, and they were all dead
in a pyre like a Viking ship funeral. But his volleys of bricks, who was
burned, what was roasted? German soldiers, certainly, but Jersey cows,
barns, sheep, Norman farmers, foxes, a wasteland of cinders where
green had been.

When he sailed home, Murdo was there to talk to him, or to
debrief him. Or to recommend he was sent to Marie's convalescent
home. There was a bottle of Haig whisky between them on the table,
which was a solace of sorts, in tumblers.

"You did a good job," Murdo said. "There wasn't too much
resistance on the beaches. Till we got near Caen."

"Did they have gas-masks?" Wallace asked. "I mean, the smell.
That fry-up – it must have been awful."

"Don't think about it. That's not up your alley. But there was
something interesting. Your ship's log. Your boat went straight across

my minefield. That's why I have been sent down to see you. You took a direct approach, but perhaps too direct."

"You want the truth or the official version?"

"As blood and kin, the truth. The official version is up to me."

"Do you believe, Murdo?"

"In God. Of course I don't go to church much. But in a war, rather more. It seems, if we have any salvation, we should look up there."

"I agree." Wallace screwed up his eyes as if searching for something inside him. "God knows why I did it. I suppose I didn't want you all to laugh at me. I had a kip, my mate lost the whole bloody D-Day fleet. So I sailed across your minefield to catch up. I should have lost my ship."

Wallace looked at him and shook his head.

"What a choice."

"The worst of my life. A *moral* choice. What is worse than that? Or was it just vanity? Hardly something to be left behind on, the whole big bang against France. I don't sleep too well now, but I am not cracking up. You will not recommend I lose my command and send me to funny farm."

Murdo gave an odd laugh, the sound of dry bracken breaking.

"I supervised that map, Wallace. That Magdalene minefield. We did not have enough mines to lay. So we drew on our charts a false minefield. It wasn't there. A figment, or a fig-leaf. But it made all the German U-boats and destroyers sail round it, as well as us. We dropped off the details for them in a dead sailor's life-jacket which washed up with him after the Dieppe raid. They believed it. So did you."

"You mean ..." Wallace tried to laugh, but he could not make it. All he managed was gasp, gasp, gasp. Murdo waited for him to speak.

"You mean, my great moral choice ... No minefield, nothing really there ... So I wasn't dicing with death ... I didn't risk my men ..." Wallace shook the greening brass badge on his navy cap. "I was safe all the time. We were just playing games."

"No," Murdo said. "You performed well at Normandy. You are confirmed as captain of your ship."

"You bastard," Wallace said.

Murdo rose to go.

"Bastards win wars. Nice guys are for the peace. Whenever."

To his Fitzrovian friends, Hamish Henry had to confess that the house in Bentinck Street was rather a buggers' muddle. Given a war on, many of the comings and goings were involuntary. With all the short leaves and sudden postings and the GIs in their tight pants and the passing sailors in their bellbottoms, romance was indeed a brief and bruising encounter. Walking past the bombed Café de Paris with its outdoor notice: DANGER – UNSAFE PREMISES by the tarnished promises of Piccadilly and Rainbow Corner to the packed Swiss and the French and the Wheatsheaf pubs with the serial groping and the rubbing in the musk of beer and gin and chit-chat, Henry still could not join in those furtive quickies. To tell the truth, he was afraid of strangers, of being hurt. He preferred to wander past the NAAFIs and hear the singing of 'Lili Marlene' and 'Deep Purple' and 'That Lovely Week-End' and outside the gay Golden Lion, 'He'll be Wearing Silk Pyjamas when he Comes.'

Back in Henry's room in Bentinck Street, he had to surrender his Bletchley know-how to Kim Philby and Guy Burgess and the other double-agents in our Intelligence, who at least found some humour in the drab fag-end of the war. Guy used to cruise almost nightly, even after he was trapped by a copper in the lavatory below Sloane Street with a somebody in a red jacket and riding britches who claimed to be a Mountie. With his charm and the bribe of a carton of Craven A, Guy sauntered from under what he said was a cloud no bigger than a man's hand.

If any conscience about spying for the Russians tweaked at Henry's nerves, he quickly shut off the irritation. Often in the house was Professor Bernal, a known Communist, who still managed to be chosen by Lord Mountbatten to work on Combined Operations with General Eisenhower. For that was what D-Day was. The Second Front had at last been opened to relieve pressure on the Russian front, where the Red Army was now advancing after Stalingrad. Henry had even been complimented by his Comrade Professor from Cambridge, the cultured Anthony Blunt, for passing on details of German air attack plans, culled from Enigma.

"You should get a Red Star and bar, dear boy. You had a lot to do with winning the tank battle of Kursk."

Henry managed to see his mother Ellen-Maeve from time to time. To stop the flat being requisitioned, she had moved into Clio's room beside Virginia and Ruth, although the three ageing women could hardly tolerate each other. Rationing and double taxation had destroyed their pretensions to superiority and class. Like everybody else, they scrabbled around to try to keep themselves warm and fed. If anyone began the litany of "Before the war," the end result was tears and curses. Ellen-Maeve was even drafted to work on an Assembly

Line of thingummibobs to make ends meet, not that they ever would meet again. Instead of cocktail sticks, her swollen fingers had to struggle with screws and fittings. She wore a turban like the rest of the girls, because she couldn't get a perm.

"Look," she said, showing her callouses and broken nails to her son. "I can't even go out with those in that state."

"There's nowhere to go out to, mother."

"You go out."

"Not where you would like to go out to."

"And I've nothing to wear. These Utility clothes they're talking about. No pleats, no pockets, straight down with a belt. Can you imagine? I in them. And they cost coupons."

Henry had to agree with her.

"It's a far cry from Fortuny."

"It doesn't matter to you. You can look like any old scruff-bag."

"Actually, I can't, at the Ministry."

"Anyway, you got your poor dead father's best clothes."

"But he was shot down in the last war."

"I know. But they made things to last then. They don't now. Do you know, I have to put blacking on my legs because I haven't any more stockings, even to darn. Have some tea."

"Yes, please. You've got some?"

"I got a food packet from Annandale. That's all I ever get from there. What an inheritance, don't you think? It was very smart of Ruby to get out there, while she still could, and live off the fat of the land. She always had her eyes on the main chance."

The tea table was new and extremely odd, being a steel oblong with wire mesh down the sides like a ferret cage.

"Don't look at it like that," Ellen-Maeve said. "It's that cowardy-cat Virginia. Ever since those buzz-bombs began falling on us, she said we had to have a Morrison shelter. Can you imagine we three old biddies squashed like sardines in that tin box? I said to her, I said, I'd rather be blown to bits by a V-1 than cuddle up to your bony knees. But Ruth doesn't mind, of course. She's been doing that to Virginia for years."

"I don't bother about those doodlebugs," Henry said. "I mean, we just carry on regardless. If their engine cuts out above you, of course, you hit the deck. But otherwise, it's more dangerous to cross the street in front of a Number 41 bus."

"Yes, Henry, but you never know where they're going to land."

"Not on you, mother. Not on you."

In spite of this reassurance, the keening of the air raid sirens flushed Ruth and Virginia out of their bedroom in their faded flowered house-coats. They scuttled in and lifted the mesh and crawled under the steel defences.

"Don't mind us," Virginia said in her withering way.

"I don't mind you at all," Henry answered. "Mother and I will finish our tea."

The whole affair was more like *Comic Cuts* than *Heartbreak House*, although a flying bomb did actually drop fairly near the two women scampering to be safe. The blast down the road blew in a window, shredding the calico across the frame with splinters of glass. Henry suffered a small cut on his left hand, but Ellen-Maeve was unscathed. She had certainly more guts than her flat-mates. All she said was, "Oh dear, more to clean up in the morning. Let's have another cup of tea."

Gillon was almost as fortunate at the Sunday Service at the Guards Chapel at Wellington Barracks by Buckingham Palace. There had been no warning as he came down to Birdcage Walk past St James's Park with all the iron railings gone to make tanks, or so it was said. Most of the ducks had vanished from the ponds, ending up in the Brigade Officers' Mess. Yet even the doodlebugs could not stop the leaves turning green, and the grass. Nature was rather stubborn, really.

The Bishop of Maidstone was officiating at Matins, while the Commanding Officer of the Grenadiers, Lord Edward Hay, was tricked out in his scarlet best to lead the congregation in their worship. Gillon was standing at the back during the First Lesson, and he heard this passage read by the Chaplain of the Brigade from Ecclesiastes:

> "To every thing there is a season, and a time to every purpose under the heaven.

> "A time to be born, and a time to die: a time to plant, and a time to pluck up that which is planted.

> "A time to kill, and a time to heal: a time to break down, and a time to build up..."

Gillon's thoughts drifted away to the low stone ceiling of the Georgian military chapel. His marriage had broken down, Rachel had left him, his son Colin was long dead, he would never see his daughter Fiona in Canada again. There was only Leah left in Palestine, and here was Ecclesiastes speaking to him with the wisdom of ancient Israel, which Leah was trying hopelessly to restore again in Jerusalem.

"A time to get, and a time to lose: a time to keep, and a time to cast away.

"A time to rend, and a time to sew: a time to keep silence, and a time to speak.

"A time to love, and a time to hate: a time of war, and a time of peace..."

What was that engine in the sky, the noise of a Jeep backing up a hill?

"What profit hath he that worketh in that..."

The chug-chug above had cut out. There were fourteen seconds left before the explosion. Everybody knew that, but no one was moving. The Chaplain had dried up in his words from the Bible. All looked at heaven, but nobody dropped down. Then there was the rush and the swoosh and the thunderbolt and the blast and the fire and the screaming and the collapse of the roof and the walls upon them in the place where God might have saved them, but He could not or did not.

Gillon found himself choking and gagging face-down under plaster and stinging clinging dust. He forced his back up against the rubble and knelt and shook himself to his feet. Round him in the shattered blocks of stone lay the bleeding dead and the crying of the dying. Spores floated through the sunbeams as far squadrons. He coughed and stumbled towards the end of the chapel. Gloved arms reached at him from a woman without legs. "Help me, help me, oh God, mercy, God..." A gory bearskin was a rugby ball at his feet. Two of the columns still stood in the fug and the fog of the débris. And on the altar, a legend: BE THOU FAITHFUL UNTO DEATH AND I WILL GIVE THEE A CROWN OF LIFE.

Gillon would never forget his luck or grace that Sunday, but time would break down for his cousin at Walcheren. Wallace's transfer from the *Firebug* did not come through so he might work on the floating Mulberry Harbour B at Arromanches. He was on duty with the surviving fireworks factories off the dank Netherlands island, where the Germans were dug in strength to stop the Allied supplies reaching Antwerp for the final push into the Reich. Also the attack had to put down the last of the launching sites of the flying bombs, the big V-2s. The sky was glum, rainstorms were wet blankets, the landing-craft were open sewers, the whole strategy was soggy. But that didn't dampen the launching of the explosive bricks. They swept in their nasty arcs through the streaming skies and lit their pyres on the mud of the island. But who were they mourning? Himself, as Wallace knew they would. The burst from the Messerschmitt which hit the rocket-ship was a torch of vengeance. The detonation might be heard as far as Dover. In that instant of incandescent apocalypse, Wallace was seared to a crisp, with nothing to say.

14

A SCALDED CASE

"Don't have illusions." Arabella Plunkett-Drax was adamant to Bridget. "Some men do marry their nurses, if they have to. But being grateful is not one of Peregrine's qualities. And anyway, my son – with a penniless colonial with two small boys. It's a joke. Why do you go on looking after him?"

Bridget's scowl set her face in a mud pack.

"Because he needs me."

"And your boys? They don't"

"I can look after three men."

"I suppose it's an extra ration-book. But I have come to take him away."

"Where to?"

"Ireland. We have no rationing there. But I do thank you for what you have done."

"I think you have come too late," Bridget said. "Peregrine will never go back to Ireland. He hates it, what you did to him there. His future is here."

"With you?"

"With or without me, he'll stay. You ask him." She called up the stairs. "Peregrine! Your mother wants to see you."

The two women sat in silence, listening to the slow clump-clump-clump down the treads outside the sitting-room. They watched the sparks make galaxies stuck on the soot at the back of the chimney and the coal fire. Then the stars went out, and Peregrine came into the room. He was wearing his old pilot's uniform with its leather jacket. His red face was smooth and veined. Only around the twists of his lips did small scars line his glossy skin.

"Mama," he said, "what an honour." Arabella rose to kiss him on the cheek, but he flinched away. "Don't touch, Arabella. Still a bit sensitive." He limped to the large chair and used the arms to lever himself down to its seat. "I'm almost human, don't you think, my darlings?"

Tears were making streaks down Arabella's mascara and powdered cheeks.

"You are looking splendid, Peregrine." Arabella dabbed at her eyes. "I have come to take you home."

"Home, mama? I haven't had one for ever and a day."

"Home is where your mother is."

"Not till now. And you don't have one, except that boghouse by the burned Big House on our old estate. Do you know what home is in a war, mama? Home is a bottle of gin, a packet of fags, one night's sleep in clean sheets in a month. Home? You can't have one till this bloody mess is all over."

"Ireland's safe. I can take you out of it until you're really well."

"I'll never be really well, mama. I never was. But what I'm going to do will make me really well."

Bridget was looking at him with her fierce blue gaze.

"I am going to fly again. It's being fixed for me. Murdo is being quite a help. I am a hero, you see, as well as a guinea-pig. I am not a Bader, that chap who flies with no legs. But I am the pink steak on your plate, which you can't get on coupons. They're going to give me the latest fighter, the Meteor, a jet plane, brand new. The Jerries have got some, and I'll take them on. Back from the dead. The new knight of the skies. Bloody wonderful propaganda, don't you know. Your son, mama, born again. As a patriotic gift to the nation."

Arabella could not see for her tears, but she managed to cough and say, "You cannot let him, Bridget. For god's sake, stop him."

"Nobody can stop Peregrine doing anything." Bridget's tone was dry. "He always does what he wants. He always has. You didn't stop him when he was a child, did you?"

Peregrine hacked out a laugh.

"Oh, shut up, you two. You can't tell a young monster like me what to do. You know what we used to sing at the Old Queen Vic Hospital at East Grinstead, when Archy MacIndoe had got through carving us up for the nth time?"

His guttural voice slurred out a song to the tune of 'The Church's One Foundation':

> "We are MacIndoe's Army,
> We are his Guinea Pigs.
> With dermatomes and pedicles,
> Glass eyes, false teeth and wigs.
> But when we get our discharge
> We'll shout with all our might –
> 'Per Ardua ad Astra,
> We'd rather drink than fight'."

Peregrine gave another grimace.

"Well, as there is no drink, I would rather fight. I'll get on those Meteors and prang a Jerry or two. And come back to –"

"What?"

"I thought I might be an MP. Not a bad spot for making things happen. And they'd have to adopt me, I mean, with my war record. And my *suffering*, if I have at all, at all."

"You are not serious," Arabella said. "Who would you stand for?"

"Hitler," Bridget said, "may not be available soon. Perhaps Churchill will do."

"No, no, no, no." Peregrine smiled. "Old Winston's going to be clobbered next time round. I am going to be a Labour candidate. We will romp home."

The words choked in Arabella's mouth, but she managed to speak.

"Dear boy, you are too absurd. With a record like yours before the war, what constituency would ever select you?"

"Wars, my darling Arabella, wipe the slate clean. All the committee members will see is a charred celebrity, fresh from the struggle in the clouds and a make-up job by Fleet Street. They will know I will mop up votes like a Hoover. Any marginal seat I fight will be a majority of thirty thousand pity votes. Any party will beg to have me on their list. And I am choosing the winning side."

"But you don't believe a word Labour's saying." Bridget's voice was faltering. "Nationalization. Take over coal and steel and the railways. You can't want that."

"I'll vote the ticket, Biddy. Then I'll have what I want. To be in power. That's the ticket for me."

"It always has been. Power for you."

"Yes. It always will be." The telephone began to ring in the hall. Peregrine slowly pushed himself upright. "That'll be for me. The Air Ministry. A training course for the jets." He moved slowly from the room, leaving the two women to look after him.

"You've ruined him," Arabella said. "He used to listen to me."

"He never did," Bridget said. "You ruined him before he left school."

There was a knocking at the front door. Bridget had a perfect excuse to get rid of Arabella.

"My boys," she said, "back from school. And I'll see they won't become sons like yours."

She fled towards the hall, where Peregrine was putting down the telephone.

"Worcester," he said. "Thursday. I'll tell you more later, when you have dealt with the brats."

He did tell her more later about his transfer, when he had whipped her with his brown leather crop, and made love to her. She bit her mouth so the boys would not hear her moan through the bedroom walls. She submitted, and she did not know why. He needed it, and so he needed her, only her. And in that need of only her lay her hope of keeping him.

Before the General Election in 1945, Peregrine had achieved what he wanted. In a Gloster Meteor of 616 Squadron, he worked out a new technique against the last of the flying bombs. Out of ammo, he flew beside a pilotless missile and flipped it out of control with his wingtip, so it missed Croydon and crashed uselessly in a hayfield, destroying some worms and a stoat. "Easy as playing tiddlywinks," he was reported to say, and his words and his grinning disfigured image in a leather helmet were plastered all over the press. His adoption as the Labour candidate for Netherbampton was a shoo-in. Relieved of duty, he hardly had to campaign when the election was called that summer. He joined a landslide Labour majority in the House of Commons, which sang 'The Red Flag' upon its victory. Peregrine did not say that he probably knew the Horst Wessel song rather better.

Although the war against Japan was grinding on, Ian Hamish was sent home after the recapture of Burma. He had tried to visit his mother Ruby, still stuck at Annandale, but there was no transport to get him there, not enough leave between his orders. He was returning to a London which he hardly knew after the defeat of Germany and the change of government from Churchill to Clement Attlee. There was a violent shift of opinion, of course, the people wanted quick answers and reconstruction, but the austerity was worse. We seemed to have lost the war about living well, and peace was a queue for the hand-outs from a bare larder.

Clio was not at home. Indeed, she seemed to have moved from his room, which was dusty and full of fug and smells. The gas and electricity were cut off. His letter to her from Burma lay unopened among the unpaid bills. She had left no forwarding address. She had done a flit. If she was to be found, he would have to look in their old stamping-grounds. Even her mother Virginia did not know where Clio was, and the Ministry had discharged her as unreliable. So Ian Hamish to the dark Soho went to trawl for his lost love.

Opposite the French pub, St Anne's Church behind its square spire had been reduced to a cesspool. On the black waters floated a miniature D-Day fleet of French letters. Inside the pub, the squash was worse than an army mess hut. And a new riff-raff was taking over. There were few Americans and Canadians now with their tight uniforms and breezy bonhomie. Ian saw strangers in slouch hats, deserters or black marketeers hiding their faces. Amputees or twitchers in the corner, running away from psychiatric hospital or discharged too soon for lack of space. And the first of the rootless demobbed in awful shiny suits, not knowing how to live or what to do, but trying to latch on to the old artistic boozers, wasting their talents on a flood of free froth.

Ian found Clio in the Marquis of Granby at a booth with a wide boy in a striped suit so loud it looked like the prophecy of prison bars. Two red flushes were flares in her pale cheeks. She was jerking about on her chair as if an electric hare on a dog track.

"Clio," Ian said, when he had squeezed himself up to them. "Long time, no see."

"Ian?" There was a glaze in Clio's extraordinary eyes. "Ian? You are Ian?"

"I was Ian. May I?" He slid onto the low bench beside her, and explained to her companion. "Old friends, we are."

"You'd better be," was the answer. "You weren't asked."

"Vic is rather touchy," Clio said. "He thinks you may be a copper or a nark – to use his language."

"Still Army," Ian said. "And did you serve?"

"Better things to do," the other bloke said. "Supplies. I'm a supplier, squire. What's missing, if you know what I mean."

"What's missing," Clio said, "is missing usually because Vic supplies it later."

"You stuck-up cow, I'll –"

As the bloke raised a hand to slap, Ian leant over and caught it. Training on reflexes in camps did have a use.

"Don't think of it," Ian said and forced the raised arm against the table. "How are you, Clio?"

"Getting by," she said. "Isn't everybody?"

"I'll do you," the bloke said, pulling his wrist free.

"Can I do you now, sir?" Ian repeated the catch phrase. "No, you can't. You'll never do me. Clio, shall we get out of here? If we can."

The press around the booth was suffocating and the din noisier than a *blitzkrieg*.

"She can't go," the bloke said. "We haven't finished our business."

"Right," Clio said. "You're back then, Ian?"

"Yes. For good, I think. Or good and bad. You left the flat and your job."

"Had to, ducks. There's a time, you know, in a girl's life – Too many shortages. You can't put up with nothing any more."

"The war has gone on a bit."

"Any more bloody coupons," Clio said, "and I would have flipped my lid. Feel my leg under the table." As Ian stroked the top of her silk stockings, his groin itched. "You've got to have some clothes. Booze – and other things. Vic's a supplier, as he says."

"Spiv. Isn't that the word now?"

"Me, you bastard." The bloke was indignant. "I'm a merchant. In the free economy. No restrictions. You want it, I get it. Cash down. What's wrong with that?"

"Nothing," Ian said, "depending on the price. What do you pay, Clio? What with?"

"Does it matter?" she said. "The war's so dreary. Let's have a laugh. Kicks. Come on, Vic. Pull it out."

From under the table as a rabbit from a hat, Vic brought up a bottle of Gordon's gin.

"Here," he said. "No hard feelings." He filled up the tumbler in front of Clio. "You share hers, if you're old pals, like you says."

Ian took a swig of the gin, which was a jolt in the mouth.

"Whoo," he said. "Who's who? Come home, Clio. We'll start again."

"Can't," Clio said. "Otherwise engaged, or I would."

"Who to?"

"Can't say."

"Where can I get you?"

"Here. Round here. No fixed abode."

"Oh, come home."

"When I can."

"There," the bloke said. "Don't push it."

"And what are you doing, Ian?" Clio asked.

"Not much," Ian said. "Until the war's really over and I get de-mobbed. But something's happened. I'm sorry to say, a slim volume." He dug in his pocket to produce a small paperback. On its maroon cover, the lettering: FROM THE BURMA FRONT by Ian Hamish Ogilvie. "Grey Walls Press. They've still got paper." He put it in Clio's hands. She flicked through the sparse pages and stopped at one poem and read out:

Their eyes run out in cheese,
And in the scented breeze,
Savouring the toast,
I smell their innards roast.

Clio slapped the book shut.

"How horrid. Do you have to shock like that to sell?"

"It was like that in Burma," Ian said. "When we pushed the Japs back. Rotting corpses all along the track."

"But do you have to tell us?"

"If you weren't there, why not? Perhaps you should know."

"I don't want to know," Clio said. "I didn't ask for there to be a war. It's all your fault. Men like you."

"Let's blow," the bloke said. "Got to see a geezer in the Wheat-sheaf." He touched his forefinger to his nose. "Hush, hush. Ta, ta for now." He rose and yanked Clio upright, her thighs pushing back the table top.

"I'm sorry," Ian said, also rising. "We didn't talk."

"Wartime departures." Clio spoke with the solemn voice of a jar too many. "They are often not on schedule."

Ian watched her struggle off in her white fur jacket as a vixen among a pack of hounds. A glass cracked in his heart.

"Hell, hell, hell," he mumbled, and he knew he was in hell, and he had long been there.

The evening of V-J Day in the flat in Bentinck Street was no celebration. The cloud no bigger than a man's hand, which had once threatened Guy Burgess, now menaced all of Russia under its spreading mushroom radiation. The Kremlin did not have an atomic bomb, while Washington did. In a confrontation, Omsk and Tomsk might suffer the fate of Hiroshima and Nagasaki. The comrades would be obliterated, the capitalists laugh all the way to the bank.

"It's utterly immoral," Hamish Henry said.

"Until we have it," Guy said and patted Henry on the knee. "Then it becomes floral. A bouquet to drop on Harry Truman –" he began to sing – "oh, what's he doin', that Harry Truman, we'll send him off to Auschwitz now."

"You are a pig, Guy. About as sensitive as a turnip."

"Insensitive? *Moi?* There's a fetching little waxwork show just down the way in Oxford Street. For only a tanner you can see 'The Horrors of the Concentration Camps' in all their gory details. That's the wonderful thing about our culture, Henry. We reduce abomination to a sideshow."

Many came through the door that morose night, the Professors Bernal and Blunt, the diplomats Donald Maclean and Kim Philby, the intelligence operators John Cairncross and Leo Long, and Jack Hewit, whom Guy had picked up when a chorus boy in *No No Nanette*. They seemed to have been summoned by their chief contact, the Czech diplomat Otto Katz, although he was unlikely to risk a meeting with so many of his chief agents and sympathizers. Yet there they all were in a huddle in the front room, assessing the disaster to come, what had to be done. Glasses were passed round. Guy even put on a red paper hat. If this Party meeting were discovered, they would have to be at a victory party.

"Gentlemen," Katz said, "we have business. You know of Tube Alloys?"

"Yes," Philby said. "It's the dummy for our nuclear fission project. I have contacts there. We have them in the Manhattan Project, do we not?"

"Not enough," Katz said. "One from here. But you, Donald, as you can arrange anything –"

"Except a change of sex," Guy said. "He'd make a wonderful old woman."

Maclean blushed at the insinuation, but said nothing.

"You, Donald," Katz went on, "you will accept what you will be offered, the post of First Secretary at your Washington embassy."

Maclean was astounded.

"How do you know I will be given the job?"

"You will," Guy said, "you will. Otto knows everything except the back of his own head, where his secret thoughts cluster, invisible to us."

"And you, young man," Otto was staring at Hamish Henry, "when your job at Bletchley is finished, you will arrange to join the nuclear physicists and Cockroft, when he is recalled from Canada to head the British programme here. You are a Cambridge man, are you not?"

"Most of us are," Hamish Henry said. "Like your Peter Kapitsa. We sent him back to you, and you kept him. For your own atomic work."

"So?" Katz said. "The proletariat never has enough scientists in the right places."

"Oh, I don't know," Guy said. "Whenever I look round this room, all I hear is scratch, scratch, scratch – the sound of other little moles wanting to burrow in and join us. After all, our victory is inevitable, isn't it? Scientifically proven by good old dialectical materialism."

Again he started singing to the tune of the Eton Boating Song.

> "Jolly Kremlin weather
> And a red harvest breeze
> We'll all betray together
> Our country between our knees ..."

"Shut up, Guy." Blunt was acidic. "Comrade Katz does not confuse ideology with your sense of humour. You need a purge. Only of your wit, of course."

So the plots and stratagems meandered on, until Hamish Henry excused himself. He had a rendezvous, he said, not with destiny, but with his cousin Ian, fresh from the Far East with all the latest intelligence. He would be early for that meeting, but he felt too sad to stick around. Even though we had a Socialist government, Ernie Bevin had been made Foreign Secretary. And as Bevin had spent his whole life battling the comrades in the Trades Unions, he wasn't going to give way to the Red Army in Europe. In power, all poachers turned gamekeepers. And given the power of the Americans, Bevin also might pull the atomic trigger on the Volga.

Henry found Ian at a table at the Café Royal once again. The time before, they had been afraid during the Phoney War, and they had deplored the Nazi-Soviet pact. Now all was noise and balloons marked *V-J DAY* and shrieks and joyful shouts and the usual surly waiters, so bitchy and anaemic that they could not be called up. Ian had managed to snaffle a whole bottle of Sancerre for them, but then he had always been better at getting hold of the drink than his own beliefs.

"Heigh ho, Henry. Have a glass."

Noise rose in splinters scraping at their talk.

"Several," Henry said and drained his first glass. "It must be a special treat for you. You were out there on the Burma front. Knocking off the Japs before you fried them at Hiroshima."

"I fry them?" Ian smiled. "I spy them. Bombing is not my personal game."

"Well, our side fried them."

"Our side? Oh, come on, Henry, don't I spy a pink persuasion still fluttering in your winds of change?"

"You were always poetical, Ian. And congratulations on your Grey Walls verses. Both gory and agreeable. We all think war is vile. We all want peace. But now we've got it, do we really want it?"

"We haven't got a peace," Ian said. "You know that. You specially would know that. And do we want what we've got? I don't think so." He filled Henry's glass from the wine bottle. "Stalin's being very difficult, even though he's been given Eastern Europe. He didn't help us against Japan, except to come in at the end and grab a few Jap islands. You can't say he's exactly the best friend of democracy, and all that."

"Oh, screw politics," Henry said. "Let's drink to victory, whatever that is. People don't know why they ever fight a war, or whose side they are on. You have to win. We did. There'll be other wars. Which side?" He emptied his glass again. "I hope there's more of this stuff. And I hope, the next war –"

"There can't be one."

"I hope the next war, Ian, we're on the same side. I'll tell you why. Blood, they say, is thicker than slaughter. We are blood and kin, at the end of the bloody day. And we are, at least, a drinking family. Can I have some more?"

Ian filled his glass again, and Henry raised it. "This is my toast, and not to V-J Day. It's to blood." He clinked his glass against his cousin's one. "Blood is thicker than even alcohol."

"I'll get some more," Ian said, "if I can ever get a bloody waiter." He rose to snap his fingers at some vanishing server. "Oh my god, Clio!"

Weaving through the carousing throng, Clio was appearing in a spangled short frock left over from the 'thirties. This was the sort of dress ripped from your shoulders in Paris as a collaborator. No coupons there, but a flaunting of your assets. Clio slammed herself down on the spare seat at the table.

"I didn't expect you to come." Ian said.

"I was invited."

"I still didn't expect you to come."

"You're a pessimist." Clio pinched Ian's cheek to make him squirm. "You hate me being outrageous."

"Oh, you know. Shocking the bourgeosie." Ian stroked his cheek to make it straight. "That's what you've always done."

He finished the bottle in his glass and gave it to Clio.

"I'll get you some more when I can."

"You've seen me perform before," Clio said. She stood and shimmied in her glitter and put her fingers in her mouth and gave a whistle like an express train. Everybody gawped at her, and a waiter shouched forward.

"Another bottle of Sancerre, my man. And shifty."

She sat down and smiled sweetly.

"As we were saying?"

"Christ, Clio," Ian said, "you make it impossible to be seen with you."

"Why, darling? The revolution's not quite come. We aren't hanging from the lampposts yet." She turned on Henry. "Your red lot is a soft lot. All those big words." She bellowed. "We are the masters now! You are lower than vermin!" Again all eyes were looking at her, but she reverted to a stage whisper. "But in your infinite mercy, Henry, we still exist. In fact, you don't dare get rid of us. You think you've won, but you've lost. History will squash you, like the beetles you are."

Ian put his hand over Clio's wrist, forcing its quiver against the table.

"You're over the top, darling."

"I always am."

The waiter was already coming back towards them with another green bottle. Perhaps he wanted to avert a scandal.

"You're very effective," Ian said to her, and to the waiter. "Thank you. And get us the bill."

"I hope you can pay for it," Clio said.

"I can't. But I will."

Ian began filling the glasses again, while Clio turned on Henry.

"What are you going to do, now the war's over."

"Back to science, I suppose. And you, Clio?"

"That's a laugh. Do what a girl's always done. Lie back, don't enjoy it, till some stupid bugger marries you. You really had it good during the war, you dozy lot. Regular pay, pub bash every night, no bloody women, no responsibility, no children, no chores, just being bloody heroes once in a blue moon when you had to fight the foe. And what were the women doing? Running the factories, bringing up the kids, starving on the rations, and no medals for it. Not even any ribbons."

"Not quite like you, Clio," Ian said. "Hardly your war."

"I quit in time," Clio said. "What are you going to do, Ian?"

"I don't know. Publishing, I think."

"Then you can publish yourself."

"Not quite. There are lots better than me."

"There's no money in it."

"None. And your spiv friends, Clio, there's no future in them."

"Shut up. We all move on. That's what it's been. That's what it will be." She lifted her glass. "Moving time. War's over. Here's to the next one. Make us all feel happy again."

She drank alone.

"And secure," she said.

She drank alone again, and put down her glass.

"Can't you see," she said. "you're only safe in a war. You know who you are. You know what you are fighting for. But this sodding peace. No jobs, no cash, no hope."

"Social insecurity," Ian said.

"That. Just that."

15

THE SIXTH COMMANDMENT

Thou shalt not kill.

That was a brute of a lesson to teach to the commandos at the end of the war. They had been trained to kill on a nudge or a noise. They would chop with the side of their swinging hand at the neck of the man who had slapped them on the back. Or they would slice with a handy knife or slam the intruder on the floor and throttle him. They did not think, they acted. They were mindless murderers on instinct. They were beasts in camouflage. And in the rehab camps in Southern India, Peg's job was to try to put them to rights, or at least to get them knowing a little right from wrong.

Her toughest case was Angus McFarlane. On a raid to Arakan, he had stopped four bullets in his belly. Supporting a wounded mate, he had made it to the boats, there to take them off. And when Peg tried to tell him how brave he was, he told her she was the brave one.

"Two weak laddies we had. Two cockneys. Didna want a wee scrap. Stretcher-bearers. Again their consciences, d'ye ken? When we pull out, they stay. With our wounded tha' couldna walk. Torture. Slow death. Certain. And they stay. Tha's men for ye."

Three months of treatment was necessary to return the commandos to civilian society. And even then, they were hardly fit for peace. That was why Peg was recalled to England, to testify in a couple of murder trials. In a Devon pub, one of her patients had been tapped on the shoulder on his bar stool, and he had killed his greeter with a chop on the gullet. The other case was of a father of a small boy, who had jumped on his daddy's back and was thrown at once through a third-floor window and broke his skull on the street.

In the courts, both men were cleared on her evidence, and in the first case the testimony came from David Niven. The film star and ultimate screen British officer was flown back from Hollywood to be a character witness. He had actually fought to win the war, while so many John Waynes who won the war in the movies never stepped further than the studio.

"We are taught to kill," Niven said. "And debriefing takes a long time. You cannot say after killing somebody, next take, please. I did not really mean to do it, sir. It is too late. The other man is dead. There can be no new take. And the killer did not mean to do it. It was his war lesson."

Returning to London, Peg went to call on her cousins, who were bunched at Virginia's flat, which in itself was something of a refugee camp. All the evacuees from the Empire appeared to be herded there, including Ruby, who had at last found transport home back from Annandale. Lodgings were impossible to find in bombed London, and Virginia had to take in much of the family along with Ellen-Maeve, even her companion Ruth's bitter parents, the aged Charles and May Seymour-Scudabright, released from their internment camp. Seeing the pasty-faced crew gathered together in an icy welcome, Peg thought that the Raj was rather reversed. She was now queening it over her poor imperial relations.

"It's the awful rations," Ellen-Maeve was complaining. "Even if you can afford to eat out, you can only pay five bob for a whole meal. There's a ceiling on the price."

"Ah, but they put it on the wine," Ruth said. "Fifteen quid for a bottle of red plonk. That makes up for what they lose on the meal and the menu. And if you don't order wine, you won't get served. And certainly, you won't ever get a table at the Ritz again."

"There is always a way around regulations," Peg said. "But what if these helped you to win the world war?"

"Those rules and regulations put us inside." Charles Seymour-Scudabright's face was as withered and dark with rage as a prune. "We won the first world war. We would have kept the Empire if we'd have made peace with Hitler in time. The Japs would never have attacked us. We'd still have Singapore."

"You still do."

"Not for long. And we will not have your India under Labour."

"It's nice to be getting one's own country back," Peg said.

"What about your son Shilendra?" Ruby's mouth seemed to have bitten on lemon peel. "Didn't he fight with the Japs to liberate India from us? What happened to him?"

Peg's expression was stretched cardboard.

"I haven't heard from him since the war was over. He may be in China."

"Which side? The Nationalists or the Commies? He's good at changing sides."

"I said I don't know. But I am sorry for all of you squashed up here with so little to eat. For once, we have rather more space and even food in India."

"You've come here to gloat, have you?" Ellen-Maeve said. "And you'll expropriate Annandale, and my little share of it."

"Well, the family took it after the Mutiny. Perhaps the locals may take it back a century on."

"After all we did for you?" Charles's grimace was a grin on a death's head. "We rescued you. We put in your roads, railways, hospitals, famine relief. I helped organize all this for you in the Civil Service. And what did we do it all for? What? To be kicked out on our backsides, when we've shed our sons' blood for you."

"It's no use, Charles," Virginia said. "Gratitude is not a word for foreign tongues. And not in families."

"I don't know," Peg said. "I looked after your wounded ones in both wars, here and in my country. But I agree with you on one thing, Charles. This time you were fighting with the Indians for India, and a free India, which will come. Your bayonets were pointing the other way. At Tokyo. The Japanese might have been worse than you."

Ellen-Maeve was looking at a hole on the knee of one of her stockings. She pulled her skirt over it.

"And we've nothing to wear. All our old clothes have worn out. Do you know what the King himself said to *that* Attlee? 'We must all have new clothes. My family is down to the lowest ebb'."

"The King." Peg began to hiccup with laughter, as she heard Virginia say, "And our family is even dowdier and ebbier."

"Do you know," Ellen-Maeve went on, "Princess Elizabeth, our next Queen, she doesn't even have enough coupons for her wedding dress."

"She is a little young," Peg said, "to be married."

"Not in *your* India. You marry at twelve, don't you? But here, we are law-abiding as always, and even Buckingham Palace can't afford anything to cover their rags."

"Silk rags?"

"One of my last friends in the Commons," Charles said, "he invited me to lunch. He managed to escape the slaughterhouse in the last election. And you talk of a five-shilling limit on a meal! Well, lunch there was one-and-sixpence. And dinner was a princely two shillings."

"Perhaps they were subsidized," Peg said.

"The food was awful. And after subsidizing our steel and railways and coalmines with public money – and having bread-rationing for the first time, and in the peace – that's why we had to take that terrible American Loan. The Yanks own us now."

"Well, they did win a revolution against you, Charles."

"As you think you have in India."

"I'll tell you what," Peg said, as she brushed her skirt, preparing to leave for the hostel provided by the grateful British government for her salvation of the lives of two of its soldiers. "India will now send you food packets and clothes. We have all the rice and cotton we need. So when I get back, I will organize the shipment of *saris*, my dears, and curries to your hearts' content. To keep the clothes on your backs and food in your bowels. For all you have done for us, of course."

The dented Chrysler truck which stopped in front of the King David Hotel in Jerusalem was on the milk round. Presumed Arabs in long robes carried in full churns towards the basement restaurant *La Régence* of the building, now taken over by the British Army and the Palestine Mandatory Service. A Royal Signals Captain Macintosh challenged the deliverymen and was shot twice in the stomach for his pains. The intruders took over the kitchens for their churns and lit the fuses on top and left for a waiting taxi, while a small bomb squad of Jewish Irgun provided covering fire. The TNT and gelignite in the metal containers, packed by an explosives expert named Gideon, took twenty minutes to detonate. When it blew up, it might have been a thousand-pounder, dropped as a blast from Jehovah.

A seven-storey wing collapsed. Marble slabs played deadly ducks-and-drakes with the people outside in the street. Bodies flew as vultures, splinters of plate glass were slicers through the air, beheading a policeman. This was not Paul, who was flung flat by the blast, bruising his nose and his jaw and his knees. He staggered up to see the ruins of the imperial headquarters in the Holy Land. He had to hear the shrieks and moans of the wounded and the dying.

"Christ," he said. It was an Armageddon too soon. "I hope it has nothing to do with that Leah."

She was in the taxi with Gideon and his squad. Such was the code name for her man Avi. He had certainly fought the battle of Jericho again, and the walls had come tumbling down in Jerusalem.

"Hey, Avi," she said, patting his knee, "we done good for our leader Begin."

And Avi began to laugh.

"Can we begin again?" he said. "Yes. And I think that blow-up was the beginning of the end for them."

For Paul and for the leader of the Jewish defence army, David Ben-Gurion, this doing was no good. To kill and wound two hundred British people in a terrorist attack was stupid. It would inflame hatred against the Jews and support for the Arab cause. Even a Labour government which backed a future Israel could not ignore such an outrage, or there would be *pogroms* at home. The general in charge, Sir Evelyn Barker, took extreme measures of segregation. All Jewish cafés and shops and restaurants and even private houses were out of bounds. British troops were forbidden any intercourse with any Jew except by way of duty. That would make contact with Leah very difficult for Paul. As his commanding officer directed him, these measures were necessary because they were "punishing the Jews in a way the race dislikes as much as any – by striking at their pockets and showing our contempt for them."

In the following curfew, Leah was arrested with six hundred other suspects. She was interrogated, but released. There was no evidence against her. Those terrorists and their sympathizers who were caught were caned or hanged. Four Irgun members had their necks broken by the noose, but the flogging policy stopped when the rebels kidnapped a major and his unit from the 6th Airborne Division and put their backs and buttocks to the lash. Tail for tail, or spine for spine, or tit for tat, was the order of the day.

Worse was to come, as it always did in a guerrilla war. A hundred Irgun members attacked the prison at Acre and blew down another wall in the ancient citadel, now converted into a prison. Two hundred prisoners, most of them Arabs, escaped, but three of the raiders were caught and hanged. In revenge, two British sergeants, spirited away by the Irgun, were found dangling their heels from ropes swung over the branches of eucalyptus trees. That was too much for the Foreign Secretary, Ernest Bevin, who was still supplying the Muslim states with weapons to confirm strategic control of oil supplies in the Middle East. The Jews would be swept away into the Levantine Sea, when we evacuated Palestine and left the mess to the United Nations after the ending of the mandate. "You must remember the British sergeants were hanged to the tree," Bevin said, referring to Christ's crucifixion, in the House of Commons, "– not by Arabs."

So the British began their quitting of the Empire in the Near East before the Far East. And as always, their role as referees and scapegoats between the warring faiths and peoples would end in a bloodbath and another evacuation. For new nations, frontiers were always the artificial creation of the occupying power. Outnumbered as Gideon and King David were in front of their enemies in the *Torah* and the Old Testament, the scratch Jewish battalions beat back their attackers to make a new Israel. Five Royal Air Force fighters were shot down, flying in from Egypt. Luckily for the family, Peregrine was no longer a pilot, but in the Commons, cheering on his Foreign Secretary's policies, so sympathetic to those of the previous idols of the MP from Netherbampton. But his cousin Leah was in the fight to reclaim the ancient Holy City of her new found land. In that time, blood was far from kin.

Siege lay within siege, as the Jewish Quarter died house by house. The last couple of thousand Jews were penned into an area a few streets wide. Fire on them was so heavy that they could move only through the catacombs and sewers. They were falling back on their last two strongpoints, the Ashkenazi and the Tiferet synagogues. Arab irregulars were swarming closer with their explosives, jacketed in the cast-offs of many Muslim wars, daggers in their belts, gelignite in their hands, lighters ready for the fuses to bring the Hebrew walls tumbling down. They had already shattered the dome of the Tiferet and opened caverns in its walls. The few snipers left in its rubble were being picked off by the Arab Legion, posted in the battlements of the Old City, laying down a covering fire. The green and checked cloths on their heads were flowers of death on the stone blocks.

"Three hundred yards. Top of the synagogue. Thirty yards left. Brown roof. Fifteen yards down. Courtyard. Five rounds rapid. Fire in your own time."

The Sandhurst voice directed the volleys of the Legion, then choked.

"Jesus," it said, "Jesus."

The voice died of wounds. Outside the walls of the Old City, some Haganah forces sniped and attacked, desperate to save the last Jews alive in Jerusalem. The Arab Legion faced both ways at the enemy within and without. But the Haganah detachments were also being encircled by closing Arab armies. Net over net over net over the Holy City.

Leah was too tired to despair. She had been fighting for three days and nights. She had killed two men and had never killed a man before. Her right cheek-bone was bloody and bruised from the stock of the Bren gun. The magazines were all empty. Her loader had tied in his guts with his shirt when a piece of mortar bomb had blown a hole in his stomach, and he wouldn't live more than an hour or two. There had been little firing in the night or at dawn. The defenders of the Jewish Quarter had little left to fire. And yet Leah could not believe that they had lost Jerusalem.

In the lull of that last morning, she watched the swallows diving and flickering, a truce now after the bombardments. Yet the birds were wise enough to wheel round the gaudy flags that flew above each coward embassy and trembling faith – the Union Jack, the Vatican Ensign, the Ethiopian banner, the Stars and Stripes. Leah swung the barrel of her Bren towards the red, white and blue crosses of Britain and cursed that she had no bullets to rip the flag-pole down. Then below her sights, she saw two old rabbis picking their way through the hillocks of rubble. White flag, twin black carriers, white flag. We have lost Jerusalem.

Leah had to admit, the Arab Legion behaved correctly. The Legionaries cut out the men, collecting a bazaar counter of prisoners of war to trade in the final exchange of men when the fighting would stop. But they allowed the women and children to pick up their bundles and drag their way down the alleys towards the Zion Gate. Leah was among the refugees, hidden in a long dusty dress, a child on one arm – in the other hand, a parcel of prayer shawls and spoons and bowls and the text of Deuteronomy.

> Then will the Lord drive out all these nations from before you, and ye shall possess greater nations and mightier than yourselves.
>
> Every place whereon the sole of your feet shall tread shall be yours: from the wilderness and Lebanon, from the river, the river Euphrates, even unto the uttermost sea shall your coast be.
>
> There shall no man be able to stand before you: for the Lord your God shall lay the fear of you and the dread of you upon all the land that ye shall tread upon, as He hath said unto you.
>
> Behold, I set before you this day a blessing and a curse ...

Beside Leah, an old man had earlocks below a flat black hat. He shook his head from side to side uncontrollably. Nay, nay, nay, nay, nay. He did not believe, he could not believe, as the final diaspora came to the Zion Gate for the scattering from Jerusalem.

The Haganah raged outside the walls. Volleys struck at the stones. Shrapnel wailed in the dark. The refugees fell to the ground, prayed, grovelled, to escape the avenging fury of their own.

Furthermore, the Lord spake unto me, saying, I have seen this
people, and, behold, it is a stiff-necked people.

Let me alone, that I may destroy them, and blot out their name
from under heaven: and I will make of thee a nation mightier
and greater than they ...

The anger of the Haganah was spent. The last whine of metal
thinned to no noise. Outside the walls, the army of Israel waited to
take away its defeated. Inside, the Jewish Quarter burned in pillars of
fire. The child on Leah's arm cried and, as she kissed away its tears,
she found herself weeping. Under Zion Gate, Leah wept and
despaired.

"What is Israel without Jerusalem? There is no Israel without
Jerusalem."

Then she hoped.

"Israel shall have Jerusalem."

Paul had sunk in his own horror, as the last of the police pulling out of
Palestine. He had been called out to Dier Yasin. There had been a
ritual cleansing there, a deterrence to scare off the Arabs over the
borders, when the war would be over. Stuffed down this village well
were two hundred and fifty bodies, old men and women and children,
stripped and shot, eyes and mouths and wounds open to flies that
went scrick scrick scrick all day long in the stench and the sun. This
was a final April in Palestine.

As he was pulling out because the Empire was finished in the
Levant as it was in India, he was surprised by a knock on his hotel
door in Tel Aviv. He opened it, his pistol at the ready. Leah had come
to call. Obviously, Israeli intelligence was better than his intelligence
now.

"Kind of you to drop in," he said. "I won't be coming back."

"We don't want you back," Leah said, yanking at the buckle of her
webbing belt which had stuck. She was imprisoned in her British
battle-dress. Then she bit her lip. There were tears in her eyes. "We
have lost Jerusalem."

"I know," Paul said. "I wish you hadn't."

"I don't know," she said. "It was all we wanted."

"To hell with it," Paul said. "Get it later. Another war. You've got
most of your homeland back. That's all anyone wants — we'd like it in
Scotland."

Leah smiled.

"For a copper, you're on the way to being sympathetic."

"Not for what you did at Dier Yasin."

Leah's face went as hard as slate.

"It wasn't us. It was the Stern Gang."

"On your side, I presume."

"They thought, that killing, it would scare off the occupiers of our land."

"I am sure it will. Millions of Arab refugees. We were cleared, you know, by deterrence, from the Highlands. We know the policy quite well. But it wasn't so nasty."

"Don't mock us, Paul. We have to have Israel back."

"But not with atrocities you learned from the Nazis. Why repeat Lidice here? Or Belsen, or Dachau?"

"Oh God," Leah said, "you had your Glencoe. There's always a necessary massacre to clear the land. You know that. What about your Crusades? When you took Jerusalem you butchered every Jew, man, woman, child and dog – to clean out our holy city."

Leah got her belt off. She swung it like a weapon. Then she sat on the hotel bed. Her sweat reeked of ammonia.

"Look," she said, "I can't excuse anything. The Arabs are running because we're advancing. Their wirelesses are telling them to. They think they'll come back behind their armies and take our land again, instead of us taking their land. If there's an incident like Dier Yasin ..."

"An incident? A slaughter."

"That's war. You never fought in one. You were just a colonial copper, trying to keep the peace, which was never there. Bystanders can be moral. Soldiers can't."

"No law now," Paul said. "I suppose there isn't. Time to go."

"Go quick," Leah said. "You saved me once. That's why I'm here. I'm returning the compliment, wise guy. You saw Dier Yasin. You were an eye-witness. Our people won't want you around."

"So see an atrocity, and you are a marked man?"

"Retire," Leah said. "And live. Fade away, as the Brits have done here. Get out. Go incognito. Or somebody will find you out for all you have done and seen."

16

A WINTER'S TALE
1946

Big Ben froze up. Time was ice. This was the worst winter for sixty-six years. Britain's economy skidded to a halt. Bare-kneed schoolchildren like Boy Keiss, now a boarder at the Dragon School in Oxford, skated on the tennis-lawn and grew chilblains as large as pink leeches on his fingers. The national coal supplies ran out, and one of God's sparrows fell rigid in flight and gashed the perm of a housewife. The Central Electricity Board met by candlelight in heavy overcoats to work out that there could be no heat or light in homes for five hours in the mornings and afternoons. Four and a half million people were out of work, and the trains did not run on schedule or at all. Shepherds tunnelled through the snow to get hay to their buried sheep, and the Minister of Power declared that the Labour Government was prepared for anything except the weather.

Murdo had been transferred to Whitehall as a special adviser on energy. The only possible policy was to expand the nationalized coal mines. The problem was that too many miners had been drafted into the forces and were not yet demobbed. And if they were, they were often in bad condition and refused to go back underground for a lunger's slow dying. So the policy was to import Jamaicans to do the dirty work. After all, what an opportunity to get out of the slavery of cutting the sugar or cane. For it was just as hot down in the narrow pits and shafts as under the Caribbean sun, although the vision was limited under that black inward roof of sky.

A poster of John Bull with his sleeves rolled up lay on Murdo's desk. The caption in bold type was: WE'RE UP AGAINST IT. WE WILL WORK OR WANT. The government believed that propaganda would also solve the peace. Slogans would enable the people to put up with shortages. Of course, these would not work. Even the Russian folk would not put up forever with another Five Year Plan, which promised a decent living only to the next generation. How could more austerity push a war-weary lot to postpone prosperity even further? Nature was not the only criminal. Perhaps the government was letting us down, too. There were fourteen-foot snow drifts in Essex. The fuses of the electric railway at Purley exploded, as if the *maquis* had hit them. Pneumatic drills were needed to dig out parsnips. But was it necessary for the Prime Minister to suspend television and the wireless Third Programme, and even greyhound racing, just to save a few megowatts? He should have acted like the Romans to keep up morale. Give them tea and circuses, not WORK OR WANT. War did not work any more. The mobs wanted peace and entertainment.

By March and the thaw, the deluge came in a storm. A cataclysm released the floods. Shrewsbury was turned into a Venice, while part of the London Underground became a pool for rats to swim in. The waters destroyed the stored potatoes and grain supplies. The cattle were mired and died in the meadows, which were now bogs. One in three of the hill sheep had to be incinerated. The roast stink of death rose over the Brecon Beacons.

Nobody listened to Murdo. Cigarette taxes went up by a half, and the only advice from the Chancellor of the Exchequer was to smoke a fag to the filter tip. This burnt offering would be better for our health. Even American films were taxed, so that Crosby and Hope and Dorothy Lamour could no longer take their audiences on the Road to Zanzibar. Anything went to get out of the country, but the foreign travel allowance was only £50, if that, while the basic petrol ration was abolished. Lighting an electric fire in summer became an offence. At least, the bad news was rationed as well. The newspapers diminished to four pages, so they could not tell this from that. And Murdo resigned from his job. He could not be party to such a white shroud dressing the corpse of his country.

In Soho, however, an alternative economy was being created, a testament to survival and ingenuity. Where governments fail, the people fill the cracks. In his wanderings as a penniless publisher through Greek and Frith, Old Compton and Wardour Streets, Ian Hamish found a thriving society. The stimulation of the pubs from the French to the Crown and Two Chairmen lingered on, as mint does after rain. Though no magazines were allowed paper or publication for two weeks during the great chill, the Grey Walls Press had cozened enough stocks of wood pulp to print on. With a cobweb of ice on his hair, Ian would drink with the wayward editor Tambimuttu and Dylan Thomas and beastly Roy Campbell in his safari hat and the cruising John Lehmann through the bars and solicit their contributions to Wrey Gardiner's eccentric publishing house, which hardly ever paid up, and never on time. As for his own contributions, these included the sighting of the best bulbous romantic poet of his time in a late-night drinking club, which would give way to the strip joints to come:

> We saw Dylan in the Gargoyle
> Very drunk and on the boil.
> 'I am dying. Are you living?
> I'm a poet. Are you spivving?
> Another drink? I'll hit the floor.
> Have I slept with you before?
> Another whisky. Make a killing
> Of a genius, who is willing.
> You can't make an old lion roar.
> We're self-destructive after war.
> When there's no enemy, you see,
> The fact is now, I'll murder me.'

In spite of the doggerel and the literary encounters, Ian could not get Clio out of his system, however many of the easy lays and slags he met. The women also had lost the wartime buzz and trade. They were not about to die, and so they could not salute you. They were hanging on through this ghastly period of cold and privation, which seemed almost as sad as the siege of Leningrad. The Russian survivors had even eaten human flesh then, but what the government was offering was worse than being a cannibal.

"I don't know if eating whalemeat," Ian was later saying to his mother Ruby in the Ivy, which seemed to have clung on with the theatricals in Shaftesbury Avenue during the war. "I don't know if it doesn't make you into a shark. And I thought whaling had gone out with Moby Dick."

"It's tough stuff." Ruby glared at the morsel of crimson stuff which she had sawed off with her toothed knife. "But if that's all we can get."

"There is snoek, mama."

"It's not on points, like sardines now."

"Only on one point, because nobody wants to buy it. Have you tasted it?"

"Not yet."

"I have. It's something between putrid tongue and Bombay Duck, which as you know is salted fish fillets stamped on by bare Indian heels."

"Where is snoek from?"

"South Africa. It's like a barracuda. It eats your tonsils before you can swallow it. Even after it is tinned, it gobbles the enamel off the plate. But the Ministry has put out a wonderful recipe for it. *Snoek piquante*, where the Boers meet chic Paris. There is so much vinegar, so many onions in the vile mix, you can't savour the fish for the trimmings."

"It's better than cat food, I suppose." So Ruby said and proved a prophet, for that is where snoek would end, and even the pussies turned their noses up at it. But not Ian, as Clio swirled into the restaurant in her long skirt with a frilled dangling petticoat, and with a well-dressed man in a tweed coat and grey flannels. He had her on his arm below the sloping shoulders of her pink waisted jacket.

"Don't look now, Ruby." Ian was shaking his head. "It's the New Look. And if you look close enough, there's Clio in it."

Ruby's head swivelled and her mouth dropped.

"So this is what you've all been getting up to here," she hissed. "While I was in India. And how can she get away with the coupons? That skirt's a year's supply."

"Perhaps she got a special grant from the government through that chap with her." Ian affected a slight smile. "After all, Princess Elizabeth was given a hundred clothes coupons for her wedding dress, when she married that Captain Philip Mountbatten, RN."

"He's Greek. That's why they got away with it. But Clio – that is the *French* look."

"I gather, mama, the bridesmaids at the royal wedding only got twenty-three coupons each. And the pages only ten coupons. Hardly enough to buy silk parachute britches. Now isn't that a fair division between the rich and the rest? The Crown and the country."

Ruby was watching Clio seating herself at the table next to them. There was no recognition yet. Perhaps that tart could not see through her long false eye-lashes. But Ian was rising to make himself known. Always the weakling, always the gentleman.

"Clio," he was saying. "Lovely to see you again. You know my mother." The two women now nodded at each other, while Ian introduced himself a little too far. "I am Ian Ogilvie, sir, a family friend."

"Hume," the man said. "Donald Hume. I was in the RAF, old chap. Now I'm getting by."

"Like we all are." Clio looked up at Ian. "Shall we move tables?"

"Why?" Ian said. "It's lovely to see you again."

Now Ruby interrupted.

"Hello. And what do you do, Mister Hume?"

"In trade, like you have to be. All these bloody regulations. None of us can stand them. They give you ribbons to pin on your old blue tunic and your wings, and nothing to live on."

"Agreed," Ian said. "Have a drink? I've got some decent wine. Clio always liked that, the good wine."

And so they talked on, although Clio was shifting in her seat to either side of her bottom in her nervousness. Ian managed to remain cool as they talked about the changes which might come in after the devastating winter. Possibly, there would be a new look in everything, for dresses to housing to design. The government decrees of Utility stuff could not continue. Rotten plywood furniture, wedgie platform-soled shoes, short squat skirts with padded shoulders and heavy hats, colours in puce and purple and bottle green, they were doomed. Any woman who had frilly knickers again would throw away the old look in the dustbins, their true destinations.

"They're quite pretty now, you know," Ian said, making small talk. "The bombsites and the rubble. They've become wildlife grottos. I mean, there are plover in the brown ponds. And the flowers – I know they are mainly weeds, dandelions and thistles and ragwort and sorrel, but you'll find willow-herb there and roses. But what's a weed but a misnamed flower?" He looked at Clio. "Gone wrong, the other side of the fence."

Clio looked aside, then up at Ian, staring him down. She was framed against the coloured diamonds of the windows, which had survived the Blitz.

"What the hell do you know? Sorry, Ruby, but we're different now. After the war, it's another snooker game. The toffs are out, and they won't be back."

"I don't know either," Ruby said. "But you haven't buried us yet." She rose, pushing back her chair with the fading width of her sensible tweed skirt. "I have to go. Please excuse me. And thank you, Ian, for showing me *your* side of London." As her son moved to peck her on the cheek, she squeezed past the other table. "Don't see me out. I know my way home."

The three of them watched Ruby sail away.

"Mothers," Ian said. "But without them, how could we be here?"

"If one could flog a mother," Hume said, "I might be able to come up with a better one for you. At a fair price."

"Impossible. I rather like the one I have. Anyway, I am hopelessly used to her. Do you have family?"

"Not now. All dead, nearly. Anyway, they're no use now. Do you remember that identity disc you got in the war? And if you were done in and had it, the CO used to have to tell your nearest and dearest. Well, that's all over now. We haven't got any identity discs any more. We've got the New Look instead."

"Donald's right." Clio's cheeks were burning bright beneath her pale make-up. "We have to re-invent ourselves. The war's knocked us flat. And we can't even emigrate to a place in the sun. We just have to do the best we can here. But I'm fed up with soldiering on. Something fresh, you know. Exciting. On the ball."

"You get around a lot," Ian said. "Don't you, Mr Hume?"

"Pilots do."

"I used to be one. Not now."

"I still fly around. Old Dakotas. Ferry the goods. It can be done still, if you know the man who can fix the licences."

"And you do."

"And I do. A chum called Setty. Stanley Setty. He's in with that Whitehall mob. All very respectable, though Stanley –" Hume snickered. "I wouldn't always take him home for dinner.'

"A lot of people have risen in the war to high places." Ian looked at the anger in Clio's eyes and hated himself for sounding so pompous. So he rose as well. "I must leave you to your meal." Then almost in despair, he found himself saying, "Clio, you still know where to find me."

"I do," Clio said. "I do. When I can."

"Can do everything," Hume said, "if you really want to."

This was the one truth of the lunch, Ian knew that on his way out to pay the bill.

17

FAREWELL, ANNANDALE

Paul was fortunate when he was returned home. Although swamped with applications from out-of-work officers with specialist skills, the Colonial Office found a spot for Paul in Rhodesia. He had experience in South and West Africa; perhaps he could be useful in police work in the east of the Dark Continent. The Empire would take time to peter out there, and probably not without a struggle from the white settlers. The posting might not be a long one, but it would certainly be the last one.

As Paul was walking towards Soho, a man was waiting for him by a bombsite. His army greatcoat was pulled over his ears and neck until it met the back of his peaked cap, a war souvenir from the Afrika Korps – you had to shoot a German's head off before you could get his hat, but the Italians threw theirs away as they ran across Libya. The rusty bayonet lying along the man's forearm in his sleeve was also a war souvenir, blooded at Monte Cassino and then again in Turin – a woman that time, she shouldn't have screamed, he'd paid her the two cigarettes. His black boots were his old best boots, now muddy and gashed at one toe, and his six missing teeth were other combat scars, broken off by a Military Policeman's club in Salerno. The war had been all right, there were always opportunities, he had stuck it through, he was British, wasn't he? But it was that long year waiting to be demobbed while all his mates were on the fiddle, he had to go Absent Without Leave, why should he march in for bloody permission to quit in peace time? Three years a deserter now and still on the lam, he was fighting his private war in the rubble left from the Blitz. His country owed him a living and he had been taught only to be a runner.

Paul was crooked by the deserter's elbow as he passed a gap in the falling bricks. Choking, he pulled at the strangling arm. Stumbling, he was thrust backwards. Jolted, he was brought up standing against a wall smelling of damp and piss. Scared, he looked at the bayonet at his throat and the fierce face of the scavenger holding the weapon that was once sported on the muzzle of a .303 Lee-Enfield rifle. Now it had its civilian point.

"Let's have it," the man said.

"When you put your penknife down," Paul said. His nerve came back with the power of speech.

"Gimme." The man's voice was hard, uncertain. His dialogue came from the gangster films which he saw to give himself courage.

"Of course," Paul said. "When you've put your penknife down. You hang for murder here. It's not worth it."

Grunting his despair, the man dropped the point of the bayonet and swung at Paul with his left fist. Paul grabbed his arm. He moved into the deserter, caught him in a hug, locking the man's elbows so that there was no chance of a stab in the back. Grotesque, joined, stomping in a war dance, Paul wrestled with the deserter. He put his left foot in, he put his left foot out, he put his left foot in and he shook it all about, he did the hokey-cokey and he turned around about, that's what it was all about. The deserter managed to try a stab with the bayonet, but only pierced the cloth of Paul's coat, which caught the point of the steel in the ripped wool and twisted it out of his attacker's hand. The deserter began to sob. He struggled a little more, losing his breath as Paul squeezed him harder and harder. He was giving up.

Paul flung the man away so that he thudded into the broken wall. He picked up the bayonet and held it towards the deserter. The man, under threat, became cocky, defiant.

"It's murder for you too," he said. "You'll swing."

"I doubt it," Paul said. "Manslaughter in self-defence. What did you want from me?"

"Tosheroons," the man said. "What else is there?"

"Going straight," Paul said. "You're a deserter?"

"What's that to you?"

"You're a deserter?"

"I heard you."

"You're a deserter?"

"I didn't spend the war on my fat arse behind a desk."

"You're a deserter?"

"So what?"

"You're a deserter?"

"Yeah," the man said. "Turn me in. It can't be worse than out here."

"It's not your fault then?"

"I tried to stick you up, didn't I?"

"The war made you do it, surely. That's what you'll plead in court."

"It's the fact," the man said. "But nobody'll listen."

"Millions of people came back from the war and went back into civilian life without fuss. You didn't. There was something wrong with you, not the war."

"Yeah," the man said, failing to snarl like Bogart. "There was something wrong. I'm *evil*." He sneered. "My mum always said I'd come to a bad end."

"There are still twenty thousand deserters on the run," Paul said. "That's not many at the end of a world war. My god, we trained a whole population to murder their fellows. Why didn't more come back to do us in?" He smiled at the deserter. "I would have thought there would have been armies of you."

"You're a cool one," the man said. "No mistake."

There was a thrash of feathers, a screech, a dying unfolding of wings. Both men looked towards the noise. One of the hawks which now hunted the bombsites was flying with slow beats, a mouse held in its claws.

"The war's still on," Paul said. "I can see that. Only you're out of date." He waved the bayonet like a conductor's baton. "Using *this*. Bayonets are over. Rusty relics, all you get from them is blood poisoning."

"You can talk," the man said. "You do talk. You'd talk a floozie out of her knickers. I never learned to talk. Not many can talk. I bet you have a job."

"Since this morning."

"Where? What? Lucky sod."

"Abroad. Africa. India's gone."

"Not bloody here. No bloody work here."

Paul smiled.

"I'm a copper," he said. "A colonial copper."

The deserter flinched.

"You mean, I tried to mug a copper."

"Just your luck. You want a beer to celebrate I'm still in business? Though not in this mess of a country."

"Piss off," the man said. He turned and began running across the bombsite. His boots tore at the green weeds and flowers growing on the rubble. He stumbled over a jagged foundation, recovered, splashed through a puddle in a hole, bolted down a crack between two leaning walls, vanished.

Paul did not move. He watched the deserter run, then he looked down at the rusty bayonet in his hand. He smiled. His souvenir of everything the war had failed to do for those who had served a long way from home.

After all the fighting and the train massacres had died down with the partition of Solomon's country into an independent India and Pakistan, he took his aunt Peg in her black robes back to Annandale, where Margaret Jardine could no longer cope. While the old Austin staggered up the overgrown drive, they could see the tea plants fallen into scrub. As they took their luggage up the verandah, a shutter sounded tick-tock-tock as it struck a window-frame in the breeze, the slight parting knell of the imperial day.

Stooped in her wicker wheelchair, Margaret extended a claw in greeting, although her fingernails were painted in crimson. One had to keep one's standards up, whatever the circumstances. She managed to croak to one of the servants, who had not fled with the rest.

"Tea now. And the cake." She was at her most polite in defeat. "I hope you had no trouble getting here."

"Most of the trains are still running," Solomon said. "And vaguely on time."

"Have they cleaned up the carriages? All that blood."

"We always had too many cleaners here," Peg said. "Our problem was, what were we cleaning, and who for?"

"That dreadful partition," Solomon said. "We should never have had it. That speed-at-all-costs Mountbatten of yours. To try to solve it all in nine weeks. Ram through a solution in a couple of months. That's what caused all the bloodshed."

"They say half a million people died." Margaret's voice was calm, even satisfied. "Six million refugees had to move over your new frontiers."

"Your fault," Peg said. "You divided us to rule us. Like the Romans."

"No, no, Peg. We united you, a bunch of squabbling petty warlords. We didn't allow the Hindus to kill off the Muslims, and the Sikhs to kill both lots of you. We kept you together. That's obvious. When you made us go – and you wanted us out as soon as poss – you got what you had before we came. Murders, local wars, migrations. Don't blame us. Blame yourselves."

The servant came in with a pewter tray. On it, porcelain Chinese cups and saucers for three, a sponge cake with a glazed cherry on top, and a silver tea pot covered by an embroidered caddy to keep it warm.

"Please be mother," Margaret said to Peg. "It will be your future role at Annandale."

As they sipped their tea with trimmings of lemon in the brew, as they picked delicately at the soggy yellow slices which had failed to rise, Solomon tried to mollify Margaret.

"Look," he said, "we do want to take over, that is true. But you can't keep going on here. You are better off back in England."

"Better off?" Margaret gave a dry cackle. "I can't export a rupee from here. I have nothing to take back to England. A few jewels, a few clothes. I cannot pay for an old folks home."

"Stay here," Peg said. "We will look after you."

"No, thank you," Margaret said. "You take it. I can't keep it. I can't stay on your charity. You understand that."

"Yes," Solomon said. "I understand that. Why did your workers go?"

"A lot of them were Muslim. They pulled out to Kashmir. I don't know how many made it. But there is trouble there, too."

"Yes. The war will go on. Jinnah's war. Pakistan against India. Gandhi was always right. Partition was intolerable and immoral."

"But you murdered Gandhi, too, for saying that. For saying the Raj was right in keeping India undivided."

"Not quite, Margaret, not quite. As I have always said, Gandhi preached the way of peace to make India free and united. Unfortunately —"

"We gave you freedom without a fight. But too quickly, as we see."

"You could not have hung on," Peg interrupted. "You did not wish to hang on. Any more, Margaret, than you can or wish to hang on at Annandale."

Margaret was silent. Her tea-cup shook in her hand as she took a sip and prepared to counter her cousins.

"Peg — Your son Shilendra — didn't he want to fight to free India? And Solomon — wasn't he with your brother Shankar, the one who died in Burma? I was so sorry about that."

"You were not sorry." Solomon's voice was ice. "You were glad when Shankar died. And as for Shilendra, can't you see auntie Peg is in black?"

"I am sorry about that, too." Margaret's irony was evident. "And what happened to him?"

"He went back to China." Peg clapped her hands together to stop them trembling. "Unfortunately, when he met his old friends, Mao Tse-Tung's government, they thought he had collaborated with the Japanese, when he was only using them to —"

"Get back to India his way. They shot him?"

"He was tried and executed."

Peg began to weep, and Solomon rose to put his hand round her shoulders.

"Except for you, Solomon," Margaret's voice was harsh,"your family hasn't done too well in getting hold of Annandale."

"There are two of us left." Solomon sounded as brisk as if he were giving orders. "We will run this place, which will be Indian again, and high time, too. We will repatriate what income we can, when we are allowed to do so. And more than that, we will arrange for your safe repatriation when you have packed. You still have a British passport, and I will see to an armed guard on the train and your passage back from Bombay. You will be treated with every consideration on your journey home."

Margaret coughed and shook her head. Her last sparse white curls could not hide her pink scalp.

"Always the old King Solomon with his excellent judgement. And always the gentleman, though we know how you learned those tricks."

"I'll take Peg up to her rooms."

"Your rooms now."

"Our rooms soon. When you are gone."

18

NO COLONY THERE

Ian Henry was wondering about his flat champagne in the Colony Room off Dean Street. The scum on the surface of his glass was so oily that the bubbles could not break through. Trapped, they looked like frogs' spawn or sago pudding. He glanced up to see the raddled owner Muriel Belcher sitting at the bar, shouting, "Hello, Miss Hitler," to the curious figure of the outlandish painter Francis Bacon. He looked like a principal boy with his hair spiky from being scrubbed in brown Kiwi polish and his pantomime girl high boots. "Sieg Heil, darling," he said, lifting his arm in a Nazi salute. "I want to get right up to here."

Too many were already dead from the band of the old regulars. The gigantic poet Anna Wickham had hanged herself out of her bedroom window because she could not find a bigger drop for her plummeting reputation. And the incontinent beggar and artist Nina Hamnet had given up her Oxo tin for pub money and had also fallen from her flat to impale herself on the railings beneath. "Always spiky, that cunty," Muriel had observed. "And she got spiked." Such vicious talk made it no surprise to Ian, when he saw the burned Peregrine enter the decaying room of what passed for present culture. There was an instant and amused recognition between the two of them.

"Finish my flat bottle," Ian said. "If you can get it down your throat."

Peregrine sat, first bringing three spare glasses from the bar. Ian filled one of them.

"Expecting company?"

"Yes," Peregrine said. "Yes, indeed. If they show up."

"Anybody I know?"

"I don't know."

Below his face which was a moonscape, Peregrine was a pin-stripe dandy, the cream lines in his suit so narrow as to be almost invisible. The cut was Savile Row, the stitches by labouring hand, the ruff on the cloth not quite pressed.

"I wouldn't expect to see you here," Ian said. "Hardly the ambience for a successful MP."

"A safe house, I'd call it." Peregrine's grin was as wicked as himself. "Only drunken artists here. They wouldn't know a Member of the House more than the seat of their trousers."

"I do know about Soho," Ian said. "Nye Bevan's got the top room at Wheeler's and the rest of the cabinet is always in the Gay Hussar or the Ivy. You've got no secrets. All your dirty washing is on the line."

"Not quite here," Peregrine said. "I fly where there are no spies. How are you getting by, cousin? You must be starving."

"On tick. Soon the clock will work. Tick-tock. How do you get by? An MP's salary couldn't possibly pay for your tastes."

"Licences. The bits of bumph which release you from regulations. You want to make a fortune, Ian?"

"Not particularly."

"Buy a bombsite for nothing. Come to cousin Peregrine for a way out of the controls. I give you permits for bricks and timber and glass, all you need. At a nice price, too. You go to the local council and say, I have the go-ahead. Give me planning permission. And slip the officer a few thou. And you are Rockefeller, with your own dinky plaza."

"Not my style," Ian said. "I will have to leave it to you."

"You are a fool, Ian. You always were out of step with what is going on. Can't you understand? Everything is run down, people are tired to death. They walk through their lives like zombies. They've been dead for ten years of nothing very much. You can't dragoon a population to fight for more than a decade. People are fed up with all this drabness thrust upon them." He stood up. "Ah, Stanley."

Through the upstairs door a character came, the stripes of his suit a little too wide, the shoes a little too patent leather. He swanned towards Peregrine and embraced him.

"You've got it for me?"

"The usual bits of loo paper. Later. This is Mr Setty. He knows his way around. He even found his way to this dump."

Ian did not shake his hand, but poured out the final drops from the champagne bottle.

"Who is the last glass for?"

"Surprise," Peregrine said. "Surprise."

"Where are them licences?" Setty said. "I want them now. I don't have the time, you know."

Out of his pocket, Peregrine fished a packet.

"Have I ever let you down, old chum?"

Setty drained his glass in a swallow.

"I never did you. The right stuff in the right place."

"Excuse me," Ian said. "What stuff where?"

"No concern of yours, old boy," Peregrine said. "Merchandise is not one of your interests."

The door to the bar swung open again. Blown on a wind, Clio skimmed in towards them. Peregrine did not rise, but she kissed him on the lips, bending towards his mouth.

"Hello, all," she said, and seeing Ian, "hello, stranger."

"I didn't expect you'd turn up here," Ian said.

"I am worse than a bad penny," Clio said, seating herself. "It's so nice seeing *everybody* I know." Then she turned to Setty. "Hey, Donald is looking for you. It's serious, he says."

"Serious?" Setty gave a fat grin. "I'm not serious. When you're around, funsome, I'm on the town."

"Shut it." Peregrine was menacing. "You have things to do."

"Yeah." Setty stood up and slid a brown envelope over the table. "You done what you done." And to Clio. "Farewell, my lovely." And he left, with Ian looking after him.

"Wasn't that a book title? Raymond Chandler?"

"We can't distinguish," Clio enunciated with the care of the drunk, "ourselves now for what we play, and who we really are."

"Pretty portentous," Peregrine said, pocketing the pay-off. "You two are acquainted?"

"Pretty well," Clio said. "I do not think Ian wants to see me back with you. You are such a bastard."

"We are who I am. Actually, Clio, I never understood why you came back to me."

"Because you are such a bastard."

"That makes some sort of weird sense."

"If you don't mind me putting my oar in," Ian said, "what happened to Bridget?"

"One of those war sacrifices," Peregrine said. "You know, the débris of the peace. A bit old-fashioned under the skin." And he began to croon –

> "Time to move on, and I can
> Time to move on, I'm your man
> Time to move on, you are glue
> Time to disappear, me too
> Needing me's a hole in the head
> Needing you, I'm better off dead –"

"Christ, shut up," Clio said. "I bet you made that up as you went along."

"I make myself up daily," Peregrine said, putting out a forefinger nail to scratch the powder off Clio's cheek. "Don't you, darling?"

"You are a bastard," Ian said. "Why the hell are you in Parliament?"

"Bastards for ever!" Peregrine raised his empty glass in a toast. "Get another bottle, old chap, and we'll drink to that. I'm not a member here, only in the Other Place. And the lady needs a drink, too."

"You're a member of nothing. Of nowhere." Ian snapped his fingers at Muriel at the bar. "Hitler *is* here. Another bottle of your foul fizz."

"OK, cunty." Muriel pointed at the barman. "Get him the usual poison."

Clio swung her head from side to side.

"I always seem to meet you, Ian, when things are not working."

Ian paused to consider what he could in his fuddled brain.

"Do you think, Clio, you make things not work? Or not work just for me."

"You want the truth, Ian?" She gave Peregrine one of her flashes, her quick smile, and jeered at him. "Ian is the man I always go back to. He will wait until you leave me again, you bastard."

19

MUSHROOM CLOUDBURSTS

1950

Hamish Henry was already under intensive investigation. Curiously enough, his chief, John Cockroft, backed his work. The man who had originally helped to split the atom believed in the free exchange of scientific endeavour. He was still communicating with Peter Kapitsa, the remarkable Russian physicist who had returned home from Cambridge with his knowledge and his laboratory. The new Cold War should not stop passing on fresh findings about the universe. Scientists were greater than politicians, who tried to prohibit the community of wisdom, as a part of the new research might be used to make weapons. Of course, the dilemma was greater now, because the developing fission bomb could now destroy the whole world in a radioactive wasteland. And so, the scientists would have to join the rest of the human race in their total obliteration, because of their curiosity.

The larger questions of the fate of humanity can be defined by silly and personal matters. Hamish Henry was packing his suitcases in Bentinck Street, when he found Guy Burgess doing the same thing. Very suspicious, Guy interrogated his wary flatmate.

"Hello, Henry. Who told you?"

"Who told me what?"

"Who told you ... um ... Going on holiday?"

"Yes. To the Far North. Cambridge. I still work there."

"It doesn't stop you having a room here."

"I need all my clothes up there. Such a cold east wind blows over the Fens. All the way from the Urals. Somewhere in Russia, I believe. And you believe."

Guy gave his full lopsided smile at Henry.

"I never suspected you of being witty before. Perhaps you also have turned."

"I learnt both sides from you, Guy. Where are you going?"

"A little trip for the good of my health."

"Is it threatened here?"

"I can never stand a draught." Guy walked towards a window and jammed down the frame onto the sill. "Too close to the wind here. I think I need to go back into the closet." He returned to his suitcase and began laying down his silk shirts as carefully as claret. "You were never one of us." He was an accuser now. "Don't betray us in our going."

Hamish Henry was feeling almost reckless. We had the atomic bomb, too, as well as America and Russia. A certain feeling for his country began stirring in his conscience.

"Going where, Guy?" he asked. "Going why? You are getting out. You've asked yourself nothing. Why did you do all this? No answer. They are onto you. That's why they kicked you back here from Washington."

"Will you help them?"

Henry shook his head.

"Of course not. I was in it, as well as you."

"Was? You say was?"

"What was it worth, Guy? This Cold War. First, the Russians join the Nazis. Then, they become our Allies. Then Stalin gobbles up all of Eastern Europe. Then we have a Cold War. Who are the imperialists now? That's why I am packing my bags."

Guy Burgess smoothed a last shirt before he closed the lid on his case.

"So you won't denounce us too soon?"

"Never. But who's us?"

"Donald Maclean. You remember?"

"Only him. There were many more moles."

"They don't have to go now. There is still work to do here. You swear you won't turn us in?"

"I swear."

Guy gave his ambiguous smile once more and picked up his case and lunged forward to kiss Henry on the cheek.

"Well, darling," he said. "I believe you. The Kremlin won't. But I won't tell on you, if you won't tell on me." He crossed his fingers. "Pax. Or you won't live on any more than I will. Bye bye, beautiful."

That was the last Henry saw of Guy Burgess before he was spirited away to Moscow. Yet as Henry carried his own bag away, he began to hear of the atomic bomb tests in Australia, which only put some British observers at risk, and all the local Aborigines, of course. The first device was loaded on an old frigate and blown off the shores of the wilderness of Oz. Unfortunately, a radioactive cloud was carried by the wind across the mainland, contaminating huge areas. This would be the first of some hundred explosions of atomic weapons with their fall-out on all life beneath their poison cloud.

With the defection of Burgess and Maclean, Henry knew his own days and job were numbered. Always amazed by the discretion of his country's intelligence system, he should have suspected that his grilling would have been an irresistible one. Actually, it took place at the Gay Hussar, with the choleric Labour junior minister, George Brown, sitting only a table away, and getting rather loud on his second bottle of Bulls Blood, which had risen to his cheeks. For Henry to find his aged cousin Gillon as the chief inquisitor was almost a relief. Confessions were more in order to somebody in the family.

Gillon came to the point over the first course of unrationed pike and beetroot. Unfortunately, the jagged jaws of the fish had been left on Henry's plate. The cheeks were meant to be delectable.

"I have been defending you too long, Henry. You have blown your cover. You know why, wise guy."

"Stupid guy. I was wrong."

"Very wrong. My ministry wanted to put you on trial, but I persuaded them you were irrelevant. And more than that, you would create a larger Cambridge scandal. You are small fry. We have top civil servants, noble lords, professors in science and economics, even an admiral, who passed through the Fens before Bentinck Street. I have put my neck on the block for you, God knows why. I have sworn you were a side-lined minor player at the big ball game."

"I owe you lunch," Henry said.

"I don't forgive you," Gillon said. "You're still under surveillance. You always will be." He tut-tutted up his nose. "We haven't bugged these seats. This is private. But walk carefully."

"I will. This is disillusion time."

"The question is, why you ever had any illusions?"

"They were better than the other side, the Fascists."

"Were they? Who will kill more, Stalin in his Siberias, or Hitler in his concentration camps? I could never make out why a free spirit like you had to go for a particularly nasty tyranny."

"I don't know either," Henry said lamely. "I wish I did."

"Have the roast duck to follow," Gillon said. "No coupons. And Victor tells me, flown in from the marshes of the Danube. But talking of changing sides, what about our cousin Peregrine, the real just-alive Labour war hero?"

"Peregrine was always too clever for me."

"He'll end too clever for himself. In one way, Henry, I agree with you. The Fascists show a super capacity for change. When Musso and Adolf went down, we found the blackshirts were all our allies under the cloth. All the war long, too. They were infiltrating to help us win, you see."

"Yes, it is amazing how defeat is a thermometer, when the mercury goes down. Didn't I hear Virginia —"

"She has taken refuge in not remembering. She claims it is Alzheimer's, but she has a lot to forget. They're a sad bunch in that flat. They even had old Margaret Jardine arrive from India, but she couldn't take it when they tried to move her to a Home. She gave up the ghost."

"And the ghastly May and Charles?"

"They have had to move on. Some retirement place in Dorset. His pension wasn't taken away in spite of his internment. The Civil Service always looks after its own, whatever its point of view, because it is not meant to have one." Gillon stuck out an arm in a Nazi salute, hitting the neck of their wine bottle, which trembled, but did not fall. He put on an OK accent. "That gesture, sir? It proves I am neutral. I am just testing to see how high the waters are."

Henry was amused.

"My mother's moved out, too. I've rather lost touch with the Nazis. Ruth must still be there."

"She may have other plans." Gillon summoned the waiter "Two duck and the trimmings."

He turned back towards his cousin, who asked: "Ruth has to look after Virginia, doesn't she? They have been so close so long."

"Too close, too long." Gillon smiled. "Even a woman doesn't know what she really wants always, until a man shows it to her. But you wouldn't think that."

"Well — I can't say I really know women."

"No, you can't. But I tell you one member of the family who really does want your advice. Boy Keiss. He's thinking of switching from Classics to Physics. He thinks neutrons are the future, not parsing Latin and Greek."

"He may well be right."

"Advise him on science, not on politics. And not on sex, don't you think?"

"I think." Henry lifted his glass. "Here's to you and security, Gillon. I must say, you do all keep me under surveillance in the most elegant way."

For Paul on the road to North Oxford, there was no conversion as on the way to Damascus. Although she was abandoned, Bridget had set her heart against him. He supposed it was her Irish blood. Most people could forgive, even if they could not forget. But the babes of Eire were like the elephants of the green. They could never forgive nor forget, even if it was they who had done you wrong.

"I came to see the boys," he said. "I haven't much leave left over before I go to Rhodesia."

"You always abandoned the boys," Bridget said. "Why should they want to see you? I brought them up."

"Not in the Gold Coast," Paul said. "When you were having your first fling with Peregrine. You sent the tots off to South Africa. Some mother. It finished off Kelso."

"How should you know? You know nothing of him."

"He was the weak one. Boy is strong. He had the luck of the cradle. He's a loner. And he's not mine. But Kelso, I fear for him, my son."

"Since when did you care so much for the children you've had nothing much to do with?"

"You know why. I had my duty. Overseas."

"That's always the excuse of you men. Duty. You know what that means? Bye bye, home. Bye bye, responsibility. Shove it on the wife."

"We are not married now. Can I see Kelso?"

"You don't know?"

"You tell me nothing."

"They've called him up. Royal Artillery. He's in the Canal Zone."

"I was in Palestine. I might have seen him. Why didn't you write? Or him?"

"We didn't hear from you. We didn't know you cared."

"I do. Give me his address."

"You can get it from the War Office."

Paul and Bridget looked at each other with the narrow eyes of hatred. How had they loved each other, had a child?

"I will. Is Boy all right?"

"The bright one. He always will be. A scholarship to Westminster. He is all paid for, except the holidays. And then, we have to do on my measly allowance —"

"I pay that. And I haven't any money. I still manage, because the courts say so."

"Always inside the law, weren't you? The rules, the bloody rules. They rule you."

"I care," Paul said. "I care for Kelso. And you. I still do."

Silent tears came from his eyes. He wiped them off with his knuckles.

"Biddy," he said. "Can we try again?"

She found herself crying with laughing, or laughing so as not to cry.

"Too late. Really. Too late."

"For the sake of the boys. I'll take you to Rhodesia. What sort of life do you have here?"

He looked round the old wallpaper and the sagging chairs and the empty fireplace, smelling of old coal.

"We scrape by," Bridget said. "My boys and I."

"Peregrine left you in the lurch."

"We parted company."

"A successful Member of Parliament. Who'd have thought it?"

"Nobody. But he never thinks, either. He acts on instinct. But always to his own advantage."

"Why did you ever fall for a swine like that?"

"You would never understand." Bridget was silent, and then she said, "Because he is a swine."

Paul rose and smoothed the creases of his trousers over his knees.

"There's nothing more to be said then, Biddy. Is there anything I can do for you and the boys?"

"Other than winning the Pools and passing on the money, nothing. Except – if you could smuggle a few bags of sugar back here without the snoopers seeing you, I would be most grateful. I haven't enough to make the jam with."

And so Paul left for the other Salisbury in East Africa. He knew he would never be able to put the sweetness in her life.

When Stanley Setty's severed head turned up bobbing in a baked beans' carton in the North Sea, Ian Hamish hoped that Clio might fly back to him. Yet she took her time before turning up at his flat door with all her possessions in a large scuffed pink handbag, which she deposited on a chair.

"Peregrine tipped off Donald," she said. "We both had to split and run for it. Anyway, it was time to go."

"It wasn't time to come here, Clio? Back to me?"

"That, too. But Donald really went too far. It was all right flogging forged petrol coupons and resprayed cars with dodgy log-books. And I didn't mind all that smuggling of planes and arms to Israel –"

"Not a bad thing," Ian said.

"And the money for the sweepstakes to Eire, and a few immigrants below the counter. But that SS knife he always had. I think that's the one he used on poor old Stanley, before he was dumped in little bits over the drink."

"You'll have to testify."

"Not bloody likely."

"You will be called as a witness in the murder trial, when they catch Donald."

"They won't. And if they do, Peregrine won't say anything because he has to keep out of it. Nor will Donald, because he doesn't know what I would say about him. Not printable, if you know what I mean. His SS knife meant Super Swine. He even made Peregrine look like Galahad."

"And I won't say anything, naturally. But why do you muck around with these scum?"

"I don't know. I wish I did. I come from a lousy family, I suppose. Wrong company too early." She flashed her dazzle of a smile at Ian. "You're the only good thing in the whole bad lot."

Ian shrugged and splayed his open hands at the worn cushions and ragged carpets of his bachelor room.

"I am very poor, you know. Publishing pays nothing, and my poems and stories, well – I can't afford to keep you."

Clio put her arms round him and laid her blonde head on his shoulder.

"You don't have to keep me, silly billy. You have to look after me."

"I am just a place to hide until things die down."

"More than that, Ian." She lifted up her mouth to kiss him. He stiffened against her. "Yes," she said. "That, too."

Later, he still doubted her, although he could not resist her, and he knew he never would. She was not only safe with him, but she was secure in her presumption that there would be no one else in his life but her, whatever she chose to do. He would never get away, and he was as jealous as a wasp wanting honey.

"Peregrine, what's he going to do? He lost his huge majority at the last election with the landslide against Labour."

"There's a point," Clio agreed, "where even the electorate won't put up with any more slippery behaviour from boiled faces."

"Attlee's only just hung on. Churchill will be back. And Peregrine hasn't got his salary now."

"He won't care. The last time I saw him, he was taking over Donald and Stanley's businesses. Import-export, without the taxes and the hassles. Do you remember that shady character Max Intrator?

Peregrine knew him, too. The big thing now is foreign currency. Everybody wants it, to go abroad. And Peregrine always has wads of it."

"But he isn't protected now by being an MP."

"He hated that. Having to dance at the local Knees-up-Mother-Brown constituency bashes with all the county frumps. Surgeries to hear the local complaints against the system, which he did not believe in and could not fix for them."

"He was a fraud."

"Always will be. But he believes what he does. Most people put on an act when they are cheating. But there are no skins on that onion. Peel him layer by layer and you'll find at the centre the same stink and crocodile tears."

"But why then – you –"

"I have you now, Ian. And I mean to stay."

Clio meant to stay, but Ian knew he would not keep her. They had no money, they scraped by. She was too restless to hold a job, although she tried as a scent saleswoman in Harrod's. In the end, she used so many of the bottles on herself and on her customers to try and sell the perfumes that she was accused of drinking them and sacked. "As if I'd swig Chanel No 5," she said. "I do prefer Moët 39."

She left at the end of the decade, saying she would be spending Christmas in Hove with her mother Virginia, who could scarcely recognize her daughter because of advancing senility, and was confined to an old folks' home.

Clio did not choose to come back, but disappeared. Yet Ian knew that she was not a bolter like the Mitford sisters. She was a returner, at least to him. Or so he comforted himself. As for changing her nature, he would be no more successful than the government, which had tried to reform the British people and failed to adopt the necessary persuasions of wartime to the weary anger of a rational peace. The slow demobilization and the continuing demoralization, the squatting and the rent and the food restrictions, had made the conditions of the conflict last the whole of the 'forties, ten years too far.

Yet Ian was clever enough not to pursue Clio. If he did, he would never succeed with her. The daily invasions of private lives, the hated inspectors, these had reduced the Labour majority in the Commons to six only. At the end of the day, the snoopers had produced the spivs, the intruders had spawned the wide boys, too many petty officers had provoked too many petty criminals, and in the never-ending battle between authority and liberty, the voters were choosing to be more free.

20

WHAT HAVE WE DONE?
1951

One hundred years had passed since the Crystal Palace with its iron and glass rising in cupolas over the trees, the sparrows dropping down on England's industrial might and Queen Victoria and the grand old Duke of Wellington, who sent up hawks after the damned defilers above, he knew how to clear a rabble out of trees or Waterloo woods. One hundred years gone since the Great Exhibition, when the godly prophets of disaster had warned of pox and plague being spread by visiting Papist hordes, of fire and brimstone smashing the domes down onto the idolaters beneath, only to see the revelation of the age of pride and assurance, steam-engines and crinolines, crankshafts and fossils, spindles and doilies, power looms and high hats, a full third of the people of England walking through the halls of glass and wonder, their vision stretching beyond the curved and skiey space that murmured with the power to girdle the globe with machines and good manners. One hundred years ago, there was an Empire on display, and now the Festival of Britain.

The rain fell for two days out of three that January and February and March, and the site on the South Bank turned into a morass, and the new pleasure gardens in Battersea which were meant to rival the Georgian elegance of Vauxhall and Ranelagh looked like the shell-holes of Passchendaele where the Tommies had drowned in the mud. Yet Marie and her brood and the millions proved that once again the British could survive their own forebodings and even their weather. At the first preview, visitors advanced into the Festival grounds as the workers retreated before them across the river, hammering a last few nails and details into their right place. The Skylon glowed in the spring light, airily astonished at being able to stand at all, a landmark as exclamation mark for the whole exhibition. Beyond, the Dome of Discovery, a concrete scallop of grandeur, enclosing radar screens and cricket-bat makers and the cogs and the sinews of British industry and invention. Dominant, the Festival Hall for the lady harpists and the tuba players beloved of postcard jokes. Not to forget the Lion and

Unicorn Pavilion, where whimsy reigned in the clutter of regality and spoofery that told of the country of Shakespeare and Edward Lear, greatness knowing its own absurdity even in its decline.

"Dog," Rosa said, pointing to the huskies which lay about the Polar Theatre, tongues licking lollipops of air. Scott, Scott, why won't they let you lie in the Antarctic ice, forgotten as a gallant failure by all posterity? Why do the British only love their losers and regard their winners as cases of indecent exposure?

"It's also a wolf," Rosabelle said, putting her daughter on the ground. "My, you're getting heavy. I won't be able to carry you any more."

"It can't be a dog and a wolf," Rosa said with the deadly truth of her age. "Dog or wolf."

"Dog and wolf," Rosabelle said. "Cross-bred."

"If you're talking about grannie," Marie said, "you can do it rather more tactfully." Then she bent her creaky neck to talk to Rosa. "A dog and a wolf went off together in my old country, Red Indian country. And they had children. And they called them huskies, just like mummy and I called you Rosa. And you have red hair, too."

Rosa thought for a little, then she said: "Why didn't you call me Pixie?"

Rosabelle laughed and said: "Well, you are a pixie or an imp, and I got your name wrong, didn't I?"

Queues were forming everywhere among the Festival crowds. The people hardly noticed they were queuing, they were so bemused by the bright colours and the towers and the music all about them, this true mirage on the South Bank among the shoddy ruins of London. One queue was waiting patiently at a locked door. There was nothing on the other side of the door. People were just used to queuing for not very much.

Rosabelle hated standing in any line, even toeing the party one. Pushing her daughter before her, she swept to the front of the people at the café, speaking loudly: "Sick child, she must lie down!" The people parted as obediently as the Red Sea for Cecil B. De Mille, for they knew the voice of authority.

"I'm not sick," Rosa cried out.

"A sick and naughty child," Rosabelle said firmly and deposited Rosa on an empty table, beating three old-age pensioners to it by a second or so. "A very sick and naughty child," Rosabelle said to the aged crones, who hobbled away, almost pleased to have been forced to do their good deed for the day. And even Marie, who hobbled up to find a seat, did not scold her own daughter. A mother had to put her child first. And anyway, they were the vanguard, were they not, of the workers? The old habit of natural command had passed on from imperial sahibs to the commissars of the left.

"May I join you ladies?" Ian Hamish had drifted up, unnoticed behind Marie; but then, she hardly had ever noticed him before. "I came to catch a glimpse of this eighth wonder of the world."

"Grab a chair, if you can," Marie said. "And have something to eat. If there is anything."

"I'm reporting the Festival for *Punch*," Ian said. "If I can find anything funny to write about this acme of comfortable mediocrity. It's a perfect case of the British middle classes patting themselves on the back without lifting their elbows."

Unseen from within the café, a balloon painted in bright colours drifted off, holding two gentlemen in Edwardian clothes and a lady in bootees and a hobble skirt. The balloon was rising to nowhere in particular and symbolized nothing of importance. As it floated higher and grew smaller, the people who watched it felt happier and sadder, filled with a nostalgia for a time that never had been. "Yes," they said to each other, "I like that, it was like that."

Within the café, Marie at last found a waitress who would serve them.

"Ice cream for the child, miss. Tea and biscuits for the rest."

"It's off," the waitress said.

"What's off?"

"Ice cream and biscuits."

"Tea and orangeade, then."

"It's off."

"What?"

"Orangeade. And there's only powdered milk with the tea."

"Well, we're off," Marie said and rose. But at Rosa's howl, she sat down again, defeated.

"Bring us what you have," she said.

"That's better, ducks," the waitress said. "Tea, peas and chips, just like everybody else."

She went off among the chattering tables.

"Everybody looks so happy," Marie said. "I just can't understand it."

"Why not?" Ian said. "We've got an atom bomb, which puts us beside America and Russia, the tom tiddler of the Big Three. We aren't going to join the rest of Europe because Europe is a bad thing – look at the mess it's got us into just because of its silly wars. We've still got a hunk of Empire, which is a lot more than most people have.

We're powerful and broke, suspicious and full of pride. Good God, even the Labour government's come to its senses and is wasting our last pennies on guns for some Asian war as irrelevant as the Crimea. So now it has to ask people to pay for their false teeth and glasses on the free Health Service. It has got its priorities just as wrong as the nation has. This is the Festival of Complacency, the jolly good show of what we think we are and soon won't be."

When the peas and chips arrived, Rosa cried and would not touch anything on her plate. Rosabelle was out of sweets to pacify these wails and out of temper for being there at all.

"You know," she said, "this tatty mirage, if that's all Labour has achieved in six years, you might as well piss in a puddle."

"Don't say that in front of Rosa," Marie said.

"She knows how to do that."

Rosa stopped crying, and smiled.

"Can I do it now? I want to go."

"So do we, darling. But wait a moment." Rosabelle turned to Ian. "We really thought there would be a revolution for the workers. You never did."

"Not I," Ian said. "Utopias are not my bag. And I don't really like all this camp and fey wit, bamboo grand vistas and rotundas and tea-houses instead of monumental arches and grand terraces. It's cut-rate cockiness, and that's not something to fight a war for."

Rosabelle looked at her daughter.

"Or something to lose a father for."

When they parted, Ian wondered if life would ever get better, or if the good times were never round the corner. Yet he knew that running down everything was a form of patriotism in England, a thwarted hope that as matters could not possibly be worse than they were, so they must improve soon. Only it was not wise to say so, in case luck or the gods thought such temerity was tempting fortune and should be punished.

Of course, the Festival of 1951 was meant to recreate the boasting of the Great Exhibition a hundred years before. Yet centuries were useless measurements, even in terms of families. Populations and kin worked in generation after generation, rather like those tables in the Old Testament, where begat followed begat and begat for many verses. What was inherited from all those ages was the insoluble question. Rather like the riddle to the Sphinx, the only answer was man, whatever that meant. And woman, too. But that was not part of the riddle. Just the fact of life.

THE PEOPLE
OF HIS
PASTURE

1

NORTH OF SUEZ

1956

These years were a time between times. It was not a war and not a peace, but a cold war. It was not a recovery and not a recession, but a restoration and a rest. It was not prosperity and not poverty, merely the illfare state. It was not so much the time of clubs or of pubs, more of coffee bars. And so, between the champagne and the warm beer, the grounds collected at the bottom of the cup; from them fortunes might be read. It was not the time of Rolls-Royces or of bicycles, rather of motor scooters. There was a median of things, a meridian and a miasma. Yet it was hardly the golden mean of the ancient Greek philosophers, the correct balance for feeling and action in the midst of extremes. It was the waiting-room at the railway station, the pause over tea and currant buns before the next train came. It was the queue at the post office to pick up the undelivered parcel from persons and points unknown. A dull expectancy pervaded the middle 'fifties. It was a time to see through.

Everything could still be faced without losing too much, even the end of an empire. Débutantes danced to the dated music of Tommy Kinsman, and the street gangs dressed exactly like Edwardian gentlemen. The rise of the teddy boys appeared to prove that the lower classes were back to aping their betters. These narrow-trousered dandies who coshed and robbed were as proud of their plumage as any aristocratic Mohock who had terrorized Georgian London. The spiv with his flash and criminal ways was gone, and social differences were apparently dying out as secretaries began to dress like ladies and thugs like Brigade of Guards officers. The welfare state seemed to have blunted the worst edges of poverty and inequality, and the Tories were too wise to revive the old class conflict which might destroy their chosen strategy of levelling up rather than breaking down. There were nasty bush wars in Kenya and Malaya and Cyprus, troubles in Iran and Egypt, but really, even Rome had never changed its empire so decently from control to commonwealth with so few skirmishes abroad and so firm a truce at home. In this strange interlude of convalescence from a great war and of patriotic complacency, everything seemed to be ticking over all right, as long as nobody looked too far ahead.

Then Colonel Nasser seized the Suez Canal, that sea vein to the Indian Empire, which was already lost. And the Prime Minister Anthony Eden saw in the Egyptian dictator another little Hitler, also born on the wrong side of the banks. So British troops and fleets were massed in Cyprus for a long hot summer, waiting for an excuse to ship over the water to Alexandria and the Nile, a crusade too late and too far. And Boy Keiss, now a scholar at Trinity College in Cambridge in his first year, was still a reservist from his National Service in the Brigade of Guards, where the Plunkett-Drax family had arranged his welcome to the scarlet tunics and bygone bearskins of the old Sinclair Highland brigades, in which his clan had once enlisted.

You do not want the state to drop its heavy hand on your shoulder as a student and force you to make a moral choice when you are trying to study. Yet that was what happened to Boy. He picked up the buff envelope at the Porter's Lodge on his way to see his moral tutor. Ensign Sinclair had been called up again. Egypt was fighting Israel, and the French and the British were ganging up with the Jews as an easy way again to get their hands on the international waterway through the sands to the Far East. And the Russians were invading Hungary to put down the popular revolution under way in the streets of Budapest. Colonial wars against Arab tyrants for God and Zion, uprisings from ex-Fascist Central Europeans taking on the Red Army with their bare hands. How was a Boy to choose between these competing causes, which all seemed out of date, given the way science was changing the world?

By the time he had reached his tutor's oak up the stairs in Nevile's Court by the Wren Library, Boy had made up his mind with the instant ignorance of the young. He couldn't defend the Empire any more. Too many of his kin had died doing that. Yet he was no coward, and he had learned to pull a trigger and toss a grenade. He would go and help the Hungarian freedom fighters, whatever their murky past, against the tanks from the Kremlin. That was a cleaner conflict, a better war. But it was an obscure war. England had ordered him to fight in the wrong place at the wrong time through a devious government for a lost cause. If he did not go to fight at Suez, he would be a deserter. How could he go, though, when he did not believe? He knew he knew more than Downing Street was stating. He was that proud, that young.

Jock Macguire was waiting for him inside. "I thought you might be coming," he said. "For other reasons." This bald and pudgy figure seemed to understand all the ages and generations, and he had even written about Africa and the Victorians. "Have they got you, Boy, have they got to you?"

"Call-up today, Jock." His tutor insisted on Christian names. "I am meant to go to bloody Suez."

"Knowing you slightly," Jock said, "you are not going."

"I am not going."

"You know the alternatives?"

"No."

"Five years in military prison as a deserter. Nasty place called Shepton Mallet. They disguise the bruises by beating you through Bibles. It would quite put paid to your distinguished career in physics at Trinity."

"Jock, I cannot go to Suez. Um – my family – um – a colonial past."

"Where will you go?"

"I am going to Hungary. At least it's a war I understand."

"No wars can be understood. They are all stupid and useless. Don't go. See it out here."

"But, Jock, if I have to fight..."

"You don't. Stay here. I'll take on the military for you." Jock put on his mocking grin. "Don't be heroic. Champions – they walk the plank. They are hoisted on the top mast. They attract flies when wrapped in shrouds. Do not join them, when you have a shred of *nous* in your tiny mind."

"So just sit here," Boy said, "and let them come and get me."

"Exactly." Jock tried to appear severe, but failed, taking another swig from his Irish whisky. "Let us defend you. The hated Establishment, though hardly myself. Jesus, you're far too young to know a thing."

Boy found himself standing. He did not know why. A dreadful pride put him on his feet. No condescending now. He knew without knowing what he had to do.

"Sorry, Jock," he said. "I have to go."

"To Hungary?"

"I suppose so."

"You don't know what you are doing."

"I am trying."

"Not very hard. And not very logically. But – I'll do what I can for you, when you know you are wrong. I will try to see you can come back here."

So they left each other, Jock and Boy, before he reached his rooms on the other side of Nevile's Court under the gables. And who would be sitting there with his instinct for intrusion but Hamish Henry. Given how things were, that cousin would be waiting for him, would he not?

"How did you get in, Henry?"

"I don't know, Boy. Porters are people, although they often pretend not to be representatives of the fading *ancien régime*."

"And what's the point? Why the honour of your presence?"

"I am rather interested how things will turn out for you." Henry crossed his legs, looked at his knees, then uncrossed his legs again. "I had rather difficult times, working out which side to back in the last war."

"So I have heard."

"Word gets around."

"In families, it tends to."

"But the thing about Cambridge is –" Now Henry put the tips of the fingers of each hand together and stared at that bony web. "We all, at Kings at least, believe in sharing knowledge, the truth in any field. Even physics." He raised the grid of his fingers as a vizor over his eyes. "I mean, there is no sin in learning from each other about nuclear fission, for instance, and helping each other. Only boring governments say nay."

"I had heard about you knowing Burgess and Maclean. And Philby too. They all skipped to Moscow."

Henry dropped his hands.

"I am as clean as a whistle," he said. "I never joined the Party. All I care for now are academic values – academic though they are."

"Well, if you're now helping in making our hydrogen bombs –"

Hamish slipped on his loose grin.

"Nobody could trust me that far. Reactors. Nuclear energy. Warmth to keep all the home fires burning for ever. Very regrettable. And a windfall for the other cousins."

"Which lot?"

"The radical ones. The landowners. Marie's red brood. There are Sinclair lands in Caithness. My people want power stations there."

"She will never sell."

"She will. There's nothing coming in from the Lothian coal mines now for her welfare schemes. The atoms can pay off her sick miners with the new energy. But that wasn't why I came to see you, Boy."

"Why, then?"

"Suez, of course."

"Damn you, Henry. Would you like the last of the sherry?"

"If that's all there is."

"You'll have to drink it out of egg-cups. I broke my last glass."

"Oh, well, Boy. I like a yolk in my Tio Pepe."

As they sipped the sweet brown mixture from the blue-ringed china, Boy tried to explain to Henry why he was going to Hungary to fight, and not to Suez. But though Boy thought he knew why, he was incoherent. The words stumbled on his tongue.

"I can't fight for Anthony Eden ... He's telling lies ... The Empire's pooh-pooh, Pooh Bear ... The Americans will squash us, anyway ... Eisenhower, he didn't fight in Europe to save our skins in the Near East ... Anyway, well, anyway ... I'm in the Brigade ... Trained soldier ... I believe in freedom ... So if I'm not here, gone away, didn't get the call-up papers, do want to fight ... well, I can shove it up Ivan's noses, not the wogs, as we call them ... And they can't get me, military prison, all that."

Henry dropped his mouth open, then closed it.

"Dear Boy, you got a scholarship here. And you cannot even string a sentence together. Well, although I am not your tutor ..."

"God forgive."

"God would not forgive that. Though I am not your tutor, let me be your mentor. How may killing a few innocent Russians advance your career here? And when you consider the ex-Blackshirts you may be killing them for, it almost makes me pick up the Hammer-and-Sickle again."

"I told you, Henry, I don't know. I really don't know. But I think it is better ..."

"Never act before you think." Henry downed the dregs of his sherry and grimaced. "Awful stuff. It must have congealed at the bottom of the barrel. My dear, you came here to think. Do nothing. Particularly at this time, when nobody can think clearly about anything. Go away to somewhere agreeable like Florence or Amalfi, drink some Chianti, and twiddle your toes. Why? You need a holiday. A small nervous breakdown. That is why you did not receive your call-up papers. Sorry, you forgot to leave an address."

Now Hamish Henry rose and yawned.

"There are no causes now, my dear Boy. Do not espouse one. You're attractive and intelligent. Do not commit at your tender age. Only connect, as our E.M. Forster said. But only to the right people. And only when you know they are the right people, or the left ones. I mean, the left-over ones."

Boy found himself on his feet, too. He had to do as he said he would do.

"I am going to Trafalgar Square tonight," he said. "I must protest."

"Mob rule, my dear, is a long gone thing. Bye, bye."

And so Henry departed for his Fellow's room in Kings College, and so Boy went towards his Waterloo, station and battleground, except that he found himself arriving at King's Cross. He did not know that a certain Magoub, the great-grandson of the Mahdi who had killed General Gordon at Khartoum, had just knocked down his moral tutor Macguire as an imperialist lackey. What Boy did find were streams of young people pouring from the northern stations towards the centre of London, shouting slogans which passed away in the smog and the drear.

The broken columns in the streets became masses in the avenues and a maelstrom in the square under Nelson's Column. The police barriers were swept away as the morass of heads seethed below the platform of the speakers. And there Boy could see a face he knew, his cousin Rosabelle, her long red hair a flamboyant oriflamme of defiance. She had linked arms with a teenage girl, again with tresses on fire, probably her daughter. Screaming into a microphone, Rosabelle was shouting: "Down with the Fascist scum! Give the Canal back to our Arab comrades! Eden out! Eden out! Eden out!"

Now the crowd took up the chant, and a surge crushed Boy, then swept him aside as mounted blue officers on greys clip-clopped forward through the crowd, dividing their huddle as the Red Sea before Moses. Boy was spewed back towards the National Gallery and ended spreadeagled against a stone balustrade. Winded, he looked up to see a pair of scarlet boots in snakeskin leggings perched on the parapet and a man's face looking down at him and shouting. "Boy, you fool, what the hell are you doing here?"

The arms of the man and the woman reached down and hauled Boy scrabbling upwards towards their roost above the mob, now shouting at the mounted police, "All coppers are bastards!" Boy could see who were his rescuers, Clio and Ian Hamish Ogilvie, come to observe the fun. His kith and kin were certainly inescapable in the twilight of the Empire.

"Got you out of that," Clio said, as Boy plumped down beside her. "Are you OK?"

"I think so."

"Were you sent down?" Ian said.

"I came up," Boy said, "for air."

Clio grinned.

"Not another duff protestor, saving our sacred land from another nice little disaster."

"No," Boy said. "Just another nice little deserter. Saving himself."

"Where are you off to?"

"Budapest. If the trains still run from Blackfriars."

"You've time for dinner," Ian said. "Or you'll be hungry all the way to Hungary. And I don't have to file my piece until tomorrow."

So Boy found himself in Chez Victor, a small French restaurant in Gerrard Street, once the police cordon had let them pass out of Trafalgar Square. He began drinking carafes of red wine as if it were blackcurrant cordial and he heard his voice spouting flotsam and jetsam about duty and country in a welter of emotional drivel, which failed even to convince his own sense and sensibility, whatever was left of them.

"You're a bloody fool," Clio said, dragging a garlicky snail from its shell with the long point of a carmine fingernail. "Sod them all. By the time you get to camp, the show will all be over. The Yanks will wag their pinkie fingers, and the old bulldog will crawl back into his kennel." She plopped the snail's body into her mouth and sucked her finger. "Or they really will gobble you up."

"Clio's right," Ian said "You're making a useless gesture."

"Posture," Clio said. "I do hate postures."

"Posture, then. Don't pose, Boy, although you think it's courage. It's just bravado."

"Heros are zeros," Clio said. She held up the empty snail shell to kiss it and pour the last drops of garlic sauce down her mouth. "Look what happened to Peregrine, our burned fighter ace. Does your mother know?"

"No," Boy said. He was squirming, for he knew that his mother Bridget and Clio had shared the missing pilot.

"Peregrine was a Fascist spy and a serial killer in his Spitfire before he became a Member of Parliament. A leading importer and exporter of every dodgy piece of merchandise. A bent pillar of the community. A gentleman who thought he was above the law, until it knocked on his door, and –"

"And?"

"He did a runner, naturally. They say he has visited most of the plastic surgeons in Mexico. And when he turns up here again, we won't know him."

"But he will know us."

"He will know you, Boy. He told me – although I couldn't do it for him – he always wanted a son."

Ian's hand scrunched over his glass of red wine and shattered it, the splinters cutting his palm. Blood and burgundy were a mix.

"Christ," Clio said, "what a way to change the subject. Open up." She spread out Ian's fingers and picked out a shard and bound her napkin round the bleeding cuts and tied a knot in the ends of the cloth. "Hold it tight till we've finished dinner, and I'll get you to Casualty at Charing Cross hospital, when the show is over."

"We should go now," Boy said. "He's hurt."

"He's a frightful masochist," Clio said. "He loves pain, especially from the people he loves. And we've got to get you to the station, too. But which one? Budapest bound? Or King's Cross and back to the Fens?"

So they argued through the rest of the meal, and Boy found his convictions slipping into a melting pot, so that impulses of generosity and fear, sacrifice and self-interest, were scrambled eggs in his skull. And when they walked away from Chez Victor towards the hospital and the station, Trafalgar Square was merely a carnage of rubbish, the broken bodies of torn placards littering the paving stones, with gloomy bobbies telling the stragglers to move on, please, move on.

"There," Ian said, holding his bandaged hand up so that the blood flowed down his arm. "We came, we saw, we did not conquer. Nor will you, dear Boy, nor will you. Your greatest act of courage will be to go home. To be called a coward and do the right thing is the bravest deed anyone can do. I know that."

And so Boy allowed himself to be persuaded and returned to Trinity. It all happened as Clio had predicted. Before he could even present himself at Wellington Barracks, the American President Eisenhower had killed off the whole Suez adventure. Anthony Eden had exceeded the grand old Duke of York. He had sailed a hundred thousand men to the Suez Canal, and sailed them back again. He fell from office with a nervous breakdown. This was, indeed, the beginning and the end of the British Empire.

Life in the African colonies soon began to expire. The new Prime Minister, Harold Macmillan, was called in to revive the corpse, although he sensibly preferred to bury it. Like any undertaker, he had to reassure the family at home with visions of fortune and future ease, while actually pickling the body before it started to stink and could be carried away. The funeral procession had to be done decently and discreetly. No wreaths or forty-gun salutes by request.

The Gold Coast was first given independence and took the new name of Ghana. The rest of the African possessions were assured that their freedom would come soon, even for Mau-Mau Kenya, if they would wait for the proper obsequies and not shoot the pall-bearers. By concentrating the eyes of the British people on the better life to come, Mac the Hearse hoped to drape a black shroud over Africa without his party or his country noticing that the white man's face was covered and gone. It was a shrewd strategy for a necessary grave. Britain could no longer afford an Algeria or an Angola, where the French and the Portuguese would not give in. And as for Rhodesia, where Boy's apparent father Paul had gone, and his brother Kelso, who might be half a one, that colony must look after its own. The family might start up again there, too.

2

FALLS

1961

"All girls being equal, e.g. two breasts and one etcetera," Paul had once said to his son, "a rich girl is just as easy to marry as a poor one."

"But all girls aren't equal," Kelso had said. "Some are prettier than others."

"Prettiness doesn't last," Paul had answered. "Your mother Bridget was the prettiest forget-me-not in all of South Africa. But disposable income, that does see a family through hard times."

Kelso had come out to Southern Rhodesia in the uneasy days of the Federation for the opportunity, but not for a marriage. Yet what could he do when he met Elizabeth Fairlie in Salisbury at some company bash in Meikles, the only good hotel in town, where he could hardly afford to stay. That pert bounce, that blonde bob, those whippet legs, that blunt approach, "Hello, stranger. Just arrived? Wet behind the ears from London?"

He knew he had been selected, but found himself saying stupidly, "Cambridge, actually."

That reply had convulsed Elizabeth, who choked and wiped her eyes on his offered handkerchief, before she could get out, "You can't believe English gents can be true. I mean, you're better than a *Punch* cartoon."

"Scottish, mainly. And *Punch* is out-of-date. You only find it in dentist's waiting-rooms along with *The Field* and *Horse and Hounds*."

"But you look so like a –"

"Waxwork."

"No, no. Cast from the old mould. The visiting inspector."

"That's my father," Kelso said. "He's in your police. I am a businessman, if I'm lucky. Kelso Sinclair."

"Elizabeth Fairlie."

"Oh, gold, tobacco. That family?"

"You have done your homework."

"We like to know a little about the natives," Kelso said drily, "before we arrive to educate them."

In spite of the disapproval of her widowed father, his only daughter Elizabeth insisted on marrying the penniless Kelso within three months. Now the supporter of his father Paul, Kelso had refused to allow his lonely mother to fly out for the wedding, and her supporter Boy did not turn up, either. Nothing widens family feuds more than family occasions. With each spring, a child was born to Elizabeth to take over the Fairlie tobacco farms and gold mines. First Kathleen arrived, to be followed by Conan and Catherine. Drilling new wells, Kelso extended by irrigation the thousands of acres of the green leaves, which would end up cured and smoked. That clean and purest of veldt air which extended to the far horizon over the plants might end in lung cancer for the millions, but during those African summers of the white Highlands, all seemed a living dream in the Elysian Fields. The native village by the great ranchhouse was a hive of content, or so it appeared. Only in Paul's territory up by the Victoria Falls were troubles brewing, as a certain militance began to sprout with the victory of the Rhodesian Front Party in the election, its policies so close south of the border to the Afrikaners, who may have lost the Boer War, but had certainly won the long peace thereafter.

Paul was watching the vervet monkeys scavenging in the bushes between the hotel fence and the Zambezi river. They were small and grey-green with black faces. A tiny hand grew on the end of each of their paws. One of the monkeys, Paul noticed, only had three hands; its fourth paw had been severed at the joint. Looking round the rest of them, Paul saw that two others had been mutilated. It hardly affected their agility or their play.

"Why are there so many three-legged monkeys round here?" In the bar, Paul asked Phil the Boatman, who took the tourists to see the hippos grazing on the water grasses above the Falls. "Crocs? Or Big Boy, the Great Dane?"

"Witchdoctors."

"What?"

"They are still very powerful here. They believe, if you cut the paw off a living thing, it will summon back the dead."

"The living thing has to stay alive?"

"Yes. Then the paw has the power of life. We've got a spirit medium round here – Alice, wife of Livingstone Pemba, the storekeeper. You can hear her sometimes howling in strange voices. Possessed. The power of the monkey's paw."

Paul remembered a story by W.W. Jacobs. A monkey's paw with the power to grant wishes. An old woman with a wrecked sailor son wishing him back from the sea. His ghastly approach, because he was still drowned and dead. The use of the last wish to get rid of him again. The monkey's paw.

Paul shivered in the muggy bar.

"It's a common belief," he said. "In China, too, a monkey's paw is bad magic. I didn't know the monkey had to stay alive to make it work."

"Two more beers," Phil said to the barman. "All of us monkeys, we've got to stay alive to make us work."

Livingstone Pemba beamed. His store was full of pink mist. In his poor vision made rich by the sun, the tins and the bags, the packets and the racks of clothes, the mealie sacks and the sausages on their hooks, all were rosy with obscure promise. Even the two men approaching him were surrounded with auras of dawn. Until they opened their mouths, they might have been messengers of hope.

"Alice, she say, we come shopping," Size Tauro said.

"We got a list, Livingstone," said his brother Lovemore.

"What you got, we got," Size said and laughed. "*Brother.*"

Livingstone Pemba no longer beamed. That was why Alice had been so good to him last night. "Come, my man," she had said, crooning like a frog. "Come in me, my man, my own man, my strong man." And she had laughed like her family, knowing his smallness, his weakness, his want of her. But she had made him feel as strong as a buffalo, as mighty as an elephant. That was the gift of her thighs. Now in the morning, he was giving gifts to her big brothers. He had paid a thousand dollars' bride price for her, but that was only the beginning. Her family was eternal blackmail.

"Let me see the list," Livingstone Pemba said.

"You can't read," Size said. "Not without yo' glasses."

Lovemore picked up Livingstone's glasses from beside the cash register. He swung them, then threw them across the store to clatter onto the floor.

"Go get 'em, boy," Lovemore said. "We got shopping to do."

"Or we tell Alice. And she won't be good fo' you. Not fo' years."

The big brothers laughed. As Livingstone crossed his store and began searching for his spectacles on hands and knees, they took two empty sacks and started to fill them with groceries and clothes. Their sister's tie with Livingstone was, for them, a licence to plunder. Her marriage was the moral sanction for looting.

Just before Size stepped on the spectacles, Livingstone found them. He settled them on his nose. Beyond Size's sturdy legs, the store became defined in all its planned tawdriness. The secret of shop-keeping was temptation, persuading the client to pick up more than he or she could afford. So colour and glitter were arranged in bright pyramids, difficult to resist. Size and Lovemore were certainly not resisting, but then, they were not paying. They were stuffing their sacks so full that the seams bulged and split.

"You'll ruin me," Livingstone said, rising to his feet.

"Wait when we try," Lovemore said, trying on a cap marked *Wankie* from the name of the distant game reserve.

"Yo' get to the till," Size said. "The Party need some cash."

"And you're the Party," Livingstone said. "Why don't you come in with guns? And hold me up."

"Our sister, she hold you up her," Lovemore said and laughed like artillery. Size joined in the barrage. Then the big brothers took Lovemore under the elbows and carried him as far as the cash register.

"Fifty dollar," Size said.

"I haven't got it."

"Show."

Livingstone turned the key and rang open the register. Inside, there were twenty-seven dollars in small notes and coins.

"Give it," Lovemore said.

"And yo' do better," Size said. "Yo' not working, brother No time now fo' capitalists when they not working in this new country."

Livingstone handed over the notes and the coins. The big brothers turned and walked towards the entrance to the store, swinging their full sacks. A small boy came into the store and stopped. He looked up at the two men with fear.

"Hey, Lookout," Lovemore said, clipping the child on the top of his curly head, "yo' got be nice to yo' daddy. He don't feel no good. He poor."

The small boy began to cry. Livingstone came round the counter and swept the little boy into his arms.

"Don't you cry, Lookout," he said softly. "Daddy loves you. Daddy'll look after you. Daddy wants to leave you something when you grow up. Or else, your family'll look after you. And you get nothing."

As if the day could get worse, the policeman now walked through the door in his khaki shorts and with his revolver at his belt.

"Hello, Livingstone," Paul said. "I just saw Alice's brothers walking out with a couple of sacks. They said they paid for it. Right?"

Livingstone shook his head, then found himself nodding.

"They say they pay."

"Will they?"

"They say."

"Do you want to press charges?"

"No. They're my wife's brothers."

"Alice. Yes, Alice. There is bad news about her."

"Bad news." Livingstone cradled his son. "She always bad news."

"Very bad news. They say she talk to the spirits. They say she say, kill the white men."

"She a foolish woman," Livingston said. "We go to church. We good Christians. You ask Father Mbdele. I give to the Mission to Save Souls."

"I don't doubt that, Livingstone. I doubt your wife."

"Nobody believe in that old stuff no more. Mumbo-jumbo, you call it. So me too."

"People still believe round here."

"More fool they."

"Look," Paul said, "you let me know. Any of this voodoo stuff, any meeting in the bush, you let me know."

"Sure, boss."

Paul handed over a form with a stamp on it.

"Your new trading licence," he said. He patted the curls of the small boy in Livingstone's arms. "You will let me know, won't you?"

The spirits were speaking through Alice. She writhed and rolled on the dirt floor, the voices of the dead gasping from deep within her. Her jerking feet kicked over the calabash of ritual beer. Her flailing hands scattered the bones of divination and banged on the gourds and drums. Her feathers and beads and amulets were broken free and scattered round the embers of the fire in the hut. The exhaled voices spoke the old language.

"Kill the whites – Mapwani speaks – The God Mapwani speaks – Kill the whites – Their bullets shall be water – Their bombs shall be rain – Your spears shall drink blood – Your bullets shall make skulls – The land shall be your land – Mapwani gives it back – Hear the God speak – Hear him – Kill the whites – Take back your land – Kill – Kill – Kill –"

The words no longer convulsed Alice. The spirits left their medium twitching on the dirt to collapse, a dead weight, hardly breathing. Her two brothers, Size and Lovemore, rose from their haunches and ran forward to revive her. They slapped her cheeks, breathed alcohol into her mouth. She did not stir. They tried to lift her, but her slack arms slipped from between their hands.

The other watchers from the village began to ululate.

"Alice – the spirits have taken her – Alice –"

But the man in the pinstripe suit strode forward and hushed them, speaking to them in the old language.

"She is not gone," Witness Nkadala said. "She is always so, after the spirits have spoken. The words of the God are true, but you shall not speak them. If you speak, you shall have your tongues cut out because you spoke. You shall have your eyes taken out because you saw. You shall have your ears cut off because you heard and spoke. So I speak, Witness Nkadala. I shall tell the Minister what the God Mapwani said through his servant Alice Pemba. And he shall tell you the day and the hour when the will of the God shall be done. I have spoken, Witness Nkadala. I shall bring millet from the Party for a great beer-drinking. Then I shall speak to you about the killing that must be done."

Witness Nkadala bent over the slack body of Alice and put his hand on her forehead. The effect was magical. Alice sat up, her face composed, and she looked about her.

"I have been to a strange country," she said. "What did the spirits speak through my mouth?"

"Enough," Witness Nkadala said. "The truth was spoken."

He helped her to her feet, then he fingered the dried monkey's paw that hung from a copper chain round her neck.

"That is powerful," he said.

"The old ways are powerful," she said. Then she looked round the hut. "That fool husband of mine is not here."

"Livingstone? We kept him from the hut." Witness Nkadala smiled without mirth. "He is such a fool he might betray us."

"Not while I am his wife." Alice laughed coarsely and touched Witness Nkadala's arm. "When the day comes, Witness, I shall come to you."

Looking at the bold glistening of Alice's eyes, Witness Nkadala felt a cold void within his ribs. The spirit medium had chosen him. He could not escape her in the world of the living and the dead. And he did not desire the fate of her husband.

Lovemore and Size and Witness went on their killing round two nights after the spirits had spoken. They knew that Paul would dine twice a week at the hotel, and then he would walk in the moonlight through the rain forest towards the edge of the thundering drop of the great river, with the spray making small rainbows under the dark branches. What they did not know was that his son Kelso had come that afternoon to ask him to go to the christening of the baby Catherine, and serve as a godfather. So it was that the two men came strolling beneath the glittering sombre traceries of the leaves towards a murder.

Size shot off his stolen sten-gun, but it jammed as Paul fell to his knees. Lovemore strode forward and swung his machete sideways and sliced off Paul's head at the neck. It jerked and squirted and hit Kelso's boots. He bent and picked up in his hands the gory face of his father. The three killers stood still and stared at Kelso, Alice's two huge brothers and the smaller Witness Nkadala, shocked at the sight of the white man in his bloodied safari suit, holding the horrible trophy. Kelso shook and turned and began to run back through the broken palisades of the wood. Behind him, he heard shouting and crashing and then nothing, as he panted into the hotel and laid Paul's head on the bar.

In the commotion, the three killers escaped. They had other work to do, the ending of Livingstone Pemba. Alice had taken him out of the store into the yard and had stunned him with an iron pot. His body was dragged to the edge of the game reserve, where lions would find him. Killed with the machete, he was scraped with Alice's leather paw with claws, as though the beasts had already killed him, although the beasts were human in this case.

When Alice heard that the dead policeman's son had escaped, she raged and shouted, "He saw you, he saw you. And he is alive. You call yourself Witness, you Nkadala fool. He is the witness. He see you hung." The men could not silence her, but they all agreed to escape into the bush. Then the inevitable British law would not find them, only Alice. And nothing could be proved against her. And the spirits would protect her, as they must.

3
REMEMBRANCE DAYS

The schoolgirls were drawn up in their ranks on the playing-fields of November. Their parents stood among them on that cold blowing day that fluttered the cloth poppies in the lapels of the brown jackets of the children and the dark coats of the men and women. In front of a solitary wooden cross stuck on the touchline of the hockey field and loaded with a wreath of more red poppies, Rosa stood. On a signal from the headmistress, she began her recitation into the wind, her hair blowing out as crimson as the flowers.

> "They shall grow not old, as we that are left grow old;
> Age shall not weary them, nor the years condemn.
> At the going down of the sun and in the morning
> We will remember them."

The words were hardly audible, although Rosa tried to shout. The sound tailed away into the Two Minutes Silence of the memorial service for the dead of the Two World Wars. Rosa was now burying the tip of her cold nose inside her scarf and looking down at the muddy grass. She did not seem to be praying or thinking of the millions of the dead who had fought for something or another that was quite irrelevant by now. She just seemed to be trying to survive as warmly as possible until she could get away.

Fifty yards to the left of her stood her grandmother Marie, while a Highland trumpeter in tartan and sporran and bearskin and bare knees sounded the Last Post. Each slow-drawn note was more clear and more cold than the wind. Marie did not want to weep, but the wind helped, driving a drop or two out of her eyes to freeze on her cheek. She did remember the seas of mud in Flanders where men had drowned in liquid earth, and the Japanese labour camps where the prisoners had crawled to death in shame and squitters, also the moment of sad absurdity on a Veterans' Parade she had seen in Birdcage Walk, when the strutting young soldiers were followed by old cripples driving their motorized chairs, and at the Eyes Right, one of the old men had turned his neck so stiffly into the salute that he had run into the kerb.

Did all the glory days have to end like that? Was the whole of the Empire a sad farce with a thin red line drawn under it? What could she tell her granddaughter, who obviously hated the slow melancholy ceremony and hadn't a clue what it was all about. Yet so many of the gallant young men had died. All those lost lives, which might have left more children to mourn their passing.

Marie took Rosa back to Ermondhaugh. Her mother Rosabelle was coming back from some Artistic Performance near Cambridge, hurling stink-bombs at the American cemetery, where the dead airmen were buried standing in neat rows, and God and his Angels flew among the Flying Fortresses in the mosaic on the chapel ceiling. The young physicist Keiss Sinclair, who was called Boy although he had grown up, would be there. He had important news for her, or so he said. Something about her property and energy, as if there were any energy in property, which just lay in the sodden earth of inheritance around her.

"Rosa," Marie said, as the taxi took them up the drive to the great house, "I'll try to explain to you that Poppy Days are worth it. A lot of splendid people died."

"Mummy says the World Wars were capitalist murder sprees."

"That, too. But Mummy isn't always right."

"I bet you thought you were always right, when you were Rosabelle's Mummy."

"I still am. But *touchée*. Mothers always know best for their daughters."

Boy had at least grown into his face. He had always looked old when he was young, but now he approached his natural years. He had the long lines of the Sinclair blood from their Viking ancestors, rather like her forebears, the Crow braves. On a drooping face with a high brow, a pair of clefts stretched from the top of the nose to the sides of the jawbone. Two deeper creases ran from the bottom of the nostrils past each lip beside the dimple in the strong chin. This was a throwback face, primitive and a proof that Darwin was right. Social justice might change the world, but genetics would always box its corner.

"Boy," she said, "how good to see you. Do you know my grand-daughter Rosa?"

"I have seen her," Boy answered. "She was standing with her mother and the lions in Trafalgar Square on Suez day. How could I ever forget her red hair?"

"You were there?" Rosa could not believe it.

"They called me up. I didn't want to go. I am not very good at armies. And orders. Particularly if I have to kill wogs. That seems like murder to me."

"These views seem to run in the family," Marie said. "Let's have lunch and talk about it."

In the private rooms of the converted miners' rest home, the three of them ate a meal of bannocks and gulls' eggs and smoked salmon, sluiced with a bottle of hock. With so few years left to her, Marie wanted to enjoy each day, or a little bit of each day. And alas, food and wine were the pleasures of the aged. She watched Boy looking shyly at Rosa, and she glancing at him and hoping he did not see her peering. And Marie smiled and said, "What did you come all this way to tell me, Boy? Enough of the niceties. Down to the mutton, or do I mean, salmon?"

"It's your land in Caithness."

"Where the Viking Sinclairs came from."

"They are going to build a nuclear processing plant on the sea. They want it at Dounreay. There are shafts there to sink the waste."

"We can't touch that," Rosa said. "Those atom bomb tests. They give you leukemia. Mummy and I, we're on the next march from Aldermaston."

"So am I," Boy said. "I'll join you."

"But you're a nuclear physicist."

"I am against the Bomb, too. But I am for nuclear energy."

"Why?"

"It's cheap. It doesn't foul the atmosphere like all those coal stations. It's efficient. It works."

"But suppose it blows up?"

"It can't, and it won't. The problem is, what to do with the waste."

"I don't want it on our clean land," Marie said. "If it went wrong, that would be the final clearance of the Highlands and the crofts."

"Hundreds of jobs for Caithness," Boy said. "And there are no jobs there. They have already had a poll with the local people. Ninety per cent want the plant to come there, so that they can live better."

"They don't know what they are in for," Rosa cried.

"They may be desperate for work," Marie said. "But nobody has told them of the risks."

"They are fully informed," Boy said. "Like your old miners at Dunesk. They needed the work. They knew what they were in for. Silicosis. Black lungs. And they are living out their misery here. And you are looking after them. And, I shouldn't say, but I know, you haven't got enough money left to keep the place going."

"But nuclear gunge at Dounreay," Rosa was wailing. "It's obscene."

"It's cleaner energy than coal. And frankly, there will be less loss of life, if we produce power that way."

"There are going to be nuclear power stations on the Firth of Forth," Marie said. "The Setons and the Douglas family used to defend us from English power. Now they have sold out to your nuclear friends. But that is power. Not waste. What do you want me to do? Allow the waste to be processed at Dounreay, so that it does not contaminate the whole of Britain and Europe?"

"That would be a good act," Boy said, "if you took the waste in and made it safe."

"The history of my life." Marie could not sit any more from the raging inside her veins. She stood and shook. Old people as her were no longer so steady on their pins. She walked to the high window and looked down at the forty old men and women wandering round her garden as ghosts in suits or unsuitable woolly jumpers. "I have always collected the waste. The waste of other lives. The waste of governments. The waste of our Empire. But what's worse — we have to collect the waste of our lives." She turned back to Boy after looking down at her dependants. "So Dunesk — and Dounreay — we are your rubbish bin. We pick up what's left over from all these great ambitions. Yes, we made industry happen here. We were the revolutionaries, we sent it across the world. And our iron ships and our coal engines, why, we — or shall I say, *you* — you dominated the globe. But there was all that waste. The waste of people, the waste of what was in the earth, the dark air, the poison in the rivers, like from our paper mills here. And now, Boy, you want me to go on with this dreadful rotting of our family. To pay for our mills and our mines, which I am trying to do, we have to take in the worst waste of all, your atomic killer dust, and rinse it clean, at the peril of the last perfect land to the north, pretty well stripped of the clan, and left to the sheep and the deer. I don't know, my dear, I don't know. How long can we go on being the servants and the cure of all the horrors our country commits?"

The debate went on through the afternoon, and tempers sparked when Rosabelle returned for tea. She was refined vitriol on the subject of the nuclear plant at Dounreay.

"Worse than the Sutherlands," she said. "Worse than the thousands dying shipped to Canada. You will blight whole generations. One leak, and nobody will have a croft left for fifty thousand years."

Boy was left trying to talk the truth of nuclear energy and the facts of its safety into three generations of passionate protestors. His reason was futile against the emotion of the women. Only one detail disconcerted them. Jobs would be on offer to the Donald and Kirsty, the children of Martha and Angus Mackenzie, who had moved to an extended croft nearby, and were teaching at the village school there.

"They'll be getting three times the salary of their father," Boy said. "I know it's shocking, and education should get much more. But here you are. Splitting the atom is a two-edged sword. Either the destruction of us all – or our salvation. Mass murder or cheap power. Graves and jobs. You must take your pick."

By dinner, because she was nearly bankrupt, and so many of the casualties of Lothian labour hung onto her skirts, Marie decided to accept this offer on the land in Caithness. At the end of the day, present lives were more important than future lives. And she had her own blood to protect, although she did not dare tell Rosabelle and Rosa about her decision – she had to put them first so that they could continue in their protests. And she had to look after the wreckage of the mines around her. And so she whispered to Boy before he left, "Tell them – you may tell them – it's all right for Dounreay. But it is against my will. And I wish you had not asked me."

Bitter about the past and the loss of her sons living their own lives away from her, Bridget was talking to herself too much. She rehearsed all the time all the things which had gone wrong for her. Why had she left Paul for Peregrine? Why was that bastard the father of Boy, which made him a bastard? Women were so unfortunate. They could not choose their conceptions. And now, in her loneliness, she had both her sons arriving to make her feel even more miserable for her bad choices. Boy and Kelso, carrying the news of the severed head of his father.

The problem was, you could never change things. You could never go back on what you had done. That idiotic French singer, the sparrow Piaf, singing that she regretted nothing. Of course, you regret. But what you regret is that you did it that way, and not another way. Then again, could she have done it any other way? She had a raging heart under her hard skin. She had to follow the dictates of her womb. She had to do what she did in bed. How regret the necessary drive of desire?

"Boy, will you have some tea? And you too, Kelso. I'm sure you would rather have whisky, but that will have to wait." Bridget passed round the china cups to her two sons. "Milk? Sugar?" She fulfilled their requests, then she smoothed her skirt over her full knees. "Now you can tell me all about it."

So Kelso told her about the murder of her husband. The police knew the identities of the three killers, but they had fled to join the rebel gangs of Nkomo or Mugabe, who were jostling Ian Smith for control of Southern Rhodesia. The guilty men would not be found, unless they were captured in the bush. There was little law and order out there now, more a question of a racial war.

"Then why are you going back?" Bridget asked.

"Family, mother," Kelso said. "And money. My wife's lot are in gold and tobacco. And they have brought in another lot we know. The Apfelsteins. They are the Joburg people, who are very rich and have most of the gold in South Africa. My lawyer is Jules Apfelstein, and he's put me onto some huge scheme to build a dam below the Victoria Falls, where Daddy was murdered."

"Them." Bridget was interested. "I knew that Jewish family. They got all the gold from the Rand."

"They are very *liberal*, mother. They have a huge charitable trust. They give money to hospitals and good causes. They hate apartheid, things like that."

"If you'd known South Africa when I was there, Kelso, you wouldn't think apartheid was that bad a thing."

"Other times, other views. Anyway, you remember, Miriam was an Apfelstein. She was the one who married the Indian doctor. Now their son Solomon and she have Annandale."

"Some of it should have come to us."

"I don't know," Kelso said. "We don't have much to do with India now."

"Or Rhodesia, then. Why are you hanging on there?"

"My wife. My family. Your three grandchildren. You must come out and visit us, Bridget."

"You took your father's side."

"He's dead. It's all over." Kelso walked across the room to where his mother was seated, and he bent her stiff neck against the comfort of his tweed jacket. "Can't we learn to love each other now?"

Bridget hated to weep, but the tears began prickling against her eyelids, then poured down. She buried her head in the rough cloth, and she put her arm round her son's waist.

"I'll come," she said. "I'll come." She raised her head and wiped off her tears with the back of her hand. "When I am ready. Not till then."

She had kept her pride, but the brothers also had to come to some kind of separate truce. They had always been jealous of each other. Which one would she give more of her love to? Which did she prefer? She had rationed her affections between them, playing one against the other, as they had played in their childish games. Now she had gone with Boy far too long since the divorce. Perhaps it was time to get Kelso back, and the three grandchildren, whom she yearned to see. They were hers, too.

"I don't think Mother," Boy was saying, "is quite ready for a visit to Rhodesia. We have things going on here, which take up her time."

Kelso looked round the shabby house in North Oxford, which was scoured down to the bindings and the threads. Unhappy women kept their nests obsessively clean. They had little else to do.

"It will be a holiday for Mother," Kelso said. "And Elizabeth and I will pay for it. And you, Boy – no children. No luck on the romantic front?"

"I've been too busy for that, brother. All this atomic energy business. They work me to the bone."

"As long as it is not to the bone marrow. Isn't that where the radiation is meant to hit you?"

"It is perfectly safe what I do, Kelso. Don't wish me into an early grave."

"You always used to squabble," Bridget said, "when you were little. You'd fight over the jelly, and I had to hit you on the head with my silver ladle. But you always loved each other, really."

"Still do," Boy said, and Kelso agreed.

They spent the rest of the day, as families do, not discussing their own relationships, which were presumed, but those of the rest of their kith and kin. Most of the ones hated by Bridget were finished. Charles Seymour-Scudabright was dead, and his wife was hanging on in a superior Old Establishment Home, soon to go herself. Virginia had lost her flat in London and moved down to Hove in the last throes of her odd way of life. But the news from Boy beggared credulity – Ruth had left her long embrace with Virginia and had joined up with Gillon in a sort of mutual desperation, the relief from their solitariness apart.

"Gillon told me that, the last time we met." Boy was revelling in the gossip. "He said, when you reach my age, you find out that everybody you know except for your children, who you never see, is dead. So you search among your acquaintances, and you see who is left. Very few now can speak the same language. In my case, there was Ruth. I had always liked her and found her very sympathetic and attractive, if she could only get away from the ghastly pretentiousness of Virginia. And she had had enough, or so Gillon told me. So when Gillon proposed to her, she accepted. As Gillon said, she was bored with feely-feely between women, and she had really preferred men all the time. This sent Virginia into an instant – and I think deserved – decline. What do you think?"

"I love it," Bridget said. "When I arrived in England, I have never had such a put down as I got from Virginia. Where's the whisky now? Let's drink to –"

"Revenge?"

"No. Waiting. And winning. Kelso, the decanter's in the sideboard. No, that side!"

As she commanded her sons, Bridget felt happy, the first time for months. All did work out in the end, if you stuck at it. She was lucky. She had two fine boys, and they had come back to her. And there were three tinies out in Rhodesia. That was a blessing and a promise.

Kelso had filled the three cut-glasses with the malt, and she raised her tipple.

"Here's to your father," she said. "Paul."

She saw Boy flinch, and Kelso smile.

"I really loved him, you know. Whatever happened, I really loved Paul."

She had to switch now and forget Peregrine. With her going on through Kelso's children, she had to make herself clear and clean the slate.

"To Paul," she repeated. "My husband."

The weary marchers stood in their tens of thousands or sat at Nelson's feet as he perched blind and high above them on his column, a roost for the pigeons of Trafalgar Square who did not care a hoot for his victory. Swollen feet, hot bodies, cold faces filled the paved acre. The statues of the lions were swarming with spectators, the barriers set up by the enclosing policemen were bending under the weight of the mass of protestors. Three days, three nights, most of the crowd had marched from Aldermaston, where the nuclear research station was. Some women had wheeled babies in prams all the way, others had carried them on their backs like papooses. The marchers had slept badly, they were hungry, their hope was high. "Ban the Bomb," they chanted, "Ban the Bomb!" Or else, "Macmillan No, Macmillan No, Macmillan No No No No No!" Now they were listening to the old beaked eagle of a philosopher with his white crest of hair, who had somehow risen from the grave and the last century to speak for the

rational progress of humanity against the dirty deaths of burst
megatons seeping invisible through the air. And by his side stood
Rosabelle, the Valkyrie of the movement, burning bright and ready to
shriek.

Boy was pressed into the pack of the crowd, squashed against Rosa,
his head blurry, hardly hearing the words of Bertrand Russell, feeling
only the warmth of the flame-haired girl at his side. This was the
second left hook that his duty had socked to him. First Suez swung at
him, and now Ban the Bomb, when he believed in nuclear energy. But
these overground tests of hydrogen bombs by the Americans and the
Russians, they were spraying the seasons with pesticides, the rays of
the sun were radiation, the dew was leukemia. Cancer was in orbit
over the Kremlin, Scorpio was spinning over Washington. Between
the crab and the spider in the Cold War, we would be sucked and
pinched and webbed into extinction.

So Boy had to march now from where he worked on a crusade for
the cradle and the bed, a crusade for the garden and the children, a
crusade for the fruits of Eden and the joy of Jerusalem. He and Rosa
must march with the thousands and tens of thousands until the people
were all marching, million on million against the rulers, saying, We
have life, all we have is our lives, Ban the Bomb, Ban the Bomb, Ban
the Bomb.

In the surge to protest at the final honeycomb of power, Boy hung
onto Rosa as a life raft. They ended squatting on the paving slabs at
the entrance to Downing Street, with three ranks of the police massed
against them. They were a trio in the final odd hundred, who had not
been split and swept away. They were holding the last thin red line
against the bully boys in blue, backed by twelve mounted coppers on
brown horses in front of the Prime Minister's door, cossacks who
could not charge at such passive resistance.

Now the sirens of the evening were squalling and the Black Marias
were parking by the Cenotaph and the police squads were picking up
the limp squatters by the armpits and hoisting them into the vans with
the barred windows to spend the night in the cells and to be on a
charge in the morning. And God knew where were the rights that Pym
and Hampden had fought for, the rights of assembly and free speech,
the duty of saying No to the tyranny of Whitehall, No, No, No, No,
No, I am a Briton, I will not, I refuse.

The raiders began to drag Rosa away, she sagging in their dark grip.
What had the anarchists sung on the long march from Aldermaston,
the old Wobbly songs and the songs of Spain and the chant to tease —
"All fuzz are bastards —" So Boy rose and smote the bluebottles on

face and chest, hip and thigh. He brought one down, he brought two low, he grappled with a third. They dropped Rosa and came in a wave on Boy. And he swung and thrust and hulked and bent and bowed and fell under their blows battering him down, but the last sight he had of Rosa was her swiping off a police helmet and yelling, "But it's for Peace!"

4

JACK THE NIPPER

The doldrums of the year of the death of the hero of his age, Winston Churchill, were the times of Jack the Nipper. The attacks were so delicate at first that the victims only discovered later that they were wounded. In a crowded or lonely place, they heard the mere noises of the street, they saw nothing unusual. Later they recollected a pat on their backs or a brushing of their skin or nape or calf no heavier than the wing of a moth. They would walk on to hear someone hurrying up, and they would turn as if this intruder were the assailant. But they met the concern of a stranger. "Do you know? You're bleeding. Badly." And they would feel behind their neck or leg, and their fingers would touch a wet and sticky slash or rent. And they would reach their red hand back in front of their eyes, disbelieving. "No," they would say. "I didn't feel it."

Jack the Nipper became bolder. The range of his rambles and his mutilations spread. He had begun in the City, lost in the press of the daily workers as he cut deftly and surgically with razor or scalpel. Now the assaults were reported on the Inner Circle of the tube that was the connecting intestine of the Underground, and even in the sad suburbs towards the end of the electric railway line, Pinner and Ongar and Tooting Broadway. No avenue was respectable enough, no thorough-fare was secure. Jack the Nipper drew his fine blade across the metropolis, invisible and undetected. One man alone in the melancholy of the year made a legend of himself. There had once been a Spring-heeled Jack, leaping on maidens and over high walls with eyes as fiery as lanterns. And there had been Jack the Ripper with his East End disembowellings. Yet this third Jack was so broadcast and expert in his two dozen petty operations that he scattered a shrapnel of suspense across the city, which had never been so scratchy with anticipation since the year of the doodle-bugs, the waiting between the time the engine of the flying-bomb cut out and its inevitable detonation.

When the first torso was found in the Thames, it was not held to be the work of Jack the Nipper. Although the arms and the legs and the head had been expertly removed, and although the body was that of a young woman, Jack was held to be only a slasher, a hit-and-run artist. The police did not rule him out, but continued to pursue their inquiries. As these inquiries led to dead ends and *cul-de-sacs* where no Nipper was to be found, the detective-inspector in charge of the case or cases began to talk of copy-cat incidents. The example and deeds of the original Jack had resulted in sinister imitations and finally in wholesale amputations. All that could be said positively was that these instances of grievous bodily harm were the work of one or more amateurs of anatomy, as in the case of the long-gone Ripper. In pubs, medical students found themselves shunned or spat at. "Are you all right, Jack?" was asked, and such remarks led to fist fights. There was even a brawl in the Coach and Horses in Soho, when some wit suggested that when another regular's Jill came tumbling down the hill, she landed on the point of his steak knife. Bar humour is never funny, but the weekly exploits of Jack the Nipper made it a deadly insult. The name was a sick joke.

A pop group, the Fleet Rats, exploited the general fear and loathing. Mass paranoia sells records. Many said that the simple lyrics for the brooding beat came from a children's song, which emerged from the playgrounds, although the Chief Rat claimed to have taught the song to the children as a reverse Pied Piper. This new nursery rhyme, spoken in rhythm to a banging shoe or a tapping stick, seemed ancient as well as modern.

> Jack the Nipper
> Was no Ripper
> But he had a little knife
> He put it in 'er
> He took it out 'er
> But the lady kept her life

> Hush and tush! Walking down the street
> All safe now! The copper's on his beat
> Hello, Mabel! Just call me Jack
> You'll get home, but I'll cut you on the back
> Hello, Doris! Lose a little hair
> To the razorman from Nowhere Square

> Jack the Nipper
> Was a kipper
> He never said a word

He put it in 'er
He took it out 'er
And then he disappeared.

Mothers are always frightened for the lives of their children, and
when the children begin playing murder games instead of hopscotch
or ring o'roses, then mothers are frightened out of their own lives,
particularly as Jack the Nipper only attacked women, and usually
young women. Now hysterical mothers, even in Islington, could not
stop themselves from flying out of garlic-scented kitchens onto rough-
tiled patios and smacking toddlers for falling over with screams of glee
when the pig-in-the-middle in rompers touched them to the final beat
of the rhyming game. "Don't sing that," they screamed, "or Jack the
Nipper *will* come and get you."

The children, too, had nightmares when a roller blind or the plastic
venetian variety fluttered in the breeze, although they were never as
scared as their young mothers were, especially when these were single
parents. It was irrational, of course. Jack the Nipper only struck on
streets or trains, in crowds or on corners, habitually out of doors. He
never invaded private homes. He seemed to relish the risk of discovery. Perversely, he appeared to want to be found out in public,
which he never was. But in the middle of the night, alone in bed when
the aspirin had worn off, what woman could not hear in the tiny
details of the darkness, the creaks and the whispers, the drips and the
rustles, the softly softly approaches of Jack the Nipper with his little
knife?

So one man and the news of him balanced London on the edge of
his blade this interminable year of mourning. And this was a city of
walkers, who could not watch their backs. On pavements of flagstones
and concrete, on roads of tarmac and cobbles, the footfalls sounded.
Scrape of toecap and shuffle of sole, rap of heel and ping of tread on
the iron decoration of a manhole cover. Hop-skip down stairs and the
swish of a secretary scampering for the bus, and the hush of her
followers in the street, their pace suspended. The walkers had their
signals for the listener and the blind man – dash and halt, linger and
scuttle, saunter and scurry. It was a language of movement, strangely
decoded. For its accompaniment became a comment, its welcome a
message of fear. The security of passers-by was suddenly the horror of
the stealth behind. The rabble of commuters in the morning was the
fright at the solitary mugger at night. Round the corner, perhaps, was
no newspaper-seller shouting – "Air-crash, package tour, read all
about it!" – but the tremor of a murderer who might be Jack.

Hark! He lurks, she listens, they are slashed. This was the grammar of a city of walkers, declining their lives in brief-case and shoe and sandal, kick and scuffle and plod to work.

In his kitchen in Camden, Ian Hamish was waiting for Clio to come home. She flitted from their place as regularly as a bat at night. He was never allowed to ask her where she had been. He was only glad when she appeared again, as he knew she would, as she always did. Her only consolation to him other than, "I do love you, too," was to say, "I have to have somewhere to leave my things, don't you know."

He had had enough of publishing and journalism, which was being a dogsbody in search of a story, which often had no bone. Now he called himself Mayhew minor, after the Victorian writer on low life. He was in search of what made London tick. To him, its society was as significant as growing up in Samoa or the Trobriand Islands or the Primate House. Its mores were its message, its displays were its decoys, it was its behaviour patterns. Like any other group, it divided into pecking orders and mating dances and burial observances. It could be dissected like the cockroach in formaldehyde which had been the outer limit of his early biological education. Its pickled parts could be arranged into legs, abdomen, thorax and associated bits. Every group of human beings had its processes, even the interlocking elites of the city. A field study could be done in the metropolitan streets. Ian's job was to do it, and he was being paid.

Before he could have his usual lonely scrambled eggs with tabasco on toast, Clio swanned in. She was dressed in a rainbow Thai silk suit of all the colours of the spectrum. She flounced down on the wooden seat at the kitchen table.

"Hell of a drag of a day," she said. "Shopping is so wearing. And to think, one has to wear what one shops for."

"Unless you throw it away."

"I think I will this." She reached into a carrier bag and brought out a flamingo-pink long shawl. "Do you think it's a mistake, Ian?"

"Depends what it's with. Or who you're with."

"Don't be jealous, darling. I'll be with you all night." She leant against the hard back of her chair. "Christ! What's that?"

Ian moved over behind her, as she bent forward. He could see a run of blood spreading over the fireworks of her jacket.

"You're bleeding," he said.

"No."

"You must have leant on a sharp edge."

"Jack the bloody Nipper."

"No. I'm sure. An accident."

"Jack the bloody Nipper. He's been following me. If I think who he is —"

"Don't be paranoiac. Hey, come and lie on the bed, face down. I'll take your jacket off, and look after the cut."

And so Ian did. The wound across her left shoulder-blade was not deep, and did not need stitches. She shrieked when he put on the iodine, but after the plaster was stuck down, she became quite calm.

"He got me all right," she said. "Of course he would have to. He never misses. Jack the Nipper."

"You can't know who he is."

"I have my suspicions."

An illumination came upon Ian as a hot iron in his belly.

"Peregrine?"

"Why not? He's disappeared. We don't know what he looks like now. He's come back to amuse himself with all of us suckers."

"It isn't likely."

"Then why me? Among millions."

"Chance. A random hit."

"It's Peregrine. Believe me. Twisted bastard. Getting his revenge."

"I don't believe you."

"It's Peregrine."

Back in their knotty-pine kitchen, Ian knew that time was passing him by. He looked round a fading French farmhouse in NW Nowhere. The walls had gone to blotched dinge, with copper-saucepans showing black bottoms hanging from their hooks, with dusty chicken-bricks and furry unglazed bowls, with horse-collars of garlic bought from the Breton on the bicycle by the pub and now moulting pungent leaves, with red heavy-duty plastic Provencal tiles cracking underfoot, with cork noticeboards displaying the faded squares of nonsense, with bean bags drooping like full rubbish bags. Why pretend to live like a Gallic peasant, when he was not?

Clio would not eat. She was getting too thin, becoming obsessive about her weight. To put on two pounds was like a crash at the Bank of England. Yet she did join him in sharing the last bottle of Gigondas from the wine-rack in the broom cupboard, where there were no brooms left.

"What at you going to do, if it is Peregrine after me?"

"You don't want me following you, do you? In our semi-detached life."

"Certainly not. But if it is Peregrine..."

"Would you go back to him?"

"Certainly not. You are the only person in my life I go back to."

"The eternal return." Ian smiled. "I'm not being awful. I am grateful. I cannot live without you – in intervals."

"I can't imagine why."

"Nor can I. But I have to have you around, from time to time. If not, all the time."

"Me, too. But this Jack the Nipper thing. Aren't you scared?"

"No. It's everywhere. We used to export all our villains. We would put them in the navy or the army to get rid of their violence on foreign breeds. They would kick the hell out of the various wogs who begin at Calais, as my mother used to say. Now, they have to get rid of their cruelty at home. They're like crabs in a bucket. Thousands of Jack the Nippers, pinching any crab who rises to the top."

"You mean the underclass drag you down? Because we can't get rid of them any more, they want to get rid of us."

"Not an underclass, because there aren't classes really now – certainly not in the Marxist sense. They're going out. The very word's offensive. Underclass suggests people without hope or ability, doomed, crushed for ever. But there is an Undercrust. It's like those big plates beneath the earth. They are usually submerged, quiet. Then suddenly they stir. The plates crunch together. Mountains are thrown up, volcanos, revolutions."

"Undercrust," Clio said. "I like that."

"Then there are the middling people, all striving to become one of the many variable elites who run us. Let's call them the Overalls. That'll do, because you have to change them all the time. The Overalls are rising and falling and replacing each other forever. They are like that vital ozone layer, shredding away because of all the gas and poisons we pump up above. Get rid of them, and we'll have a greenhouse effect in society, even more of the anarchy and violence we have now. They're necessary, the Overalls, but expendable. What do you think?"

"I don't see democracy needing Overalls –"

"Every society has elites. They're necessary evils. The question is – who are they? How control them? How change them?"

Clio put her hand across the scrubbed pine kitchen table top and took Ian's fingers, long and knobbled at the joints, the nails trimmed back beyond the arcs of flesh at the ends, broad hands, worker's hands, the hands she allowed to touch her.

"You'll write a wonderful book," she said. "I know it. And it was so lucky you got a grant for it. But there is one thing. Your Undercrust

– the occasional earthquake – don't you feel the tremor now? All this violence. No motives in it. Look what happened to me. Stabbed, and I didn't even see it." She shook a little on her wooden seat. "It was Jack the Nipper."

"He's a fiction of the press," Ian said. "They have made him the embodiment of a social phenomenon. There is a lot of violence – fights in pubs, street attacks, roughing up policemen, sheer aggression. But not *one* person doing it all. He's like Robin Hood – not real. Jack the Nipper is a public fear of rapists and burglars. There are hundreds of Jacks, not just one."

"But one Jack hurt me."

"Yes, but one of many. It's like all these scares – Legionnaire's Disease, you get it from your air-conditioner, so switch it off. Salmonella, so don't eat eggs. Ovine and bovine madness, so no mutton chops or steaks. There's a fad for diseases, dieting, which is part of the general paranoia about food and health, disease and death. Actually our stomachs are bin-liners for bacteria, while you're much more likely to die from cancer than from Jack the Nipper."

"But he might creep up on me again."

"It's an idea, that's all." Ian's sudden enthusiasm gushed out. Clio loved to see in him, the quick vitality. "That would be worth doing. *The Fads of Fear*. Showing that what people were scared of – at any one time – diagnosed the sickness of their society. The fear was the symptom of the social disease."

"So we deserve to feel bad about Jack the Nipper."

"He is the creation and the result of our fears."

"I don't know, Ian." Clio shook a little again in their knotty-pine kitchen. "Jack may not exist. We may have had to invent him. But he did cut me in the back. And that is real. It is evil."

That night, because she was hurt, Clio wanted Ian to hurt her more, yet to make her feel secure in the lock of his arms. She guided her hand towards the wound in her back. "Now," she said, "now." She screamed as he pierced her. Her thighs slipped away as two eels, then they locked round his waist in a soft vice. Her heels clamped his spine. "Yes," she said. "I'll always be here for you. You keep me."

Ian knew he was trapped with an ageing woman, who grew more vital by the night.

Boy stood in the queue which was one and a half miles long. Its tail began at County Hall and the people slowly moved west in front of the doomed five brick cakes of St Thomas's Hospital with the river on their right, doing no Lambeth Walk as far as the bridge over the Thames, but a shuffle of grief over the water, turning back to the east with the river on their right hand as they wound round towards the brown sugar pinnacles of Westminster and its Hall, where the Grand Old Man lay in state. The people did not question why they were there, after all, it would be enough to say in the years to come, I was alive in Churchill's time, I heard him say on the wireless, We shall fight them on the beaches even if that fight never came, blood toil sweat and tears and we had a lot of that, let me tell you, what with the blitz and the V-2s and the coupons. I was alive in Churchill's time and it was his time, you know, the last of the great men he was, we shall not see his like again, and for that reason I am standing here in this great worm of sorrow that is passing through the Hall where he lies. He saved us once, he did. He said we saved ourselves and that's true, but it was really him after Dunkirk. We're here to pay our respects. He'd like that.

Frost and bitter wind, snow to sleet to January rain, and the queue still inched on with the almost lost patience of the war. Feet frozen, hands cold as far as the knuckles, heart the only beat of warmth under huddle of overcoat, nose a nubbin of ice, the people still waited in line, moved on, waited, moved, waited, moved, waited with Boy among them. They had come from the corners of the island, they had come from over the Channel and the seas, they had come to say to themselves, I was there, he spoke to me once, I heard him plain, I never spoke to him, but he knew I was there fighting with him, he knew, so now I am here to meet him, I must. Boy trembled in the chill, but he found himself wedged between the fat cleaning-woman behind, incense of sweat and Guinness, and the hatted schoolgirls in front, as they urged him as far as the Hall of Westminster. There the carpets at last soothed the drag of the feet and the six jerky candle-flames made a hundred bright leaves and berries of mistletoe on the grove of bronzes above, and the four Horseguardsmen of the apocalypse bowed their shining plumed helmets to consider their sabre-hilts and the points of their steel digging between their black high boots. Beyond them on its raised steps stood the red and white and the blue flag, garish and grooved over the Old Man's coffin under the gold crucifix that should not have been there to bless this preserver of his people and destroyer of his enemies.

Better he should lie under the shadow of a Spitfire, a Hurricane, a Repulse, a Revenge, a Blenheim bomber than under this cross of gold that never hurled back the stormtroopers, or the Old Guard or Armada at any Trafalgar or Malplaquet or El Alamein. We kill more than we get killed, we last longer than you last, we lose only to win in the end, this island has not fallen since the Normans and it will not fall again, we shall strike back across the seas and we shall bring in our hands the Gotterdammerung that you have seen many times before and before that. I am a Churchill and there were Churchills before me and before the Duke of Marlborough, and if the Hitlers go back in history only to primitive insignificance, why, that is where they will go back again while I shall live in honour and memory and family. Sir Winston Churchill, with the people and their children plodding by in their queues of mourning, yea, for the glory that has departed with me and the people who are staying on...

Marie, Countess of Dunesk, was seated on her old bones at the back of St Paul's Cathedral behind all the witnesses of the ending of the Empire from Palestine to Central Africa. Mr Ben-Gurion was there with Dr Erhard and another Aristotle, now called Onassis, and Earl Warren, The Grand Duke of Luxemburg, Marshal Korniev, General de Gaulle, Paul Reynaud, Mr Kishi, Mr Krag and old uncle Moise Tshombe and all. The Queen was there and the royal family and Lord Avon and Lord Attlee and the old soldiers like Alexander and Slim, but these were the figures of the past. What did Sir Winston want to do, but lie embedded in his coffin drawn on a gun-carriage by an escort of blue-jackets with steps solemn mournful and slow all the way from Westminster to this City cathedral saved from the incendiary bombs by his order and God's mercy? Or did Sir Winston want to live to stop the protests of herself and Rosabelle and Rosa against the Cold War continuing with its nuclear poisons, which were no deterrents, except for everybody who was still alive?

The congregation was singing now at the great burial service under the dome of St Paul's where the chanted echoes were trapped for the eardrum of God, who hearest all.

> "There's no discouragement
> Shall make him once relent
> His first avowed intent
> To be a pilgrim..."

As Bunyan's hymn said, the Old Man did have courage, the British usually had courage, they muddled ahead in what they thought they had to do, but why did they have to wait until their backs were against the sea before they would fight? Why wait that long to forget their grumbling and distrust of those who were set to rule over them? Why did they have to be in the last ditch to accept greatness? Old Sir

Winston had been twenty years in the wilderness before the trumpets of defeat had called him back to his grudging country's service. And he would have stayed out in the cold until his forgotten burial in his village church, short of a Second World War that gave him an old man's opportunity.

Now Marie heard everybody singing some other song, which was written in the wrong place at the wrong time of Civil War.

> "Glory, glory, halleluiah
> Glory, glory, halleluiah
> Glory, glory, halleluiah
> For his soul goes marching on..."

Too cheery, really, the Battle Hymn of the Republic for the ceremony in St Paul's. Odd that the Old Man had been half American, perhaps that was why de Gaulle would persist on calling us Anglo-Saxons and keeping us out of the Common Market and Europe. Old Generals do have such a personal view of things. Yet, as always, there was something in that ancient French prophet's ravings. English was displacing French as the common language of the world, the shared culture. Galling for Paris to see itself lose at last the Nine Hundred Years War against England that had begun so well for France at the Battle of Hastings. One might call it a Two Thousand Years War since Julius Caesar first brought Latin speech across the Channel. Empires fade, languages remain, for in the long run, words survive better than power or glory. Sir Winston was right to polish his phrases, de Gaulle right to fear the Anglo-Saxon tongue. In the beginning was the word — and in the end, too.

> "God save our gracious Queen
> Long live our noble Queen
> God save the Queen
> Send her victorious
> Happy and glorious..."

The cranes all dipped their necks and the shrill pipes blew as the launch called *Havengore* took the body downriver from the Tower with the swans and the black-hulled policeboats all about as far as the Festival Hall Pier where Gillon and Ruth stood waiting with the last thin line of the faithful and the unforgetting and the watching to see the Old Man taken off the water, taken from the Thames to the slow train home from Waterloo to lie at last in his grave at St Martin's at

Bladon down the fields from Blenheim, the names of the battles no more than the marks on stations and houses now, and the old warrior six feet under the turf and cypress tree, never to rise again like King Arthur from his magic cave at the country's final hour. For Britain would never have the time to call again in that brief flash of the cloud and the rays and the megatons and the final burning of London for the likes of you, Winston Churchill, not any more now.

"That was the end of an age," Gillon said, holding onto his wife's arm. He could see she was weeping, and dammit, there was a prickle in his own eyes.

"I didn't trust him." Ruth was sobbing. "I went against Winston. He saved us. I'll never forgive myself."

"It doesn't matter what we did during the war," Gillon said. He pulled a creased handkerchief out of his pocket and began to wipe Ruth's eyes. "You finish off. I'm smudging all your make-up." He handed over the bit of linen. "We all got it wrong before the war. Or there would not have been one."

As he watched Ruth wipe the cold cream and powder off her face, he could see the young woman in her appearing, tearful and ready to please, with pink cheeks. She had been prettier than a thousand pictures, then. Only her bond with the ghastly Virginia and his own marriage had stopped him pouncing on her before. And now, they were together. And memories did not matter, even for the great dead.

"Darling," Gillon said, "we have only got a future. I helped to win the last war, and you did very little to try and lose it. We were all deluded. I agree it might have been the last just war. Fascism was horrible. So is Communism now with its labour camps killing millions of Russians. But we're not responsible for the bad beliefs of our time. Only for each other, me and you."

Ruth was still dabbing at her eyes.

"Why did you come and pick me up? Such a mess with Virginia. And you got me out."

"I thought I knew you better than her."

"You do, you do."

"It's not that blood will tell, and all that. It's just –" Gillon smiled and peered into her eyes. "Here's looking at you, kid."

On their long walk home, for there were no taxis to be had, they ran into Boy coming down Whitehall by the Cenotaph among the crowds. He seemed in a daze, as if he did not know where he was. He almost bumped into them. Gillon had to put a hand on his chest to stop him.

"Oh, hello," Boy said. "You have seen the event."

"The passing away," Gillon said. "What brought you there?"

"I don't know," Boy said. "It was not curiosity. More like a legacy, I suppose."

"What did Winston leave for you?"

"Some sort of heritage, perhaps."

"Not for you," Ruth said. "Physics. He knew nothing of science."

"Yes, he did. He knew who to advise him."

"You're right," Gillon said. "After all, I was a minor one of them. Do you miss him, though, in your brave new world?"

"I do," Boy said. "But I shouldn't. I don't know why. You know how it is – though it's usually somebody in the family you love. They die. There is a gap in nature. There is somebody who can't be replaced."

"Yes," Gillon said. "I agree." He looked past Boy's shoulder to see a curious figure close behind him wearing a dun mackintosh and a grey trilby hat. The face was so smooth that it might have been cut from a glossy magazine. The features reminded Gillon of everybody and nobody. Only the irises of the eyes slid from side to side, two blobs on a see-saw.

"Do you want to come back with us, Boy?" Gillon asked. "A drink, a meal."

"I must wander," Boy said. "I am not really off duty."

"Our duty is to be here." Ruth was making amends for her past. She clung to Gillon's arm. "Isn't he a wonderful man?"

"Yes," Boy said. "He is."

And so they parted at the ritual of the burial of the Great Leader of his country. Yet the man in the mackintosh and trilby hat stayed behind Boy, as he struggled towards Piccadilly. And under the silver statue of Eros, Boy was tapped on the shoulder. And the stranger with mischief in his voice said:

"Hello, son. Or that's what we say in the Americas."

Boy swung round to consider the blank of the face of the man he did not know.

"Who are you?"

"You are Keiss Sinclair. Called Boy, though you are not a boy now."

"I am. And you?"

"We'll talk about it in a place which has some resonance for me." The man indicated the Café Royal across the circus. "I have seen and heard of some action over there."

Boy knew that he should not have gone with the other fellow, but he was intrigued. Not until they were seated at a table in the balcony room did he notice the man's clenched hands. Boy was looking for them, for he knew they indicated true age. They could not be disguised. Yet these were hairless and smooth, with a few blue veins running up to the broken knuckles, which had curious red scars on their bumps.

"I see you are interested in my grasp, Boy." Now the man spread out his two hands on the table top. All the nails were trimmed, except on his little fingers. Two white extensions were the blades of small chisels. "What are you looking for?"

Boy could not answer, while the man called a waiter and demanded a bottle of Château Talbot.

"If I might ask —" Boy said.

"You may."

"Those two fingernails of yours, what are they for?"

"Ladies," the man said. "They always like that extra sensation. A tickle in places of interest. Something not quite usual. I am sure you know what I mean."

Boy stammered, "Of course."

"No, you don't know what I mean. On the other hand, or should I say little finger, you have little of me in you."

"Who are you?"

"Your father," the man said. "You know that already."

"Peregrine?"

"It used to be my name."

"You really are?"

"I am, thou art, she, your mother Bridget is. So we are. I love declining. We all do."

"But you don't look like —"

"You? Of course not. All those little scalpels, far more efficient than my hand jobs. I have had so much surgery that I wouldn't call it cosmetic. I'd call it tragic. A sort of serial representation."

"But you had to leave the country. Why have you come back?"

"To see you, dear Boy. Who else?"

"Are you going to see Mother?"

"How banal. Of course not. And —" The waiter arrived to open the bottle of red wine with his corkscrew levered against the glass rim. He poured out a sip for Peregrine, who said, "Tolerable. Distinctly tolerable. Decant on."

Boy reached for his glass and gulped something down.

"You were saying," he spluttered.

"Savour," Peregrine said. "Don't swig. It's bad for the indigestion. What I was saying was – Do not tell *anybody* – and I mean anybody – that I am here."

"But why come?"

"That is my business." Peregrine's eyes were quicksilver, his stretched mouth a caricature of a grin. "Never ask people their business. As I said, I came to see how you are getting on. My only son, my heir. You will be discreet. And you will inherit more than you know."

Boy gulped down the rest of his wine.

"This meeting," he said, "it is odd. You must have been following me."

"Indeed."

Now Boy noticed a dark red rim under one of Peregrine's long little fingernails.

"Are you good at following people?"

"What a question, dear boy. If I can keep up with them, as I have managed to keep up with you."

And so Boy and his father chatted until they had finished the Talbot. Sworn to secrecy again, Boy asked when was their next rendezvous, only to hear, "I'll keep in touch. In very close touch."

5

THE SUMMER OF QUESTION

1968

All he had fought for, Gillon thought, had been put in question. This was the year of the children's crusade when the old people as himself were put on trial. They might have won two World Wars, but what colonial revenge could justify the napalm in Vietnam, the massacre of the villagers and the Yankee body bags? Black youth was being shunted from the drugged murder slums of Chicago and New Orleans to be amputated or die on the killing fields of a country without any use to the West. Idiocy was foreign policy now, patriotism was plain murder, the kids were right to revolt, as they were doing in nearly all the capitals of Europe and the Americas.

And Ruth, what of her? She had left him when Virginia was dying, to be with her love from the past. Gillon had never known what women talked about when they were intimate. This was a foreign language, feelings beyond his understanding. He had thought that he had weaned Ruth away from her bad female influence, he had brought her back into the family, which still leeched together, in spite of all its scatterings. Yet he had lost. Ruth had stayed away for months until Virginia had died, and then she had not returned, suddenly stricken herself. Of course, nobody died of broken hearts any more, but the doctors could never satisfactorily diagnose Ruth's complaint. She was under observation, when she had contacted what was called 'hospital disease', a form of viral pneumonia. He was at her bedside when she died, but she would hardly recognize him before she was taken away.

Gillon had been rejected twice by both his wives. Yet his daughter Leah had called him back to Salzburg, and that was why he was going to that Austrian city of music and ambiguous memories. He could hardly understand why she was there. She must be in army Intelligence, even the Mossad. She had brought her mother Rachel and her sister from Canada over to live with her in Tel Aviv, and she had even found Fiona a job in the new Apfelstein hospital there, funded by a grant from the huge trust set up by the Jewish family from Johannesburg. Again, cousins were at work, for the one who had married the deceased Indian doctor Seaforth, was Miriam Apfelstein, still the support of the surviving Indian members of the family at Annandale.

When Leah met him at the airport, Gillon found that she had grown into her beauty. She was superb now. Age had fleshed her out and fined her down. The bones of her cheeks carried her brown face as exultantly as the wings carry a hawk. Her body was full and proud, her walk arrogant as she took her father to the waiting limousine. She looked at the shaven neck of the chauffeur with her fine eyes, then her lids fell over them in disdain. She might have been a conqueror wondering why the defeated natives were allowed to share a vehicle with herself. Gillon could not keep back the compliments.

"You are a miracle," he said. "You make age drop in its tracks. What's happened?"

"We have Jerusalem," Leah said. "I told you we would. I told cousin Paul that before, when he was in your rotten police in Palestine. That's why I brought you over, to celebrate it. You've even got a role in the Sedeh, what you call the Passover feast."

"Passover here?" Gillon was incredulous. "But it's the heart of the Nazi part of Upper Austria. We're just off Hitler's eyrie at Berchtesgaden."

"That's the point, father. Hurt them back where it really hurts. Besides, I have business here. The service is in English. I deal with the Americans, who will be there."

The nineteen hundred years of losing and lamentation were past. The Jews had taken back Jerusalem by act of war. The crusaders of Israel now held the Holy City, and they wanted witnesses of their victory. As Gillon ate the Matsoh bread and shank of lamb and egg, and bitter herbs dipped in salt water and washed down with wine, all brought in by angry waiters with shaven skulls, he listened to the Hebrew and the English words, spoken or sung by the sixty guests.

"Blessed art thou, O Lord, our God! King of the universe, who makest a distinction between sacred and profane; between light and darkness; between Israel and other nations and between the seventh day and the six days of labour ..."

Each had been given his or her part down to the smallest child, who joined in the nursery games at the end. But as he heard or read the text of the Hagadah, Gillon found that the words no longer matched the facts. History had overtaken the ceremony. Listen to the

imported Rabbi from Brooklyn as he held the unleavened bread and
spoke:

"Behold! this is the bread of affliction, which our ancestors ate in
the land of Egypt: let all those who are hungry enter and eat thereof;
and all who require, come and celebrate the Passover. At present we
celebrate it here, may we celebrate it next year in the land of Israel.
This year we are here in exile, but next year we hope to be free men in
the land of Israel ..."

Exile? Voluntary exile now, paid exile? Next year to be free men in
Israel? Free men already fought for Israel and now the Egyptians ate
the bread of affliction. The wailing was by the enemies of Israel; the
wandering was for the refugees fleeing from greater Israel; the Sinai
Desert and the Red Sea had swallowed up the beaten hosts of Egypt.

"Now," the Rabbi said, "the question of the Wicked Son at the
Passover."

And Gillon read:

"What mean YOU by this service? By using the word YOU I
intend to exclude myself: and thus withdrawing from all the duties
belonging to every member of the community I reject the faith of the
Jews."

"And now," the Rabbi said, "the answer to the Wicked Son."

And Leah spoke, her voice like a warning bell.

"This is done because of that which the Lord did for ME, when I
went forth from Egypt. For ME, but not for you; for had you been
there, you would not have been redeemed."

So superb, Leah, so strong in the sting of her rebuke that Gillon
felt ashamed, idiotically ashamed, for the words put into his lips. He
opened his mouth to protest in earnest, forgetting that he was playing
a part, but already the Wise Son was asking, "What is this?" and
already the reply was being given by the Rabbi, "With a strong hand
did the Lord bring us out of Egypt, from the house of bondage." So
Gillon settled back to drink his wine at the due time and watch the
guests flushed with conquest after their centuries of regret, their
millennia of oppression, their faith eternal in scripture and in God's
promise to the Jews that was now writ on the Rock of the Holy City
itself. Listen to the prayers of the Rabbi exultant:

"O Lord, our God! Have mercy upon us, on thy people Israel, and
on thy city Jerusalem, and on Mount Zion, the residence of thy glory,
and the great and holy Temple, which is called by thy name. Our
Father! Feed us, nourish us, sustain us, provide for us, grant us
abundance, and relieve us speedily from all our anxieties, and let us
not, O Lord, our God, stand in need of the gifts of mankind, nor of

their loans; for their gifts are small, and their reproach is great; but let our dependence be only on thine hand, which is full, ample, rich and open; so that we may not be put to shame in this world, nor be confounded in the world to come. Restore also speedily in our days, the Kingdom of the House of David, thine anointed, to its ancient state ..."

When Leah had taken him back to his hotel room, Gillon did ask her what was the ancient state of the Kingdom of David.

"Now you have Jerusalem and the West Bank and the Golan Heights and Sinai, where will you ever end? Were there not Jews once in Babylon, in Egypt, in Damascus? If Jerusalem had only been enough – but now you want Zion, and Zion stretches over the whole Near East."

"We have enough now," Leah said. "We have Jerusalem and we can defend our frontiers."

"The British, who have been another wandering race and have often confused themselves with the Old Testament and the Israelites, should have had enough when they reached the Isle of Wight. But it didn't stop them grabbing a whole Empire that girdled the globe, in the name of Christ and the King. They didn't know when to stop. There was always another strategic route to protect. Once India was had, Africa had to be had to protect the route to India. And then we had to have Egypt to protect the Suez Canal. Now you have one bank of the Suez Canal, won't you want the other, in the name of Zion?"

"No," Leah said, "never. We want peace. Peace and Jerusalem."

"You want Zion," Gillon said. "That is the worm in your Promised Land."

"Jerusalem is all," Leah said. "Believe me. Just Jerusalem and peace. No doubt about it."

"We have lost," Gillon said, "you have won. Our Empire has gone back to London, yours begins at Jerusalem."

"Israel stops at Jerusalem." Leah was getting angry now. "That is the end of our state, God's city on earth. No more. No more, I tell you, or I shall take up arms against Israel. We stop at Jerusalem."

"You won't stop," Gillon said. "We never did. And look where it has got us." And then his curiosity got the better of his discretion. "And why are you doing the Passover here?"

Leah shrugged.

"I can't tell you, as you know, you in British Intelligence in the last war. Let's just say, the CIA are in Austria in strength, and we have to deal with them, against the Russians. After all, that terrible crushing of

Czech freedom fighters in Prague. I know the Americans support us, but they need us too."

"To protect the oil in the Middle East."

"As you did. The Empire."

"As we did. And don't any more." He smiled at Leah. "You know, my dear, the Scots and the Jews get on very well together. And as you're half-half, that's the very best mix. And you know why? We are both tribal people. Clannish. We stick to our own. And don't you ever forget it."

Before he left in the morning, Gillon had a telegram from Marie. She feared for her grand-daughter Rosa, who was fighting with the students in Paris. Her daughter Rosabelle had tried to get Rosa out, but she could not be found. Could Gillon do anything to help? And as he had nothing much else to do or to live for in his retirement, Gillon decided to hire a car and play Galahad for the last time for the sake of his family, what was left of it.

He had read of the street-fighting and the troubles in France, and he took the precaution of buying full cans of petrol at the Swiss frontier to carry with him through to the Channel. Yet as he drove past the manufacturing towns on his way to the capital, he saw sights that he had only imagined – red flags flying over factories with their gates welded together and with lines of silent workmen in their blue denims looking out through the bars, ready for any attack – the leaders of the country, pleading on television like whipped boys to the masses – the fact that authority could just disappear overnight, and the people wake up to the knowledge that all government was only a confidence trick. But the old General de Gaulle was watching and listening. And as Gillon drove towards Paris up the Autoroute du Sud, already the armed policemen were searching the cars, and the lorries filled with troops were waiting down the sideroads, and somewhere, like a storm on the horizon, the rolling of the tracks of the tanks.

Yet in Paris itself, the theatre was in the streets and the streets in the theatre. Gillon drove to the Odéon with its black and red flags flying high, the slogan painted on the stone, ex-THEATRE DE FRANCE, the banner blazoning overhead, ODEON EST OUVERT, and inside, the day-and-night free debate that had run longer than any political discussion since the French revolution, with the students and the workers filling the elegant seats, and the orators haranguing from the boxes and the stalls, anyone with a tongue delivering his or her plans for tomorrow's France. But Gillon could already see the police agent in his new student clothes snapping the faces of the speakers with his Minox, evidence for the retribution that would surely come, the outrage raining from the Palais de Justice, the truncheons splitting the skulls, the interrogations, the solitary cells, the slow despair of losing, of having lost, the post mortems in the back room.

Outside now, Gillon walked through the streets to the Sorbonne, the roads curiously empty and expectant, the citizens staying in their rooms, watching through the cracks in the lace curtains or from the upper windows, already withdrawing from the students at the sight of the burnt-out cars, the broken glass, the trees cut down to make barricades, the destruction of the normal for battle against the riot police. Of course, when the barricades had first gone up with the students digging up the cobblestones to lob at the *flics*, the whole of Paris had skipped back to the lessons of the *lycée*, the great days of the fall of the Bastille, the mobs in the streets, the *aristos à la lanterne*, the people drunk with power, and again in the Liberation, the songs of revolution first on the children's lips after the nursery rhymes.

Then the young began burning up property, and everybody had his pension, her savings, and an auto. Everybody had property. Property was not robbery. Robbery was destroying and taking property. And, after all, somebody had to see that thieves did not break in, somebody had to be the government, and the old General de Gaulle was still up there, remember the war, the free French, the *maquis*, de Gaulle, Gaul, France, *gloire*, Napoleon, the Fourteenth of July with the big parade from the Arc de Triomphe, French tanks, French aeroplanes, remember, remember, for the revolution would take it all away.

As a Canadian, with the French-speaking Quebec still so separate from the Commonwealth, yet still inside, Gillon could understand why Paris was changing its mind, giving up its brief plunge into the hot blood of memories. The streets were empty and foreboding as he walked towards the Sorbonne and the centre of the revolt. Paris was waiting for the General to come back, and he was coming, surely.

"Gillon," a voice said in the corridors of the university, now sprawling with students in sleeping-bags or huddling over the free-food counters and trestle tables stacked with leaflets. Gillon hadn't been so shoved and hustled since the trains of the Second World War.

Clio was coming towards him, dressed in a tailored combat outfit, chic guerrilla gear. "What the hell are you doing here?"

"And what the hell are *you* doing here? This isn't a fashion show."

"Oh, I don't know," Clio said. "Simply everybody's here who is anybody. We are all radicals now."

"Speak for yourself. I came to look for Rosa. Is Ian here?"

"Wandering the boulevards. Writing one of his awful poems. Or working out the sociology of the revolution, whatever that's meant to be, except kids throwing cobbles at the CRS. Equals the local SS. As riot police go, they stink."

Gillon felt a violent blow in his back that smashed him against the wall. Swaggering by, a black-jacketed crop-headed gorilla, swinging an iron chain in his hand.

"*Fiche le camp, crapouillot*," the gorilla said and went on.

"*Ah, les Congolais*," Clio said and shrugged.

"This may be a free university," Gillon said, rubbing his bruises. "But it's too much of a free-for-all for me."

"We can't fight the SS police without the *Congolais*. They don't like de Gaulle either. He betrayed them too. They learnt how to smash the *flics* in Saigon, Algeria, the Congo. With them we can beat the SS."

"Don't they beat you?"

Clio laughed at him.

"Some of us girls don't mind that, as love goes."

Now there was a weirder apparition at the back of Clio. Where had Gillon seen that face before, the unknowable face which he already knew? These were the features of infinite recognitions, yet they could never be given a name or a place. Something had been done to them, so Gillon could not say, "You. Who are you? I have seen you before."

The man seemed to slice his hand across Clio's back. A strand of the blonde helmet of her hair flaked down.

"Stop," Gillon said. "I've seen you. In Whitehall. That time of Winston's funeral. With Boy."

"I hardly think so," the man said. "I do not know you. Nor this young *poule*." He swung Clio round to face him. "You would not know me, would you?"

Clio looked at the man in the manicured mask of skin and shook her head.

"No," she said, "I do not know you. But you must be Serge."

"A *nom-de-plume*," he said.

"The white leader of the *Congolais*. You get them their weapons."

"A little exchange of arms is a wonderful thing. We all become bosom pals."

"But your voice. You are English."

"I try not to be. A world traveller, you might say."

"Wanted," Gillon said, "in all the countries of the world."

The man looked at him with his glancing eyes, which could never hold straight.

"Wanted, indeed, everywhere. Those who supply what people want –" he touched the Smith & Wesson pistol stuck into his belt –

"they are the desirable ones." He turned to Clio. "And you, *petite*, come to a party with me. Among the ruins."

"No," Clio said. "I'm fighting. Have you seen *une amie*? Answers to the name of Rosa."

"Ah, *l'ecossaise*." The man smiled a thin grin as a crack in his smooth face. "I have seen her. My people molest her. She is too young to be in this situation."

"Damn you," Gillon said. "I'll go and have a look." And he left the two of them.

An hour later, wandering through the fetid labyrinths of the Sorbonne, now bunkers of resistance rather than classrooms, he saw Rosa huddled at the end of a bench, her arms clasped around her knees, her head sunk down, deep asleep.

"Thank the Lord," he said to himself. Then he went forward and shook her awake by the shoulder.

"No," she screamed thickly, "bloody you!" Then she saw who was assaulting her. "Oh, Uncle Gillon." She fell towards him. "It's pretty bloody here."

"I bet it is. I've come to get you out."

"Wait. Have you got a cigarette?"

Gillon produced a pack of *Gitanes* he had picked up on the way.

"Thanks, Gillon." She lit up. "I don't know. I have to stay."

"You've lost. The tanks are coming in. The Communists and the unions have deserted you. No hope now."

"I have to stay. See it through."

"No. Retreat. Fight again. Win the victory later."

Rosa looked round the room. In a corner, a *Congolais* was yanking his chain round the neck of a student girl. "*Eh, Marianne*," he was saying. "*nous partons. Une examination, encore.*" And they went.

"They're pigs," Rosa said. "They're bigger shits than the *flics* outside."

"That's the problem," Gillon said. "The guys you hire to defend you are worse than the guys you fight."

"I don't know." Rosa said. "I'm so tired. Clio's here, and Ian."

"I've seen her. Not him."

"He's quite someone. I like him. He makes sense, among all this shit."

"I like him," Gillon said. "Almost alone in the family, he's always made some sense."

Rosa agreed to come to Gillon's hotel in the Rue des Beaux Arts the next morning. He would ferry her back to England with the hidden petrol cans in his hired car. She did not tell him why she was lingering for more abuse. Actually, she was waiting for Ian to come in from the dangerous streets, where the CRS was waiting to ambush them with batons and tear gas.

When Ian came, evening had already drifted its soot over the black uniforms of the riot police, waiting in their dark wedges outside the university. He found her crouched under a desk, her nerve gone.

"Hello, angel," he said. "What are you doing down there?"

She let him help her up to her feet.

"I'm shaky," she said.

"Quite right," he said. "So am I. I've come to take you out."

"Too late. I've got a rescuer. Uncle Gillon. We leave from the Beaux Arts tomorrow morning."

"Perhaps I'll hitch a lift."

"What about Clio?"

"Oh, she'll do her own thing. She always does."

"Don't you worry about her?"

"If I did, I'd have worried myself to death long ago. I never know where she is, or what she is doing. She never tells me."

"You can't go on like that."

"I have to."

That night, Ian took Rosa to an Algerian restaurant in the Saint Germain quarter The food would be horrible, but they were safer there, within the ring of the black enforcers outside. After their couscous with everything, and a bottle of red wine from anywhere, Rosa began to speak her mind. Perhaps it was the fear of the past week, perhaps she began to doubt the dictates of her Red mother, perhaps she was learning to appreciate the hangdog look and blue gaze of this older cousin in front of her, so gentle when all the others were so rough.

"Why do you put up with Clio?" she asked. "She's such a devil, so impossible."

"I really don't know," Ian said. "She says I'm too bloody tolerant. Give or take a mile, I probably am."

"Too tolerant. That can't be a sin."

"It is to her. She likes the vicious."

"Not me." Her shoulders in her thin blouse were suddenly cold with dried sweat. Rosa clasped them with both hands. "It's nice to feel somebody is caring for you."

"That's what Clio says. But she only comes back for this welfare state from time to time, when she's badly bruised."

"So what do you feel?"

"I've always wanted her."

"You can't be such a wet mat."

"No." Ian looked down at the red-and-white check tablecloth to consider where and who he was. "I am not a wet mat. A sponge, perhaps. I can take in what people do. That's why I try to write, try to describe. What did Auden say about the writer? In his own weak person, if he can, he must absorb all the wrongs of man."

Rosa put out her hand across the table. She took Ian's palm in hers, and left it there.

"I like you. I really like you. You're different. You try to see things as they really are. You don't listen to all this silly talk. You can love too, can't you?"

"What's that?"

"Putting somebody else before yourself."

"Yes," Ian said. "I can do that."

"What about me?"

Ian shook his head and smiled.

"I am far too old for you, Rosa. You are looking for the father you never had. Hamish Gordon. Went down on that convoy to Russia."

"No, I'm not. I'm looking for someone like you. I don't like the young that much. They are too far out. You are the alternative."

"Like death is the alternative to life?"

Rosa gave a grimace.

"Don't be smart. Don't put yourself down. You're not that old." She squeezed his hand now. "I'll wait a bit for you, if we get out of here in the morning. But don't ask Clio along, too. She can look after herself."

Ian pulled away his hand.

"I am sure she can," he said. "Let's have some more plonk."

"Oh, you plonker." Rosa took back her hand and kissed the palm, which had held his. "Why do you have to be pursued? Anyway, tell me what you have been writing."

"Rubbish, as usual."

"Tell me."

"You insist?"

"I insist."

"All right, but you'll hate me."

"I might love you more."

"All right."

So Ian read to Rosa his verses on the events of 1968, which seemed to make some sense to both of them.

"London's burning, Prague is burning,
Paris burning, Chicago burns.
Call the engines, call the tanks in,
Call the bullets, it's your turn.
Pour on water, pour on slaughter.
Students all will rape your daughter.

Buenos Aires, Rome are burning.
Saigon's burning, Tokyo burns.
Call the engines, call the troops in,
Call the truncheons, it's your turn.
Old men use fear to kill the new.
It is their love to murder you.
            Ho, ho, Mao."

"You're not so much for the revolution, then," Rosa said. "You think the young will be screwed again."

"Yes. I'm not so much for it now."

"Why do you write like that?"

"I don't know. The words just come out that way. Then I know I believe them."

Rosa smiled.

"That's very honest. I don't know what I think, either, until I see what I do. You will come to London with me and Gillon in the morning?"

"I will. Count on me."

Peregrine declared himself to Clio after Gillon and Rosa had left them in the Sorbonne. She was hardly surprised. She knew he would find her again. He slashed her naked back with his fingernails, stretching her out on a concrete floor. More stimulation, he said, than jealousy. Anyway, she would get far worse treatment from his *Congolais*. His suave brutality relit her desire for him. It had only been banked. And, as always, in the morning, when the stormtroopers smashed into the Sorbonne, he had his way out for them. He would always escape with her. Or without her, if he did not care to take her along.

6

THE POISONED LAND

There is a tiredness in the affairs of men which is the grimace of governments. Harold Wilson and his cabinet were stumbling in office, and as the nonsense poem noticed, gunpowder was running out of the heels of his shoes. His puff of a 'classless, dynamic new Britain' merely blew smoke over a long industrial and imperial decline. He postured on a world stage where the house lights were being killed one by one. His long combat against the Establishment and the mandarins of Whitehall was a sapping series of skirmishes. Through experience rather than disillusion, he was losing the belief in being able to change things very much. The bright hope of the 'sixties was turning to the long evening of the next decade. Wilson would not win the next election which heralded the inconsiderable ten years to come. Even his return, five years later, would only be to resign at the bitter end.

His slow sinking was posted by the plots of the security services against him. His authority was ended by their actions and their innuendos. Those who lived by conspiracy could only see the lives of others as conspiracies. With his realistic view of the economics of Britain, if not its global politics, Wilson was falling foul of the War Office and the Pentagon. To President Lyndon Johnson, and Richard Nixon with his Communist-baiting past, Wilson and his country were becoming suspect in the 'special relationship' with the United States. They would not send troops to Vietnam or maintain all their military and intelligence bases in the Near and Far East. They would not supply arms to South Africa or break-away Rhodesia, both fighting black 'socialist' rebellions. A vital police station for oil and the Persian Gulf was abandoned in Aden, although the unsinkable aircraft-carrier islands of Diego Garcia were being handed over to American control. In its rush out of Empire, the British government seemed to be chucking away its remaining responsibilities. It had thrown away the baby and let out the bathwater, but it could not even be bothered to clean the tub. There might even be a plot there.

"It is so boring," Hamish Henry was telling Boy Keiss in his rooms at Kings College in Cambridge. "Once you are on the black list, or should I say on the reds under the bed list, you are never struck off."

"They can't still suspect you of peddling nuclear secrets."

"They do. The sins of youth. You are never allowed to outgrow them."

"But you're a professor now. A senior don."

"Promotion does not imply compassion. The higher you rise, the harder you may fall. And the more you are distrusted, because you are presumed to know more. Which you don't, of course." He filled up Boy's glass of Gaelic peat whisky. "You can taste the smoke in that brew. Well, the fire in me has long since gone out. How's our work for the Atomic Authority going?"

"Well," Boy said. "We'll soon be providing a tenth of our energy needs. I'm going up to see our nuclear plants in Scotland soon."

"Not our submarines in the Clyde?"

"Now I couldn't tell you, could I?"

Hamish Henry laughed.

"Family trust, Boy. I can see you still don't have too much of it. Will you be seeing Marie at Dunesk, the matriarch of our bit of the clan? How on earth did you ever persuade her to sell the land to you at Dounreay for your atomic horrors?"

"She had to keep her Miners' Old Home going. But it was over the dead bodies of Rosabelle and Rosa."

"Whom you fancy?"

"Who told you that?"

"Birds of a feather. I do admire those two women still waving the red flag. I never did, even when I believed."

"But you must have been told to go underground."

"A mole is a coward." Hamish Henry considered the amber glow in his tumbler and drained it. "To stay in a burrow and subvert has no glory. But to go out on the streets and demonstrate, that is guts."

"But you were meant to organize, not be a cheerleader."

"Now, what do I do?" The host turned his back on Boy to go to the window and stare across the quad at the illuminated spires of the chapel, pointing its curlycue spires as rockets at the night sky. "I educate the young in the sciences, which will rule the world. But I cannot tell them what to do with their knowledge. That would be called indoctrination or subversion. I put into their podgy hands and tiny minds the means of unimaginable destruction. So they swagger out of here staggering under the weight of their grenades and tommy-guns, with brains like unbaked doughnuts."

"Isn't that better," Boy asked, "than telling them the wrong things to do with all that power?"

"No, it's worse. The aimless use of scientific knowledge will be the end of us all. The refusal of physicists like us *not* to make the hydrogen bomb has condemned us to the horrific stalemate of the Cold War. I admit, once I would prefer Russia to have won, but now, I would rather all of us who knew how to make those diabolical nuclear weapons had said, 'No, no, no, we will not, we will never make them'."

"That is impractical, and you know it. And rather idealistic, Henry, for you."

Henry turned back to Boy and shook his shoulders and spread his hands.

"Oh, traitors," he said, "can be idealists. In fact, that is often the reason. Particularly, when you are not paid for it."

That year of 1969, the seas began to stink, too.

Off Devon, a trawler winched in a heavy catch. Then the brine began to boil and bubbles a yard wide exploded and the air burned and the sailors coughed and their tongues swelled and their mouths blistered and the Captain cut the trawl free with a hacksaw and the gases boiled down beneath the waves and the trawler went back to port.

In the North Sea, the crab-legged drilling platforms walked out to the middle of the grey waters and dropped their drills and took out of the depths natural gas and oil to pipe to the mainland. Yet not all the tapped juices of the earth would stay in the pipes. Some began to spread over the surface of the waves. The spokesman of the companies of exploration said: "The North Sea is beginning to change its colour."

On the beaches, the towels were full of tar and the oil slicks came floating in, dropped off the tankers, and Dunkirk fleets of small boats went out to blanket the oil with detergents and to soak it up with straw, and still the oil came floating in with the dying gulls screaming their clogged deaths in its wake.

Down the rivers that flow into the sea came the wastes of industries and cities, arsenic, mercury, copper, piss, acid, ammonia, nitrates. The fish died and the waterfowl. Only the rats thrived and the noble swans which, like Mithridates, ate poisons to become immune and to prolong their white-winged glory.

In a brook near a nuclear-power station, school children found three-headed tadpoles, frogs with seven legs, newts with thirteen, and other deformed pond life. They showed their teacher who showed the nuclear power people who took away the evidence and stopped the leak and went on making the mess that altered life itself.

The great red salmon that leapt the rocks and rapids of the Scots and Irish rivers began to die of a wasting disease, and the young salmon were trapped in their shoals by nets off Greenland and their numbers fell until they were hardly seen, and people said the red salmon would never be found again in three years or so.

The land also had its blight.

Vietnam came to the hedgerows with defoliants called weed-killers which made mice bear legless babies, and, if mice, what of men?

The animals and fowl penned in the batteries and breeding factories began to suffer like those who ate them and who chose to herd themselves into cities. Cows, maddened by artificial insemination, took to leaping on one another like bulls. Rams, prisoned together, learnt the art of buggery. Calves in wooden cages grew soft hooves, as they did not need to walk; their keepers provided them with shoes. The meat of hens which never moved from their cages became white and tasted of chemicals and sponge cake. Old farmers did not like these new habits of the animals in their concentration camps; but the young farmers did not care and the people in the cities did not mind where their food came from as long as it was cheap enough.

At Porton Down, a scientist touched his lip with a rubber glove that had touched a toxic compound he had been making as a deterrent against biological warfare. When he was alive, he believed that Britain should make diseases so horrible that nobody else would dare to attack it with their man-made diseases. When he was dead within two minutes after the glove touched his lips, one of his colleagues said: "If he had sneezed, there went Birmingham."

The sky had its vapours.

Lead fell on Milwall from the chimneys and the few trees which reminded people in the docks of the old forests all wilted and perished.

Thunder cracked the clean air in Wales. It came from the high Concorde, flying faster than the sound that lagged behind it to rattle the glass in Saint David's Cathedral and to lay to rest God's palms. For why should He bother to clap up storms, now men could make their own?

When the wind dropped, smog filled the High Streets from the car exhausts and the lungs of the old people gave way and none called it murder except for a mad barrister who filed a suit for massacre against Henry Ford, forgetting that Ford was dead.

At Dounreay in Caithness, where Marie Dunesk had sold the site to the Atomic Energy Authority, a nuclear park had been created, where plutonium could be processed, then used in Fast Reactors to provide electricity, then reprocessed in a Materials Testing Reactor. This completed a fuel cycle, the first in that particular world. The provision of power appeared to be a self-contained matter, harming nobody. Or so Boy was still telling Marie Dunesk in her 'eighties. But with cancer in her own body, she feared that she might have contaminated all the body politic of the old Sinclair lands to the north. The effects up there had not been read yet as hers were on radiographic scans in the Edinburgh wards. And if she went, what would happen to the family and the castle on the Esk and Ermondhaugh, where most of the old miners and their families had died or were dying, as she was?

"You promise me, there will be no radiation in Caithness?"

"Very unlikely," Boy said. "But there is radiation everywhere. We get it from the ground, from the granite here. The question is, how much? Look, they are using radiation to cure you."

"To treat me," Marie said. "And to kill me. Just more slowly."

Boy had to admit that she looked as if she were dying. Her face was a web of lines, her cheeks shrunken, her hands skeletal. She had lost nearly all the sweep of her red hair. Only a few dark strands trickled down from the plaid bonnet on her head.

"They will cure you." Boy failed to speak strongly. "You will bury us all."

"I have buried too many. It is my turn now." A downward grin split the spokes into her lips. "They say that we Indians know when we are going to die. I know. Next spring. I will have time to tidy up, as you say. Put all in order. I am not going back to your rays and your machines."

"But they are helping you."

"I doubt it. They kill the good cells with the bad cells. I need the good cells I have left to do what I will do before I go."

"But you must go back to the hospital."

"Must?" Marie's laugh was a dry crackle of bracken. "Must is my choice. I am that I am. And I will do what I must for me, and for us all, in the time that I have left. What are you doing in the time you have left, Boy?"

"I am going to Rosyth by Edinburgh and the Clyde Base by Glasgow to check our nuclear fleet there."

"Those awful submarines which launch those Polaris missiles, which we buy from America? Rather worse than Colonel Custer's six-guns, I am told. You might meet up with Rosabelle. She's always protesting out there with her street theatre. Nearly naked, she wallows around in tomato ketchup. She'll catch her death of cold."

"Not from radiation, then. Is Rosa with her?"

"She said she had met you. She's just back from Paris, and now you'll find her scrapping away in London, as usual. Old Gillon got her out of the Sorbonne, which was good of him. She met another cousin there, Ian Hamish. She said she liked him very much."

A strange stab of jealousy passed through Boy. But Rosa could never go for such a middle-aged sponge-bag, not at her age, which was more like his. Then Marie's question cut him as a whip.

"You're not going to your nuclear station at Torness?"

"No, not this time."

"Those other lairds round here, they should never have sold that land. It's far too close to home. I told them that. They wouldn't listen." Now she spoke with the disconnection of the old. "I put it in the fridge."

"What is the fridge?"

"Torness. It's poisoning the Esk."

"It can't. It's well away. It's down the Firth of Forth."

"It must be the tides."

"They can't go upstream."

"The salmon do. You'll see it in the fridge."

"What then?"

"A poisoned salmon. I found it belly-up in a pool by the bank. You will see what it died of. It is your radiation –"

"Salmon are full of disease. Lice, salmonella – It won't be radiation. Torness is safe."

"You check it for me, you hear, Boy."

Marie sounded as if she were commanding a servant, but Boy meekly accepted her authority.

"I'll pick it up from the fridge before I go," he said. "Thank you for putting me up."

Then suddenly, with that unexpected grace which had always been her hallmark, Marie opened her arms to him, and when he came over to her, she hugged him with frail bones no bigger than coathangers, and said:

"Thank you for putting up with me."

Seconded to the Military of Defence, Boy had been asked to check on the reactors in two of the nuclear submarines docked in the Scots lochs. He could find nothing wrong within their vast cigar-cases, launching pads for the Polaris missiles, as well as the torpedos of old naval wars. These silent diving monsters were as elusive in their oceans as Nessie in her depths, giant killer eels of stealth and myth. But dangers still came to him on the way home by conventional methods, as they always had, and still would.

Boy stood by the great hole in the belly of Glasgow. He could not say that the guts had been ripped out of the city. The city had never had any guts, just ulcers, hernias, wens. Round the hole, the dark granite of the old offices tagged away into the closemouths of the slums, with the sluttish mothers and the chibmen and the far-from-bonny hairies hanging out on the street corners. Yet the great hole was not for housing but for motorways, concrete leggy tapeworms criss-crossing high and low, firth and forth, to make foul intestines for the city centre, evacuating the lorries and limousines to the south and the airport from the maw of the great void called Glasgow. Once sheep ate men, now cars ate men, but men could eat sheep. Cars were a harder diet and their breath was bad.

Yet as Boy turned towards the north-west, he was lost in a glory of evening. There was a gold scar flung across the hills towards Loch Lomond. Out of the brightness two black thunderheads threw up their dark feathery turbans into the pale sky. Soot seemed to be dusting the air, the stone walls were blotters to the late light, so that the spires of the churches were dark dirks at God's shiny throat. The heavy blocks of terrace houses were warts on the cheeks of heaven, the galleries of cranes along Clydeside were chains to the arms of the last of the sun.

"Ya sully bastart," the chib-man said behind Boy. "Whau'rs yur wullit? Mibbe ye'll no want a face like a pun' o' mince."

Boy turned. Behind him, a squat heavy man with crossed slashes on his right cheek, in his eyes glims of madness or whisky. His right hand held his open chib, steel streak of slash and run. A hard case from the Gorbals, a nutter.

"Gie us some cash or Ah'll cut ye fae earhole tae arsehole."

Boy transferred his parcel from his left hand to his right hand and took out his wallet. It held a few pounds. He gave it to the hard case.

"Reight, Santy Claus. Noo gie us the wee parcel."

"It's only got a dead fish in it," Boy said. "A poisoned fish. It's no good except to throw at politicians."

"Doan't ye gie me tha'." The chib-man snatched the parcel with his free hand. "Naebuddy but a nutter would hump a stinkin' fish tae Glesca. We've the Macfisheries alreidy." He looked to right and left. People were coming. He closed the chib. "An' doan't be stoappin' tae

talk tae ony polis, or Ah'll cut off yer heid an' hit ye in the face wi' it."
And so he ran off, hunched and scuffling as a broken-wing tern.

Boy looked after him, smiling. His father Paul had told him once of
being robbed by a deserter on a bomb-site; but this Gorbals hard case
was no deserter; chance had deserted him. All that risk for a few quid
and a rotten fish. For the parcel did only contain Marie's poisoned
salmon.

Boy faced once more to the north-west. Now the pitchy shapes of
kirk and slum and crane had nearly joined the gloamed dusk except
where a scrap of final sun capped the hills in a red cockade. Chill
now, time for a wee drop in the pub, a dram to keep the warm in, a
fug of sweat and plain talk of work and wages and Celtic and Rangers,
a barmaid that had long lost hers, a Scots folk found again in the hot
dens where people herded against neglect and the night.

7

ARM'S LENGTH

The crocodiles were graded in sizes. In one trough, the nippers fresh from the egg, no bigger than your hand, but sharp enough in the tooth to bite off your little finger. Then the yearlings, lying in intimate piles as wet airline baggage, inert in their pen. And so on through the age groups, a kindergarten of crocodiles segregated by their birth-dates, two-year-olds all together, threes, fours up to fives.

"Mobile handbags we call them," the crocodile farmer was explaining to Kelso. "We used to call them flat dogs, 'cos they can go fifty miles inland if they're hungry. Now they're just product as we got a use for them. At five years' old, we cull them. We get the best quality skin out of their tummies and the rest of the hide goes for belts and things. Croc steaks we export – they're Afrodisiacs in Asia. Or we recycle the croc meat – if there's one thing a croc loves, it's eating his mother. Me, I don't like the taste – it's not fish and not flesh. The only part of the croc we don't use is the teeth. They drive dentists crazy."

The sixty crocodiles in the fives pen were splaying out their fangs – broken, awry, discoloured, criss-crossed, innumerable, lethal. Sometimes they left their jaws agog in an interminable yawn, expecting their fortnightly dinner. Comatose, they seemed to accept their reptilian fate.

"You wouldn't think you'd want to farm crocodiles," Kelso said. "It's worse than silk from a sow's ear."

"They get their own back," the farmer said. "Come and see Big Pope." He took Kelso round to a small enclosed lagoon where an enormous brute as long as a cricket pitch slumbered among eight mates a quarter of its length. "Big Pope ate five people before we caught him. There are so many crocs in the Zambezi they eat a person a day, so the villagers say."

"Why don't you control them?"

"We got a war on, so crocs are our second problem. I wouldn't say life was cheap in the tribal lands, but death by crocs or lions, it's natural. Expected even. Part of life. They may be ancestors, anyway. Witchdoctors like Alice. We did shoot out most of the Zambezi crocs some years ago. Then what happened? The big barbel at the bottom of the river ate all the fish spawn, so we didn't get any bream or tigerfish. So there wasn't any protein for the villagers. So we had to let the crocs back to eat the barbel to get the same fish again."

"And lose a human being a day?"

"That's ecology."

"You could call it genocide," Kelso said.

"Nature," the crocodile farmer said, "is not something we should rise above." He looked round the pens of his enterprise where buyers on high iron bridges overlooked their future belts and shoes. "We must live with nature and off it. But not interfere with it."

"I don't know," Kelso said. "I still have an old-fashioned feeling – man is better."

"Some crazy American scientist brought in one plant here to see if it would grow. It grew all right. It covered the whole Zambezi and choked it up – Kariba weed. It was so thick the elephants could walk on it from one bank to the other. Luckily, the hippos loved it. We were letting the Affs carve them up for meat, but we stopped that. Now there are hippos everywhere, eating that weed, the kings of the river with the crocs. And the Zambezi flows free, full of fish."

"What I like about your nature stories," Kelso said, "there's no moral in them."

"Keep off the grass," the crocodile farmer said, "if you can't eat it."

As he left the track by the Zambezi, Kelso saw an elephant in a minefield, a solitary bull with good tusks. It confronted the high wires bearing a sign:

DANGER – MINES

Huge ears flapped their warning. The dark bulk was so threatening that Kelso knew it could crush the wires and his Jeep with hardly the effort of a charge. Yet it stood with its trunk raised under a msasa tree, watching the watching man. Then the elephant turned and crashed away through the bush, not turning back to the safety of the river, but seeking the burst of the unexploded mines. As Kelso drove away, the brown dust from his wheels making a cloud of powder behind him, he listened for the thump of the charge that would mangle the old bull. But there was no explosion. The great beast was fortunate or fated to live a while longer.

Back under the thatched roof of the hotel by the Victoria Falls, Kelso found himself a celebrity. He was the man who had brought in his father's head and put it on the bar. Now Rhodesia was independent and fighting the terrorists, Kelso was a folk hero. "Have a drink," so the strangers would say in their shorts with their revolvers at their belts. "You some man, man." As for the endangered elephants, he was told, "There's a lot of caketins out there. It's the cheap way of clearing them. We have to cull elephants anyway. They knock down a tree a day each. If we didn't cull them, they'd starve."

Kelso knew it was a matter of survival now for everybody. He had asked Elizabeth and the children to join him up at the Falls for their half-hols. He couldn't put a finger on it, but he felt he was losing her. He was too much away on business, and the children could not occupy her time, now they were away at local boarding schools. Yet he was only doing what was wanted by her family, the Mackenzies, trading gold for arms to keep Southern Rhodesia free, or free of black power.

He did not know who was coming to meet him. The code name was Serge. And sure enough, as he sat alone at dinner, an anonymous man with a conventional smooth look in a beige safari suit appeared at his table. The stranger was wearing long brown chamois leather gloves, even in the heat. He did not take them off, nor the dark glasses over his eyes.

"Kelso Sinclair," he said. "Serge Whoever. Glad to meet you."

He held out his gloved right hand. The little finger was curled down, so that it brushed Kelso's palm in the shake.

"Pleased as well," Kelso said. "The menu's not great. Antelope and croc's tails. Occasionally, Zambezi trout with a lot of bones in them. If you like, tomorrow, we can go and catch some. They're actually called tigerfish."

"We'll do that," Serge said, "if we can do some business." He pulled out of the briefcase at his side a bottle of Dom Perignon champagne and of Courvoisier brandy. "I never travel without reinforcements. Do they run to ice here? The home brew is not for me."

So they drank well and ate badly, the meat a rough toothbrush to their gums and lumps in their guts. The deal was straightforward. Six Alouette helicopters with grenade launchers, fifty 3-inch mortars with ten thousand bombs, two hundred thousand rounds of ammo for the old .303 rifles and sten and bren guns of the police and army, two thousand personnel mines, and ten flame-throwers, although Serge could not promise these.

"Of course, with the embargo," Kelso said, "how do you bring them in?"

"My problem," Serge said. "As a friend of mine once said, you can divide everything into a simple declension. My problem. Your problem. His or her problem. Your problem is to leave gold bars worth ten point five million Swiss francs in this designated deposit in Berne." He handed over a slip of paper. "That is, before the shipment reaches here. My problem is to deliver the goods."

"And how?"

"From the Congo. I have friends there."

"Do you give them arms, too?"

"It helps friendships, doesn't it, like ours."

Kelso smiled at the polished mask across the table.

"Do you supply the Terrs here as well? I mean, do you sell to both sides?"

"None of your concern. I provide materials for those who pay in gold."

"And diamonds."

"And diamonds. And unmarked dollars. Nothing else. I try to keep it simple."

"You mentioned two other problems. His problem. Her problem."

"So I did." Now Serge took off his sunglasses to reveal eyes which never kept still, but wandered, looking for people who might be looking for him. "His problem, what is that, I will tell you. You know why I knew you when I came in? I know your family from a long time ago. His problem is also your problem. He is your brother Keiss or Boy. He is your problem, because you don't know how to deal with him."

Kelso was astounded.

"How the hell can you know so much?"

"That's my job, not my problem. I have to know everything about the man I am dealing with. Especially when so much money and *trust* is at stake. Does that pass?"

Kelso swallowed.

"I suppose so. You won't say more."

"No. We are meant to be super discreet."

"And so, what is her problem?"

"Your wife Elizabeth's problem."

"You dare say –"

"I say nothing, friend. Ask her. She is *your* wife."

"She's coming here tomorrow with the children."

"In the afternoon." Serge shook his head and moved his mouth and said nothing.

"You know that too?"

"Well," Serge said, "it will give us time to catch our tigerfish in the morning."

Kelso put on the bait, with Serge sitting beside him. He pushed the barb through the eyes of the tiny dead fish, threading six on the curve of the hook, silver pendants with tails. He rose in the flat boat, pulled back the wire catch of his reel, gathered the slack of the nylon line in his free hand, and cast with a sideways flick of his wrist. The sinker and bait flew out beside the whitened trees which stuck up their broken branches from the water by the lake shore. As the weight plopped and ringed the still surface, a fish eagle screamed from its nest of twigs at the hope of fish rising.

Kelso reeled in, the point of his thin rod bending low by the side of the boat. There was a strike within seconds. He struck back once, twice, three times. Tigerfish, he was told, had to have the hook jerked home. The rod bent, the line snagged and loosened, and he began reeling in, keeping up the pull and the pressure. Behind him, Boniface the boatman crouched with the net.

The fish came up fast and twisting on the hook, black-speckled back, red fins on white belly turning, rising to the net as to a lure of death. Boniface brought it out threshing in the meshes and grabbed it, a forefinger and thumb rammed into its gills. He forced the fish's mouth open, showing its needle teeth.

"He bite yo' finger off, boss," Boniface said. "He a big one. Three pound."

Kelso had caught his first tigerfish. In the next two hours, Serge and he caught a dozen more. There were strikes nearly every time the lines were cast. The two men only had to get the fish and bring them to the side of the boat. But every time the fanged snappers were thumped into the scuppers, every time the bait was threaded on the hook, every time the line was flung out by the fossil trees, Kelso felt his excitement ooze away into the hot sweat briefly cooling on his skin under the bronze sun.

"Let's have a beer," he said, putting down his rod. "It's almost too easy, catching tigerfish."

"Nothing's too easy," Serge said, "when it's a matter of killing something."

"Yo' lucky first time, boss," Boniface said. He took a beer bottle from a kaolite cooler and bumped off its cap on the edge of an oil drum. "Many time tiger don't bite. Then the bosses don't want to pay. No tip."

Kelso took the beer, which was already warm. The cooler could not cope with the heat.

"And one for my friend Serge," he said. "We'll have fresh tigerfish tonight. At the hotel, when my family come in. Why wasn't it on the menu?"

"Too top bone. Six hour boil and then bone soft. Eat them then." Boniface smiled. "We eat them. But not on menu. Not for white people. You can't swallow them bone."

Kelso took two more swallows of warm beer. There was no more point in catching tigerfish. What was hunting without eating the prey? What was sport when there was pointless killing in it?

"We'll go back," he said, turning to Serge. "If that's all right with you."

"Spot on," Serge said. "I have a shipment to make. You, too."

Boniface smiled again.

"Fifty dollar," he said, "and they stuff yo' big tigerfish. Yo' take it home. Show yo' mighty hunter, boss."

Kelso stared at Boniface, but he could detect no irony in the black boatman. Only a smile of ingratiation or superiority. And his habit of saying 'boss' as a Cockney street-trader said 'squire', to have you on.

"Let's go," he said, and he went to sit in the bows.

Lake Kariba was filling up, as the game moved out to the dry high ground. He would help to make the biggest lake in Africa, several hundred miles long and fifty miles wide, all penned in by a concrete dam across a narrow gorge. They had mounted an Operation Noah to save the wild animals marooned on the islands in the rising flood. Most would survive and thrive on the edge of the waters, along with the crocodiles and the bilharzia. On that burning afternoon, the heat haze confused lake and sky until Kelso felt himself suspended on a machine flying through purgatory between heaven and hell. He had come to the lake to find peace. Instead, it had been a good day for tigerfish.

When they landed by the hotel, Serge took his string of the catch. He had been silent throughout the morning, his black stare through his glasses as meaningless as drain covers.

"Why do you take the fish?" Kelso asked. "You can't use them."

"I always take whatever the deal is," Serge said. "Don't forget. Put the gold bars in the bank. And your goods will arrive. A deal is a deal is a deal. Or you're a poor old tigerfish on a prong. You see, Kelso, I know you, all about you. And you do not know me." He held out a hand. On its long fingernail, there was a shred of brown hair. "Yours, I think."

Kelso took the sample.

"Is that mine?"

"It is now."

"You took it. I never noticed."

"To seal the deal."

"I have never met anyone like you, Serge, if that's who you are."

"No. And I would not recommend it again." Serge ducked his head in a little bow. "I won't keep you from your family, which I know a little, too."

While Kelso was waiting for Elizabeth and the children to come along for dinner, the hippopotamus lumbered out of the lake to eat the hotel flowers. The water beast had a passion for poinsettias. Chopping down the giant boxing-glove of its head, it devoured the scarlet petals and green branches. The sound of a large specimen of fauna crunching flora was louder than a Derby and Joan Club using its dentures on rock cake. Nature, Kelso thought, was noisy.

Below Kelso on the terrace, the hotel gardener watched the devastation of his bright bushes. He did not seem to mind too much under his jungle camouflage hat, as the hippopotamus moved on to the purple joys of bougainvillea.

"He's just having his tea," Kelso said, sipping his Malawi Sunrise, the bitters so tart on top of the orange and ginger ale.

"He come two, three time a week. Eat my garden. You want photo?" The gardener appeared eager to turn the devastation to his advantage.

"No," Kelso said. "Wild life isn't my bag." It was everybody else's. The other guests were running to ring the hippopotamus at a safe distance, their cameras ready to shoot. "Still he's quite an attraction."

"Yo' come here fo' the birds?"

No, not the birds for Kelso. The weaver birds hanging upside down from their hundred little nests in the jacaranda tree by the dining room were the most cantankerous, whistling chatterboxes any businessman could hope to avoid.

"I came for the people," Kelso said, not saying he came for the arms.

The answer confused the gardener. He turned his seamed face towards Kelso, his zigzag hat reflecting his puzzlement.

"Yo' come to see the people. Nobody come here see the people."

"I do," Kelso said. "And the flowers."

The hippopotamus finished his tea by swallowing a bed of petunias. Then he waddled back to the lake shore, waded in and pushed off into the shining waters. Where the low sun laid its glittering scimitar on the ripples, the great beast turned onto its back, presenting its four squat legs and domed belly to the last of the light. Such was the grand finale. The cameras clicked like locusts. Kelso smiled.

"Africa," he told the gardener, "is theatre." He looked up to see his wife and his brood coming towards him. "Darlings," he said, "you have come to the end of the show."

"No, daddy," the boy Conan said, "there's a show down the road nobody is seeing. And it's the best. You have to see it. Promise."

"I promise." Kelso rose and kissed his two daughters, Kathleen and Catherine. They seemed to flinch from him, and only offer him a cheek for his lips. He had never embraced them enough when he was home, or else their mother was turning them away. As for kissing Elizabeth, all he got was a peck in air and an explanation, "Love you, darling, but I've got a cold sore on my mouth."

During the early dinner, Kelso could see what a marvellous mother Elizabeth had been, bringing up her three little blonde children as advertisements for Lux soap and the healthy life. At their age, of course, as they grew to puberty and beyond, they never knew quite where they were, their voices high and low, their manners brash and shy, or giggle and silence. As for Elizabeth, she was non-committal, talking entirely about school events and the atrocities of the War of Independence, which had not much affected their lives in Salisbury.

"I suppose it was like this for your mother Bridget in the last war in England – shortages, rations. All because of your Labour government's bloody sanctions. It doesn't matter to us, really. We get all we want from South Africa. Those Afrikaners, they understand us. It's like the Boer War again to them."

"I bet it is," Kelso said.

"We built this country from nothing," Elizabeth said, "and we don't want it taken away."

"Agreed," Kelso said. "And I'm trying to help, aren't I? That's why I'm away from home, missing you lot so much. I'm trying to help the Mackenzies keep all they have worked for."

"You're away too much," Elizabeth said. "All of us think that."

"I do, daddy," Conan said. "We can see the show after dinner? I can show you."

"A promise is a promise," Kelso said to his son.

"How many broken promises," Elizabeth said, "about seeing the girls' first communions and sports days?"

"I have to earn the money," Kelso said. "It's very difficult, getting round the regulations. Forgive me, but I do my best. I'd rather be with you all the time."

The eyes of his wife and daughters looked at Kelso with distrust. There was the sound of a kudu horn shrieking in the distance. So his boy piped up again:

"That's them. They're starting. I've finished. Can we see the show? Will you take me?"

"Of course." Kelso crushed his paper napkin and stood up and took Conan's hand. "Please forgive us. We'll see you."

When Kelso and his son entered the little straw enclosure outside the hotel, the warriors were already charging. Their sandals pawed the ground, their nylon grass skirts flailed above their battered denim shorts, their wildebeeste caps reared above their naked chests. Even Conan felt no fear. He knew the warriors would stop short before trampling him down. And they did halt, the fearsome Shangaans. One of them stuck out a hand and Conan shook it. Then they returned to their wild crying, stamping, leaping and pouncing. "This Pointy-Pointy dance," their hopeful manager explained.

At the end of the caper, the dancers dropped on their bellies to the red earth, panting like hunted game. Their manager explained in his check shirt and patched jeans and bare feet.

"As you see," he said, "they play very hard. They very strong men. They strong on *sadza*, mealie meal. The next dance the Iron Bar dance. The little man, he lift it in his teeth. He dance. All over, we are number one for traditional dance. Always number one. All we need is promoter. Then we travel the world, always number one."

The manager was looking directly at Kelso, so he looked behind him. There were four more people in the audience, perched on their uncomfortable planks. There was a French woman and her young son. Also two smart Coloureds from the Cape, seeking the freedom of an independent African country and the sense of superiority in seeing the consequences.

"Only promoter," the manager of the Shangaans said, fixing Kelso with yearning eyes. "And we be number one in London, Maputo, New York, Havana, Blackpool. You see how hard they play. Now the Iron Bar dance."

The smallest of the dancers did pick up a section of railway line between his teeth and dance with it. The strain made his muscles quiver in a thousand tremblings, the sweat ran in a dozen trickles between the hollows of his ribs.

Kelso and Conan had each paid five dollars to watch the performance. That meant a take of thirty dollars. Two dollars each for the ten dancers, Kelso calculated, and five for the manager. And five dollars for the electric light would pay for the three weak bulbs strung from the wire which was stretched across the enclosure. Two dollars was enough for four beers to replace the sweat. Kelso wished he were a promoter, not a man dealing in arms. When the Shangaans had charged the machine-guns of Cecil Rhodes, the war was real, and Rhodes took the later profits. Now the assault of the warriors was a show, and he had not the money to repay: the cash had gone on new weapons, to kill them all, perhaps.

The thin small man dropped the iron bar from between his teeth, rasping for breath. The six onlookers clapped their hands to the sound of the drum beat. Behind Kelso, the French woman gave her son her verdict on the dancers.

"*Ils ont du charme,*" she said.

In bed that night with Elizabeth, Kelso found her tepid. They had not made love for months, and he had not found anyone else on his travels. She responded to his want in the way that the soldiers described their sleeping partners. "Mattresses," the women staying at home were called, "mattresses." Perhaps that was what war and fear did to women, leaving them cold and unfeeling. They did not want to risk loving men who might never come back. Yet he was not fighting in the front line. He was procuring arms so others could kill. But what had the mysterious Serge meant when he said that Elizabeth had her problem? What was it? He had meant to ask her, but when he had come to nothing – he could not call it love-making – his wife had turned away into a false sleep, leaving him on his back staring at the slow flip-flop of the revolving fan above, and wondering why he could never face up to anything he did not understand.

Ian Hamish was writing in his North London kitchen:

> Erasure is the worst problem of our technological civilization. It is worse than the problem of refugees or missing people, those who have left society or dropped out of it or disappeared. It was Herman Hesse who wrote that, if memory was the most important thing for man, forgetfulness was the second most important thing. We must be able to delete the unnecessary and

the unpardonable from our minds. But erasure is the ultimate weapon against the modern citizen. It consigns him to total oblivion. If his particulars are wiped from the memory bank of his new computer society, he ceases to exist. For the state, it is as though he has never been, a still-birth in the silence of his facts.

Erasure is the pleasure of electronics. We may store memories with an effort by punching SAVE on the keys; but we may erase memories easily or even unwillingly through a technical fault, and we are not then saved. We may neither recall nor move nor act, when the computer is down.

Our culture of amnesia encourages instant erosion of the past. Who may remember any of the ceaselessly changing images on television? What coherence lies in switching from one channel to another? We live now only to forget immediately. This is the end of history. It may be worse for a society to be unable to forget, as the Northern Irish cannot forget and still are fighting the Battle of the Boyne after three hundred years. But it is bad enough to have minds wiped clean by gadgets, when stored memory is the advance of civilization.

The KKK of memory and erasure is King Lear, Kafka's Castle and Krapp's Last Tape. They deal with the madness and sadness of a recall. In Krapp, the tape is even better than a truthful wife as a witness. It records wholly. We may trust the memory of a wife — every slur, every bullying, every boast of being the best man — they are remorsely retold. But electronic information is lethal, if retrieved. Now we do not need a Judgement Day. The tape is kaput and will condemn us utterly. Erase, erase, erase. That is the heroin that scatters all sense. That is the cocaine of ceasing to be.

Ian Hamish looked up from his sociological scribblings, as Clio slurped into the kitchen seat, opposite. She seemed to be quite on the heroin and the cocaine, but she had not quite erased him from her life.

"Well," he said, "you did make it back from Paris, I see."

"You ran away," she managed to say. She put a small red paper napkin to the residue running from her nose. "With Rosa. I heard."

"We lost you," Ian said. "But then, you wanted to be lost. With somebody who wasn't me?"

"What are you writing about, darling?"

"The usual rubbish. This is about wiping out. Everything that's happened. History. The past. Starting again. Living only for the minute, because that's all that is possible."

"Suits me."

"Yes, it would. But Clio, look at you."

Clio looked down at her slashed skin-tight white leather jeans, now as dirty as old car tyres. Her purple and vermilion space jacket was stained with acid or blood. Her yellow hair straggled as a mop.

"I look all right," she said.

"To you, you do."

"To me, I do."

"You look like shit," Ian said. "I don't know what you did. I don't know who you met ..."

"Jack the Nipper," Clio said. She began laughing wildly, out of control. "Do you know who ..."

"Shut up." Ian rose and slapped Clio across the face. This was the first time he had hit a woman in his life. "You don't know what you're saying. I'm putting you to bed. Then I'm out. I'm really out."

"Darling."

Clio stretched up loose arms at him. He caught their waving, then he clutched her at the waist and staggered and fell with her up the stairs, where he laid her out on the kelim rug which covered their bed. Almost at once, she was away into some nirvana beyond his knowing. The shy smile on her face was that of a little girl who had been naughty, but even if she were to be found out, she knew she would get away with it.

Rosa had been calling Ian Hamish to meet again after their flight from Paris, but Ian had resisted a rendezvous, for fear he might give way. Now he found himself bleating on the telephone like a lamb, begging to see her. They fixed it for that night at the Terrazza in Soho, the Italian place to be, if you were not in Rome.

"How can you afford it?" Rosa asked, when Ian had sent the waiters scurrying around after their Pinot Grigio and prosciutto and hot olives with everything. "You can't earn a thing. You can't live off Clio."

"No, I can't. And I would not. Not me." Ian was pink at the accusation. "I graft a bit. Old newspaper jobs. Some friends. As well as what's left of my grant for my sociology of London."

"Money's too much, isn't it? You can buy anything."

"Don't be so cynical, because you're so young."

Rosa was that in her Guevara sweatshirt, Che's eyes defining her hidden nipples, Che's beard upon the tiny shelf of her belly, as he was laying across so many young hopes. Ian had come here in a fever, now a fatigue tugged at his eyelids. She was too far and too late for him.

"Well, Ian, money is everything in our world."

"You'd rather be in Cuba with the comrades?"

"I didn't say that. We're losing, you know, over here. I tell you, the old men will win, like me."

"You're not *that* old. Anyway, you're a poet. You don't have to commit."

"Lorca did, and he got shot. I won't, so I'll be here to pay the bill."

As they talked over their spaghettini and vongole, Rosa turned out to be too inquiring to take all her mother's hard left beliefs aboard. On a tape, Bob Dylan was singing, 'The Times They Are A-Changing'. In this case, in the wrong direction. This was a curious child, who took on her no dogmas as extra luggage. She felt free to move wherever the wind blew, as long as she trusted her fellow voyager, to advise her where to go. And she had chosen Ian by some instinct of survival or reproduction. She wanted to live with him, she wanted to live through him. He did not know why, but she was sure she was right.

"Clio's no good for you. Look what happened in Paris."

Ian looked more hangdog than usual as he tried to defend his lover.

"She came back. She's sleeping. Do you know, she was so far out, she said she had met Jack the Nipper —"

"You didn't believe her?"

"Of course not."

"Perhaps you should. Perhaps she did. What do you think of him?"

"As a sociologist?"

"Yes."

"He's the post-product of imperialism. Once we put pathological killers into our redcoat regiments. They could slaughter and torture as they pleased. Now we have to take them in at home. So they take it out on us. They torment us for what they have lost, the liberty to indulge their viciousness and walk away."

Rosa's eyes were new-penny bright.

"That's why I love you, Ian," she said. "Sometimes you get it spot on."

"But Clio could only have met one Jack the Nipper. There are thousands around, who we can't send to the colonies now."

"Perhaps he's the real one. The one they all copy. Perhaps she knows him, and you know him."

"I can think of one."

"That one Mummy told me about from Ireland. Clio always liked being beaten up. What was his name?"

"Peregrine. He was a sod."

"What happened to him?"

"Disappeared, or ran away. Very shady. But Clio was in love with him, and others."

"And not you?"

"Rosa, I don't know. She always comes back."

"When she has nowhere else to go."

"Perhaps, but —"

Rosa put her gnawed fingernails across the table and took Ian's bony hand in her clasp.

"Look," she said, "you've always run after an impossible woman, who doesn't really want you. Why run away from me?"

"You're too young. It wouldn't possibly work."

"She's far too old for you. Try me."

"I can't."

"Try."

That was all there was to it. They went back to the bedroom, which Rosa had borrowed from a girlfriend for the afternoon, and they made love. In his life, Ian had never had such delight. The touchings, the turnings, the twistings, the smotherings, the facings so supple, the backings so firm, the rearings, the lying so close that there was only one body, the skin fusing to skin, the escape from the solitude he could never escape, except through this time, except in her.

"You'll never go now," Rosa said.

"You've only got this place for the afternoon. I'll have to go back, clear things up."

"Then you'll be back to me, with me, for ever."

"Then. For ever."

Yet when Ian returned to North London and Clio, he found her blue in the face and choking on her own vomit. He had her taken to the St George Hospital off Hyde Park Corner, and he sat up with her for days and nights, when he was allowed to visit. She was saved with transfusions and saline drips. Her blood was so infected that she needed sixteen pints, before it flowed clean again. The doctors also found a cyst on an ovary, which they had to remove. She would never have a child now, although well past it. She dropped to ninety-five pounds in weight. She seemed a wraith on the stacked pillows, when Ian brought her grapes and cream meringues, all she would eat.

"Hi," she said, "I'm sorry. I seem to have blown up. Or shrunk."

"My favourite explosion," Ian said and stayed with her.

With Ian's desertion, Rosa began to see the desperate Boy Keiss again. He was earnest and dedicated to his work, reasonably good-

looking, with something of Ian in the family's long Scots face. Yet he
was so simple and fearful of her. After three excursions to see the
latest Jean-Luc Godard productions at the National Film Theatre, Boy
did not even dare to hold her hand, let alone try and kiss her. When he
did, she merely brushed her lips against his. And then when he asked
her to marry him soon afterwards, she had to speak to him as to a
child.

"Boy, I do like you very much, but –"

"Liking turns to loving. They all say that. I love you."

"You really don't know."

"Is there somebody else?"

"Not now."

"There was."

Rosa did not choose to answer, but she decided on the best way to
turn him down. She was practical.

"You'll have to wait. You don't have enough money to buy a house
or support me. And you can't afford to have children, which you
would want, wouldn't you?"

"You don't want a budget from me, do you? A proposal with
numbers on."

"No, not at all. I am just being realistic. I am lucky. I can count on
something from Granny Marie. But you only have your job with the
Atomic Energy people. You're always travelling. You may get sick.
You can't offer marriage, if you don't have the means."

Boy shook his head and rolled his eyes in mock despair.

"And there speaks the romantic radical."

"And there speaks the woman and mother to be."

Of course, Rosa was not speaking the truth. Any squat or croft
would do with Ian Hamish. But she was seeking a way to let Boy
down gently, because she was fond of him. And money, or the lack of
it, was the answer to all declarations of love. Cash was the true heart
of their metropolis.

So the day ended in money as it had begun in money. From the
time before sunrise, when the street lamps had counted out their light
on the night-workers, to the grudging pennies of dawn casting their
coppers on the commuters cold as bank statements on the platforms
of the electric lines, through the adding machines of the day, Oxford
Street ringing with the take from the shoppers, the tills sending forth
their peals and the bells of the city churches silent as the clerks at the
discount brokers, money had been in every eye, mouth, pocket and
purse. In the pubs, the beer was as warm and heartening as money.

On the corners, the evening papers were as strident and plucking as money. In the garages, the cars were as bright and hoarse as money.

Money fitted every adjective and every purpose, for it fulfilled every need and was everywhere. Indeed, it was self-perpetuating, for money bred money. The only people who could not endure London were those without money, but even the penniless survived in hope of it. The very people who denounced the capitalism that made the money used its notes and coined it. Mercy itself was measured in money in the Inns of Court. And when the sun went down on the mercenary City going home in its hundreds of thousands, packed tight as wallets, it dropped over the horizon like a golden guinea going down a drain, paying no interest at all.

8

A FAMILY PORTRAIT

The morning that Marie was not there, she was meant to be unable to leave her bed. Crippled by her arthritis, she had to be turned over to be washed. Yet when Rosa came in carrying the breakfast tray, she found her grandmother was missing. The window was open, but looking out of it, Rosa could see no body lying below. And Marie could not be found in any of the bathrooms, slumped or passed out. So the search for her shifted to the woods of the estate, which led to the old coal mines and the Esk river. And there she was found by her daughter Rosabelle about midday. She was lying on the top of an old cairn of mossy stones. Stretched out, her face to the sky, death had refined her beauty, drawing away the lines from her bronze cheeks, undoing the webs of the years, restoring the proud definitions of her countenance. She had laid her old buffalo-hide leggings over her, as she came to meet her withdrawal at its destined time according to the spirit within her.

Rosabelle kissed her mother's chill hand. She did not weep. She admired. What a way to meet the inevitable. There was no hope in her matching Marie's role in keeping the family together. She had not got that quality of strong diplomacy, nor of angry compassion. She had her own extreme feelings, and she shared in the fight against injustice. Yet perhaps she would change herself. Having property was said always to alter the proprietor. She would not give her legacy away, for she had a daughter to look after. That was the terrible trap of inheritance. It was the snare of conviction.

There had to be an awful family reunion before Marie's ashes were scattered at her request on the Pentland Hills. Each relative was given a small envelope with a few cinders from the tanned body for a walk upon the slopes, where Marie had so often ridden on her pony. Up there, the remains were to be cast on the turf within sight of the great house and castle below in the glen. Boy took his packet to the edge of a mysterious old oak copse planted in the shape of the Templar Cross above Rosslyn, the old Sinclair stronghold and chapel. There he opened his brown flap and shook out the black flakes and grey dust, which blew away on the wind over the moor.

Boy was on his way to Dounreay, and he did not know what Rosabelle would do about the land sold for the Atomic Energy reactors there. She could not take it back, but she still had the neighbouring acres, where their cousin Martha had moved with her husband Angus Mackenzie and her two children. A sort of pale of protest could be erected round the nuclear power station, as had once happened round Dublin to keep out the Irish. Boy also feared the family wake over Marie, because Ian Hamish was coming up to Ermondhaugh with Clio, recovered from her long stay in hospital, apparently. What Rosa still felt for Ian, she would not tell Boy. These were the sharp moments between the two of them, when she told him not to be so bloody suffering and hangdog. She did not feel guilty about anything. She could look after her own affairs, thank you very much, and he could look after his. Even if the two of them were having an affair, it did not rule out all other possibilities at their age.

Boy returned to an extraordinary set-up. Clio had managed to arrange the survivors of their branch of the Sinclairs in a formal family portrait. The old Gillon stood by Ellen-Maeve with her son Hamish Henry, and the aged Murdo. Boy's mother Bridget was dwarfed by his brother Kelso, over from Rhodesia, with Ian Hamish at his side. The Caithness cousins, the Mackenzies, were not there, nor the Indian ones, Miriam and Peg and Solomon, nor the ones in Israel, Rachel and Leah and Fiona, nor the vanished Peregrine. Yet with Rosabelle and Rosa in the centre of the picture in front of Ermondhaugh, a new dynasty was being created, and Boy was proud to join it.

"Come on, Boy, come on. Get next to your mother," Clio was shouting. "It's no good my trying to become a bloody snapper, if I can't even get any cooperation from my nearest and dearest. Get in behind Bridget by your brother."

So Boy found himself in the position of the furthest and distant from the old rosewood camera on its tripod with its glass slides. This portrait would be a museum piece. Perhaps the family was already, as it tried to cling together in a cabinet of curiosities, when all the forces of the twentieth century were forcing the cousins apart in their divergences. Then he felt a sudden cold prickle in his spine. Somebody was behind him. Something wrong. He swung round. Nobody there. Only Clio yelling, "Look at me, idiot, look at me."

Boy found both his ancient cousins, Gillon and Murdo, to be supporters of his atomic energy job. They reckoned they would be the last of the Kipling breed of engineers and tinkerers, which had kept the British Empire ticking over for a couple of centuries, but now nuclear research was producing new brands of submarines and rockets and shells, which would deter the more powerful disguised empires of America and Russia from any assault on the remnants of the thin red line.

"Now you have the whole Home Fleet in the hull of a Resolution sub with its Polaris missiles," Murdo said.

"When you think of that lumbering Swordfish bi-plane with its wonky slung torpedo – you needed a squadron of them to sink the Bismarck, if any got through."

"I remember radar coming in," Gillon said. "Detection of enemy planes by electronics, not carrier pigeons. It was magic at the time. And now, nuclear engines, deep-sea missile systems that can stay under the Arctic for three months, then bob up and destroy Moscow with one warhead better than all of Napoleon's Old Guard or Hitler's panzer armies. In fact, what are armies for now? They are out of date."

Hamish Henry was welcoming, too, although he had his work cut out looking after his twittering mother, whose buttercup curls with white roots were disarranged round her broken saucer of a face.

Boy's mother Bridget had dyed auburn hair and a stiff perm, but her bluebell eyes and energy still brought out the girl in her, particularly as she was playing her old power game of which of her sons did she love the best, and who would get what particular stick of furniture.

"Well, Keiss, I thought you should have the bureau and Kelso the sideboard, but now I think it should be the other way, and Kelso will have the bureau, and you the sideboard. He is the elder, you know, so he deserves the best."

"Mother," Boy said, "you'll live for ever," but he could not cut off her in full flow, as she revised her will in her head and on her tongue, as remorseless as the tidal wave of the Severn Bore.

Kelso was popular again with Bridget because Elizabeth had said she was thinking of a separation. He was away too much on his gold and arms business in Europe. She needed somebody to look after her during the war of independence in Rhodesia. And now that Kelso might become hers again and his father Paul was dead, Bridget was changing sides, because her first son would surely need his mother now.

"Well," she was saying between the inventory of her household goods, "I never really trusted that Elizabeth, if you know what I mean."

"But you always said you adored her," Kelso had to protest.

"Well, saying and doing –" Now Bridget touched the side of her nose with her forefinger. "Those are ham and eggs. Two different things. I like people who say 'I Do' to my son to stick to it."

Yet even harder for Boy would be the meeting with Rosabelle and Rosa. He did not know what the mother and daughter had said to each other about him. Presumably everything. He remembered seeing the two of them shrieking from the plinth in Trafalgar Square during the Suez misery, and they must judge him harshly now for Dounreay, however much they pretended to love him.

"Marie left everything to Rosa and me." Rosabelle was aggressive. "I hope none of the family think –"

"Only the best of you," Boy said. "It's what you would expect."

"I've looked at the sale of Dounreay. It is not a lease."

"Freehold."

"So we can't take it back. Except, of course, if it is still clan common land. After all, the chiefs seized the land at the time of the Clearances, when we all went to Canada. Until then, they only held it in trust for their clans. Supposing a court found that seizure was illegal now ..."

"And restore the whole of Scotland to the crofters?" Boy smiled. "Lovely idea. But the law always supports property rights."

"Ach," Rosabelle said. "You are going up there?"

"On a tour of inspection."

"You will find Martha and Angus Mackenzie there. You will not miss them."

"Are they on our land?"

"No, on the land that is still ours."

"I may go up to Caithness too," Rosa said.

"Good," Boy said. "With me?"

"With you," Rosa said, "and without you. Anyway, the same way to the north."

"But you'll take the high road, and I'll take the low road –"

"And I'll be in Dounreay before ye."

Now Boy chucked all restraint to the four corners of the room.

"Rosabelle, if I asked Rosa to marry me again, and she actually said yes for a change, would you approve?"

Rosabelle was amused.

"She doesn't need my consent."

"That's not what I asked."

"You're a fair young man, that's true. With your head and your job in the wrong place. That's also true."

"If I gave up my job. Became a physics don like Hamish Henry."

"Then you wouldn't fancy Rosa. All those donnish lives, looking after young men with sherry and caresses."

"Cambridge isn't all like that."

"It was when I went there," Rosabelle said, "and met Hamish Henry's friends. Anyway, it's for Rosa to say, as I said."

Now Boy knew he had dug himself into his own grave.

"Rosa, well, er ... will you –"

"Don't be more of a fool than ever, Boy. You can't ask me in front of Mummy."

"I didn't mean to. It just came out."

"As things do with you, Boy. As they do."

Rosabelle had given her daughter and Boy separate bedrooms, although she knew they were sleeping together in London. She was certainly modern enough to accept the fact, but the thought of a strange man in the hallowed place where she had rocked Rosa's cradle and changed her nappies was too much for her. So Boy found himself excluded from his desires and wandered lonely along the corridors of the great house, now empty of all except the funeral guests, for the last of the dependent miners were departed. So it was that he reached the walled garden beyond the kitchens, and heard Clio's voice sharp with anger.

"You bloody pervert! Where did you materialize from?"

Then a curious voice, fluting and modulated, gave an answer. It was familiar and remote. Boy thought he had heard it before, but he could not identify the source.

"They seek me here, they seek me there," Boy heard over the wall. "Those coppers seek me everywhere. But I nip her here, and I nip her there –"

There was a slight shriek, and Boy started forwards towards the gate into the enclosed garden.

"Oh, do shut up, Clio." The words were a drawl now. "They must have taught you that at school. Suffer in silence. Particularly when you enjoy it."

There was no noise now, so Boy stood where he was. Clio was speaking.

"How long have you been around? Why didn't we see you?"

"Is he in heaven or on the scene? That damned elusive Peregrine."

Now Boy knew the answer. He should have known before.

"You may even find me in the picture, Clio, the family portrait. Like that Scrooge business, the ghost of Christmas past. What do they say about photographs? There may be developments."

"You weren't in it. You couldn't have been. Nobody saw you. I didn't."

"Well, if I wasn't, you can always superimpose me. A sort of wraith at the window. Didn't you hear of our famous ancestor, Doctor Harry Lamb, who married the redoubtable great nurse Mary? Lots of people thought he was Jack the Ripper. Now he's come back to haunt you."

"You certainly bloody have!"

As Clio's voice soared over the wall, Boy could see Ian Hamish strolling towards him from the great house. He had no time to think. He did not want to protect Clio, but he found himself shouting, "Ian! Splendid to see you."

When Ian came up to him, he seemed surprised.

"I thought I heard you talking. But you're alone."

"Probably talking to myself," Boy said. "I can't find worse company. But I have to talk to you."

"Let's go in the rose garden," Ian said. "More private. Have you seen Clio?"

Again Boy raised his voice. "No! Let's do that. Go in the garden."

When he and Ian passed through the gate, they only found the damask roses trailing from their arbours, planted in their quarters round a central trickling fountain. There was nobody else there. The far gate to the fields was closed.

"This is a garden of paradise," Ian said. "A garden of Eden. That fountain in the middle is the river of life. And it flows away in the Tigris and the Euphrates, the Ganges and the Nile. Or it's meant to."

"All I can see," Boy said, "is a criss-cross of gravel paths. Though I'd love to have your vision. In a way, poets see more than physicists. Though whether it's quite true, practical ..."

Ian sat down on the bench in the little pavilion at the top of the garden, and Boy joined him.

"You mean Rosa and me," Ian said. "It can't lead to anything. You want to marry her."

"She's told you, then."

"Yes. I've always told her that I'm hopeless for her. But she won't believe me."

"Then don't see her."

"I don't have that sort of willpower. She's very beautiful, as you know. And she likes what I do, pushing a few words around. She hates what you do."

"I said I'd change. I'd become a don, not a doer."

Ian stood up abruptly.

"Well, those who can, do, those who can't, teach. I can neither do nor teach, only scribble. And I must find Clio, or I'll never make up my mind – although she hardly helps me do so. She wasn't here?"

"Not that I know of," Boy said, saving his eavesdropping for some later confrontation. What was jealousy doing to him?

"On with the search, then."

So Ian left by the far gate to the fields, although by now he would be too late to discover anything. And Boy left to pack for his departure for Dounreay. With or without Rosa, he had to go and do his duty. The only odd thing was that Kelso wanted to come with him as far as Edinburgh. He had a business meeting there, he said, with a man called Serge. A very important meeting, for the Rhodesian government as well as himself. Could he hitch a lift?

"Of course, big brother, of course you can."

The dome at Dounreay was the biggest golf ball in Scotland. It housed the new commercial Prototype Reactor. It had not quite fallen down the biggest hole in Scotland. Nuclear waste, surrounded by Polyfilla to make it safe, was now being dumped down a vast shaft. Boy thought that such Do-It-Yourself kit might not be suitable to contain radioactive plutonium waste. Perhaps it was all right in the Second World War to patch up bullet holes in Mustang wings with chewing gum, because nothing better was on offer. Yet radiation risks should perhaps be treated more seriously.

Certain, this was the endeavour outside the guards and the iron security gates of the Atomic Energy Authority plant. The worst fears of Boy were housed in a psychedelic caravan, painted with all the colours which dazzled the eye beyond the rainbow. The roof was crowned by a huge poster: STOP NUCLEAR WASTE KILLING KIDS. And, as he expected, there Boy found Rosa squatting along with their young Mackenzie cousins, Donald and Kirsty. The three of them were polite enough when he came to visit them, offering him the traditional tea and scones and butter of a mild welcome.

"Well," Rosa said, "it's good of you to cross the barricades."

"A surrender the now," Kirsty said.

"I hae me doots," Donald said.

"No surrender," Boy said. He gave the three protestors a folder each of printed material. "It's all explained here," he said. "What the reactors do. How safe they are. The amount of energy they provide. And the jobs." He gave Donald a hard look. "They're still recruiting. And there are no other jobs here."

"Except for the stags and the gillies," Rosa said.

"Wha' the wages?" Donald was interested.

"Very good," Boy said. "All clothing provided. Three weeks' holiday and festivals. Pensions. Here." He pushed another folder over to Donald. "Join the New Age."

"Don't give him that propaganda," Rosa said and reached out to take the material. Yet Donald held onto it.

"Ach, awa'," he said.

"Don't you come, Boy, seducing the young with money."

"And security," Boy said.

"Insecurity. They're doing leukemia tests round here. There may be a cluster like at Sellafield. We used to march against that when we met. Leukemia, don't you remember? From overground testing of H-Bombs. You've turned."

"Not at all, Rosa. Everything here is underground. Compressed. In leak-proof containers. Nothing can be contaminated."

"Kirsty tells me the news is a plutonium fuel rod disappeared in a waste dump. And you haven't been able to find it."

"We're still looking."

"I hope you don't get irradiated while you look."

"Our suits are wholly protective."

"And your Intermediate Level nuclear waste shaft. It's unshielded, and it exploded. It can contaminate the ground around for fifty thousand years."

"We're dealing with that," Boy said. "We're shutting down the Experimental Fast Breeder Reactor. We've got a better model now, under the golf ball. But the first one was brilliant. As it produced all that lighting for your homes in Caithness, it also produced more nuclear fuel."

"How? What?"

"Well, uranium. And plutonium. And waste sludge."

"Which you popped down the hole, untreated."

"Which we sunk."

"And sunk us with it. I mean, the next thousand future generations here."

"Don't exaggerate," Boy said. "You always do. Can't you understand the paradox? What can kill us all can give us all the energy we need. Look, we're born to die. We know that. But we're finding a way without much risk to power us for ever. It's a challenge I would take."

Donald put down the folder he was reading.

"All tha' money?"

"Aye," Boy said. "All that money."

"I can apply?"

"I'll recommend you," Boy said.

"Ye canna." Kirsty rose, her cheeks red and righteous. "Or I'll scratch ye to bits."

Now Donald was on his feet.

"I'll do wha' I'll do."

"Surely you will." Boy rose as well. "Rosa, will you come with me to eat oysters in Scrabster tonight, and we'll talk it out?"

"No uranium shellfish for me," she said. "And nothing to talk about. I'll be home at the croft with Angus and Martha, when they're back from teaching at the school. But what have you done? You've gone on with what the English have always done up here. You've bought Donald like you bought the clans. You're paying gold to someone to split the family, split the clan. You pay off and divide."

"The future," Boy said. "It is the future. Donald should have it, too."

9

DRESSING DOWN

Dressing up among males is a customary tribal practice. In the Americas and Polynesia, Australasia and Africa, body-painting is normal, also circumcision and tattooing, as is sticking bones and pins and rings through noses and ears, also wearing feathers and bracelets and pouches to cover the private parts. It is no different among the tribes of London. The buttons on the suits of the Pearly Kings are matched by the red robes and jewelled headpieces of the Sovereign. No concoction on the aborigine skull can exceed the hats at Ascot or the bearskins upon the Brigade of Guards. The love of male plumage is common to birds, beasts, savages, soldiers and Etonians. At times of ceremony, this love goes on display – top hats in grey or black, silk scarves or cravats at the neck, frock coats with penguin's tails, pepper-and-salt trousers to camouflage and accentuate the length of the legs.

Yet these shows are only on Grand Occasions. For the English male is forced by discretion to hide his passion for the gaudy. Sometimes, the rites of panoply are reserved for secret societies or private gatherings – the Masons with their aprons and regalia, the Knights of the Garter with their britches and plumes, the exclusive dances in special colours and manners – Please come in RED AND BLACK AND GOLD, EN TENUE DE CHASSE or DE SADE, as THE CHAMBER OF HORRORS or THE GARDEN OF EDEN.

This love of costume is enshrined in games at festivals – HOMO LUDENS, as the phrase goes – MAN THE PLAYER. Charades are played, particularly at Christmas. There is a dressing-up chest, which is plundered for unlikely trans-sexual costumes. The mark of the Christmas pantomime is that older men dress up as women, Dames and Widows and Ugly Sisters, while young women dress up as principal boys, Dandini and Prince Charming. The change of sexes as well as costumes provokes extraordinary public mirth. Some male actors have made their careers on their extravagant female characteristics and outfits. What Danny La Rue was to the stage of yesteryear, Barry Humphries is today. To seek humiliation at the talons and tongue of Dame Edna Everage is the chosen attitude of abasement of most celebrities. The man dressed as a woman is the only dominatrix who may publicly flagellate the elites of England for their stupidity and lack of wits.

There is always a private side to public spectacle. There are those leaders of society who hire prostitutes to chain them like dogs to tables or whip them or make them wear maid's uniforms before they are disciplined. There are those tycoons who put on their wives' clothing and cruise the pubs looking for rough trade to rip it off. These secret dressers use costume as a revelation of their hidden needs, as a provocation towards their discovery, as an incitement to others to fulfil the desires which they can hardly admit to themselves. In their habits official and unofficial, the elites of London reveal far more about themselves than they know that they show.

Significantly, the most pervasive phenomenon of present London, Jack the Nipper, is invisible. Nobody has seen him, nobody knows how he dresses. A conclusion is that violence is so widespread and aimless now that it has no coat on its back. It is classless. It may come from peer or pauper, banker or bourgeois or beggar. If Jack had no clothes, he would be known. By costume, we identify ourselves...

Ian put down his ball-point pen. He had not seen Clio for three days and nights, ever since she had shown him the Scots family portrait with a strange apparition in the background, a whitish figure at a window in the great house. She could not explain the stranger in the background, another Banquo's ghost at Macbeth's feast after Marie's funeral. The streets of London were like that now, full of faceless danger. A city-wide contagion of callousness and indifference infected rational analysis. It subverted reasonable hypothesis. It certainly made the working methods of sociology and anthropology look like guidelines and guyropes, trying to control a falling Big Top or a tumbling Communications Tower of Babel. London induced a great confusion, and Ian no longer knew what he believed or what he thought he was doing at all.

Yet the field study had to go on, and the leg work. That was the discipline in writing as a profession. That was the puritan conscience in Ian's agnostic mind. He had even taken a grant for this work. By the act of taking public money, he was forced to produce something.

He was condemned to his research. He found the situation rather ironical, in a way. For his sympathies were with the workless, who took the dole by right, and with the deprived, who should be given money by the government and were not. Why did he feel so bad if he did not earn his grant? Surely he deserved it for trying to survive as a poet and author for decades on low pay. And yet – and yet, he felt he must work off his debt to society in whatever rotten state it was now.

Clio burst through the door in her normal mayhem, dragging behind her a youngish skinhead with a pug face, dressed in army surplus grunge and swinging cameras on their straps as dried heads slung around his neck.

"This is Blossom," Clio announced. "Robin Blossom. He's teaching me all the tricks of the trade."

"What tricks exactly?" Ian asked too precisely. "And what trade?"

"Taking photos, you ass. Where's the scotch?"

"It's tea-time."

"Then we'll put the Glenlivet in our Earl Grey."

"Nah," Robin said, "it spoils the char. Hi, squire."

"Hello," Ian said. "I'll put the kettle on."

"Clio tells me you're doing a book on London. Like I'm doing, only I'm snapping it."

"I'm trying." Ian placed the kettle on the hot hob. "I'm not succeeding."

"Pictures don't lie, guv. Words do. You listen to those sodding politicians."

"Pictures lie, too. It depends on the angle. Clio's just taken one, and she doesn't even know who the intruder is. Or she says she doesn't."

"Oh, don't you go on about that," Clio said. "Boring, boring, boring. But Robin is Superman. He never asks the people he takes. He stalks them, catches them with their pants down. Snap, crackle, pop it in the darkroom. And all is revealed, the true downside of London. He's teaching me. Now I'm so old I'm not worth looking at, I want to take nasty pictures of others."

"You're a sort of thief in the night, then," Ian said. "You steal your images when no one is looking."

"Nah," Robin said. "Everybody's chuffed when they get their pix in the papers. The more they run away from you, the more they want to be a celeb."

"And is it profitable?"

"It took me from Wapping to a Bentley. I'll do better than Bailey, I will. Fastest lens in the west."

"And what do you shoot, generally?"

"The nobs and the slobs. High life, low life, no life. The whole muck-up from the creche to the cemetery."

"And what do you learn from it?"

"You'd better screw me first before I screw you. You get your wages if you do as I say. Rock 'n roll, but don't rock the boat. I'm all right, Jack, and I don't mean the Nipper. Churn and burn the suckers, and skive off scot-free. Stop the shit before it hits the moving object."

Clio laughed, and even Ian was amused.

"And with a philosophy like that, how the hell do you think you'll be accepted?"

"He can get in anywhere," Clio said. "I met him at Anabel's. And he could gate-crash Buck House."

"Yah," Robin said. "But I don't want to be one of you. That's the problem. You're let in too easy now. You forget your mates, and you wake up, and you find you've *altered*. Like them alien films — you're took over – and you don't even know it. Suddenly you're up there with the nobs and you don't know who the fuck you are. You're not the lad you started with, and you're not the man you wanted to be. You're a sort of a thing from the outer slums. You're processed, and you haven't even noticed. And you can't get back, because you've forgotten how."

"What I'm writing," Ian said, "makes me agree with you. I think society mutilates you here. It operates on you. Of course, you're under an anaesthetic, so you don't notice the surgery and the amputations. What are the drugs? Mass sport, mass media, television the opium of the people, pubs always open, intellectuals and education a bad joke, profit making, all the usual shit and explanations. But there's something deeper than that. Why does a child accept the scalpel from the state school? Why does a young man take dirty jobs for low pay? Everybody's ill with materialism and the Have-Nots only want what the Haves already have. So advertising must be the disease, really – mass demand for the better material life – and expectations always kept going by the government one step ahead of disappointment. That's the universal drug – the feeling that you too can get on."

"Right," Robin said. "And I do, and I do good. I'd only pick up a brick to chuck when I'm down and out."

"Then you'll be too down and weak to chuck it."

"Right again, guv. Right on."

And so they talked and tended to agree and grew towards a mutual respect. This was odd, yet true, for they were chalk and cheese. But in the quick shifts of the time, where the greasy pole could be climbed as quickly as falling down it, a certain recognition was growing between the middling and the striving, the learned and the learning, between the elites and the socially mobile, with only the Undercrust excluded into aimless violence and angry resignation. So successful had been the structuring of the new economic man in the new Britain of the 'eighties that he did not heed the changes done to him over the process of time. He was transformed and ignorant of it. He was operated upon and forgetful of the knife. His occasional reminders of his state were notorious, yet subliminal – the acts of Jack the Nipper, the muggings in the streets. All else was erasure and immediate gratification. O ye of little memory, Ian thought, how shall you know who you are or what is done to you in the name of your country?

The Golden Harrow was named after the agricultural rake, not the public school. As he went into the Soho pub, Hamish Henry found himself surrounded by bicyclists, fresh apparently from the Milk Race of the Tour de France. They wore skin-tight black rubber shorts with lurid side stripes of purple and red and yellow for identification. Their attractions were delineated behind. Their tops were variable, ranging from fringed matadors' jackets to clinging string vests and chiffon blouses. Particularly ambiguous were their bother boots with uppers painted in pastel shades of pink and green above steel-tipped toes. Among them, the man called Serge stood out in a silver-spangled body stocking, wearing a black-and-scarlet silk dressing-gown sporting a stiletto in the shape of a corkscrew and the legend, CHAMPION OF THE UNDERWORLD. As he raised a hand in greeting, light flashed from a long glazed fingernail.

"You're rather underdressed," Serge said, looking at Henry's dark suit. "I did say – Confer first. Then go cruising for a bruising."

"Wait," Henry said. "I've got a change of gear in my shoulder bag. I couldn't come from the Fens looking like a tart."

When he emerged from the STUDS ONLY, Henry wore lipstick and rouge and a diamantée dangle from his left ear above a coachman's overcoat in dark green and pink bootees.

"You blend now," Serge said. "Though we're all wondering what's under that lawn you're wearing. I've got you a *kir royal* and a corner table. But you really are a jumbo with the rouge. And you put on lipstick like Vincent van Gogh in the asylum."

"This isn't my scene, really," Henry said. "I come here so rarely. And I hardly know you. Meeting you with Kelso up in Edinburgh over this arms thing for Rhodesia. What do you want of me?"

"It's what you want." Serge's eyes were almost as spangled and glancing as his body armour. "A lot of money, I presume. To do what you want to do. Everybody wants that. The guns and stuff I sell to Kelso are small beer, and the cause is lost. After the Salisbury agreements, Mugabe will win the elections and keep the White Front away. But there's a state I know wants a bit of weapons grade plutonium. You have access to it, so does Boy. They reprocess the stuff up at Dounreay. The thing is, Boy seems to me like that old Robespierre, a sea-green incorruptible. While you, dear Henry, with your dodgy past, are open to inducements, if nobody wants to be reminded of what you did."

"Why do you know so much about me?" Henry asked. "And wasn't it you in Clio's portrait? The odd guy in the window."

"I am never where they say I am." Serge's short laugh was a snapping trap. "Don't you know the secret of life? You must be anonymous and superfluous. Then you are free to do what you want to do."

Henry looked round at the barman with a ruby ring in his pierced ear and at the young cyclists in their cheek-tight rubbers, which had never pedalled a machine.

"Not much freedom there," he said. "They used to call those pants bum-freezers in the old army. You wore them in the mess. You could hardly sit down in them. They kept you in, and your desires. That's how we ran the Empire on repression."

"I don't think that's quite the case here. You don't need a tin-opener to get what you desire. But suppose I said, Henry, half a million quid in a Swiss account for a wee case of the old plutonium. You could retire, you know, from those dreaming spires, that dreadful Kings, where you are underpaid, undervalued, and under nobody you'd wish to be under."

Henry smiled and said, "We don't take an oath, but academic integrity is part of the parcel."

"I am only gilt-wrapping it. What you may do is not even illegal these days. I know you were concerned with nuclear secrets passing to Russia in the bad old red era. You did it for the ideology – sounds like a mouth-wash now. And you didn't do it for the money. And because ideology is dead and gone to market forces, why not make the switch?"

"Why do you know so much about me?"

"Homework is the essence of my trade. Suppose I tell you, Henry, our clients are not all bad. In fact, another of them is a cousin of yours."

"I don't believe it."

"Leah. Israeli intelligence. They're developing their own little nuclear deterrence, as they call it. Rather like keeping fleas off a dog. I'm sure she'll have a go at Boy, and he'll find her harder to resist than me. That's why I came to you. The profit motive, I always think, is superior to every argument."

"I don't know," Henry said. "I don't know if I can get the stuff."

"Of course you can. You know the sources."

"They still have a folder on me in MI6."

"Which makes you perfect. Now you are a straight don at Cambridge – or should I say not too bent – you are my mark. Does not a retirement in the Shangri-La non-Sheraton of your choice appeal to you?"

"Certainly. But, um – I'll have to think."

"Don't. Take it or leave it." The quicksilver eyes of Serge locked in a metal. "Or you may have problems."

"What? Are you saying –"

"Say yes. Do what you can."

"I will not."

"Oh dear," Serge said. "Lessons is it?" He jerked his protruding nail at an odd figure at the bar, dressed as a bald Pierette designed by an action painter. All her stripes had become splotches, and her little skirt was tinged with crimson. Long black stockings did not hide the muscles in her legs, nor did foundation cream conceal a strong blue chin.

"Hello, trick artists!"

"Hello, Patsy," Serge said. "I am very put out. This object –" He slashed short of Henry's check with his razor of his fingernail – "he's a spy. A journalist, I think. Not one of us."

Patsy was weeping now, black tears from her false eyelashes.

"He doesn't care. He's a reporter. And my Buddy's just dead."

"He doesn't care," Serge said. "He's a spy. He's dressed up just to deceive us."

"You don't care," Patsy said. "You don't feel. All these people – our buddies – a slow horrible death – and you're Squire Spy!" Patsy hammered a tattoo of taps with her finger on Henry's chest. "You'd ask somebody for a doctor's certificate before you'd shack up with him! Certified AIDS-free like a bloody British lion stamped on an egg to say it won't give you salmonella. Safe sex! You want it wrapped in plastic and deodorised. You don't want life. And you don't care about death." More tears began to streak the powder on Patsy's face, and she left the tapping on Henry's ribs to smear them away. "You're an undertaker! You don't feel and you don't mind about us at all."

Henry was stung by the justice of Patsy's words. He did not feel or mind enough. He felt he should console this stricken bald creature, now so smudged with weeping. He put a hand on Patsy's shoulder, only to have it shaken off violently.

"Traitor!" Patsy said. "Don't pretend!"

"I'm not."

"You are. Oh, you are. Julie – " Patsy was addressing the barman. "You've never seen *him* before –"

"No," the barman said.

"What do you think?"

The barman examined Henry's appearance as if he were trying to smuggle cocaine in his cheeks through the Customs.

"Unreal. He changed in the toilet."

"He isn't, is he?"

"He's seriously unreal."

"What's his game?"

"This is a bar," Julie said. "Any creep can come in."

"Pansy!" Patsy was calling across the chatter of the pub. "We've got a right one here."

"Coming!

Henry turned on the shout behind him to see an iron barrel in leather and chains charging through the bicyclists on the attack. Then an arm swung from the back across his throat. While he choked and struggled, Pansy launched a flying kick at his stomach. Its force doubled him up and dropped him on the floor.

"Dear, dear," he heard a voice saying above him. "Can't hold his drink."

"Give him the bum's rush," another voice said, and suddenly there was a chant of, "Out, out, out, out, OUT!" And hands were lifting him and fists were pounding him and feet were kicking him. And he was thrust and ferried to the door of *The Golden Harrow* and flung out onto the street. And the pastel boots flailing at his ribs suddenly withdrew and were replaced by a pair of black and shining toe-caps. And from the night sky, the voice of authority spoke, "What's this here?" Blinded by his tears now, Henry pulled himself to his feet by clutching onto a lamp-post. He found himself blinking at a City policeman with the local black-and-white check tea-towel round his cap, looking like the latest in Op Art.

"Had an argy-bargy with her mates, did she?" the policeman mused, viewing Henry's sorry state. "A tiff in the ladies' room?"

"A minor misunderstanding." Serge was now standing on the pavement. "I don't think there will be any complaints, officer. I know the man. He merely came where he wasn't wanted."

"And you, sir?"

"Serge. Ask at the station about me."

"I will."

"I think the incident is better forgotten." Now Serge turned on Henry. "You do not wish to press charges, do you? As you provoked the incident –"

"Nothing," Henry said. "A misunderstanding, that's all."

"You see," Serge said to the policeman. "Nothing happened."

"A breach of the peace," the policeman said. "And it wasn't there." Then he turned sternly on Henry. "Right you! Off home. Or you'll spend the night at the station."

"Thank you, officer," Henry said humbly.

"And I don't want to see you again either," Serge said, "until you recognize what you have to do." He slung Henry's shoulder bag at him. "Put on some decent clothes. And reflect."

"Yes," Henry said. "Of course."

He limped away down the street towards Kings Cross Station. His ribs hurt, his lungs wheezed. The passers-by stepped away from him as if he had the plague. They wanted nothing to do with this damaged exotic piece of walking wounded. After a while, he came to a square, where a Tudor cottage stood in the middle behind iron railings and beside the eroded statue of some ravaged monarch. Henry stood holding onto the blunt spear-points of the black iron fence, trying to catch his breath. He was ashamed. He had intruded on a world that hid its private grief by public display. He had put on a false front and had been detected and punished for it. He had been selling himself to Serge. He was the venal one. He had to mount the railings and change into his dark suit and pretend a respectability which he hardly had. His gaudy identity had deserved a smiler with the knife, another Jack the Nipper in a fragile city with sufficient pain and fear abroad already.

Henry looked at the scarred and pitted face of the stone king in the square and knew the disease of time. And he lurched over the points of the railings to put on the disguise of who he really was.

10

BEARING WITNESS

Kelso was flying into Harare, which was once called Salisbury. Changing names mean changing control. Once there was a map of enterprise which covered a quarter of the globe, and there was a lot of red on it. Now there was only a severed head and a bit of spilled blood to take into the new government, which had asked him to bear witness against one of its own.

He need not bear witness, he knew that. Yet he was the only witness. He had caught his father's head and put it on the hotel bar at Victoria Falls. Even if he knew he should not return to Southern Rhodesia, now called Zimbabwe, he was flying back. He had gapped it before it was too late. Now he was coming to bear witness. Although he might be murdered for it, he still believed in law and order. And he still had family there.

The wheels of the landing aeroplane blundered and made Kelso shudder in his seat. Faults in the runway or an inexperienced pilot. Both were the gifts of recent independence – potholes and hasty promotion. The roadblocks were removed at the cost of the road. As the Party rose swiftly, safety standards fell. The future was satisfied at the risk of the present. For some, it was like a new heaven on earth. Only heaven on earth had little to do with the many.

Unshaven and bleary, Kelso took his turn to descend the gangway and cross the tarmac towards the passenger entrance of the airport. An African dawn reddened the sky, bands of crimson and scarlet and orange bandaging the horizon beyond the military aircraft and the control tower. The queues at the immigration desks were longer, the questions on the entry form had trebled, the faces of the officials were all black except for one white survivor. Reverse tokenism, called national reconciliation.

Kelso declared that the purpose of his visit was tourism. Bearing witness did not mean confessing at immigration. At Heaven's Gate, Kelso doubted that he would tell St Peter the whole truth. Even the new government had not put him on the list of prohibited visitors. That did not mean that he was welcome.

His luggage arrived on a conveyor belt, scaled with cracked rubber. On a pink slip, he declared the foreign currency in his pocket. Money normally meant liberty – yet here, as the pink slip declared, money mishandled meant bondage. Kelso's bags were searched with enthusiasm. He hardly protested when a roll of film was confiscated for closer inspection.

"We will return it, sah, if you apply tomorrow."

"But it hasn't been exposed."

"So we will expose it and return it."

There was no way Kelso would apply tomorrow. He had nothing to lose, considering what was in his head. His lawyer, Jules Apfelstein, was waiting to welcome him among the noisy family groups, greeting their long-lost relatives. Jules could not hide his relief. He seized Kelso's hand between two wet palms and chattered to hide his nervousness. For a small compact man, he was large in manner, effusive with intensity.

"I didn't think you'd be on that flight. I really didn't. I checked you were on the passenger list. But I thought you'd back out at the last minute. You're safe in London –"

"Safe in London –" Kelso said. "The Irish blew up the bandstand in Regent's Park. With the band on it. Greenjackets. Now they're red-coats."

"If you think you're coming back to Shangri-La, you aren't. You don't know what's been happening here. And I'm not telling you in the airport." Jules bent to test the weight of Kelso's large suitcase and settled for the flight bag. "What are you carrying? Ammunition?"

"When is the hearing of the final appeal?"

"In a fortnight."

"And my evidence is the key evidence?"

"You know that."

"That's why I bit the bullet. And here I am."

Jules had a new Mercedes saloon parked outside. As they drove out of the airport, they passed a bus stop. A woman in a red dress with a baby tied to her back, an oil-drum balanced on her head, and two small children in tow, waved to the car with a limp wrist.

"We can stop for them," Kelso said. "We've got the room."

"Take on one, you take on all," Jules said. "They've no sense of restraint – possibility. You should see the pirate taxis pull up at a bus stop. Twenty-five people climb into room for two. The taxis navigate sideways like crabs. They're a menace."

The Mercedes passed other Africans walking towards the city. Many waved without looking back, using the gesture of the broken hand. Jules kept driving at a steady sixty miles an hour. He cruised beneath a new coloured concrete arch, stating:–

WEL
TO
ZIM

Half of the arch had fallen down and was stacked by the side of the road.

"That was the Victory Arch," Jules said "Somebody blew it up four months ago. The Ministry said it was bad construction and termites – concrete-eating termites. They're going to put it up again, when they have the money."

"Is there much subversion?"

"None, officially. A few bandits down south. A bit of destabilization from South Africa. But the papers never report it. The paper, I should say. It's government-controlled now, like the radio and the television. We hear all the news that's fit to hear."

"Have they reported on our case?"

"Not much. There's no bail for Witness Ndkala. Special Detention Order of the Home Minister. It's a new emergency law. No Habeas Corpus or bail if it's a matter of security."

"It's a matter of murder, not security."

Jules took his eyes off the road to look at Kelso. Behind him, red flamboyants blazed in front of the bungalows outside the city.

"It's a matter of a Minister who's a murderer," Jules said. "You have come back to testify. You're a brave man, Kelso."

"Look at the road," Kelso said. The Mercedes swerved as Jules brought it back into the left lane. "Let's stay alive. He killed my father."

Jules stopped the Mercedes in front of iron gates. A security guard in a green uniform and an orange helmet opened the grilles and saluted.

"You went because of Elizabeth," Jules said.

He drove through the gates past flowering bougainvillea and poinsettia, garish in the early morning light. He stopped the car in front of a large bungalow. A brick wall with tasteful loopholes hid the swimming pool from the drive.

"I didn't take the gap because of Elizabeth," Kelso said. Then he heard himself ask what he had not meant to ask. "And how is she?"

Jules stared at him, trying to gauge his feelings.

"Happy," he said. "She tells everybody she's very happy."

The rat that had lived in Kelso's belly for the past six months bit and worried at him. He denied it in his face and voice.

"I'm glad for her," he said.

He lied, and he had come to bear witness.

Jules showed Kelso to the spare bedroom with its mukwa suite and copper reliefs of charging elephants on the walls. After a shower and a change of clothes, Kelso went to be told the situation.

The problems were the problems of all African states after independence, but they were worse since Kelso had left. The Prime Minister, who came from the majority tribal group, was pressing for a One Party state. The leaders of the smaller tribes were demanding local self-government. The national army was disintegrating into factions, and thousands of soldiers were deserting and taking to the bush with their arms to be guerrillas again for no cause. The main ammunition dump had been blown up, either by South African agents or by a careless watchman, who insisted on smoking cheroots near leaky gas canisters. Lawlessness in the cities was increasing with armed bandits terrorizing storekeepers and stopping buses to loot and rape in the name of fighting for freedom. The government could not fulfil its promises of full employment for Party members, so gangs of disappointed young men were turning to riot and actual revolution, not its appearance. And they wanted to take back the stolen land, particularly the profitable tobacco farms, the big Mackenzie plantations.

Faced with this anarchy, the government was reacting with panic. Raids had been made on the properties of the leaders of the opposition groups. When caches of arms were found, accusations of subversion were made. Rumours of coups flew nightly round the city, like bats. Special security guards rode behind the wailing sirens of the ministerial cars, shooting at everyone and everything that did not get out of the way. The Home Minister carried a book of detention orders in his pocket and issued them on the spot to any man who annoyed him. He had personally beaten up a white woman who happened to bump his car. He was above the law because he refused to obey the law. For reasons of security, he had people detained without trial, he claimed immunity for selected officials, he had the press censored and journalists arrested.

"We always thought it wouldn't happen here," Jules said. "But it's happening."

"Then why stay?"

"Because we can't live as well anywhere else as we can here. And I have to look after the family trust and the gold mines. Anyway, it's not the Prime Minister. It's the people he has around him."

"The King does no evil," Kelso said. "It is always his servants."

"We still have judges," Jules said. "And attorneys, and all the due process of law. But if a Minister breathes the word Security, then there's no law."

"Then there's no point in my coming back to testify."

"Yes, there is. Why do you think they let you back in?"

"I was surprised," Kelso said. "I quite expected to be stopped at immigration and sent back to London. Persona non bloody grata."

"The Prime Minister is very shrewd. He never dismisses anyone. He lets the bad ones dig their own graves, then gives them a little push with his finger – and in they fall. Witness Ndkala is still in the cabinet because he's got a following among the Party radicals. He wants a real revolution now, redistribution of all wealth, and he'll kill for it. You know that, they know that, but the Prime Minister doesn't feel strong enough to give him the push until it's proved impossible to keep him on."

"So the government wants me to testify against Witness so they can get rid of him?"

"That's what I hear."

"If I get as far as the Appeal Court," Kelso said. "Alive."

"You'll get there," Jules said "It's not as bad as all that."

"You've just been telling me it's worse than all that."

Jules spread his palms, seeking for stigmata. His eyes were liquid with false innocence.

"I agree. On the television, they do pronounce Law and Order as Low and Odour. But it doesn't stink that much yet. Would I ask you to stay in my home if I thought you were in the slightest danger?"

"True," Kelso said. "You wouldn't want to get hit, too."

Jules rose.

"I must go to the office and do some work. Can you amuse yourself until lunch?"

"May I use your telephone?"

"Please do." Jules stopped by the door. "You want to ring Elizabeth? Do you think that's wise?"

"That's my affair," Kelso said. "Or should I say, her affair. My wife."

The telephone rang for Kelso, and he heard:

"We shouldn't meet."

"I've come back."

"Not for me."

"For you, too."

"There'd be no point in it."

Elizabeth's voice was unfamiliar. Kelso knew it so well, but the instrument or their estrangement made her tone remote. He could imagine her trying to control her panic at his return, and so pretending a coolness to show that she did not care. Or perhaps, simply, she did not care now.

"I have to see you," he said. "I have to know."

"You already know. I'm in love with Robert. I'm with him. I want to be with him."

"But it's only been months. Or longer. What's that against fifteen years of love?" There was a silence on the telephone. "You do still love me?"

"Yes," Elizabeth said. "Bless you. You have all my affection ..."

"Damn your affection. I want your love."

"Love, then. But it's over, Kelso. There's no point in our meeting."

"As you love me still, I want to meet."

"If you insist. It won't do any good."

"All those years, Beth. All those memories, those shared times only we know. Those oaths – sacred – we took at our wedding. A family. I'm still in love with you. Faithful to you."

"Don't be. It's no use now."

"I want to be." Chastity was his revenge. "You're the only woman in my life. I love you."

"Kelso –"

He knew her voice, the crack in it, the sudden care sounding. He was glad he had provoked the sound, even if it didn't do any good.

"The Rendezvous," he said. "Dinner. Tomorrow."

"I can't do dinner. Robert wouldn't let me. Not with you. Lunch."

"Lunch, then. It's ironic, isn't it, that I can't ask my own wife out to dinner." There was the silence again, and in the silence, Kelso tasted cruelty on his sour lips. "My wife in the sight of God and man. My wife who is making a fool of me, a public cuckold. Cutting my balls off, isn't that what they say now?"

"Don't, Kelso. You shouldn't have left me alone so much. It had to happen sooner or later. I couldn't stand the loneliness. He came. He loved me. He was always there. You weren't."

"My faithful wife. You never gave me a chance. You never said, Kelso, keep me with you, I'm falling in love with another man, hold me. You deceived me. You agreed with him to deceive me, betray me, not tell me –"

"We were trying not to hurt you."

"You hurt me. I had to find out. I did. And then you said it was too late. I never had a chance."

"We've been through all this a hundred times, Kelso. Don't let's go through it again."

"Every day, every night, I go through it again and again. Come back to me, Beth. We'll forget it, start again. I'll always be with you. I swear."

"It's over, Kelso. Let's cancel that lunch."

"I insist. You said so. Don't betray me on that."

There was the silence again.

"If you wish."

"I do, Beth. You owe me that, at least."

"I owe you. You always told me that. He doesn't. That's why I'm with him." She swore suddenly. "All that bloody gratitude." It was not like her.

"I don't want your gratitude. I want your love."

"I'll be at the Rendezvous tomorrow. Good-bye."

"Good-bye, Beth. I love you."

Kelso heard the click on the receiver as his wife put down the telephone. He had his small triumph. He had caused some pain in return for his great pain. He had provoked a meeting. He felt worse than ever.

Kelso had reserved a table at the windows of the Rendezvous. He could look down at the flower-sellers, ranged along the side of the square, where the trees were blossoming imperially in rows of red, white and blue. A car stopped by the stalls. The sellers rushed upon it, thrusting their bunches of lilies and roses, sweet peas and chrysanthemums at the woman driver. They pushed and struck at each other. One man cuffed a boy and sent him sprawling, feathery ferns flying. Although the plate glass of the window cut off the sounds of the quarrel, Kelso could see the jabber and the jostle. The woman driver did not get out of her car, but drove off. Trade was bad. Even buying flowers became a little war.

As Kelso looked away, he saw Elizabeth coming towards his table. She was handsome now rather than beautiful. Her body was fuller under her pink and grey dress, but her face was more scalloped with age and assurance. Her eyes were the same, looking for amusement or advantage, a blue glance flickering above the thin sensuality of her lips that were never still even when she was listening.

"How lovely to see you," Kelso said, rising. His mouth sought hers, but she turned her cheek to him, so that his lips hardly brushed her skin.

"Lovely to see you too," she said, sitting at the table without allowing him the time to pull out her chair for her. Thwarted in courtesy, he took his place opposite her. She would not be obliged to him.

"You're more beautiful than ever."

"You look good too." She leaned across the table.

"You shouldn't be here, Kelso. You're in danger."

"How do you know?"

"I heard it from a friend of Jules."

"He shouldn't speak. He's a lawyer."

"This is a small town which calls itself a city. Everybody knows everything. You're going to identify Witness Ndkala for killing your father."

"He did. I will do it. It is against the law. That's all."

Elizabeth scanned Kelso's face, searching for evidence.

"You were never so set on the law, Kelso. When you left, you didn't want to hurt the government in the first stage of national reconciliation. You thought one or two bloody crimes were inevitable at the end of a long war and a takeover."

"I left because of you, Beth. I couldn't stay here near you and Robert. As you say, it's a small town. He couldn't leave because of his job. So I did."

"Don't blame me for everything. I suppose I made you come back, too."

"I couldn't stop thinking about you in London. There is a law, Beth. A moral law. A wife is a wife for ever. Love is love for ever. I want to testify to the truth of that. And when Jules said I could speak about who killed my father, I felt I couldn't refuse. It would be wrong not to speak out. It's wrong not to speak out against a wrong. Especially if there is family involved."

"You didn't care that much about Paul until he was killed."

"I did, and I want his murderers in their grave. Anyway, I don't care too much about living right now, Beth. I'd rather speak out."

"You've become very moral, Kelso, because it suits you."

"What else have I got?"

"Only the law. Poor you. I've been to lawyers. I can divorce you without your consent."

"In five years. Unless you want to allege some unreasonable grounds."

"You've been to lawyers, too."

"To defend myself."

The waiter came to take their order. They did not care about what they were eating. Their meal was only the occasion for their confrontation. Kelso chose the inevitable bream rather than the inescapable kingklip, while Elizabeth chose a Caesar Salad. They both agreed on a dry white wine, the limit of their agreement.

"Kelso, believe me," his wife said, "before I came here, I meant to be loving. I meant to be sweet and reasonable and good. But seeing you, talking to you, it all goes wrong. We don't get on any more. We say hurtful things we don't mean."

"It's your guilt speaking."

"Yes, things like that. What do you want me to do? Get down on my knees? Weep? Beg your pardon? Or tell you the truth? You did leave me alone too much. I'm a woman. Someone else loved me. You lost me."

"I had to earn the money for us. I could only earn it away from you. Horribly, with gold and weapons. There was a war on. I couldn't take you with me. You couldn't come anyway because of our children."

"You left me alone. I fell in love."

"Who cares who is right? What about our children?"

With tears in her eyes, Elizabeth said, "I am glad you came round to them. Kathleen and Catherine, they're beautiful girls as you know. All they want is tennis and husbands."

"Who will take them out of here, I hope."

"They like it here. And Conan, he's become a young undertaker."

"That is odd."

"He says it is a trade with prospects, given how things are now."

"Don't you think – with this terrible war – our children need their father, too? I can swear, I can be around all the time."

"Too late, Kelso, too late. You always were too late."

"This is the worst time for me, Beth. Couldn't you have chosen another time to leave me?"

"There's no timing in love. It always seems to happen at the wrong time, the worst time."

"But all those fifteen years together. Couldn't you have waited – couldn't you wait now – till I can bear it?"

"No, Kelso. He needs me. His sister's got cancer. He's afraid he might have it too. He needs me"

"But my need. After fifteen years of love."

"No. I'm sorry."

"You throw away that for an affair. A thing of the flesh. With a man you can't even be sure will stay with you. You discount fifteen years of love, endurance, looking after you, helping to make you into the most desirable, wonderful woman in the world. And I have to give you up to a casual stranger. Doesn't the past mean anything? All we had, and have –"

"If you go on speaking like that, Kelso, I must go. I can't come back to you."

"You will not. You have choice. Moral choice. So has he. He can walk away."

"I cannot. I must be with him."

"You will not. You've got the hots for him."

"Don't be crude."

She rose to go, but he held her by the hand, pulling her down.

"I'm sorry, Beth. Please stay."

"Can we talk of anything except ourselves?"

"I'll try."

So they talked of what had happened in the city and in the country in the many months that he had been away. How everything had deteriorated slowly, very slowly – law and order in general – and their love in particular, which they had agreed not to mention. And he said he would wait for them always in England, if they had to flee their home in the new Zimbabwe. As the country went, so might they return.

Waiting for the car to come to take him to the trial, Kelso sat in the coffee shop at Meikles, where he had first met Elizabeth. Still serving there were black waiters in red pageboy uniforms, giving him his cheese omelette and salad with French dressing. Otherwise the decor was now intercontinental, tiles and square wooden tables, formica counters and paper napkins. The blown-up photographs on the walls were in place and out of time. They showed the hotel in the days of the pioneers and the first settlers, a low building with Dutch gables and a pillared porch shadowing the dirt pavement and horses attached to hitching-posts. Seventy years ago. The old man at the corner table with a face like a survey map would remember that.

There was a thump nearby. Kelso's plate rattled on his table. A cobweb was shaken off the ceiling and deposited on his cheek. He brushed off the gossamer and addressed a waiter.

"Do you have earthquakes here?"

"No. Never, sir."

THE PEOPLE OF HIS PASTURE

"Then what was that?"

"What?" the waiter said. "Nothing."

A white youth in a Mickey Mouse T-shirt and sandals ran into the room. He could not hide his joy.

"They blew it," he said to a group of three other young men, drinking cola. "Party HQ. They've blown the whole building into the street."

His three friends smiled. One let out a rebel yell. The fat one stretched out his meaty knees that showed plumply between high tan socks and bush shorts. On one knee, the Union Jack was tattooed; on the other, the skull and crossbones. As he crossed his legs, the flags waved.

"Did they get the PM and the Comrade Ministers?"

"No such luck. Lunch hour. Everyone was out."

"No one hurt then."

"Only three Affs in the street. No one."

Kelso rose from his able and walked towards the lobby. He had to bear witness or was that no longer worth it? The wars of revenge were still going on. Yet he had to testify, to identify the Minister Witness Ndkala. He had to state in court who killed his father, the police officer. Yet the quiet small man in a green sweatshirt and black pants, who put the Mauser pistol to his head and killed him with two bullets and ran away down the road would never be identified. In this society of crime without consequence, of murder without offence, who could get into any dock and swear to tell the truth, the whole truth, and nothing but?

11

POLL TAX

Outside in Piccadilly, the windows were smashing and the Porsches burning. "I smell posh!" the young shouted and looted the luxury stores. The protest was against a poll tax, which had led to a peasants' revolt six hundred years ago. This was a tax on heads. Now other heads would roll. What Ian Hamish called the Undercrust was furious, destroying the things of affluence and the symbols of power. The government called the tax the 'community charge', but a group called Class War defined the charge as "a brick in your hand with a pig in your sights." The deprived and the homeless took their revenge on hundreds of police men and women, who were injured with bottles and iron bars and cobble stones. 'Tax-busters' they yelled they were, and they assaulted the costly and authority. The eruption through the West End was a seething stew boiling over and scalding the body politic. Violence was the way to change, and mob rule the method.

Ian was there to observe, as he always did. But he was soon out of action with cracked ribs from a protestor flailing a scaffold pole. And Robin Blossom was there with his camera. He was more protected. He went with his old mate from art school, Sid the Lid Mackenzie, not known for keeping the lid on it, but for taking it off. Sid had progressed from making caricatures of the celebrities for Spitting Image and copies of models for The Other Self to hanging from nylon ropes his effigies of Margaret Thatcher and the Royal Family and dousing them with petrol and burning them to spark riots. He was both a creator and a destroyer, an inspired satirist and a crude arsonist. He had started fires in new Dockland developments and had smashed Mercedes with sledgehammers in a 'Bash the Rich' campaign; but equally he could catch a quirk and delineate a deformity of character with hard and cruel wit. Presently, he was kicking in plate-glass windows with his Doc Marten boots in flying leaps worthy of the Kirov Ballet, recorded by Robin from a back angle to protect his mate's identity. Afterwards they were meant to proceed to the battle of Downing Street, where the crowd was trying to break down the new guardian railings and upend the police horses and the Prime Minister.

"Nah," Sid said, kicking aside the cascades of glass and emerging with a red-white-and-blue patriotic Ghetto Blaster, "tea break. Let's have a pint and let someone else get their sodding heads knocked in."

Taking a breather and a glass on the leather seats edged with brass of the Sub Rosa bar of the New Cavendish Hotel, Robin noticed the mixed loathing and respect of the aliens from outer Europe and Asia cowering there to escape from the mayhem without. For none of these foreigners knew whether Sid the Lid was a rock star or a punk mugger with his blond hair permed into foot-long spikes and his Designer Gear of a heavy metal jacket festooned with miniature skulls and grenades and Uzi submachine-guns in chrome. He must be a pop personality, or else why would he be lounging in the discreet luxury of the hotel off Jermyn Street? He did look like the yobbos outside, indulging in their bit of bother and putting the boot into the tourist trade. Their outrage was a kick up the arse to invisible earnings, a bunch of fives to the balance of payments. And yet England was a free country, and anyone who had the price of a beer could drink it in the Cavendish bar with the ghost of its founder Rosa Lewis cackling at this new mixture of cockney and class.

"It won't work, Rob," Sid the Lid conceded. "But it'll open doors. Raise the threshold. Make Maggie bring down the barriers and give the pigs guns. And then, and then, oh my brother, do we have class war!"

"Class farce," Robin said. "Don't you know, dickhead, that's all over. Two in three, yeah, two in three own their own place now. Mortgages, it's a way of life –"

"Way of death."

"Yeah, but they own it while they can pay. They got property. And you jokers in your squats –"

"Can't pay, won't pay, don't pay, never will pay. Why should we? Don't want pigs, don't want fascist schools, don't want nothing but us to say what we want. Class war."

"There aren't no classes no more," Robin sighed. "You're a time warp, Sid. Ever heard of social mobility? Trading up? East Europe's gone to the supermarket. And you, you're still in Anarchist Alley. On every page, book-Marx."

"You're buying the beer," Sid the Lid said. "You'll get millions from Murdoch or Maxwell for those smashing pix of me you've got. Think of that safe little thrill in every bourgeois hearth and home as they watch somebody else doing what they secretly all want to do – kick the shit out a pig or Lillywhite's windows."

"Don't be so sure," Robin said, while the waiter handed them their two glasses of beer as if it were an arm's length transaction. "They may just feel fear and loathing."

"I dig hate," Sid said. "I live on it. Cor, look at that —"

Across the back of the Armani jacket of a young Japanese woman, a slow red stain was spreading. The waiter saw it, other waiters saw it, Sid and Robin saw it.

"Jack," Robin said in awe. "How do you like that? Jack's at it again!"

There was birdsong in the air as the waiter rushed up with his napkin, and other voices twittered and condoled. Sid smiled and turned back to Robin and his beer.

"He's better than Nechayev, really," Sid said. "Class enemy number one."

"The Robin Hood of the slashing people —"

"Well, good old Jack, he has got this whole city in a twist. He must have been out there with the lads, having his bit of fun. And come in here, invisible. 'Cos he's like one of them, nobody would notice him."

"Jack the Nipper. I dunno — there may be hundreds of Jacks now."

"Maybe. And maybe it's a better way —"

"What?"

"You don't have to smash it — not these big demos —"

"You mean, sneak up on the inside. Pat them on the back, then they find they're bleeding. Shake them by the hand, then they've lost a finger. Give them a hug and crack their ribs. Kiss them on the cheek and bite their ear off."

"Nice, Robin, nice."

"Well, it's more effective, innit? Undercover violence. Not bashing the rich, but stroking them with flick-knives."

"Know what we used to do with scabs? In the dark we'd lob spuds in their faces. And in the spuds, old razor-blades. Very nice."

"The pigs will win today," Robin said, "because they can see you coming. But if they didn't see you coming, if they thought you were pig-friendly — until they got a blade in the back."

"Nice," Sid said and drained his beer. "He's really brill, that old Jack. Maggie should make him Minister of Education. Teach us a thing or two. Bottoms up, Rob — and let's go and do her in Downing Street."

As they left the Cavendish bar, Sid could not resist the last word to the stricken Japanese girl. "Well," he said, "you do it to sushi, don't you?"

Robin hustled him away. "I may want to come back here," he said.

"Socially bloody mobile, aren't you?" Sid said. "A yuppie on skate-boards." And by the time they arrived at Downing Street, the party was over and the blue-lamp vans were driving away the arrested and the police horses stood high and mighty above the debris of smashed bottles and broken planks. And when Sid screeched, "Cossacks! Nazis!," he had to scarper with Robin scuttling to one side to take his shots of the black horsemen riding after his friend, running for his dear angry life.

Old as it was, London was no longer scared of its history or of foreigners, who were much more scared now of Londoners at football matches away and abroad. London was afraid of its own children. The riots were only the flash of the danger. The tap on the shoulder might not be Jack the Nipper or the police, but a sturdy beggar demanding money with menaces. The bulging carrier bag at the bus station might be an Irish bomb, the car abandoned for a week an imminent bang. What was the plumber there to fix? Or the meterman to read? Or the milkman to deliver? In each pipe or dial or bottle, the threat was of the fire this time. The everyday led to the explosion and the hereafter.

And there were the Missing, who were not just the runaway children, the fifty thousand young people who left their homes for the streets and the hard dreams of the metropolis. Missing were the husbands vanished without trace and maintenance payments, the wives gone away to begin their lives all over again. One of our planes, they used to announce in the last war, is missing. After a battle, servicemen, who could not be accounted for, were said to be missing. Even now in the age of the computer and the credit card, the poll tax and the register, many were still missing, lost for a while, or presumed dead, though the fact was that they simply could not pay their bills.

For Ian Hamish, Clio was regularly missing, though never quite lost for ever. In his sociology of London, he called the problem of missing persons, 'Unsocial Mobility without roots. Progress without leaving a wake or a motive.' Yet he missed Clio, as he always did. There was a gnawing in his stomach as though there was a rat in it in his restless nights. Sometimes he swore at her and nothing, when she was away, "Bitch! Bitch! Bloody bitch!" Then when she returned, he was grateful and quiet.

He suspected she was with her young photographer and tutor, Robin Blossom She was determined to be another Koo Stark or Gina Lollobrigida, trading her fading beauty for recording other celebrities.

Yet he could not trace where she had gone. Actually, she had joined in the reverse migration to the East End. Once the best way from Stepney and Whitechapel had been the gold rush west to Piccadilly and Mayfair. But after the tiny beginnings of Lord Snowdon's studio in Rotherhithe and David Owen's Limehouse Declaration with the Gang of Four from his riverside house in Narrow Street, the opportunity of huge work spaces in renovated warehouses overlooking the Thames had attracted artists back to Wapping and the Docklands, just as converted ragtrade lofts had spawned a renaissance in Lower Manhattan.

Clio was to be discovered in Robin's pad, a vast room with scraped brick walls and pitch-pine floors, red-painted tubular furniture with black leather seats, Hockney posters on the walls, and a vast circular bed set under a ceiling mirror, ornamented with the signs of the zodiac. Lying back on the cover of false polar-bear fur and looking up beyond her lover's shoulder, Clio felt disoriented under the gilt symbols inlaid on the reflecting glass. She was a long-gone Virgo, and she thought it was the wrong sign for that night.

Robin stripped her with unexpected skill. He knew what hook met what eye, which way zips unzipped, and how to ease buttons from holes. He unrolled her tights in one long pull with the expertise of a stroke in the Boat Race, while Clio lifted her legs in the air to aid his facility. And then he fell upon her in a fury, thrusting into her, piercing her, lunging and groaning, until she cried out in pain and want, and as he cleft her to the depths and shuddered at the mouth of her womb, she crooked her leg and dug her heels behind his pumping buttocks to draw him into her as far as he would go.

"Bloody hell," Robin said, flopping over her right leg to lie beside her on the pseudo-arctic fur and look up at his sign, Aquarius, "you're better than a Magimix."

"You're more like a riveter, Robin."

"Worked on a road-gang once. Pile-driver."

"I can imagine. Well, Robin," Clio rolled over and propped herself on one elbow, "you are penetrating."

"Yeah," Robin said. "But what I say is, a hole is a hole is a hole, but some holes are man-holes."

"For some women."

"For some men, too. Tell me, don't Ian worry when you flit?"

"He's got used to it. I'm a bat in the night. I don't stay home."

"They don't get used to it, you know, men. They say they do. But I bet Ian wants to do me for you. You're his old lady."

"Old is the word," Clio said. "Too bloody old for you."

Ian did not know, as he sat in his kitchen, scribbling and detaching
himself from his jealousy.

> Gaul may have been divided into three parts and Britain has
> always been divided into two parts. but these parts are variable.
> They may be North and South, Celts and Saxons, Rich and
> Poor, White and Black, Have and Have-nots, Men and Women,
> State and Public School, Posh and Plebs, English and Other
> Races, but there have ever been two nations in twin Britains.
> Except, perhaps, in the Second World War when, during the
> blitz, it was Us and Them trying to invade the island. The real
> division now in the minds of the government is the Mobile and
> the Immobile, the Ambitious and the Unemployed. The Prime
> Minister's belief is that all can rise, if they pull their socks and
> stockings up. But she has forgotten one thing. The Room at the
> Top is not expandable, which is why the Mess at the Bottom is
> expendable. There is only space for a few elites here, and the
> rest can rot where they are.

A skewer seemed to turn in Ian's ribs. These were still badly
bruised from the scaffold pole which had hit him at the Poll Tax riot
and made him crawl home. He had never known research to be so
painful. There must be less lacerating methods of doing it. What were
the ricked necks and blurred eyes of sessions in the university library
to the bumps and contusions of street violence? He had particularly
admired the photographs of Parisian low life by Brassai, because of
how the Frenchman had secured them. He would enter a bar with his
rosewood camera, take one shot as the pimps and Apaches rushed at
him, throw the camera back to an accomplice behind, and then let
himself be beaten to a pulp while she ran away. Still, that was a hard
row to hoe. Ian did not know if he had the guts for it.

There was another way, through the grand voyeur, television. No
evening was free without an awards ceremony, where grotesque
statuettes with Christian names were presented to assorted writers and
singers and apparent artistes. You did not have to attend in person to
watch the tribal rites of the celebrities. You could watch them with
tens of millions of other viewers from the safety of your own armchair. These orchestrated occasions made the dominant few accessible
to the curiosity of the many, who could enjoy the fanfares and
costumes and self-congratulation of the mafia of the Communications

System at interminable Film and Drama Prize Shows, Arts Festivals, Pop Telethons. Only once so far had this celebration by mass hypnosis choked on its own fame. During the revolutions of Eastern Europe this past year, the state channel which had propagated the profligate Romanian dictator and his wife portrayed them really shot, riddled with bloody holes from a firing squad. For once, the medium was the executioner, not the entertainer. The two leading players had to bite the bullet and were seen no more. That they were succeeded by their ilk did not matter. Like a starving sow, the box had devoured her own.

With a sigh and a twinge, Ian Hamish pressed the plastic buttons of his remote control and conjured the dark screen into sound and image. And the lead words were, "...Soccer hooligans in a fight with police disrupted..." The first image was of a shaven scarface draped in a huge Union Jack. So Ian pressed the box into black silence. His legwork would have to continue, plod by pain. There was really no alternative.

Rosa was missing, too. Even her mother Rosabelle could not find her, let alone Boy, who was having fears of his own. With Kelso's murder in Zimbabwe, his mother Bridget had become inconsolable and scatty. She would hardly eat, she put the kettle on five times over for tea, she did not even know who he was, calling him Paul or the postman. "What, no letters today? I am expecting a very important one from South Africa. I know the government, I do." And she did not.

Boy tried to do something about her incipient Alzheimer's disease, but she would not budge into a Home, holding fiercely onto her independence as she always had. He had some money to spare, so he secretly deposited it in her Savings Book, as he knew she was beyond counting now. He, however, had begun to reckon his days, how many of them were left. The tumour under his left armpit was as big as a golf-ball, and growing. He thought he knew what it was, and he had to take the treatment. He was afraid.

He was actually visiting Ian Hamish to demand if he knew where Rosa had gone, when she came into the Camden kitchen to find both of the men there. A stray ambiguous grin warped her face, and she looked down at her shoes.

"I didn't expect to see the two of you here," she said.

"Sit down," Ian said. "Glass of wine?"

"Several. A bottle might do."

She sat on a pine chair and took her glass of claret and drank it at a gulp and held it out again. She was aggressive.

"I'm not going to tell you where I've been."

"We didn't ask," Ian said.

"None of your business, anyway."

"I don't know," Boy said. "I love you. So it is my business."

"*Your* business?" Rosa was spitting at him. "What about my business? You stupid oafs. What did you care? You didn't, you didn't."

The barrier broke. A flood of tears. Ian scraped back his chair and put an arm round her shoulders. She shook it off, but he put it on again. And she let his hand rest on her shaking neck.

"Don't tell us now," Ian said. "Just stay till you can. Or don't tell us at all. And just stay with us."

After a while, Rosa did speak.

"Of course, I got preggie. So I had to go away. I didn't know which of you it was. So I had to go away. I mean, I couldn't come to you, Ian, and say, It's yours. Or you, Boy. It's yours. I didn't know. So I ran away to have it by myself. Then it was mine, all mine. I was so lonely, out there, waiting in that bloody wet Dorset cottage I'd borrowed from a girl-friend. Then I began to bleed, and the hospital took me in, and they couldn't save her. It was going to be a her, and I was going to call her Marie. Because she was the only one who really loved me and my mother. Not you. Men. You just love your bloody selves. Babies. You don't know about having babies."

"That is our greatest loss," Ian said. "We can't have babies. The fact is, life can only come out of you. It's the greatest gift of God. And women have it. What do we have? Books, ha."

"And doing in Creation," Boy said. "Until it does us in."

Rosa stayed for supper, while Clio remained a missing person. And lost along with her was the dead infant Marie, the victim of a miscarriage.

"I'll always blame myself," Rosa was saying. "I went on smoking, drinking a bit. I should have stopped. I didn't."

"Mothers are always too guilty, even if they have children," Ian said. "They worry that everything the children do is really their fault. Bringing up kids is the mother always admitting to mistakes she hasn't done."

"Anyway," Boy said, "you can have another child."

Rosa had recovered a little of her hard edge.

"And you gentlemen will assist me?"

"As long as we know who the father is," Ian said.

"It does help," Boy said.

"Sorry, boys," Rosa said. "There's been a mix-up in my fallopian tubes, or thereabouts. No more babies up the spout, I'm afraid."

And now she began to weep again so uncontrollably that she needed a tea-towel to dry her tears. Boy and Ian put her to bed in the spare room, but she did not want them to leave her alone. So they took turns through the night in sitting beside her and holding her hand, while she babbled on about how all the family was dying out, and she was part of the destruction.

"The old ones are all going, Gillon and Murdo. And Miriam's gone in India my mother told me, the last time I saw her."

"I heard from Solomon," Boy said. "He's coming over to London on a diplomatic mission He's high in Culture, now."

"High time they exported some culture back to us," Rosa said. "We need it. But my baby, she was the future. The fourth of us single women. Marie and Rosabelle and me. And nobody now."

Her tears were softer, as the dew. Boy held her hand in a warm lock.

"Can I tell you something now? You know I lost my brother?"

"Yes. You, too."

"Now it's me. You were right. Up in Dounreay. I've got a tumour under my arm. I know what it is. A radiation leak. Somewhere, somehow. I don't know, but it's bad. I'll have to go in for radiation treatment. That's an irony, isn't it? I always told you, nuclear energy — it gives you life and power, and it kills you."

"Boy, I'm so sorry. I really am."

"Don't be. I believed in it. I did what I wanted. I thought it was good for us all."

"You shouldn't have let Donald Mackenzie work up there."

"Oh, he'll be all right. Procedures are much safer now. I was in the early days, when they didn't bother so much about protecting us."

"It's not too late. They can cure you. Cobalt, isn't it? They bombard you with cobalt rays."

"Something like that. Death rays, life rays, like in the comic books. But one thing, Rosa —"

"Yes."

"Try to love me a little before I go."

"Of course, darling Boy, of course."

"I know you love Ian better, but it's hopeless. Clio —"

"I know."

"He can't look after you."

"Can you now?"

"Yes, better. Though not much better." Boy rubbed his lower teeth against his top lip. "Families are funny, aren't they? They grow so big, your cousins seem to cover the whole earth. Then they shrink, and there are hardly enough to fill a tea-cup."

"Quite a few of us struggling on."

Rosa put up her face for Boy to kiss her on the lips.

"Don't worry, darling. I'll be with you. You can go now. I'll sleep."

As Boy left the bedroom and Rosa turned on her side, she knew she would sleep. The troubles of others could be soothing, if they were worse off than she was. Count your blessings, wasn't that it? And counting everybody else's misfortunes made her more sure of her arithmetic.

At his first radiation therapy, Boy discovered that a whole wing of the cancer hospital had been donated by the Apfelstein Trust. The migrant Jews to England had taken the inspiration of the Tory leader Benjamin Disraeli, Lord Beaconsfield, on to the Rand, but with their immense fortunes from the gold reef of all the world, they had chosen to endow the hospitals for the colonial children, whose fathers had made all that lucrative empire possible. Anyway, Boy could hardly dispute the Apfelstein choices as he was the beneficiary of them. So was his cousin Solomon, who was meeting him for lunch at the Savoy with its theatre. "So many references there," Solomon said over the telephone. "Gilbert and Sullivan, HMS Pinafore, the Mikado. We used to sing along in our school in India, although I have to prefer Bollywood now."

In his dark silk jacket buttoned up to the neck in the Congress style, Solomon put Boy to shame in his check shirt with a scruffy paisley tie. He did not drink himself, nor did he disapprove of Boy's choice of lager beer with the menu in inscrutable French and occasional English. He was a vegetarian, he said, not by religion, but by choice. The house beef, though, was excellent. Solomon was tolerance magnified. A Buddhist serenity shone from his face.

"I come here on a strange research mission," he said. "Alexander the Great and his brief entrance into India. And a double bill, as I think it is called. The Indian Mutiny, or should I say, Resistance."

"I'm not a historian," Boy said. "I can atomize your bones, but I cannot help your mind. I'll have the beef. Medium. Rare isn't my line."

"Well, I have been assigned by the Ministry to make films of the better sort, I hope. A certain Parsee gentleman called P.K. Zoroastaram has decided to put his considerable fortune into creating epics of the screen. He has an obsession with the past. He claims to come from much older people than you are. His ancestors worshipped fire and are still eaten by vultures. I am meant to advise him, for my sins. And to keep some measure of historical truth."

A waiter came up with a silver trolley holding a bleeding haunch of bullock. He spoke to Boy.

"Your beef, sir. It is better off the bone."

"The edges, please. The brown edges. This isn't an operating room."

"No, sir. We carve. We are more delicate." He struck a long knife to a grinder, then he sliced the darker meat off the huge joint. He did his job, thinly and cleanly, and he laid the portions on a heated china plate with flowered rims. "Horseradish sauce, sir? And the trimmings?"

"And the trimmings," Boy said, watching Solomon receive a *toupée* of lettuce and an onion tart. Perhaps he was right, after all. Eating meat was rather off-putting, sometimes.

"I have to go to the British Museum," Solomon was saying, "to inquire into all the artefacts you have taken from us – I won't say stolen – and from the Greeks. We want to be authentic in our reproductions of reality. You have something of the Parthenon, I believe, and Alexander the Great went there. And the amount of loot you removed from Delhi in the Mutiny – well, well."

"At least we preserved them," Boy said. "Most conquerors wouldn't."

"True. The museum is the conscience of the bandit classes. But that doesn't mean you shouldn't give the treasures back."

"I'm with you there."

"Perhaps I may set an example. As you know, my mother Peg has passed away. And Miriam, too. I am the only one who was left at Annandale, although I have moved on."

"Yes, I had heard that."

"What else had you heard?"

"You have given back the estate to the local people. What did you do with the house?"

"Miriam wanted it to become a country hospital. And of course, with the Apfelstein Trust, all is possible."

"All is possible. With the Trust."

"There is something else, though, which may surprise you." Solomon fished in the side pocket of his elegant jacket, where there was a slight bulge. He produced a large square-cut emerald with a dark flaw in it, mounted on an ornate gold ring.

"Miriam and Peg wanted this to go to Rosa, although my great-uncle Iain took it from us. They have always admired what Marie and Rosabelle and now Rosa have tried to do here. So as we are giving gems to the British — and manners —"

Solomon's smile was so supercilious that Boy could almost have flicked it off his face.

"Keep it," he said. "Don't patronize me."

"I apologise," Solomon said. "We have been patronized so long, we seem to have caught the bad habit. Certainly, I agree. The sins of the fathers should not be visited on the children. Take the ring. It is not yours to refuse. Give it to Rosa, if you have any contact with her."

"I do. I do."

Boy took the ring and looked into its green core, where light fell back against the dark flow.

"Thank you," he said. "You're a wonderful man, Solomon."

"Now you flatter me."

"I don't think I do," Boy said, and the rest of the lunch passed in amity and peace.

12

EASTWARD HO!

The ball-boy ran ahead, cut off at the waist by the steam rising from the grass. At first light, the hopeful Solomon was waggling his driver on the first tee of the Hillingdon Golf Club in Bombay. He anchored himself on his shoes, pointed his chin down the shaft, and swung lazily. He hit the ball respectably forward at the invisible green.

"Good shot," said the film producer P.K. Zoroastaram. "Pity you will not play a thousand rupees a hole. You win for sure, and jolly good luck too."

The little man in horn-rimmed spectacles, which gave him the eyes of owls, teed up. His bony knees divided his long khaki shorts from long khaki socks. He swung as steady as a metronome.

"You see," he said, "the fog lift in a minute. But if we do not play now, it is too hot, you see. Too bloody hot."

When Solomon reached his ball-boy, the little legs were already visible, as was the flag ahead. The surface water was being sucked away rapidly into the hot air. By the bunkers, men in loincloths were squatting, picking up weeds by hand from the coarse grass. The surrounding slums of the thirsty city pushed up their sack and tarpaulin and tin roofs. Solomon coughed in the humid reek and selected a wedge from his bag, which was almost as long and large as his slender caddie. His looping shot found a bank to the right of the green.

"Off target," he heard PKZ piping behind him, and then a low iron drove a ball to nestle by the pin. "Spot on," was the whistle in no wind.

The low smoke lifted as they putted out. "One down," PKZ said, marking a card meticulously with his pencil. "You from the Sinclair family. Your national game. And you let me beat you."

"Not yet," Solomon said, placing his ball on its little red peg on the second tee. "Though you are on home ground. It's your course now."

He hooked his drive towards where a high fence barred the unlikely grass fairway from the squalid yellow mud walls outside. His ball-boy ran ahead and covered his poor shot with a little cloth.

"What's that for?" Solomon could not understand.

"You see him?" PKZ pointed to a large bird hovering above. "Vulture. He like golf balls very much. But not with a cloth on. Not his cup of tea."

Again the tiny film producer hit a drive without much length, but straight down the middle. "I give you three strokes, Solomon, if you play two thousand rupees a hole."

"No," Solomon said. "I would lose all my consultancy money on Alexander and the Mutiny. Why are these vultures here? Not much to eat."

"You see that?" PKZ pointed towards a round building just over the fence on the third hole. "That is our Tower of Silence. We have records of the dead there, and they go back to Her Majesty Queen Elizabeth the First. God bless her."

"But the British hadn't even arrived then."

"I know. But we were here before the British, you see."

"And the vultures eat your dead in your Tower of Silence."

"The corpus. Then the soul may rise to the sun."

As Solomon hacked his way towards the pin on the second hole, he knew that the Parsees were the heirs of the Raj, even if he was not. They had inherited the Hillingdon Club and its imperial traditions. They were maintaining the waste of water on this sweating golf course in the middle of a city under drought. Privilege was hardly ever destroyed, it was passed on.

On the third hole, Solomon's drive was so fierce and hooked that it flew over the fence and struck the wall of the open burning *ghat*, over which the vultures were circling in a parasol.

"Out of bounds," PKZ said with satisfaction.

"Indeed," Solomon said.

Two strokes down, yet Solomon won his only hole of the match with two inspired shots and a long putt. Back in the club-house as the heat rose to an extra Turkish bath, he passed by the entrance a large sepia photograph of Lord Hillingdon, wasted and white-whiskered in the long elegance of his cavalry uniform, the ultimate skeletal essence of the departed Raj, still continuing here with its notices for whist and housey-housey, and a painting of the young Queen of England after her coronation.

"A whisky, Solomon?"

"Not before breakfast."

"Bacon and eggs, then? The coffee is good. And we still have the silver, you see. You eat on good things."

"Just coffee," Solomon said. "I will admire the pot. And then we must get back to work."

"Yes," PKZ said. "You will read the scripts so far. I want the real history and the melodramatic moment."

These were not to be found in the old Bombay film centre. Opposite a squatter's shack encampment, a flamboyant 'thirties cinema facade hid the two hundred and sixty offices of what PKZ called 'The Fishmarket'. Solomon followed his master down rotting corridors stinking of entrails with all the electric fittings ripped out, to enter an advertising throne room, where the past successes of FIRESUN PRODUCTIONS plastered the silk walls in spangles and stardust. From his circular desk, larger than King Arthur's Round Table, PKZ selected two screenplays in ornate covers, showing battle scenes, one with chariots and elephants, the other with howitzers and rifles. Two nymphs in rainbow *saris* fluttered and scraped about their boss, as mating butterflies.

"This is Solomon," PKZ shrilled. "He give me what I want. The Shakespeare language, so intellect, so beautiful. Yet everyone in the world will understand. Because we have so few words after the songs. We have action. Action. Action!"

Solomon was staying at his producer's residence, FireSun House, a large construction with two stories near the shore. Only the hum of the air-conditioner broke his concentration on the first of the scripts he had been given. If he looked up past the green quilts on the walls and the waxed funereal flowers in their urns, he could see a high hedge, seething with azaleas and humming-birds, with the kite-hawks swooping above. In the street, coffee-sellers squatted with their few brass pots, enticing dark women with one paste diamond struck in a nostril, as they strolled by, a coiled pad on their head beneath a loaded flat basket. Green glittered in bangles on their stick wrists and purple *saris* were hitched between their strong down-driving thighs.

Further down the road, the women were picking up the ripped tarmac to carry away on their heads and dump it. Eight long hours through the heat of the sun until the sweat stuck their clothes in a bright glaze to their skin-and-bone frames, heavy only at the hip so they could push out more babes for this hard labour. Solomon bent back to his pages, to see if there was any enlightenment in them. Was this present injustice really the product of the past? When Alexander the Great and Clive of India brought the West to the East, was their legacy too great a burden? Were they responsible for tar baskets and boiling toil?

The instructions for the battle scenes were certainly impressive.

A huge army of 20,000 elephants look as if some dark clouds landed up the Earth. The cavalry is agile and satisfactory. The bowers are fatal. With chaos and clamour filling the atmosphere, the massed servitors are flung down. Alexander waits impatiently to jump into the war-grounds.

In the battle on the Ganges, which the Indian king Pruthusa won in this revisionist version of history, Solomon read of a chariot attack by Alexander on his antagonist:

Both of them race in equal force and line and collide each other. Alexander is red with anger and his callous expression turns on his face. He experience a convulsion and fall out of his chariot. Pruthusa grips his knot hand, speeds his chariot and hauls Alexander with great force, until his body is ensanguined. With a jerk and cry he fall unconscious to the ground. Dragoons pace forward. Pruthusa strike them, then cutting the reins, capers on one of the horses. Trumpets blow. Pruthusa defending and offending lacerates among the crowd and flaunts away gaily.

In terms of action, action, action, Solomon had read better scripts. But then action scenes were wordless. The dialogue, however, did count for something in this mighty encounter between West and East. As Solomon skimmed through the pages, he focused on certain declarations.

PRUTHUSA: Alexander is unbrawny, can be ountnumbered...
             Messengers with invitation cards commence towards Kalinga. Success awaits us. Must be fortitude. If they unaccept, disposition will be made...
             A rebel is only crushed by severe chastization. To be strong is always in disfavour of the enemy. You must be constance decided. Unmanly and loose Ethics can push a Kingdom in a whirlpool.

Indeed, Solomon thought. Empires also went down in unmanly and loose ethics. He could hardly put it better himself. What would be the response of Alexander the Great?

ALEXANDER: In what controversy was I entangled in a tiger's claw? Coming to India, I can tell you...

Compelling, you see, is disliked by me. Although I am fortitudinal, I am full of lackness. But war is the only weapon to crush the poisonous element of foulness. Yet I must not be discourteous or the result will be drastic. It would not be an intelligence to create the disaster of such big man slaughter...

Yet Alexander, after his overthrow in his chariot, was given dialogue which PKZ expected Solomon to bring up to the level of Hamlet.

ALEXANDER: I am not a cruel demon, besieger, tyrant in a human form. I am unable to bear these allegations. My own pride and prejudice are hurting me. I can feel my inner perplexity. I am desperately deserted inwardly. I tremble with the scare-crow of war.

There was no time before lunch for Solomon to begin on the scenario about the Indian Mutiny, which would doubtless end in happy Sepoys firing their pig-fat cartridges in the air and singing, 'God Save Memsahib Queen'. Yet Solomon decided on diplomacy, telling his producer, "I don't know if I can add too much to the present Alexander script."

The two men were sitting cross-legged at a low table, eating with *chapattis* as scoops in their hands, digging into vegetable messes and sweet curds.

"The script," Solomon went on, "is so extraordinary and literary in its language, it cannot be improved."

"You can do it, Solomon."

"There is an alternative. You could junk it."

"Junket. That is a pudding."

"Throw it away."

"But I have worked it myself."

"Then it needs no more work. You came to the Ministry for our advice on whether this was a case when West met East."

"Yes, an eastern western."

"It would be the first Indian world-wide blockbuster?"

"Yes. We play Alexander as Clint Eastwood, John Wayne, Sir Laurence Olivier. Depend on availability, of course."

"Of course. Once you have the star, you have the budget."

"A hundred *lakhs*, more. What is a *lakh*, more or less."

"But you see," Solomon said, "you do not have the right script. In my poor judgement, of course."

"You do the script. You have a *lakh* of rupees, you see. You are the proudest writer in the world."

"But it must stay true to your original intentions?"

"Yes. You do the words. I do the rest."

"It is only a matter of style, then."

"Yes." PKZ was jubilant. "Style. I like that. Class. Then Action!"

"Yes, actions." Solomon carefully wiped his fingers on his napkin, disentangled his feet and stood. "Excuse me. I always take a walk after lunch to settle the stomach."

"Then you write?"

"Then I write."

What Solomon knew he would write was a letter of farewell and have his things sent after him from FireSun House. He walked past the amputee beggar children and the sad police in their yellow-and-blue caps set above their faded shorts with puttees wound round their bare legs over their sandals, keeping no order in the honking maelstrom of the streets with the garish lorries announcing, HORN, PLEASE. By this cacophony of poverty, the matchbox skyscrapers rose from the reclaimed ground off Cuffe Parade. And then Solomon eventually reached the three arches and four turrets of the brick Gateway to India, where the Raj had once come in and gone out. The Taj Hotel behind looked like St Pancras Station, only with a dome or two on top, but it would have notepaper and a glass with ice-cubes and gin, something to clear his adieus in.

After dismissing his producer briefly, he wrote a memorandum to the Ministry, explaining his decision to abandon any cooperation on the film of Alexander the Great.

> Style was the Greek Empire, as it was the Roman, and the Mughal, and the British Empire. More important than power and ceremonial is a way with words. We get words wrong at our peril. We have been unified by the British language, even if many of us prefer Hindi. It is no longer the language of the occupier, who has left. We have made up an Indian English, which is our own. But if it is to go on the wide screen to all the eyes and ears of the world, it has to translate to a universal English, if there is such a speech.
>
> I fear that the film of Alexander the Great will not be a message in how the West met the East and was civilized by our Indian virtues, as Islam once civilized the barbarous Crusaders. I

fear that the film will never be distributed outside our continent, or if it is, it will drown in a thousand giggles. However misguided they were, we cannot hold up past invaders to ridicule. All of them left something behind, which we have mutated to present India — palaces, water-courses, railways, and a world language. In respect of that, I cannot complete my mission, and I request another assignment.

13

RED NOSES

Today was red-nose day. To raise money for hungry children, the people of London were smitten by the pox. An acne of plastic lumps disfigured them. Tory ministers wore red noses over pained lips, bronze military statues bloomed with red noses, taxis sported red noses on their bonnets. Good sports among women bought red noses, but they soon banished the carbuncles to hang on their handbags. Drunks in the pubs put on red noses to hide their own. The marathon relay of humourists, Comic Relief, announced that it had raised twenty million pounds by this contagion of humiliation.

This was charity as idiocy. The Prime Minister did not announce the obvious, "We have become a nation of clowns," but she used the personal and the plural to reveal, "We have become a grandmother." She was certainly in need of a red nose in the House of Commons to match the colour of her face. "Obviously we are not amused," the Leader of the Opposition said to laughter. Her Majesty the Queen was certainly not amused, as saying "We" and "It pleases Us" was reserved for Her to say. Moreover, the Prime Minister was rushing to the bedside of victims of the daily train disasters faster than protocol on greased wheels. "Our concern..." was being voiced by the Iron Lady in condolences all over the country, quite forgetful that there was Her Majesty with a claim to be uniquely greater than We, Prime Minister.

Two red noses caged the vital organs of two performance artists posing by a concrete wall on the South Bank. The rest of their naked bodies was covered with silver glitter-paint, except for their lips, which were outlined in black. They changed their poses and their props every few minutes – now the Thinker and the Toilet Squatter – now the Discus Thrower and the Petrol-bomb Hurler – now the Charioteer and the Graffiti-Artist. Ancient and Modern they called themselves, otherwise Thesis and Antithesis, Text and Subtext, Yin and Yang, or Patsy and Pansy. Patsy's shape looked like a small pear balanced on a large gourd supported by twin beanpoles, while Pansy was a body sculpture rampant in argent, muscles swelling far beyond their due, pectorals like turkey breasts, thighs as hawsers. Patsy's skull was shaven, while Pansy's dark hair was slicked back and caught in a pig-tail. Occasionally, they uttered:

"Meaning?"

"Meaning."

"Meaning?"

"Meaning."

Pause.

"Meaning?"

"Meaning."

"Meaning?"

"Yuk."

Long pause.

"Piss."

"Off."

"Piss."

"Off."

Longer pause. Just like Beckett or Pinter really.

"Piss."

"Off."

"Piss."

"All right."

And Pansy elevated his red nose and pissed on the wall. A stain ran down the woodgrained concrete.

"Public."

"Nuisance."

"Public."

"Nuisance."

Silence.

"Public."

"Nuisance."

"Public."

"All of us. People. Nuisance."

Longer silence, and the child in the small crowd around the wall said, "What are those funny men doing?" And Robin Blossom, capturing them on camera, laughed and answered, "Pissing on a wall."

"Art is —"

"Meaning."

"Art is —"

"Piss."

"Art is —"

"Public nuisance."

"Art is —"

"Us."

The two artists broke up their final pose as the Two Graces, and they presented their cupped hands to the audience for contributions to the charity of Comic Relief or themselves. "As I am touching you," Patsy said, "touch me. Where you want. Lower, please." While Pansy now struck the poses of the body builder, making great snakes ripple under his silver skin and a haggis swell from his glossy bicep. But all the time he kept one hand outstretched for donations. And as Robin tried to slope off with discretion, he was not surprised to hear a shrill alarm of menace sound behind him. "Here, you! No pix if you don't pay." Robin nearly legged it, but the thought of pursuit by a shiny piece of naked beefcake made him pause. He fished out the bronze blob that was now worth a quid and flipped it across to Pansy, whose fist closed round it in mid-air like a salmon taking a lure.

"Where do you work out, angel?"

"The Golden Harrow."

"See you there."

Robin walked on past the litter of packing-cases and plastic bags which were the houses of the street people at night. Only three of the derelicts were there in the afternoon, and one old man with a stained yellow beard and greasy tam o'shanter was arguing with Ian Hamish, the lover of Clio when Robin wasn't, the old sociology fart.

"You what?" the old man was spitting out of bare gums. "I were old soldier. Fuckin' cardboard barracks now."

"Do you have no alternative?" Ian was saying.

"Dinna sleep rough if I had ten quid –"

"You wouldn't drink it?"

"Gi' me a fuckin' drink or fuck off."

"I just wanted to know –"

"Know! Know!" The old man howled in rage. "Do it! Gimme! Fuckin' askin'! Gimme." And he caught Ian by the arm and shook him. "Get it out!" And Robin saw Ian put his free hand in his pocket to find some coins. And he smiled to himself. There were no freebie pictures or interviews now. In the age of communications, all information cost a bit.

"Hi, Ian," he said. "Research ain't for nowt these days. It sets you back a packet. But you got a grant."

"Long gone. I'll tell you what," Ian said, considering his rival, "we could do a deal."

"What about? Clio?"

"No, a book. Your photos, my text. London, Now and Then. The publishers would snap it up."

Robin laughed.

"Snap it up? Me and you?" Then he paused. "Maybe you've got something."

"Of course. In our audio-visual world, the picture-book is king. And what your low-life shots need is bottom. They need bottom. A real text."

"Yeah. Though where I come from, blokes don't read."

"And where you don't come from, they still do."

"What sort of dosh are we looking at?"

"I don't know. At least a five thousand advance, split both ways. Ten per cent royalties. Only UK and Commonwealth. Foreign rights ours. What do you say?"

"Not bad," Robin said. "You want to work with me, not kill me?"

Ian smiled and juggled with invisible weights in the palms of his hands.

"What do I have here? In the left scale, revenge. In the right scale, commerce. Hate, here. Greed, there. Heart, here. Head there." The left palm shot up and hit Ian under the chin. "Greed wins." He bent down and brought up his heavy right hand to shake Robin's grip. "Deal?"

"Deal. You're a performance artist. Better than Patsy and Pansy."

"Now we're friends," Ian said, "you don't happen to have seen Clio lately?"

"Nah," Robin said. "She's sloped off. Some big charity gig. Suddenly there's a helluva lot of dosh around for AIDS. Barrows of the stuff for putting on shows to raise more barrows of the stuff. She's hooked. Got some big backer. She's taking all the pix, and she won't cut me in."

"I hate it," Ian said. "Charity chic. Charity is the fast track of the villain. Ninety per cent of what they take goes in the big balls they put on. It's a lucky hospice which gets its ten per cent."

"Yeah," Robin says, "as long as you get yours, who the hell cares?"

When he returned home to Camden, Ian found himself more confused than ever. The notes for his thesis had become personal. He began to write in some agitation,

> Doing good was always just doing good until I came to London. But here it is doing well for oneself. Charity seems a hypocrisy. One of my best sources, Robin Blossom, even opposes the green movement, which is demonstrably doing nothing but good for our quality of life and the future of life on earth itself. He sees its adherents as doing very well for

themselves, thank you very much. And it is very difficult to see
how we shall save trees and whales and beasts and birds before
we save other human beings first. How shall we face creation
without first saving mankind? The human disaster we have
made of our societies is the primary error we have to correct.
The rest of life on earth may have to wait.

Living well for the dying, slimming for the starving, keeping in trim
for the sick, viewing those present for the blind; giving a hand to the
limbless, chatting on behalf of the deaf and dumb, being seriously
bright for the mentally retarded, kicking a leg for the spastics; saving
children by leaving the babies with nanny, preserving animals and
holidays by boarding pets in kennels, hugging trees to save forests
while reading fashion mags to waste more paper, using limousines not
to walk and pedalling on bike-machines in health clubs; playing
Samaritan in Valentino and Chanel, bestowing alms in Cartier
bracelets, aiding Africa in Mayfair, begging for the needy and
attention. This was a charity lunch and Clio was there among the good
ladies. They were not near enough the top table for the value of their
tickets, two hundred pounds a cheque, which Clio had not paid for.
Position was measured in inches from the relevant Royal, and She was
twenty yards off.

"I don't know who did the *placements*," some rouged old bag said in
Clio's ear, "But I thought when I bought Number Two table, it wasn't
in Siberia. It's fraud. Low numbers here mean you are further off.
We're a long way from Her."

"Perhaps that's a good thing," Clio said, looking at a discus of a
pink hat above the shoulders of a *sumo* wrestler. "You never know
your luck."

She knew who her backer was, and the backer of this AIDS gala
lunch. Peregrine seemed to have initiated or contracted most of the ills
of the century, and AIDS was no exception. He could not be seen, he
said now. Anyway, he had always been the alien and undetectable man.
He had left her a million dollars in a Swiss bank account to promote
her career, he stated, although it was her old age pension. The pay-off
was to become a charity lady, particularly for AIDS. This would give
her all the photo-opportunities she craved. Peregrine had insisted that
his donation was not blood money or a guilt offering. He had nothing
to be sorry for, he was dying, he had nobody to leave his gains to,
however ill-gotten, except for his son Boy, who would also get his
dues, if he would accept them.

He was also Disgusted, West End. He was the original Jack the Nipper, the phenomenon and marker of his time. He had initiated the assaults, the unseen slash in a woman's jacket or dress or skirt with the chisel edge of his thumb. But the fun soon went out of the game. He spawned copycats and proper murderers. His little declaration turned into stabbing and mutilation of whole bodies. Now dozens or even hundreds of Jacks crept and hacked and stole away. Imitation was the sincerest form of thuggery and also the curse of the modern age. Peregrine was a designer of the surreptitious cut and the invisible wound, and his artifices were now as common as Habitat goods.

No man is an island, and Peregrine was sure of that. His copycat in New York — for Jack's style had crossed the Atlantic — blew darts through long straws into the tight arses of white women; but the black Dartsman was making an economic point, not a sexual one. The women of Manhattan had been forced to return to the girdle and the corset to protect themselves from the random pricks of outrageous fortune. And as for the recent Acidman of East London, who sprayed hydrochloric spirits from old Coca-Cola cans on female bottoms so that the wet shock became the future burn, he was a traitor to instant retaliation. Even so, English and foreign women in Mayfair and Piccadilly still refused to wear body armour to avoid the light slashes of the one and only original Jack the Nipper. Pity, he could not have a trademark or a logo, but only a rent or a slash.

There was another reason to be Jack the Nipper. However sympathetic most straight women and so few straight men were about the plague of AIDS, Peregrine knew that they could not feel as he did. The only true parallel was the feeling the soldiers had for each other in the trenches in the First World War when myriads of mates died all the time and the survivors lived in a dullness of grief. Stricken as he was now, he could only campaign after his death for the tens of millions who were already dying in Africa. Even his dealing in weapons had only killed in tens of thousands, while AIDS was decimating a whole continent.

There was still hunger, too. The Ethiopians were dominating the glossies and famine relief of that year. The proud emaciated girls stared from the pages of the magazines with their hair braided in myriads of plaits and barbaric jewellery bolted round their thin necks and drapes of beige and white and pitchblende billowing round their forms slimmer than aerials, while on the television news, babies with eyes spilling from their sockets and stomachs as bloated as watermelons sucked at the dried breasts of their mothers, too tired to brush away the flies that feasted upon their sunken flesh. On the catwalk, in the padded samurai jackets and the slit long skirts that showed each stride in a streak of brown limb, the Abyssinians were superb in their lean grace. And as for the millions left starving at home, the creator of the working model of ET had used just such a shrunken child's face and the eyes of a Siamese cat to project the forlorn aspect of the extra-terrestrial. Meagre was in, the look of the time.

Peregrine had arranged for Clio and Boy to be that evening at the Natural History Museum, where the African models were pleading their stuff to save the planet, backed by the huge Apfelstein Trust. He would be there, he said, but unidentifiable. They needed the last of his banking details, if they were to be rich, and so help others, if they could. At the occasion, the future of the world itself was introduced by a maestro of the air waves. "We are all on trial," he intoned gloomily. "Tonight fashion makes a statement." And so it did, on a catwalk constructed round the reconstructed skeleton of a giant *Diplodocus*, which was too aerated to bellow what it thought.

The models were dressed as trees and bushes, flowers and fishes and rain forest canopies. They wore the leaves and fronds and petals and fins of green chic or ethnic chic, the consciousness of the fresh decade taking over from the greedy and polluting 'eighties. They looked ghastly to Boy, as if they were struck by the seven plagues of Egypt. Brussels sprouts stuck on them in gangrenous boils, strings of pearls hanging from black umbrellas shrouded them in the glitz of mourning veils, birds had nested in their hair and left their broken eggs, while lianas festooned their limbs like muscles grown on steroids. Human beings were made to look like a creepy herbivarium. Even the cloth dyes were natural, derived from mugwort and deadly nightshade, while the cotton was free of pesticide and shape, and the coarse silk was rougher than a sharkskin. Everything was worn loose and was full of wrinkles with haphazard creases. The colours were jungle moss or desert sand or dust bowl beige with hardly a relieving red berry to pep them up. If nature was so drab, why would we bother to imitate it?

Boy found Clio at her camera, with her shutter open. She was snapping a model more spare than a dinosaur's rib-bone. "Hi, baby," Clio was calling, and as the model turned to the cry, she was caught in her chrysalis of biodegradable non-vinyl, ready to shed it and become the dark butterfly of the night. "Ta for now," Clio cried again. "Fly, baby, fly!"

"We're meant to be at this jungle dinner," Boy said. "Will you come with me, Clio?"

"Yup," Clio said. "I've snapped my ass off. It'll be quite fun." She shouldered her camera on its strap. "We'll see the invisible man, or not. What does a blank look like? Tell me. The vacuum in the cleaner."

They sat down to what was called A RAINFOREST MENU, which had plundered far-flung fish and fowl – no fur, by request. Flora and fauna were its accoutrements. Swamp and wetland paid their homage. The vegetable kingdom took a bow in the atrium, decorated with coconut-palm fronds and preserved baobab trunks. A Vichychoisse topped by an olive shaped into a tree frog was followed by lime-soaked parrotfish from the Amazon with fresh samphire and *haricots verts*, then kiwi fruit and grass-bright sorbet, followed by *tisane* and *petits fours* with glazed facets shiny as emeralds. "You can't say," Boy observed to Clio, "that you don't get herbage in the eye."

"It's so so clever," Clio said. "And it's too too green. A friend of mine, Robin Blossom, once took me to a St. Patrick's Day dinner with the friendly neighbourhood IRA in Kentish Town. In between blowing up kids' military bands and Tory politicians, they gave these greenfeasts, in which every morsel flew their hue – lettuce, dandelion or nettle soup, an appalling meat in green jelly with mint-peaked potatoes, a bog-vivid ice-cream, and a herbal tea with sups of crème de menthe on the side, or else dyed kerosene which was a wonderful compliment to the evening and the old sod."

"You must have choked."

"I did."

"Have you ever thought, if everything is green, what's going to happen to all the other colours? Poor old spectrum. Where does the rainbow go?"

Boy never got an answer, because a tap brushed off the chip on his shoulder. He looked around to see a scarecrow in a flopping dinner jacket, with a frog-mask over his face.

"Checking, checking," the apparition said. "Hello, Clio, too. Have you got all you wanted?"

A hand in a green tight leather glove passed over an envelope to Clio.

"Those are the keys of the kingdom, my dear. The last entrance to Aladdin's Cave, c/o Suisse Bankverein, Bern. Don't blow it, except on good causes, like yourself."

"Oh, Peregrine," Clio said, before the frog prince put his other glove across her mouth.

"Walls have ears," he said. "Do shut up. Boy and I have to have a little natter before I disappear for good or bad. Whatever."

Boy rose to the invitation.

"Over by that babbling fountain," Peregrine said. "That jungle nook with breeze-block rocks. It won't be bugged. As you know, I am not too popular here."

There was a ferro-concrete bench stained a delicate shade of oak. There Boy sat down with his father, reducing the level of noise from the dinner table to a mere babble.

"As long as we can hear each other speak," Peregrine said, "we may be able to get something done. You're looking good."

"Not so well, actually," Boy said.

"Nor I. They give me three months at the most. This AIDS is rather speedy, you know."

"I have a few years," Boy said. "A rather greedy cancer."

"From all those bombs you're making?"

"From all those nuclear energy stations I am making."

"Same awful stuff. Same results. We die of it." The man in the frog-mask took another envelope out of his pocket. "Here's your slice, Keiss, my son. I don't mind what you do with it. You can even look after your mother."

"No good now," Boy said. "She's passed away. A stroke. A cerebral haemorrhage."

"Ah." Peregrine was silent for a while. The water dripped from the false fountain. "Did she tell you the truth about me and her before she died?"

"No. She was too proud."

"I thought the truth was always known in the end. It catches up with us."

"Not with you. Look at you. Or can I look at you?"

Boy put out his hand towards the frog mask.

"Father, can I look at you?"

"You will see a Dorian Grey."

"Are you too vain to show me?"

"It has collapsed."

"Surgery does."

"And running away. I suppose so."

The green gloves clawed at the side of the frog mask and lifted it on its elastic. Below was a face of a thousand seams and wrinkles with red eyes. The mask was dropped again.

"Satisfied, Keiss?"

"I would never —"

"You are such a puritan, you think I have got my deserts. My sins show on my good looks at last. Well, when you are dying, you really don't care a hoot. Let it go, let it go, let it go. If you have to pay for it, you do."

"But they never caught you, Jack the Nipper."

"No. My only success."

"But why did you do it? I never understood."

"What else was there to do? The Second World War was easy. You pranged a few Jerries, got burned, became a hero, ran the country. Then we lost everything. Empire, respect, the whole show. So what could you do to protest? A sort of home guerrilla war. Well, you put a fingernail into pomposity. You cut up hypocrisy. And you were so smart they couldn't find you. Always one step ahead, when they thought they could get you. I liked that."

"A rather pitiful protest, don't you think?"

"Rather a good one, really. I have become a public ikon, though anon. A wizard show, really."

"I can't take your money, you know," Boy said.

"Yes, you will, and you can. You can make amends for your father. Cancer research?" Peregrine gave a dry cackle. "Come on. Do something for what condemns you."

"You're strange. Couldn't you think of a better bad cause than giving your money to me?"

"There's Clio. She's got her whack."

Both of the men looked over to the table, where Clio's blonde bob was floating as a buoy above the soft hubbub.

"If I loved anyone," Peregrine said, "I loved her. But then it ruined her. And it's too late for money to put her to rights."

His bones managed to rise within his black dinner suit, the green mask riding above.

"Good-bye, Keiss," he said. "You won't see me again. I have only one thing to tell you. We all do what we can do in this weary world. We do not have much of a choice."

14

HONOUR AND PORTRAITS

Aaron Arteban, the Pope of the publishers, was launching Ian's book, *A City Anatomy*, with photographs by Robin Blossom, at the National Portrait Gallery. Able to arrange eclipses and the music of the spheres as well as other events, Aaron had also fixed a celebrity portrait show of Clio's pictures, *Style in Giving: the Art of the Patron*. Since everybody lived on subsidies or grants now, the publicity was the payback of generosity. To give was to receive a glossy portrait, or even one in oils, on permanent show.

As he passed through the throng in the halls of the gallery, Ian Hamish looked at the paintings of the literary dead. Doctor Johnson did not look particularly surprised to be there. Nor did John Keats, reading with his hand on his head, nor Lord Byron resplendent in Albanian turban, nor Wordsworth pensive and the Brontë sisters pastel under the brush of brother Branwell, nor Dickens with his firm grasp on his daily manuscript, nor Elizabeth Barrett Browning saturnine under flowing black locks, nor Landseer carving a gigantic lion and Ellen Terry sniffing a red camellia, nor Aubrey Beardsley in auburn locks and Rupert Brooke in a slouch-hat, nor T.S. Eliot in Cubist camouflage and Paul McCartney in a halo of bouquets and Dirk Bogarde soft in egg tempera. None of the artists of the ages was glaring at the living who wanted to join them. But paintings cannot condemn or blackball like club members. They can only wait for the proscription of modern times to winnow out the famous who had let failure go to their heads.

Aaron Arteban had given the book launch and exhibition in his usual princely manner, taken from his publishing losses. His address book read like the Almanach de Gotha combined with the Dictionary of National Biography. His firm prospered from one heiress to another. Looking like an all too palpable *eminence grise*, he moved from compliment to congratulation, giving each guest the seconds or the minutes they merited from their distinctions. His uncanny memory conjured up a fleeting reassurance singly to the crush. In the space of an hour, he must have suggested a dozen books that would never see the light of type. Everyone felt part of this spread web of culture and communication which only this supreme spider could spin – omniscient, prescient, confidential to all and sundry.

The agents were shouting yen and percentages and Finnish serial rights beside the bar table too loudly to hear the speeches from the rostrum in the adjoining gallery. Only a few chestnuts rebounded across the roar – "Rule One – Books on South America don't sell. Rule Two – Books on the Royal Family always sell. Rule Three – There aren't any more. You're a publisher now."

With relief, Ian saw Robin Blossom snapping and flashing as always. He was taking pictures of the Field Marshals and the Prime Ministers, the cavalcade of past history, the Duke of Wellington and the two Pitts, Gladstone and Disraeli, and even dumpy Queen Victoria Herself.

"Like a shooting gallery, innit?" he said to Ian. "And I'm shooting."

"They can't shoot back," Ian said. "Though we're very good targets."

"Talking of the nobs, not my usual subject, you may have missed one." Robin nodded to a Whistler in a corner. "One of your lot, innit?"

So Ian saw a portrait of Marie, Countess of Dunesk. The Edwardian artist was having his fun. She rode on her pony in her Indian leggings, but an ermine red cloak swept back behind her, and a tiara enclosed the eagle feathers stuck in her bonnet. Her proud fierce face blazed from the canvas and the soft Lothian hills in the background. Ian laughed to see Rosa's grandmother, who had reached this hall of fame in the end.

"She was a right one, all right," he said.

Leaving behind those set in their gilt frames in their heavy diadems and their jewels, their frock coats and their red uniforms, the two men descended to another gallery to find their mistress and her evidence. Clio had used a fish-eye lens and grease to distort the rich and the generous, the great and the good. She had none of the paid mercy of the portrait painters upstairs, who had been hired to flatter their subjects. She had shown the clutching of charity, the grasp of celebrity. Pushing forward with puffed cheeks and avid lips, pushy fingers clawed at the camera. Or else the lords and the ladies lolled on restaurant couches, sagging behind the champagne glasses and the canapés in a recline of luxury, expecting acclaim to come with the waiters.

"Those who toil not certainly don't spin" Ian said. "Or they would never have allowed these pictures to be took."

Now Clio was with them in her diamanté white jeans and natural sloughed snakeskin top. She looked as if she had taken a portrait of herself. Her lips seemed to pout from hollow cheeks. Her eyes glittered with an adrenalin desire. A lick of blonde hair split her forehead as far as one inch-long eye-lash. Her breasts were as pointed as two mortar bombs, her nails hooked in vermilion talons. And she quivered, as intense as a long jet of gas flame. She denied all age.

"Hi, hi," she said. "One blossom, one thorn in my side. Am I your Rose of Clio?"

"You're looking divine," Ian said, kissing her and smudging her cheek. "And what a show. A revelation. You'll be stoned with Rolexes and Cartier bracelets. Strangled with Chanel scarves. Condemned to a thousand years of venal servitude. The very wealthy will never forgive such an exposure."

"I shoot what I see."

"Bang, bang, "Robin said. "Straight between their true-blue eyes."

"Pow-wow, darling. How was your show upstairs?"

"We came downstairs to see you."

"Slumming, are you?"

"Some slum."

There was a strange contrast, Ian thought, between the pillars and arches of the gallery, and these black-and-white rapacious faces of power. Truly, the greedy had always ruled the planet, but they had not allowed their naked lust to be demonstrated until now. They might still get away with it in the name of art. Yet not for long. The worm in the bud ended by shrivelling the flower of the land.

"Something you better see, Ian," Clio said. "A family portrait, which you know. And a blow-up."

There Peregrine stood in his final appearance. By the Sinclair family group, which Clio had taken at Ermondshaugh, hung an enlargement of the wraith at the window. The blood seemed to be drained out of the man he was supposed to be, if he were a thing of no existence. The grainy face was posed and pitted. His clothes were a shroud where the moths had been. He seemed more an impression on the place than a substance there. He was not to be believed. Yet the placard below him read: BENEFACTOR.

"Well, he did me good," Clio explained. "Before he faded away. And he left a bomb to his son Boy."

"Boy's fading away, too." Ian said. "The cancer is incurable. He's turning to mystic solutions, I gather."

"They always do," Robin said, "if they can afford it. What about you, Clio? Now you're rich and famous, I mean."

"Well, I can afford to do without you two berks for a start," Clio said. "And that's a relief."

"Emotionally, too?" Ian asked.

"Why use a long word when a short one will do, Ian. You always did."

"Like piss off?"

"Exactly, Robin. You are always pithy. So pith off."

"Till we meet again, kiddo."

Robin left with his cameras as trophies slung around his neck. Clio rested her hand on Ian's shoulder.

"Pity," she said. "Talent and no vision. I wouldn't have thought your book worked with Robin. He can snap, but he can't see."

"That's why it works, if it does," Ian said. "His pictures are the raw thing itself. No art in them. You believe them. Because they are just there. As it is."

"But you're a wordsmith. You hammer out those paragraphs. You have to get them right. You strike them into horseshoes. You cobble away. And in the end, it works. But it doesn't flow for you."

"No, it doesn't flow." Ian waved his arm round the National Portrait Gallery. "I have to find words for all this, now. All these lords and ladies and admirals and generals and braid and plumes and medals and honours and centuries. What it's all about. But you, my darling Clio, just come home. We're too old now not to settle for each other."

"Yea, soon." Clio's smile was a flash of summer lightning. "I'm not a rolling stone, needs to come to rest right now, gather a bit of Kate Moss. I'm a fading meteor. A little more space to move and burn. Before – before I fizzle out in you. Happily –"

"Perhaps I can't wait."

"You'll wait."

Clio pecked Ian on the mouth with a quick kiss and was away, leaving him to the sad business of signing books and going back to solitary in Camden. Of course, books never came to an end. There was always a post-script to them, which he would have to work out. And as he went upstairs and again passed the still ranks of all those soldiers and sailors and statesmen reigning above the indifferent chatting mob below, Ian knew he hadn't the style to describe their courage and their dignity any more. For heroics were out of fashion. Caesar was the name of a poodle, Achilles was a tortoise, Alexander a hair-dresser. Superiority was mockery, the elite was shite. So what were the words for these occasions and memories? Could their style be reproduced in his? Ian doubted it, for the new aristocracy deserved only the sneer and the innuendo, not the old poetry of praise. Ichabod, Ichabod, with Churchill's death, the glory was departed.

And so, when Ian staggered to the north after signing and selling twenty copies of *A City Anatomy* – "and, remember, lad, a signing is a sale, it can't be returned" – he found himself composing at his wooden kitchen table a final paragraph for the second edition of his book, which would never be printed. He would have liked to rewrite all his text to describe the history of London, the suffering in the Blitz, the pride of the fighter pilots, the cries of the people, the endurance of the Thames river and the docks. But his was the generation of satire and irony, of unbelieving. His words were crumbs fallen from the table of the feast of the brave dead. So he found himself with his pencil once more, unable to hymn the greatness of the past. He could only use his scalpel on the pawkiness of the present.

> In the distribution of Honours and the fight to obtain Honours lies the secret of this society. There is none other, for the getting of wealth is simply not good enough. Yet the gaining of titles and significant letters before and after your name, that is a crowning achievement. Pity the republican country without the capacity to grant Honours, for the only glory in serving it may lie in the gold braid and the medals and the ribbons of a military career. In London particularly and Britain generally, the granting of honours twice a year is the cement of the monarchy and the true glue of the government. The dual Matronage of Queen and Prime Minister knows that the many squabbling and restless groups climbing up the greasy pole of ambition can only be satisfied for failing to reach the pig at the top by being flung a peerage here, a baronetcy there, and innumerable orders naming them Companions or Dames of a British Empire on which the sun has long set.

Yet one legend lived on, honoured by the young. Now that Jack the Nipper had disappeared, the metropolis may have become quieter, and the sale of padded jackets and corsets gone into decline. But the children remembered and played a new game on the streets and in the schoolyards. There were fresh words to it and the words were their own. Two of the boys would crook a little finger and intertwine each of these and pull one against another until a finger slipped out or lost hold. The other children would circle them in a ring and chant to the rhythm of a banging shoe or a tapping stick:

"Jack the Nipper
Was no Ripper
But he had a little knife
He put it in 'er
He took it out 'er
But the lady kept her life

"Hush and tush! Walking down the street
All safe now! For Jack is off his beat
Like the Ripper, Jack put his chopper down
He's gone to blazes and left London town
Hello, chicken! When you carve the bird –
Crackerjack the wishbone, your wish is heard –"

And so Jack's exploits were preserved as a rhyme and a game and a hope. And the lips of the innocent sang, and their hands pulled and broke apart, and the winner half-believed he would get what he wanted. And the spines of women no longer crawled at the footfall behind their own feet. And Jack the Nipper joined Spring-heeled Jack and the Ripper in the annals of unsolved crime. He had brought a brief fear to the city, but the city would outlive him as it had survived all its invaders for a thousand years. The rebels and the highwaymen, the pamphleteers and the pickpockets, the burglars and the stabbers in the back, these were the sturdy beggars of its history. Their protests were pitiful, their force in vain. This final Jack had strolled the streets and caused a petty havoc so minimal in terms of the ten million Londoners that his fame was out of all proportion to his misdeeds. Yet in some dark artery or nerve of the metropolis, he lurked invisible and inscrutable and present, withdrawn to the alley of his last walk.

Knowing he was dying sent Boy to Mahintale in Ceylon, now named Sri Lanka. He had not seen enough of the wonders of the world, and he had seen too much of the radiation rooms of the hospitals, which were slowly killing him along with his cancerous cells. He had heard that Solomon had retired from his official duties, as only the Indians could manage from time to time. Retiring from the world to meditate seemed perhaps the best cure left for Boy. He could not think of a better alternative. And now he had much of Peregrine's loot to spend, before he gave away his father's spotty legacy.

The approaches to the shrine were rocks, rounded, humped, conical, fallen, creased and bright with lichen. The roots of satinwood and rain trees curled in still snakes in the crevasses. Leaves shook in the whirr of crickets from their forked lightning twigs in the hill breeze. Manna fell from heaven in the five-petalled blossom of the frangipani. Monkeys screamed and leapt by the hard path, their chatter overtaken by the anxious hum of a hundred other pilgrims in yellow and white costumes, afraid to be solitary in these weird grottos.

Boy had expected to find Solomon a hermit in the pursuit of peace, not near the steps to the great stupa built in honour of Prince Mahindra, who had converted the King of Ceylon to the worship of the Buddha. Above Boy stood the unicorn ringed top of the cupola of the temple, the shape of the universe. Only he could not contemplate that, given the questions of the curious all about him. "Sir? You alone? Sir?"

Boy was not alone, and he desired to be alone. He lurched up the rock steps polished by a million bare soles to the high look-out where Prince Mahindra had sat for years, waiting for a deer to bring the King of Ceylon to him and hear that it was better to respect life than to kill it. Buddhist chants were playing on a loudspeaker to destroy any hope of meditation. Then there was a tap on Boy's shoulder, and he turned to see a brownish face of a man in a straggly halo of white hair and beard, a sepia blanket pinned about the nakedness of the body below.

"Keiss," the holy man said. "I knew you would be here."

"I did not tell you I was coming," Boy said.

"I knew you would be here. Follow."

So Boy followed Solomon down the far side of the mountain towards the ruins of temples and palaces and dry gardens. Red and yellow flowers glared and reared by a waterless bath with an eroded lion cut into the stone above it. Steps led through square archways supporting invisible walls and the sky. Solomon passed through towards a baobab tree, a curled maze of wood houses and serpentine branches. He vanished into its depths, and Boy followed him, hitting his head on the tangle of holy trinkets hanging from the leafy roof above.

In the cool gloom, Solomon was sitting on crossed legs, waiting for Boy to blunder and kneel and dispose of his weight on his bottom.

"I knew you were coming," Solomon said for the third time.

"I believe you," Boy said. "You were there. I won't ask you how."

"Those of my friends who find me," Solomon said, "they ask me if I will visit them. Send me a postage stamp from your country, I say. Then I will look at it and meet you there."

"Don't mystify me, Solomon. You were a civil servant. Against all this hocus-pocus."

"It is merely a different level of communication," Solomon said. "A radar of the spirit. The cyber space of the soul."

"A message I do not understand. Not quite yet."

"Yet. I know why you have come here."

"Of course, you know. I am dying of cancer. There is no cure."

"Except in the spirit."

"Exactly. I have always thought that cancer was half a disease and half a lack of will, morale, whatever. What do you think?"

"It is irrelevant, as the body is irrelevant. Only the soul matters."

"And the body, while you still have to drag it around?"

"Then don't. Sit under the tree of life, as I do." Solomon passed a hollowed gourd over to Boy. "Drink it. A sort of sour yoghurt. The villagers bring it to me."

"Why?"

Boy drank the white sharp mixture and sneezed.

"They think I have solutions," Solomon said, "which I do not have."

"They think you can cure them?"

"I can help them to cure themselves."

"Is that all you have to tell me? I have come a long way to hear you."

"You have come a very short way, if you want to cure yourself. That is the long way."

Boy smiled and shook his head.

"I don't have that long to live. I only have short cuts now."

"You will live as long as you find the right way to do so. It is not dying slowly as you are now."

Boy looked at the gnarled canopy about him with its wooden coils.

"Tell me, Solomon," he said, "how did you ever have the guts to give up Annandale and all and come and live here on charity?"

"Easy," Solomon said. "That was the easy thing. And I had someone to follow. Prince Mahindra. His father Asoka had made the first Indian Empire. He chose to withdraw here and convert Ceylon to peace."

"But he was a Buddhist. Aren't you a Hindu?"

"That is also irrelevant. A Christian college, a Hindu mother, Buddhist by inclination, when all the ways to God are rambles in the

same direction. God is our spirit, our Creation. We only have to find
our own way there."

"You gave up our British Empire a long time ago," Boy said.

"So did you," Solomon said. "More recently."

"We've done it quite well," Boy said. "But I don't know if I can be
a Buddhist Prince like you."

"You don't understand. I am not the Prince. I must find the way
only for myself. If I can pass it on, so be it."

"And can you, to me?"

"The next step. Only that."

"Then the next step."

"There's a lesson there. But you have to find it."

"How?"

"History. And the lessons are in history."

"And faith."

"At the Lion Rock at Sigiriya, there was a king who killed his
father —"

"My father didn't kill me," Boy said, "though he killed a lot of
other people."

"The King fortified the Lion Rock and waited for his brother to
come out of India to kill him."

"My brother was killed in Africa," Boy said. "And only cancer is
coming to kill me."

"Do not be so literal. Go to the Lion Rock. Climb it at dawn
before anyone rises there. Look down on the pleasure gardens below
that face north towards India. And be the eyes of the king who killed
his father. And he will speak to you."

"I — the eyes of a corpse and a rock."

"As I am the eyes of this Bo-tree." Solomon spread his arms and
touched the green bark around him. "Buddha sat under this tree. He
speaks to me. Be the place. Hear the voice of those who sat there.
They give the answers. I can give you no more."

And so, Boy to the Lion Rock came, past the sacred rock caves of
Dambuila. In there, forty yellow Buddhas in scarlet robes were carved
from a single stone. Some stood in tents which seemed to come from
Brighton Beach, all painted with blue-and-white stripes, as beautiful as
candy floss. Other Buddhas reclined or sat in front of blazing scallop
shells of fire and light. Behind them, the rock walls had chequer
boards drawn on them above long rows of disciples shining as flames
with lotus-flower patterns below. The King of Ceylon rode on a white
elephant against the King of India on a black elephant, while their
enemies surrounded them with lopped heads and limbs, and in the

depths, great fish swam. The sign of peace was the Buddha's upheld hand, four red circles drawn on his palm.

In the Rest Home at Sagiriya, Boy was woken at lemon pale dawn by faint chants and the rustle of sleeping servants. He found them sprawled on the red plaster floors outside his room, their long shirts hiding their nakedness. As he stepped out towards the Lion Rock, he saw a dog-fight between two curs, suddenly separated by a man in huge spectacles riding his bicycle. Already, children were trudging to school with their satchels, some in little English uniforms of black and white.

Boy would never know how he made it up the thousand stairs of the Lion Rock. As he was expiring with dragging breaths, he came cross the famous maidens in their low guard chamber. Fresco'd on the curving rocks, the girls stood with lotus in still pools. Their heads were bowls for jasmine, their breasts were pillows for milk and kapok. Their waists were the stems of lilies, the cloths on their hips were bright clay, as they offered pineapples and flowers to the sentinels of the high places, who, if they fell asleep on duty, would be dashed to death on their long rockfall.

Higher was a dry lawn, which led through two gigantic limbs towards the top citadel. These two vast and trunkless legs of stone on either side of the stairway were greater than those of the fabled Ozymondias, King of kings. Boy remembered Shelley's lines from his *Dragon Book of Verse*:

> 'Look on my works, ye Mighty, and despair!'
> Nothing beside remains. Round the decay
> Of that colossal wreck, boundless and bare
> The lone and level sands stretch far away.

And so they did, when Boy reached the eyrie of the ancient King of Ceylon, who had killed his father. That ruler had waited eighteen years for revenge to blow in dust and elephants from the south of India into his refuge, with the dry plains then irrigated by his spreading tanks beneath his gaze. There were still the outlines of the pleasure gardens beneath the soar of the rock, but they looked to Boy as a dead man on his back with two dried pools for the sockets of his countenance.

Now the eyes of the parricide were Boy's eyes. He was seeing as in the hindsight of the long departed King. And a voice and strange questions were sounding in his ears:

"What if they pass the gates and the moat, where the lotus leaves meet the waters? What if they scale the low ridges and burn the temples and bring down the walls? How shall they climb the Lion Rock? How pass between its paws, its three-nailed feet larger than elephants'? How scale the warped rock, its hide scaly as dragons? How reach the peak of my palaces, my cisterns, my rice-chambers, my goats?

"Yet the rock is as orange as old blood. It is as black as the Death God Kali of India. Even the fish-eagle dies on the cliff. And the eye of Buddha looks down on the eyes of the father I walled alive in the garden.

"The army has come from India. Call my elephants, my companions! We shall fight in the marshes by the tanks of the Great Kings. We shall put to flight the frogs in the sluices. Hear the trumpets of the elephants! We shall go out as gongs between the lion's paws! As brass through the vermilion gates to match my brother!

"There is no God and He is Buddha. There is Buddha and He is no God. The dust from India chokes the sun. We march into the clouds. I have waited long. I have waited too long. I cannot stay and wait longer. This is the time to lose gladly."

When the next tourists reached the peak of the Lion Rock, they saw Boy walking away with a smile on his face. He had left his body. He had entered the place. He had learned how to be defeated in his long wait for death. He would lose gladly.

15

HIGHLAND MILLENNIUM

Boy never understood what kept him alive until the last gathering of the clan in Caithness. Perhaps Solomon had given him a touch of faith, had shown him a path up from the Bo-tree. Perhaps sinking back on the mercy of a God, whose ways were more mysterious than ever, had allowed Boy to reach old age and the millennium. Sitting in the Café Royal in Edinburgh at an empty table, Boy could see in the stained glass windows and the bright Old Doulton tiles from Lambeth the futility of invention and of sporting with mortality. Man proposed, indeed, but God disposed. We played, and He displayed our power-lessness in His Creation.

Sipping at his *kir*-red champagne, Boy looked at the pictures of the Edwardian games which still held the Commonwealth together, a cricketer in his striped cap wielding his bat as a lance, a rugby full-back in britches, a tennis coach with a pear-drop racket, a man playing lozenge bowls and another casting a fly or drawing a bow or blowing a horn for the hunt. These were once the fathers of that industrial revolution which had bound the red quarters of the globe in a web of steel and a cloud of coal, Robert Peel working out how to print calico, Michael Faraday experimenting with electro-magnetism and George Stephenson with a model of the first steam train, *The Rocket*. And brighter than the colour pictures in Boy's nursery book, *Highroads of History*, there blazed James Watt and Matthew Boulton with the Condensing Engine, and the fleet to carry all these manufactures and goods world-wide, a steam-and-sail vessel after Isambard Kingdom Brunel's *Great Britain*, and a cargo ship with two funnels chuntering up the Firth of Forth.

Now there were Rosa and Rosabelle, the first of Boy's guests on the way to the north and a long past home. The years had not flecked Rosa's fire of beauty, in Boy's eyes, but Rosabelle limped now on a silver-topped cane, the sunken face of a falcon under a hood of severe streaked snow. Boy was hurting in his chest as he got to his feet and kissed the women on each cheek and helped them into their chairs.

"Only for you, Boy," Rosabelle sighed as she sat down. "Only for you would I come to that Tattoo for the old lady."

"I agree," Boy said. "You are far too young for that."

Rosa laughed.

"I never took you for a flatterer, Boy. But it's true. The Queen Mum is a hundred now, and Mummy and I still have a little catching up to do."

"Very little," Rosabelle said. "If at all."

"Before we go up the Rock to the Castle to see the Tattoo," Boy said, "you will have a wonderful meal. Oysters, champagne, the works."

"But you haven't any money," Rosa said. "You're ill. You haven't been working."

"Peregrine's money. He'll pay."

"He never did," Rosabelle said. "He got off everything. How could you take anything from him?"

"What I don't spend here," Boy said, "I'll spend up in the Highlands, where we all go on. I haven't much further to go."

"Oh, Boy." Rosa clasped his hand. "You'll bury us all."

"We'll see. Ah —"

Pins and needles pierced Boy's shoulders as he rose again to meet two more cousins, who had driven up together, Ian Hamish and Hamish Henry. He seated them between the women, but there was still an empty chair, and a question.

"Clio didn't come?"

"No," Ian Hamish said. "It's the Season in London. And she is still recording that archaic event, as though it had any meaning now."

"Now we have our own parliament," Rosabelle said, "London has no meaning at all."

"It took nearly three centuries," Ian Hamish said, "to repeal the Act of Union. And you haven't got real independence yet."

"We will, we will," Rosa said. "As sure as Scots are Scots."

"She's a Scot, too," Boy said. "The old Queen Mother. And the regiments marching for her, they are Scots. Like it or not, that's what we've done for the Crown for a long time. And we're still marching."

"Not much longer, Boy."

"Oh, I don't know. We're all going up to the Sinclair Games. If we're not going home, we're visiting it. What's bringing us all there? Some clutch, some pull, some tradition, something we helped to make for the British Crown."

Ian Hamish grinned and fished a piece of paper from his pocket.

"Can I throw a red rag to you bulls?" he said. "I came upon this G.K. Chesterton poem, when I was finishing my sociology of

London." He hooted at Rosabelle. "I knew you would love it, darling." Then he read:

> "The earth is a place on which England is found,
>   And you find it however you twist the globe round;
>   For the spots are all red and the rest is all grey,
>   And that is the meaning of Empire Day."

"You're being bloody impossible," Rosabelle snapped.

"He's taking the mickey," Rosa said. "Calm down, mum."

"I'm not going to that bloody Tattoo up the hill."

"Order," Boy said, "Order."

"A few glasses of bubbly," Hamish Henry said, "and we'll float up there. The remedy for all problems is to study the menu. So study. And Boy, incidentally, I'd hoped to fill that empty chair. I asked Leah to come along."

"But she's in Tel Aviv."

"No. She would have come. But there's another crisis in Israel. Now I come to think of it, there is always a crisis in Israel. Ever since the Flood."

"I know why you know Leah," Boy said. "Through my father, Peregrine."

"Yes," Hamish Henry said. "He said he was going to recruit you, too."

"Those nuclear bomb tests between Israel and South Africa? I wouldn't help. Did you?"

"He made it attractive. But you got the bulk of his money, didn't you?"

"I didn't have to earn it," Boy said. "Not by betraying any secret or any one."

"Ouch," Hamish Henry said, then he turned on the charm of youth, which still strayed across his sagging face. "No shop in the mess, isn't that it? And anyway, I am a reformed character. Look at me, here, at the military Tattoo for the Queen Mother. A pillar under the throne."

"Right," Ian Hamish said. "Right. I'll have Lock Fyne oysters, then grilled cod, if there is any left of it under the quotas and the North Sea."

And so the ordering began of the meal, and with it, the forgetfulness of the errors of time past. For in the end, families could achieve reunion, if not oblivion. They were here to celebrate only one thing, that they had lived to tell their tales of who was gone and what was gone. Their part in their going was no longer significant.

Boy had put his love Rosa on his right. He had to ask her why he had lost her, and Ian Hamish as well.

"It's not your fault," she said. "It is mine. It's probably our tradition. Three generations of single women at Dunesk, Marie and Mummy and me. It's not that we don't love you men, because we do. It just seems we're stronger, we can do what we feel we must do, if we are on our own."

"I suppose so," Boy said. "But the line ends with you."

"Line? What's a line?" Rosa was angry. "We're part of a whole people. We have to put our work into them. Not our blood, every time."

"No," Boy said. "But you can take time off for a bit of private happiness."

"Yes, indeed. How ill are you, Boy?"

"I don't know when I have to go. Today, tomorrow, next week. Certainly soon. But it doesn't matter. I've just got to give something away."

"What? Peregrine's loot?"

"Yes. You'll get it all. The crofters. Their Association."

"Our friends, the Mackenzies. Up at Dounreay?"

"Which is closing down, too."

"Yes," Rosa smiled. "We might have been together except for that."

"I know," Boy said. "Don't let's talk about it. You can't go back. I've learned that. Only forward, into whatever. I hear there's even a queue for crofts now."

"Yes. All this Greenpeace stuff. And Desert Island Discs. Back to the land. So the crofts are all being rebuilt and the rights given back by our new government. And the Sinclairs can go home."

"If we want to. You will come that far with me?"

"I will, Boy, I will. If we only hadn't met at Dounreay on opposite sides of the barricades."

"My fault. I was wrong."

"Cousin Donald is still working there in the job you got him."

"Is it killing him? Like me?"

"Not yet. And he has his wages. But that's your fault, Boy. Your fault, too."

Rosa turned away to speak to Ian Hamish on her right, Boy's rival, but no longer now. Women did seem to forgive you from time to time, Boy thought, but forgive and forget was not a pair of words to apply to them. Women forgave male perversity and brutality almost too easily, as with his father Peregrine. They loved the prolonged pleasures of reconciliation; but they never forgot their forgiveness, let alone the trespasses against them. They would bring up the subject and the crime, which was best forgotten, time after time and year after year. Then they could forgive and forgive and forgive *ad nauseam*. An act of indemnity and oblivion did not lie in their nature, and their pardon was without end.

Rosabelle did forgive and forget just enough to allow herself to be transferred up the Rock to the Royal Tattoo for the Hundredth Birthday of Elizabeth, the Queen Mother. She had been the Colonel of the Black Watch for two-thirds of her long reign over the Empire, and the Union Jack still flew over the battlements of the castle, where the seats were stacked in serial rows round the parade ground. The marching bands came from Calgary and New Zealand and South Africa as well as from the Highlands. Some of them even wore the old khaki tunics and bush hats of forgotten colonial conflicts. The drum majors flaunted real leopard skins with scarlet trimmings beneath their huge drums, pregnant on their spotted stomachs. Their black-and-white drumsticks were muffled to the soft beat which moved their white spats. They were led by a Gold Stick in a velvet jockey cap and blanco'd leggings. His pointers and pirouettes led their lines in and out of each other as a cat's cradle, which never collapsed.

Now two soldiers in combat gear wheeled out a podium for a fat old fart in a busby to mount and conduct the massed bands, no longer imperial but rather archival. But after they had played 'Old Lang Syne' and the lone piper on the tower had played the 'Lament', Boy could hardly see through his tears. There had only ever been three tunes on the Highland bagpipes – the charge, the dance, and the lament for the dead. And now the orphan soldier girls from the Queen Victoria School at Dunblane were kicking and twirling in their short kilts and soft leather shoes. Then they were as rigid as Guardsmen, hearing the National Anthem, before the tribute to the old Queen Mother, who had spanned the whole century. Played on a penny-whistle, it seemed to Boy a fair last squeak for the greatest show on earth of the past age.

He had not told his guests of his rendezvous after the Tattoo. He let them make their way back to Ermondhaugh or their hotels on Princes Street before he sought out the changing-rooms of the Cape Town Highlanders Pipes and Drums. He had thought he had seen his nephew Conan bursting his cheeks on the parade ground as he manipulated his pig's belly and tubes by the huge black kilted

drummer to his side. And here Boy found Conan and took him away
to a bar by the Castle and its guests, departing.

"You know we've arranged for your whole band to go up to the
Highlands," Boy said. "To play for us at our show there."

"I know," Conan said, his ruddy cheeks sunken now in his lean
long face. "We're chuffed. Jolly good show, and all that."

"You couldn't bring your mother Elizabeth over and your sisters?"

"They wouldn't come, uncle. A lot to do out there."

"But the blacks are seizing your farms. Taking back what they lost."

"What we developed. And we still have all the industry, and the
gold."

"How much longer do you think your family will stay out there?"

Conan grinned and drained his pint of beer.

"You know how it is with the Sinclairs? We're still waiting for the
final Clearances from Rhodesia. When they come, we'll go. Not till
then."

"But you've already gone."

"I'm in a good trade."

"An undertaker."

"An undertaker. Grandad and dad killed a few Terrs, before they
got done. I reckoned death could be a better business. I'm not burying
the past, like. I'm earning from it"

"There's a lot of death in Africa."

"Sure is. It's not so much the wars now, all that tribal stuff we
stopped. It's AIDS. Tens of millions are croaking now. We call it the
Monkey's Revenge. We ate bush meat, and now we're the meat for the
bush."

"So," Boy said, "dying is your way of life."

"Good trade, uncle."

"You may have to bury me," Boy said. "Up at the Highland
Games. But let's have another beer first, and settle the future of the
world, if we can't settle our own."

Even with a Labour government in by a landslide at the end of the
century, class was not dead yet in England. Its requiem was often sung
now. Surely all was a matter of merit. Yet the Season still persisted.
The June was wet, as most Junes in England are. With a touching faith
in Nature, which did not return the compliment, or a magnificent
disdain for the weather and the spectator, the sporting events of the
year were scheduled as usual in the open air, drizzle, rain and storm.

So Clio followed the Season, as it progressed in damp delights. The touts at the gates of Wimbledon and the hospitality tents of the companies offered Centre Court tickets and Buck's Fizz to the favoured rich. Business entertainment services created a whole village of marquees outside the international tennis competition on grass. Inside these canvas spaces, ceiling fans swung their lazy propeller blades, while houris in turquoise tottered over Persian rugs to serve their chilled concoctions. At Henley Regatta, few left the big tops and the off-duty air hostesses and the Pimms to watch the rowing, because the sight of one, two, four or eight men sweating at the oars of a flimsy boat was neither aesthetic nor amusing, although the pink blazers and socks of the Leander Club certainly were. Cowes, perhaps, resisted the market most; but even there, the brash plutocrats in their power boats had penetrated the Royal Yacht Squadron.

For the paradox remained constant. All the events of the Season were based on exclusion, yet big business could always buy a place or a seat within. The Enclosures at Ascot and Henley, the Royal and the Stewards': the Squadron at Cowes and the All England Lawn Tennis and Croquet Club: these had thrived on restricted access. And yet each year such bulwarks of caste were scaled by the ambitious and the corporate until one might rub elbows with anybody in the old citadels of the few. The enclosure was now a freebie pasture, the club an open sesame to the gilded key.

Sport now seemed to have little to do with it, and the wise and the jaded took to flight to preserve their sense of superiority. They could always watch the events, anyway, on that ubiquitous intruder, the television screen. Ensconced in the safety of their considerable drawing-rooms, the owners of the larger homes of England could attend the grand occasions without discomfort. And so Clio found herself at a considerable pile in Gloucestershire, where a peer of the new aristocracy, the leader of the band called the Oik Boys, had decided to hold his strictly private wedding to the third daughter of the Duke of Featheringby. A fee of half a million pounds had been negotiated with *Hello!* magazine for the coverage, and Clio was part of the cover.

She thought of her only constant lover, Ian Hamish, and she wished he were there rather than the inescapable Robin Blossom, who was now haunting her. Ian would relish the supreme tatty flash of it all, and why the Oik Boys and the pop stars would never be acceptable, however many stately homes their royalties could buy. The secret of old England was that it relished the old. Wealth was not to be flaunted, but disguised. Brand names were the things to avoid.

Only the outsiders wore Burberry tartan macs, or foreigners who knew no better. Watch all the owners at Ascot and see them in the same beige-white riding rainproofs. Black umbrellas were *de rigeur*, even when they had to be unrolled – except for the beloved Queen Mother, who could put up a see-through cloche to give her visibility in a downpour at the races. But only royalty could change the game with impunity. Otherwise, avoid the designer labels and the advertised smartnesses that studded the pages of blockbuster novels, seeking hopelessly for *ersatz* class and achieving only *kitsch*.

For class in England was the avoidance of it. Shun the Chelsea Flower Show, because of the firms who came to transplant primroses in spring and Cape violets in summer and the ineffable geranium all the time. Attendance might prove your riches, but also that you derived from window-boxes and not from gardens, which needed gloves and personal care and decades to grow. Never wear an old school tie, and certainly not as a bow-tie. Pale blue stripes on a black butterfly at the neck meant social death by a thousand cuts. In bathrooms no gold taps as in this great house, but mottled chrome, while lavatory seats had to be worn to rubbed wood from a past procession of fond bottoms.

As for those who left supermarket price labels on the gold metal tops of their Bollinger or Moët, didn't they have wine merchants? Dust on the bottle and the grimy *château* label, or better no label at all, denoted a cellar of antiquity. Leather patches sewed onto the elbows of old Harris tweed, dinner-jackets handed on to grateful grandsons with bottle-green lustre on their lapels, yellow heirloom lace constricting the pink faces of yelling infants at christenings, this was continuity, this was age, this was the recognition of birth and time. And no Johnny or Jane-come-lately could achieve that worn stuff, that bequeathed use.

Robin Blossom himself a wearing a pair of slashed and faded combat trousers that seemed to date from the Falklands and Gulf Wars, but were straight out of the acid bath.

"You don't understand," Clio told him. "That sell-by look doesn't work, unless it's the real old gear. You can't forge it. You have it, or you don't."

"You have it, darling," Robin said, "in your face. And I have it now." He clicked his camera open and took out a roll of film. "Sod the past. Clickety-click, and bingo."

"You have to develop that rubbish, you know. And yourself, along with it."

"Oh, come off it, Clio. I taught you a trade. You're a top society *paparazza* now. You're the gumrot of the salivating classes. You're the X-ray of the cancer of power. And all because of me."

"You don't think I did a little myself."

"Yeah, but –" Robin was loading his Leica again, unrolling the end of the spool of film into the cogs of the camera interior. "You knew how it worked up top, but you didn't know how to expose it. You had the *entrée*, but not the savvy. That's where Yours Truly came in."

Robin closed the back of his camera and pressed a button and choom, choom, choom, the first shot clicked into place.

"Ready to go," he said. "Kick off in fifteen mins. Got to get a good spot near the head Oik."

Gilt thrones had been set up under purple velvet awnings for the bride and groom, who were dressed in satin *à la crème* and scarlet crêpe. A seven-foot wedding-cake in the shape of St Paul's Cathedral lay ready to cut with a sabre; its gold hilt was modelled on the Speaker's Mace of the House of Commons. Amid a barrage of flashes like the ack-ack of the Blitz, the head Oik and his bride tossed his crown and her tiara to the gorgeous and gawping comrade stars of the pop firmament. One of them wore a sleeveless morning coat in the colours of the Union Jack: the tattoos on his bare arms were a Heart and Anchor and a Sea Serpent, very like Nelson, really. So Clio found herself running, running, running, towards some refuge in the Far North, where there might be a meaning behind all this expanse of glitz in a waste of shame. Yes, lust in action, that it was. She had to flee for her life and her death, too. A final return.

As Boy lay on his bed, dying, Rosa came to him at Scrabster. In his room above the old fishing port and ferry to Orkney, she put her hand and her mouth upon him, and she pricked him in the middle and put him into her. She settled over him as the sea mist of the dawn, the har of Caithness. She seemed to draw the last of his spirit from him. He shuddered and spoke.

"I want to die now. I will never be so happy again."

"Later, Boy. Still a boy, you are. Die later."

As she rose from him to leave, the gold emerald ring from Annandale streaked on her finger as the green flash Boy had once seen in a tropic sunset. And he had a dream when she was gone as his dream at the Lion Rock. He was in a time almost before time in Orkney, where the Vikings had lived in their round stone brochs for thousands of years. And this was his dream of his trial, as he wrote it in the morning.

The har seeps from the sea. The fog is a grey bonnet on the circle of standing stones. Within, another circle of men stand about Astir and Rognar. Silent, they watch the trial of the pair, stripped to the waist, their heads bare. Astir raises his broadsword as long as himself with his two hands. He swings it to meet the weapon of Rognar. The blades cross above them near the stabbing point. They lock. One slip, and a skull will split. Now the two on trial circle, slow, slowly. Not yet does one tall blade force the other down for the slice from the side that will sever the head at the neck from the body. Rognar staggers but has high hold. Astir is strong as an Orkney crab. Time, too, is on hold. The har lifts in the vault of the morning.

The tips of Astir's fingers burst under his nails. The bright blood bathes the back of his palms. Scarlet streams run down his arms. His grip is numb. Stop the shudder in the sinew that seizes the sword. Heave and hoist hour upon hour. Lay him low.

Rognar's blade slides and screeches down. It crashes on the other's hilt. Sparks crack and fly. Astir begs his bones to strike to the left, but they are set. Rognar lifts his blade halfway into a Celtic cross. More thrust now, and more hurt. Much more cannot be, but must.

Who throws the stone? Nobody will know. It strikes Astir on the brow. He falls on one knee. His sword droops, drops. Rognar's blade slices across to sever. Astir bows his head. Sharp iron scalps his skin and hair. Gush of blood swills his back. He swings his blade into Rognar's side. He hears the smack of rib-wreck.

Astir rises. He stoops. Tears are the guilt in his eyes. He has bent his head to live. The point of his sword pushes the hilt of Rognar's blade into that stricken hand.

How does Rognar rise? The wound at his waist gives him red legs. The broadswords clash and cross and thrust on. The two men lurch and right themselves. A long groan moans from the waiting men. The blood ebbs from the two on trial. Aloft, the weapons waver as in wind. Rognar's sword slumps sudden. Astir heaves to the right, cleaving a skull from a spine.

The men are a ring around Astir in accusal. The shame of his living makes him bend at the neck, as if for the blow. "He stole my black cow," he says. The words are thick in his throat. "I did not steal his cow."

The circle of men part. Astir steps through the gap. His sword drags on the grass. The spittle of hate is grit on his wounds. The stones do not move for him. They watch the verdict. Better to die at the time of trial. Worse to survive in a long wrong.

His had been the long wrong, Boy knew that. If the Clearances had been the longer wrong to the Sinclairs, the coming of the nuclear power to the clean ocean and the cliffs was a long wrong, only now to begin to be cleared away. What was the time-scale of that second clearance? Fifty thousand years and more, before the moors would be truly clean again of all the residue. There had been the leukaemia cluster around Dounreay with a dozen children catching his wasting disease, when there should only have been one or none. Of course, sixteen hundred people were still working there, including cousin Donald Mackenzie. And they would go on working. Although the plant would accept no more nuclear waste, it had already had sixteen thousand tips of the stuff over eighteen years. A decommissioning of this toxic legacy would cost two and a half billion pounds and take another century to complete. There were a lot of wages in that, if you could survive the job.

Too late now for regret. Boy had to reach the Highland Games at Halkirk, where the clan gathering was taking place, and he would meet his lawyers and hand over the money from his father's trade in weapons to the Crofters' Association. This was no restitution. There could never be a recompense for the bad things which had been done, the sufferings, the casualties, the graves. But it was a beginning, and without a beginning, how could there be a follow-on?

As Boy rose, another love-making took place at breakfast in Thurso. Clio had come back to Ian Hamish on the dawn train. Hardly awake, fuddled in the head, Ian had answered the rapping at his hotel door to find his hysterical old lover in his arms.

"I'll never run away," she sobbed. "Never, never, never, never, never. It's so awful out there. All gold and vomit. Piss and paste diamonds. Darling, *you* never leave me now. I'm sticking to you like a plaster on your bunion. Cherish me."

So Ian also reached the pitch of his desire with Clio, before they had their slices of haggis and eggs and bacon, the full breakfast for the day ahead. There was a twist in her thighs, a nervous pump between her legs, that took all the sense out of him. And he lay back, groaning and saying, "Damn you, Clio, but I could never get away, and I won't ever. We're too old for this now. And parting."

Her smile was almost smug as she sank back on the pillow.

"No, you won't ever now. Because you've got a leech in your bed."

The Halkirk Highland Games were the remembrance and the acting now. Boy and Ian Hamish and Clio came out among the Land Rovers and the caravans parked around the edges of the recreation ground. Heats were being held for the best piper, with five judges in kilts looking as dark as doom at every blowing contestant. And in the middle, the children's games were happening at all ages in the races. Some of them fell over and burst into tears and were rescued by their mothers' arms. One wee thing won a race and was called Mackenzie. "We'll hope that's Kirsty's brat," Boy said to himself. And larger girls cross-stepped across drawn swords. Then a red-haired lass stepped on a blade and flounced off, strutting and yelling, "It's no fair."

Yet fair it was, and the procession of the Sinclairs marched round the ground. Their chieftain, the aged Margaret, Viscountess Thurso, led the long line behind, with Lord Thurso and Malcolm, the Earl of Caithness, their long eagle plumes nodding on their bonnets. The Sinclairs had come back here from all over the globe, where they had been scattered, from Canada and New Zealand, from Australia and South Africa. And they were followed by the Grampian Police Pipe Band, led in its finery by the Pipe Major Drew Sinclair. And behind came the players whom Boy had seen at the Edinburgh Tattoo, the Cape Highlanders in their kilts with Conan the undertaker, the black and the brown and the white of them, the true skins and colours of the Empire without the red and the blue.

All of the clan met for lunch in a tent which had been donated by another wild colonial boy, Niven Sinclair, an officer in the King's African Rifles who had to flee his peanut ranch in Tanganyika after independence, only to found a fleet of Mercedes to fuel and ferry the British Broadcasting system near the White City. He was aiding the Earl to restore Girnigoe, that magnificent ruin on the sea which the World Monument Fund had declared the only castle in all the world to deserve preservation. Boy found himself at a trestle table with the cousins he knew. He had reserved a plastic carton of red wine for them, and a bottle of Glenfarclas which seemed more of the right stuff.

Donald and his father Angus Mackenzie were there, and Boy signed over one and a half million pounds to their Crofters' Association. They did not seem particularly grateful, but then it was never in the nature of the Sinclairs to be able to express gratitude, except by a nod.

"I'll tell ye the numbers," Angus said, creasing the cheque in half and placing it in his sporran. "Thirty-three thousand crofters back on near two million acres. And they are hammerin' on the corn bykes to come back, noo the law is wi'us agen."

"But there's no living in the crofts," Boy said.

"There's nae livin' wi'out them. Nae guid livin'."

So Boy turned to his strange reconciliation. Rosa had come back to him at last, and her old mother Rosabelle was smiling at him beyond her. At her advanced age, Clio was crawling all over Ian Hamish in public, as she had never done before, licking his ear and embarrassing him. And beyond them sat Conan, the undertaker from Africa in his tartan pride, waiting to bury them all, in good time, of course.

Uncontrollably, Boy found himself on his feet, staggering on the rough turf floor.

"I have to say," he said, then he forgot himself. "I have to say – or I will try to say – it seems to me – there is a strange cycle in things."

"Hear, hear," Ian Hamish said.

"They used to talk about a music of the spheres. And in what I did, physics, we didn't like chaos. We ended with strings, which held us together. Or returned us somehow, however far we went –"

Outside the tent, the skirl of the bagpipes challenged the sky.

"I mean to say, music is repetitious. The chords come round again, even in the stars. And time, well, I know it repeats itself. I have dreams now, the old Vikings we were, the soldiers and the engineers. I even dream of Indian empires we never helped to make. It's strange when you have a vision at the end, and you know it's true. You can't do much, given the way things happen. You can change things a little, sometimes for the worse. But not much. All you can do is to go to the unknowable flow, and when you know that, don't resist. Beg for mercy. Ask forgiveness for what we have done. Amen."

A silence fell at the table at the end of Boy's words. Then there was a shout from the grounds outside at the throwing of the hammer. And then Conan lifted his glass and said, "Bottoms up."

As he waited to give dinner to their clan matriarch, Rosabelle, Boy saw a weird sunset, yellow and pink to the east, dark to the west. He had not felt that illumination since he had seen Solomon, but now he was summoned home to Caithness for his final accounting. He was fit to burst in a last thrombosis, a terminal jolt to the heart. Yet he would hang on through the dragging night to the church service in the morning, the hallowing of the clan. And perhaps the clouds of grey towards Orkney were the wings of the dove of grace, which would enable him to get through dinner.

"I want to talk to you alone, Boy," Rosabelle said as she sat down in front of her plate of whitebait, "because you seem to be the only one of our folly family to make any sense."

"I don't think I make too much sense to myself," Boy said. "I have dreams of Viking ancestors and Indian ones I never had. They tell me I have failed, but now I am dying, I must do it gladly." He pushed an envelope over the table. "That's for you and Rosa. For your good causes. That's the last of my father's loot, thank God. Do take it."

Rosabelle looked with her sunken eyes at the white paper. Then she reached out a crooked hand and took it.

"When I believed in the cause," she said, her hoarse voice clear on the sudden, "I wouldn't have taken capitalist gold, certainly not arms' cash. But – there's so much good we can do with it. So much good Rosa –"

"Rosa," Boy said. "Rosa."

"I'm sorry, Boy. I really am. You loved her best. I wanted to tell you that, before –"

"Before."

"She couldn't. She couldn't say to you how much she wanted – she wished it could have been you. She sent me to tell you."

"She showed me."

"Not enough. And this strange legacy." Rosabelle ran a fingernail along the envelope, scoring it. "Like you, Boy, I failed at all my causes. But if one does a little, as best one can – we do have Scots independence now, the crofters are coming home, and the workers are better off, and if I'm a landowner, which I didn't choose to be –"

Rosabelle's voice trailed away, and she looked into her lap. Boy left her to think in silence.

"There's a great irony or mystery," she said. "We believe we can change things, but we can't much. Yet we try. And forces beyond us, they –"

Her voice sank again, and Boy came to the rescue.

"The service tomorrow in Thurso," he said. "Are you going?"

"Yes," Rosabelle said. "I never believed in God. But enough of our lot do for me to turn out and support them."

Boy shook his head.

"I've always found the churches here divide people. They don't bring them together. The problem with any kirk, and there are so many of them from the Wee Frees to the Church of Scotland, is always the sheep and the goats."

"Like the proletariat and the bourgeoisie. Can't get on, can they?"

"Yes and no. It's true, in the parables, God prefers the sheep and sends the goats out to the desert."

"We and they."

"We and they."

"You don't know who you are until you know who your enemy is."

"Yes. Clan still fights clan. Kirk still opposes kirk. Their flocks may be chosen sheep, but *your* flock is especially chosen. The other kirks contain the goats, or worse, the beasts of the field, or devils. But now I'm off, I don't know where, I find all these feuds so futile, so bloody, just like the feuds among the twelve tribes of Israel. And ten of them got lost."

"Yes," Rosabelle said. "I never did see God as Stalin turned out to be – a bloody-minded herdsman. Sheep or gulags. Where do I put you? Even if you've done nothing to deserve your fate."

The ecumenical service at Thurso West Church the next Sunday morning began with the trooping of the Clan Sinclair banners with their ragged or engrailed crosses upon them, held up by the chiefs. Yet these crusading flags were denied by an extraordinary trio of preachers, the Anglican minister and the Catholic Bishop of Aberdeen and a woman preacher and professor of law from Belfast, where the clans were still warring with each other over different ways to God, as they had done for the past three hundred years. Looking round the pews and the benches at the pink faces of his blood kin in their tartans and their bonnets, Boy felt that perhaps all might still be possible in a truce under heaven. And though the three sermons mentioned a clan system gone sour in Northern Ireland, Boy hoped at last that all these terrible choices, which some called divine, were over. There were so many byways to paradise. Did it matter which one was taken? But still the minister could not resist claiming from the Bible and the Gospel of St John that the best were in his church. His texts were:

He calleth his own sheep by name and leadeth them out.

Other sheep I have which are not to this fold.

Boy had to sit on his hands and stop himself rising and calling out to the minister. Could he not understand? After all their trials and tribulations, His people were returning from the far corners of the earth. His people had taken their strength from the hills and carried it over His seas and were in His pasture again, his flock coming home. There was room for all now, not just for this scrap of His people, but for all of his peoples, not just in this dollop of land, but in all the lands, not in the Sinclair castaways at last reaching a rest, but in all the refugees trying to find a passing place somewhere, before they might return to their ancestral earth. Wherever it was between the will of the Almighty and their own endeavours, people hung on, if other people would have them in for a while, before they might return as Ulysses to their right and their bed.

"Amen," Boy said to his private prayer "Amen."

That afternoon, Boy sailed out in a hired dinghy to die. If he had never been a Beowulf and fought the monsters that preyed on his own, he could end as the Viking princes who had ruled over Caithness. There was a long continuity in dying as well as in living. The rituals of birthing and burial passed through the millennia, from the swaddling in the bands to the going down in the stone tomb and in the north seas. Whatever the *wyrd* was, whatever his destiny, Boy knew that his past was played out. As Marie had known when she had laid herself on her cairn, he knew the last ceremony of his little ship.

Out in the bay, Boy furled the sail with the ebb of his strength, so little was left now. Out of his case, he drew the petrol in the bottle with the wick, and he lit it, and he set the flame to the rope against the mast. Then he took out the syringe with the lethal fluid in it, for he was not brave enough to die as Joan of Arc or in a *suttee*, and he pressed the point into his vein. Above him, he heard a strange humming, which seemed to throb into a harmony. Was this the distant sound of a thousand puffins, or of the singing seals which were the drowned dead? The melody of nature? The music of the spheres?

From Scrabster towards Orkney, a small pyre on the water made a bright shield for the passing of Boy Sinclair. As for the family and the clans, they would continue, as they always had, as they always did, whatever. Only the Empire was gone, forever.

THE END